Raves for Tanya Huff:

"If you enjoy contemporary fantasy, Tanya Huff has a distinctive knack, one she gives full vent in her detective mystery, *Blood Trail*. There's a strong current of romance . . . a carefully thought out pattern of nonhuman family life . . . an unexpected serious theme that helps raise it above the crowd . . . funny, often lighthearted and highly entertaining . . . more than just another 'light' fantasy."
—*Locus*

"No one tickles the funnybone and chills the blood better than Tanya Huff."
—*Romantic Times*

"Huff tells a great story, but never takes herself or it too seriously. She consciously borrows elements from other books as well as movies, comics and mythology and combines them with her own great imagination to make a thoroughly satisfying story."
—*SF Site*

"Huff is one of the best writers we have at contemporary fantasy, particularly with a supernatural twist, and her characters are almost always the kind we remember later, even when the plot details have faded away."
—*Chronicle*

"The author of the 'Blood' novels has once again proven herself a master of urban fantasy."
—*Library Journal*

"This story is a gruesome romp through mystery, horror, and the occult. The author takes it seriously enough that it succeeds, but she also injects some delightful humor."
—*Voya*

THE BLOOD BOOKS, VOLUME 1

BLOOD PRICE
BLOOD TRAIL

Tanya Huff

DAW BOOKS, INC.
DONALD A. WOLLHEIM, FOUNDER
375 Hudson Street, New York, NY 10014

ELIZABETH R. WOLLHEIM
SHEILA E. GILBERT
PUBLISHERS
http://www.dawbooks.com

Introduction

Although *Blood Price* came out in May 1991, I actually got the contract for the book back on August 24, 1989. I offered the outline for *Price* and *The Fire's Stone* at the same time, half assuming DAW wouldn't want the former since they hadn't, at that point, published any urban fantasy. To my surprise, they wanted them both and since I knew that *Price* was the beginning of a series, I wrote *The Fire's Stone* first. Thus, the delay.

Why a vampire book?

Well, at the time I was working at Bakka—a science fiction bookstore in Toronto—and I noticed that vampire readers are very loyal. In a desperate search for something decent to read they'll cross their fingers and pick up just about anything with fangs on the cover. We were thinking of buying a house in the country and so would need a mortgage and vampire books came with a large—and, as I mentioned, loyal—fanbase built in.

So I wrote the first chapter of my "vampire book" and it just wasn't working. The beloved read it and said, "You know, instead of writing a *vampire book*, why don't you write a Tanya Huff book with a vampire in it."

And so that's what I did.

Vicki is in probably the closest to me of any of my characters. Okay, I was never a police officer, I'm a little nearsighted but otherwise my eyes are fine and she's in better shape but other than that . . . She even lives in my old apartment. The Retinitis Pigmentosa came about because I needed a good reason for her to have left a job she loved and excelled at. I also liked the parallels between her and Henry—she can't work at night, he can't work in the daytime.

Henry Fitzroy was a real person. I thought I was fairly well versed in the Tudor age but as astonished to discover that not only did King Henry VIII have an illegitimate son but that the son died suddenly at seventeen—in three months he went from healthy young man to the grave. There was also some controversy around the disposal of the body.

Michael Celluci is, essentially, the straight man for Vicki and Henry. I always saw him as Joe Coffee in an early season of Hill Street Blues. He's a good cop and a good guy, and is far too well grounded to have his world view overturned by vampires or demons. Vicki's the only one who's ever managed to knock him off balance.

I have no memory of the why's and wherefore's of my antagonist but it *has* been almost twenty years. (Recently a British review pointed out that the Blood books have aged very well, the only obvious way they hint at their date of original publication is that there isn't a cell phone in sight.)

Honesty forces me to admit that *Blood Price* is not the name on the contract but rather *Ninety-Eight Point Six*, which is, of course, body temperature. And a terrible title.

Blood Trail was originally called *A Canadian Werewolf in London, Ontario*—seriously, that's what's on the contract. The fun part of *Trail* was taking wolf society and combining it in a believable way with human society to create a blend of both. Because if you have vampires, why wouldn't you have werewolves? My werewolves live in packs made up of family units, they hunt rats, they flunk algebra, they sing opera. I thought the sheep farm was a nice touch.

And you don't need to use a silver bullet to kill them. Unfortunately lead works fine.

—Tanya Huff
November 2005

BLOOD PRICE

One

Ian shoved his hands deep in his pockets and scowled down the length of the empty subway platform. His hands were freezing, he was in a bitch of a bad mood, and he had no idea why he'd agreed to meet Coreen at her apartment. All things considered, neutral ground might have been a better idea. He shifted his scowl to the LED clock hanging from the ceiling. 12:17. Thirteen minutes to get from Eglinton West to Wilson Station, six blocks worth of bus ride, and then a three block run to Coreen's. It couldn't be done.

I'm going to be late. She's going to be pissed. And there goes our chance to make up. He sighed. It had taken two hours of arguing on the phone to get her to agree to a meeting. Maintaining a relationship with Coreen might be time-consuming, but it sure as hell wasn't boring. Lord, but the woman had a temper. . . . His lips curled up into a smile almost without him willing the motion; the flip side of that temper made all the effort of staying on the roller coaster worthwhile. The smile broadened. Coreen packed a lot of punch for a woman barely five foot two.

He glanced up at the clock again.

Where the hell was the train?

12:20.

Be there by 12:30 or forget it, she'd said, completely ignoring the fact that on Sunday the Toronto Transit Commission, the ubiquitous TTC, drastically cut back on the number of trains and at this hour he'd be lucky to get the last one they ran.

Looking at the bright side, when he finally got there, given the time of night and the fact that they both had an eight o'clock class, he'd have to stay over. He sighed. *If she'll even let me into her apartment.*

He wandered down to the southernmost end of the platform and peered into the tunnel. No sign of lights, but he could feel wind against his face and that usually meant the train wasn't far. He coughed as he turned away. It smelled like something had died down there; smelled like it did at the cottage when a mouse got between the walls and rotted.

"Big mother of a mouse," he muttered, rubbing his fist against his nose. The stench caught in his lungs and he coughed again. It was funny the tricks the mind played; now that he was aware of it, the smell seemed to be getting stronger.

And then he heard what could only be footsteps coming up the tunnel, out of the darkness. Heavy footsteps, not at all like a worker hurrying to beat the train after a day's overtime, nor like a bum staggering for the safety of the platform. Heavy footsteps, purposefully advancing toward his back.

Ian gloried in the sharp terror that started his heart thudding in his chest and trapped his breath in his throat. He knew very well that when he turned, when he looked, the explanation would be prosaic, so he froze and enjoyed the unknown while it remained unknown, delighted in the adrenaline rush of fear that made every sense more alive and made the seconds stretch to hours.

He didn't turn until the footsteps moved up the half dozen cement stairs and onto the platform.

Then it was too late.

He almost didn't have time to scream.

*   *   *

Tucking her chin down into her coat—it might be April but it was still damp and cold, with no sign of spring—Vicki Nelson stepped off the Eglinton bus and into the subway station.

"Well, that was a disaster," she muttered. The elderly

gentleman who had exited the bus right behind her made an inquiring noise. She turned a bland stare in his general direction, then picked up her pace. *So I'm not only "lousy company, and so uptight I squeak," but I also talk to myself.* She sighed. Lawrence was pretty, but he wasn't her type. She hadn't met a man who was her type since she'd left the police force eight months before. *I should've known this was going to happen when I agreed to go out with a man significantly better looking than I am. I don't know why I accepted the invitation.*

That wasn't exactly true; she'd accepted the invitation because she was lonely. She knew it, she just had no intention of admitting it.

She was halfway down the first set of stairs leading to the southbound platform when she heard the scream. Or rather the half-scream. It choked off in mid-wail. One leap took her to the first landing. From where she stood, she could see only half of each platform through the glass and no indication of which side the trouble was on. The south was closer, faster.

Bounding down two, and then three steps at a time she yelled, "Call the police!" Even if no one heard her, it might scare off the cause of the scream.

Nine years on the force and she'd never used her gun. She wanted it now. In nine years on the force she'd never heard a scream like that.

"What the hell do you think you're doing?" the more rational part of her brain shrieked. *"You don't have a weapon! You don't have backup! You don't have any idea of what's going on down there! Eight months off the force and you've forgotten everything they ever taught you! What the hell are you trying to prove?"*

Vicki ignored the voice and kept moving. Maybe she was trying to prove something. So what.

When she exploded out onto the platform, she immediately realized she'd chosen the wrong side and for just an instant, she was glad of it.

A great spray of blood arced up the orange tiles of the station wall, feathering out from a thick red stream to a delicate pattern of crimson drops. On the floor below, his eyes and mouth open above the mangled ruin of his throat, lay a young man. No: the body of a young man.

The dinner she'd so recently eaten rose to the back of Vicki's throat, but walls built during the investigations of other deaths slammed into place and she forced it down.

The wind in the tunnel began to pick up and she could hear the northbound train approaching. It sounded close.

Sweet Jesus, that's all we need. At 12:35 on a Sunday night it was entirely possible that the train would be nearly empty, no one would get off, and no one would notice the corpse and the blood-spattered wall down at the southernmost end of the northbound platform. Given the way of the world, however, it was more likely that a group of children and a little old lady with a weak heart would pile out of the last carriage and come face-to-face with the staring eyes and mutely screaming mouth of a fresh corpse.

Only one solution presented itself.

The roar of the train filled the station as, heart pounding and adrenaline singing in her ears, Vicki leaped down onto the southbound tracks. The wooden step over the live rail was too far away, almost centered in the line of concrete pillars, so she jumped, trying not to think of the however many million volts of electricity the thing carried turning her to charcoal. She tottered for a moment on the edge of the divider, cursing her full-length coat and wishing she'd worn a jacket, and then, although she knew it was the stupidest thing she could do, she looked toward the oncoming train.

How did it get so close? The light was blinding, the roar deafening. She froze, caught in the glare, sure that if she continued she'd fall and the metal wheels of the beast would cut her to shreds.

Then something man-height flickered across the northbound tunnel. She didn't see much, just a billowing shadow, black against the growing headlight, but it jerked her out of immobility and down onto the track.

Cinders crunched under her boots, metal rang, then she had her hands on the edge of the platform and was flinging herself into the air. The world filled with sound and light and something brushed lightly against her sole.

Her hands were sticky, covered with blood, but it wasn't hers and at the moment that was all that mattered. Before the train stopped, she'd flung her coat over the body and grabbed her ID.

The center-man stuck his head out.

Vicki flipped the leather folder in his direction and barked, "Close the doors! Now!"

The doors, not quite open, closed.

She remembered to breathe again and when the centerman's head reappeared, snapped, "Have the driver get the police on the radio. Tell them it's a 10-33 . . . never mind what that means!" She saw the question coming. "They'll know! And don't forget to tell them where it is." People had done stupider things in emergencies. As he ducked back into the train, she looked down at her card case and sighed, then lifted one gory finger to push her glasses back up her nose. A private investigator's ID meant absolutely nothing in a case like this, but people responded to the appearance of authority, not the particulars.

She moved a little farther from the body. Up close, the smell of blood and urine—the front of the boy's jeans was soaked—easily overcame the metallic odors of the subway. A lone face peered out through the window of the closest car. She snarled at it and settled down to wait.

Less than three minutes later, Vicki heard the faint sound of sirens up on the street. She almost cheered. It had been the longest three minutes of her life.

She'd spent them thinking, adding together the spray of blood and the position of the body and not liking the total.

Nothing that she knew of could strike a single blow strong enough to tear through flesh like tissue paper and fast enough that the victim had no time to struggle. Nothing. But something had.

And it was down in the tunnels.

She twisted until she could see into the darkness beyond the end of the train. The hair on the back of her neck rose. What did the shadows hide, she wondered. Her skin crawled, not entirely because of the cold. She'd never considered herself an overly imaginative woman and she knew the killer had to be long gone, but *something* lingered in that tunnel.

The distinctive slam of police boots against tile brought her around, hands held carefully out from her sides. Police called to a violent murder, finding someone covered in blood standing over the body, could be excused if they jumped to a conclusion or two.

The situation got chaotic for a few minutes, but fortunately four of the six constables had heard of "Victory" Nelson and after apologies had been exchanged all around, they got to work.

". . . my coat over the body, had the driver call the police, and waited." Vicki watched Police Constable West scribbling madly in his occurrence book and hid a grin. She could remember being that young and that intense. Barely. When he looked up, she nodded at the body and asked, "Do you want to see?"

"Uh, no!" After a second he added, a little sheepishly, "That is, we shouldn't disturb anything before homicide gets here."

Homicide. Vicki's stomach lurched and her mood nose-dived. She'd forgotten she wasn't in charge. Forgotten she was nothing more than a witness—first on the scene and that only because she'd done some pretty stupid things to get there. The uniforms had made it seem like old times but homicide . . . her department. No, not hers any longer. She pushed her glasses up her nose with the back of her wrist.

PC West, caught staring, dropped his gaze in confusion. "Uh, I don't think anyone would mind if you cleaned the blood off your hands."

"Thanks." Vicki managed a smile but ignored the unasked question. How well she could see, or how little she could see, was nobody's business but hers. Let another round of rumors start making its way through the force. "If you wouldn't mind grabbing a couple of tissues out of my bag. . . ."

The young constable dipped a tentative hand into the

huge black leather purse and actually looked relieved when he removed it holding the tissue and still in possession of all his fingers. Vicki's bag had been legendary throughout Metro and the boroughs.

Most of the blood on her hands had dried to reddish brown flakes and the little that hadn't the tissue merely smeared around. She scrubbed at it anyway, feeling rather like Lady MacBeth.

"Destroying the evidence?"

Celluci, she thought. *They had to send Celluci. That bastard always walked too quietly.* She and Mike Celluci had not parted on the best of terms but, by the time she turned to face him, she managed to school her expression.

"Just trying to make life more difficult for you." The voice and the smile that went with it were patently false.

He nodded, an overly long curl of dark brown hair falling into his face. "Always the best idea to play to your strengths." Then his eyes went past her to the body. "Give your statement to Dave." Behind him, his partner waved two fingers. "I'll talk to you later. This your coat?"

"Yeah, it's mine." Vicki watched him lift the edge of the blood-soaked fabric and knew that for the moment nothing existed for him but the body and its immediate surroundings. Although their methods differed, he was as intense in the performance of his duties as she was— *had been,* she corrected herself silently—and the undeclared competition between them had added an edge to many an investigation. Including a number neither of them were on.

"Vicki?"

She unclenched her jaw and, still scrubbing at her hands, followed Dave Graham a few meters up the platform.

Dave, who had been partnered with Mike Celluci for only a month when Vicki left the force and the final screaming match had occurred, smiled a little self-consciously and said, "How about we just do this by the book?"

Vicki released a breath she didn't know she'd been

holding. "Sure, that'd be fine." Taking refuge from emotions in police procedure—a worldwide law enforcement tradition.

While they talked, the subway train, now empty of passengers, pulled slowly out of the station.

". . . responding to the scream you ran down onto the southbound platform, then crossed the tracks in front of a northbound train to reach the body. While crossing the tracks . . ."

Inwardly, Vicki cringed. Dave Graham was one of the least judgmental men in existence, but even he couldn't keep his opinion of that stunt from showing in his voice.

". . . you saw a man-shaped form in what appeared to be a loose, flowing garment cross between you and the lights. Is that it?"

"Essentially." Stripped of all the carefully recorded details, it sounded like such a stupid thing to have done.

"Right." He closed the notebook and scratched at the side of his nose. "You, uh, going to stick around?"

Vicki squinted as the police photographer snapped off another quick series of shots. She couldn't see Mike, but she could hear him down in the tunnel barking commands in his best "God's gift to the Criminal Investigations Bureau" voice. Down in the tunnel . . . the hair on the back of her neck rose again as she remembered the feeling of *something* lingering, something dark and, well if she had to put a name to it, evil. She suddenly wanted to warn Celluci to be careful. She didn't. She knew how he'd react. How *she'd* react if their positions were reversed.

"Vicki? You sticking around?"

It was on the tip of her tongue to say no, that they knew where to find her if they needed further information, but curiosity—about what the police would find, about how long she could remain so close to the job she'd loved and not fall apart—turned the no into a grudging, "For a while." She'd be damned if she'd run away.

As she watched, Celluci came up the stairs onto the platform and spoke to the ident man, sweeping one arm back along the tracks. The ident man protested that he

needed a certain amount of light to do his job, but Celluci cut him off. With a disgusted snort, he picked up
his case and headed for the tunnel.

Charming as ever, Vicki thought as Celluci scooped
her coat off the floor and made his way toward her,
detouring slightly around the coroner's men who were
finally zipping the body into its orange plastic bag.
"Don't tell me," she called as soon as he was close
enough, her voice carefully dry, almost sarcastic, and
hopefully showing no indication of the churning emotions that had her gut tied in knots. "The only prints on
the scene are mine?" There were, of course, a multitude
of prints on the scene, none of which had been
identified—that was for downtown—but the bloody hand-
prints Vicki had scattered around were obvious.

"Dead on, Sherlock." He tossed her the coat. "And
the blood trail leads into a workman's alcove and stops."

Vicki frowned as she reconstructed what had to have
happened just before she reached the platform. "You
checked the southbound side?"

"That's where we lost the trail." His tone added,
Don't teach Grandpa to suck eggs. He held up a hand
to forestall the next question. "I had one of the uniforms
talk to the old man while Dave was dealing with you,
but he's hysterical. He keeps going on about Armageddon. His son-in-law's coming to pick him up and I'll go
see him tomorrow."

Vicki shot a glance across the station where the old
man who had followed her off the bus and down the
stairs sat talking to a policewoman. Even at a distance
he didn't look good. His face was gray and he appeared
to be babbling uncontrollably, one scrawny, swollen-
knuckled hand clutching at the constable's sleeve. Turning her attention back to her companion, she asked,
"What about the subway? You closed it for the night?"

"Yeah." Mike waved toward the end of the platform.
"I want Jake to dust that alcove." Intermittent flashes
of light indicated the photographer was still at work.
"It's not the sort of case where we can get in and out
in a couple of minutes." He shoved his hands into his
overcoat pockets and scowled. "Although the way the

transit commission squawked you'd think we were shutting it down in rush hour to pick up someone for littering."

"What, uh, sort of case is it?" Vicki asked—as close as she could get to asking if he, too, felt it, whatever *it* turned out to be.

He shrugged. "You tell me; you seem to have gone to a great deal of trouble to land right in the middle of this."

"I was here," she snapped. "Would you have preferred that I ignore it?"

"You had no weapon, no backup, no idea of what was going down." Celucci ticked off an identical litany to the one she'd read herself earlier. "You can't have forgotten everything in eight months."

"And what would you have done?" she spat through clenched teeth.

"I wouldn't have tried to kill myself just to prove I still could."

The silence that fell landed like a load of cement blocks and Vicki gritted her teeth under its weight. Was that what she'd been doing? She looked down at the toes of her boots, then up at Mike. At five ten she didn't look up to many men but Celluci, at six four, practically made her feel petite. She hated feeling petite. "If we're going to rehash my leaving the force again, I'm out of here."

He held up both hands in a gesture of weary surrender. "You're right. As usual. I'm sorry. We're not going to rehash anything."

"You brought it up." She sounded hostile; she didn't care. She should've followed her instincts and left the moment she'd given her statement. She had to have been out of her mind, putting herself in this position, staying in Celluci's reach.

A muscle in his jaw jumped. "I said I was sorry. Go ahead, be superwoman if you want to, but maybe," he added, his voice tight, "I don't want to see you get killed. *Maybe,* I'm not willing to toss aside eight years of friendship. . . ."

"Friendship?" Vicki felt her eyebrows rise.

Celluci drove his hands into his hair, yanking them through the curls, a gesture he used when he was trying very hard to keep his temper. "Maybe I'm not willing to toss aside four years of friendship and four years of sex because of a stupid disagreement!"

"Just sex? That's it?" Vicki took the easy way out, ignoring the more loaded topic of their *disagreement.* A shortage of things to fight about had never been one of their problems, "Well, it wasn't just sex to me, Detective!"

They were both yelling now.

"Did I say it was just sex?" He spread his arms wide, his voice booming off the tiled walls of the subway station. "It was great sex, okay? It was terrific sex! It was . . . What?"

PC West, his fair skin deeply crimson, jumped. "You're blocking the body," he stammered.

Growling an inaudible curse, Celluci jerked back against the wall.

As the gurney rolled by, the contents of the fluorescent orange bag lolling a little from side to side, Vicki curled her hands into fists and contemplated planting one right on Mike Celluci's classically handsome nose. Why did she let him affect her like this? He had a definite knack for poking through carefully constructed shields and stirring up emotions she thought she had under control. *Damn him anyway.* It didn't help that, this time, he was right. A corner of her mouth twitched up. At least they were talking again. . . .

When the gurney had passed, she straightened her fingers, laid her hand on Celluci's arm and said, "Next time, I'll do it by the book."

It was as close to an apology as she was able to make and he knew it.

"Why start now." He sighed. "Look, about leaving the force; you're not blind, Vicki, you could have stayed. . . ."

"Celluci. . . ." She ground his name through clenched teeth. He always pushed it just that one comment too far.

"Never mind." He reached out and pushed her glasses up her nose. "Want a lift downtown?"

She glanced down at her ruined coat. "Why not."

As they followed the gurney up the stairs, he punched her lightly on the arm. "Nice fighting with you again."

She surrendered—the last eight months had been a punitive victory at best—and grinned. "I missed you, too."

                    *   *   *

The Monday papers had the murder spread across page one. The tabloid even had a color photograph of the gurney being rolled out of the station, the body bag an obscene splotch of color amid the dark blues and grays. Vicki tossed the paper onto the growing "to be recycled" pile to the left of her desk and chewed on a thumbnail. Celluci's theory, which he'd grudgingly passed on while they drove downtown, involved PCPs and some sort of strap-on claws.

"Like that guy in the movie."

"That was a glove with razor blades, Celluci."

"Whatever."

Vicki didn't buy it and she knew Mike didn't really either, it was just the best model he could come up with until he had more facts. His final answer often bore no resemblance to the theory he'd started with, he just hated working from zero. She preferred to let the facts fall into the void and see what they piled up to look like. Trouble was, this time they just kept right on falling. She needed more facts.

Her hand was halfway to the phone before she remembered and pulled it back. This had nothing to do with her any longer. She'd given her statement and that was as far as her involvement went.

She took off her glasses and scrubbed at one lens with a fold of her sweatshirt. The edges of her world blurred until it looked as if she were staring down a foggy tunnel; a wide tunnel, more than adequate for day to day living. So far, she'd lost about a third of her peripheral vision. So far. It could only get worse.

The glasses corrected only the nearsightedness. Nothing could correct the rest.

"Okay, this one's Celluci's. Fine. I have a job of my

own to do," she told herself firmly. "One I *can* do."
One she'd better do. Her savings wouldn't last forever
and so far her caseload had been embarrassingly light,
her vision forcing her to turn down more than one potential client.

Teeth gritted, she pulled the massive Toronto white
pages onto her lap. With luck, the F. Chan she was looking for, inheritor of a tidy sum of money from a dead
uncle in Hong Kong, would be one of the twenty-six
listed. If not . . . there were over three full pages of
Chans, sixteen columns, approximately one thousand,
eight hundred and fifty-six names and she'd bet at least
half of those would have a Foo in the family.

Mike Celluci would be looking for a killer right now.

She pushed the thought away.

You couldn't be a cop if you couldn't see.

She'd made her bed. She'd lie in it.

*   *   *

Terri Neal sagged against the elevator wall, took a
number of deep breaths, and, when she thought she'd
dredged up a sufficient amount of energy, raised her arm
just enough so she could see her watch.

"Twelve seventeen?" she moaned. *Where the hell has
Monday gone, and what's the point in going home? I've
got to be back here in eight hours.* She felt the weight of
the pager against her hip and added a silent prayer that
she would actually get the full eight hours. The company
had received its pound of flesh already today—the
damned beeper had gone off as she'd slid into her car
back at 4:20—so maybe, just maybe, they'd leave her
alone tonight.

The elevator door hissed open and she dragged herself
forward into the underground garage.

"Leaving the office," she murmured, "take two."

Squinting a little under the glare of the fluorescent
lights, she started across the almost empty garage, her
shadow dancing around her like a demented marionette.
She'd always hated the cold, hard light of the fluorescents, the world looked decidedly unfriendly thrown into
such sharp-edged relief. And tonight. . . .

She shook her head. Lack of sleep made her think crazy things. Resisting the urge to keep looking over her shoulder, she finally reached the one benefit of all the endless hours of overtime.

"Hi, baby." She rummaged in her pocket for her car keys. "Miss me?"

She flipped open the hatchback, heaved her briefcase—*this damn thing must weigh three hundred pounds!*—up and over the lip, and slid it down into the trunk. Resting her elbows on the weather stripping, she paused, half in and half out of the car, inhaling the scent of new paint, new vinyl, new plastic, and . . . rotting food. Frowning, she straightened.

At least it's coming from outside my car. . . .

Gagging, she pushed the hatchback closed and turned. Let security worry about the smell tomorrow. All she wanted to do was get home.

It took a moment for her to realize she wasn't going to make it.

By the time the scream reached her throat, her throat had been torn away and the scream became a gurgle as her severed trachea filled with blood.

The last thing she saw as her head fell back was the lines of red dribbling darkly down the sides of her new car.

The last thing she heard was the insistent beep, beep, beep of her pager.

And the last thing she felt was a mouth against the ruin of her throat.

* * *

On Tuesday morning, the front page of the tabloid screamed "SLASHER STRIKES AGAIN." A photograph of the coach of the Toronto Maple Leafs stared out from under it, the cutline asking—not for the first time that season—if he should be fired, the Leafs being once again at the very bottom of the worst division in the league. It was the kind of strange layout at which the paper excelled.

"Fire the owner," Vicki muttered, shoving her glasses up her nose and peering at the tiny print under the headline. "Story page two," it said, and on page two, complete with a photo of the underground garage and a hysterical account by the woman who had found the body, was a description of a mutilated corpse that exactly matched the one Vicki had found in the Eglinton West Station.

"Damn."

"Homicide investigator Michael Celluci," the story continued, *"says there is little doubt in his mind that this is not a copycat case and whoever killed Terri Neal also killed Ian Reddick on Sunday night."*

Vicki strongly suspected that was not at all what Mike had said, although it might have been the information he imparted. Mike seldom found it necessary to cooperate with, or even hide his distaste for, the press. And he was never that polite.

She read over the details again and a nameless fear ran icy fingers down her spine. She remembered the lingering presence she'd felt and knew this wouldn't be the end of the killing. She'd dialed the phone almost before she came to a conscious decision to call.

"Mike Celluci please. What? No, no message."

And what was I going to tell him? she wondered as she hung up. *That I have a hunch this is only the beginning? He'd love that.*

Tossing the tabloid aside, Vicki pulled the other city paper toward her. On page four it ran much the same story, minus about half the adjectives and most of the hysteria.

Neither paper had mentioned that ripping a throat out with a single blow was pretty much impossible.

If I could only remember what was missing from that body. She sighed and rubbed at her eyes.

Meanwhile, she had five Foo Chans to visit. . . .

*   *   *

There was something moving in the pit. DeVerne Jones leaned against the wire fence and breathed beer fumes into the darkness, wondering what he should do about it. It was his pit. His first as foreman. They'd be starting the frames in the morning so that when spring finally arrived they'd be ready to pour the concrete. He peered around the black lumps of machinery. And there was something down there. In his pit.

Briefly he wished he hadn't decided to swing by the site on his way home from the bar. It was after midnight and the shape he'd seen over by the far wall was probably just some poor wino looking for a warm place to curl up where the cops would leave him alone. The crew could toss the bum out in the morning, no harm done. Except they had a lot of expensive equipment down there and it might be something more.

"Damn."

He dug out his keys and walked over to the gate. The padlock hung open. In the damp and the cold, it sometimes didn't catch, but he'd been the last man out of the pit and he'd checked it before he left. Hadn't he?

"Damn again." It had just become a very good thing he'd stopped by.

Hinges screaming in protest, the gate swung open.

DeVerne waited for a moment at the top of the ramp, to see if the sound flushed his quarry.

Nothing.

A belly full of beer and you're a hero, he thought, just sober enough to realize he could be walking into trouble and just drunk enough to not really care.

Halfway down into the pit, his eyes growing accustomed to the darkness, he saw it again. Man-shaped, moving too quickly to be a wino, it disappeared behind one of the dozers.

As silently as he was able, DeVerne quickened his pace. He'd catch the son-of-a-bitch in the act. He made a small detour and pulled a three foot length of pipe from a pile of scrap. No sense taking chances, even a cornered rat would fight. The scrape of metal against metal rang out unnaturally loud, echoing off the sides of the pit. His presence announced, he charged around the dozer, bellowing a challenge, weapon raised.

Someone was lying on the ground. DeVerne could see the shoes sticking out of the pool of shadow. In that pool of shadow—or creating it, DeVerne couldn't be sure—crouched another figure.

DeVerne yelled again. The figure straightened and turned, darkness swirling about it.

He didn't realize the figure had moved until the pipe was wrenched from his hand. He barely had time to raise his other hand in a futile attempt to save his life.

There's no such thing! he wailed silently as he died.

*   *   *

Wednesday morning, the tabloid headline, four inches high, read: "VAMPIRE STALKS CITY."

Two

He lifted her arm and ran his tongue down the soft flesh on the inside of her wrist. She moaned, head back, breath coming in labored gasps.

Almost.

He watched her closely and when she began to go into the final climb, when her body began to arch under his, he took the small pulsing vein at the base of her thumb between the sharp points of his teeth and bit down. The slight pain was for her just one more sensation added to a system already overloaded and while she rode the waves of her orgasm, he drank.

They finished at much the same time.

He reached up and gently pushed a strand of damp mahogany hair off her face. "Thank you," he said softly.

"No, thank *you*," she murmured, capturing his hand and placing a kiss on the palm.

They lay quietly for a time; she drifting in and out of sleep, he tracing light patterns on the soft curves of her breasts, his fingertip following the blue lines of veins beneath the white skin. Now that he'd fed, they no longer drove him to distraction. When he was sure that the coagulant in his saliva had taken effect, and the tiny wound on her wrist would bleed no more, he untangled his legs from hers and padded to the bathroom to clean up.

She roused while he was dressing.

"Henry?"

"I'm still here, Caroline."

"Now. But you're leaving."

"I have work to do." He pulled a sweater over his head and emerged, blinking in the sudden light from the bedside lamp. Long years of practice kept him from recoiling, but he turned his back to give his sensitive eyes a chance to recover.

"Why can't you work in the daytime, like a normal person," Caroline protested, pulling the comforter up from the foot of the bed and snuggling down under it. "Then you'd have your nights free for me."

He smiled and replied truthfully, "I can't think in the daytime."

"Writers," she sighed.

"Writers," he agreed, bending over and kissing her on the nose. "We're a breed apart."

"Will you call me?"

"As soon as I have the time."

"Men!"

He reached over and snapped off the lamp. "That, too." Deftly avoiding her groping hands, he kissed her good-bye and padded silently out of the bedroom and through the dark apartment. Behind him, he heard her breathing change and knew she slept. Usually, she fell asleep right after they finished, never knowing when he left. It was one of the things he liked best about her, for it meant they seldom had awkward arguments about whether he'd be staying the night.

Retrieving his coat and boots, he let himself out of the apartment, one ear cocked for the sound of the dead bolt snapping home. In many ways, this was the safest time he'd ever lived in. In others, the most dangerous.

Caroline had no suspicion of what he actually was. For her, he was no more than a pleasant interlude, an infrequent companion, sex without guilt. He hadn't even had to work very hard to have it turn out that way.

He frowned at his reflection on the elevator doors. "I want more." The disquiet had been growing for some time, prodding at him, giving him little peace. Feeding had helped ease it but not enough. Choking back a cry of frustration, he whirled and slammed his palm against the plastic wall. The blow sounded like a gunshot in the enclosed space and Henry stared at the pattern of cracks radiating out from under his hand. His palm stung, but the violence seemed to have dulled the point of the disquiet.

No one waited in the lobby to investigate the noise and Henry left the building in an almost jaunty mood.

It was cold out on the street. He tucked his scarf a little more securely around his throat and turned his collar up. His nature made him less susceptible to weather than most, but he still had no liking for a cold wind finding its way down his back. With the bottom of his leather trench coat flapping about his legs, he made his way down the short block to Bloor, turned east, and headed home.

Although it was nearly one o'clock on a Thursday morning, and spring seemed to have decided to make a very late appearance this year, the streets were not yet empty. Traffic still moved steadily along the city's east/ west axis and the closer Henry got to Yonge and Bloor, the city's main intersection, the more people he passed on the sidewalk. It was one of the things he liked best about this part of the city, the fact that it never really slept, and it was why he had his home as close to it as he could get. Two blocks past Yonge, he turned into a circular drive and followed the curve around to the door of his building.

In his time, he had lived in castles of every description, a fair number of very private country estates, and even a crypt or two when times were bad, but it had been centuries since he'd had a home that suited him as well as the condominium he'd bought in the heart of Toronto.

"Good evening, Mr. Fitzroy."

"Evening, Greg. Anything happening?"

The security guard smiled and reached for the door release. "Quiet as a tomb, sir."

Henry Fitzroy raised one red-gold eyebrow but waited until he had the door open and the buzzer had ceased its electronic flatulence before asking, "And how would you know?"

Greg grinned. "Used to be a guard at Mount Pleasant Cemetery."

Henry shook his head and smiled as well. "I should've known you'd have an answer."

"Yes, sir, you should've. Good night, sir."

The heavy glass door closed off any further conversation, so as Greg picked up his newspaper Henry waved a silent good night and turned toward the elevators. Then he stopped. And turned back to face the glass.

"VAMPIRE STALKS CITY."

Lips moving as he read, Greg laid the paper flat on his desk, hiding the headline.

His world narrowed to three words, Henry shoved the door open.

"You forget something, Mr. Fitzroy?"

"Your paper. Let me see it."

Startled by the tone but responding to the command, Greg pushed the paper forward until Henry snatched it out from under his hands.

"VAMPIRE STALKS CITY."

Slowly, making no sudden movements, Greg slid his chair back, putting as much distance as possible between himself and the man on the other side of the desk. He wasn't sure why, but in sixty-three years and two wars, he'd never seen an expression like the one Henry Fitzroy now wore. And he hoped he'd never see it again, for the anger was more than human anger and the terror it invoked more than human spirit could stand.

Please, God, don't let him turn it on me. . . .

The minutes stretched and paper tore under tightening fingers.

"Uh, Mr. Fitzroy . . ."

Hazel eyes, like frozen smoke, lifted from their reading. Held by their intensity, the trembling security guard had to swallow once, twice, before he could finish.

". . . you can, uh, keep the paper."

The fear in Greg's voice penetrated through the rage. There was danger in fear. Henry found the carefully constructed civilized veneer that he wore over the predator and forced it back on. "I hate this kind of sensationalism!" He slapped the paper down on the desk.

Greg jumped and his chair hit the back wall, ending retreat.

"This playing on the fears of the public is irresponsible

journalism." Henry sighed and covered the anger with a
patina of weary annoyance. Four hundred and fifty years
of practice made the false face believable regardless of
how uncomfortable the fit had grown lately. "They make
us all look bad."

Greg sighed in turn and wiped damp palms on his
thighs, snatching at the explanation. "I guess writers are
kind of sensitive about that," he offered.

"Some of us," Henry agreed. "You sure about the
paper? That I can keep it?"

"No problem, Mr. Fitzroy. I checked the hockey
scores first thing." His mind had already begun to dull
what he had seen, adding rationalizations that made it
possible, that made it bearable, but he didn't slide his
chair back to the desk until the elevator door had closed
and the indicator light had begun to climb.

Muscles knotted with the effort of standing still, Henry
concentrated on breathing, on controlling the rage rather
than allowing it to control him. In this age his kind survived by blending in, and he'd made a potentially fatal
mistake by letting his reaction to the headline show.
Allowing his true nature to emerge in the privacy of an
empty elevator could do little harm, but doing so before
a mortal witness was quite another matter. Not that he
expected Greg to suddenly start pointing his finger and
screaming vampire. . . .

Helping to dampen the rage was the guilt he felt at
terrifying the old man. He liked Greg; in this world of
equality and democracy it was good to meet a man willing to serve. The attitude reminded him of the men
who'd worked on the estate when he was a boy and took
him back, for a little while at least, to a simpler time.

Barriers firmly in place, he got off the elevator at the
fourteenth floor, holding the door so Mrs. Hughes and
her mastiff could get on. The big dog walked past him
stiff-legged, the hairs on the back of his neck up, and a
growl rumbling deep in his throat. As always, Mrs.
Hughes made apologetic sounds.

"I really don't understand this, Mr. Fitzroy. Owen is
usually such a sweet dog. He never . . . Owen!"

The mastiff, trembling with the desire to attack, settled for maneuvering his huge body between his owner and the man in the door, putting as much distance as possible between her and the perceived threat.

"Don't worry about it, Mrs. Hughes." Henry removed his hand and the door began to slide closed. "You can't expect Owen to like everybody." Just before the door shut completely, he smiled down at the dog. The mastiff recognized the baring of teeth for what it was and lunged. Henry managed a slightly more honest smile as the frantic barks faded down toward the lobby.

Ten minutes alone with the dog and they could settle what stood between them. Pack law was simple, the strongest ruled. But Owen always traveled with Mrs. Hughes and Henry doubted Mrs. Hughes would understand. As he had no wish to alienate his neighbor, he put up with the mastiff's animosity. It was a pity. He liked dogs and it would take so little to put Owen in his place.

Once in the condo, with the door safely closed behind him, he looked at the paper again and snarled.

"VAMPIRE STALKS CITY."

The bodies of Terri Neal and DeVerne Jones had been found drained of blood.

The headline appeared to be accurate.

And he knew he wasn't doing it.

With a sudden snap of his wrist he flung the paper across the room and took a minor satisfaction in watching the pages flutter to the floor like wounded birds.

"Damn. Damn. DAMN!"

Crossing to the window, he shrugged out of his coat and tossed it on the couch, then yanked back the curtains that blocked the city from view. Vampires were a solitary breed, not seeking each other out nor keeping track of where their brothers and sisters roamed. Although he suspected he shared his territory with others of his kind, there could be a score moving, living, feeding among the patterns of light and shadow that made up the night and Henry would be no more aware of it than the people they moved among.

And worse, if the killer *was* a vampire, it was a child, one of the newly changed, for only the newly changed needed blood in such amounts and would kill with such brutal abandon.

"Not one of mine," he said to the night, his forehead resting against the cool glass. It was as much a prayer as a statement. Everyone of his kind feared that they would turn loose just such a monster, an accidental child, an accidental change. But *he'd* been careful; never feeding again until the blood had had a chance to renew, never taking the risk that his blood could be passed back. He would have a child someday, but it would change by choice as he had done and he would be there to guide it, to keep it safe.

No, not one of his. But he could not let it continue to terrorize the city. Fear had not changed over the centuries, nor had people's reactions to it and a terrorized city could quickly bring out the torches and sharpened stakes . . . or the twentieth century laboratory equivalent.

"And I no more want to be strapped to a table for the rest of my life than to have my head removed and my mouth stuffed with garlic," he told the night.

He would have to find the child, before the police did and their answer raised more questions than it solved. Find the child and destroy it, for without a blood bond he could not control it.

"And then," he raised his head and bared his teeth, "I will find the parent."

* * *

"Morning, Mrs. Kopolous."

"Hello, darling, you're up early."

"I couldn't sleep," Vicki told her, making her way to the back of the store where the refrigerators hummed, "and I was out of milk."

"Get the bags, they're on sale."

"I don't like the bags." Out of the corner of one eye she saw Mrs. Kopolous expressing a silent and not very favorable opinion of her unwillingness to save forty-nine cents. She grabbed a jug and brought it back to the counter. "Papers not out yet?"

"Yeah, yeah, they're right here, dear." She bent over

the bundles, her stocky body hiding the headlines. When she straightened, she slapped one copy of each morning paper down by the cash register.

"SABERS DOWN LEAFS 10–2."

Vicki let out a lungful of air she hadn't known she was holding. If the tabloid made no mention of another murder—besides the slaughter in the division play-offs— it looked like the city had made it safely through the night.

"Those terrible things, you're mixed up in them, aren't you?"

"What terrible things, Mrs. Kopolous?" She scooped up her change, then put it back and grabbed an Easter cream egg instead. What the hell, there was reason to celebrate.

Mrs. Kopolous shook her head, but whether it was at the egg or life in general, Vicki couldn't tell. "You're making faces at the paper like you did when those little girls were killed."

"That was two years ago!" Two years and a lifetime.

"I remember two years. But this time it's not for you to get involved with, these things sucking blood." The register drawer slammed shut with unnecessary force. "This time it's unclean."

"It's never been *clean*," Vicki protested, tucking the papers under her arm.

"You know what I mean."

The tone left no room for argument. "Yeah. I know what you mean." She turned to go, paused, and turned back to the counter. "Mrs. Kopolous, do you believe in vampires?"

The older woman waved an expressive hand. "I don't not believe," she said, her brows drawn down for emphasis. "There are more things in heaven and earth. . . ."

Vicki smiled. "Shakespeare?"

Her expression didn't soften. "Just because it came from a poet, doesn't make it less true."

When Vicki got back to her apartment building, a three-story brownstone in the heart of Chinatown, it was 7:14 and the neighborhood was just beginning to wake up. She considered going for a run, before the carbon monoxide levels rose, but decided against it when an experimental breath plumed in the air. Spring might have officially arrived, but it'd be time enough to start running when the temperature reflected the season. Taking the stairs two at a time, she thanked the lucky genetic combination that gave her a jock's body with a minimum amount of maintenance. Although at thirty-one who knew how much longer that would last. . . .

Minor twinges of guilt sent her through a free weight routine while she listened to the 7:30 news.

By 8:28 she'd skimmed all three newspapers, drunk a pot and a half of tea, and readied the Foo Chan invoice for mailing. Tilting her chair back, she scrubbed at her glasses and let her world narrow into a circle of stucco ceiling. More things in heaven and earth. . . . She didn't know if she believed in vampires, but she definitely believed in her own senses, even if one of them had become less than reliable of late. Something strange had been down that tunnel, and nothing human could have struck that blow. A phrase from Wednesday's newspaper article kept running through her head: *A source in the Coroner's Office reports that the bodies of Terri Neal and DeVerne Jones had been drained of blood.* She knew it was none of her business. . . .

Brandon Singh had always been at his desk at the Coroner's Office every morning at 8:30. He had a cup of tea and a bagel and was, until about 8:45, perfectly approachable.

Although she no longer had any sort of an official position to call from, coroners *were* government appointments and she *was* still a taxpayer. She reached for her address book. *Hell, after Celluci how bad could it be?*

"Dr. Singh, please. Yes, I'll hold." *Why do they ask?* Vicki wondered, shoving at her glasses with her free hand. *It's not like you have a choice.*

"Dr. Singh here."

"Brandon? It's Vicki Nelson."

His weighty Oxford accent—his telephone voice—lightened. "Victoria? Good to hear from you. Been keeping busy since you left the force?"

"Pretty busy," she admitted, swinging her feet up on

a corner of the desk. Dr. Brandon Singh was the only person since the death of her maternal grandmother back in the seventies to call her Victoria. She'd never been able to decide whether it was old-world charm or sheer perversity as he knew full well how much she disliked hearing her full name. "I've started my own investigations company."

"I had heard a rumor to that effect, yes. But rumor . . ." In her mind's eye, Vicki could see his long surgeon's hands cutting through the air. ". . . rumor also had you stone blind and selling pencils on a street corner."

"Not. Quite." Anger leached the life from her voice.

Brandon's voice warmed in contrast. "Victoria, I *am* sorry. You know I'm not a tactful man, never had much chance to develop a bedside manner. . . ." It was an old joke, going back to their first meeting over the autopsy of a well-known drug pusher. "Now then," he paused for a swallow of liquid, the sound a discreet distance from the receiver, "what can I do for you?"

Vicki had never found Brandon's habit of getting right to the point with a minimum of small talk disconcerting and she appreciated him never demanding tact when he wouldn't give it. *Don't waste my time, I'm a busy man,* set the tone for every conversation he had. "That article in yesterday's paper, the blood loss in Neal and Jones, was it true?"

The more formal syntax returned. "I hadn't realized you were involved in the case?"

"I'm not, exactly. But I found the first body."

"Tell me."

So she did; information exchange was the coin of favors among city employees even if she no longer exactly qualified.

"And in your professional opinion?" Brandon asked when she finished, his voice carefully neutral.

"In my professional opinion," Vicki echoed both words and tone, "based on three years in homicide, I haven't got a clue what could have caused the wound I saw. Not a single blow ripping through skin and muscle and cartilage."

On the other end of the line, Brandon sighed. "Yes, yes, I know what happened and frankly, I have no more idea than you do. And I've been dealing with this sort of thing considerably longer than three years. To answer your original question, the newspaper story was essentially true; I don't know if it was a vampire or a vacuum cleaner, but Neal and Jones were drained nearly dry."

"Drained?" Not just massive blood loss, then, of the kind to be expected with a throat injury that severe. "Oh my God."

She heard Brandon take another swallow.

"Quite," he agreed dryly. "This will, of course, go no further."

"Of course."

"Then if you have all the information you require. . . ."

"Yes. Thank you, Brandon."

"My pleasure, Victoria."

She sat staring at nothing, considering implications until the phone began to beep, imperiously reminding her she hadn't yet hung up, jerking her out of her daze.

"Drained . . ." she repeated. "Shit." She wondered what the official investigation made of that. *No, be honest. You wonder what Mike Celluci made of it.* Well, she wasn't going to call and find out. Still, it was the sort of thing that friends might discuss if one of them was a cop and one of them used to be. *Except he's sure to say something cutting, especially if he thinks I'm using this whole incident as an excuse to hang around the fringes of the force.*

Was she?

She thought about it while she listened to the three-year-old upstairs running back and forth, back and forth across the living room. It was a soothing, all-is-right-with-the-universe kind of sound and she used its staccato beat to keep her thoughts moving, to keep her from bogging down in the self-pity that had blurred a good part of the last eight months.

No, she decided at last, she was not using these deaths as a way of trying to grab onto some of what she'd had to give up. She was curious, plain and simple. Curious the way anyone would be in a similar circumstance, the difference being that she had a way to satisfy her curiosity.

"And if Celluci doesn't understand that," she muttered as she dialed, "he can fold it sideways and stick it up his. . . . Good morning. Mike Celluci, please. Yes, I'll hold." *Someday,* she tucked the phone under her chin and tried to peel the paper off a very old Life Saver, *I'm going to say no, I won't hold, and send somebody's secretary into strong hysterics.*

"Celluci."

"Morning. It's Vicki."

"Yeah. So?" He definitely didn't sound thrilled. "You complicating my life with another body or is this a social call at . . ."

Vicki checked her watch, during the pause while Celluci checked his.

". . . nine oh two . . ."

"Eight fifty-eight."

He ignored her. ". . . on a Thursday morning?"

"No body, Celluci. I just wondered what you'd come up with so far."

"That's police information, Vicki, and in case you've forgotten, you're not a cop anymore."

The crack hurt but not as much as she expected. Well, two could play at that game.

"Come to a dead end, eh? A full stop?" She flipped over pages of the newspaper loud enough for him to hear the unmistakable rustle. "Paper seems to have come up with an answer." Shaking her head, she held the receiver away from her ear in order not to be deafened by a forcefully expressed opinion of certain reporters, their ancestors, and their descendants. She grinned. She was definitely enjoying this.

"Nice try, Mike, but I called the Coroner's Office and that report was essentially correct."

"Well, why don't I just read *my* report to you over the phone. Or I could send someone over with a copy of the file and no doubt you and your Nancy Drew detective kit can solve the case by lunch."

"Why don't we discuss this like intelligent human beings over dinner?" *Over dinner? Good God, was that my mouth?*

"Dinner?"

Oh, well. In for a penny in for a pound as Granny used to say. "Yeah, dinner, you know, where you sit down in the evening and stuff food in your mouth."

"Oh, dinner. Why didn't you say so?" Vicki could hear the smile in his voice and her mouth curved up in answer. Mike Celluci was the only man she'd ever met whose moods changed as quickly as hers. Maybe that was why. . . . "You buying?" He was also basically a cheap bastard.

"Why not. I'll deduct it as a business expense; consulting with the city's finest."

He snorted. "Took you long enough to remember that. I'll be by about seven."

"I'll be here."

She hung up, pushed her glasses up her nose, and wondered just what she thought she was doing. It had seemed, while they talked—*All right, while we indulged in the verbal sparring that serves us for conversation*—almost like the last eight months and the fights before hadn't happened. Or maybe it was just that their friendship was strong enough to pick up intact from where it had been dropped. Or maybe, just maybe, she'd managed to get a grip on her life.

"And I hope I haven't bitten off more than I can chew," she muttered to the empty apartment.

Three

Stumbling to the right to avoid annihilation by a loaded backpack, Norman Birdwell careened into a stocky young man in a leather York University jacket and found himself back in the corridor outside the lecture hall. Shifting his grip on the plastic handle of his attaché, he squared his narrow shoulders and tried again. He often thought that exiting students should be forced to move in orderly rows through the left side of the double doors so that students arriving early for the next class could enter unopposed through the right.

By sliding sideways between two young women, who, oblivious to Norman's presence, continued discussing the sexist unfairness of birth control and blow-dryers, he made it into the room and headed for his seat.

Norman liked to arrive early so he could sit in the exact center of the third row, his lucky seat ever since he'd written a perfect first year calculus paper in the spot. He was taking this evening sociology class because he'd overheard two jocks in the cafeteria mention it was a great way to meet girls. So far, he wasn't having much luck. Straightening his new leather tie, he wondered if perhaps he shouldn't ask for a jacket.

As he slid into his seat, his attaché jammed between two chair backs in the second row and jerked out of his hand. Bending to free it, his mechanical pencil slid free of his pocket protector and rolled back into the darkness.

"Oh, fuck," he muttered, dropping to his knees. He'd been experimenting with profanity lately, hoping it would make him sound more macho. There'd been no noticeable success.

There were legends about what lurked under the seats in York University lecture halls but all Norman found, beside his pencil—which he'd only had since Sunday night and didn't want to lose—was a neatly rolled copy of Wednesday's tabloid. Clipping the pencil back where it belonged, Norman spread the paper on his knee. The professor, he knew, would be up to fifteen minutes late; he'd have plenty of time to read the comics.

"VAMPIRE STALKS CITY!"

With trembling fingers, he opened it to the story.

"Get a load of Birdwell." The thick-necked young man elbowed his companion. "He's gone white as a ghost."

Rubbing bruised ribs, the recipient of this tender confidence peered down at the solitary figure in the third row of the hall. "How can you tell?" he grunted. "Ghost, geek; it's all the same."

"I never knew," Norman whispered down at the black type. "I swear to God, I never knew. It wasn't my fault."

He . . . no, it, had said it had to feed. Norman hadn't asked where or how. Maybe, he admitted now, because he hadn't wanted to know. *Don't let anyone see you,* had been his only instruction.

He peeled damp palms up off the newsprint and raised them, smudged and trembling, into the air as he vowed, "Never again, I promise, never again."

*   *   *

The gong sounded for another order of Peking Duck and while it reverberated through the restaurant, a mellow undertone to the conversations occurring in at least three different languages, Vicki raised a spoonful of hot-and-sour soup to her lips and stared speculatively at Mike Celluci. He'd been almost charming for this, the first half hour of the evening, and she'd had about as much of it as she could take.

She swallowed and gave him her best *don't give me*

any bullshit, buddy, I'm on to you smile. "So. Still holding tight to that ridiculous angel dust and Freddy Kruger claws theory?"

Celluci glanced down at his watch. "Thirty-two minutes and seventeen seconds." He shook his head ruefully, a thick brown curl dropping down over his eyes. "And here I bet Dave you couldn't last a half an hour. You just lost me five bucks, Vicki. Is that nice?"

"Quit complaining." She chased a bit of green onion around the edge of her bowl. "After all, I'm paying for dinner. Now, answer the question."

"And here I thought that you were after the pleasure of my company."

She really hated it when his voice picked up that sarcastic edge. Not having heard it for eight months hadn't lessened her dislike. "I'm going to pleasure your company right into the kitchen if you don't answer the question."

"Damn it, Vicki." His spoon slammed into the saucer, "Do we have to discuss this while we eat?"

Eating had nothing to do with it; they'd discussed every case they'd ever had, singly and collectively, over food. Vicki pushed her empty bowl to one side and laced her fingers together. It *was* possible that now she'd left the force he wouldn't discuss the homicides with her. It was possible, but not very likely. At least, she prayed it wasn't very likely. "If you can look me right in the eye," she said quietly, "and tell me you don't want to talk about this with me, I'll lay off."

Technically, he knew he should do exactly that—look her in the eye and tell her he didn't want to talk about it. The Criminal Investigations Bureau took a dim view of investigators who couldn't keep their mouths shut. But Vicki had been one of the best, three accelerated promotions and two citations attested to that, and more importantly, her record of solved crimes had been almost the highest in the department. Honesty forced him to admit, although he admitted it silently, that statistically her record was as good as his, he'd just been at it three years longer. *Do I throw away this resource?* he wondered as the silence lengthened. *Do I refuse to take*

*advantage of talent and skill just because the possessor of
those talents and skills has become a civilian?* He tried
to keep his personal feelings out of the decision.

He looked her right in the eye and said quietly,
"Okay, genius, you got a better idea than PCPs and
claws?"

"Difficult to come up with a worse one," she snorted,
leaning back to allow their waitress to replace the bowls
with steaming platters of food. Grateful for the chance
to regain her composure, Vicki toyed with a chopstick
and hoped he didn't realize how much this meant to her.
She hadn't realized it herself until her heart restarted
with his answer and she felt a part of herself she thought
had died when she'd left the force slowly begin to come
back to life. Her reaction, she knew, would have been
invisible to a casual observer but Mike Celucci was anything but that.

*Please, God, just let him think he's picking my brain.
Don't let him know how much I need this.*

For the first time in a long time, God appeared to
be listening.

"Your better idea?" Mike asked pointedly when they
were alone with their meal.

If he'd noticed her relief, he gave no sign and that was
good enough for Vicki. "It's a little hard to hypothesize
without all the information," she prodded.

He smiled and she understood, not for the first time,
why witnesses of either gender were willing to spill their
guts to this man. "Hypothesize. Big word. You been
doing crossword puzzles again?"

"Yeah, between tracking down international jewel
thieves. Spill it, Celluci."

If anything, there had been fewer clues at the second
scene than at the first. No prints save the victim's, no
trail, no one who saw the killer enter or exit the underground garage. "And the scene was hours old by the
time we arrived. . . ."

"You said the trail at the subway led into a workman's alcove?"

He nodded, scowling at a snow pea. "Blood all over

the back wall. The trail led into the alcove, but nothing led out."

"Behind the back wall?"

"You thinking of secret passageways?"

A little sheepishly, she nodded.

"All things considered, *that* would be an answer I could live with." He shook his head and the curl dropped forward again. "Nothing but dirt. We checked."

Although DeVerne Jones had been found with a scrap of torn leather clutched in his fist, dirt was pretty much all they'd found at the third site. Dirt, and a derelict that babbled about the apocalypse.

"Wait a minute . . ." Vicki frowned in concentration, then shoved her disturbed glasses back up her nose. "Didn't the old man at the subway say something about the apocalypse?"

"Nope. Armageddon."

"Same thing."

Celluci sighed with exaggerated force. "You trying to tell me that it's not one guy, it's four guys on horses? Thanks. You've been a lot of help."

"I suppose you've checked for some connection between the victims? Something to hang a motive on?"

"Motive!" He slapped his forehead with the heel of his hand. "Now why didn't I think of that?"

Vicki stabbed at a mushroom and muttered, "Smart ass."

"No, no connections, no discernible motive. We're still looking." He shrugged, a succinct opinion of what the search would turn up.

"Cults?"

"Vicki, I've talked to more weirdos and space cases in the last few days than I have in the last few years." He grinned. "Present company excepted, of course."

They were almost back to her apartment, her hand tucked in the crook of his arm to guide her through the darkness, when she asked, "Have you considered that there might be something in this vampire theory?"

She dug her heels in at his shout of laughter. "I'm serious, Celluci!"

"No, I'm Serious Celluci. You're out of your mind."
He dragged her back into step beside him. "Vampires
don't exist."

"You're sure of that? 'There are more things . . .' "

"Don't," he warned, "start quoting Shakespeare at
me. I've had the line quoted at me so often lately, I'm
beginning to think police brutality is a damned good
idea."

They turned up the path to Vicki's building.

"You've got to admit that a vampire fits all the parameters." Vicki no more believed it was a vampire than
Celluci did, but it had always been so easy to rattle his
cage. . . .

He snorted. "Right. Something's wandering around
the city in a tuxedo muttering, 'I vant to drink your
blood.' "

"You got a better suspect?"

"Yeah. A big guy on PCPs with clip-on claws."

"You're not back to *that* stupid theory again."

"Stupid!"

"Yeah. Stupid."

"You wouldn't recognize a logical progression of facts
if they bit you on the butt!"

"At least I'm not so caught up in my own cleverness
that I'm blind to outside possibilities!"

"Outside possibilities? You have no idea of what's
going on!"

"Neither do you!"

They stood and panted at each other for a few seconds
then Vicki shoved her glasses up her·nose and dug for
her keys. "You staying the night?"

It sounded like a challenge.

"Yeah. I am."

So did the response.

Sometime later, Vicki shifted to reach a particularly
sensitive area and decided, as she got the anticipated
inarticulate response, that there were times when you
really didn't need to *see* what you were doing and night
blindness mattered not in the least.

*   *   *

Captain Raymond Roxborough looked down at the lithe and cowering form of his cabin boy and wondered how he could have been so blind. Granted, he had thought young Smith very pretty, what with his tousled blue-black curls and his sapphire eyes, but never for a moment had he suspected that the boy was not a boy at all. Although, the captain had to admit, it was a neat solution to the somewhat distressing feelings he'd been having lately.

"I suppose you have an explanation for this," he drawled, leaning back against his cabin door and crossing sun-bronzed arms across his muscular chest.

The young lady—girl, really, for she could have been no more than seventeen—clutched her cotton shirt to the white swell of bosom that had betrayed her and with the other hand pushed damp curls, the other legacy of her interrupted wash, off her face.

"I needed to get to Jamaica," she said proudly, although her low voice held the trace of a quaver, "and this was the only way I could think of."

"You could have paid for your passage," the captain suggested dryly, his gaze traveling appreciatively along the delicate curve of her shoulders.

"I had nothing to pay with."

He straightened and stepped forward, smiling. "I think you underestimate your charms."

"Come on, Smith, kick him right in his windswept desire." Henry Fitzroy leaned back in his chair and rubbed at his temples. Just how much of a shit did he want the captain to be? Should the hero's better nature overcome his wanton lust or did he even have a better nature? And how much of a hero would he be without one?

"And frankly, my dear," he sighed, "I don't give a damn." He saved the night's work, then shut down the system. Usually he enjoyed the opening chapters of a new book, getting to know the characters, warping them to fit the demands of the plot, but this time. . . .

Rolling his chair back from the desk, he stared out his office window at the sleeping city. Somewhere out there, hidden by the darkness, a hunter stalked— blinded, maddened, driven by blood lust and hunger.

He'd sworn to stop it, but he hadn't the slightest idea how to start. How could the location of random slaughter be anticipated?

With another sigh, he stood. There'd been twenty-four hours without a death. Maybe the problem had taken care of itself. He grabbed his coat and headed out of the apartment.

The morning paper should be out by now, I'll grab one and . . . Waiting for the elevator, he checked his watch. 6:10. It was much later than he'd thought. . . . *and trust I can make it back inside without igniting.* Sunrise was around 6:30 if he remembered correctly. He wouldn't have much time, but he had to know if there had been another killing. If the load of completely irrational guilt he carried for not finding and stopping the child had gotten any heavier.

The national paper had a box just outside his building. The headline concerned a speech the Prime Minister had just made in the Philippines about north/south relations.

"And I bet he works on the south until at least mid-May." Henry said, drawing his leather trench coat tighter around his throat as a cold wind swept around the building and pulled tears from his eyes.

The tabloid's closest box was down the block and across the street. There wasn't really any need to look for the other local paper, Henry had every faith in the tabloid's headline. He waited at the light while the opening volley of the morning rush hour laid a nearly solid line of moving steel along Bloor Street, then crossed, digging for change.

"LEAFS LOSE BIG."

Death of playoff hopes, perhaps, but not a death Henry need worry about. With a sense of profound relief—lightly tinted with exasperation; the Leafs were in the worst division in the NHL, after all—he tucked the paper under his arm, turned, and realized the sun was about to clear the horizon.

He could feel it trembling on the edge of the world and it took all his strength not to panic.

The elevator, the red light, the headlines, all had taken more time than he had. How he had allowed this to happen after more than four hundred and fifty years of racing the sun to safety was not important now. Regaining the sanctuary of his apartment was the only thing that mattered. He could feel the heat of the sun on the edges of his consciousness, not a physical presence, not yet, although that and the burning would come soon enough, but an awareness of the threat, of how close he stood to death.

The light he needed was red again, a small mocking sun in a box. The pounding of his heart counting off the seconds, Henry flung himself onto the street. Brakes squealed and the fender of a wildly swerving van brushed against his thigh like a caress. He ignored the sudden pain and the driver's curses, slammed his palm against the hood of a car almost small enough to leap, and dove through a space barely a prayer wider than his twisting body.

The sky turned gray, then pink, then gold.

Leather soles slamming against the pavement, Henry raced along shadow, knowing that fire devoured it behind him and lapped at his heels. Terror fought with the lethargy that daylight wrapped around his kind, and terror won. He reached the smoked glass door to his building seconds before the sun.

It touched only the back of one hand, too slowly snatched to safety.

Cradling the blistered hand against his chest, Henry used the pain to goad himself toward the elevator. Although the diffused light could no longer burn, he was still in danger.

"You all right, Mr. Fitzroy?" The guard frowned with concern as he buzzed open the inner door.

Unable to focus, Henry forced his head around to where he knew the guard would be. "Migraine," he whispered and lurched forward.

The purely artificial light in the elevator revived him a little and he managed to walk down the corridor dragging only a part of his weight along the wall. He feared for a moment that the keys were beyond his remaining dexterity, but somehow he got the heavy door open, closed, and locked behind him. Here was safety.

Safety. That word alone carried him into the shelter of the bedroom where thick blinds denied the sun. He swayed, sighed, and finally let go, collapsing across the bed and allowing the day to claim him.

* * *

"Vicki, please!"

Vicki frowned, a visit to the ophthalmologist never put her in what could be called a good mood and all this right-eye, left-eye focusing was giving her a major headache. "What?" she growled through gritted teeth—only incidentally a result of the chin rest.

"You're looking directly at the test target."

"So?"

Dr. Anderson hid a sigh and, with patience developed during the raising of two children, explained, not for the first time, her tone noncommittal and vaguely soothing. "Looking directly at the test target negates the effects of the test and we'll just have to do it all over again."

And they would, too. Over and over again if necessary. Holding back a sharp comment behind the thin line of her lips, Vicki attempted to cooperate.

"Well?" she prodded at last as Dr. Anderson flicked off the perimeter light and motioned for her to raise her head.

"It hasn't gotten any worse. . . ."

Vicki leaned back, watching the doctor's face. "Has it gotten any better?" she asked pointedly.

This time, Dr. Anderson didn't bother to hide the sigh. "Vicki, as I've told you before, retinitis pigmentosa doesn't get better. Ever. It only gets worse. Or," she rolled the perimeter back against the wall, "if you're very lucky, the degeneration reaches a point and goes no further."

"Have I reached that point?"

"Only time will tell. You've been pretty lucky already," she continued, raising a hand to forestall Vicki's next comment, "in many cases, this disease is accompanied by other types of neurodegenerative conditions."

"Deafness, mild retardation, premature senility, and truncal obesity." Vicki snorted. "We went through all this in the beginning, and none of it changes the fact that I have effectively no night vision, the outside edge of my peripheral vision has moved in twenty-five degrees, and I've suddenly become myopic."

"*That* might have happened anyway."

Vicki shoved her glasses up her nose. "Very comforting. When can I expect to go blind?"

The nails of Dr. Anderson's right hand beat a tattoo against her prescription pad. "You may *never* go blind and, in spite of your condition, at the moment you have perfectly functional vision. You mustn't let this make you bitter."

"My condition," Vicki snarled, standing and reaching for her coat, "as you call it, caused me to leave a job I loved that made a difference for the better in the slime-pit this city is becoming and if it's all the same to you, I think I'd rather be bitter." She didn't quite slam the door on the way out.

* * *

"What's the matter, darling, you don't look happy?"

"It hasn't been a great day, Mrs. Kopolous."

The older woman clicked her tongue and shook her head at the family size bag of cheese balls Vicki had laid on the counter. "So I see, so I see. You should eat real food, darling, if you want to feel better. This stuff is no good for you. And it makes your fingers orange."

Vicki scooped up her change and dropped it into the depths of her purse. Soon she'd have to deal with the small fortune jangling around down there. "Some moods, Mrs. Kopolous, only junk food can handle."

The phone was ringing when she reached her apartment.

"Yeah, what?"

"There's something about the sound of your dulcet tones that makes this whole wretched day worthwhile."

"Stuff a sock in it, Celluci." Phone balanced under her chin, Vicki struggled out of her coat. "Whadda you want?"

"My, my, sounds like someone's wearing the bishop's shoes."

Against every inclination, Vicki grinned. His use of that particular punch line in conversation always did it to her. He knew it, too. "No, I did not get up on the wrong side of the bed this morning," she told him, hooking her office chair over and throwing herself down into it. "As you very well know. But I did just get back from a visit to the ophthalmologist."

"Ah." She could picture him leaning back, his feet up on the desk. Every superior he'd ever had had tried to break him of the habit with no noticeable success. "The eye doctor of doom. Is it any better?"

If he'd sounded sympathetic, she'd have thrown the phone across the room but he only sounded interested. "It doesn't get any better, Celluci."

"Oh, I don't know; I read this article that said large doses of vitamin A and E can improve the visual field and enhance dark adaptation." He was obviously quoting.

Vicki couldn't decide whether to be touched or furious that he'd been reading up. Given her mood. . . . "Do something more useful with your time, Celluci, only abetalipoproteinaemia RP includes biochemical defects," he hadn't been the only one reading up, "and that isn't what I've got."

"Abetalipo*protein*aemia," he corrected her pronunciation, "and excuse me for caring. I also found out that a number of people lead completely normal lives with what you've got." He paused and she heard him take a drink of what was undoubtedly cold coffee. "Not," he continued, his voice picking up an edge, "that you ever lived what could be called a normal life."

She ignored the last comment, picked up a black marker and began venting frustrations with it on the back of her credit card bill. "I'm living a completely normal life," she snapped.

"Running away and hiding?" The tone missed sarcasm but not by very much. "You could've stayed on the force. . . ."

"I *knew* you'd start again." She spat the words from between clenched teeth, but Mike Celluci's angry voice overrode the diatribe she was about to begin and the bitterness in it shut her up.

". . . but oh no, you couldn't stand the thought that you wouldn't be the hot-shit investigator anymore, the fair-haired girl with all the answers, that you'd just be a part of the team. You quit because you couldn't stand not being on the top of the pile and if you weren't on top, if you couldn't be on top, you weren't going to play! So you ran away. You took your pail and your shovel and you fucking quit! You walked out on me, Nelson, not just the job!"

Through all the fights—after the diagnosis and after her resignation—*that* was what he'd wanted to say. It summed up the hours of arguing, the screaming matches, the slammed doors. Vicki knew it, knew it the way she knew when she found the key, the little seemingly insignificant thing that solved the case. Everything about that last sentence said, *this is it.*

"You'd have done the same thing, Celluci," she said quietly and although her knuckles were white around the receiver, she set it gently back on the phone. Then she threw the marker in her other hand across the room.

Her anger went with it.

He really cares about you, Vicki. Why is that such a problem?

Because lovers are easy to get and friends good enough to scream at are a lot rarer.

Running both hands through her hair, she sighed. He was right and she'd admitted as much by her response. As soon as he realized she was right as well, they could go on building the new parameters of their relationship. Unless, it suddenly occurred to her, last night had been the farewell performance that enabled him to finally come clean.

If it was, she pushed her glasses up her nose, *at least I had the last word.* As such things went, it wasn't much of a comfort.

* * *

"Well, if it isn't old Norman. How you doing, Norman? Mind if we sit down?" Without waiting for an

answer the young man hooked a chair out from under
the table and sat. The four other members of his party
noisily followed his lead.

When the scramble for space ended, Norman found
himself crammed between the broad shoulders of two
jocks he knew only as Roger and Bill, the three of them
staring across the round table at three young ladies. He
recognized the blonde—he usually saw her hanging on
Roger's arm—and as the girl next to Bill was being awfully friendly he supposed she was with him. That left
one extra. He grinned wolfishly at her. He'd been practicing the grin in his bathroom mirror.

She looked puzzled, then snorted and turned away.

"It was real nice of old Norman to keep this table for
us, wasn't it, Bill?"

"It sure was." Bill leaned a little closer and Norman
gasped for breath as his available space narrowed drastically. "If it wasn't for old Norman, we'd be sitting on
the floor."

Norman looked around. The Friday night crowd at the
Cock and Bull had filled the basement pub. "Well, I,
uh. . . ." He shrugged. "I, uh, knew you were coming."

"Of course you did." Bill grinned at him, a little dis-
concerted to find that the Birdwell-nerd was at least as
tall as he was. "I was saying to Roger here before we
came in, it wouldn't be Friday night if we didn't spend
part of it with old Norman."

Roger laughed and all three of the girls grinned. Norman didn't get the joke, but he preened at the attention.

He bought the first round of beer. "After all, it's my
table."

"And the only empty one in the place," the blonde
muttered.

He bought the second round as well. "Because I've
got lots and lots of money." The wad of twenties he
pulled out of the pocket of his windbreaker—five thousand dollars in small unmarked bills had been the third
thing he'd asked for—caused a simultaneous dropping
of jaws around the table.

"Jesus Christ, Norman, what did you do, rob a bank?"

"I didn't have to," Norman said airily. "And there's plenty more where that came from."

He insisted on buying the third and fourth rounds and on switching to imported beer. "Imported beer is classier," he confided to the shoulder of Roger's leather jacket, Roger having moved his ear out of range. "It really gets the chicks."

"Chicks?" The echo had a dangerous edge to it.

"Consider the source, Helen." Bill deftly removed the glass from her hand—both hand and glass having been threateningly raised—and drained it. "You'd just be wasting the beer."

The five burst out laughing again and again, not understanding, Norman joined in. No one would think he wasn't with it.

When they started getting up, he rose with them. The room swayed. He'd never had four beers in quick succession before. In fact, he wasn't entirely certain he'd ever had four beers before. "Where we going?"

"*We* are going to a private party," Bill told him, a beefy hand pushing him back into his seat.

"You just stay here, Norman," Roger patted him on the other shoulder.

Confused, Norman looked from one to the other. They were leaving without him?

"Jesus, it's like kicking a puppy," Bill muttered.

Roger nodded in agreement. "Uh, look, Norman, it's invitation only. We'd bring you if we could. . . ."

They *were* leaving without him. He pointed across the table, his voice an accusatory whine, "But she's supposed to be for me."

Expressions of guilty sympathy changed to disgust and Norman quickly found himself alone, Helen's voice drifting back from the door, somehow audible in spite of the noise level in the pub. "I'd give him back his beer if I didn't hate vomiting so much."

Trying unsuccessfully to flag the waitress, Norman scowled into the beer rings on the table. She *was* supposed to be for him. He knew she was. They were cheating him. With the tip of a shaking finger, he drew a five pointed star in the spilled liquid on the tabletop, his vows of the day before forgotten. He'd show them.

His stomach protested suddenly and he lurched toward the bathrooms, hand clutched over his mouth.

I'll show them, he thought, his head dangling over the toilet. *But maybe . . . not tonight.*

* * *

Henry handed the young man seated just inside the door a twenty. "What's on for tonight?" He didn't quite have to yell to make himself heard over the music but, then, the night was young.

"The usual." Three rolls of tickets were pulled from the cavernous left pocket of the oversized suit jacket while the money slid into the right. A number of after-hours clubs had been switching to tickets so that if, or more likely when, they were busted they could argue that they hadn't been selling drinks. Just tickets.

"Guess it'll have to be a usual, then."

"Right. Two trendy waters." The pair of tickets changed hands. "You know, Henry, you're paying a hell of a lot for piss and bubbles."

Henry grinned down at him and swept an arm around the loft. "I'm paying for the ambience, Thomas."

"Ambience my ass," Thomas snorted genially. "Hey, I just remembered, Alex got a case of halfway decent burgundy. . . ."

It wouldn't have taken a stronger man than Henry Fitzroy to resist. "No thanks, Thomas, I don't drink . . . wine." He turned to face the room and, just for a moment, saw another gathering.

The clothes, peacock bright velvets, satins, and laces turned the length of the room into a glittering kaleidoscope of color. He hated coming to Court and would appear only when his father demanded it. The false flattery, the constant jockeying for position and power, the soul destroying balancing act that must be performed to keep both the block and the pyre at bay; all this set the young Duke of Richmond's teeth on edge.

As he made his way across the salon, each face that turned to greet him wore an identical expression—a mask

*of brittle gaiety over ennui, suspicion, and fear in about
an equal mix.*

Then the heavy metal beat of Anthrax drove "Green-
sleeves" back into the past. The velvet and jewels spun
away into black leather, paste, and plastic. The brittle
gaiety now covered ennui alone. Henry supposed it was
an improvement.

I should be on the street, he thought, making his way to
the kitchen/bar, brushing past discussions of the recent
killings and the creatures they had been attributed to. *I
will not find the child up here. . . .* But the child hadn't
fed since Tuesday night and so perhaps had passed
through the frenzy and moved to the next part of its
metamorphosis. *But the parent. . . .* His hands clenched
into fists, the right pulling painfully against the bandage
and the blisters beneath it. *The parent must still be
found.* That he could do up here. Twice before in Alex's
loft he had tasted another predator in the air. Then, he
had let it go, the blood scent of so many people made
tracking a competitor a waste of time. Tonight, if it happened again, he would waste the time.

Suddenly, he noticed that a path was opening before
him as he made his way across the crowded room and
he hastily schooled his expression. The men and women
gathered here, with faces painted and precious metals
dangling, were still close enough to their primitive begin-
nings to recognize a hunter walking among them.

*That's three times now; the guard, the sun, and this. You'll
bring the stakes down on yourself if you're not more careful,
you fool.* What was the matter with him lately?

"Hey, Henry, long time since you bin by." Alex, the
owner of the loft wrapped a long, bare arm around Henry's shoulders, shoved an open bottle of water into his
hand, and steered him deftly away from the bar. "I got
someone who needs to see you, mon."

"Someone who *needs* to see me?" Henry allowed himself to be steered. It was the way most people dealt with
Alex, resistance just took too much energy. "Who?"

Alex grinned down from his six-foot-four vantage
point and winked broadly. "Ah, now, that would be tel-
lin'. Whach you do to your hand?"

Henry glanced down at the bandage. Even in the dim light of the studio it seemed to glow against the black leather of his cuff. "Burned myself."

"Burns is bad stuff, mon. Were you cookin'?"

"You could say that." His lips twitched although he sternly told himself it wasn't funny.

"What's the joke?"

"It'd take too long to explain. How about you explaining something to me?"

"You ahsk, mon. I answer."

"Why the fake Jamaican accent?"

"Fake?" Alex's voice rose above the music and a half a dozen people ducked as he windmilled his free arm. "Fake? There's nothing fake about this accent, mon. I'm gettin' back to my roots."

"Alex, you're from Halifax."

"I got deeper roots than that, you betcha." He gave the shorter man a push forward and, dropping the accent, added, "Here you go, shrimp, delivered as ordered."

The woman sitting on the steps to Alex's locked studio stood considerably shorter even than Henry's five six. Her lack of height, combined with baggy jeans and an oversized sweater, gave her a waiflike quality completely at odds with the cropped platinum hair and the intensity of her expression.

Sliding out from Alex's arm, Henry executed a perfect sixteenth century court bow—not that anyone in the room could identify it as such. "Isabelle," he intoned gravely.

Isabelle snorted, reached out, grabbed his lapels, and yanked his mouth against hers.

Henry returned the kiss enthusiastically, skillfully parrying her tongue away from the sharp points of his teeth. He hadn't been certain he was going to feed tonight. He was certain now.

"Well, if you two are going to indulge in such rampant heterosexuality, in *my* house yet, I'm going." With an exaggerated limp-wristed wave, Alex sashayed off into the crowd.

"He'll change personalities again before he gets to the

door," Henry observed settling himself on the step. The length of their thighs touched and he could feel his hunger growing.

"Alex has more masks than anyone I know," Isabelle agreed, retrieving her beer bottle and picking at the label.

Henry stroked one finger along the curve of her brow. It had been bleached near white to match her hair. "We all wear masks."

Isabelle raised the brow out from under his finger. "How profound. And do we all unmask at midnight?"

"No." He couldn't stop the melancholy from sounding in his voice as he realized the source of his recent discontent. It had been so long, so very long, since he'd been able to trust someone with the reality of what he was and all that meant. So long since he'd been able to find a mortal he could build a bond with based on more than sex and blood. And that a child could be created out of the deepest bond that vampire and mortal could share, then abandoned, sharpened his loneliness to a cutting edge.

He felt Isabelle's hand stroke his cheek, saw the puzzled compassion on her face, and with an inward curse realized his mask had slipped for the second time that night. If he didn't find someone who could accept him soon, he feared the choice would be taken from him, his need exposing him whether he willed it or not.

"So," with an effort, he brought himself back to the moment, "how was the gig?"

"It was March. It was Sudbury." She shrugged, returning to the moment with him, if that was how he wanted it. "Not much else to add."

If you can't share the reality, there are worse things than having someone to share the masks. His gaze dropped to a faint line of blue disappearing beneath the edge of her sweater and the thought of the blood moving so close beneath the surface quickened his breath. It was hunger, not lust, but he supposed in the end they were much the same thing. "How long will you be in town?"

"Only tonight and tomorrow."

"Then we shouldn't waste the time we have."

She twined her fingers in his, carefully ignoring the bandage, and pulled him with her as she stood. "I thought you'd never ask."

* * *

Saturday night, at 11:15, Norman realized he was out of charcoal for the hibachi and the only local store he'd been able to find it in had closed at nine. He considered substitutions and then decided he'd better not mess with a system that worked.

Saturday night passed quietly.

Sunday night. . . .

* * *

"Damn. Damn! DAMN!"

Mrs. Kopolous clicked her tongue and frowned. Not at Vicki's profanity, as she might have on any other day, but at the headline of the tabloid now lying on her counter.

"VAMPIRE KILLS STUDENT: Young man found drained in York Mills."

Four

"Good God, would you look at old Norman."

"Why?" Roger pulled his head out of his locker and turned around. He could feel his jaw quite literally drop. " 'Good God' doesn't quite cover it, my man. I wish Bill were here to see this."

"Where is he?"

Roger shrugged, not taking his eyes from the sartorial splendor of Norman Birdwell. "Beats me. But he'll shit if he misses this."

Norman, conscious of eyes upon him, threw a bit more of a swagger into his walk. The chain hanging from his new black leather jacket chimed softly against the small of his back. He squinted down at the sterling silver toe caps on his authentic style cowboy boots and wondered if maybe he shouldn't have gotten spurs as well. His new black jeans, tighter than he'd ever worn before, made an almost smug shik shik sound as the inseams rubbed together.

He'd shown them. Thought he wasn't cool, did they? Thought he was some kind of a nerd, did they? Well, they'd be thinking differently now. Norman's chin went up. They wanted cool? He'd show them *cold*. Tonight he was going to ask for a red Porsche. He'd learn to drive later.

"What the hell is that?"

Roger grinned. "Now aren't you glad you weren't any later?" he asked, shoving a friendly elbow into Bill's ribs. "Kinda takes your breath away, doesn't it?"

"If you mean it makes me want to gag, you're close."

Bill sagged against his locker and shook his head. "How the hell is he paying for all of that?"

"So go ask him."

"Why not. . . ." Bill straightened and stepped away from his locker just as Norman passed by.

Norman saw him, allowed their eyes to meet for a second, then moved on, chortling silently to himself, *"Ha! Snubbed you. Let's see how you like it."*

The question of payment dead in his mouth, Bill stood staring until Roger moved up beside him and slugged him in the arm.

"Hey, what's wrong?"

Bill shook his head. "There's something different about Birdwell."

Roger snorted. "Yeah, new threads and an attitude. But underneath he's the same old Norman the Nerd."

"Yeah, I guess you're right." But he wasn't. And it wasn't something Bill could explain. He felt as though he'd reached under the bed and something rotten had squished through his fingers—a normal, everyday action gone horribly awry.

Norman, aware he'd made an impression—Norman, who in a fit of pique had decided he didn't care if a stranger had to die—Norman strutted on.

* * *

"Victoria Nelson?"

"Yes?" Vicki peered down at the young woman—*girl, really, if she's out of her teens it's by hours only*—standing outside her apartment door. "If you're selling something. . . ."

"Victoria Nelson, the Private Investigator?"

Vicki considered it a moment before answering and then said slowly, "Yes. . . ."

"I have a job for you."

The words were delivered with the intensity only the very young can muster and Vicki found herself hiding a smile.

The girl tossed unnaturally brilliant red curls back off her face. "I can pay, if that's what you're worried about."

As the question of money hadn't even begun to cross Vicki's mind, she grunted noncommittally. They locked eyes for a moment—*tinted contacts, I thought so. Well, they go with the hair.*—then she added, in much the same noncommittal tone, "Most people call first."

"I thought about it." The shrug was so minimal as to be almost nonexistent and her voice was completely non-apologetic. "I figured the case would be harder to turn down in person."

Vicki found herself holding the door open wider. "I suppose you'd better come in." Work wasn't so scarce she had to take jobs from children, but it wouldn't hurt to hear what the girl had to say. "Another thirty seconds in the hall and Mr. Chin'll be showing up to see what's going on."

"Mr. Chin?"

"The old man who lives downstairs likes to know what's going on, likes to pretend he doesn't speak English."

Sliding past Vicki in the narrow hall, the girl sniffed, obviously disapproving. "Maybe he *doesn't* speak English," she pointed out.

This time, Vicki didn't bother to hide her smile. "Mr. Chin has been speaking English a lot longer than both of us have been alive. His parents came to Vancouver in the late 1880s. He used to teach high school. He still teaches English as a Second Language at the Chinese Community Center."

Bright green eyes narrowed accusingly and the girl glared up at Vicki. "I don't like being patronized," she said.

Vicki nodded as she closed the door. "Neither do I."

During the silence that followed, Vicki could almost hear their conversation being replayed, each phrase, each word tested for nuance.

"Oh," the girl said at last. "Sorry." Then her brow unfurrowed and she grinned as she offered a compromise. "I won't do it anymore if you'd don't."

"Deal." Vicki led the way through her tiny living room, pushing her leather recliner back upright as she passed, to her equally tiny office. She'd never actually had a client, or potential client, in the office before and there were a couple of unanticipated problems. "I'll, uh, get another chair from the kitchen."

"It's okay. This is fine." Shrugging out of her coat she settled both herself and it on Vicki's weight bench. "Now, about this job. . . ."

"Not yet." Vicki pulled her own chair out from the desk and sat down. "First, about you. Your name is?"

"Coreen, Coreen Fergus." She continued on the same breath, obviously feeling that her name covered all the necessary details. "And I want you to find that vampire that's been terrorizing the city."

"Right." It was too early on a Monday and the latest death was too close. "Did Michael Celluci put you up to this?"

"Who?"

"Never mind." Shaking her head, Vicki stood. "Look, I don't know *who* put you up to this but you can go back to them and. . . ."

"Ian Reddick was my . . ." She frowned, searching for a word that would give the relationship its proper weight. ". . . lover."

"Ian Reddick," Vicki repeated and sat down again. Ian Reddick, the first victim. The body she'd found mutilated in the Eglinton West subway station.

"I want you to find the thing that killed him."

"Look, Coreen," her voice dropped into the professional "comfort tone" that police officers worldwide had to master, "I recognize how upset you must be, but don't you think that's a job for the authorities?"

"No."

There was something utterly intractable in that "no." Vicki pushed her glasses up her nose and searched for a response while Coreen continued.

"They insist on looking for a man, refusing to acknowledge that the paper might be right; refusing to consider anything outside their narrow little world view."

"Refusing to consider that the killer might actually be a vampire?"

"Right."

"The paper doesn't really believe it's a vampire either, you know."

Coreen tossed her hair back off her face. "So? The facts still fit. The blood is still missing. I bet Ian would have been drained dry if he hadn't been found so quickly."

She doesn't know it was me. Thank God. And again she saw him, his face a clichéd mask of terror above the gaping red wound that was his throat. Gaping red wound . . . no, more as though the whole front of his throat had been ripped away. Not ripped through, ripped away. *That* was what had been missing; the incongruity that had been nagging at her for over a week now. Where was the front of Ian Reddick's throat?

". . . so will you?"

Vicki slowly surfaced from memory. "Let me get this straight. You want me to find Ian's killer, working under the assumption that it really is a vampire? Bats, coffins, the whole bit."

"Yes."

"And once I've found it, I drive a stake through its heart?"

"Creatures of the night can hardly be brought to trial," Coreen pointed out reasonably but with a martial light in her eye. "Ian must be avenged."

Don't get sad, get even. It was a classic solution to grief and one Vicki didn't altogether disapprove of. "Why me?" she asked.

Coreen sat up straighter. "You were the only female private investigator in the yellow pages."

That, at least, made sense and explained the eerie coincidence of Coreen showing up in the office of the woman who'd found Ian's body. *"Out of all the gin joints in all the. . . ."* She couldn't remember the rest of the quote but she was beginning to understand how Bogart had felt. "It wouldn't be cheap." *What am I cautioning her for? I am not going vampire hunting.*

"I can afford the best. Daddy pays me a phenomenal amount of guilt money. He ran off with his executive assistant when I was in junior high."

Vicki shook her head. "Mine ran off with his secretary

when I was in sixth grade and I never got a cent out of
him. Times change. Was she young and pretty?"

"He," Coreen corrected. "And yes, very pretty.
They've opened a new law practice in the Bahamas."

"As I said, times change." Vicki pushed her glasses
up her nose and sighed. Vampire hunting. Except it
wouldn't have to be that. Just find whoever, or whatever,
killed Ian Reddick. Exactly what she'd be doing if she
were still on the force. Lord knew they were underman-
nned and could use the help.

Coreen, who had kept her gaze locked on the older
woman's face, smiled triumphantly and dug for her
checkbook.

* * *

"Michael Celluci, please."

"One moment."

Vicki tapped her nails against the side of the phone
as she waited for the call to be put through. Ian Reddick's throat had been missing and Celluci, the arrogant
shit, hadn't thought to mention whether it had been
found or if the other bodies were in the same condition.
She didn't really care at this point if he wasn't speaking
to her 'cause she was bloody well going to speak to him.

"Criminal Investigation Bureau, Detective-Sergeant
Graham."

"Dave? It's Vicki Nelson. I need to talk to Celluci."

"He's not here right now, Vicki. Can I help?"

From her brief experience with him, Vicki knew Dave
to be, if possible, a worse liar than she was. And if he
couldn't lie convincingly for important things he certainly couldn't do it just to protect his partner's ass.
Trust Celluci to get out before the heat came down. "I
need a favor."

"Shoot."

The wording became crucial here. It had to sound like
she knew more than she did or Dave might clam up and
retreat to the official party line. Although, with luck,
the acquired habit of answering her questions could last
around the department for years. "The hunk of throat
missing from the first body, did anyone ever find it?"

"Nope."

So far so good. "What about the others?"

"Not a sign."

"Not even last night's?"

"Not yet anyway. Why?"

"Just sitting here wondering. Thanks, Dave. Tell your partner from me that he's a tight-lipped horse's ass." She hung up and stared at the far wall. Maybe Celluci had been holding the information back to ensure he had bargaining power in the future. Maybe. Maybe he quite honestly forgot to tell her. Ha! Maybe pigs would fly, but she doubted it.

Right now, she had more important things to consider. Like what kind of creature walked off with six square inches of throat as well as twelve pints of blood?

The subway roared out of Eglinton West toward Lawrence and, with the station momentarily deserted, Vicki strode purposefully for the workman's access at the southern end of the northbound platform. This was now her case and she couldn't stand working with second-hand information. She'd see the alcove where the killer allegedly disappeared for herself.

At the top of the short flight of concrete stairs, she paused, her blood pounding unnaturally loudly in her ears. She had always considered herself immune to foolish superstitions, race memories, and night terrors, but faced with the tunnel, stretching dark and seemingly endless like the lair of some great worm, she was suddenly incapable of taking the final step off the platform. The hair on the back of her neck rose as she remembered how, on the night Ian Reddick had died, she'd been certain that something deadly lingered in the tunnel. The feeling itself hadn't returned, but the memory replayed with enough strength to hold her.

This is ridiculous. Pull yourself together, Nelson. There's nothing down in that tunnel that could hurt you. Her right foot slid forward half a step. *The worst thing you're likely to run into is a TTC official and a trespassing charge.* Her left foot moved up and passed the right. *Good God, you're acting like some stupid teenager*

in a horror movie. Then she stood on the first step. The
second. The third. Then she was on the narrow concrete
strip that provided a safe passage along the outside rail.

See. Nothing to it. She wiped suddenly sweaty palms
on her coat and dug in her purse for her flashlight, then,
with the satisfyingly solid weight of it in her hand,
flooded the tunnel with light. She would have preferred
not to use it, away from the harsh fluorescents of the
station, the tunnel existed more in a surreal twilight than
a true darkness, but her night-sight had deteriorated to
the point where even twilight had become impenetrable.
The anger her condition always caused wiped away the
last of the fear.

She rather hoped something was skulking in her path.
For starters, she'd feed it the flashlight.

Pushing her glasses up her nose, her gaze locked on
the beam of light, Vicki moved carefully along the access
path. If the trains were on schedule—and while the TTC
wasn't up to Mussolini, it did all right—the next one
wouldn't be along for another, she checked the glowing
dial of her watch, eight minutes. Plenty of time.

She reached the first workman's alcove with six minutes remaining and sniffed disapprovingly at the evidence of police investigation. "Sure, boys," she muttered,
playing the light around the concrete walls, "mess it up
for the next person."

The hole Celluci's team had dug was about waist level
in the center of the back wall and about eight inches in
diameter. Stepping over chips of concrete, Vicki leaned
forward for a better look. There was, as Celluci said,
nothing but dirt behind the excavation.

"So if he didn't come in here," she frowned, "where
did he. . . ." Then she noticed the crack that ran the
length of the wall, into and out of the exploratory hole.
A closer look brought her nose practically in contact
with the concrete. The faint hint of a familiar smell had
her digging for her Swiss army knife and carefully
scraping the edges of the dark recess.

The flakes on the edge of the stainless steel blade
showed red-brown in the flashlight beam. They could
have been rust. Vicki touched one to the tip of her

tongue. They could have been rust, but they weren't. She had a pretty good idea whose blood she'd found but brushed the remaining flakes into a plastic sandwich bag anyway. Then she squatted and ran the blade up under the crack at the top edge of the hole.

Even as she did it, she wasn't sure why. Most of Ian's blood had been sprayed over the subway station wall. There could not have been enough blood on the killer's clothes to have soaked all the way through a crack in six inches of concrete even if he'd been wearing paper towels and had remained plastered against the wall for the entire night.

When she pulled out the knife, mixed in with dirt and bits of cement, were similar red-brown flakes. These went into another bag and then she quickly repeated the procedure at the bottom edge of the hole with the same results.

The roar of the subway became a welcome, normal kind of terror for the only explanation Vicki could come up with, as the alcove shook and a hundred tons of steel hurtled past, was that whatever killed Ian Reddick somehow passed through the crack in the concrete wall.

And *that* was patently ridiculous.

Wasn't it?

As a large producer and wholesaler of polyester clothing, Sigman's Incorporated didn't exactly run a high security building. Since the murder of Terri Neal in the underground parking lot, they'd tried to tighten things up.

In spite of four and a half pages of new admittance regulations, the guard in the lobby glanced up as Vicki strode past, then went back to his book. In gray corduroy pants, black desert boots, and her navy pea jacket she could have been any one of the hundreds of women who came through the area every day and he was neither expected nor encouraged to stop all of them. She certainly wasn't the press—the guard had grown adept at spotting the ladies and gentlemen of the fifth estate and herding them off to the proper authorities. She didn't look like a cop, and besides, cops always checked in.

She looked like she knew where she was going, so the guard decided not to interfere. In his opinion, the world could use a few more people who knew where they were going.

At 2:30 in the afternoon, the underground parking garage was empty of people which explained pretty much exactly why Vicki was there at that time. She stepped off the elevator and frowned up at the whining fluorescent lights. *Why the hell don't they have security cameras down here?* she wondered as the echoes of her footsteps bounced off the stained concrete walls.

Even without the scuffed and faded chalk marks she could tell where the body had fallen. The surrounding cars had been crammed together, leaving an open area over three spaces wide, as if violent death were somehow contagious.

She found what she'd come looking for tucked almost under an ancient rust and blue sedan. Her lower lip caught between her teeth, she pulled out her knife and knelt beside the crack. The blade slid in its full six inches, but the bottom of the crack was deeper still. The red-brown flakes that came up on the steel had most certainly not dropped off the wreck.

She sat back on her heels and frowned. "I really, really don't like the looks of this."

Fishing a marble from the bottom of her bag, she placed it on one of the remaining chalk marks and gave it a little push. It rolled toward the wall, moving away from the crack at almost a forty-five degree angle. Further experiments produced similar results. Blood, or for that matter anything else, could not have traveled from the body to the crack in any way that might be called natural.

"Not that there's anything even remotely natural about any of this," she muttered, tucking this third sandwich bag of dried blood in beside the others and crawling after her marble.

Rather than go back through the building, she climbed up the steeply graded driveway and out onto St. Clair Avenue West.

"Excuse me?"

The attendant in the booth looked up from his magazine.

Vicki waved a hand back down the drive in the general direction of the underground garage. "Do you know what's under the bottom layer of concrete?"

He looked in the direction she indicated, looked back at her, and repeated, "Under the concrete?"

"Yeah."

"Dirt, lady."

She smiled and eased around the barricade. "Thanks. You've been a great help. I'll show myself out."

The chain link fence protested slightly and sagged forward under Vicki's weight as she peered down into the construction site. It was, at the moment, little more than a huge hole in the ground filled with smaller holes, filled with muddy water. All the machinery appeared to have been removed and work stopped. Whether because of the murder or the weather, Vicki had no way of knowing.

"Well," she shoved her hands down into the pockets of her coat, "there's definitely dirt." If there was any blood, it was beyond finding.

"No problem, Vicki." Rajeet Mohadevan tucked the three sandwich bags into the pocket of her lab coat. "I can run them through before I head home tonight with no one the wiser. Are you going to be around the building?"

"No." Vicki saw the flicker of sympathy across the researcher's face but decided to ignore it. Rajeet was doing her a favor, after all. "If I'm not at home, you can leave a message on the machine."

"Same number?"

"Same number."

Rajeet grinned. "Same message?"

Vicki found herself grinning back. The last time the police lab had called her at home had been in the worst of the fights between her and Celluci. "Different message."

"Pity." Rajeet gave an exaggerated sigh of disappointment as Vicki headed for the door. "I've forgotten a few of the places you told him to stuff his occurrence book." She sketched a salute—a reminder of the old days, when Vicki had been an *intense* young woman in a uniform— and returned to the report she'd been filling out before the interruption.

Walking down the hall, the familiar white tiles of the corridor wrapping around her like an old friend, Vicki considered heading through the tunnel to headquarters and checking to see if Celluci were at his desk. She could tell him about the cracks, find out if he'd been withholding any more information from her, and . . : no. Given his mood the last time they'd talked and given that he hadn't called over the weekend, if she showed up now she'd just interfere with his work and that was something neither of them ever did. The work being what it was, the work came first and the cracks were added questions, not answers.

She was out of the building entirely when she realized that the thought of seeing another cop sitting at what had been *her* desk had not influenced her decision one way or another. Feeling vaguely like she'd betrayed her past, she hunched her shoulders against the late after- noon chill and started for home.

For years Vicki had been promising to buy herself a really good encyclopedia set. For years she'd been put- ting it off. The set she had, she'd bought at the grocery store for five dollars and ninety-nine cents a volume with every ten dollars worth of groceries. It didn't have a lot to say about vampires.

"Legendary creatures, uh huh, central Europe, Vlad the Impaler, Bram Stoker. . . ." Vicki pushed her glasses up her nose and tried to remember the characteristics of Stoker's Dracula. She'd seen the play years ago and thought she might have read the book in high school— only a lifetime or two back.

"He was stronger, faster, his senses were more acute. . . ." She flicked the points off on her fingertips. "He slept all day, came out at night, and he hung around with a guy who ate flies. And spiders." Making a disgusted face she turned back to the encyclopedia.

"The vampire," she read, *"was said to be able to turn into bats, wolves, mist, or vapor."* The ability to turn to mist or vapor would explain the cracks, she realized. The victim's blood, being heavier, would precipitate out to coat the narrow passageway. "And a creature that rises from the grave should have no trouble moving through earth." Marking her place with an old phone bill, she heaved herself out of the recliner and turned the television on, suddenly needing sound in the apartment.

"This is crazy," she muttered, opening the book again and reading while she paced. Fantasy and reality were moving just a little too close for comfort, definitely too close for sitting still.

The remainder of the entry listed the various ways of dealing with the creatures, from ash stakes through mustard seed to the crucifix, going on in great detail about staking, beheading, and burning.

Vicki allowed the slender volume to fall closed and raised her head to look out the window. In spite of the street light glowing less than three meters from her apartment, she was very conscious of the darkness pressing against the glass. For a legendary creature, the methods of its destruction seemed to be taken very seriously indeed.

* * *

Behind the police barricade, something crouched low over the piece of sidewalk where the fourth body had been found. Although the night could hide no secrets from him and, unlike the others who had searched, he knew what to search for, he found nothing.

"Nothing," Henry murmured to himself as he stood. "And yet there should be something here." A child of his kind might be able to hide its tracks from human hunters but not from kin. He lifted his head and his nostrils flared to check the breeze. A cat—no, two—on hunts of their own, rain that would fall before morning, and. . . .

He frowned, brows drawing down into a deep vee. And what? He knew the smell of death in all its many manifestations and laid over the residue of this morning's slaying was a faint miasma of something older, more foul, almost familiar.

His memories stretched back over four hundred and fifty years. Somewhere in there. . . .

The police car was almost up on him before he saw it and the tiny sun in the heart of the searchlight had begun to glow before he moved.

"Holy shit! Did you see that?"

"See what?" Auxiliary Police Constable Wojtowicz stared out her window at the broad fan of light spilling out from the top of the slowly moving car.

"I don't know." PC Harper leaned forward over the steering wheel and peered past his partner. "I could've sworn I saw a man standing inside the barricades just as I flipped the light on."

Wojtowicz snorted. "Then we'd still be able to see him. Nobody moves that fast. And besides," she waved a hand at the view out the window, "there's nowhere to hide in that." That included the sidewalk, the barricades, and an expanse of muddy lawn. Although black shadows streamed away from every irregularity, none were large enough to hide a man.

"Think we should get out and look around?"

"You're the boss."

"Well. . . ." Nothing moved amid the stark contrast of light and shadow. Harper shook his head. The night had been making him jumpy lately; exposing nerves and plucking at them. "I guess you're right. There's nothing there."

"Of course I'm right." The car continued down the block and she reached over to shut the searchlight off. "You're just letting all this vampire stuff in the press get to you."

"You don't believe in vampires, do you?"

"Course not." Wojtowicz settled more comfortably into her seat. "Don't tell me you do?"

It was Harper's turn to snort. "I," he told her dryly, "have been audited."

Back on the lawn, one of the shadows lay, face pressed against the dirt, and remembered. The scent was stronger here, mixed a third part with earth and blood, and it brushed away the centuries.

It was London, 1593. Elizabeth was on the throne and had been for some time. He'd been dead for fifty-seven years. He'd been walking back from the theater, having just seen the premiere presentation of *Richard the Third.* On the whole, he'd enjoyed himself although he had a feeling the playwright had taken a few liberties with the personality of the king.

Out of a refuse-strewn alleyway, a young man had stumbled—thin and disheveled but darkly handsome, very drunk, and, clinging about him like his own personal bit of fog, had been that same smell.

Henry had already fed from a whore behind the theater, but even if he hadn't, he would not have fed from this man. The scent alone was enough to make him wary, the not quite sane glitter in the dark eyes had only added further warning.

"Most humbly, I beg your pardon." His voice, the voice of an educated man, had been slurred almost beyond understanding. "But I have been in Hell this night and am having some small difficulty in returning." He'd giggled then, and executed a shaky bow in Henry's direction. "Christopher Marlowe at your service, milord. Can you spare a few coppers for a drink?"

"Christopher Marlowe," Henry repeated softly into a night more than four hundred years after that unhappy man had died. He rolled onto his back and gazed up at the clouds closing ranks over the stars. Although he had read the play just after its posthumous publication in 1604, he wondered tonight for the first time just how much research Marlowe had done before writing *The Tragical History of Dr. Faustus.*

*   *   *

"Vicki, it's Rajeet. Sorry to call so late—uh, it's 11:15, Monday night, I guess you've gone to bed—but I figured you'd want to know the results of the tests. You have positive matches with both Ian Reddick and Terri Neal. I don't know what you've found, but I hope it helps."

Five

". . . *although the police department refuses to issue a statement at this time, the Coroner's Office has confirmed that Mark Thompson, the fifth victim, has also been drained of blood. A resident, who wishes to remain nameless, living in the area of Don Mills Road and St. Dennis Drive, swears he saw a giant bat fly past his balcony just moments before the body was found.* Jesus H. Christ." Vicki punched the paper down into a tightly wadded mass and flung it at the far wall. "Giant bats! No surprise he wants to remain nameless. Shit!"

The sudden shrill demand of the phone lifted her about four inches out of her chair. Scowling, she turned on it but at the last instant remembered that the call might be business and modified her response accordingly. A snarled, "What!" seldom impressed potential clients.

"Private investigations, Nelson speaking."

"Have you seen this morning's paper?!"

The voice was young, female, and not instantly identifiable. "Who is this, please?"

"It's me. Coreen Fergus. *Have* you seen this morning's paper?"

"Yes, Coreen, I have, but. . . ."

"Well, that proves it then, doesn't it."

"Proves what?" Tucking the phone under her chin, Vicki reached for her coffee. She had a feeling she was going to need it.

"About the vampire. There's a witness. Someone saw it!" Coreen's voice had picked up a triumphant tone.

Vicki took a deep breath. "A giant bat could be anything, Coreen. A blowing garbage bag, the shadow of an airplane, laundry falling off another balcony."

"And it could also be a giant bat. You are going to talk to this person, aren't you?"

It wasn't really a question and although Vicki had been deliberately not thinking about trying to find an unnamed source in the rabbit warren of apartments and town-houses around St. Dennis Drive, talking to "this person" was the next logical step. She reassured Coreen, promised to call the moment she had any results, and hung up.

"Like looking for a needle in a haystack." But it had to be done; a witness could break the case wide open.

She finished her coffee and checked her watch. There was one thing she wanted to check before she hit the pavement. 8:43. Cutting it close, but Brandon should still be at his desk.

He was.

After greetings were exchanged—perfunctory on one side at least—Vicki slid in the reason for her call. ". . . and you and I both know you've found things that you haven't told the papers."

"That's very true, Victoria." The coroner didn't even pretend not to understand. "But, as you know very well, I won't be able to tell these *things* to you either. I'm sorry, but you're no longer a member of the constabulary."

"But I have been hired to work on the case." Quickly, she outlined the pertinent parts of Coreen's visit for him, leaving out any mention of the young lady's personal belief as to the supernatural identity of the killer as well as the latest phone call.

"You've been hired as a private citizen, Victoria, and as such you have no more right to information than any other private citizen."

Vicki stifled a sigh and considered how best to approach this. When Brandon Singh meant no, he said it, straight out with no frills. And then he hung up. As long as he remained willing to talk he remained willing to be convinced. "Look, Brandon, you know my record. You know I have as good a chance as anyone in the city of solving this case. And you *know* you want it solved. I'll stand a better chance if I have all available information."

"Granted, but somehow this smacks of vigilantism."

"Vigilantism? Trust me, Brandon, I am not going to dress up in some silly costume and leap around making the city safe for decent people." She doodled a bat symbol on her notepad, then hastily crumpled the page up and tossed it away. Under the circumstances, bats were not a particularly apt motif. "All I'm doing is investigating. I swear I'll hand over everything I turn up to Violent Crimes."

"I believe you, Victoria." He paused and Vicki, fidgeting with impatience, jumped into the silence.

"With a killer of this caliber on the loose, can the city afford not to have me on the case, even in an auxiliary position?"

"Think highly of yourself, don't you?"

She heard the smile in his voice and knew she had him. Dr. Brandon Singh believed in using every available resource and while he personally might have preferred a less intuitive approach than hers, he had to admit that "Victory" Nelson represented a valuable resource indeed. If she thought highly of herself, it wasn't without cause.

"Very well," he said at last, his tone even more portentous than usual as though to make up for his earlier lapse. "But there's very little the papers don't have and I don't know what use you'll be able to make of it." He took a deep breath and even the ambient noise on the phone line seemed to fall silent to listen. "We found, in all but the first wound, a substance very like saliva. . . ."

"Very like saliva?" Vicki interjected. "How could something be *very like saliva?*"

"Something can't. But this was. What's more, every body so far, including that of young Reddick, has been missing the front half of the throat."

"I'd already discovered that."

"Indeed." For a moment, Vicki was afraid he'd taken offense at her interruption, but he continued. "The only other item kept from the press concerns the third body—

the large man, DeVerne Jones. He was clutching a torn piece of thin membrane in his hand."

"Membrane?"

"Yes."

"Like a bat wing?"

"Remarkably similar, yes."

It was Vicki's turn to breathe deeply. Something very like saliva and a bat wing. "I can see why you didn't tell the papers."

* * *

Celluci hung up the phone and reached for the paper. He couldn't decide whether the apology had been made easier because Vicki was out of her apartment or harder because he'd had to talk to her damned machine. Whatever. It was done and the next move was hers.

A second later Dave Graham barely managed to snatch his coffee out of harm's way as his partner slammed the paper down on the desk.

"Did you see this bullshit?" Celluci demanded.

"The, uh, giant bat?"

"Fuck the bat! Those bastards found a witness and didn't see fit to let us know!"

"But we were heading out to St. Dennis this morning. . . ."

"Yeah," Celluci shrugged into his jacket and glared Dave up out of his chair, "but we're heading down to the paper first. A witness could blow this case wide open and I don't want to piss away my time if they've got a name."

"A name of someone who sees giant bats," Dave muttered, but he scrambled into his own coat and followed his partner out into the hall. "You think it really could be a vampire?" he asked as he caught up.

Celluci didn't even break stride. "Don't you start," he growled.

"Who is it?"

"It's the police, Mr. Bowan. We need to talk to you." Celluci held his badge up in line with the spy-eye and waited. After a long moment, he heard a chain being pulled free and two—no, three—locks snapped off. He stepped back beside his partner as the door slowly opened.

The old man peered up at them through rheumy eyes. "You Detective-Sergeant Michael Celluci?"

"Yes, but . . ." Surely the old man's eyesight hadn't been good enough to read that off his ID.

"She said you'd probably show up this morning." He opened the door wider and moved back out of the way. "Come in, come in."

The detectives exchanged puzzled looks as they entered the tiny apartment. While the old man relocked the door, Celluci looked around. Heavy blankets had been tacked up along one wall, over the windows and the balcony door, and every light in the place was on. There was a Bible on the coffee table and a water glass beside it that smelled of Scotch. Whatever the old man had seen, it had caused him to put up the barricades and reach for reassurance.

Dave settled himself carefully on the sagging couch. "Who said we'd be here this morning, Mr. Bowan?"

"Young lady who just left. In fact, I'm surprised you didn't pass her in the parking lot. Nice girl, real friendly."

"Did this nice, real friendly girl have a name?" Celluci asked through clenched teeth.

The old man managed a wheezy laugh. "She said you'd react like that." Shaking his head, he picked a business card off his kitchen table and dropped it into Celluci's hand.

Leaning over his partner's shoulder, Dave barely had a chance to read it before Celluci closed his fist.

"What else did Ms. Nelson say?"

"Oh, she seemed real concerned that I cooperate with you gentlemen. That I tell you everything I told her. Course I had no intention of doing otherwise, though I've got no idea what the police can do. More a job for an exorcist or maybe a pri. . . ." A yawn that threatened to split his face in half cut off the flow of words. "S'cuse me, but I didn't get much sleep last night. Can I get either of you a cup of tea? Pot's still hot." When both men declined, he settled himself down in a worn armchair and looked expectantly from one to the other. "You going to ask me questions or you just want me to start at the beginning and tell it in my own words?"

"Start at the beginning and tell it in your own words." Celluci had heard Vicki give that instruction a thousand times and had no doubt he was hearing her echo now. His anger had faded into a reluctant appreciation of her ability with a witness. Whatever mood Vicki had found him in, she'd left Mr. Bowan well primed for their visit. "Use your own words, we'll ask questions if we need to."

"Okay." Mr. Bowan rubbed his hands together, obviously enjoying his second captive audience of the morning in spite of his fright of the night before. "It was just after midnight, I know that 'cause I turned the TV off at midnight like I always do. Well, I was on my way to bed so I turned off the lights, then I thought I might better step out on the balcony to have a look around the building, just in case. Sometimes," he confided, leaning forward, "we get kids fooling around in the bushes down there."

While Dave nodded in understanding, Celluci hid a grin. Mr. Bowan, no doubt, spent a great deal of time out on his balcony checking out the neighborhood . . . and the neighbors. The binocular case on the floor by the armchair bore mute witness.

Last night, he'd barely stepped outside before he knew something was wrong. "It was the smell. Like rotten eggs, only worse. Then there it was, big as life and twice as ugly and so close I could've reached out and touched it—if I was as senile as my daughter-in-law seems to think I am. The wings were spread out seven or eight feet." He paused for effect. "The giant bat. Nosferatu. Vampire. You find his crypt, gentlemen, and you'll find your killer."

"Can you describe the creature?"

"If you mean could I pick it out in a lineup, no. Tell you the truth, it went by so awfully fast I saw mostly outline. But I'll tell you this much," his voice grew serious and a note of terror crept in, "that thing had eyes

like I've never seen on any living creature and I hope
to God never to see again. Yellow they were and cold,
and I knew that if they looked back at me I wouldn't
last much beyond the first glance. It was evil, gentlemen,
real evil, not the diluted kind of evil humanity is prey
to but the cold uncaring kind that comes from old Nick
himself. Now, I'm old and death and me's gotten pretty
chummy over the last few years; nothing much scares
me anymore but this, this scared the holy bejesus out of
me." He swallowed heavily and searched both their
faces. "You can believe me or not—that reporter fella
didn't when I went down to see what the sirens were
about—but I know what I saw and I know what I felt."

As much as he wanted to side with the reporter, who
had described Mr. Bowan as an entertaining old coot,
Celluci found himself unable to dismiss what the old
man had seen. And what the old man had felt. Something in his voice or his expression raised the hair on
the back of Celluci's neck and although intellect argued
against it, instinct trembled on the edge of belief.

He wished he could talk this over with Vicki, but he
wouldn't give her the satisfaction.

*   *   *

"God, I hate these machines." The heavy, exaggerated
sigh that followed had been recorded in its annoyed entirety. "Okay. I'd have reacted much the same way.
Probably been an equal pain in the ass. So, I'm right,
you're right, we're both right, let's start over." The tape
hissed quietly for a few seconds while background
noises—the rumble of two deep voices arguing, the staccato beat of an old, manual typewriter, and the constant
ringing of other phones—grew louder. Then Celluci's
voice returned, bearing just enough edge to show he
meant what he said. "And stop hustling my partner for
classified information. He's a nice man, not that you'd
recognize nice, and you give him palpitations." He hung
up without saying good-bye.

Vicki grinned down at her answering machine. Mike
Celluci was no better at apologizing than she was. For
him, that was positively gracious. And it had obviously

been left before he talked to Mr. Bowan and found she'd been there first. Any messages left *after* that would have had a very different tone.

Finding the tabloid's unnamed source had actually been surprisingly easy. The first person she'd spoken to had snorted and said, "You want old man Bowan. If anyone sees anything around here it's him. Never minds his own fucking business." Then he'd jerked his head at 25 St. Dennis with enough force to throw his mohawk down over his eyes.

As to what old man Bowan had seen. . . . As much as Vicki hated to admit it, she was beginning to think Coreen might not be as far out in left field as first impressions indicated.

She wondered if she should call Celluci. They could share their impressions of Mr. Bowan and his close encounter. "Nah." She shook her head. Better give him time to cool off first. Spreading the detailed map of Toronto she'd just bought out over her kitchen table, she decided to call him later. Right now, she had work to do.

It was easy to forget just how big Toronto was. It had devoured any number of smaller places as it grew, and it showed no signs of stopping. The downtown core, the image everyone carried of the city, made up a very small part of the whole.

Vicki drew a red circle around the Eglinton West subway station, another around the approximate position of the Sigman's building on St. Clair West, and a third around the construction site on Symington Avenue where DeVerne Jones had died. Then she frowned and drew a straight line through all three. Allowing for small inaccuracies in placing the second and third positions, the line bisected all three circles, running southwest to northeast across the city.

The two new deaths appeared to have no connection to the first three but seemed to be starting a line of their own.

And there was more.

"No one could be that stupid," Vicki muttered, digging in her desk for a ruler.

The first two deaths were essentially the same distance

apart as the fourth and the fifth; far from exact by mathematical standards but too close to be mere coincidence.

"No one could be that stupid," she said again, smacking the ruler against her palm. The second line ran northwest to southeast and it measured out in a circle that centered at Woodbine and Mortimer. Vicki was willing to bet any odds that between midnight and dawn a sixth body would turn up to end the line.

Just west of York University, the lines crossed.

"X marks the spot." Vicki pushed her glasses up her nose, frowned, and pushed them up again. It was too easy. There had to be a catch.

"All right. . . ." Tossing the ruler onto the map, she ticked off points on her fingers. "First possibility; the killer wants to be found. Second possibility; the killer is just as capable of drawing lines on a map as I am, has set up the pattern to mean nothing at all, and is sitting in Scarborough busting a gut laughing at the damn fool police who fell for it." For purposes of this exercise, she and the police were essentially the same. "Possibility three"; she stared at the third finger as though it might have an answer, "we're hunting a vampire even as the vampire is hunting us and who the hell knows how a vampire thinks."

Celucci was as capable as she of drawing lines on a map, but she reached for the phone anyway. Occasionally, the obvious escaped him. To her surprise, he was in. His reaction came as no surprise at all.

"Teach your grandmother to suck eggs, Vicki."

"So can I assume Toronto's finest will be gathered tonight at Mortimer and Woodbine?"

"You can assume whatever you want, I've never been able to stop you, but if you think you and your little Nancy Drew detective kit are going to be anywhere near there, think again."

"What are you going to do?" How dare he dictate to her. "Arrest me?"

"If I have to, yes." His tone said he'd do exactly that. "You are no longer on the force, you are virtually blind at night, and you are more likely to end up as the corpse than the hero."

"I don't need you babying me, Celluci!"

"Then act like an adult and stay home!"

They slammed the receivers down practically simultaneously. He knew she'd be there and she knew he knew it. Moreover, she had no doubt that if their paths crossed he'd lock her away on trumped up charges for her own safety. Better than even odds said that, having been forewarned, he'd lock her up now if he thought he could get away with it.

He was right. She was virtually blind at night.

But the police were hunting a man and Vicki no longer really believed a man had anything to do with these deaths. Blind or not, if she was there, she might even the odds.

Now, what to do until dark? Maybe it was time to do a little detecting and find out what the word was on the street.

"At least he didn't scream about Mr. Bowan," she muttered as she shrugged back into her coat.

"Yo, Victory, long time no see."

"Yeah, it's been a couple of months. How've you been, Tony?"

Tony shrugged thin shoulders under his jean jacket. "I've been okay."

"You clean?"

He shot her a look out of the corner of one pale blue eye. "I hear you ain't a cop no more. I don't got to tell you."

Vicki shrugged in turn. "No. You don't."

They walked in silence for a moment, threading their way through the crowds that surged up and down Yonge Street. When they stopped at the Wellesley lights, Tony sighed. "Okay, I'm clean. You happy now? You going to bugger off and leave me alone?"

She grinned. "Is it ever that easy?"

"Not with you it ain't. Listen," he waved a hand at a corner restaurant, less trendy than most of its competitors, "you're going to take up my time, you can buy me lunch."

She bought him lunch, but not the beer he wanted, and asked him about the feeling on the street.

"Feeling about what?" he asked, stuffing a huge fork-ful of mashed potatoes into his mouth. "Sex? Drugs? Rock'n'roll?"

"Things that go bump in the night."

He threw his arm up in the classic Hammer films tradition. "Ah, the wampyre."

Vicki took a swallow of tepid coffee, wondered how she'd survived drinking it all those years on the force, and waited. Tony had been her best set of eyes and ears on the street. He wasn't exactly a snitch, more a barometer really, hooked into moods and feelings, and although he never mentioned specifics, he'd pointed her in the right direction more than once. He was nineteen now. He'd been fifteen when she first brought him in.

"Feelin' on the street. . . ." He methodically spread the last roll a quarter inch thick with butter. "Feelin' on the street says, paper's right with this one."

"A vampire?"

He peered up at her from under the thick fringe of his eyelashes. "Killer ain't human, that's what the street says. Sucks blood, don't it? Vampire's a good enough name for it. Cops won't catch it 'cause they're lookin' for a guy." He grinned. "Cops in this city ain't worth shit anyway. Not like they used to be."

"Well, thank you very much." She watched him scrape his plate clean, then asked, "Tony, do *you* believe in vampires?"

He flicked a tiny crucifix out from inside his shirt. "I believe in stayin' alive."

Outside the restaurant, turning collars up against the wind, she asked him if he needed money. She couldn't get him off the street, he wouldn't accept her help, so she gave him what he'd take. Celluci called it white-middle-class-guilt-money. While admitting he was probably right, Vicki ignored him.

"Nah," Tony pushed a lock of pale brown hair back off his face. "I'm doing okay for cash."

"You hooking?"

"Why? You can't arrest me anymore; you wanna hire me?"

"I want to smack you. Haven't you heard there's an epidemic going on?"

He danced back out of her range. "Hey, I'm careful. Like I said," and just for an instant he looked much, much older than his years, "I believe in stayin' alive."

"Vicki, I don't care what your curbside guru says and I don't care what the 'feeling on the street is'; there are no such thing as vampires and you are losing your mind."

Vicki got the phone away from her ear before Celluci slammed his receiver down. Shaking her head, she hung up her own phone considerably more gently. All right, she'd told him. She'd done it against her better judgment and knowing full well what his reaction would be. No matter what went down tonight, *her* conscience was clear.

"And it's not that *I* believe in vampires," she pointed out to the empty apartment, pushing back to extend the recliner. "*I* believe in keeping an open mind." *And,* she added silently, grimly, her mind on Tony and his crucifix, *I, too, believe in stayin' alive.* Beside the chair, her bag bulged with the afternoon's purchases.

At 11:48, Vicki stepped off the northbound Woodbine bus at Mortimer. For a moment, she leaned against the window of the small garden store on the corner, giving herself time to grow used to the darkness. There, under the street lamp, her vision was functional. A few meters away, where the overlap of two lights created a double-shadowed twilight, she knew she wouldn't be able to trust it. It would be worse off the main street. She fished her flashlight out of her bag and held it ready, just in case.

Across a shadow-filled distance, she saw a traffic signal work through its tiny spectrum and decided to cross the street. For no reason really, the creature could appear on the east side of Woodbine just as easily as on the west, but it seemed like the thing to do. Moving had always been infinitely preferable to waiting around.

Terry's Milk Mart on the north side of Mortimer appeared to be open—it was the only building in the immediate neighborhood still brightly lit—so she crossed toward it.

I can ask a few questions. Buy a bag of chips. Find out. . . . SHIT! Two men from homicide were in the store talking to a surly looking teenager she could only assume was not the proprietor. Eyes streaming from the sudden glare of the fluorescents, she backed down the six stairs much more quickly than she'd gone up them. She spotted the unmarked car south across Mortimer in the Brewers Retail parking lot—*trust the government to light a square of asphalt at almost midnight*—and headed in the opposite direction, willing to bet long odds that Celluci had included her in his instructions to his men.

If she remembered correctly, the houses that lined the street were small, virtually identical, detached, two-story, single family dwellings. *Not the sort of neighborhood you'd think would attract a vampire.* Not that she expected the creature to actually put in an appearance on Woodbine; the street was too well lit, too well traveled, with too great a possibility of witnesses. No, she was putting her money on one of the quiet residential streets tucked in behind.

At Holborne, for no reason she could think of, she turned west. The streetlights were farther apart here and she hurried from one island of sight to the next, trusting to bureaucracy and city planning to keep the sidewalk under her feet. She slipped at one point on a pile of dirt, her bag sliding off her shoulder and slamming hard edges against her knees. Her flashlight beam played over a tiny construction site where a skinny house was rising to fill what had once no doubt been a no larger than average side yard. The creature had killed under circumstances like these once before, but somehow she knew it wouldn't again. She moved on.

The sudden scream of a siren sent her heart up into her throat and she spun around, flashlight raised like a weapon. Back at the corner, a fire engine roared from the station and, tires squealing, turned north up Woodbine.

"Nerves a bit shot, are they, Vicki?" she muttered to herself taking a long, calming breath. Blood pounded in her ears almost loud enough to echo and sweat glued her gloves to her palms. Still a bit shaky with reaction, she made her way to the next streetlight and leaned back against the pole.

The spill of light reached almost to the house, not quite far enough for Vicki to see the building. The bit of lawn she could see looked well cared for—in spite of the spring mud—and along one edge roses, clipped short to survive the cold, waited for spring. It was a working class neighborhood, she knew, and, given the lawn, Vicki was willing to bet that most of the families were Italian or Portuguese as both cultures cared about—and for— the land. If that was the case, many of the houses would be decorated with painted icons of saints, or of the Madonna, or of Christ himself.

She wondered how much protection those icons would offer when the killer came.

Up the street, two golden circles marked a slow moving car. To Vicki, they looked like the eyes of some great beast for the darkness hid the form that followed and the headlights were all she could see. But then, she didn't need to see more to identify it as a police car. Only police on surveillance ever drove at that precise, unchanging speed. She'd done it herself too many times to mistake it now. Fighting the urge to dive out of sight, she turned and strode confidently up the walk toward the house, digging in her bag for an imaginary set of keys.

The car purred by behind her.

Making her way back to the sidewalk, Vicki doubted that her luck could last. Celluci had to have saturated this area with his men. Sooner or later, she had to run into someone she knew—probably Celluci himself—and she wasn't looking forward to explaining just what she was doing roaming about in the middle of a police manhunt.

She continued west along Holborne, marshaling her arguments. *I thought you could use an extra pair of eyes.* But then, so could she. *I doubted you'd be prepared to deal with a vampire.* True, but it'd go over like rats in the drunk tank. *You have no right to keep me away.* Except that they/he did. Every right. It was why there were laws against suicide.

So what am I doing out here anyway? And is this more or less stupid than charging down into a subway station to single-handedly challenge God knows what. The darkness pressed close around her, waiting for an answer. *What am I trying to prove?*

That in spite of everything I can still be a fully functioning member of society. She snorted. *On the other hand, there're a number of fully functioning members of society I'm not likely to run into out here tonight.*

Which brought the silent interrogation back around to "just what was she trying to prove," and Vicki decided to leave it there. Things were tough enough without bogging them down further in introspection.

At the corner of Woodmount, she paused. The triple line of streetlights disappeared into the distance to either side and straight ahead. The suspended golden globes were all she could see. Casting about like a hound for a scent, she drew in a deep lungful of the cold night air. All she could smell was earth, damp and musty, freshly exposed by the end of winter. Normally, she liked the smell. Tonight, it reminded her of the grave and she pulled her jacket tighter around her to ward off a sudden chill. In the distance, there was the sound of traffic and farther off still, a dog barked.

There seemed little to choose between the directions, so she turned to her left and headed carefully back south.

A car door slammed.

Vicki's heart slammed up against her ribs in response. This was it. She was as sure of it as she'd ever been of anything in her life.

She started to run. Slowly at first, well aware that a misstep would result in a fall or worse. Her flashlight remained off; she needed the stations of the streetlights to guide her and the flashlight beam confined her sight. At Baker Street, she rocked to a halt.

Where now? Her other senses strained to make up for near blindness.

Metal screamed against wood; nails forced to release their hold.

East. She turned and raced toward it, stumbled, fell, recovered, and went on, trusting her feet to find a path she couldn't see. Fifty running paces from the corner, shadow sight marked something crossing her path. It slipped down the narrow drive between two buildings and when Vicki followed, responding to the instinct of the chase, she could see red taillights burning about a hundred yards away.

It smelled as if something had died at the end of the lane. Like the old lady who'd been found the third week of last August but who'd been killed in her small, airless room around the first of July.

She could hear the car engine running, movement against the gravel, and a noise she didn't want to identify.

The evil that had lingered in the subway tunnel had been only the faintest afterimage of the evil that waited for her here.

A shadow, its parameters undefined, passed between Vicki and the taillight.

Her left hand trailing along a wall of fake brick siding and her right holding the flashlight out before her like the handle of a lance, Vicki pounded up the drive paying no attention to the small, shrill voice of reason that demanded to know just what the hell she thought she was doing.

Something shrieked and the sound drove her back a half dozen steps.

Every dog in the neighborhood began to howl.

Ignoring the cold sweat beading her body and the knot of fear that made each breath a labored fight, Vicki forced herself to move forward again; the six steps regained, then six more. . . .

Half sprawled across the trunk of the car, she turned on the flashlight.

Horror flickered just beyond the beam's farthest edge

where a wooden garage door swung haphazardly from a single twisted hinge. Darkness seemed to move within the darkness and Vicki's mind shied away from it so quickly and with such blind panic that it convinced her nothing lingered there at all.

Caught in the light, a young man crouched, one arm flung up to shield his eyes from the glare. At his feet, a body; a bearded man, late thirties, early forties, blood still draining from the ruined throat, thickening and congealing against the gravel. He had been dead before he hit the ground, for only the dead fall with that complete disregard of self that gives them the look of discarded marionettes.

All this Vicki took in at glance. Then the crouching man stood, his open coat spreading and bracketing him like great black leather wings. He took a step toward her, face distorted and eyes squinted nearly shut. Blood had stained his palms and fingers a glistening crimson.

Scrambling in her purse for the heavy silver crucifix she'd acquired that afternoon—and not really, God help her, expected to need—Vicki drew breath to scream for backup. Or maybe just to scream. She never found out which for he took another step toward her and that was all she saw for some time.

Henry caught the young woman as she fell and eased her gently to the gravel. He hadn't wanted to do that, but he couldn't allow her to scream. There were too many things he couldn't explain to the police.

She saw me bending over the body, he thought as he snapped off the flashlight and shoved it into her purse. His too sensitive eyes welcomed the return of night. They felt as though they'd been impaled with hot irons. *Got a good look at me, too. Damn.* Common sense said he should kill her before she had a chance to expose him. He had strength enough to make it look no different from the other deaths. He would be safe again then.

Henry turned and looked past the body—meat now, nothing more—into the torn earthen floor of the garage where the killer had fled. This night had proven the deaths were in no way his responsibility.

"Damn!" He said it aloud this time as approaching sirens and a car door slamming at the end of the drive reminded him of the need for immediate action. Dropping to one knee, he heaved the unconscious young woman over a shoulder and grabbed up her bag in his free hand. The weight posed no problem; like all of his kind he was disproportionately strong, but her dangling height was dangerously awkward.

"Too damn tall in this century," he muttered, vaulted the chain link fence that bordered the back of the yard, and disappeared with his burden into the night.

Six

Dumping the contents of the huge black purse out on his coffee table, Henry dropped to his knees and rummaged through the mess for something that looked like ID; a wallet, a card case, anything. Nothing.

Nothing? Impossible. These days no one traveled without identification, not even those who traveled only the night. He found both card case and wallet at last in the bag itself, tucked in a side pocket, accessible without having to delve through the main compartment.

"Victoria Nelson, Private Investigator." He let out a breath he hadn't been aware of holding as he went through the rest of her papers. *A private investigator, thank God.* He'd been afraid he'd run off with some sort of un-uniformed police officer, thereby instigating a citywide manhunt. He'd observed, over the centuries that the police, whatever else their failings, took care of their own. A private investigator, though, was a private citizen and as such had probably not yet been missed.

Rising to his feet, Henry looked down at the unconscious woman on his couch. Although he found it distasteful, he would kill to protect himself. Hopefully, this time, it wouldn't be necessary. He shrugged out of his coat and began to compose what he'd say to her when she woke up . . .

. . . if she woke up.

Her heartbeat filled the apartment, its rhythm almost twice as fast as his own. It called to him to feed, but he held the hunger in check.

He glanced at his watch. 2:13. Sunrise in four hours. If she was concussed. . . .

He hadn't wanted to hit her. Knocking someone out with a single blow wasn't easy no matter what movies and television suggested. Sporadic practice over the years had taught him where and how to strike, but no expertise could change the fact that a head blow slammed the brain back and forth within the skull, mashing soft tissue against bone.

And it's quite an attractive skull, too, he noted, taking a closer look. *Although there's a definite hint of obstinacy about the width of that jaw.* He checked her ID again. Thirty-one. Her short dark blond/light brown hair—he frowned, unable to make up his mind—had no touch of gray but tiny laugh wrinkles had begun to form around her eyes. When he'd been "alive," thirty-one had been middle-aged. Now, it seemed to be barely adult.

She wore no makeup, he approved of that, and the delicate, pale gold down on her cheeks made her skin look like velvet.

And feel like velvet. . . . He drew back his hand and clamped the hunger tighter. It was want, not need, and he would not let it control him.

The tiny muscles of her face shifted and her eyes opened. Like her hair, they were neither one color nor the other; neither blue, nor gray, nor green. The tip of her tongue moistened dry lips and she met his gaze without fear.

"Son of a bitch," she said clearly, and winced.

Vicki came up out of darkness scrambling desperately for information, but the sound of blood pounding in her ears kept drowning out coherent thought. She fought against it. Pain—and, oh God, it hurt—meant danger. She had to know where she was, how she'd gotten there. . . .

A man's face swam into view inches above her own, a man's face she recognized.

"Son of a bitch," she said, and winced. The words, the movement of her jaw, sent fresh shards of pain up

into her head. She did what she could to ignore them.
The last time she'd seen that face, and the body it was
no doubt attached to, it had risen from slaughter and
attacked her. Although she had no memory of it, he
had obviously knocked her out and brought her here;
wherever here was.

She tried to look past him, to get some idea of her
surroundings, but the room, if room it was, was too dark.
Did she know *anything* she could use?

*I'm fully clothed, lying on a couch in the company of
an insane killer and, although the rest of my body appears
to be functional, my head feels like it's taken too many
shots on goal.* There seemed to be only one thing she
could do. She threw herself off the couch.

Unfortunately, gravity proved stronger than the idea.

When she hit the floor, a brilliant fireworks display
left afterimages of green and gold and red on the inside
of her eyelids and then she sank into darkness again.

The second time Vicki regained consciousness, it happened more quickly than the first and the line between
one state and the next was more clearly delineated. This
time, she kept her eyes closed.

"That was a stupid thing to do," a man's voice observed from somewhere above her right shoulder. She
didn't argue. "It's entirely possible you won't believe
this," he continued, "but I don't want to hurt you."

To her surprise, she did believe him. Maybe it was the
tone, or the timbre, or the ice pack he held against her
jaw. Maybe her brains had been scrambled, which
seemed more likely.

"I never did want to hurt you. I'm sorry about," she
felt the ice pack shift slightly, "this, but I didn't think I
had time to explain."

Vicki cracked open first one eye and then the other.
"Explain what?" The pale oval of his face appeared to
float in the dim light. She wished she could see him better.

"I didn't kill that man. I arrived at the body just before you did."

"Yeah?" She realized suddenly what was wrong.
"Where are my glasses?"

"Your . . . oh." The oval swiveled away and returned a moment later.

She waited, eyes closed, as he pushed the ends in over her ears, approximately where they belonged, and settled the bridge gently against her nose. When she opened her eyes again, things hadn't changed significantly. "Could you turn on a light?"

Vicki could sense his bemusement as he rose. So she wasn't reacting as he expected; if he wanted terror, she'd have to try for it later, at present her head hurt too much to make the effort. And besides, if it turned out he was the killer, there wasn't a damn thing she could do about it now.

The light, although it wasn't strong enough to banish shadows from far corners, helped. From where she lay, she could see an expensive stereo system and the edge of a bookshelf with glass doors. Slowly, balancing her head like an egg in a spoon, she sat up.

"Are you sure that's wise?"

She wasn't. But she wasn't going to admit it. "I'm fine," she snapped, closing her throat on a wave of nausea and successfully fighting it back down. Peeling off her gloves, she studied her captor from under beetled brows.

He didn't look like an insane killer. *Okay, Vicki, you're so smart, in twenty-five words or less, describe an insane killer.* She couldn't tell what color his eyes were, though an educated guess said light hazel, but his brows and lashes were redder than his strawberry-blond hair-coloring that freckled in the sun. His face was broad, without being in the least bit fat—the kind of face that got labeled honest—and his mouth held just the smallest hint of a cupid's bow. *Definitely attractive.* She measured his height against the stereo and added, *But short.*

"So," she said, settling carefully back against the sofa cushions, keeping her tone conversational. *Talk to them,* said the rule book. *Get their trust.* "Why should I believe you had nothing to do with ripping that man's throat out?"

Henry stepped forward and handed her the ice pack.

"You were right behind me," he told her quietly. "You must have seen. . . ."

Seen what? She'd seen the body, him bending over it, the lights of the car, the ruined garage door and the darkness beyond it. *Darkness swirled against darkness and was gone.* No. She shook her head, the physical pain the action caused a secondary consideration. *Darkness swirled against darkness and was gone.* She couldn't catch her breath and began to struggle against the strong hands that held her. "No. . . ."

"Yes."

Gradually, under the strength of his gaze and his touch, she calmed. "What. . . ." She wet dry lips and tried again. "What was it?"

"A demon."

"Demons don't . . ." *Darkness swirled against darkness and was gone.* "Oh."

Straightening, Henry almost smiled. He could practically see her turning the facts over, accepting the evidence, and adjusting her worldview to fit. She didn't look happy about it, but she did it anyway. He was impressed.

Vicki took a deep breath. *Okay, a demon.* It certainly answered all the questions and made a kind of horrific sense. "Why were *you* there?" She was pleased to note her voice sounded almost normal.

What should he tell her? Although she wasn't exactly receptive—not that he blamed her—she wasn't openly hostile either. The truth, then, or as much of it as seemed safe.

"I was hunting the demon. I was just a little too late. I kept it from feeding but couldn't stop the kill." He frowned slightly. "Why were *you* there, Ms. Nelson?"

So he's found my ID. For the first time, Vicki became aware that the contents of her bag were spread out over the smoked glass top of the coffee table. The garlic, the package of mustard seed, the Bible, the crucifix—all spread out in plain, ridiculous sight. She snorted gently. "I was hunting a vampire."

To her surprise, after one incredulous glance down at the contents of her bag, as if he, too, were seeing them for the first time, her captor, the demon-hunter, threw back his head and roared with laughter.

*   *   *

Henry, Duke of Richmond, had felt her speculative gaze on him all through the meal. Whenever he glanced her way she was staring at him, but every time he tried to actually catch her eye she'd drop her lids and look demurely at her plate, the long sweep of her lashes—lashes so black he was sure they must be tinted—lying against the curve of an alabaster cheek. He thought she smiled once, but that could have been a trick of the light.

While Sir Thomas, seated to his left, prated on about sheep, he rolled a grape between his fingers and tried to figure out just who the lady could be. She had to be a member of the local nobility invited to Sheriffhuton for the day for surely he would have remembered her if she'd been with the household on the journey north from London. The little bit he could see of her gown was black. Was she a widow, then, or did she wear the color only because she knew how beautifully it became her and was there a husband lurking in the background?

For the first time in weeks he was glad that Surrey had decided against journeying to Sheriffhuton with him. *Women never look at me when he's around.*

There, she smiled. I'm sure of it. He wiped the crushed grape off against his hose and reached for his wine, emptying the delicate Venetian glass in one frantic swallow. He couldn't stand it any longer.

"Sir Thomas."

". . . of course, the best ram for the purpose is. . . . Yes milord?"

Henry leaned closer to the elderly knight; he didn't want the rest of the table to hear, he got enough teasing as it was. He'd barely managed to live down the ditty his father's fool, Will Sommers, had written about him; *Though he may have his sire's face/He cannot keep the royal pace.*

"Sir Thomas, who is that woman seated next to Sir Giles and his lady?"

"Woman, milord?"

"Yes, woman." It took an effort, but the young duke kept his voice level and calm. Sir Thomas was a valued retainer, had been a faithful chamberlain at Sheriffhuton all the long years he'd been away in France, and by age alone deserved his respect. "The one in black. Next to Sir Giles and his lady."

"Ah, next to Sir Giles. . . ." Sir Thomas leaned forward and squinted. The lady in question looked demurely at her plate. "Why that's old Beswick's relic."

"Beswick?" This beautiful creature had been married to Beswick? Why the baron was Sir Thomas' age at least. Henry couldn't believe it. "But he's old!"

"He's dead, milord." Sir Thomas snickered. "But he met his maker a happy man, I fancy. She's a sweet thing though, and seemed to take the old goat's death hard. Saw little enough of her when he was alive and less now."

"How long were they married?"

"Month . . . no, two."

"And she lives at Beswick Castle?"

Sir Thomas snorted. "If you can call that moldering ruin a castle, yes, milord."

"If you can call this heap a castle," Henry waved a hand at the great hall, relatively unchanged since the twelfth century, "you can call anything a castle."

"This is a royal residence," Sir Thomas protested huffily.

She did smile. I saw her clearly. She smiled. At me. "And where *she* dwells, it would be heaven come to earth," Henry murmured dreamily, forgetting for a moment where he was, losing himself in that smile.

Sir Thomas gave a great guffaw of laughter, choked on a mouthful of ale, and had to be vigorously pounded on the back, attracting the attention Henry had been hoping to avoid.

"You should be more careful of excitement, good sir knight," chided the Archbishop of York as those who had hurried to the rescue moved back to their places.

"Not me, your Grace," Sir Thomas told the prelate piously, "it's our good duke who finds his codpiece tied too tightly."

As he felt his face redden, Henry cursed the Tudor

coloring that showed every blush as though he were a maiden and not a man full sixteen summers old.

Later, when the musicians began to play up in the old minstrel's gallery, Henry walked among his guests, trying, he thought successfully, to hide his ultimate goal. They'd be watching him now and one or two, he knew, reported back to his father.

As he at last crossed the hall toward her, she gathered her black and silver skirts in one hand and headed for the open doors and the castle courtyard. Henry followed. She was waiting for him, as he knew she would be, on the second of the broad steps; far enough away from the door to be in darkness, close enough for him to find her.

"It, uh, it is hot in the hall, isn't it?"

She turned toward him, her face and bosom glimmering pale white. "It *is* August."

"Yes, uh, it is." They weren't, in fact, the only couple to seek a respite from the stifling, smoky hall but the others discreetly moved away when they saw the duke appear. "You, uh, aren't afraid of night chills?"

"No. I love the night."

Her voice reminded him of the sea, and he suspected it could sweep him away as easily. Inside, under torchlight, he had thought her not much older than he, but outside, under starlight, she seemed ageless. He wet lips gone suddenly dry and searched for something more to say.

"You weren't at the hunt today."

"No."

"You don't hunt, then?"

In spite of the darkness, her eyes caught and held his. "Oh, but I do."

Henry swallowed hard and shifted uncomfortably—his codpiece was now, indeed, too tight. If three years at the French Court had taught him nothing else, he had learned to recognize an invitation from a beautiful woman. Hoping his palm had not gone damp, he held out a hand.

"Have you a name?" he asked as she laid cool fingers across his.

"Christina."

* * *

"Vampire?" Henry stared at Christina in astonishment. "I was making a joke."

"Were you?" She turned from the window, arms crossed under her breasts. "It is what Norfolk calls me."

"Norfolk is a jealous fool." Henry suspected his father had sent the Duke of Norfolk to keep an eye on him, to discover why he continued at Sheriffhuton, a residence he made no pretense of liking, into September. He also suspected that the only reason he hadn't been ordered back to Court was because his father secretly approved of his dalliance with an older, and very beautiful, widow. He wasn't fool enough to think his father didn't know.

"Is he? Perhaps." Ebony brows drew down into a frown. "Have you never wondered, Henry, why you only see me at night?"

"As long as I get to see you. . . ."

"Have you never wondered why you have never seen me eat or drink?"

"You've been to banquets," Henry protested, confused. He had only been making a joke.

"But you have never seen me eat or drink," Christina insisted. "And, this very night, you yourself commented on my strength."

"Why are you telling me this?" His life had come to revolve around the hours they spent in his great canopied bed. She was perfect. He wouldn't see her otherwise.

"Norfolk has named me vampire." Her eyes caught his and held them although he tried to break away. "The next step will be to prove it. He will say to you, if I am not as he names me, then surely I will come to you by day." She paused and her voice grew cold. "And you, wondering, will order it. And either I will flee and never see you again, or I will die."

"I, I would never order you. . . ."

"You would, if you did not believe me vampire. This is why I tell you."

Henry's mouth opened and closed in stunned silence, and when he finally spoke his voice came out a shrill caricature of his normal tone. "But I've seen you receive the sacrament."

"I'm as good a Catholic as you are, Henry. Better perhaps, as you have more to lose while the king's favor wanes toward the Mass." She smiled, a little sadly. "I am not a creature of the devil. I was born of two mortal parents."

He had never seen her in daylight. He had never seen her eat or drink. She possessed strength far beyond her sex or size. But she received the sacraments and she filled his nights with glory. "Born," his voice had almost returned to normal, "when?"

"Thirteen twenty-seven, the year that Edward the Third came to the throne. Your grandfather's grandfather had not yet been conceived."

It wasn't hard to think of her as an ageless beauty, forever unchanging down through the centuries. From there, it wasn't hard to believe the rest.

Vampire.

She saw the acceptance on his face and spread her arms wide. The loose robe she wore dropped to the floor and she allowed him to look away now that she was sure he would not. "Will you banish me?" she asked softly, casting the net of her beauty over him. "Will you give me to the pyre? Or will you have the strength to love me and be loved in return?"

The firelight threw her shadow against the tapestries on the wall. Angel or demon, Henry didn't really care. He was hers and if that damned his soul to hell so be it.

He opened his arms in answer.

As she buried herself in his embrace, he pressed his lips against the scented ebony of her hair and whispered, "Why have you never fed from me?"

"But I have. I do."

He frowned. "I've never borne your mark upon my throat. . . ."

"Throats are too public." He could feel her smile against his chest. "And your throat is not the only part of your body I have put my mouth against."

Even as he reddened, she slid down to prove her point and somehow, knowing that she fed as she pleasured him lifted him to such heights that he thought he could not bear the ecstasy. Hell would be worth it.

"This was your idea, wasn't it?"

The Duke of Norfolk inclined his head. His eyes were sunk in shadow and the deep lines that bracketed his mouth had not been there a month before. "Yes," he admitted heavily, "but it is for your own good, Henry."

"My own good?" Henry gave a bitter bark of laughter. "For your good more like. It does move you that much closer to the throne." He saw the older man wince and was glad. He didn't really believe Norfolk used him to get closer to the throne; the duke had proven his friendship any number of times, but Henry had just come from a painful interview with his father and he wanted to lash out.

"You will wed Mary, Norfolk's daughter, before the end of this month. You will spend Christmas with the Court and then you will retire to your estates at Richmond and you will never go to Sheriffhuton again."

Norfolk sighed and laid a weary hand on Henry's shoulder. His own interview with the young duke's father had been anything but pleasant. "What he does not know, he suspects; I offered this as your only way out."

Henry shook the hand free. Never to go to Sheriffhuton again. Never to see her again. Never to hear her laugh or feel her touch. Never to touch her in return. He clenched his teeth on the howl that threatened to break free. "You don't understand," he growled out instead, and strode off down the corridor before the tears he could feel building shamed him.

"Christina!" He ran forward, threw himself to his knees, and buried his head in her lap. For a time, the world became the touch of her hands and the sound of her voice. When at last he had the strength to pull away, it was only far enough to see her face. "What are you doing here? Father and Norfolk, at least, suspect and if they find you. . . ."

She stroked cool fingers across his brow. "They won't

find me. I have a safe haven for the daylight hours and we will not have so many nights together that they will discover us." She paused and cupped his cheek in her palm. "I am going away, but I could not leave without saying good-bye."

"Going away?" Henry repeated stupidly.

She nodded, her unbound hair falling forward. "It has become too dangerous for me in England."

"But where. . . ."

"France, I think. For now."

He caught up her hands in both of his. "Take me with you. I cannot live without you."

A wry smile curved her lips. "You cannot exactly *live* with me," she reminded him.

"Live, die, unlive, undie." He leapt to his feet and threw his arms wide. "I don't care as long as I'm with you."

"You're very young."

The words lacked conviction and he could see the indecision on her face. She wanted him! Oh, blessed Jesu and all the saints, she wanted him. "How old were you when you died?" he demanded.

She bit her lip. "Seventeen."

"I shall be seventeen in two months." He threw himself back on his knees. "Can't you wait that long?"

"Two months. . . ."

"Just two." He couldn't keep the triumph from his voice. "Then you will have me for all eternity."

She laughed then and pulled him to her breast. "You think highly of yourself, milord."

"I do," he agreed, his voice a little muffled.

"If your lady wife should come in. . . ."

"Mary? She has rooms of her own and is happy to stay in them." Still on his knees, he pulled her to the bed.

Two months later, she began to feed nightly, taking as much as he could bear each night.

Norfolk posted guards on his room. Henry ordered them away, for the first time in his life his father's son.

Two months after that, while revered doctors scratched their heads and wondered at his failing, while

Norfolk tore the neighborhood apart in a fruitless search, she pulled him to her breast again and he suckled the blood of eternal life.

* * *

"Let me get this straight; you're the bastard son of Henry VIII?"

"That's right." Henry Fitzroy, once Duke of Richmond and Somerset, Earl of Nottingham, and Knight of the Garter, leaned his forehead against the cool glass of the window and looked down at the lights of Toronto. It had been a long time since he'd told the story; he'd forgotten how drained it left him.

Vicki looked down at the book of the Tudor age, spread open on her lap, and tapped a paragraph. "It says here you died at seventeen."

Shaking off his lethargy, Henry turned to face her. "Yes, well, I got better."

"You don't look seventeen." She frowned. "Mid-twenties I'd say, no younger."

He shrugged. "We age, but we age slowly."

"It doesn't say so here, but wasn't there some mystery about your funeral?" One corner of her mouth quirked up at his surprised expression, the best she could manage considering the condition of her jaw. "I have a BA in history."

"Isn't that an unusual degree for a person in your line of work?"

He meant for a private investigator, she realized, but it had been just as unusual for a cop. If she had a nickel for every time someone, usually a superior officer, had dragged out that hoary old chestnut, *those who fail to learn from history are doomed to repeat it,* she'd be a rich woman. "It hasn't slowed me down," she told him a little pointedly. "The funeral?"

"Yes, well, it wasn't what I'd been expecting, that's for certain." He clasped his hands together to still their shaking and although he fought it, the memories caught him up again. . . .

* * *

Waking—confused and disoriented. Slowly, he became aware of his heartbeat and allowed it to pull him back to full consciousness. He'd never been in a darkness so complete and, in spite of Christina's remembered reassurance, he began to panic. The panic grew when he tried to push the lid off the crypt and found he couldn't move. Not stone above him, but rough wood embracing him so closely that the rise and fall of his chest brushed against the boards. All around, the smell of earth.

Not a noble's tomb but a common grave.

Screaming until his throat was raw, he twisted and thrashed through the little movement he had but, although the wood creaked once or twice, the weight of earth was absolute.

He stopped then, for he realized that to destroy the coffin and lie covered only in the earth would be infinitely worse. That was when the hunger began. He had no idea how long he lay, paralyzed with terror, frenzied need clawing at his gut, but his sanity hung by a thread when he heard a shovel blade bite into the dirt above him.

*   *   *

"You know," he said, scrubbing a hand across his face, terror still echoing faintly behind the words, "there's a very good reason most vampires come from the nobility; a crypt is a great deal easier to get out of. I'd been buried good and deep and it took Christina three days to find me and dig me free." Sometimes, even four centuries later, when he woke in the evening, he was back there. Alone. In the dark. Facing eternity.

"So your father," Vicki paused, she had trouble with this next bit, "Henry VIII, really did suspect?"

Henry laughed, but the sound had little humor. "Oh, he more than suspected. I discovered later that he'd ordered a stake driven through my heart, my mouth stuffed with garlic and the lips sewn shut, then my head removed and buried separately. Thank God, Norfolk remained a true friend until the end."

"You saw him again?"

"A couple of times. He understood better than I thought."

"What happened to Christina?"

"She guided me through the frenzy that follows the change. She guarded me during the year I slept as my body adapted to its new condition. She taught me how to feed without killing. And then she left."

"She left?" Vicki's brows flew almost to her hairline. "After all that, she left?"

Henry turned again to look out at the lights of the city. She could be out there, he'd never know. Nor, he had to admit a little sadly, would he care. "When the parent/child link is over, we prefer to hunt alone. Our closest bonds are formed when we feed and we can't feed from each other." He rested his hand against the glass. "The emotional bond, the love if you will, that causes us to offer our blood to a mortal never survives the change."

"But you could still. . . ."

"Yes, but it isn't the same." He shook himself free of the melancholy and faced her again. "That also is tied too closely to feeding."

"Oh. Then the stories about vampiric . . . uh . . . ."

"Prowess?" Henry supplied with a grin. "Are true. But then, we get a lot of time to practice."

Vicki felt the heat rise in her face and she had to drop her gaze. Four hundred and fifty years of practice. . . . Involuntarily, she clenched her teeth and the sudden sharp pain from her jaw came as a welcome distraction. *Not tonight, I've got a headache.* She closed the book on her lap and carefully set it aside, glancing down at her watch as she did. 4:43. *I've heard some interesting confessions in my time, but this one. . . .* The option, of course, existed to disbelieve everything she'd heard. To get out of the apartment and away from a certified nut case and call for the people in the white coats to lock Mr. Fitzroy, bastard son of Henry VIII, etcetera, etcetera, away where he belonged. Except, she did believe and trying to convince herself she didn't would be trying to convince herself of a lie.

"Why did you tell me all this?" she asked at last.

Henry shrugged. "The way I saw it, I had two options.

I could trust you or I could kill you. If I trusted you first," he spread his hands, "and discovered it was a bad idea, I could still kill you before you could do me any harm."

"Now wait a minute," Vicki bridled. "I'm not that easy to kill!" He was standing at the window; ten, maybe twelve feet away. Less than a heartbeat later he sat beside her on the couch, both hands resting lightly around her neck. She couldn't have stopped him. She hadn't even seen him move. "Oh," she said.

He removed his hands and continued as though she hadn't interrupted. "But if I killed you first, well, that would be that. And I think we can help each other."

"How?" Up close, he became a little overwhelming and she had to fight the desire to move away. Or move closer. *Four hundred and fifty years develops a forceful personality,* she observed, shifting her gaze to the white velvet upholstery.

"The demon hunts at night. So do I. But the one who calls the demon is mortal and must live his life during the day."

"You're suggesting that we team up?"

"Until the demon is captured, yes."

She brushed the nap of the velvet back and forth, back and forth, and then looked up at him again. *Light hazel eyes. I was right.* "Why do you care?"

"About catching the demon?" Henry stood and paced back to the window. "I don't, not specifically, but the papers are blaming the killings on vampires and are putting us all in danger." Down below, the headlights of a lone car sped up Jarvis Street. "Until just recently, even I thought it was one of my kind; a child, abandoned, untrained."

"What, purposefully left to fend for itself?"

"Perhaps. Perhaps the parent had no idea there was a child at all."

"I thought you said there had to be an emotional bond."

"No, I said the emotional bond did not survive past the change, I didn't say that it had to exist. My kind can create children for as many bad or accidental reasons as yours. Technically, all that is needed is for the vampire to feed too deeply and for the mortal to feed in return."

"For the mortal to feed in return? How the hell would that happen?"

He turned to face her. "I take it," he said dryly, "you don't bite."

Vicki felt her cheeks burn and hurriedly changed the subject. "You were looking for the child?"

"Tonight?" Henry shook his head. "No, tonight I knew and I was looking for the demon." He walked to the couch and leaned over it toward her, hands braced against the pale wood inlaid in the arm. "When the killings stop, the stories will stop and vampires will retreat back into myth and race memory. We prefer it that way. In fact, we work very hard to keep it that way. If the papers convince their readers we are real, they can find us—our habits are too well known." He caught her gaze, held it, and grimly bared his teeth. "I, for one, don't intend to end up staked for something I didn't do."

When he released her—and she refused to kid herself, she couldn't have looked away if he hadn't allowed it— Vicki swept the stuff on the coffee table back into her bag and stood. Although she faced him, she focused on the area just over his right shoulder.

"I have to think about this." She kept her voice as neutral as she could. "What you've told me . . . well, I have to think about it." Lame, but the best she could do.

Henry nodded. "I understand."

"Then I can go?"

"You can go."

She nodded in turn and reaching into her pocket for her gloves, made her way to the door.

"Victoria."

Vicki had never believed that names held power nor that speaking names transferred that power to another, but she couldn't stop herself from pivoting slowly around to face him again.

"Thank you for not suggesting I tell all this to the police."

She snorted. "The police? Do I look stupid?"

He smiled. "No, you don't."

He's had a long time to perfect that smile, she reminded herself, trying to calm the sudden erratic beating of her heart. She fumbled behind her for the door, got it open, and made her escape. Despite proximity, she took a moment on the other side to catch her breath. *Vampires. Demons. They don't teach you about this sort of shit at the police academy. . . .*

Seven

Because the streets in the inner city were far from dark, and as she'd managed so well out at Woodbine with much less light, Vicki decided to walk home. She turned her collar up against the wind, shoved her gloved hands deep in her pockets, more out of habit than for additional warmth, and started west along Bloor Street. It wasn't that far and she needed to think.

The cool air felt good against her jaw and seemed to be easing the pounding in her head. Although she had to be careful about how heavily her heels struck the pavement, walking remained infinitely preferable to the jostling she'd receive in the back of a cab.

And she needed to think.

Vampires and demons; or *a* vampire and *a* demon at least. In eight years on the police force, she'd seen a lot of strangeness and been forced to believe in the existence of things that most sane people—police officers and social workers excepted—preferred to ignore. Next to some of the cruelties the strong inflicted on the weak, vampires and demons weren't that hard to swallow. And the vampire seemed to be one of the good guys.

She saw him smile again and sternly stopped herself from responding to the memory.

At Yonge Street, she turned south, waiting for the green more out of habit than necessity. While not exactly ablaze with light, the intersection was far from dark and the traffic was still infrequent. She wasn't the only person around, Yonge Street never completely emptied, but the others whose business or lifestyle kept them out in the hours between midnight and dawn stayed carefully, unobtrusively, out of her way.

"It's 'cause you walk like a cop," Tony had explained once. "After a while, you guys all develop the same look. In uniform, out of uniform; it doesn't matter any more."

Vicki saw no reason to disbelieve him, she'd seen the effect for herself. Just as she saw no reason to disbelieve Henry Fitzroy; she'd seen the demon for herself as well.

Darkness swirled in darkness and was gone. She'd seen no more than the hint of a shape sinking into the earth, and for that she gave thanks. The vague outline she remembered held horror enough and her mind kept shying away from the memory. The smell of decay, however, she remembered perfectly.

It had been neither sight nor smell that had convinced her Henry spoke the truth. Both could be faked, although she had no idea of how or why. Her own reaction convinced her. Her own terror. Her mind's refusal to clearly recall what she had seen. The feeling of evil, cloying and cold, emanating out of the darkness.

Vicki pulled her jacket tighter, the chill that pebbled her flesh having nothing to do with the temperature of the night.

Demon. At least now they knew what they were looking for. They knew? No, *she* knew. She cracked a smile as she thought of explaining all this to Mike Celluci. He hadn't been there, he'd think she was out of her mind. *Hell, if I hadn't been there, I'd think I was out of my mind.* Besides, she couldn't tell Celluci without betraying Henry. . . .

Henry. Vampire. If he wasn't what he claimed, why would he go to all the trouble of creating such a complicated story?

Never mind, she chided herself. *Stupid question.* She'd known pathological liars, had arrested a couple, had worked with one, and why was never a question they concerned themselves with.

Henry's story had been so complicated, it had to be the truth. Didn't it?

At College Street, she paused on the corner. Only

a block to the west, she could see the lights of police headquarters. She could go in, grab a coffee, talk to someone who understood. *About demons and vampires, right.* Suddenly, the headquarters building seemed very far away.

She could walk past it, keep walking west to Huron Street and home, but, in spite of everything, she wasn't tired and didn't want to enclose herself with walls until she had banished all the dark on dark from the shadows. She watched a streetcar rattle by, the capsule of warmth and light empty save for the driver, and continued south to Dundas.

Approaching the glass and concrete bulk of the Eaton's Center, she heard the bells of St. Michael's Cathedral sound the hour. In the daytime, the ambient noise of the city masked their call but in the still, quiet time before dawn they reverberated throughout the downtown core. Lesser bells added their notes, but the bells of St. Michael's dominated.

Not really sure why, Vicki followed the sound. She'd chased a pusher up the steps of the cathedral once, years ago when she'd still been in uniform. He'd grabbed at the doors claiming sanctuary. The doors had been locked. Apparently, not even God trusted the night in the heart of a large city. The pusher had fought all the way back to the car and he hadn't thought it at all funny when Vicki and her partner insisted on referring to him as Quasimodo.

She expected the heavy wooden doors to be locked again, but to her surprise they swung silently open. Just as silently, she slipped inside and pulled them closed behind her.

Quiet please, warned a cardboard sign, mounted in a gleaming brass floor stand, *Holy Week Vigil in progress.*

Her rubber soled shoes squeaking faintly against the floor, Vicki moved into the sanctum. Only about half of the lights were on, creating an unreal, almost mythical twilight in the church. Vicki could see, but only just and only because she didn't attempt to focus on anything outside the specific. A priest knelt at the altar and the first few rows of pews held a scattering of stocky women dressed in black, looking as though they'd been punched out of the same mold. The faint murmur of voices, lifted in what Vicki assumed was prayer, and the fainter click of beads, did nothing to disturb the heavy hush that hung over the building. Waiting; it felt like they were waiting. For what, Vicki had no idea.

The flickering of open flame caught her eye and she slipped down a side aisle until she could see into an alcove off the south wall. Three or four tiers of candles in red glass jars rose up to a mural that gleamed under a single spotlight. The Madonna, draped in blue and white, held her arms wide as though to embrace a weary world. Her smile offered comfort and the artist had captured a certain sadness around the eyes.

Like many of her generation, Vicki had been raised vaguely Christian. She could recognize the symbols of the church, and she knew the historical story, but that was about it. Not for the first time, she wondered if maybe she hadn't missed out on something important. Peeling off her gloves, she slid into a pew.

I don't even know if I believe in God, she admitted apologetically to the mural. *But then, I didn't believe in vampires before tonight.*

It was warm in the cathedral and the nap she'd had that afternoon seemed very far away. Slowly she slid down against the polished wood and slowly the Madonna's face began to blur. . . .

In the distance something shattered with the hard, definite crash that suggested to an experienced ear it had been thrown violently to the floor. Vicki stirred, opened her eyes, but couldn't seem to gather enough energy to move. She sat slumped in the pew, caught in a curious lassitude while the sounds of destruction grew closer. She could hear men's voices shouting, more self-satisfied than angry, but she couldn't catch the words.

In the alcove the spotlight appeared to have burned out. Wrapped in shadow, illuminated only by the tiers of flickering candles, the Madonna continued to smile sadly, holding her arms out to the world. Vicki frowned. The candles were squat and white, the wax dribbling down irregular sides to pool and harden in the metal holders and on the stone floor.

But the candles were enclosed . . . and the floor, the floor was carpeted. . . .

A crash, louder and closer than the others, actually caused her to jerk but didn't break the inertia holding her in the pew.

She saw the ax head first, then the shaft, then the man holding it. He charged up the side aisle from the front of the church, from the altar. His dark clothes were marked with plaster dust and through the gaping front of his bulging leather vest Vicki thought she saw the glint of gold. Candlelight glittered off colored bits of broken glass caught in the folded tops of his wide boots. Sweat had darkened his short hair, blunt cut to follow the curve of his head, and his lips were drawn back to reveal the yellow slabs of his teeth.

He rocked to a halt at the entrance to the alcove, caught his breath, and raised the ax.

It stopped short of the Madonna's smile, the haft slapping into the upraised hand of the young man who had suddenly appeared in its path. The axman swore and tried to yank the weapon free. The ax stayed exactly where it was.

From Vicki's point of view it appeared that the young man twisted his wrist a gentle half turn and then lowered his arm, but he must have done more for the axman swore again, lost his grip, and almost lost his footing. He stumbled back and Vicki got her first good look at the young man now holding the ax across his body.

Henry. The tiers of flickering candle flame behind him brought out the red-gold highlights in his hair and created almost a halo around his head. He wore the colors of the Madonna; wide bands of snowy white lace at collar and cuff, a white shirt billowing through the slashed sleeves of his pale blue jacket. His eyes, deep in shadow, narrowed and his hands jerked up.

The ax haft snapped. The sound of its shattering reverberated through the alcove, closely followed by the rattle of both pieces striking the floor. Vicki didn't see Henry move, but the next thing she knew he had the axman hanging from his fist by the front of his vest, feet dangling a foot off the marble floor.

"The Blessed Virgin is under my protection," he said, and the quiet words held more menace than any weapon.

The axman's mouth opened and closed, but no sound emerged. He hung limp and terrified. When dropped, he collapsed to his knees, apparently unable to take his eyes from Henry's face.

To Vicki, the vampire looked like an avenging angel, ready to draw a flaming sword at any moment and strike down the enemies of God. The axman apparently agreed, for he moaned softly and raised trembling hands in entreaty.

Henry stepped back and allowed his captive to look away. "Go," he commanded.

Still on his knees, the axman went, scrambling backward until he moved from Vicki's line of sight. Henry watched him go a moment longer, then turned, made the sign of the cross, and knelt. Above his bowed head, Vicki met the painted eyes of the Madonna. Her own grew heavy and, of their own volition, slid slowly closed.

When she opened them again a second later, the spotlight had returned, the candles were back in their red glass containers, and a red-gold head remained bowed beneath the mural.

The inability to move seemed gone, so she pulled herself to her feet and slid out of the pew heading toward the alcove. "Henry. . . ."

At the sound of his name, he crossed himself, stood, and turned to face her, pulling closed his black leather trenchcoat as he moved.

"Wha . . ."

He shook his head, put his finger to his lips, and taking her arm gently in one hand, led her out of the sanctum.

"Did you have a pleasant nap?" he asked, releasing her arm as the heavy wooden door closed behind them.

"Nap?" Vicki repeated, running a hand up through her hair. "I, I guess I did."

Henry peered up into her face with a worried frown. "Are you all right? Your head took a nasty blow earlier."

"No, I'm fine." Obviously, it had been a dream. "You don't have an accent." He'd had one in the dream.

"I lost it years ago. I came to Canada just after World War I. Are you sure you're all right?"

"I told you, I'm fine." She started down the cathedral steps.

Henry sighed and followed. He seemed to remember reading that sleeping after a concussion was not necessarily a good thing, but he'd entered the church right behind her and she hadn't been asleep very long.

It was just a dream, Vicki told herself firmly as the two of them headed north. *Vampires and demons I can handle, but holy visions are out.* Although why she should dream about Henry Fitzroy defending a painting of the Virgin Mary from what looked like one of Cromwell's roundheads she had no idea. *Maybe it was a sign.* Maybe it *was* the blow she'd taken on the head. Either way, her few remaining doubts about his ex-royal bastard highness seemed to have vanished and while she was more willing to bet on her subconscious working it out than on God intervening, she decided to keep an open mind. Just in case. *Wait a minute. . . .*

"You followed me!"

Henry smiled guardedly. "I'd just told you a secret that could get me killed. I had to see how you were dealing with it."

In spite of her pique, Vicki had to admit he made sense. "And?"

He shrugged. "You tell me."

Vicki pushed the strap of her bag back up on her shoulder. "I think," she said slowly, "that you're right. We could accomplish more working together. So, for now, you've got yourself a partner." She stumbled over a dark crack in the pavement, righted herself before Henry could help, and added dryly, "But I think you should know that generally, I only work days." It wasn't the time to tell him why. Not yet.

Henry nodded. "Days are fine. I myself, being a little sensitive to sunlight, prefer to work nights. Between us, we have the entire twenty-four hours covered. And speaking of days," he shot a quick glance to the east where he could feel dawn approaching, "I have to go. Can we discuss this tomorrow evening?"

"When?"

"About two hours after sunset? It'll give me time to grab a bite."

He was gone before she had time to react. Or agree.

"We'll see who plays straight man to whom tomorrow night," she snorted and turned west toward home.

The sun had cracked the horizon by the time she reached her apartment, and with yawns threatening to rip her jaw from her face, she fell straight into bed.

Only to be rudely awakened about forty-five minutes later. . . .

"Where! Have! You! Been!" Celluci punctuated each word with a vigorous shake.

Vicki, whose reactions had never been particularly fast when first roused from sleep, actually let him finish the sentence before bringing her arms up between his and breaking his grip on her shoulders.

"What the hell are you talking about, Celluci?" she demanded, shielding her eyes against the glare from the overhead light with one hand and grabbing her glasses off the bedside table with the other.

"One of the uniforms saw a woman who looked like you being bundled into a late model BMW, just after midnight, and not more than five blocks from the latest body. You want to tell me you weren't in the Woodbine area tonight?"

Vicki leaned back and sighed, pushing her glasses up her nose. "What makes that any business of yours?" There was no point in trying to reason with Celluci until he calmed down.

"I'll tell you what makes it my business." He threw himself off the bed and began to pace the length of the bedroom; three steps and turn, three steps and turn. "You were in the middle of a police investigation, that's what makes it my business. You were. . . ." Suddenly, he stopped. His eyes narrowed and he jabbed an accusing finger in Vicki's direction. "What hit you?"

"Nothing."

"Nothing does not put a black and blue lump the size of a grapefruit on your jaw," Celluci growled. "It was him, wasn't it? The guy loading you into his car." He sat back down on the bed and reached out to turn Vicki's face into the light.

"You are out of your mind!" She knocked his hand away. "Since you obviously aren't going to let me get back to sleep until you satisfy your completely irrational curiosity; I *was* in the area. And, as you keep telling me, I don't see so well in the dark." She smiled with scorpion sweetness. "You were right about something. Make you feel better?"

He responded with an identical smile and growled, "Get on with it."

"I went with a friend. When I walked my face into a post, he took me back to his place to make sure I was all right. All right?" She waved a hand at the door and threw herself back on the pillows. "Now get out!"

"The hell it's all right." He slammed his palm against the bed. "Next to my partner, you are the world's worst liar and you are throwing some grade A bullshit in my direction. Who's this friend?"

"None of your business."

"Where did he take you?"

"Also none of your business." She sat back up and shoved her face close to his. "You jealous, Celluci?"

"Jealous? Damn it, Vicki!" He raised his hands as if to shake her again but let them fall as her eyes narrowed and her own hands came up. "I've got six dead bodies out there. I don't want you to be the seventh!"

Her voice dropped dangerously low. "But *you* should be able to throw yourself in the line of fire?"

"What does that have to do with anything? I had half the fucking force out there with me. You were alone!"

"Oh." She grabbed the front of his jacket and dragged him suddenly forward until their noses touched. "So you were worried?" she ground the words out through clenched teeth. It hurt her jaw, but at least it kept her from ripping his throat out.

"Of course, I was worried."

"THEN WHY DIDN'T YOU SAY SO INSTEAD OF ALTERNATELY ASSAULTING AND ACCUSING ME!" She pushed him backward so hard she flung him off the bed and he had to scramble to get his feet under him.

"Well?" she prodded when he'd regained his balance again.

He pushed the heavy curl of hair off his forehead and shrugged, actually looking a little sheepish. "It . . . I . . . I don't know."

Folding her arms over her breasts, Vicki settled carefully back against the pillows. Given that she'd have done exactly the same thing under similar circumstances she supposed she'd have to let it pass. Besides, her jaw hurt, her whole head hurt, and now she had enough adrenaline in her system to keep her awake for a week.

"You been home yet?" she asked.

Celluci rubbed a weary hand across his eyes. "No. Not yet."

Settling her glasses back on the bedside table, she patted the sheet beside her.

A little later, something occurred to her.

"Wait a minute—watch my jaw—you gave me back your key to my apartment months ago." He'd thrown it at her as a matter of fact.

"I had a copy made."

"You told me there were no copies!"

"Vicki, *you* are a lousy liar. *I* am a very good one. Ow, that hurt!"

"It was supposed to."

"No, Mom, I'm not sick. I was just up late last night working on a case." Vicki wedged the phone between her shoulder and her ear and poured herself a mug of coffee.

On the other end of the line she heard her mother sigh deeply. "You know, Vicki, I had hoped that when you left the force I'd be able to stop worrying about you. And here it is, three in the afternoon and you're not out of bed yet."

What the second observation had to do with the first, escaped Vicki entirely. "Mom, I'm up. I'm drinking coffee." She took a noisy swallow. "I'm talking to you. What more do you want?"

"I want you to get a normal job."

As Vicki was well aware how proud her mother had been of her two police citations, she let this pass. She knew that in time, if it hadn't happened already, the phrase "my daughter the private investigator" would begin peppering her mother's conversations much the way "my daughter the homicide investigator" had.

"And what's more, Vicki, your voice sounds funny."

"I walked my face into a post. I got a bit of a bump on my chin. It hurts a little when I talk."

"Did this happen last night?"

"Yes, Mom."

"You know you can't see in the dark. . . ."

It was Vicki's turn to sigh. "Mom, you're beginning to sound like Celluci." On cue, Celluci came out of the bedroom, tucking his shirt into his pants. Vicki waved him at the coffeepot, but he shook his head and stuffed his arms into his overcoat. "Hold on for a minute, Mom." She covered the receiver with one hand and looked him over critically. "If we're going to keep this up, you'd better bring a razor back over. You look like a terrorist."

He scratched at his chin and shrugged. "I have a razor at the office."

"And a change of clothes?"

"They can live with yesterday's shirt for a few hours." He bent down and kissed her gently, careful not to put too much pressure on the spreading green and purple bruise. "I don't suppose you'll listen if I ask you to be careful?"

She returned the kiss as enthusiastically as she was able to and said, "I don't suppose you'll listen if I ask you to stop being a patronizing son of a bitch?"

He scowled. "Because I ask you to be careful?"

"Because you assume I won't be. Because you assume I'm going to do something stupid."

"All right." He spread his arms in surrender. "How about, don't do anything I wouldn't do?"

She considered saying, *"I'm paying a call on a vampire tonight, how do you feel about that?"* but decided against it and said instead, "I thought you didn't want me to do anything stupid?"

He smiled. "I'll call you," he told her, and left.

"You still there, Mom?"

"They won't let me go home until five, dear. Where else would I be? What was that all about?"

"Mike Celluci was just leaving." She tucked the phone under her arm and with the extra long cord trailing behind her, got up to make toast.

"So you're seeing him again?"

The last piece of bread was a little moldy around the edges. She tossed it in the garbage and settled for a bag of no-name chocolate chip cookies. "I seem to be."

"Well, you know what they say about spring and a young man's fancy."

She sounded doubtful, so Vicki changed the subject. Her mother had liked Celluci well enough the few times they'd met, she just thought that temperamentally they'd both be better off with someone calmer. "It's spring?" Gusts of wind slapped what could've been rain but looked more like sleet against the windows.

"It's April, dear. That makes it spring."

"Yeah, what's your weather like?"

Her mother laughed. "It's snowing."

Vicki brushed cookie crumbs off her sweatshirt and got herself more coffee. "Look, Mom, this is going to be costing the department a fortune." Her mother had worked for eighteen years as the private secretary of the head of Life Sciences at Queen's University, Kingston and she abused the privileges that had accumulated as often as possible. "Although you know I enjoy talking to you, did you have an actual reason for calling?"

"Well, I was wondering if you might be coming down for Easter."

"Easter?"

"It's this weekend. I won't be working tomorrow or Monday, we could have four whole days together."

Darkness, demons, vampires, and six bodies, the life violently ripped from them.

"I don't think so, Mom. The case I'm on could break at any time. . . ."

After listening to a few more platitudes and promising to stay in touch, Vicki hung up and went to her weight bench to work off equal parts of cookies and guilt.

*   *   *

"Henry, it's Caroline. I've got tickets to the *Phantom* for May fourth. You said you wanted to see it and now's your chance. Give me a call in the next couple of days if you're free."

It was the only message on the machine. Henry shook his head at his vague sense of disappointment. There was no reason for Vicki Nelson to call. No reason he should want her to.

"All right," he glared at his reflection in the antique mirror over the telephone table, "you tell me why I trusted her. Circumstance?" He shook his head. "No. Circumstance said I should have disposed of her. A much neater solution with much less risk. Try again. She reminded you of someone? If you live long enough, and you will, *everyone* will remind you of someone."

Turning away from the mirror, he sighed and ran his fingers through his hair. He could deny it all he wanted but she did remind him of someone, not in form perhaps but in manner.

Ginevra Treschi had been the first mortal he had trusted after the change. There had been others with whom he had played at trust but in her arms he was himself, not needing to be anything more. Or less.

When he found he could not live in Elizabeth's England—it was both too like and too unlike the England he had known—he had moved south, to Italy and finally to Venice. Venice had much to offer one of his kind for the ancient city came alive at night and in its shadows he could feed as he chose.

It had been carnival, he remembered, and Ginevra had been standing by San Marco, at the edge of the square, watching the crowd surging back and forth before her like a living kaleidoscope. She'd seemed so very real amidst all the posturing that he'd moved closer. When she left, he followed her back to her father's house then spent the rest of the night discovering her name and situation.

"Ginevra Treschi." Even three hundred years and many mortals later it still sounded in his mouth like a benediction.

The next night, while the servants slept and the house was quiet and dark, he'd slipped into her room. Her heartbeat had drawn him to the bed and he'd gently pulled the covers back. Almost thirty and three years a widow, she wasn't beautiful, but she was so alive—even asleep—that he'd found himself staring. Only to find, a few moments later, that she was staring back at him.

"I don't wish to hurry your decision," she'd said dryly. "But I'm getting chilled and I'd like to know if I should scream."

He'd intended to convince her he was only a dream but he found he couldn't.

They had almost a year of nights together.

"A convent?" Henry raised himself up on one elbow, disentangling a long strand of ebony hair from around the back of his neck. "If you'll forgive me saying so, *bella,* I don't think you'd enjoy convent life."

"I'm not making a joke, Enrico. I go with the Benedictine Sisters tomorrow after early Mass."

For a moment, Henry couldn't speak. The thought of his Ginevra locked away from the world struck him as close to a physical blow. "Why?" he managed at last.

She sat up, wrapping her arms around her knees. "I had a choice, the Sisters or Giuseppe Lemmo." Her lips pursed as though she tasted something sour. "The convent seemed the better course."

"But why choose at all?"

She smiled and shook her head. "In your years out of the world you have forgotten a few things, my love. My father wishes me for Signore Lemmo, but he will graciously allow me to go to God if only to get his overly educated daughter out of his house." Her voice grew serious and she stroked a finger down the length of Henry's bare chest. "He fears the Inquisition, Enrico. Fears that I will bring the Papal Hounds down upon the family." Her lips twisted. "Or that he will be forced to denounce me."

Henry stared at her in astonishment. "The Inquisition? But you've done nothing. . . ."

Both her eyebrows rose. "I am lying with you and for some, even not knowing what you are, that would be enough. If they knew that I willingly give myself to an Angel of Darkness . . ." She turned her wrist so that the small puncture wound became visible. ". . . burning would be too good for me." A finger laid against his lips stopped him when he tried to speak. "Yes, yes, no one knows but I am also a woman who dares to use her mind and that is enough for these times. If my husband had died and left me rich or if I had borne a son to carry on his name. . . ." Her shoulders lifted and fell. "Unfortunately . . ."

He caught up her hand. "You have another choice."

"No." She sighed. The breath quavered as she released it. "I have thought long and hard on this, Enrico, and I cannot take your path. It is my need to live as I am that places me in danger now, I simply could not exist behind the masks you must wear to survive."

It was the truth and he knew it, but that made it no easier to bear. "When I was changed . . ."

"When you were changed," she interrupted, "from what you have told me, the passion was so great it left no room for rational thought, no room to consider what would happen after. Although I am fond of passion," her hand slid down between his legs, "I cannot lose myself in it."

He pushed her back onto the pillow, trapping her beneath him. "This doesn't have to end."

She laughed. "I know you, Enrico." Her eyes half closed and she thrust her hips up against him. "Could you do *this* with a nun?"

After a moment of shock, he laughed as well and bent his mouth to hers. "If you are sure," he murmured against her lips.

"I am. If I must give up my freedom, better to God than to man."

All he could do was respect her decision.

It hurt to lose her, but in the months that followed the hurt eased and it was enough to know that the Sisters kept her safe. Although he thought of leaving, Henry lingered in Venice, not wanting to cut the final tie.

Chance alone brought him news that the Sisters had not been able to keep her safe enough. Hushed whispers overheard in a dark café said the Hounds had come for Ginevra Treschi, taken her right from the convent, said she had been consorting with the devil, said they were going to make an example of her. She had been with them three weeks.

Three weeks with fire and iron and pain.

He wanted to storm their citadel like Christ at the gates of hell, but he forced himself to contain his rage. He could not save her if he threw himself into the Inquisitor's embrace.

If anything remained of her to be saved.

They had taken over a wing of the Doge's palace— the Doge being more than willing to cooperate with Rome. The smell of death rolled through the halls like fog and the blood scent left a trail so thick a mortal could have followed it.

He found her hanging as they'd left her. Her wrists had been tightly bound behind her back, a coarse rope threaded through the lashing and used to hoist her into the air. Heavy iron weights hung from her burned ankles. They had obviously begun with flogging and had added greater and more painful persuasions over time. She had been dead only a few hours.

". . . confessed to having relations with the devil, was forgiven, and gave her soul up to God." He rubbed his fingers in his beard. "Very satisfactory all around. Shall we return the body to the Sisters or to her family?"

The older Dominican shrugged. "I cannot see that it makes any difference, she. . . . Who are you?"

Henry smiled. "I am vengeance," he said, closing the door behind him and bolting it.

*   *   *

"Vengeance." Henry sighed and wiped damp palms on his jeans. The Papal Hounds had died in terror, begging for their lives, but it hadn't brought Ginevra back. Nothing had, until Vicki had prodded at the memories. She was as real in her own world as Ginevra had been and unless he was very careful, she was about to become as real in his.

He'd wanted this, hadn't he? Someone to trust. Someone who could see beneath the masks.

He turned again to face his reflection in the mirror. The others, men and women whose lives he'd entered over the years since Ginevra, had never touched him like this.

"Keep her at a distance," he warned himself. "At least until the demon is defeated." His reflection looked dubious and he sighed. "I only hope I'm up to it."

*   *   *

The girl darted behind the heavy table, sapphire eyes flashing. "I thought you were a gentleman, sir!"

"You are exactly right, Smith." The captain bowed with a feline grace, never taking his mocking gaze from his quarry. "Or should that be Miss Smith? Never mind. As you pointed out, I was a gentleman. You'll find I surrendered the title some time ago." He lunged, but she twisted lithely out of his way.

"If you make one more move toward me, I shall scream."

"Scream away." Roxborough settled one slim hip against the table. "I shan't stop you. Although it would pain me to have to share such a lovely prize with my crew."

"Fitzroy, what is this shit?"

"Henry, please, not Fitzroy." He saved the file and

shut off the computer. "And this shit," he told her, straightening, "is my new book."

"Your what?" Vicki asked, pushing her glasses up her nose. She'd followed him from the door of the condo into the tiny office even though he'd requested that she wait a minute in the living room. If he was going back to close his coffin, she had to see it. "You actually read this stuff?"

Henry sighed, pulled a paperback off the shelf above the desk, and handed it to her. "No. I actually write the stuff."

"Oh." Across the cover of the book, a partially unclothed young woman was being passionately yet discreetly embraced by an entirely unclothed young man. The cover copy announced the date of the romance as "the late 1800s" but both characters had distinctly out of period hair and makeup. Cursive lavender script delineated both the title and the author's name; *Destiny's Master* by Elizabeth Fitzroy.

"Elizabeth Fitzroy?" Vicki asked, returning the book.

Henry slid it back on the shelf, rolled the chair out from the desk, and stood, smiling sardonically. "Why *not* Elizabeth Fitzroy? She certainly had as much right to the name as I do."

The prefix "Fitz" was a bastard's signifier and was given to acknowledged accidental children. The "roy" identified the father as the king. "You didn't agree with the divorce?"

The smile twisted further. "I was always a loyal subject of the king, my father." He paused and frowned as though trying to remember. He sounded less mocking when he started speaking again. "I liked her Gracious Majesty Queen Catherine. She was kind to a very confused little boy who'd been dumped into a situation he didn't understand and he didn't ever much care for. Mary, the Princess Royal, who could have ignored me or done worse, accepted me as her brother." His voice picked up an edge. "I did not like Elizabeth's mother and the feeling was most definitely mutual. Given that all parties concerned have now passed to their eternal reward; no, I did not agree with the divorce."

Vicki glanced back at the shelf of paperbacks as Henry politely but inexorably ushered her out of his office. "I suppose you've got a lot of material to use for plots," she muttered dubiously.

"I do," Henry agreed, wondering why some people had less trouble handling the idea of a vampire than they did a romance writer.

"I suppose you can get even with any number of people in your past this way." Of all the strange scenarios Vicki had imagined occurring during this evening's conference with the over four century old, vampiric, bastard son of Henry VIII, none had included discovering that he was a writer of—*what was the term?*—bodice rippers.

He grinned and shook his head. "If you're thinking of my relatives, I got even with most of them. I'm still alive. But that's not why I write. I'm good at it, I make a very good living doing it, and most of the time I enjoy it." He waved her to the couch and sat down at the opposite end. "I could exist from feeding to feeding—and I have—but I infinitely prefer living in comfort than in some rat-infested mausoleum."

"But if you've been around for so long," Vicki wondered, settling down into the same corner she'd vacated early that morning, "why aren't you rich?"

"Rich?"

Vicki found his throaty chuckle very attractive and also found herself speculating about. . . . A mental smack brought her wandering mind back to the business at hand.

"Oh, sure," he continued, "I could've bought IBM for pennies in nineteen-oh-whenever, but who knew? I'm a vampire, I'm not clairvoyant. Now," he picked a piece of lint off his jeans, "may I ask you a question?"

"Be my guest."

"Why did you believe what I told you?"

"Because I saw the demon and you had no logical reason to lie to me." There was no need to tell him about the dream—or vision—in the church. It hadn't had much to do with her decision anyway.

"That's it?"

"I'm an uncomplicated sort of a person. Now," she

mimicked his tone, "enough about us. How *do* we catch a demon?"

Very well, Henry agreed silently. *If that's how you want it, enough about us.*

"We don't. I do." He inclined his head toward her end of the couch. "You catch the man or woman calling it up."

"Fine." Tackling the source made perfect sense to Vicki and the farther she could stay from that repulsive bit of darkness the happier she'd be. She perched her right foot on her left knee and clasped both hands around the ankle. "How come you're so sure we're dealing with a single person, not a coven or a cult?"

"Focused desire is a large part of what pulls the demon through and most groups just can't achieve the necessary single-mindedness." He shrugged. "Given the success rate, the odds are good it's just one person."

She mirrored his shrug. "Then we go with the odds. Any distinguishing characteristics I should look for?"

Henry stretched his arm out and drummed his fingers against the upholstery. "If you're asking does a certain type of person call up demons, no. Well," he frowned as he reconsidered, "in a way, yes. Without exception, they're people looking for an easy answer, a way to get what they want without working for it."

"You just described a way of life for millions of people," Vicki told him dryly. "Could you be a little more specific?"

"The demon is being asked for material goods; it wouldn't need to kill if it remained trapped in the pentagram answering questions. Look for someone who's suddenly acquired great wealth, money, cars. And demons can't create so all that has to come from somewhere."

"We could catch him for possession of stolen goods?" They couldn't mark every bit of cash in existence, but luxury cars, jewels, and stocks all were traceable. Vicki's pulse began to quicken as she ran over the possibilities now open to investigation. *Yes!* Her hands curled into fists and punched the air triumphantly. It was only a matter of time. They had him. Or her.

"One more thing," Henry warned, trying not to smile

at her—what did they call it? Shadow boxing? "The more contact this person has with demonkind, the more unstable he or she is going to get."

"Yeah? Well, it's another trait to look for, but you've got to be pretty damned unstable to stand out these days. What about the demon?"

"The demon isn't very powerful."

Vicki snorted. "You might be able to rip a person's throat out with a single blow . . ." She paused and Henry nodded, answering the not-quite-asked question. ". . . but no one else I know could. This demon is plenty powerful enough."

Henry shook his head. "Not as demons go. It has to feed every time it's called in order to have an effect on things in this world."

"So the deaths were it feeding? Completely random?"

"They didn't mean anything to the person controlling the demon if that's what you're asking. If the demon had been killing business or personal rivals of a single person, the police would have found him or her by now. No, the demon chose where and whom to feed on."

Vicki frowned. "But there *was* a definite external pattern."

"My guess is that the demon being called is under the control of another, more powerful demon and has been attempting to form that demon's name on the city."

"Oh."

Henry waited patiently while Vicki absorbed this new bit of information.

"Why?" Actually, she wasn't sure she wanted to know. Or that she needed to ask.

"Access; uncontrolled access for the more powerful demon and however many more of its kind it might want to bring through."

"And how many more deaths until the name is completed?"

"No way of knowing."

"One? Two? You must have some idea," she snapped. With one hand he gave her hope, with the other he took it away. The son of a bitch. "How many deaths in a demon's name?"

"It depends on the demon." As Vicki scowled, he rose, walked to the bookcase, and slid open one of the glass doors. The book he removed was about the size of a dictionary, bound in leather that might have once been red before years of handling had darkened it to a worn and greasy black. He sat back down, closer this time, twisted the darkly patinaed clasp, and opened the book to a double page spread.

"It's hand-written," Vicki marveled, touching the corner of a page. She withdrew her finger quickly. The parchment had felt warm, like she'd just touched something obscenely alive.

"It's very old." Henry ignored her reaction; his had been much the same the first time he'd touched the book. "These are the demonic names. There're twenty-seven of them and no way of knowing if the author discovered them all."

The names, written in thick black ink in an unpleasantly angular script, were for the most part seven or eight letters long. "The demon can't be anywhere near finished," she said thankfully. She still had time to find the bastard behind this.

Henry shook his head, hating to dampen her enthusiasm. "It wouldn't be laying out the entire name, just the symbol for it." He flipped ahead a few pages. The list of names was repeated and beside each was a corresponding geometrical sign. Some were very simple. "Literacy is a fairly recent phenomenon," Henry murmured. "The signs are all that are really needed."

Vicki swallowed. Her mouth had gone suddenly dry. Some of the signs were *very* simple.

Silently, Henry closed the book and replaced it on the shelf. When he turned to face her again, he spread his arms in a helpless gesture. "Unfortunately," he said, "I can't stop the demon until after it kills again."

"Why not?"

"Because I have to be there ready for it. And last night it completed the second part of the pattern."

"Then it could have completed . . ."

"No. We'd know if it had."

"But the next death, the death that starts the pattern again, it could complete . . ."

"No, not yet. Not even the least complicated of the names could be finished so quickly."

"You were ready for it last night." He'd been there, just as she had. "Why didn't you stop it, then?" But then, why didn't she?

"Stop it?" The laugh had little humor in it. "It moved so fast I barely saw it. But the time after next, now that I know what I'm facing, I'll be waiting for it. I can trap it and destroy it."

That sounded encouraging, if there *was* a time after next. "You've done this before?"

She needed reassurance but Henry, who knew he could make her believe anything he chose to tell her, found he couldn't lie. "Well, no." He'd never been able to lie to Ginevra either, another similarity between the two women he'd just as soon not have found.

Vicki took a deep breath and picked at the edge of her sweater. "Henry, how bad will it get if the named demon gets free?"

"How bad?" He sighed and sagged back against the bookcase. "At the risk of being considered facetious, all hell will break loose."

Eight

Norman glanced around the Cock and Bull and frowned. Thursday, Friday, and Saturday nights, the nights he'd set aside for seriously trying to pick up chicks, he arrived early to be sure of getting a table. So far, this had meant by 9:30 or 10:00, someone would have to share with him. Tonight, the Thursday before the long Easter weekend, the student pub was so empty it looked as if he'd have no company all night.

It isn't cool to go home for Easter, he thought smugly, running a finger up and down the condensation on his glass of diet ginger ale. His parents had been disappointed, but he'd been adamant. The really cool guys hung out around the university all weekend and Norman Birdwell was now really cool.

He sighed. They didn't, however, apparently hang out at the Cock and Bull. He'd have given up and gone home long ago except for the redhead who held court at the table in the corner. She was absolutely beautiful, everything Norman had ever wanted in a woman, and he had long adored her from across the room in their Comparative Religions class. She wasn't very tall, but her flaming hair gave her a presence and inches in other areas made up for her lack of height. Norman could imagine ripping off her shirt and just gazing at the softly mounded flesh beneath. She'd smile at him in rapt adoration and he'd gently reach out to touch. His imagination wasn't up to much beyond that, so he replayed the scene over and over as he stared across the room.

A beer or two later and voices at the corner table began to rise.

"But I'm telling you there's evidence," the redhead exclaimed, "for the killer being a creature of the night."

"Get real, Coreen!"

Her name was Coreen! Norman's heart picked up an irregular rhythm and he leaned forward, straining to hear more clearly.

"What about the missing blood?" Coreen demanded. "Every victim sucked dry."

"A pyscho," snorted one of her companions.

"A giant leech," suggested another. "A giant leech that slimes along the streets of the city until it finds a victim and then . . . SLURP!" He sucked back a beer, suiting the action to the word. The group at the table groaned and buried him in thrown napkins and then Coreen's voice rose over the babble.

"I'm telling you there was nothing natural about these deaths!"

"Nothing natural about giant leeches either," muttered a tall, blonde woman in a bright pink flannel shirt.

Coreen turned on her. "You know what I mean, Janet. And I'm not the only person who thinks so either!"

"You're talking about the stories in the newspapers? Vampire stalks city and all that?" Janet sighed expansively and shook her head. "Coreen, they don't believe that bullshit, they're just trying to sell papers."

"It isn't bullshit!" Coreen insisted, slamming her empty mug down on the table. "Ian was killed by a vampire!" Her mouth thinned into an obstinate line and the others at the table exchanged speaking glances. One by one, they made excuses and drifted away.

Coreen didn't even look up as Norman sat down in Janet's recently vacated chair. She was thinking of how foolish all her so-called friends would look when her private investigator found the vampire and destroyed him. They'd soon stop laughing at her then.

Norman, after taking a few moments to work out the best things to say, tried a tentative, "Hi." The icy stare he received in response discouraged him a little, but he swallowed and went on. He might never get another chance like this. "I just, uh, wanted you to know that, uh, I believe you."

"Believe what?" The question was only slightly less icy than the stare.

"Believe, well, you. About the vampires." Norman lowered his voice. "And stuff."

The way he said *"and stuff"* sent chills down Coreen's back. She took a closer look and thought she might vaguely remember him from one of her classes, although she couldn't place which one. Nor could she be sure if her lack of clear memory had more to do with him or with the pitcher of beer she'd just finished.

"I know," he continued, glancing around to be sure that no one would overhear, "that there's more to the world than most people think. And I know what it's like to be laughed at." He ground out the last words with such feeling that she had to believe them and believing them, to believe the rest.

"It doesn't matter what we know." She poked him in the chest with a fingernail only a slightly less brilliant red than her hair. "We can't prove anything."

"I can. I've got completely incontestable proof in my apartment." He grinned at her look of surprise and nodded, adding emphasis. *And the best part of it is,* he thought, almost rubbing his hands in anticipation, *it isn't a line. I do have the proof and when I show her, she'll fall into my arms and. . . .* Once again, his imagination balked but he didn't care that fantasy failed him; soon he'd have the reality.

"You can help me prove that a vampire murdered Ian?" The brilliant green eyes blazed and Norman, transfixed, found himself stammering.

"V-vampire. . . ." Caught up in the proof he could offer her, he'd forgotten she expected vampires.

Coreen took the repetition as an affirmation. "Good." She practically dragged him to his feet and then out of the Cock and Bull. She wasn't very big, Norman discovered, but she was pretty strong. "We'll take my car. It's out in the lot."

Her headlong charge slowed a little as they reached

the doors and stopped completely by the row of pay phones. She frowned and came to a sudden decision.

"You got a quarter?"

Norman dug one out of his pocket and handed it over. He wanted to give her the world; what was twenty-five cents? As Coreen dialed, he inched toward her until by the time she started to speak he stood close enough to hear perfectly.

"Hi, it's Coreen Fergus. Oh, I'm sorry, were you asleep?" She twisted to look at her watch. "Yeah, I guess. But you've gotta hear this. Of course, it's about the vampire. Why else would I call you? *Look,* I met a guy who says he had incontestable proof . . . in his apartment. . . . Give me a break. You're my detective, not my mother." The receiver missed being slammed back onto its cradle by the narrowest of margins.

"Some people," she muttered, "are just so bitchy when you wake them up. Come on." She gave him a little push in the direction of the parking lot. "Ian's death will be avenged even if I have to do it all myself."

Norman, suddenly realizing that he and not the vampire Coreen seemed fixated on had been in some small part responsible for Ian's death, wondered what he should do next. *Nothing,* he decided, hurriedly buckling his seat beat as Coreen pulled out with a squeal of rubber. *She's coming to my apartment, that's the main thing. Once she's there, I can handle the rest.* His chest puffed out as he thought of what he'd achieved. *When I show her, she'll be so impressed she'll forget about the vampire and Ian both.*

Norman's apartment was in a cluster of identical high rises perched on the flatland west of York University and completely out of sync with their surroundings. He pointed out the visitors' parking and with one eye on the York Regional Police car that had been following her for the last quarter mile Coreen pulled into the first empty spot and shut the motor off. The police car kept going and Coreen, well aware she shouldn't have been driving at all after sharing three pitchers of beer, heaved a sigh of relief.

While Norman fumbled with his keys, she stared through the glass doors at the beige and brown lobby and wondered how he could tell he was in the right building. In the elevator, she drummed her fingers against the stainless steel wall. If she hadn't been feeling so sorry for herself back in the pub that her mind had been on hold, she'd have never gone anywhere with Norman Birdwell. She'd realized who he was the moment she saw him under the bright lights in the parking lot. If York University had a definitive geek, he was it.

Except . . . She frowned, remembering. Except he'd really sounded like he knew something, and for Ian's sake she had to follow every lead. Maybe there was more to him than met the eye. She glanced at Norman, who was smiling at her in a way she didn't like, and realized suddenly where he fit in. He was the vampire's Renfield! The human servant who not only eased his master's way in the modern world but who, on occasion, procured. . . .

Her hand went to her throat and the tiny gold crucifix her grandfather had given her at her first communion. If Norman "The Geek" Birdwell thought he was procuring her as a late night snack for his undead master, he was in for a bit of a surprise. She patted her purse and the comforting bulge of a squirt gun filled with holy water. She wasn't afraid to use it either and she'd seen enough vampire movies to know what the effect would be. Holy water wouldn't affect Norman, of course, but then Norman wasn't much of a threat.

"When I started this, I wanted to change to the four-teenth floor," Norman told her, managing to get his keys in the lock in spite of his trembling hands. *I'm actually bringing a girl back to my apartment!* "Because the four-teenth floor is really the thirteenth, but they didn't have any empties so I'm still on nine."

"There's a lot of psychic significance in the number nine," Coreen muttered, pushing past him into the apartment. The entrance way, with its coat closet and plastic mat, opened into one big room that didn't appear to contain a coffin. An old sofa, covered in a handmade afghan, was pushed up against one wall and a blue metal trunk served as a coffee table. Tucked over in a corner, by the door that led to the balcony, was a square plastic fan and a tiny desk buried beneath computer equipment. At the other end of the room, stove, fridge, and sink made a half turn around a chrome and vinyl table with two matching chairs.

Coreen's nose wrinkled. The whole place looked spotless but there was a distinctly funny smell. Then she noticed that every available flat surface held at least one solid air freshener: little plastic mushrooms, shells, and fake crystal candy dishes. The combined effect was somewhat overpowering.

"Can I take your coat?" He had to raise his voice to be heard over the noise of the stereo in the apartment upstairs.

"No." She sneezed and dug a tissue out of her pocket. "Do you have a bathroom?" All the beer seemed to have suddenly passed through her system.

"Oh, yes." He opened a door that led to both a walk-in closet and the bathroom. "In here."

She's freshening up! he thought, almost dancing as he neatly hung up his own coat. *There's a girl in my bathroom and she's freshening up!* He cleaned the apartment every Thursday just in case this happened. And now it had. Wiping damp palms against his thighs, he wondered if he should get out the chips and dip. *No,* he decided, trying to settle himself in a nonchalant position on the sofa, *that would be for later. For after.*

Coming out of the bathroom, Coreen had a look around the huge closet. Still no coffin; it looked like she was safe. Norman's clothes were hung neatly by type, shirts together, pants together, a gray polyester suit hanging in solitary splendor. His shoes, a pair of brown loafers and a pair of spotless sneakers, were lined up toes to the wall. Although she didn't quite have the nerve to check his dresser drawers, Coreen figured Norman as the type who'd fold his underwear. Tucked into one corner, looking very out of place, was a hibachi perched across the top of a plastic milk crate. She would have investigated the contents of the crate except the smell behind the smell of plastic roses seemed to originate from that corner and, mixed with the beer, it made her feel a little ill.

Probably some lab project he's working on at home. Her mind produced a vision of Norman in a long white coat attaching wires to the electrodes in the neck of his latest creation and she had to stifle a giggle as she came out into the main room.

She didn't like the look that crossed Norman's face as she perched on the other end of the couch and she began to think she'd made a big mistake coming up here. "Well?" she demanded. "You said you had something to show me, something that would prove the existence of the vampire to the rest of the world." If he wasn't Renfield, she had no idea what he was up to.

Norman frowned. Had he said that? He didn't think he'd said that. "I, I, uh, do have something to show you, but it's not exactly a vampire."

Coreen snorted and stood, heading for the door. "Yeah, I bet." Something to show her indeed. If he showed it to her, she'd cut it off.

"No, really." Norman stood as well, tottering a little on the heels of his cowboy boots. "What I can show you will prove that supernatural forces are at work in this city. It can't be a very big step from that to vampires. Can it?"

"No." In spite of the whiny tone, he really did sound like he knew what he was talking about. "I suppose not."

"So won't you sit down again?"

He took a step toward her and she took three steps back. "No. Thanks. I'll stand." She could feel her grip on her temper slipping. "What do you have to show me?"

Norman drew himself up proudly and, after a little fumbling, managed to slip his thumbs behind his belt loops. This would impress her. "I can call up demons."

"Demons?"

He nodded. She'd be his now and forget all about her dead boyfriend and her stupid vampire theory.

Coreen added a conical hat with stars and a magic wand to her earlier vision of Norman and the monster and this time couldn't stop the giggle from escaping.

Nerves, as much as anything, prompted the reaction for despite his reputation she almost believed he spoke the truth and was ready to be convinced.

Norman had no way of knowing that.

She's laughing at me. How dare she laugh at me after I was the only one who didn't laugh at her. How dare she! Incoherent with hurt and anger, Norman dove forward and grabbed Coreen's shoulders, thrusting his mouth at hers with enough force to split his upper lip against her teeth. He didn't even feel that small pain as he began to grind his body, from mouth to hips, down the soft yielding length of her. He'd teach her not to laugh at him!

The next pain forced the breath out of him and sent him staggering backward making small mewling sounds. Tripping on the edge of the trunk, he sat, clutching his crotch and watching the world turn red, and orange, and black.

Coreen jabbed at the elevator button for the lobby, berating herself for being so stupid. "Calling up demons, yeah, right!" she snarled, kicking at the stainless steel wall. "And I almost believed him. It was just another pickup line." Except that, just for a moment, as he grabbed her, his face had twisted and for that moment she'd been truly afraid. He almost hadn't looked human. And then the attack became something she had long ago learned to deal with and the moment passed.

"Men are such bastards," she informed the elderly, and somewhat surprised, East Indian gentleman waiting at the ground floor.

At the door, she discovered that one of her new red leather gloves had fallen out of her jacket pocket during the scuffle and was still in Norman's apartment. "Great, just great." She considered going back for it—she knew she could take Norman in a fight—but decided against it. If she got the opportunity to close her hands around his scrawny neck, she'd probably strangle him.

Shoulders hunched against the wind, she stomped out to her car and soothed her lacerated feelings by burning rubber the length of the parking lot.

* * *

As the pain receded, the anger grew.

She laughed at me. I shared the secret of the century with some stupid girl who believes in vampires, and she laughed at me. Carefully, not certain his legs would hold him, Norman stood. *Everyone always laughed at me. Last one chosen to play baseball. Never wearing quite the same clothes as the other kids. They even laughed when I got perfect marks on tests.* He'd stopped telling them all about it eventually; about the A plus papers, about the projects used as study aids by the teachers, about winning the science fair three years in a row, about reading *War and Peace* over the weekend. They weren't interested in his triumphs. They always laughed.

Just like she *laughed.*

The anger burned away the last of the pain.

Knees carefully apart, Norman shoved the trunk up against the wall, then grabbed the afghan off the sofa and hung it on the half dozen hooks he'd put over the apartment door. The heavy wool would trap most of the odors before they could reach the hall. For the rest, he opened the balcony door about two inches and used one of the mushroom shaped air fresheners to keep it from slamming closed. Ignoring the sudden stream of cold air and the increase in noise from above, he pushed the fan up tight against the crack and turned it on.

Then he went into the closet for the hibachi and the plastic milk crate.

The tiny barbecue he set up as close as he could to the fan. He built a pyramid of three charcoal briquets, soaked them in starter fluid and dropped in a match. The fan and the high winds around the building took care of almost all of the smoke and, as he'd disconnected his smoke detector and the four that covered the ninth floor hallway, he didn't worry about the small amount of smoke that remained. He let the fire burn down while he got out the colored chalks to draw the pentagram.

No-wax tile flooring doesn't hold chalk well, so Norman actually used chalk pastels. It didn't seem to make a difference. At each of the five corners of the pentagram, he set two candles; a black one nine inches high,

and a red one six inches high. He'd had to cut them
both down from twelves and eights and had discovered
that a few of the blacks were actually dark purple. That
hadn't seemed to matter either.

Candles lit, he knelt before the now glowing coals and
began the steps to call the demon.

He'd bought six inches of the eighteen karat gold
chain at a store in Chinatown. With a pair of nail scissors, he clipped off three or four links and let them fall
into the glowing red heart of the charcoal briquettes.
Norman knew that the hibachi couldn't possibly deliver
enough heat to melt even that little bit of gold but, although he sifted the remaining ash every time, there was
never an answering gleam of metal.

The frankincense came from a trendy food store on
Bloor Street West. He had no idea what other people
used the bright orange flakes for—he couldn't imagine
eating them although he supposed they might be a spice.
The half handful he threw on the heat ignited slowly,
creating a thick, pungent smoke that the fan almost managed to deal with.

Coughing and rubbing the back of one hand across
watering eyes, he reached for the last ingredient. The
myrrh had come from a shop specializing in essence oils
and the creation of personal, signature perfumes. Ounce
for ounce it had been more expensive than the gold.
Carefully, using the plastic measuring set his mother had
given him when he moved out, he dribbled an eighth of
a teaspoon over the coals.

The heavy scent of the frankincense grew heavier still
and the air in the apartment picked up a bitter taste that
coated the inside of Norman's mouth and nose. The first
night he'd tried this, he'd almost stopped with the myrrh,
had almost been unable to get past the weight of history
that came with it. For centuries myrrh had been used to
treat the dead, and all those centuries of death were
released every time the oil poured over the coals. By
the second time, he could shrug aside the dead with the
knowledge of worse to come. By this, the seventh calling, it no longer distracted him from the task at hand.

The sterile pins, identical to the ones the Red Cross

used to take the initial drops of blood from donors, he'd bought at a surgical supply house. Usually he hated this part, but tonight the anger drew him through it without pause. The small pain spread down from his fingertip until it joined the throbbing between his legs and the sudden sexual tension almost threw him out of the ritual. His breathing ragged, he somehow managed to maintain control.

Three drops of blood onto the coals and as each drop fell, a word of calling.

The words he'd found in one of the texts used in his Comparative Religions class. He'd created the ritual himself, made it up out of equal parts research and common sense. *Anyone could do it,* he thought smugly. *But only I have.*

The air over the center of the pentagram shivered and changed as though something were forcing it aside from within. Norman stood and waited, scowling, as the smell of the burning spices gave way to a fetid odor of rot and the beat of his neighbor's stereo gave way to a sound that throbbed inaudibly in brain and bone.

The demon, when it came, was man-sized and vaguely man-shaped and all the more hideous for the slight resemblance.

Norman, breathing shallowly through his mouth, stepped to the edge of the pentagram. "I have called you," he declared. "I am your master."

The demon inclined its head and its features shifted with the movement as if it had no skull beneath the moist covering of skin. "You are master," it agreed, although the fleshy hole of a mouth didn't adapt its constant motion to utter the words.

"You must do as I command."

The huge and lidless yellow eyes scanned the perimeters of its prison. "Yes," it admitted at last.

"Someone laughed at me tonight. I don't want her to ever laugh at me again."

The demon waited silently, awaiting further instruction, its color changing from muddy-black to greenish-brown and back again.

"Kill her!" There, he'd said it. He clenched his hands

to stop their trembling. He felt ten feet tall, invincible. He'd taken charge at last and accepted the power that was his by right! The throbbing grew more powerful until his whole body vibrated with it.

"Kill who?" the demon asked.

The mildly amused tone dragged him back to earth, shaking with fury. "DON'T LAUGH AT ME!" He stepped forward and, remembering just in time, twisted his foot at an awkward angle to avoid crossing the pentagram.

The demon's answering lunge brought them almost nose to nose.

"Hah!" Norman spat the word forward even as he retreated back. "You're just like them! You think you're so great and you think I'm shit! Well, just remember you're in there and I'm out here. I called you! I control you! I AM THE MASTER!"

Unmoved by the stream of vitriol, the demon settled back in the center of the pentagram. "You are master," it said placidly. "Kill who?"

The amusement remained in the creature's voice, driving Norman almost incoherent with anger. Through the red haze, he realized that screaming *Kill Coreen!* at the demon would accomplish nothing. He had to think. How to find one person in a city of over three million? He stomped to the far wall and back, caught the heel of his right boot and almost fell. When, after much tottering, he'd regained his balance, he bent and picked up the bit of scarlet leather that had nearly brought him down.

"Here!"

The demon speared the glove out of the air with a six inch talon, the loose folds of skin hanging between its arm and body snapping taut with the motion.

Norman smiled. "Find the glove that matches this one and kill the person who has it. Don't let anyone else see you. Return to the pentagram when you've finished."

The odor of decay lingered in the air after the demon had disappeared, a disgusting aftereffect that only time would remove. Sucking the finger he'd pricked, Norman strutted to the window and looked out at the night.

"No one," he vowed, "is ever going to laugh at me

again." No more toys, no more clothes, no more computers; he'd taken up his power tonight and when the demon returned, well-fed on Coreen's blood, he'd send it out after a symbol of that power. Something the world would be forced to respect.

The throbbing beat grew more powerful and Norman rubbed against the windowsill, hips jerking to its rhythm.

*   *   *

Still seething, Coreen pulled into the MacDonald's parking lot. Norman Birdwell. She couldn't believe she'd even spoken to Norman Birdwell let alone gone back to his apartment with him. He'd sounded so damned believable back in the pub. She shook her head at her own credulity. Of course, she hadn't realized who he was back at the pub, but still. . . .

"I hope you appreciate this, Ian," she said to the night, slamming the car door and locking it. "When I vowed to find your killer, I never counted on having to deal with geek lust." It had gotten colder and she'd reached in her pocket for her gloves before she remembered that she now possessed only glove, singular. Grinding her teeth, she headed inside. Some moods only a large order of fries could deal with.

On her way to the counter, she spotted a familiar face and detoured.

"Hey, Janet. I thought you were all going over to Alison's?"

Janet looked up and shook her head. "Long story," she muttered around a mouthful of burger.

Coreen snorted and tossed her remaining glove down on top of the junk piled on a neighboring seat. Under the fluorescents it looked almost obscenely bright. "Yeah? Well, I've got a longer one. Don't go away."

Sometime later, Janet was staring at Coreen in astonishment, an apple pie poised forgotten halfway to her open mouth.

". . . so I kneed him in the balls and split." She took a long swallow of diet cola. "And I bet I'm never going to see my other glove again either," she added sadly.

Janet closed her mouth with an audible snap. "Norman Birdwell?" she sputtered.

"Yeah, I know." Coreen sighed. She should never have told Janet. Thank God they were heading into a long weekend; it might slow the spread of the story. "Like majorly stupid. It must've been the beer."

"There isn't enough beer in the world—no, in the universe—to make me go anywhere with that creep," Janet declared, rolling her eyes.

Coreen mashed the onions she'd scraped off her burger into a pureed mess. "He said he knew something about the creature that killed Ian," she muttered sheepishly. She *really* shouldn't have told Janet. What could she have been thinking of?

"Right," Janet snorted, "another fearless vampire hunter and you fell for it."

Coreen's eyes narrowed. "Don't make fun of it."

"Fun of it? You're just as likely to find Norman's demon killed Ian as some stupid vampire." She knew the words were a mistake the moment they left her mouth, but by then it was too late.

"Vampires have been documented historically and all the facts fit. . . ."

Twenty-three minutes later—Janet had been timing the lecture with barely concealed glances at her watch—Coreen stopped suddenly and stood. "I have to go to the bathroom," she said. "Wait for me. I'll be right back."

"Not bloody likely," Janet muttered the second Coreen disappeared down the stairs to the basement. Digging her gear free of the pile, she headed for the door, shrugging into her jacket as she went. She liked Coreen, but if she heard one more word about vampires she was going to bite somebody herself. Any vampire Coreen ran into was going to be able to claim self-defense.

At the door, she discovered she'd picked up Coreen's remaining red glove. *Damn! I take it back and it's more of the Count Dracula power hour.* She stood there for a moment, slapping the leather fingers into her palm, torn between doing the right thing and running to save her sanity.

Sanity won.

As the bright lighting turned the top of Coreen's ascending head to flame, Janet shoved the glove into her pocket, spun on her heel, and escaped into the night. *If I run,* she thought and matched the action to it, *I could be clear of the parking lot lights before Coreen looks out the window.* In the darkness beyond, she'd be safe.

* * *

It came up through the ground. It preferred to travel that way, for then it need waste no energy on remaining unseen. And until it fed, it had little energy to waste. It sensed the prey above it, but it waited, following, until no other lives could be felt.

Then it emerged.

The urge to kill was strong, nearly overpowering. It had been so commanded by its "master" and its nature called it to feed. Only fear of what failure would bring managed to deflect the killing stroke that instinct had begun so that it struck bone and not soft tissue.

The prey cried out and crumpled, silent now but sill alive.

It longed to lap at the warm blood that filled the night with the scent of food but it knew that feeding, once begun, could not be stopped and that this was not the place marked for death. Gathering the prey up, it turned its face to the wind and began to run, using all three of its free limbs. It could not take the prey to the earth, nor could it take to the sky with so heavy a burden. It must trust to speed to keep it unseen.

The prey would die. It would obey its "master" in that, but it would obey an older master as well and the prey would die in the pattern.

Unnoticed, the crushed red glove lay just beyond the edge of the parking lot lights. Beside it was a splash of darker red, already freezing.

Nine

"And repeating our top story, the strange deaths in the Toronto area continue with the seventh body, found early this morning by police on Foxrun Avenue, just south of the Oakdale Golf and Country Club. Homicide investigators at the site have confirmed only that death occurred after a violent blow to the throat and will not say if this victim had also been drained of blood. Police are withholding the victim's name pending notification of the next of kin.

"Weather for southern Ontario will be colder than the seasonal norm and. . . ."

Vicki stretched out an arm and switched off the radio then lay for a moment on the weight bench, listening to the sounds of the city, convincing herself that the rumble of a distant truck was not the tread of a thousand clawed feet and that a high-pitched keening to the east was only a siren.

"So far, no demonic hordes." She reached down and pressed her palm against the parquet floor. "Touch wood." It looked like she still had time to find the bastard dealing out these deaths and break every bone in. . . .

Cutting off the thought, she stood and went into the living room where she'd taped the map of the city to the wall. Vengeance was all very well, but dwelling on it obscured the more pressing problem: finding the scum.

The first six deaths had occurred on Sunday, Monday and Tuesday nights, a week apart. This Thursday night killing broke the pattern. Squinting at the map, Vicki circled Foxrun Avenue. She had no idea how this fit geographically or if it fit geographically or if it broke that pattern to pieces as well.

She pushed her glasses up her nose and forced her teeth to unclench.

Henry could play connect the dots this evening when he woke; she had other leads to follow.

If Henry was right, and the person calling the demon was receiving stolen goods for each life, those goods had to have been reported missing. Find the goods, find the demon-caller. Find the demon-caller, stop the killing. It was all very simple; she only had to check every occurrence report in the city for the last three weeks and pull out unusual and unexplained thefts.

"Which," she sighed, "should only take me about two years." And at that, two years of searching was infinitely better than another second sitting on her ass, helpless. Trouble was, with eighteen divisions in Metro, where did she start?

She tapped the map with her pencil. The morning reports at 31 Division would have details on the death the radio hadn't released. Details Henry might need to pin down the next site, the next killing. Also, the two lines from the previous six deaths intersected in 31 Division. That might be meaningless now, but it was still a place to begin.

Clutching the bag containing the four doughnuts—two strawberry jelly and two chocolate glazed—in one hand and the bag with the accompanying coffees in the other, Vicki lowered her head and rounded the corner onto Norfinch Drive. With the York-Finch hospital at her back, nothing stood between her and a vicious northwest wind but the police station and a few square miles of industrial wasteland. Squat and solid, 31 Division made a lousy windbreak.

A patrol car rolled out of the station parking lot as she approached and she paused to watch it turn east on Finch Avenue. At 9:20 on Good Friday morning, traffic was sparse and it would be easy to get the mistaken impression that the city had taken this opportunity—a

religious holiday observed by only about a third of its
population—to sleep in. The city, as Vicki well knew,
never did anything that restful. If traffic complaints were
down, then domestic complaints would be up as loving
families spent the entire day together. And in the Jane-
Finch corridor, the direction the car had been heading,
where there were few jobs to take a holiday from and
tempers teetered on the edge on the best of days. . . .

Back when she was in uniform, she'd spent almost a
year working out of 31. Remembering certain highlights
as she continued toward the station, she found she didn't
miss police work at all.

"Well, if it isn't 'Victory' Nelson, gone but not forgotten. What brings you out to the ass-end of the city?"

"Just the thought of seeing your smiling face, Jimmy."
Vicki set the two bags on the counter and pushed her
glasses up her nose with frozen fingers. "It's spring and,
like the swallows, I'm returning to Capistrano. Is the
Sarge around?"

"Yeah, he's in the . . ."

"None of her damned business what he's in!" The
bellow would have shaken a less solidly constructed
building and following close behind it, Staff-Sergeant
Stanley Iljohn rolled into the duty area, past Jimmy, and
up to the counter. "You said you'd be here by nine," he
accused. "You're late."

Silently, Vicki held up the bag of doughnuts.

"Bribes," the sergeant snorted, the ends of his beautifully curled mustache quivering with the force of the
exhalation. "Well, stop standing around with your thumb
up your ass. Get in here and sit. And you," he glared
down at Jimmy, "get back to work."

Jimmy, who was working, grinned and ignored him.
Vicki did as she was told, and as Sergeant Iljohn settled
himself at the duty sergeant's desk, she pulled up a chair
and sat across from him.

A few moments later, the sergeant meticulously
brushed a spray of powdered sugar off his starched shirt
front. "Now then, you know and I know that allowing
you to read the occurrence reports is strictly against department regs."

"Yes, Sarge." If anyone else had been on duty, she probably wouldn't have been able to manage it without pulling in favors from higher up.

"And we both know that you're blatantly trading on the reputation you built as a hotshot miracle worker to get around those regs."

"Yes, Sarge." Iljohn had been the first to recommend her for an advanced promotion and had seen her arrest record as proof of his assessment. When she'd left the force, he'd called her, grilled her on her plans, and practically commanded her to make something of her life. He hadn't exactly been supportive, but his brusque goodwill had been something to lean on when Mike Celluci had accused her of running away.

"And if I catch shit over this, I'm going to tell them you used the unarmed combat you private investigators are supposed to be so damned good at to overpower me and you read the reports over my bleeding body."

"Should I slap you around a little?" Although he stood barely over minimum height for the force, rumor had it that Stanley Iljohn had never lost a fight. With anything.

"Don't be a smart ass."

"Sorry, Sarge."

He tapped one square finger against the clipboard lying on his desk and his face grew solemn. "Do you really think you can do something about this?" he asked.

Vicki nodded. "Right now," she told him levelly, "I have a better chance than anyone in the city."

Iljohn stared at her for a long moment. "I can draw lines on a map, too," he said at last. "And when you line up the first six deaths, x marks the spot just north of here. Every cop at this station is watching for something strange, something that'll mark the killer, and you can bet these reports," a short, choppy wave indicated the occurrence reports of the last couple of weeks which were hanging on the wall by the desk, "have been gone through with several fine toothed combs. Gone through by everyone here and by the boys and girls from your old playground."

"But not by me."

He nodded acknowledgment. "Not by you." His palm slapped down on the papers on his desk. "This last death, this was in my territory and I'm taking it personally. If you know something you're not telling, spit it out now."

There's a demon writing a name in blood across the city. If we don't stop it, it will be only the beginning.

How do you know?

A vampire told me.

She looked him right in the eye, and lied.

"Everything I know, I've told Mike Celluci. He's in charge of the case. I just think it'll help if I look myself."

Iljohn's eyes narrowed. She could tell he didn't believe her. Not completely.

Slowly, after a moment that stretched into all the time they'd ever worked together, he pushed the clipboard across the desk. "I want this to be the last death," he growled.

Not as much as I do, Vicki thought.

How many deaths in a demon's name?

She bent her head to read.

"Victims one and seven were both students at York University. Not much of a connection to base an investigation on."

Celluci sighed. "Vicki, at this point I'd base an investigation on ties a lot more tenuous. Did you call to give me a hard time or did you have something constructive to say?"

Vicki twisted the phone cord around her fingers. Late in the afternoon, arriving at 52 Division, her search had actually turned something up. One of the uniforms coming in off shift change had overheard her talking to the duty sergeant about unusual cases and had filled her in on one he'd taken the call for. Trouble was, she couldn't figure out how to present the information to Celluci. "So you'll be concentrating the search at York?" she asked instead.

He sighed again. "Yeah. For now. Why?"

She took a deep breath. There really wasn't an easy way to do this. "Don't ask me how I know, because you wouldn't believe me, but there's a very good chance the person you're looking for will be wearing a black leather jacket. A nine-hundred-dollar black leather jacket."

"Jesus Christ, Vicki! It's a university. Half the fucking people there will be in black leather jackets."

"Not like this one. I've got a full description for you."

"And where did you get it? Out of a fortune cookie?"

Vicki opened her mouth then closed it again. This was just too complicated. "I can't tell you," she said at last. "I'd be compromising my sources."

"You hold back information on me, Vicki, and I'll compromise sources you never knew you had!"

"Listen, asshole, you can choose to believe me or not, but don't you dare threaten me!" She spit out the description of the jacket and slammed the receiver down. All right. She'd done her duty by telling the police what she knew. Fine. They could act on it or not. And Mike Celluci could go straight to hell.

Except that was what she was desperately trying to prevent.

Grinding her teeth in frustration, she kicked a kitchen chair into the living room and, panting slightly, stood looking down at the twisted piece of furniture.

"Life used to be a lot simpler," she told it, sighed, and went back to the phone. York University was the only connection they had and Coreen Fergus was a student there. She probably wouldn't be able to help—Celluci was right, the irritating s.o.b., finding one leather jacket on campus would be like finding one honest politician—but it certainly couldn't hurt to check.

"Coreen Fergus, please."

"I'm sorry, but Coreen's not in right now. Can I take a message?"

"Do you know when she'll be back?"

" 'Fraid not. She left this morning to stay with friends for a few days."

"Is she all right?" If that child had gotten herself hurt going up to some strange man's apartment. . . .

"Well, she's a little shook; she was like really good friends with the girl whose body they found last night."

Bad enough, coming so soon after Ian, but thank God

that was all it was. "When she comes home, could you tell her Vicki Nelson called?"

"Sure thing. That all?"

"That's all."

And that was all, unless Henry had come up with something concrete.

"This one, this one, or this one." Henry looked from the map to the page of symbols.

"Can you find the next point in the pattern?" Vicki bent over the table, as far away as possible from the grimoire. She hesitated to say the ancient book exuded an aura of evil—that sounded *so* horror novel cliché— but she noticed that even Henry touched it as infrequently as possible.

Henry, busy with protractor and ruler, laughed humorlessly. "The next three points in three possible patterns," he pointed out.

"Great." Vicki straightened and shoved her glasses up her nose. "More complications. Where do we do first?"

"Where do I go first," Henry corrected absently. He straightened as well, rubbing his temples. The bright light that Vicki seemed to need to function was giving him a headache. "It had better be this area here." He tapped the map just east of the Humber River between Lawrence and Eglinton Avenues. "This pattern continues the least complicated of the three. Theoretically, it will be the first finished."

"Theoretically?"

Henry shrugged. "This is demon lore. There aren't any cut and dried answers. Experts in the field tend to die young."

Vicki took a deep breath and let it out slowly. There were *never* any cut and dried answers. She should know that by now. "So you've never actually done this sort of thing before."

"Not actually, no. 'This sort of thing' doesn't happen very often."

"Then if you don't mind my asking," she flicked a finger at the grimoire, still carefully keeping her distance, "why do you own one of these?"

Henry looked down at the book although Vicki could tell from his expression he wasn't really seeing it. "I took it from a madman," he said harshly. "And I don't wish to speak of it now."

"All right." Vicki fought the urge to back away from the raw anger in Henry's voice. "You don't have to. It's okay."

With an effort, he put the memory aside and managed what he hoped was a conciliatory smile. "I'm sorry. I didn't mean to frighten you."

She stiffened. "You didn't."

The smile grew more genuine. "Good."

Well aware she was being humored, Vicki cleared her throat and changed the subject. "You said the other night we had no way of knowing if these were all the demonic names."

"That's right." He'd been trying not to think of that.

"So these deaths might be spelling out a name that's not in the book."

"Right again."

"Shit." Arms wrapped around herself, Vicki walked over to the window and rested her forehead against the cool glass. The points of light below, all she could see of the city, looked cold and mocking. A thousand demonic eyes in the darkness. "What are we supposed to do about it?"

"Exactly what we are doing." It could have been a rhetorical question, but sometimes Henry felt even they needed answering and he wanted to give her what comfort he could. "And we hope and we pray and we don't give up."

Vicki's head rose and she turned to face him. "I never give up," she said testily.

He smiled. "I never thought you did."

He really does have a phenomenal smile, Vicki thought, appreciating the way his eyes crinkled at the corners. She felt her own lips begin to curl in answer and gave herself a mental shake, forcing her face to give no indication of a sudden strong wave of desire. *Four hundred and fifty years of practice, a body in its mid-twenties, supernatural prowess. . . .*

Henry heard her heart speed up and his sensitive nose caught a new scent. He hadn't fed for forty-eight hours and he would need to soon. *If she wants me, it would be foolish to deny her.* . . . Having long since outgrown the need to prove himself by forcing the issue—he knew he could take what he wanted—he would allow her to make the first move. *And what of vows to stay uninvolved until after the demon has been dealt with?* Well, some vows were made to be broken.

Her heartbeat began to slow and, while he applauded her control, he didn't bother to hide his disappointment.

"So." The word caught and Vicki cleared her throat. *This is ridiculous. I'm thirty-one years old. I'm not seventeen.* "I learned a few things up at 31 Division that might have some bearing on the case."

"Oh?" Henry raised a red-gold brow and perched on the edge of the table.

Vicki, who would have given her front teeth to be able to raise a single brow without her entire forehead getting involved, frowned at the picture he made. To give him credit, she didn't think he was aware of how the light from the chandelier burnished his hair, and how the position stretched the brown corduroy pants he wore tight over muscular thighs. With an effort, she got her mind back on track. This was *not* the time for that sort of thing; whatever sort of thing it might end up to be later on. "Several people, mostly employees of the local MacDonald's, reported a foul smell lingering around the parking lot at the Jane-Finch Mall. Sulfur and rotting meat. The gas company sent someone around, but they found no leaks."

"The demon?" Henry bent over the map, trying to ignore his growing hunger. It was difficult with her so close and physically, at least, so willing. "But the body was found. . . ."

"There's more. Someone reported a bear running along the shoulder of Jane Street. The police didn't bother investigating because the caller said he'd only caught a glimpse of it as it passed his car doing about a hundred kilometers an hour."

"The demon." This time it wasn't a question.

Vicki nodded. "Odds are good." She returned to the table and the map. "My best guess is that it picked up the body here and carried it over here to kill it. Why? There had to be people closer."

"Perhaps this time it was told who to kill."

"I was afraid you were going to say that."

"It's the only logical answer," Henry said, standing. "But look at the bright side."

"There is no bright side," Vicki snarled. She'd finished her day with the coroner's report.

"At the risk of sounding like a Pollyanna," Henry told her dryly, "there's always a bright side. Or at least a side that's less dark. If the demon was instructed to kill this young woman, perhaps the police can find the link between her and its master."

"And if it was just indulging in demonic perversity?"

"Then we're no farther behind than we were. Now, if you'll excuse me, with the timetable shattered, I'd better get out to the Humber in case the demon is recalled tonight."

At the door, Vicki stopped, a sudden horrific thought bleaching the color from her face. "What's stopping this thing from showing up inside someone's house? Where you can't see it? Where you can't stop it?"

"Demons," Henry told her, smiling reassuringly as he secured the belt of his trenchcoat, "are unable to enter a mortal's home unless expressly invited."

"I thought that referred to vampires?"

With one hand in the small of her back, Henry moved her firmly out into the hall. "Mr. Stoker," he said, as he locked the door to the condo, "was indulging in wishful thinking."

Henry leaned against the cemetery fence and looked out over the small collection of quiet graves. They were old stone slabs for the most part, a uniform size and a uniform age. The few marble monuments looked pretentious and out of place.

To the west, the cemetery butted against the Humber River park system, and the muttering of the swollen river filled the night with sound. To the north lay residential areas. To the east and south, vacant land. He wondered if the cemetery had something to do with the lack of development. Even in an age of science, the dead were often considered bad neighbors. Henry couldn't understand why; the dead never played Twisted Sister at 130 decibels at three in the morning.

He could feel, not the pattern, but the anticipation of it. A current of evil waiting for its chance, waiting for the final death that would anchor it to the world. This feeling, which raised the hair on the back of his neck and made him snarl, was strong enough to convince him that he'd chosen correctly. This name would be the first to finish; this demon lord the first to break free of the darkness and begin the slaughter.

He must stop the lesser demon in the few seconds between its appearance and the killing blow, for once the blood struck the ground he'd have its demonic master to contend with. Unfortunately, the pattern allowed for a wider area than he could watch all at once, so he'd done the only thing he could—walking a pentagram well outside the boundaries the pattern demanded, leaving the last six inches unclosed. When the demon entered, to attack a life within it or carrying a life in from outside, he'd close it. Such an ephemeral prison wouldn't last more than a few seconds but should give him control long enough to get to the demon and . . .

". . . and stop it." Henry sighed and turned up the collar of his coat. "Temporarily." Trouble was, the lesser demons were pretty much interchangeable. If he stopped this one, there was nothing stopping its "master" from calling up another. Fortunately, these demons, like most bullies, weren't fond of pain and he might be able to convince it to talk.

"If it *can* talk." He shoved his hands in his pockets and sagged against the fence. Rumor had it that not all of them could.

There was an added complication he hadn't mentioned to Vicki because he knew she'd scoff. Tonight, all over the world, millions of people were crying that Christ was dead. This century might have lost its ability to see the power in believing, but Henry hadn't. Most religions had marked a day of darkness on the calendar and, given the spread of the Christian church, this was among the most potent. If the demon returned before Christ rose again, it would be stronger, more dangerous, harder to stop.

He checked his watch. 11:40. Bound by centuries of tradition, the demon would be called—if it was called at all tonight—at midnight. According to Vicki, all the previous deaths had occurred between midnight and one o'clock. He wondered how the police had missed such an obvious clue.

The wind snapped his coat around his knees and lifted bright strands of his hair. Like all large predators, he could remain motionless for as long as the hunt required, senses straining for the first sight or sound or scent of prey.

Midnight passed.

Henry felt the heart of darkness go by and the current of evil strengthened momentarily. He tensed. He would have to move between one heartbeat and the next.

Then the current began to fade.

When it had sighed away to a mere possibility, Henry checked his watch again. 1:20. For tonight, for whatever reason, the danger was past.

Relief caused him to sag against the fence, grinning foolishly. He hadn't been looking forward to the battle. He was grateful for the reprieve. He'd head back downtown, maybe drop in on Caroline, get something to eat, spend the hours until sunrise not worrying about being ripped to pieces by the hordes of hell.

"Peaceful, isn't it?"

The white-haired man never knew how close he came to dying. Only the returning surge of the pattern, sensing death, stopped Henry's strike. He forced his lips back over his teeth and shoved his trembling hands in his pockets.

"Did I frighten you?"

"No." The night hid the hunter while Henry struggled to resecure his civilized mask. "Startled me, that's all." The wind from the river had kept him from scenting the blood and the sound of the water had muffled the approach of crepe-soled shoes. It was excusable that he'd been taken by surprise. It was also embarrassing.

"You don't live around here?"

"No." As he came closer, Henry revised his original impression of the man's age. No more than fifty, and a trim, athletic fifty at that, with the weathered look of a man who worked outside.

"I thought not, I'd have remembered you." His eyes were pale blue and just beyond the edge of a gray down jacket, a vein pulsed under tanned skin. "I often walk at night when I can't sleep."

Hands hanging loose beside his faded jeans, he waited for Henry's explanation. Ridged knuckles testified to past fights and somehow Henry doubted he'd lost many of them.

"I was waiting for someone." Remaining adrenaline kept him terse although amusement had begun to wash it away. "He didn't show." He answered the older man's slow smile with one of his own, captured the pale blue gaze, and held it. Leading him into the shadows of the cemetery, allowing his hunger to rise, he considered this ending to the few last hours and, stifling slightly hysterical laughter, Henry realized there was truth in something he'd always believed; *The world is not only stranger than you imagine, it's stranger than you can imagine—a vampire, waiting for a demon, gets cruised in a graveyard. Sometimes I love this century.*

* * *

"Detective? I mean, Ms. Nelson?" The young constable blushed at his mistake and cleared his throat. "The, uh, sergeant says you might want to hear about the call I had this morning."

Vicki glanced up from the stack of occurrence reports and pushed her glasses up her nose. She wondered when they'd started allowing children to join the force. Or when twenty had started looking so damned young.

Standing a little straighter, the constable began to read from his notes. "At 8:02 this morning, Saturday, 23rd of March, a Mr. John Rose of 42 Birchmont Avenue reported an item missing from his gun collection. Said collection, including the missing item, was kept in a locked case behind a false wall in Mr. Rose's basement. Neither the wall nor the lock appeared to have been tampered with and Mr. Rose swore that only he and his wife knew the combination. The house itself showed no signs of forced entry. All papers and permits appeared to be in order and . . ."

"Constable?"

"Yes, ma'am?"

"What item was Mr. Rose missing?"

"Ma'am?"

Vicki sighed. She'd had a sleepless night and a long day. "What kind of gun?"

"Oh." The constable blushed again and peered down at his handwriting. "The, uh, missing item was a Russian assault rifle, an AK-47. With ammunition. Ma'am."

"Shit!"

"Yes, ma'am."

* * *

"I don't believe it!" Norman kicked the newspaper box, the toe of his running shoe thudding into the metal with a very satisfactory boom. He'd stopped to read the front page story about the seventh victim and discovered that the stupid demon had killed the wrong girl. What was worse, it had killed the wrong girl Thursday night and here it was Saturday before he found out.

Coreen had been walking around alive for two extra days!

The throbbing, which had not disappeared with the demon as it always had before, grew louder.

He dug his change purse out of his pants' pocket, muttering, "A decent country would have a decent information service." If he'd known about this yesterday, he'd have called the demon back last night instead of spending the time on the net, looking for someone who could tell him how to operate his new equalizer. *Too bad I couldn't take* that *to class. They'd all notice me then.* What really made him angry was that the demon had come back on Thursday and then gone off and gotten him the rifle without ever letting on it had screwed up.

When he saw a Saturday paper cost a dollar twenty-five, he almost changed his mind, but the story was about him, in a way, so, grumbling, he fed coins into the slot. Besides, he needed to know what the demon had done so he could find a way to punish it tonight. As long as he had it trapped in the pentagram, there must be something he could do to hurt it.

Paper tucked under his arm—he'd have taken two, but a single weekend edition was bulky enough on its own—he continued into the small corner store for a bag of briquettes. He had only one left and he needed three for the ritual.

Unfortunately, he was seventy-six cents short.

"What!"

"The charcoal is three dollars and fifty-nine cents plus twenty-five cents tax which is coming to three dollars and eighty-four cents. You have only three dollars and eight cents."

"Look, I'll owe it to you."

The old woman shook her head. "Sorry, no credit."

Norman's eyes narrowed. "I was born in this country. I've got rights." He reached for the bag, but she swept it back behind the counter.

"No credit," she repeated a little more firmly.

He was halfway around the counter after it, when the old woman picked up a broom and started toward him. Scooping up his money, he beat a hasty retreat.

She probably knows kung fu or something. He shifted the paper under his arm and started back to his apartment. On the way past, he kicked the newspaper box again. The closest bank machine closed at six. He'd never make it. He'd have to head into the mall tomorrow to find an open one.

This was all that old lady's fault. After he worked out a suitable punishment for the demon and made sure that Coreen got hers, maybe he'd do something about the immigrant problem.

The throbbing grew louder still.

*　　*　　*

"Look at this!"

Scrubbing at her face with her hands, Vicki answered

without looking up. "I've seen it. I brought them over, remember?"

"Is the entire city out of its mind?"

"The entire city is scared, Henry." She put her glasses back on and sighed. Although she had no intention of telling him, she'd slept last night with the bedroom light on and still kept waking, heart in her throat, drenched with sweat, sure that something was climbing up the fire escape toward her window. "You've had since 1536 to come to terms with violent death. The rest of us haven't been so lucky."

As if to make up for the lack of news over Good Friday, all three of the Saturday papers carried the seventh death as a front page story, emphasized that this body, too, had been drained of blood, and all three, the staid national paper finally jumping on the bandwagon, carried articles on vampires, columns on vampires, historical and scientific exploration of vampires—all the while claiming no such creature existed.

"Do you know what the result of all this will be?" Henry slapped the paper he held down on the couch where the pages separated and half of it slithered to the floor.

Vicki swiveled to face him as he moved out of her limited field of vision. "Increased circulation?" she asked, covering a yawn. Her eyes ached from a day spent reading occurrence reports and the news that their demon-caller had turned to more conventional weapons had been all she needed to hear.

Henry, unable to remain still, crossed the room in four angry strides, turned, and came back. Bracing his hands on the top of the couch, he leaned toward her. "You're right, people are afraid. The papers, for whatever reasons, have given that fear a name. Vampire." He straightened and ran one hand back through his hair. "The people writing these stories don't believe in vampires, and most of the people reading these stories don't believe in vampires, but we're talking about a culture where more people know their astrological sign than their blood type. Somewhere out there, somebody is taking all this seriously and spending his spare time sharpening stakes."

Vicki frowned. It made a certain amount of sense and she certainly wasn't going to argue for the better natures of her contemporaries. "One of the local stations is showing *Dracula* tonight."

"Oh, great." Henry threw up both hands and began to pace again. "More fuel on the fire. Vicki, you and I both know there's at least one vampire living in Toronto and, personally, I'd rather not have some peasant, whipped into a frenzy by the media, doing something I'll regret based on the tenuous conclusion that he never sees me in the daytime." He stopped and drew a deep breath. "And the worst of it is, there's not a damned thing I can do about it."

Vicki pulled herself to her feet and went to stand beside him at the window. She understood how he felt. "I doubt it'll do any good, but I have a friend who writes a human interest column at the tabloid. I'll give her a call when I get home and see if she can defuse any of this."

"What will you tell her?"

"Exactly what you told me." She grinned. "Less the part about the vampire actually living in Toronto."

Henry managed a crooked grin in return. "Thank you. She'll likely think you're losing your mind."

Vicki shrugged. "I used to be a cop. She thinks I lost my mind ages ago."

Her eyes on their reflection in the glass, Vicki realized, for the first time, that Henry Fitzroy, born in the sixteenth century, stood four inches shorter she did. At least. An admitted snob concerning height, she was a little surprised to discover that it didn't seem to matter. Her ears as red as the young constable's had been that afternoon, she cleared her throat and asked, "Will you be going back to the Humber tonight?"

Henry's reflection nodded grimly. "And every night until something happens."

*   *   *

Anicka Hendle had just come off an exhausting shift in Emergency. As she parked her car in the lane behind her house and stumbled up the path, all she could think of was bed. She didn't see them until she'd almost reached the porch.

Roger, the elder brother, sat on the top step. Bill, the younger, stood in the frozen garden, leaning against the house. Something—it looked like a hockey stick although the light was too bad to really tell—leaned against the wall beside him. The two of them, and an assortment of "friends," rented the place next door and although Anicka had complained to their landlord on a number of occasions, about the noise, about the filth, she couldn't seem to get rid of them. They'd obviously spent the night drinking. She could smell the beer.

"Morning, *Ms.* Hendle."

Just what she needed, a confrontation with Tweedle-dee and Tweedledum. "What can I do for you, gentle-men?" They were usually too dense, or too drunk, for sarcasm to have any effect, but she hadn't given up hope.

"Well . . ." Roger's smile was a lighter slash across the gray oval of his face. "You can tell us why we never see you in the daytime."

Anicka sighed; she was too tired to deal with whatever idiot idea they had right now. "I am a night nurse," she said, speaking slowly and enunciating clearly. "There-fore, I work nights."

"Not good enough." Roger took another long pull from the bottle in his left hand. His right hand continued to cradle something in his lap. "No one works nights all the time."

"I do." This was ridiculous. She strode forward. "Now go back where you came from before I call . . ." The hands grabbing her shoulders took her completely by surprise.

"Call who?" Bill asked, jerking her up against his body.

Suddenly frightened, she twisted frantically trying to free herself.

"Us three," Roger's voice seemed to come from a distance, "are just going to stay out here till the sun comes up. Then we'll see."

They were crazy. They were both crazy. Panic gave

her the strength she needed, and she yanked herself out of Bill's grip. She stumbled on the porch stairs. This couldn't be happening. She had to get to the house. In the house she'd be safe.

She saw Roger stand. She could get by him. Push him out of the way.

Then she saw the baseball bat in his hand.

The force of the blow knocked her back onto the lawn.

She couldn't suck enough air through the ruin of her mouth and nose to scream.

Her face streaming blood, she scrambled up onto her elbows and knees and tried to crawl back toward the house. *If I can get to the house, I'll be safe.*

"Sun's coming up. She's trying to get inside."

"That's good enough for me."

The hockey stick had been sharpened on one end and with the strength of both men leaning on it, it went through jacket and uniform and bone and flesh and out into the ground.

As the first beam of sunlight came up over the garage, Anicka Hendle kicked once more and was still.

"Now we'll see," Roger panted, retrieving his beer.

The sunlight moved across the yard, touched a white shoe, and gently spread out over the body. The blood against the frozen dirt burned with crimson light.

"Nothing's happening." Bill turned to his brother, eyes wide in a parchment-pale face. "She's supposed to turn to dust, Roger!"

Roger took two steps back and was noisily sick.

Ten

"All stand for the word of the Lord. We read today from The Gospel According to St. Matthew, Chapter twenty-eight, Verses one to seven."

"Praised be the word of the Lord."

"In the end of the Sabbath, as it began to dawn toward the first day of the week, came Mary Magdalene and the other Mary to see the sepulchre. And, behold, there was a great earthquake: for the angel of the Lord descended from heaven, and came and rolled back the stone from the door, and sat upon it. His countenance was like lightning, and his raiment white as snow: and for fear of him the keepers did shake, and became as dead men. And the angel answered and said unto the women, Fear not ye: for I know that ye seek Jesus, which was crucified. He is not here: for he is risen, as he said. Come, see the place where the Lord lay. And go quickly, and tell his disciples that he is risen from the dead; and, behold, he goeth before you into Galilee; there shall ye see him: lo, I have told you. Thus endeth the lesson."

The Gloria almost raised the roof off the church and just for that moment the faith in life everlasting as promised by the Christian God was enough to raise a shining wall between the world and the forces of darkness.

Too bad it wouldn't last.

*   *   *

"Back up, please. Move aside."

Hands cuffed behind them, the brothers were brought out through the police barricade and into the alley. Curious neighbors surged forward, then back, like a living sea breaking against a wall of blue uniforms. Neither man noticed the onlookers. Roger, smelling of vomit, dry retched constantly and William cried silent tears, his eyes almost closed. They were shoved, none too gently, into one of the patrol cars, shutters clicking closed in a half dozen media cameras.

Ignoring the reporters' shouted questions, two of the constables climbed into the car and, siren hiccuping, maneuvered the crowded length of the back lane. The other two added their bulk to the living wall that blocked the view of the yard. *"No one speaks to the media,"* the investigator in charge of the case had told them, his tone leaving no room for dissension.

The body came out next, the bouncing of the gurney moving it in a macabre parody of life within the body bag. A dozen pairs of lungs exhaled, the shutters closed again, and over it all a television reporter droned in on-the-spot coverage. The faint antiseptic smell of the coroner's equipment left an almost visible track through the damp morning air.

"I seen her before the cops stuffed her in the bag," confided a neighbor to an avidly listening audience. She paused, enjoying the feeling of power, and cinched her spring coat more tightly over her plaid flannel nightgown. "Her face was all bashed in and her legs were apart." Nodding sagely, she added, "You know what *that* means."

Listeners echoed her nod.

As the coroner's wagon drove away, the police barricade broke up into individual men and women who hurriedly stepped out of the way as Mike Celluci and his partner came out of the yard.

"Get statements from anyone who saw something or who thinks they saw something," Celluci ordered. At any other time he would have been amused at the reaction that invoked in the crowd as half of them preened and the other half quietly slipped away, but this morning he was far beyond amusement. The very senselessness of this killing wrapped him in a rage so cold he doubted he'd ever be warm again.

The reporters, for whom the *story* had more reality than what had actually happened, surged forward, demanding some sort of statement from the police. The two homicide investigators pushed through them silently until they got to their car, a rudimentary instinct of self-preservation keeping the reporters from actually blocking their way.

As Celluci opened his door, Dave leaned forward and murmured, "We've got to say something, Mike, or God knows what they'll come up with." Celluci glowered at his partner, but Dave refused to back down. "I'll do it if you'd rather not."

"No." Scowling, he looked out at the pack of jackals. "Anicka Hendle is dead because of the asinine stories you lot have been spreading about vampires. You're as much responsible as those two cretins we took away. Quite the story. I hope you're proud of it."

Sliding in behind the wheel, he slammed his car door closed with enough force to create echos between the neighboring houses.

A single reporter moved out of the stunned mass, microphone raised, but Dave Graham shook his head.

"I wouldn't," he suggested quietly.

Microphone still in the air, the reporter stopped and the whole pack of them watched as the two investigators drove away. The unnatural stillness lasted until the car cleared the end of the alley then a voice behind them prodded the pack back into action.

"I seen her before the cops stuffed her in the bag."

*   *   *

"You still have that friend at the tab?"

"Celluci?" Vicki settled back into her recliner, lifting the phone onto her lap. "What the hell are you talking about?"

"That Fellows woman, the one who writes for the tabloid, are you still seeing her?"

Vicki frowned. "Well I'm not exactly *seeing* her. . . ."

"For Chrissakes, Vicki, this is no time to be coy! I'm not asking if you sleep with her; do you talk to her or not?"

"Yeah." In fact, she'd been going to call her that very afternoon to see what could be done to ease Henry's fears about peasant hordes with stakes and garlic. What weird serendipity had Celluci thinking about Anne Fellows on the same day? They'd only met once and hadn't hit it off, had spent the entire party circling each other like wary dogs looking for an exposed throat. "Why?"

"Get a pen and paper, I've got some things I want you to tell her."

His tone sent Vicki scrabbling in the recliner's side pocket and by the time he started to talk she'd unearthed a ballpoint and a coffee-stained phone pad. When he finished, she swore softly. "Jesus-God, Mike, can I assume the higher-ups don't know you're passing this along?" She heard him sigh wearily and before he could speak, said, "Never mind. Stupid question."

"I don't want this to happen again, Vicki. The papers started it, they can finish it."

Vicki looked down at the details of Anicka Hendle's life and death, scrawled across three sheets of paper in her precisely readable handwriting, and understood Celluci's anger and frustration. An echo of it brushed her spine like a cold finger. "I'll do what I can."

"Let's hope it's enough."

She recognized the finality in that statement, knew he was hanging up, and yelled his name. The seconds she had to wait before she knew he'd heard her were the longest she'd faced in a while.

"What?" he growled.

"I'll be home tonight."

She could hear him breathing so she knew he was still on the line.

"Thanks," he said at last and the click as he put down the receiver was almost gentle.

From where she sat by Druxy's back wall, Vicki could see the door as well as most of Bloor and Yonge through the huge windows. She'd decided this story was too important to chance a possible misunderstanding over the phone and had convinced Anne to meet her here for lunch. Face-to-face, she knew she'd have a better chance of convincing the columnist that the press had a responsibility to ensure that there wouldn't be another Anicka Hendle.

She picked at the rolled cardboard edge of her coffee cup. Henry wanted the press coverage of the "vampire situation" stopped to protect himself, and Vicki had been willing to do what she could. She should have realized that Henry wasn't the only one in danger. The cardboard ripped and she swore as the hot coffee spilled over her hand.

"Some detective. I could've smacked you on the head with a two by four and you'd never even have noticed I was there."

"How . . . ?"

"I came in the little door in the east corner, O Investigative One." Anne Fellows slid into the seat across from Vicki and dumped the first of four packages of sugar into her coffee. "Now, what's so important you had to drag me out in the rain?"

Prodding at her pickle with a stir stick, Vicki wondered where to begin. "A woman got killed this morning. . . ."

"I hate to burst your bubble, sweetie, but women get killed every morning. What's so special about this one that you've decided to share it with me?"

"This one's different. Have you talked to your paper today? Or heard the news?"

Anne rolled her eyes over the edge of her corned beef on a kaiser. "Give me a break, Vicki. It's Easter Sunday and I'm off. It's bad enough I have to wallow in this shit all week."

"Well, then, let me tell you about Anicka Hendle." Vicki glanced down at her notes, more to settle her thoughts than for information. "It started with the newspapers and their vampire stories. . . ."

"Not you, too! You wouldn't believe the nut cases that've been calling the paper the last couple of weeks." Anne took a swallow of coffee, frowned and put in another sugar packet. "Don't tell me—the kids are scared and you want me to write that there's no such thing as vampires."

Vicki thought of Henry, hidden away from daylight barely two blocks from the deli, and then of the young woman who'd been impaled with a sharpened hockey stick, the force of the blow not only killing her but nailing her to the ground like a butterfly on a pin. "That's exactly what I want you to write," she said through clenched teeth. She laid out each gruesome detail of Anicka's story as if she were on the witness stand, all emotion leeched from her voice. It was the only way she could get through it without screaming or throwing something.

Anne put down her sandwich early on and never picked it back up again.

"The press started this," Vicki finished. "It's up to the press to end it."

"Why call me? There were reporters at the scene."

"Because you told me once that the difference between a columnist and a reporter is that the columnist has the luxury to not only ask why but to try to answer it."

Anne's eyebrows went up. "You remember that?"

"I don't forget much."

The two women looked down at the notes and Anne snorted softly. "Lucky you." She scooped them up and at Vicki's nod stuffed them in her backpack. "I'll do what I can, but I'm not making any promises. There's screwballs all over this city and not all of them read my stuff. I suppose I can't ask where you got this information?" Much of it had been minutia not normally released to the press. "Never mind." She stood. "I can work around it without mentioning Celluci's name. I hope you realize that you've ruined my Sunday?"

Vicki nodded and crushed her empty cup. "Happy Easter."

"Henry Fitzroy is not able to come to the phone at the moment, but if you leave your name and number and a reason for your call after the tone, he'll get back to you as soon as possible. Thank you. If that's you, Brenda, I'll have it done by deadline. Stop worrying."

As the tone sounded, Vicki wondered who Brenda was and what *it* referred to. Then she remembered Captain Macho and the young lady with the heaving bosoms. The concept of a vampire with an answering machine continued to amuse her even as she recognized its practicality—creatures of the night, welcome to the twentieth century. "Henry, it's Vicki. Look, there's no point in me coming over tonight. We don't know anything new and I certainly can't help with your stakeout. If something happens, call me. If not, I'll call you tomorrow." She frowned as she hung up. Something about talking to machines made her voice sound like Jack Webb doing narration for old *Dragnet* episodes. "I had a cheese danish," she muttered, pushing her glasses up her nose. "Friday had a cruller."

Grabbing up her jacket and her bag, she headed for the door. When Celluci left the station, he'd be expected at his grandmother's to spend Easter Sunday with assorted aunts, uncles, cousins, and offspring. It happened every holiday and there wasn't an excuse good enough to get him out of it if he wasn't actually working. If he couldn't get what he needed from them, and, given what had happened to Anicka Hendle, she doubted he could—however supportive and loving his family was, they didn't, couldn't understand the anger and the frustration—he'd be over no earlier than eight. She had time to go through at least a division's worth of occurrence reports this afternoon.

As she locked the door, the phone began to ring. She paused, staring into the apartment through the six inch gap. It couldn't be Henry. It wouldn't be Celluci. Coreen was still out of town. It was probably her mother. She closed the door. She wasn't up to the guilt.

". . . as well as all cables, a power bar, and a surge suppressor. In short, a complete system." Vicki tapped the occurrence report with the end of her pencil. What she knew about computers could be easily copied onto the head of a pin and still leave room for a couple of angels to tango but, if she read these numbers correctly, the system that had been lifted out of the locked and guarded computer store made her little clone back at the apartment look like an abacus.

"Well, well, well. If it isn't the Winged Victory."

Vicki's lips drew back in a snarl. She shifted the snarl a millimeter at both ends, almost creating a smile. "Staff-Sergeant Gowan, what an unexpected pleasure."

Not bothering to hide his own snarl, Gowan snatched the reports up off the desk and swung his bulk around to face the duty sergeant. "What the fuck is this civilian doing here?" He shook the fistful of papers. "And where did she get the authorization to read these?"

"Well, I . . ." the duty sergeant began.

Gowan cut him off. "Who the fuck are you? This is my station and I say who comes in and who doesn't." He shoved his gut in Vicki's direction and she hurriedly stood, before he moved the desk so far she was trapped behind it. "This *civilian* has no fucking business being anywhere near this building, no matter what kind of a hot-shit investigator she used to be."

"Don't give yourself a coronary, Staff-Sergeant." Vicki shrugged into her jacket and slung her bag over her shoulder. "I'm just leaving."

"Fucking right, you're leaving, and you won't be back either, Nelson, remember that." The veins in his throat bulged and his pale eyes blazed with hatred. "I don't care who you had to blow to get your rank, but you don't have it now. Remember that, too!"

Vicki felt a muscle jump in her jaw with the effort of maintaining control. In her right hand, the pencil snapped, the crack of the splintering wood ringing through the quiet station like a gunshot. The radio operator jumped, but neither she nor the duty sergeant made a sound. They didn't even seem to be breathing. Moving with brittle precision, Vicki dropped both pieces of pencil in the waste basket and took a step forward. Her world centered on the two watery blue circles under silver-gray brows that glared down at her. She took another step, teeth clenched so tightly the force hummed in her ears.

"Go ahead," he sneered. "Take a shot at me. I'll have

you cuffed so fast your ass'll be in holding before your head knows what happened."

With tooth and claw, Vicki managed to hold onto her temper. Losing it would accomplish nothing and, as much as she hated to admit it, Gowan was right. Her rank no longer protected her from him nor from the system. Maneuvering somehow through the red haze of her fury, she managed to get out of the station.

On the steps, she began to tremble and had to lean against the brick until it stopped. Behind her, she could hear Gowan's voice raised again. The duty sergeant would be catching the force of his anger and it infuriated her that there was nothing she could do to stop it. Had she known the staff-sergeant would be dropping in at the station on his day off, not even the hordes of hell could've gotten her out there.

Desperate to be a detective, Gowan had never made it out of uniform. Ignoring the fact that in many respects the staff-sergeants ran the force, he wanted to be an inspector so bad he could taste it, but he'd been passed over twice for promotion and knew he'd never make it now. He hated Vicki on both counts and hated her more because she was a woman who'd beaten the boys at their own game and he hated her finally and absolutely for having him reprimanded after having come upon him roughing up a kid in the holding cells.

Vicki returned the sentiment. *Power always attracts those who will abuse it.* She'd never forgotten that line from the orientation lecture at the police academy. Some days, it was easier to remember than others.

Too strung out to take transit, she flagged down a taxi, thinking, and damn the twenty bucks it would probably cost to get her home.

The afternoon hadn't been a total loss. She'd call a friend who knew computers with the information on the stolen system and see if he could pinpoint what a setup like that would be used for. Just about anything, she suspected, but it never hurt to ask and maybe they'd pick up another handle on the demon-caller.

She hunched down into the stale smelling upholstery

as the rain splattered against the taxi's grimy windows.
*After all, how many hackers with black leather jackets,
assault rifles, and their own personal demons can there
be in Toronto?*

*   *   *

Celluci showed up just after nine.

Vicki took one look at his expression and said, "They
treated you with kid gloves."

"Like they were walking on eggshells," he agreed,
scowling.

"They mean well."

"Don't tell me what they mean." He threw his coat
over a chair. "I *know* what they mean!"

The fight that developed left them both limp and
wrung out. When it was over, and when its inevitable
aftermath was over, Vicki pushed damp hair off Celluci's
forehead and kissed him gently. He sighed without opening his eyes, but his arms tightened around her. Snagging
the duvet with the tip of one finger, she tugged it over
them both, then stretched again and flicked off the light.

There was a very good reason a lot of cops turned to
substance abuse of one kind or another. Throughout the
four years of their relationship, until Vicki had left the
force, she'd acted as Mike Celluci's safety valve and he'd
done the same for her. Just because the situation had
changed, *that* didn't need to. She didn't know what he'd
done during the eight months they hadn't been speaking.
She didn't want to know either.

Shifting his weight a little, she closed her eyes. Besides, all things considered, she'd just as soon not sleep
alone. It would be nice to have someone warm to hold
on to when the nightmares came.

*   *   *

The trees surrounding the graveyard bent almost double
in the wind, their silhouettes wild and ragged. Henry
shivered. Three nights of waiting had left him edgy and
longing for a confrontation of any kind. *Even losing
would be better than much more of this.* Demonic lore

left large pieces to the imagination and his imagination obligingly kept filling them in.

The path of power, still waiting for an anchor, pulsed sullenly, damped down by Easter Sunday and the symbolic rising of Christ.

Then it changed.

The pulse quickened, the darkness deepening into something other than night.

Somewhere, Henry knew, the pentagram had been drawn, the fire had been lit, and the call had begun. He tensed, senses straining, ready to close his own pentagram at the first sign. This was it. The lesser demon then, if he couldn't stop it, the greater and with it the end of the world. His right hand rose in the sign of the cross. "Lord, lend your strength," he prayed.

The next thing he knew, he was kneeling on the damp ground, tears streaming from light sensitive eyes as afterimages danced in glory on the inside of his lids.

*   *   *

The third drop of blood hit the coals, and the air over the pentagram shivered and changed. Norman sat back on his heels and waited. This afternoon, he'd found where Coreen lived—the student records at York had been almost insultingly easy to hack into. Tonight, there would be no more mistakes and she'd pay for what she'd done to him.

The throbbing in his head grew until it seemed the entire world thrummed with it.

He frowned as the shimmering grew more pronounced and a hazy outline of the demon appeared. It almost seemed to be fighting against something, lashing out against an invisible opponent. Its mouth opened in a soundless shriek and abruptly the pentagram was clear.

At that same instant, the coals in the hibachi blazed up with such power that Norman had to throw himself backward or be consumed. The throbbing became a high-pitched whine. He clawed at his ears, but it went on and one and on.

After three or four seconds of six-foot flames, the tempered steel of the hibachi melted to slag, the flames disappeared, and a gust of wind from the center of the pentagram not only blew the candles out but threw them against the far wall where they shattered.

"That isn't p-possible," he stammered into the sudden silence. His ears still rang with echoes, but even the throbbing had died, leaving an aching emptiness where it had been. While a part of his mind cowered in fear, another disbelieved the evidence of his eyes. Heat enough to melt the cast iron hibachi should have taken the entire apartment building with it.

He reached out a trembling hand and touched the pool of metal, all that remained of the tiny barbecue. His fingertips sizzled and a heartbeat later he felt the pain.

It hurt too much to scream.

* * *

When his sight finally returned, Henry dragged himself to his feet. He hadn't been hit that hard in centuries. Why he hadn't assumed it was the Demon Lord breaking through he had no idea, but he hadn't, not even during that first panicked instant of blindness.

"So what was it?" he asked, sagging against a concrete angel and brushing mud off his knees. He could just barely feel the power signature of the naming. It had retreated as far as it could without returning to hell altogether. "Any ideas, mister, miss . . ." he asked, turning to read the name off the headstone. Carved into the stone at the angel's feet was the answer.

CHRISTUS RESURREXIT! *Christ is risen.*

Henry Fitzroy, vampire, raised a good Catholic, dropped back to his knees and said a Hail Mary—just in case.

Eleven

Coreen slipped through the double doors moments before the class was about to begin and made her way across the lecture hall to a cluster of her friends. Her eyes had the fragile, translucent look of little sleep and much crying. Even the bright red tangle of her hair seemed dimmed.

The cluster opened and let her in, seating her in the safety of their circle, offering expressions of shock and sympathy. Although Janet had been a friend to all of them, Coreen had seen her last and that gave her grief an immediacy theirs couldn't have.

None of them, Coreen least of all, was aware of the expression of hatred that crossed Norman Birdwell's face every time he glanced in their direction.

How dare she still live when I said she was to die.

The throbbing had returned sometime during the night, each pulse reassuring Norman that the power was still his, each pulse demanding that Coreen pay.

Coreen had become the symbol for everyone who had ever laughed at him. For every slut who'd spread her legs for the football team but not for him. For every jock who pushed him aside as if he wasn't there. Well, he was there, and he'd prove it. He'd turn his demon loose on the lot of them—but first Coreen had to die.

Very carefully, he moved his bandaged hand from his lap to the arm of the chair. After spending a virtually sleepless night, he'd stopped by the student medical center before class. If that's what his student funds paid for, he wasn't impressed. First, they'd made him wait until two people who'd arrived before him went in—even though he was obviously in more pain—and then the stupid cow had hurt him when she'd taped down the gauze. They hadn't even wanted to hear the story he'd made up about how he did it.

Briefcase awkwardly balanced on his knees, he pulled out the little black book he'd bought in high school to keep girls' phone numbers in. The first four or five pages had been raggedly torn out and on the first remaining page, under the word Coreen, he wrote, *the Student Medical Center.*

From here on, Norman Birdwell was going to get even.

He didn't understand what had gone wrong the night before. He'd performed the ritual flawlessly. Something had interfered, had stopped the demon, had stopped *his* demon. Norman frowned. Obviously, there were things around stronger than the creature he called to do his bidding. He didn't like that. He didn't like that at all. How dare something be able to interfere with him.

He could see only one solution. He'd have to get a stronger demon.

After the lecture, he made his way to the front of the class and planted himself between the professor and the door. Over the years he'd learned that the best way to get answers was to block the possibility of escape.

"Professor Leigh? I need to talk to you."

Resignedly, the professor set his heavy briefcase back by the lectern. He tried to be available when his students needed him, recognizing that a few moments of answering questions could occasionally clarify an entire semester's work, but Norman Birdwell would corner him for no better reason than to prove how clever he was. "What is it, Norman?"

What was it? The throbbing had grown so loud again it had become difficult to think. With an effort, he managed to blurt out, "It's about my seminar topic. You said earlier that as well as a host of lesser demons there were also Demon Lords. Can I assume that the Demon Lords are the more powerful?"

"Yes, Norman, you can." He wondered briefly what

the younger man had done to his fingers. *Probably got them caught in a metaphorical cookie jar. . . .*

"Well, how can you tell what you're going to get? I mean if you call up a demon, how can you ensure that you're going to get a Demon Lord?"

Professor Leigh's brows rose. This sounded like it was going to be one hell of a seminar topic. So to speak. "The rituals for calling up one of the demon kind are very complicated, Norman. . . ."

Norman hid a sneer. The rituals were nonspecific but hardly complicated. Of course, he'd never be able to convince the professor that. Professor Leigh thought *he* knew everything. "How do they differ for a Demon Lord?"

"Well, just for starters, you need a name."

"Where do I find one?"

"I am not going to do your research for you, Norman." The professor picked up his briefcase and headed for the door, expecting Norman to move out of his way. Norman stayed right where he was. Faced with a shoving match or surrender, Professor Leigh sighed and surrendered. "I suggest you have a word with Dr. Sagara at the University of Toronto's Rare Book Room. She might have something that can help."

Norman weighed the worth of that information for a moment then nodded, stepping back against the blackboard. It was less than he wanted, but it was a beginning and he still had ten hours until midnight.

"Fine. I'll call Dr. Sagara and tell her you'll be coming down." Once safely out in the corridor, the professor grinned. He almost wished he could be there to see the irresistible force come up against the immovable object. Almost.

A few flakes of snow slapped wetly against his face as Norman stood waiting for the bus. He shifted his weight from foot to foot, glad he'd worn his sneakers—cowboy boots, he'd discovered, had next to no insulation against the cold. The black leather jacket kept him reasonably warm, although the fringe kept flapping up and whipping him in the back of the neck.

When he saw the bus approaching, he moved to the

curb, only to be engulfed by the waiting pack of students and pushed back almost to the end of the line. All his efforts to regain his place met with failure and finally he gave in, shuffling forward with the line and fuming.

Just wait.... Norman shifted his grip on his briefcase, ignoring the way it cracked against the shins of the person next to him. *When I have my Demon Lord, there'll be no more lines, no more buses, no more sharp elbows.* He glared at the back of the tall skinny young man attached to the elbow in question. As soon as he got a chance, that guy was going on the list.

* * *

Vicki allowed herself to be caught up in the rush of students and carried with them out through the back doors of the bus. Intensive eavesdropping during the long trip had taught her two things; that nothing had changed much since she'd gone to university and that the verb "says" seemed to have disappeared from common usage.

". . . so then my dad goes, if you're going to take the car out I gotta know where you're going like and . . ."

And what's really depressing is that she's probably an English major. Out on the sidewalk at last, Vicki fastened her jacket and took a quick look back at the bus. The doors were just closing behind the last of the students fleeing the campus and, as she watched, the heavily loaded vehicle lumbered away. Well, that was that, then; no changing her mind for another forty minutes.

She felt a little foolish, but this was the best idea she could come up with. With any luck, the head of the computer science department would be able—and willing—to tell her who'd be likely to own and use the stolen computer system. Coreen might have had information that could help sort the living needle out of the haystack, after all, she was a student out here, but when Vicki'd called her apartment at about 8:30 there'd been no answer.

Pushing her glasses up her nose, she started across the parking lot, watching for black leather jackets. As Celluci had pointed out, there were a number of them on males

and females both. Vicki knew full well that physical characteristics had nothing to do with the ability to commit crime,
but she looked anyway. Surely a demon-caller must show
some outward manifestation of that kind of evil.

*   *   *

Norman pushed into the first available seat. His injured
hand should've entitled him to one the moment he got
on the bus but not one of his selfish, self-centered fellow
students would get up although he'd glared at all and
sundry. Still sulking, he fished his calculator out of his
shirt pocket, and began to work out the time he'd need
to spend downtown. He was, at that very moment, missing an analytical geometry class. It was the first class
he'd ever skipped. His parents would have fits. He didn't
care. As much as he'd hoarded every A and A plus—
he had a complete record of every mark he'd ever
received—he'd realized in the last couple of days that
some things were more important.

Things like getting even.

When the bus finally wheezed into the subway station, Norman was deep in a pleasant fantasy of rear-
ranging the world so that jocks and their sort were put
where they belonged and he got the recognition and
the women he deserved. Chin up, he strutted down to
the trains, oblivious to the raised brows and the snick-
ers that followed him. A Norman Birdwell-run world
would be set up to acknowledge the value of Norman
Birdwell.

"Dr. Sagara?"

"What?"

Norman was a little surprised at the vehemence in the
old lady's voice; he hadn't even asked her for anything
yet. "Professor Leigh said I should talk to you."

"What about?" She glared up at him over the edge
of her glasses.

"I'm doing a project on demons. . . ."

"The ones on the Board of Directors?" She sniggered,
then shook her head at his complete lack of reaction.
"That was a joke."

"Oh." Norman peered down at her, annoyed at the lack of light. Bad enough that the Rare Book Room itself was so dark—a few banks of fluorescents would be a decent start until the whole smelly mess could be transcribed onto a mainframe—but it really was unnecessary to carry the conceit over into the offices. The brass lamp threw a pool of gold onto the desk, but Dr. Sagara's face itself was in shadow. He looked around for a wall switch but couldn't see one.

"Well?" Dr. Sagara tapped the fingers of one hand against her desk blotter. "What does Professor Leigh think your project has to do with me? He was singularly nonspecific on the phone."

"I need to find out about Demon Lords." His voice picked up the rhythm of the throbbing.

"Then you need a grimoire."

"A what?"

"I said," she spoke very slowly and distinctly as though to an idiot, "you need a grimoire; an ancient, practically mythological book of demon lore."

Norman bent forward, squinting a little as he came within the sphere of the desk lamp. "Do you have one?"

"Well, your Professor Leigh seems to think I do."

Grinding his teeth, Norman wished U of T paid more attention to its retirement regulations. The old lady was obviously senile. "Do you?"

"No." She laced her fingers together and leaned back in her chair. "But if you really want one, I suggest you contact a young man by the name of Henry Fitzroy. He came to visit me when he first moved to Toronto. Spitting image of his father as a young man. His father had a great love of antiquities, books in particular. Donated a number of the books we have in our collection here. God knows what young Henry inherited."

"This Henry Fitzroy has a grimoire?"

"Do I look like God? *I* don't know what he has, but he's your best bet in the city."

Norman pulled his electronic address book out of his briefcase. "Do you have his number?"

"Yes. But I'm not going to give it to you. You have

his name, look it up. If he's not in the phone book, he obviously doesn't want to be bothered."

Norman stared at her in astonishment. She couldn't just not tell him, could she? The throbbing became a kettledrum between his ears.

Yes, she could.

"Good afternoon, young man."

Norman continued to stare.

Dr. Sagara sighed. "Good afternoon," she repeated more firmly.

"You have to tell me. . . ."

"I don't have to tell you anything." Whining topped her rather considerable list of character traits she couldn't abide. "Get out."

"You can't talk to me like that!" Norman protested.

"I can talk to you any way I like, I have tenure. Now are you going to leave or am I going to call library security?"

Breathing heavily through his nose, he whirled and stamped toward the door.

Dr. Sagara watched him go, brows drawn down and two vertical lines cutting into her forehead. Professor Leigh would be hearing from her about this. Obviously, he still bore a grudge for that C minus.

She'll be sorry. Norman charged through the dim quiet of the Rare Book Room and careened off the entrance turnstile. *They'll all be sorry!* The exit was on the other side of the guard's desk. *If anyone laughs at me, they're dead.*

He slammed into the exit bar and got his briefcase caught between it and the desk. The grinding noise brought a startled exclamation from the guard.

"No, I don't need your help!" Norman snarled. Bandaged hand waving, he yanked at the case and jammed it more tightly. "This is all your fault," he growled as the guard came around to see what could be done. "If you built these things properly, there'd be room!"

"If you were more careful going through them. . . ." the guard muttered, jiggling the mechanism and hoping he wasn't going to have to call building maintenance.

"You can't talk to me like that. It wasn't *my* fault."
In spite of his awkward position, Norman drew himself
up and looked the guard right in the eye. "Who's your
supervisor?"

"Wha. . . ." The guard, who had never considered
himself an imaginative man, had the strangest feeling
that something not the least human studied him from
behind the furious gaze of the young man. The muscles
in his legs felt suddenly weak and he wanted desperately
to look away.

"Your supervisor, who is he? I'm going to register a
complaint and you'll lose your job."

"And I'll what?"

"You heard me." With a final heave, the briefcase
came free, deeply scored down one side. "You just
wait!" Norman backed out the door, almost running
down two students trying to enter. He scowled at the
confused guard. "You'll see!"

He felt better by the time he'd walked to Bloor Street.
With every step, he imagined pulling one of those stupid
so-called rare books off the shelves, throwing it on the
sidewalk in front of him, and kicking it out into traffic.
Still breathing a little heavily, he went into the phone
booth at the gas station and looked up the name the
crazy old woman had given him.

Henry Fitzroy had no listed number.

Letting the phone book fall, Norman almost laughed.
If they thought a minor detail like *that* could stop
him. . . .

On the way back to his apartment, he added Dr. Sagara, the library guard, and a surly TTC official to his
black book. He didn't worry much about the lack of
names; surely a Demon Lord would be powerful enough
to work without them.

Once home, he added his upstairs neighbor. On principle more than anything else, for the heavy metal beat
pounding through his ceiling only seemed to enhance
the beat pulsing in his head.

Breaking into the phone system took him less time
than he'd anticipated, even considering that he had to
type one-handed.

The only Henry Fitzroy listed lived at 278 Bloor Street East, unit 1407. Given the proximity to Yonge and Bloor, Norman suspected the building consisted of expensive condominiums. He glanced around at his own tiny apartment. As soon as he called the Demon Lord, *he'd* have that kind of address and be living in the style he deserved.

But first, he'd have to get the grimoire he was certain Henry Fitzroy had—that wacko old lady was obviously just being coy.

Of course, Henry Fitzroy wouldn't lend it to him, no point in even asking. People who lived in those kinds of buildings were too smug about what they owned. Just because they had lots of money, the world was below their notice and a perfectly reasonable request to borrow a book would be denied.

"He probably doesn't even know what he has, thinks it's just some old book worth money. *I* know how to use it. That makes it mine by right." It wouldn't be stealing to take a book that by rights should be his.

Norman turned and looked down at the pool of metal that had been the hibachi. There was only one way to get his property out of a high security building.

* * *

"Anything much happen today?" Greg asked sliding into the recently vacated chair. He should've waited a little longer. It was still warm. He hated sitting in a chair warmed by someone else's butt.

"Mr. Post from 1620 stalled his car goin' up the ramp again." Tim chuckled and scratched at his beard. "Every time he tried to put it in gear he'd roll backward, panic, and stall again. Finally let it roll all the way down till it rested on the door and started from there. I almost split a gut laughing."

"Some men," Greg observed, "are not meant to drive standards." He bent over and picked up a package from the floor by the desk. "What's this?"

The day guard paused, half into his hockey jacket, his uniform blazer left hanging on the hook in its place. "Oh that—it came this afternoon, UPS from New York. For that writer up on fourteen. I rang his apartment and left a message on his machine."

Greg put the package back on the floor. "Guess Mr. Fitzroy'll be down for it later."

"Guess so." Tim paused on the other side of the desk. "Greg, I've been thinking."

The older guard snorted. "Dangerous that."

"No, this is serious. I've been thinking about Mr. Fitzroy. I've been here four months now and I've never seen him. Never seen him come down for his mail. Never seen him take his car out." He waved a hand in the general direction of the package. "I've never even been able to get him on the phone, I *always* talk to his machine."

"I see him most nights," Greg pointed out, leaning back in his chair.

"Yeah, that's my point. You see him nights. I bet you never see him before the sun sets."

Greg frowned. "What are you getting at?"

"Those killings where the blood was sucked out; I think Mr. Fitzroy did it. I think he's a vampire."

"I think you're out of your mind," Greg told him dryly, allowing the front legs of his chair to come to ground with a thud. "Henry Fitzroy is a writer. You can't expect him to act like a normal person. And about those vampires. . . ." He reached down and pulled a copy of the day's tabloid out of his old leather briefcase. "I think you better read this."

With the Leafs actually winning the division playoffs after the full seven games, the front page was dedicated to hockey. Anicka Hendle had to settle for page two.

Tim read the article, brows drawn down over some of the larger words. When he finished, Greg raised a hand to cut off his reaction and turned the page. Anne Fellows' column didn't attempt to appeal to the reason of her readers, she played Anicka Hendle's death for every ounce of emotion it held. She placed the blame squarely in the arms of the media, admitting her own involvement, and demanding that the scare tactics stop. *Are there not enough real terrors on our streets without creating new ones?*

"They made up all that stuff about vampires?"

"Looks that way, doesn't it?"

"Just to sell papers." Tim shook his head in disgust. He pushed the tabloid back across the desk, tapping the picture on the front page. "You think the Leafs are going to go all the way this year?"

Greg snorted. "I think there's a better chance that Henry Fitzroy's a vampire." He waved the younger guard out of the building then came around the desk to hold the door open for Mrs. Hughes and her mastiff.

"Get down, Owen! He doesn't want your kisses!"

Wiping his face, Greg watched as the huge dog bounded into the elevator, dragging Mrs. Hughes behind him. The lobby always seemed a little smaller after Owen had passed through. He checked that the lock on the inner door had caught—it was a little stiff, he'd have to have a word with maintenance—before returning to the desk and picking up his paper.

Then he paused, memory jogged by the smell of the ink or the feel of the newsprint, suddenly recalling the first night the vampire story had made the paper. He remembered Henry Fitzroy's reaction to the headline and he realized that Tim was right. He'd never seen the man before sunset.

"Still," he shook himself, "man's got a right to work what hours he chooses and sleep what hours he chooses." But he couldn't shake the memory of the bestial fury that had shone for a heartbeat in the young man's eyes. Nor could he shake a feeling of disquiet that caressed the back of his neck with icy fingers.

*　　*　　*

As the light released its hold on the city, Henry stirred. He became aware of the sheet lying across his naked body, each thread drawing a separate line against his skin. He became aware of the slight air current that brushed his cheek like a baby's breath. He became aware of three million people living their lives around him and the cacophony nearly deafened him until he managed to push through it and into the silence once again. Lastly, he became aware of self. His eyes snapped open and he stared up into the darkness.

He hated the way he woke, hated the extended vulnerability. When they finally came for him, this was when it would happen; not during the hours of oblivion, but during the shadow time between the light and dark when he would feel the stake and know his death and be able to do nothing about it.

As he grew older, it happened earlier—creeping closer to the day a few seconds at a time—but it never happened faster. He woke the way he had when he was mortal—slowly.

Centuries ago, he'd asked Christina how it was for her.

"Like waking out of a deep sleep—one moment I'm not there, the next I am."

"Do you dream?"

She rolled over on her side. *"No. We don't. None of us do."*

"I think I miss that most of all."

Smiling, she scraped a fingernail along his inner thigh. "We learn to dream while we wake. Shall I show you how?"

Occasionally, in the seconds just after he woke, he thought he heard voices from his past, friends, lovers, enemies, his father once, bellowing for him to get a move on or they'd be late. In over four hundred years, that was as close as he'd come to what the mortal world called dreaming.

He sat up and paused in mid-stretch, suddenly uneasy. In absolute silence he moved off the bed and across the carpet to the bedroom door. If there was a life in the apartment, he'd sense it.

The apartment was empty, but the disquiet remained.

He showered and dressed, becoming more and more certain that something was wrong—worrying at the feeling, poking and prodding at it, trying to force an understanding. When he went down to the desk to pick up his package, the feeling grew. The civilized mask managed to exchange pleasantries with Greg and flirt a little with old Mrs. McKensie while the rest of him sorted through a myriad of sensations, searching for the danger.

Heading back to the elevator, he felt the security guard's eyes on him so he turned and half smiled as the doors opened and he stepped inside. The closing slabs of stainless steel cut off Greg's answering expression. Whatever was bothering the old man, he'd have to deal with later.

* * *

"Private Investigations. Nelson." As she had no way of knowing what callers were potential clients, she'd decided to assume they all were. Her mother objected, but then her mother objected to a number of things she had no intention of changing.

"Vicki, it's Henry. Look, I think you should come over here tonight."

"Why? Have you turned up something new we should talk about before you head out?"

"I'm not heading out."

"What?" She swung her feet down off her desk and glared at the phone. "You better have a good reason for staying home."

She heard him sigh. "No, not exactly. I've just got this feeling."

Vicki snorted. "Vampire intuition?"

"If you like."

"So you're just going to stay home tonight because you're got a *feeling?*"

"Essentially, yes."

"Just letting demons run loose all over the city while you ride a hunch?"

"I don't think there'll be any demons tonight."

"What? Why not?"

"Because of what happened last night. When the power of God reached out and said, 'No.' "

"Say what?"

"I don't really understand myself. . . ."

"What happened last night, Fitzroy?" She growled out the question through clenched teeth. She'd interviewed hostile witnesses who'd been more generous with details.

"Look, I'll tell you when you get here." He did not want to explain a religious experience to a woman raised in the twentieth century over the phone. He'd have enough trouble convincing her of what had happened face-to-face.

"Does this *feeling* have anything to do with what happened last night?"

"No."

"Then why. . . ."

"Listen, Vicki, over time I've learned to trust my feelings. And surely you've ridden a few hunches in the past?"

Vicki pushed her glasses up her nose. She didn't have much choice when it came right down to it—she had to believe he knew what he was doing. Believing in vampires had been easier. "Okay, I've got a few things to take care of here, but I'll be over as soon as I can."

"All right."

He sounded so different than he had on other occasions that she frowned. "Henry, is something wrong?"

"Yes. . . . No. . . ." He sighed again. "Just come over when you can."

"Listen, I have a . . . damn him!" Vicki stared at the receiver, the loud buzz of the dial tone informing her that Henry Fitzroy didn't care what she had. And yet she was supposed to drop everything and hurry over there because he had a feeling. "That's just what I need," she muttered, digging around in her bag, "a depressed vampire."

The list the computer science professor had finally given her held twenty-three names, students he figured would actually be able to make use of the potential of the stolen computer system. Although, as he'd pointed out, the most sophisticated of home systems were often used for no better purpose than games. *"And even you could run one under those parameters,"* he'd added. He had no idea which ones of the twenty-three wore black leather jackets. It just wasn't the sort of thing he paid attention to.

"Have any of them been acting strangely lately?"

He'd smiled wearily. *"Ms, Nelson, this lot doesn't act any way but strangely."*

Vicki checked her watch. 9:27. How had it gotten so

damned late? On the off chance that Celluci might finally be at his desk—he hadn't been in since she'd started trying to reach him around four in the afternoon—she called headquarters. He still wasn't there. Nor was he at home.

Leaving yet another message, she hung up. "Well, he can't say I didn't *try* to pass on all relevant information." She tacked the list to the small bulletin board over the desk. Actually, she had no idea how relevant the names were. It was the slimmest of chances they'd mean anything at all, but so far it was the only chance they had and these twenty-three names at least gave her a place to start.

9:46. She'd better get over to Henry's and find out just what exactly *had* happened the night before.

"The hand of God. Right."

Demons and Armageddon aside, she couldn't even begin to guess at what would make such an impression on a four hundred and fifty year old vampire.

"Demons and Armageddon aside. . . ." She reached for the phone to call a cab. "You're getting awfully blasé about the end of the world."

Her hand was actually on the plastic when the phone rang and her heart leapt up into her throat at the sudden shrill sound.

"Okay." She took a deep breath. "Maybe not so blasé after all." By the third ring she figured she'd regained enough control to answer it.

"Hi, honey, have I called at a bad time?"

"I was just on my way out, Mom." Another five minutes and she'd have been gone. Her mother had a sixth sense about these things.

"At this hour?"

"It isn't even ten yet."

"I know that, dear, but it's dark and with your eyes. . . ."

"Mom, my eyes are fine. I'll be staying on well lighted streets and I promise I'll be careful. Now, I really have to go."

"Are you going alone?"

"I'm meeting someone."

"Not Michael Celluci?"

"No, Mom."

"Oh." Vicki could practically hear her mother's ears perk up. "What's his name?"

"Henry Fitzroy." Why not? Short of hanging up, there was no way she was going to get her mother off the phone, curiosity unsatisfied.

"What does he do?"

"He's a writer." As long as she stuck to answering her mother's questions, the truth would serve. Her mother was not likely to ask, *Is he a member of the bloodsucking undead?*

"How does Michael feel about this?"

"How should he feel? You know very well that Mike and I don't have that kind of relationship."

"If you say so, dear. Is this Henry Fitzroy good looking?"

She thought about that for a moment. "Yes, he is. And he has a certain presence. . . ." Her voice trailed off into speculation and her mother laughed.

"It sounds serious."

That brought her back to the matter at hand. "It is, Mom, very serious, and that's why I have to go now."

"Very well. I was just hoping that, as you couldn't make it home for Easter, you might have a little time to spend with me now. I had such a quiet holiday, watched a bit of television, had supper alone, went to bed early."

It didn't help that Vicki was fully aware she was being manipulated. It never had. "Okay, Mom. I can spare a few moments."

"I don't want to put you out, dear."

"Mother. . . ."

Almost an hour later, Vicki replaced the receiver, looked at her watch, and groaned. She'd never met anyone as capable as her mother at filling time with nothing at all. "At least the world didn't end during the interim," she muttered, squinting at Henry's number up on the corkboard and dialing.

"Henry Fitzroy is not able to come to the phone at the moment. . . ."

"Of all the nerve!" She hung up in the middle of the message. "First he asks me to come over and then he buggers off." It wasn't too likely he'd met an untimely end while her mother had held her captive on the phone. She doubted that even vampires had the presence of mind to switch on their answering machines while being dismembered.

She shrugged into her jacket, grabbed up her bag, and headed out of the apartment, switching her own machine on before she left. Moving cautiously, she made it down the dark path to the sidewalk, then pointed herself at the brighter lights that marked College Street half a block away. She'd been going to call for a taxi, but if Henry wasn't even at home, she'd walk.

Her mother attempting to call attention to her disability had nothing to do with the decision. Nothing.

*   *   *

Henry grabbed for the phone, then ground his teeth when the caller hung up before the message had even finished. There were few things he hated more and that was the third time it had happened this evening. He'd turned the machine on when he sat down to write, more out of habit than anything, with every intention of picking up the receiver if Vicki chanced to call. Of course, he couldn't tell who was calling if they didn't speak. He looked at his watch. Ten past eleven. Had something gone wrong? He dialed her number and listened to her complete message before hanging up. It told him nothing at all.

Where was she?

He considered going to her apartment and trying to pick up some kind of a trail but discarded the idea almost immediately. The feeling that he should stay in the condo was stronger than ever, keeping him in a perpetual sort of twitchy unease.

As long as he had to hang around anyway, he'd been attempting to use that feeling in his writing.

Smith stepped backward, sapphire eyes wide, and snatched the captain's straight razor off his small shaving

*stand. "Come one step closer," she warned, an intriguing
little catch in her voice, "and I'll cut you!"*

It wasn't going well. He sighed, saved, and turned off
the computer. What was taking Vicki so long?

Unable to remain still, he walked into the living room
and peered down at the city. For the first time since he'd
bought the condo, the lights failed to enthrall him. He
could only think of them going dark and the darkness
spreading until the world became lost in it.

He moved to the stereo, turned it on, pulled out a
CD, put it back, and turned the stereo off. Then he
began to pace the length of the living room. Back and
forth, back and forth, back. . . .

Even through the glass doors of the bookcase he could
feel the presence of the grimoire but, unlike Vicki, he
named it evil without hesitation. A little over a hundred
years ago it had been one of the last three true grimoires
remaining in the world, or so he'd been told, and he had
no reason to doubt the man who'd told him—not then,
not now.

*   *   *

"So you're Henry Fitzroy." Dr. O'Mara gripped Henry's
hand, his large pale eyes gleaming. "I've heard so much
about you from Alfred here, I feel that I already know
you."

"And I you," Henry replied, stripping off his evening
gloves and carefully returning exactly the amount of
pressure applied. The hair on the back of his neck had
risen and he had a feeling that appearing stronger than
this man would be just as dangerous as appearing
weaker. "Alfred admires you a great deal."

Releasing Henry, Dr. O'Mara clapped Alfred on the
shoulder. "Does he now?"

The words held an edge and the Honorable Alfred
Waverly hastened to fill the silence that followed, his
shoulder dipping slightly under the white knuckled grip.
"It's not that I've told him anything, Doctor, it's just
that. . . ."

"That he quotes you constantly," Henry finished with
his most disarming grin.

"Quotes me?" The grim expression eased. "Well, I suppose one can't object to that."

Alfred beamed, eyes bright above slightly flushed cheeks, the expression of terror that had caused Henry to intervene gone as though it had never existed.

"If you will excuse me, Mr. Fitzroy, I have a number of things I must attend to." The doctor waved an expansive hand. "Alfred will introduce you to the other guests."

Henry inclined his head and watched his host leave the room through narrowed eyes.

The ten other guests were all young men, much like the Honorable Alfred, wealthy, idle, and bored. Three of them, Henry already knew. The others were strangers.

"Well, what do you think?" Alfred asked, accepting a whiskey from a blank-faced footman after introductions had been made, the proper things said, and they were standing alone again.

"I think you've grossly misled me," Henry told him, refusing a drink. "This is hardly a den of iniquity."

Alfred's smile jerked up nervously at the corners, his face paler than usual under the flickering gaslight. "Dash it, Henry, I never said it was." He ran his finger around the edge of his whiskey glass. "You're lucky to be here, you know. There's only ever twelve invited and Dr. O'Mara wanted you specifically after Charles . . . uh, had his accident."

Accident; Charles was dead, but Alfred's Victorian sensibilities wouldn't let him say the word. "I've been meaning to ask you, why did Dr. O'Mara want me?"

Alfred flushed. "Because I told him all about you."

"*All* about me?" Given the laws against homosexuality and Alfred's preferences, Henry doubted it, but to his surprise the young man nodded.

"I couldn't help myself. Dr. O'Mara, well, he's the kind of person you tell things to."

"I'm sure he is," Henry muttered, thanking God and all the Saints that Alfred had no idea of what he actually was. "Do you sleep with him, too?"

"I say, Henry!"

The bastard son of Henry VIII, having little patience

with social conventions, merely asked the question again. "Are you sleeping with him?"

"No."

"But you would. . . ."

Managing to look both miserable and elated, Alfred nodded. "He's magnificent."

Overpowering was closer to the word Henry would have used. The doctor's personality was like a tidal wave, sweeping all lesser personalities before it. Henry had no intention of being swept, but he could see how he might be if he were the idle young man he appeared to be; could see how the others in the room had been, and he didn't like it.

Just after eleven, the doctor disappeared and a gong sounded somewhere in the depths of the house.

"It's time," Alfred whispered, clutching at Henry's arm. "Come on."

To Henry's surprise, the group of them, a dozen young men in impeccable evening dress, trooped down into the basement. The huge central room had been outfitted with torches and at one end stood what appeared to be a stone block about waist high, needing only a knight lying in effigy on its top to complete the resemblance to a crypt. Around him, his companions began stripping off their clothes.

"Get undressed," Alfred urged, thrusting a loose black robe in Henry's direction. "And put this on."

Suddenly understanding, Henry had to bite back the urge to laugh. He'd been brought in as the twelfth member of a coven; a group of juvenile aristocrats dressing up in black bedsheets and capering around in a smoky basement. He allowed Alfred to help him change and he remained amused until Dr. O'Mara appeared behind the altar.

The Doctor's robe was red, the color of fresh blood. In his right hand he carried a human skull, in his left an ancient book. He should have looked as foolish as his sycophants. He didn't. His pale eyes burned and his personality, carefully leashed in the drawing room, blazed forth, igniting the chamber. He used his voice to whip the young men to a frenzy, one moment filling the room with thunder, the next dropping it low, wrapping it about them, and drawing them close.

Henry's disgust rose with the hysteria. He stood in the deepest shadows, well away from the torches, and watched. A sense of danger kept him there, a pricking up and down his spine that told him no matter how ludicrous this looked, the doctor, at least, played no game and the evil that spread from the altar was very real.

At midnight, two of the anonymous, black clad bodies held a struggling cat upon the stone while a third wielded the knife.

"Blood. Blood! BLOOD! BLOOD!"

Henry felt his own need rise as the blood scent mixed with the smell of smoke and sweat. The chant grew in volume and intensity, pulsing like a heartbeat and pounding against him. Robes began to fall, exposing flesh and, surging just below the surface, blood . . . and blood . . . and blood. His lips drew back off his teeth and he stepped forward.

Then, over the mass of writhing bodies between them, he met the doctor's eyes.

He knows.

Terror broke through the blood lust and drove him from the house. Clad only in the robe, and more frightened than he'd been in three hundred and fifty years, he made his way back to his sanctuary, gaining it just before dawn, falling into the day with the memory of the doctor's face before him.

The next night, as little as he wanted to, he went back. The danger had to be faced. And eliminated.

"I knew you'd return." Without rising from behind his desk, Dr. O'Mara waved Henry to a chair. "Please, sit down."

Senses straining, Henry moved slowly into the room. Except for the sleeping servants on the third floor the doctor was the only life in the house. He could kill him and be gone with no one the wiser. He sat instead, curiosity staying his hand. How did this mortal know him and what did he want?

"You blend quite well, vampire." The doctor beamed

genially at him. "Had I not been aware already of the existence of your kind, I would have disregarded young Alfred's babblings. You made quite an impression on him. And on me. The moment I realized what you were, I had to have you with me."

"You killed Charles to make room for me."

"Of course I did. There can never be more than twelve." At Henry's utterance of disgust, he only laughed. "I saw your face, vampire. You wanted it. All those lives, all that blood. Fresh young throats to rip. And they'd have given themselves joyously to your teeth if I commanded it." He leaned forward, pale eyes like cold flames. "I can give you this, each and every night."

"And what do I give you?"

"Eternal life." Hands became fists and the words rang like a bell. "You will make me as you are."

That was enough. More than enough. Henry threw himself out of the chair and at the doctor's throat.

Only to slam up against an invisible barrier that held him like a fly in a web. He could thrash about where he stood, but he could move neither forward nor back. For a moment he fought against it with all his strength and then he hung, panting, lips drawn back, a soundless growl twisting his face.

"I rather suspected you would refuse to cooperate." The doctor came around the desk, standing so close Henry could feel his breath as he spoke. "You thought I was a posturing fool, didn't you, vampire? You never thought I would hold real power; power brought out of dark places by unspeakable means, gained by deeds even you would quail to hear. That power holds you now and will continue to hold you until you are mine."

"You cannot force me to change you." Raw fury kept the fear from his voice.

"Perhaps not. You are physically very strong and mentally almost my match. Nor can I bleed you and drink, for a touch would release the bonds." Turning, the doctor scooped a book up off the desk and held it up to Henry's face. "But if I cannot force you, I have access to those who can."

The book covered in greasy red leather, was the same

one he'd held the night before during the ceremony. At such close quarters, the evil that radiated from it struck Henry with almost a physical blow and he rocked back against the unseen chains that held him.

"This," said Dr. O'Mara, caressing it lovingly, "is one of the last true grimoires left. I have heard there are only two others in the world. All the rest are but pale copies of these three. The man who wrote it sold his soul for the information it contains, but the Prince of Lies collected before he could use the knowledge so dearly bought. If we had the time, dear vampire, I would tell you what I had to do to make it mine, but we do not—you must be mine as well before dawn."

The naked desire in his eyes was so consuming that Henry felt sick. He began to struggle, fighting harder when he heard the doctor laugh again and move away.

"From months of ceremonies, I have drawn what I need to control the demon," the doctor remarked conversationally, rolling up the carpet before the fire. "The demon can give me anything save life eternal. You can give me that so the demon will give me you." He looked up from the pentagram cut into the floor. "Can you stand against a Lord of Hell, vampire? I think not."

His mouth dry and his breath coming in labored gasps, Henry threw all his strength against the binding. Muscles straining and joints popping, he fought for his life. Just as it seemed he could no longer contain a wail of despair, his right arm moved.

The candles lit and a foul powder burning on the fire, Dr. O'Mara opened the book and began to read.

His right arm moved again. And then his left.

A shimmering began in the center of the pentagram.

Power fed into the calling bled power away from the bindings, Henry realized. They were weakening. Weakening. . . .

The shimmer began to coalesce, falling into itself and forming. . . .

With a howl of rage, Henry tore free and flung himself across the room. Before the doctor could react, Henry grabbed him, lifted him, and threw him with all his remaining strength against the far wall.

The doctor's head struck the wooden wainscoting and the wood proved stronger. The thing in the pentagram faded until only a foul smell and a memory of terror remained.

Weak and trembling, Henry stood over the body. The light in the pale eyes had gone out, leaving them only a muddy gray. Blood pooled at the base of the wall, hot and red and Henry, who desperately needed to feed, thanked God that dead blood held no call. He'd have starved before he'd have fed from that man.

His skin crawling at the touch, he picked the grimoire up from the floor and staggered into the night.

*   *   *

"I should have destroyed it." Palms flat against the glass doors of the bookcase, Henry stared at the grimoire. He never asked himself why he hadn't. He doubted he wanted to hear the answer.

*   *   *

"Yo, Victory!"

Vicki turned slowly in the open phone booth, her heart doing a pretty fair impersonation of a jackhammer.

Tony grinned. "My, but we're jumpy. I thought I heard you didn't work nights no more."

"Any more," Vicki corrected absently, while her heart slowed to a more normal rhythm. "And do I look like I'm working?"

"You always look like you're working."

Vicki sighed and checked him out. Physically, he'd didn't look good. The patina of dirt he wore told her he'd been sleeping rough, and his face had the pinched look that said meals had been infrequent of late. "You don't look so great."

"Things have been better," he admitted. "Could use a burger and some fries."

"Why not." Henry's answering machine insisted he still wasn't available. "You can tell me what you've been doing lately."

He rolled his eyes. "Do I look like I'm crazy?"

Twelve

"Do you know what a grimoire is?"

"Yes, master." It hunched down in the exact center of the pentagram, still leery after the pain that had flung it back from the last calling.

"Good. You will go here."

The master showed it a building marked on a map. It translated the information to its own image of the city, a much more complex and less limited view.

"You will go to this building by the most direct route. You will get the grimoire from unit 1407 and you will bring it immediately back to the pentagram using the same route. Do not allow people to see you."

"Must feed," it reminded the master sullenly.

"Yeah, okay, then feed on the way. I want that grimoire as soon as possible. Do you understand?"

"Yes, master." In time it would feed on this one who called it. It had been promised.

It could feel the Demon Lord it served waiting. Could feel the rage growing as it moved farther from the path of the name. Knew it would feel that rage more closely still when it returned from the world.

There were lives in plenty on its route and as it had so many from which to pick and choose, it fed at last where the life would end to mark the name of another Demon Lord. The name would take another four deaths to finish, but perhaps this second Lord would protect it from the first on the chance that it would control the gate.

It did not know hope, for hope was foreign to the

demonkind, but it did know opportunity and so it did what it could.

It fed quickly, though, and traveled warily lest it attract the attention of the power that had broken the calling the night before. The demonkind had battled this power in the past and it had no desire to do so now, on its own.

It could feel the grimoire as it approached the building the master had indicated. Wings spread, it drifted lower, a shadow against the stars, and settled on the balcony. The call of the book grew stronger, the dark power reacting to one of the demonkind.

It sensed a life close by but did not recognize it; too slow to be mortal, too fast to be demon. It did not understand, but then, understanding was not necessary.

Sniffing the metal around the glass, it was not impressed. A soft metal, a mortal metal.

Do not be seen.

If it could not see the street, then the lives on the street could not see it. It sank its claws into the frame and pulled the glass from its setting.

*   *   *

Captain Roxborough stepped closer, his hands out from his sides, his gray eyes never leaving the blade. "Surely, you don't think . . ." he began. Only lightning reflexes saved him as the razor arced forward and he jumped back. A billowing fold of his shirt had been neatly sliced, but the skin beneath had not been touched. With an effort, he held his temper. "I am beginning to lose patience with you, Smith."

Henry froze, fingers bent over the keyboard. He'd heard something on the balcony. Not a loud sound—more like the rustle of dead leaves in the wind—but a sound that didn't belong.

He reached the living room in less than seconds, the overpowering smell of rotting meat warning him of what he'd face. Two hundred years of habit dropped his hand to his hip although he had not carried a sword since the early 1800s. The only weapon he owned, his service revolver, was wrapped in oilcloth and packed away in the basement of the building. *And I don't think I have time to go get it.*

The creature stood, silhouetted against the night, holding the glass door between its claws. It almost filled the tiny solarium that linked the dining room to the balcony.

Woven like a red cord through the stench was the odor of fresh blood, telling Henry the demon had just fed and reminding him how long it had been since he had done the same. He drew in a long, shuddering breath. *I was a fool not to have protected the apartment!* An open pentagram like the trap he'd prepared by the Humber. . . . *I should have known.* Now, it all came down to this.

"Hold, demon, you have not been asked to enter!"

Huge, lidless, yellow eyes turned in his direction, features reshaping to accommodate the movement. "Ordered," it said, and threw the door.

Henry dove forward and the glass crashed harmlessly to the floor where he had been. He twisted past talons, leapt, and slammed both clenched fists into the demon's head. The surface collapsed upon itself like wet cork, absorbing the blow and reforming. The demon's backswing caught him on the way down and flung him crashing through the coffee table. He rolled, narrowly avoiding a killing blow, and scrambled to his feet with a metal strut in his hand, the broken end bright and sharp.

The demon opened Henry's arm below the elbow.

Biting back a scream, Henry staggered, almost fell, and jabbed the strut into its hip.

A flap of wing almost held him then, but panic lent him strength and he kicked his way free, feeling tissue give beneath his heels. His shoulder took the blow meant for his throat. He dropped with it, grabbed above a misshapen foot, and pulled with all he had left. The back of the demon's head proved more resilient than Henry's television, but only just.

* * *

"Down, Owen! Be quiet!" Mrs. Hughes leaned back against the leash, barely managing to snag her door and close it before Owen, barking hysterically, lunged for-

ward and dragged her down the hall. "Owen, shut up!"
She could hardly hear herself think, the dog was so loud.
The sound echoed, louder even than it had been in the
confines of her apartment, and no matter how extensive
the soundproofing between units, noise always seemed
to carry in from the hall. She had to get Owen out of
the building before he got them thrown out by the resi-
dents' committee.

A door opened at the end of the corridor and a neighbor she knew slightly emerged. He was a retired military
man and had two small dogs of his own, both of whom
she could hear barking through the open door—no
doubt in response to Owen's frenzy.

"What's wrong with him?" he yelled when he was
close enough to make himself heard.

"I don't know." She stumbled and almost lost her
footing when Owen suddenly threw his powerful body
up against Henry Fitzroy's door, scrabbling with his
claws around the edges and when that didn't work, trying to dig his way under. Mrs. Hughes attempted to pull
him away without much success. She wished she knew
what her Owen had against Mr. Fitzroy—of course, at
the moment she'd settle for knowing they weren't going
to be evicted for disturbing the peace. "Owen! Sit!"
Owen ignored her.

"He's never acted like this before," she explained.
"All of a sudden he just started barking, like he'd been
possessed. I thought if I got him outside. . . ."

"It'd be quieter, anyway," he agreed. "Can I give you
a hand?"

"Please." Her voice had become a little desperate.

Between the two of them, they dragged the still barking mastiff into the elevator.

"I don't understand this," she panted. "He usually
wouldn't hurt a fly."

"Well, he hasn't hurt anything but a few eardrums,"
he reassured her, moving his blocking knee out of the
way as the doors closed. "Good luck!"

He could hear Owen's deep chested bark still sounding up the elevator shaft, could hear the frenzied barking
of his own two. Then, as suddenly as it began, it stopped.

He paused, frowning, heard one final whimper, and then complete and utter silence. Shaking his head, he went inside.

* * *

Dribbling viscous yellow fluid from a number of wounds, it snatched up the grimoire and limped out onto the balcony. The names and incantations made the book of demon lore an uncomfortable weight, by far the heaviest item it had yet retrieved. And it hurt. The not-mortal it had fought had hurt it. Much of its surface changed sluggishly back and forth from gray mottled black to black mottled gray and its right wing membrane had been torn.

It must return the grimoire to the master, but first it needed to feed. The injured membrane could carry it from this high dwelling to the ground and once there it must quickly find a life to heal it. There were many lives around. It did not think it would have difficulty finding one to take.

It dropped off into the night, yellow fluid glistening where it had been standing.

* * *

Mrs. Hughes smiled as she listened to Owen bounding around in the bushes. To her intense relief, he'd calmed down in the elevator and had been a perfect lamb ever since. As if aware of her thought, he backed out into a clearing, checked to see where she was, wuffled happily, and bounded off again.

She knew she was supposed to keep him on the leash, even in the ravine, but when they came down at night with no one else around she always let him run—both for his enjoyment and for hers. Neither one of them was happy moving at the other's pace.

Tucking her hands into her pockets, she hunched her shoulders against a sudden chill wind. Spring. She was certain it had arrived before Easter when she was a girl and they'd never had to wear gloves sixteen days into April. The wind made a second pass and Mrs. Hughes wrinkled her nose in distaste. It smelled very much like something at least the size of a raccoon had died over

to the east and was now in an advanced stage of decay.
What was worse, from the way the bushes were rustling,
Owen had already found it and was no doubt preparing
to roll.

"Owen!" She advanced a couple of steps, readying the
leash. "Owen!" The fetid smell of rotting meat grew
stronger and she sighed. First the hysteria and now
this—she'd be spending the rest of the night bathing the
dog. "Ow. . . ."

The demon ripped the second half of the word from
her throat, caught the falling body in its other hand, and
pulled the wound up to the gaping circle of its mouth.
Sucking noisily, it began to ingest the blood it needed
to heal. It staggered and almost dropped its meal as a
heavy weight slammed into it from the back and claws
dragged lines of pain from shoulders to hip. Snarling,
drooling red, it turned.

Owen's lips were drawn back, his ears were flat
against his skull, and his own snarl was more a howl as
he threw himself forward again. He twisted in midair,
spun around by a glancing blow, and landed heavily on
three legs, blood staining his tan shoulder almost black.
Maddened by the demon's proximity, he snarled again
and struck at the dangling bit of wing, crushing it in his
powerful jaws.

Before the dog could bring his massive neck and
shoulder muscles into play, the demon kicked out. One
long talon drove through a rib and dragged six inches
deep through the length of the mastiff's body, spilling a
glistening pile of intestines into the dirt.

With one last, feeble toss of his head, Owen managed
to tear the already injured wing membrane further, then
the light blazing in his eyes slowly dimmed and with a
final hate-filled growl, he died.

Even in death, his jaws kept their hold and the demon
had to rip them apart before it could be free.

Ten minutes later, a pair of teenagers, searching for a
secluded corner, came down into the ravine. The path
had a number of steep and rocky spots and with eyes
not yet adjusted to the darkness it was doubly treacher-
ous. The young man walked a little out in front, trailing

her behind him at the end of their linked hands—not from any chivalrous need to test the path, he was just the more anxious to get where they were going.

When he began to fall, other arm windmilling, she cast the hand she held away lest she be dragged down, too. He hit the ground with a peculiar, damp sound and lay there for a moment, staring into shadows she couldn't penetrate.

"Pat?"

His answer was almost a whimper and he scrambled backward and onto his feet. Both his hands and knees were dark as though he'd fallen into mud. She wrinkled her nose at a smell she could almost but not quite identify.

"Pat?"

His eyes were wide, whites gleaming all around, and although his mouth worked, no sound emerged.

She frowned and, after taking two very careful steps forward, squatted. The ground under her fingertips was damp and slightly sticky. The smell had grown stronger. Gradually her eyes adjusted and, not bound by any social expectations of machismo, she screamed. And continued to scream for some time.

* * *

Vicki squinted, trying desperately to bring the distant blur of lights into focus. She knew the bright white beam pouring down into the ravine had to be the searchlight of a police car, although she couldn't actually see the car. She could hear an excited babble of voices but not make out the crowd they had to be coming from. It was late. She should be at Henry's. But there might be something she could do to help. . . . Keeping one hand on the concrete wall surrounding the ManuLife head office, she turned onto St. Paul's Square and aimed herself at the light.

It never failed to amaze her how quickly an accident of any kind could draw a crowd—even at past midnight on a Monday. Didn't any of these people have to be at work in the morning? Two more police cars screamed past and a couple of young men running up the street to watch nearly knocked her down. She barely noticed either of them. Past midnight. . . .

Fingers skimming along the concrete, she began to move faster until one of the voices rising out of the babble stopped her in her tracks.

". . . her throat gone just like the others."

Henry had been wrong. The demon had killed again tonight. Although why here, practically at the heart of the city, miles from any of the possible names? Henry, and the *feeling* that kept him at his apartment tonight. . . .

"Damn!" Trusting her feet to find their own path, Vicki turned and started to run, thrusting her way through the steadily arriving stream of the curious. She stumbled over a curb she couldn't see, clipped her shoulder against an ill-defined blur that might have been a pole, and careened off at least three people too slow to move out of her way. She had to get to Henry.

As she reached his building, an ambulance raced by and a group of people surged up the circular drive and after it, trailing along behind like a group of ghoulish goslings as it squealed around the corner onto St. Paul's Square. The security guard must've been among them for when Vicki pushed through the doors and into the lobby, his desk was empty.

"God *double* damn!"

She reached over and found the switch that opened the inner door but, as she'd feared, he'd locked it down and taken the key with him. Too furious and too worried even to swear, she gave the door a vicious yank. To her surprise it swung open, the lock protesting as a metal tongue that hadn't quite caught pulled free. She dashed through, took a second to shut it carefully behind her— old habits die hard—raced across the inner lobby and jabbed at the elevator buttons.

She knew full well that continued jabbing would do no good, but she did it anyway.

The ride up to the fourteenth floor seemed to take days, months even, and adrenaline had her bouncing off the walls. Henry's door was locked. So certain was she that Henry was in trouble, it never even occurred to her to knock. Scrambling in her bag, she pulled out her lock picks and took a few deep breaths to steady her hands. Although fear still screamed *Hurry!* she forced herself to slowly insert the proper probe and more slowly still work on the delicate manipulations that would replace the key.

After an agonizingly stretched few moments during which she thought the expensive lock was beyond her skill, just about when she was wishing Dirty Harry would show up and blow the door off its hinges, the last of the tumblers dropped. Breathing again, thanking God the builders hadn't gone with electronics, she threw the picks into her bag and yanked open the door.

The wind whistling in from the balcony had blown away much of the stench, but a miasma of rot lingered. Again she thought of the old woman they had found six weeks dead in high summer, but this time her imagination gave the body Henry's face. She knew the odor came from the demon, but her gut kept insisting otherwise.

"Henry?"

Reaching behind her, she tugged the door closed and groped for a light switch. She couldn't see a damned thing. Henry could be dead at her feet and she'd never. . . .

He wasn't quite at her feet. He lay sprawled over the tipped couch, half covered in torn upholstery. And he wasn't dead. The dead have a posture the living are unable to imitate.

Impossible to avoid, glass glittered in the carpet like an indoor ice field. The balcony door, the coffee table, the television—the part of Vicki trained to observe in the midst of disaster inventoried the different colored shards as she moved. Henry appeared to be in little better shape than his apartment.

She wrestled the solarium door closed, forcing it through drying, sticky puddles of yellow fluid, then dropped to one knee by the couch and pressed her fingers against the damp skin of Henry's throat. His pulse was so slow that each continuing beat came almost as an afterthought.

"Is that normal? How the hell am I supposed to tell what's normal for you?"

As gently as possible, she untangled him from the upholstery and discovered that, miraculously, no bones seemed broken. His bones were very heavy, she noticed, as she carefully straightened arms and legs and she wondered wildly if he'd gotten them from the vampirism or from a more mortal heredity—not that it mattered much now. He'd been cut and gouged in a number of places, both by the shards of glass and by what she had to assume were the demon's talons.

The wounds, even the deepest, bled sluggishly if at all.

His skin was cool and damp, his eyes had rolled back, and he was completely unresponsive. He was in shock. And whatever the validity of the vampire legends, Vicki knew they were wrong about one thing. Henry Fitzroy was no more undead than she was; he was dying now.

"Damn. Damn! DAMN!"

With one hand guiding Henry's body so that it slid down onto the torn cushions, she heaved the couch back upright, knelt again beside it and reached for her bag. The small blade of her Swiss Army knife was sharpest— she used it less frequently—so she set its edge against the skin of her wrist. The skin dimpled and she paused, sending up a silent prayer that this would work, that whatever the legends were wrong about, they'd be right about this.

It didn't hurt as much as she expected. She pressed the cut to his lips and waited. A crimson drop rolled out the corner of his mouth, drawing a line in red across his cheek.

Then his throat moved, a small convulsive swallow. She felt his lips mold themselves to her wrist and his tongue lap once, twice at the flowing blood. The hair on the back of her neck rose and, almost involuntarily, she pressed the wound harder against his mouth.

He began to feed, sucking frantically at first, then more calmly when something in him realized he wasn't going to be denied.

Will he know when to stop? Her breathing grew ragged as the sensations traveling up her arm caused answering sensations in other parts of her body. *Will I be able to stop him if he doesn't?*

Two minutes, three, she watched him feed and during that time it was all he was—hunger, nothing more. It reminded her of an infant at the breast and under jacket, sweater, and bra, she felt her nipples harden at the thought. She could see why so many stories of vampires tied the blood to sex—this was one of the most intimate actions she'd ever been a part of.

*   *   *

First there was pain and then there was blood. There was nothing but blood. The world was the blood.

*   *   *

She watched as consciousness began returning and his hand came up to grasp hers, applying a pressure against that of his mouth.

*   *   *

He could feel the life that supplied the blood now. Smell it, hear it, recognize it, and he fought the red haze that said that life should be his. So easy to give in to the hunger.

*   *   *

She could see the struggle as he swallowed one last time and then pushed her wrist away. She didn't understand. She could feel his need, feel herself drawn to it. She raised her wrist back toward his mouth, crimson drops welling out from the cut.

He threw it away from him with a strength that surprised her, the marks of his fingers printed white on her arm. Unfortunately, it was all the strength he had, his body going limp again, head lolling against her shoulder.

The pain of his grip helped chase the fog away, although it was still desperately difficult to think. She shifted position. The room slid in and out of focus and she realized as she swam up out of the darkness why he'd forced himself to stop. She couldn't give him all the blood he needed, not without giving herself in the process.

"Shit, shit, shit!" It wasn't very creative, but it made her feel better.

Settling him back onto the couch, she patted him down and pulled his keys from his pants' pocket—if she was to save Henry's life she had no more time to waste on picking locks. *He needs more blood. I have to find Tony.*

The sudden rise to her feet turned out to be a bad idea, the world slipped sideways and her run for the door became more of a stumble. *How could he have taken so much in such a short time?* Breathing heavily, she moved out into the hall and jogged for the elevator.

*   *   *

"Good lord, that's Owen!"

Owen? Greg pushed his way through to the front of the crowd. If Owen had been hurt, Mrs. Hughes might need his help.

Owen had been more than hurt. Owen's jaws had been forced so far apart his head had split.

And Mrs. Hughes was beyond any help he could give.

*   *   *

She had to get to Yonge and Bloor but her body was not cooperating. The dizziness grew worse instead of better and she careened from one solid object to another, stubbornly refusing to surrender to it. By Church Street, surrender became a moot point.

"Yo, Victory."

Strong hands grabbed her as she fell and she clutched at Tony's jean jacket until the sidewalk stopped threatening to rise up and smack her in the face.

"You okay, Victory? You look like shit."

She pushed away from him, changing her grip from his jacket to his arm. *How the hell am I supposed to put this?* "Tony, I need your help."

Tony studied her face for a moment, pale eyes narrowed. "Someone been beating on you?"

Vicki shook her head and wished she hadn't. "No, that's not it. I. . . ."

"You been doing drugs?"

"Of course not!" The involuntary indignation drew her up straighter.

"Then what the fuck happened to you? Twenty minutes ago you were fine."

She squinted down at him, the glare from the street light adding to her difficulty in focusing. He looked more angry than concerned. "I'll explain on the way."

"Who says I'm going anywhere?"

"Tony, please. . . ."

The moment he took to make up his mind was the longest she'd known for a long time.

"Well, I guess I don't got anything better to do." He let her drag him forward. "But the explanation better be good."

*　　*　　*

Wide-eyed, Greg stared over the shoulder of the burly police constable. All he could see of Mrs. Hughes was running shoe, the upturned sole stained red, and a bit of sweatpant-covered leg—the coroner blocked his view of the actual body. Poor Mrs. Hughes. Poor Owen.

"No doubt about it." The coroner stood and motioned for the ambulance attendants to take care of the body. "The same as the others."

An awed murmur rippled through the crowd. The same as the others. Vampire!

At the sound, one of the police investigators turned and glared up the hill. "What the hell are these people doing down here? Get them back behind the cars! Now!"

Greg moved with the others, but he paid no attention to the speculations that buzzed around him, caught up in his own thoughts. In spite of the hour, he recognized a number of tenants from his building in the crowd. Henry Fitzroy wasn't among them. Neither were a great many others, he acknowledged, but Mr. Fitzroy's absence had suddenly become important.

Owen, who had liked everyone, had never liked Henry Fitzroy.

Unable to forget the expression that had surfaced in the young man's eyes or the terror it had evoked, Greg had no doubt Mr. Fitzroy could kill. The question became, had he?

Weaving his way through to the edge of the crowd, Greg hurried back to Bloor Street. It was time for some answers.

*   *   *

Vampires. Demons. Tony flicked his thumbnail against his teeth and studied Vicki's face, his expression warily neutral. "Why tell *me* this kind of a secret?"

Vicki sagged against the elevator wall and rubbed at her temples. Why, indeed? "Because you were closest. Because you owe me. Because I trust you not to betray it."

He looked startled, then pleased. It had been a long time since someone had trusted him. Really trusted him. He smiled and suddenly appeared years younger. "This is for real, isn't it? No shit?"

"No shit," Vicki agreed wearily.

Picking his way carefully through the glass, Tony walked over to the couch and stared down at Henry, his eyes wide. "He doesn't look much like a vampire."

"What were you expecting? A tuxedo and a coffin?" There'd been no change while she'd been gone and if he looked no better, at least he looked no worse.

"Hey, chill out. Victory. This is all kind of weird, you know."

She sighed and brushed a lock of red-gold hair back off Henry's forehead. "I know. I'm sorry. I'm worried."

"S'okay." Tony patted her arm as he came around the couch. "I understand worried." He took a deep breath and rubbed his palms against his jeans. "What do I have to do?"

She showed him where to kneel, then put the point of her knife against his wrist.

"Maybe I'd better do it myself," he suggested when she hesitated.

"Maybe you had."

His blood looked very red against the pale skin and Vicki felt his hand tremble as she guided the cut to Henry's mouth.

What the hell am I doing? she wondered as he began to suck and Tony's expression became almost beatific. *I'm pimping for a vampire.*

* * *

Blood again but this time the need was not as great and it took much less to become aware of the world beyond it.

* * *

"He's really doing it. He's really. . . ."

"A vampire. Yeah."

"It's, uh, interesting." He shifted a little, tugging at the leg of his jeans.

Remembering the feeling, and thankful Tony couldn't see her blush, she shrugged out of her jacket and headed for the bathroom, wondering if the modern vampire kept anything useful in his medicine cabinet. The extent of Henry's wounds were beyond the tiny first aid kit she carried in her bag although she'd improvise if she had to.

To her surprise, the modern vampire owned both gauze and adhesive tape. Gathering it up, along with two damp washcloths, a towel, and the terry cloth dressing gown she'd found hanging on the door, she hurried back to the living room, leaning on walls and furniture whenever possible.

She'd take care of the one deep cut on Henry's arm, and then she'd rest. Maybe for a couple of days.

* * *

Fumbling a little with his keys, Greg opened the locker in the recreation room and pulled the croquet stake out of its box.

"It's just a precaution," he told himself, studying the point. "Just a sensible precaution."

*   *   *

Trying not to think of the depth or the damage, she washed out the wound and, pressing the edges of torn skin and muscle as close together as they'd go, bound them in place with the gauze. Henry's arm trembled, but he made no attempt to pull away.

Tony carefully kept his eyes averted.

*   *   *

With awareness of self came confusion. Who was he feeding from? Vicki's scent was unmistakable, but he didn't know the young male.

He could feel his strength returning, could feel his body begin to heal as the blood he took was no longer necessary for the mere sustaining of life. Now all he needed was time.

*   *   *

"I think he's finished."

"Has he stopped, then?"

Tony held up his wrist. "That's usually what finished means." The cut gaped a little, but only one tiny drop of blood rolled down under the grimy sleeve of the jean jacket.

Vicki leaned forward. "Henry?"

"Half a mo, Victory." Tony rocked back on his heels and stood. "If you're going to wake him, I'm out of here."

"What?"

"He doesn't know me and I don't think I oughta be here while you convince him I ain't going to tell."

A second's reflection convinced Vicki that might not be such a bad idea. She had no concept of how Henry was going to take the betrayal of his secret to a complete stranger. In his place, she'd be furious.

She followed Tony to the door. "How do you feel?"

"Horny. And a little dizzy," he added before she could say anything. "I don't think he took as much from me as he did from you. Course, I'm younger."

"And mouthier." She reached out and grasped his shoulder, shaking it gently. "Thanks."

"Hey, I wouldn't have missed it." For a second his face was open, vulnerable, then the cocky grin returned. "I wanna hear how this all comes out."

"You'll hear." She pulled a handful of crumpled bills out of her pocket and pressed it into his hand. "Drink lots of liquids over the next little while. And Tony, try not to let the guard see you on the way out."

"Teach granny to suck eggs, Victory."

* * *

In the elevator, Greg slapped the two and a half foot length against his leg. He didn't really believe Henry Fitzroy was a vampire, not really, but then, he didn't really believe Mrs. Hughes was dead and she undeniably was. Belief, he had come to realize over the course of a long life, had little to do with reality.

At the fourteenth floor, he squared his shoulders and stepped out into the corridor, determined to do his duty. He didn't consider himself to be a particularly brave man but he did have a responsibility to the tenants in his building. He hadn't faltered against the Nazis, he hadn't faltered in Korea, he wouldn't falter now.

At Henry Fitzroy's door, he checked to be sure his pant leg covered the stake—he wouldn't use it if he didn't have to—and knocked.

* * *

"Damn!" Vicki glanced from Henry to the door. It didn't sound like the police—a police knock was unmistakable—but ignoring it might still be the worst thing to do. If someone on the street had seen the demon on Henry's balcony. . . .

The fisheye showed her a distorted view of the old security guard from the front desk. As she watched, he raised his hand and knocked again. She didn't know what he wanted, she didn't really care. He couldn't talk to Henry and she had to get rid of him without allowing him to see the battlefield in the living room. If the guard had suspicions—and from his expression he certainly

wasn't happy about something—she had to leave him no
doubt as to what Henry'd spent the last couple of hours
doing. And if the guard had no suspicions, it was important he not acquire any.

*   *   *

This is crazy, Greg realized suddenly. *I should be here
after sunrise, when he's sleeping.* His fingers moved nervously up and down the ridges on the croquet mallet. *I
can get the passkey, and be sure, one way or another
and. . . .*

The door opened and his mouth with it as he stared
at the tousle-haired woman who gazed sleepily out at
him, a man's bathrobe more or less clutched around her.

Vicki had turned off all the lights except the one directly behind her in the front hall, hoping its dazzle
would block anything her body didn't. She filled the
space between the door and the molding, leaning on
both, and just to be on the safe side, let the upper edge
of the bathrobe slide a little lower. She wasn't intending
to blind the guard with her beauty, but if she read the
elderly man correctly this was exactly the kind of situation that would embarrass him most.

So maybe it was a stupid idea. It was also the only
thing she could come up with.

"Can I help you?" she asked, covering a not entirely
faked yawn.

"Um, no, I, that is, Is Mr. Fitzroy home?"

"He is." Vicki smiled and pushed her glasses up her
nose. The robe shifted a little further of its own volition.
"But he's sleeping. He's kind of . . ." She paused just
long enough for the guard's ears to finish turning scarlet.
". . . exhausted."

"Oh." Greg cleared his throat and wondered how he
could gracefully get out of this. It was obvious that
Henry Fitzroy hadn't been out of his apartment in the
last few hours. It was equally obvious he hadn't been
driving fangs into this young woman's neck, or most
other parts of her anatomy. Which Greg wasn't looking
at. "I just, uh, that is, there was an *incident* in the ravine
and I just thought he might have seen something, or

heard something as he's usually up at night. I mean, I know his windows don't face that way. . . ."

"I don't think he noticed anything. He was . . ." Again the pause. Again the blush rose on the guard's face. ". . . busy."

"Look, I'm real sorry I bothered you. I'll talk to Mr. Fitzroy another time."

He looked so depressed, Vicki impulsively put out a hand. "This incident, did it happen to someone you knew?"

Greg nodded, responding to the sympathy in her voice. "Mrs. Hughes and Owen. Owen was her dog. They lived just down at the end of the hall." He pointed and Vicki's breath caught in her throat when she saw what was in his hand.

He followed her gaze and grew even redder. The brightly painted stripes on the top of the croquet stake seemed to mock him. He'd forgotten he was carrying it. "Kids," he hurriedly explained. "They leave stuff lying around all over. I'm just taking this back where it goes."

"Oh." With an effort she forced her gaze away from the stake. Showing too much interest in it would ruin everything and ripping it out of his hand and throwing it down the elevator shaft—which is what she wanted to do—could probably be considered showing too much interest. "I'm sorry about the woman and her dog," she managed.

He nodded again. "So am I." Then he straightened and Vicki could practically see duty and responsibility settling back onto his shoulders. "I've got to get back to my post. I'm sorry I bothered you. Good night, ma'am."

"Good night."

He waited until he heard her turn the lock and then he headed back to the elevator. As the doors slid closed behind him, he looked down at the stake and shook his head. The last time he'd been so embarrassed he'd been nineteen, it was World War II, and he'd wandered into the WRENS' bathroom by mistake. "Vampires, ha! I must be getting senile."

Vicki sagged against the inside of the door, reaction weakening her knees. That had been too close. Flipping the living room light back on, she picked her way carefully back to Henry.

His eyes were open and he had flung one arm up to shield them from the glare.

"Feeling better?" she asked.

"That depends . . . better than what?" He swung his legs off the couch and dragged himself up into a sitting position. He hadn't felt this bad in a very long time.

Vicki reached out and steadied him when he almost toppled. "Apparently Mr. Stoker didn't exaggerate when he mentioned the recuperative powers of vampires."

Henry tried a smile. It wasn't particularly successful. "Mr. Stoker was a hack." He rotated his shoulders and stretched out both legs. Everything seemed to work, although not well and not without pain. "Who was the boy?"

"His name's Tony. He's been on the street since he was a kid. He's very good at accepting people for what they are."

"Even vampires?"

She studied his face. He didn't look angry. "Even vampires. And he knows what it's like to want to be left alone."

"You trust him?"

"Implicitly. Or I'd have thought of something else. Someone else." Although what or who she had no idea. She hadn't even thought of Celluci. Not once. *Which only goes to prove that even half-conscious, I'm smarter than I look.* Celluci's reaction would not have been supportive. *I suppose I could've robbed the Red Cross.* "You needed more, but you wouldn't . . ."

"Couldn't," he interrupted quietly. "If I'd taken more, I'd have taken it all." His eyes below the purple and green bruise that marked his forehead were somber. "Too much blood from one person, and we risk losing control. I could feel your life, and I could feel the desire rising to take it."

She smiled then, she couldn't help it.

"What?" Henry saw nothing to smile about. They'd both come very close to death this night.

"A line from a children's book just popped into my

head, *it's not like he's a tame lion.* You're not at all tame, are you? For all you look so civilized."

He thought about it for a moment. "No, I guess by your standards I'm not. Does that frighten you?"

Both brows went up and fell again almost immediately. She was just too tired to maintain the expression. "Oh, please."

He smiled then and lifted her hand, turning the wrist to the light. "Thank you," he said, one finger softly tracing the line of the vein.

Every hair on Vicki's body stood on end and she had to swallow before she could speak. "You're welcome. I'd have done the same for anyone."

Still holding her hand, his smile grew slightly puzzled. "You're wearing my dressing gown."

Pushing her glasses up her nose, Vicki tried not to glance at the pile of clothing dumped on the dining room table. "It's a long story." She let him pull her down beside him and nervously wet her lips. Her skin throbbed under his hand. *And he's not even touching anything interesting.*

Then his expression changed and she twisted to see what had caused such a look of horrified disbelief. One door of the wall unit, glass still surprisingly intact, swung open.

"The demon," Henry told her, his voice echoing his expression, "has the grimoire."

Thirteen

Henry lurched to his feet and stood swaying. "I must. . . ."

Vicki reached up and guided him down onto the couch as he fell. "Must what? You're in no shape to go anywhere."

"I must get the grimoire back before the Demon Lord is called." He shook off her hands and stood again, shoulders set. "If I begin now, I might be able to track the demon, In order to carry the grimoire it must maintain a physical form."

"Track it how?"

"Scent."

Vicki glanced at the balcony and back to Henry. "Forget it. It has wings. It'll be flying. I don't care what you are, you can't track something if there's nothing for it to leave its scent *on*."

"But . . ."

"But nothing. If you weren't what you were, you'd be dead. Trust me. I may not have seen the centuries of death you have, but I've seen enough to tell."

She was right. Henry walked to the window and rested his forehead gently against the glass. Cool and smooth, it helped to ease the ache in his head. Everything worked, but everything hurt. He couldn't remember the last time he'd felt this weak or in this much pain and his body, now that the initial rush of energy that came with feeding had passed, was insisting he rest and allow it to heal. "You saved my life," he admitted.

"Then don't throw it away." Vicki felt a faint echo of

warmth surging up from the cut on her wrist. She ignored it. Maybe they'd get a chance to continue where they'd left off, but this certainly was not the time. *And anything more energetic than heavy petting would probably kill both of us.* Scooping up her clothes, she moved into the kitchen and pulled one of the louvered doors closed. "You did what you could, now let someone else take over."

"You."

"You see anyone else around?"

Henry managed half a smile. "No." She was right about that as well. He'd had his chance and failed.

"Fine." She zipped up her jeans and shrugged out of the bathrobe. "You can join me after sunset if you're mobile by then."

"Give me a day of rest and I should be back to normal. Okay, not quite normal," he amended at Vicki's snort of disbelief, "but well enough to function."

"That'll do. I'll leave a message on your machine as soon as I know where I'm likely to be."

"You've got less than twenty-four hours to find the person with the grimoire in a city of three million people. You may have been a good cop, Vicki. . . ."

"I was the best," she informed him, carefully stretching the neck of her sweatshirt around her glasses.

"All right. You were the best. But you weren't *that* good. No one is."

"Maybe not," her tone argued the point even if her words didn't, "but while you were spending your nights waiting for the demon to strike, I haven't been spending my days just sitting on my butt." Carefully picking her way through the glass, she came back to the couch and sat down to put on her shoes. "One of the items the demon picked up was a state of the art computer system. Apparently, they don't make them smarter or faster than this particular machine. I went out to York University today—enough bits and pieces have pointed in that direction to convince me there's a connection—and spoke to the head of the Computer Science Department. He gave me a list of twenty-three names, students who could really make a system like that sing." She straightened and pushed her glasses up her nose. "So instead of one in three million, I've got one in twenty-three in about twenty thousand."

"Terrific." Henry tore off the ruin of his shirt as he walked back across the room. Dropping carefully onto the couch, he tossed the ball of fabric at the destroyed face of the television. "One in twenty-three in twenty thousand."

"Those aren't impossible odds. What's more I won't have to deal with all twenty thousand. The men and women on the list are part of a pretty narrowly defined group. If I can't find them, I think I can flush them out."

"In a day? Because if that grimoire is used tomorrow night, that's all the time you have before the slaughter begins."

Her chin rose and her brows drew down. "So what do you suggest? I give up because you don't think it can be done? You thought you could defeat the lesser demon, remember?" Her eyes swept over his injuries. "You're not exactly infallible where this stuff is concerned."

Henry closed his eyes. Her words cut deeper than any other blow he'd taken tonight. She was right. It was his fault the grimoire had been taken, his fault the world faced pain and death on a scale few mortal minds could imagine.

"Henry, I'm sorry. That was uncalled for."

"But true." She'd moved closer. He could feel her heartbeat tremble the air between them. Her hand closed lightly around his, and he waited for the platitudes that would do nothing to ease his guilt.

"Yes," she agreed.

His eyes snapped open.

"But you wouldn't have lived as long as you have if you hadn't figured out how to learn from your mistakes. When I find this person, I'm going to need you for backup."

"Well, thank you very much." Just what he needed, being patronized by someone whose ancestors had no doubt been grubbing out a living on a peasant's plot when he'd been riding beside a king. He pulled his hand out from under hers and tried not to wince when the motion twisted the wound in his arm.

"Before you get snooty, Your Royal Highness, perhaps you should consider who the hell else I can use? Trust me on this one, suspicion of demon-calling is not likely to impress the police. I don't even think it's a crime."

"What about young Tony?"

"Tony goes his own way. Besides, this isn't the sort of thing he can help me with."

"So I'm the only game in town?"

"We're the only game in town."

They locked eyes for a moment and Vicki suddenly realized that was a stupid thing to do—all the stories, all the movies about vampires warned against it. For a moment, she felt herself teetering on the edge of an abyss and she fought against the urge to throw herself into the depths. Then the moment passed, the abyss replaced with a pair of tired hazel eyes and she realized, her heart beating a little more quickly, that it had been the man, not the vampire she'd been reacting to. Or perhaps the man as vampire. Or the vampire as man. Or something. *Wonderful. The city—the world even—is about to go up in flames and I'm thinking with my crotch.*

"I'm going to need an early start. I'd better get going."

"Perhaps you had."

There were several dozen things left unsaid.

He watched her shrug into her jacket, the sound of her heartbeat nearly overpowering. Had he taken even a little more blood from her, he wouldn't have been able to stop himself from taking her life as well. That feeding was the sweetest of all to his kind and acquiring a taste for it had brought down many a vampire. Bringing him the boy had saved them both. She truly was a remarkable woman, few other mortals would have had the strength to resist the pull of his need.

He wanted more. More of her. If they survived the next twenty-four hours. . . .

She paused on her way to the door, one hand clutch-

ing a chair back for support. "I just remembered, where
were you earlier? I kept calling and getting your
machine."

"That was why you came so late?"

"Well, no point in coming over if you weren't here."

"I was here. I turned on the machine to screen calls."
His brows went up as hers went down. "You don't do
that?"

"If I'm home, I answer the phone."

"If I had, and you'd been here when the demon
arrived. . . ."

"We'd both be dead," she finished.

He nodded. "Vicki?"

Her hand on the knob, she turned back to face him.

"You do realize that there's a very good chance we'll
fail? That you may come up blank or nothing we can
do will stop the Demon Lord?"

She smiled at him and Henry discovered with a slight
shock that he wasn't the only predator in the room.

"No," she said, "I don't realize any such thing. Get
some rest." Then she was gone.

*   *   *

*The city streets ran with blood and all of the wailing
people who dragged themselves through it looked to her
for their salvation. She raised her hands to help them and
saw that the blood poured out through great ragged
gashes in her wrists.*

*"He's coming, Vicki." Henry Fitzroy dropped to his
knees before her and let the blood pour over him, his
mouth open to catch the flow.*

*She tried to step back and found she couldn't move,
that hardened concrete covered her feet to the ankles.*

*"He's coming, Vicki," Henry said again. He leaned for-
ward and began to lap at the blood dribbling down her
arms.*

*A cold wind blew suddenly on her back and she could
hear the sound of claws on stone as something huge
dragged itself toward her. She couldn't turn to face it;
Henry's hands and the concrete held her in place. She
could only fight against her bonds and listen to it coming*

closer, closer. The smell of rot grew more intense and when she looked down, it wasn't Henry but the old woman's decomposing corpse whose mouth had clamped onto her wrist. Behind her stood what was left of Mike Celluci.

"Why didn't you tell me?" he asked through the ruin of his mouth. "Why didn't you tell me?"

*   *   *

Vicki groped for the light switch and sat panting in the sudden glare, her heart drumming painfully. The dream that wakened her had been only the latest in a series. Fortunately, she remembered none of the others in detail.

Hands trembling, she pushed the arms of her glasses over her ears and peered at the clock. 5:47. Almost three hours sleep.

She turned off the useless alarm—she'd set it for 6:30—and swung her legs out of bed. If the demon-caller followed the established pattern, the Demon Lord would show up at midnight. That gave her eighteen hours to find him or her and stuff the grimoire down his or her throat one page at a time. The dreams had terrified her and nothing made her more angry than fear she could do nothing about.

Slowly, carefully, she stood. The liter of orange juice and the two iron supplements she'd taken after arriving home might have helped to offset the blood loss, but she knew she wasn't going to be in top condition. Not today. Not for some time. The cut on her wrist appeared to have almost healed although the skin around it was slightly bruised and a little tender. The memory of the actual feeding had become tangled up with the memory of the dream, so she set them both aside to be sorted out later. There were more important things to worry about at the moment.

She'd have stayed in the shower longer, trying to wash the dream away, but she couldn't shake the feeling that something was behind her. With sight and sound blocked by the spray, she felt too vulnerable and exposed to linger.

With the coffee maker on, and another liter of orange

juice in her hand, she stood for a moment staring out at the street. One or two other windows were lit and as she watched, young Edmond Ng came yawning out onto his porch and started down to the corner to pick up his route's copies of the morning paper, completely unaware this might be his last trip. In eighteen short hours, the hordes of hell could be ripping the city and its people apart.

"And the only thing in the way is one half-blind ex-cop and the bastard son of Henry VIII." She took a long pull at the jug of juice and pushed her glasses back up her nose. "Kind of makes you think, doesn't it?" Except she didn't like what it made her think about.

Find one in twenty-three in twenty thousand. Actually, as far as a lot of police work was concerned, the odds weren't all that bad. Even if she could get the students' addresses out of the administration of the university—and frankly, without a badge she doubted she could—talking with the students themselves would likely get her further. The top of the heap usually knew who shared the view with them and if one of the twenty-three was the person she was looking for, then at least one of the others should be able to point the finger.

Of course, the possibility existed that she'd assembled all the bits and pieces into the wrong picture. That she was not not only barking up the wrong tree but searching in the wrong forest entirely.

Sweat prickled along her spine and she resisted the urge to turn. She knew the apartment was empty, that nothing stood behind her, and she wasn't going to give in to phantoms—there were enough real terrors to spend fear on.

There was time for breakfast before she headed up to York; no point in arriving empty at an empty campus. At 6:35, scrambled eggs eaten and a second cup of coffee nearly gone, she phoned Mike Celluci, let it ring three times, and hung up. What was she going to tell him? That she thought she knew who the killer was? She'd known that since the night out at Woodbine when she'd met Henry. That one of twenty-three computer geniuses out at York University was calling up demons in his or her spare time and that if not stopped was going to call up more than he or she could handle and destroy the world? He'd think she'd flipped.

"Everything comes back to the demon. Everything. Shit." The computer that pointed, however tenuously, to one of those twenty-three students had no tie to the murders Celucci worked on except through the demon. "And how do I know about the demon? A vampire told me." She drained the mug and set it down on the table with more force than was absolutely necessary. The handle broke off in her hand. With a quick jerk of her arm, she threw the piece across the room and listened with satisfaction as it smashed into still smaller pieces against the wall.

The satisfaction faded a heartbeat later.

"One half-blind ex-cop and the bastard son of Henry VIII," she repeated, as it sank in, really sank in, that she wasn't a cop anymore. In spite of everything—her eyes, her resignation—for the last eight months she'd still thought of herself as a police officer. She wasn't. There'd be no backup, no support. Until sunset she was completely on her own and if anyone needed to have complete information, it wasn't Mike Celuci, it was Henry Fitzroy.

"Damn." She rubbed her sleeve across her eyes and slammed her glasses back down on her nose. It didn't make her feel any better to know that she couldn't have gotten this far if she'd still been on the force, that rules and regulations—even as flexible as the top brass tried to be—would have tied her hands. Nor could she have gotten this far if she'd *never* been on the force, the information just wouldn't have been available to her. "I seem to be exactly what the situation calls for—a one-woman chance of stopping Armageddon."

She took a deep breath and her jaw went out. "So, let's get on with it." The eggs sat like a lump of lead in her stomach and her throat had closed up into an aching pillar that bore little relation to flesh. That was okay. She could work around it. With luck, there'd be time to sort her feelings out later.

She should've taken a copy of the list to Henry's the

night before. She didn't want to take the time now—not to copy it, not to drop it off.

"Henry, it's Vicki." Fortunately, his machine took an unlimited message because the list of names and her plans for the day used over five minutes of tape. "When I know more, I'll get back to you."

Five to seven. Seventeen hours. Vicki threw the list into her bag, grabbed her jacket, and headed for the door. An hour to get out to York would leave her only sixteen hours to search.

She was already at the door, fumbling with its lock, when the phone rang. Curious about who'd be calling so early, she waited while her message ran through and the tone sounded.

"Hi, Ms. Nelson? It's Coreen. Look, if you've been trying to reach me, I'm sorry I wasn't around, but I've been staying with some friends."

The lock slipped into place. She'd talk with Coreen later. One way or another, by midnight the case would be closed.

"It's just I was pretty upset because the girl who got killed, Janet, was a good friend of mine. I can't help but think that if I hadn't been so stupid about Norman Birdwell she'd have waited for me to give her a ride home."

"Shit!" The lock proved as difficult to reopen as it had been to close. Norman Birdwell was one of the names on the list.

"I guess if you find the vampire that killed Ian you'll find the one that killed Janet, too, won't you? I want it found now more than ever."

She paused and her sigh was almost drowned out in the rattle of the chain falling free.

"Uh, I'll be at home all day if you want to call. . . ."

"Coreen? Don't hang up, it's me, Vicki Nelson."

"Oh. Hi." She sounded a little embarrassed, caught talking to a machine. "Did I wake you up? Look, I'm sorry I'm calling so early, but I've got an exam today and I want to get over to the library to study."

"It's no problem, trust me. I need you to tell me about Norman Birdwell."

"Why? He's a geek."

"It's important."

Vicki could almost hear the shrug. "Okay. What do you want to know?"

"How well do you know him?"

"Puh-leese, I said he was a geek. He's in my Comparative Religions Class. That's all."

"How were you stupid about him?"

"What?"

"You said earlier if you hadn't been so stupid about Norman Birdwell, Janet might have waited for a ride home."

"Yeah, well. . . . I wouldn't have gone with him if I hadn't had the beers, but he said he could prove that vampires existed and that he knew who killed Ian. Well, I guess he didn't really say that . . . but something like that. Anyway, I went up to his apartment with him, but all he wanted to do was score. He had nothing to do with vampires."

"Did you happen to notice if he had a computer system? A fairly large and complicated setup."

"He had a system. I don't know how complicated it was. I was busy trying not to get squeezed and being fed some bull about calling up demons."

The world stopped for a moment.

"Ms. Nelson? You still there?"

"Trust me, I'm not going anywhere." Vicki fell into her desk chair and rummaged for a pen. "This is very important, Coreen, where does Norman live?"

"Uh, west of the campus somewhere."

"Can you give me his exact address."

"No."

"NO?" Vicki took a deep breath and tried to remember that yelling wouldn't help. Tucking the receiver under her chin, she heaved the white pages up off the floor by the desk. Bird . . . Birddal . . . Bird of Paradise. . . .

"But if it's so important I could probably take you there. Like, I drove that night so I could probably find it again. Probably."

"Probably's good enough." There was no Birdwell listed in the phone book. It made sense, he'd probably

moved into his apartment in the fall, at the beginning of
the school year, and new numbers were listed around
the end of May. "I'll be right there. Where can you
meet me?"

"Well, I can't meet you until five. Like I said, I've got
an exam today."

"Coreen, this is important!"

"So is my exam." Her tone showed no willingness
to compromise.

"Before the exam. . . ."

"I *really* have to study."

Okay, 5:00, was still early enough. A little over two
hours until sunset and still seven hours until midnight.
They had a positive identification and seven hours would
be plenty of time. And besides, yelling wouldn't help.
"5:00, then. Where?"

"Do you know where Burton Auditorium is?"

"I can find it."

"Meet me outside the north doors."

"All right. 5:00 pm, at the north doors of Burton Auditorium, I'll see you then."

Vicki hung up the phone and sat for a moment just
staring at it. Of all the possible situations that could have
developed, up to and including one last desperate confrontation with the Demon Lord itself, this had not occurred to her—that someone would just drop the answer
in her lap. She pushed her glasses up her nose and shook
her head. It shouldn't, she supposed, come as much of
a surprise; once the right questions were dredged up out
of the abyss the right answers usually followed.

Doodling on the cover of the phone book, she dialed
directory assistance—just in case. "Hi, I'm looking for a
new listing for a Norman Birdwell. I don't have an address, but he's somewhere up by York University."

"One moment, please. We have a new listing for an
N. Birdwell. . . ."

Vicki scribbled the number across the cover artist's
conception of a telephone operator. "Could I possibly
trouble you for the address as well?"

"I'm sorry, but we're not permitted to give out that
information."

"You'll be sorrier if the world comes to an end," Vicki muttered, cutting the connection with her thumb. That it was the anticipated answer made it no less annoying.

At the Birdwell number, an open modem screamed on the line and Vicki hurriedly cut if off.

"Looks like we're back to Coreen."

8:17. She yawned. She could spend the rest of the day trying to get through to N. Birdwell—who might or might not be Norman—but what she really needed was another four or five hours sleep. The blood loss combined with the late night—she'd always been more of an early to bed early to rise type—had really knocked her on her ass. She should probably still go out to York, still speak to the others on the list, but now that the opportunity to catch up on sleep had been dumped in her lap, her body seemed to be making an independent decision to take advantage of it.

Staggering into the bedroom, she tossed her clothes on the floor and managed to stay awake only long enough to reset her alarm for one o'clock. Her eyes closed almost before her head hit the pillow. Coreen's call had banished the uncertainty, defined the threat, and with it Vicki had a weapon to fight the nightmares if they came again.

"Sometimes we win with greater firepower, through sheer numbers or more powerful weapons, but for the most part it's knowledge that defines our victories. Know something and it has lost its power over you."

Vicki woke with the words of one of her cadet instructors ringing in her head. He'd been much given to purple prose and almost Shakespearean speeches, but what had redeemed him in the eyes of the cadets was not only that he'd believed strongly in everything he said but that most of the time, he was right.

The monster had a name. Norman Birdwell. Now, it could be beaten.

After a bowl of soup, a toasted tomato sandwich, and another iron supplement, she called Henry.

". . . so the moment Coreen gets me to some kind of an address, I'll call and let you know. From the sound of it, he's not going to be that difficult to take care of if there's no demon around. I'll have Coreen take me back to York and I'll wait for you there."

With her finger on the disconnect, she sat listening to the dial tone, staring off into the distance, trying to make up her mind. Finally she decided. "Well, it can't hurt." Whether he believed her or not, it was still information he should have.

"Mike Celluci, please. Yes, I'll hold."

He wasn't in the building and the young man on the other end of the phone was significantly unhelpful.

"If you could let him know that Vicki Nelson called."

"Yes ma'am. Is that all?" The young man obviously had never heard of her and he wasn't impressed.

Vicki's tone changed. She hadn't reached her rank at her age without acquiring the ability to handle snot-nosed young men. The words came out parade ground clipped. "Tell him he should check out a student at York University, name of Norman Birdwell. I'll tell him more when I know more."

"Yes, sir! I mean, ma'am."

She grinned a little sadly as she hung up. "Okay, so I'm not a cop anymore," she told an old photo of herself in uniform that hung over the desk. "That's no reason to throw the baby out with the bath water. Maybe it's time to forge a whole new relationship with the police department."

As she had the time, and nothing much else to do with it, Vicki took transit up to York. A childhood spent pinching pennies kept her out of taxis as much as possible and although she bitched and complained about the TTC along with most everyone else in Toronto, she had to admit that if you weren't in a screaming rush or too particular about who you spent time crammed up against, it got you where you needed to go more or less when you needed to get there.

During the long ride up to the university, she pulled everything she knew into one long, point-form report. By the time she'd reached her final transfer, she'd also reached a final question. When they had Norman Bird-wel, what did they do with him?

So we take the grimoire away and get rid of the imme-

diate threat. She stared out the window at a gray stretch of single-story industrial buildings. *What then? The most he can be charged with is possession of stolen property and keeping a prohibited weapon. A slap on the wrist and a few hours of community service work—if they don't throw the whole thing out of court on a technicality—and he'll be back calling up demons again.* He had, after all, managed to kill seven people before even getting his hands on the grimoire. There had to be an answer beyond the only permanent—and completely out of the question—solution she could think of. *Maybe if he tells the court where he got the computer and the jacket and the various and sundry, he'll be ruled insane.*

Find him.

Get the grimoire.

Let the police deal with the rest.

She grinned at her translucent reflection. Let the police deal with it—it had a certain attraction from where she now sat.

Coreen was waiting outside the main doors of Burton Auditorium, red hair a blazing beacon in yet another drizzly, overcast spring afternoon. "I finished the exam faster than I thought I would," she called as Vicki approached. "Good thing you're early; I would have been bored spitless out here much longer. My car's parked in the back." As Vicki fell into step beside her, she pushed a curl back off her face with a clash of day-glo plastic bangles and sighed. "I'm never sure whether finishing in the minimum time is a good thing or not. Like it means you either knew everything cold, or you didn't know squat and you just thought you knew everything cold."

She didn't appear to need a response, so Vicki kept silent, thinking, *I was never that young.*

"Personally, I think I aced it. Ian always said, there was no point in thinking you'd failed when it was too late to do anything about it." She sobered suddenly, remembering Ian, and said nothing more until they were in the car and out on Shoreham Drive.

"Norman's really doing it, isn't he?"

Vicki glanced over at the younger woman whose knuckles were white on the steering wheel. "Doing what?" she asked, more to stall for time than because she didn't know what Coreen meant.

"Calling up demons, just like he said. I was thinking about it after I talked to you. There's no reason that it couldn't have been a demon instead of a vampire that killed Ian and Janet. That's why you're out here, isn't it?"

Considering her options, Vicki decided that the truth would have to serve. Coreen was obviously not going to think she'd flipped, and all things considered, that was of dubious comfort. "Yes," she said quietly, "he's really doing it."

Coreen turned the car north onto Hullmar Drive, tires squealing faintly against the pavement. "And you're here to stop him."

It wasn't a question, but Vicki answered it anyway. "No, I'm just here to find him."

"But I know where he—four, five, six—is." She pulled into the parking lot of a four building apartment complex. "That's his building right there." She stopped the car about three lengths from the door and Vicki jotted the number down.

"Do you remember his apartment number?" she asked, peering toward the smoked glass of the entrance.

"Nine something." Coreen shrugged. "Nine's a powerful number. It probably helped him in his incantations."

"Right." Vicki got out of the car and Coreen followed. "I say we should take him out right now."

Stopped in mid-stride, Vicki stared down at her companion. "I beg your pardon?"

Coreen stared defiantly back. "You and me. We should take him out right now."

"Don't be ridiculous, Coreen. This man is very dangerous."

"Norman? Dangerous?" She snorted derisively. "His demon might be dangerous, but Norman is a geek. I can take him out myself if you're not interested." When she started walking again, Vicki stepped in front of her.

"Hold it right there, this is no time for amateur heroics."

"Amateur heroics?" Coreen's voice rose an octave.

"You're fired, Ms. Nelson!" Turning on one heel, she circumvented Vicki's block and stomped toward the building.

Sighing, Vicki followed. She'd save actual physical restraint as a last resort. *After all, she can't even get into the building.*

The inner door to the lobby was ajar and Coreen barged through it like Elliot Ness going after Capone. On her heels, Vicki reached out to stop her.

"Coreen, I. . . ."

"Freeze, both of you."

The young man who emerged from behind the potted palm was unprepossessing in the extreme. Tall and thin, he carried himself as though parts of his body were on loan from someone else. A plastic pocket protector bulged with pens and his polyester pants stopped roughly two inches above his ankles.

Coreen rolled her eyes and headed directly for him. "Norman, don't be such a. . . ."

"Coreen," Vicki's hand on her shoulder rocked her to a halt. "Perhaps we'd better consider doing as Mr. Birdwell suggests."

Grinning broadly, Norman raised the stolen AK-47.

Vicki had no intention of betting anyone's life on the very visible magazine being empty, not when the police report had included missing ammunition.

One of the building's four elevators was in the lobby, doors open. Norman motioned the two women into it.

"I was looking out my window and I saw you in the parking lot," he told them. "I knew you were here to stop me."

"Well, you're right . . ." Coreen began but fell silent as Vicki's grip on her arm tightened.

Vicki had very little doubt that she could get the gun away from Norman without anyone—except possibly Norman—getting hurt, but she sure as hell wasn't going to do it in an elevator with what appeared to be stainless steel walls. Forget the initial burst—the ricochets would rip all three of them to shreds. She kept her grip on Coreen's arm as they walked down the hallway to Norman's apartment, the barrel of the Russian assault rifle waving between them like some sort of crazed indicator switch.

Don't let anyone open their door, she prayed. *I can handle this if everyone just stays calm.* As she couldn't count on neighbors not diving suddenly into the line of fire, she'd have to wait until they were actually in the apartment before making her move.

Norman's place was unlocked. Vicki pushed Coreen in ahead of her. *The moment he closes the door. . . .* She heard the click, dropped Coreen's arm, spun around, and was pushed to one side as Coreen charged past her and threw herself at their captor.

"Damnit!"

She ducked a wildly swinging elbow and tried to shove Coreen down out of the line of fire. The dark, almost blue metal of the barrel scraped across her glasses. She caught one quick glimpse of Norman's fingers white around the pistol grip. Coreen clutched at her shoulder. She didn't see the steel reinforced butt arc around outside her limited periphery. It missed the thinner bone of her temple by a hair—smashing into her skull, slamming her up against the wall, plummeting her down into darkness.

*   *   *

Brows drawn down into a deep vee, Celluci fanned the phone messages stacked on his desk, checking who they were from. Two reporters, an uncle, Vicki, the dry cleaners, one of the reporters again . . . and again. Growling wordlessly, he crumpled them up and shoved them into his pocket. He didn't have time for this kind of crap.

He'd spent the day combing the area where the latest victim and her dog had been found. He'd talked to the two kids who'd found the body and most of the people who lived in a four block radius. The site had held a number of half obliterated footprints that suggested the man they were looking for went barefoot, had three toes, and very long toenails. No one had seen anything although a drunk camped out farther down in the ravine had heard a sound like a sail luffing and had smelled rotten eggs. The police lab had just informed him that between the mastiff's teeth were particles identical to the bit of whatever-it-was that DeVerne Jones had been holding in his hand. And he was no closer to finding an answer.

Or at least no closer to finding an answer he could deal with.

More things in heaven and earth. . . .

He slammed out of the squad room and stomped down the hall. The new headquarters building seemed to deaden sound, but he made as much as he could anyway.

This place needs some doors you can slam. And Shakespeare should have minded his own goddamned business!

As he passed the desk, the cadet on duty leaned forward. "Uh, Detective, a Vicki Nelson called for you earlier. She seemed quite insistent that you check out. . . ."

Celluci's raised hand cut him off. "Did you write it down?"

"Yes, sir. I left a message on your desk."

"Then you've done your job."

"Yes, sir, but. . . ."

"*Don't* tell me how to do mine."

The cadet swallowed nervously, Adam's apple bobbing above his tight uniform collar. "No, sir."

Scowling, Celluci continued stomping out of the building. He needed to be alone to do some thinking. The last thing he needed right now was Vicki.

Fourteen

Henry stepped out of the shower and frowned at his reflection in the full-length mirror. The lesser cuts and abrasions he'd taken the night before had healed, the greater were healing and would give him no trouble. He unwrapped the plastic bag from around the dressing on his arm and poked gently at the gauze. It hurt and would, he suspected, continue to hurt for some time, but he could use the arm if he was careful. It had been so many years since he'd taken a serious wound that his biggest problem would be remembering it before he caused himself more pain.

He turned a little sideways and shook his head. Great green splotches of fading bruises still covered most of his body.

"Looks familiar, actually. . . ."

*   *   *

The lance tip caught him under the right arm, lifting him up and out of the saddle. For a heartbeat, he hung in the air, then as the roar of the watching crowd rose to a crescendo, he crashed down to the ground. The sound of his armor slamming against the packed earth of the lists rattled around inside his head much as his head rattled around inside his helmet. He almost wouldn't mind the falls if only they weren't so thrice-damned loud. He closed his eyes. *Just until all the noise stops. . . .*

When he opened them again, he was looking up into the face of Sir Gilbert Talboys, his mother's husband.

Where the devil did he come from? he wondered. *Where did my helmet go?* He liked Sir Gilbert, so he tried to smile. His face didn't seem to be functioning.

"Can you rise, Henry? His Grace, the King, is approaching."

There was an urgency in Sir Gilbert's voice that penetrated the ringing in Henry's ears. Could he rise? He wasn't exactly sure. Everything hurt but nothing seemed broken. The king, who would not be pleased that he had been unseated, would be even less pleased if he continued to lie in the dirt. Teeth clenched, he allowed Sir Gilbert to lift him into a sitting position then, with help, heave him to his feet.

Henry swayed but somehow managed to stay standing, even after all supporting hands had been removed. His vision blurred, then refocused on the king, resplendent in red velvet and cloth of gold, advancing from the tournament stand. Desperately, he tried to gather his scattered wits. He had not been in his father's favor since he had unwisely let it be known that he considered Queen Catherine the one true and only Queen of England. This would be the first time his father had spoken to him since he had taken up with that Lutheran slut. Even three years later, the French Court still buzzed with stories of her older sister, Mary, and Henry could not believe that his father had actually put Anne Boleyn on the throne.

Unfortunately, King Henry VIII had done exactly that.

Thanking God that his armor prevented him from falling to one knee—he doubted he'd be able to rise or, for that matter, control the fall—Henry bowed as well as he was able and waited for the king to speak.

"You carry your shield too far from your body. Carry it close and a man cannot get his point behind it." Royal hands flashing with gold and gems lifted his arm and tucked it up against his side. "Carry it here."

Henry couldn't help but wince as the edge of his coutel dug into a particularly tender bruise.

"You're hurting, are you?"

"No, sire." Admitting to pain would not help his case.

"Well, if you aren't now, you will be later." The king chuckled low in his throat, then red-gold brows drew down over deep set and tiny eyes. "We were not pleased to see you on the ground."

This would be the answer that counted. Henry wet his lips; at least the bluff King Hal persona was the easiest to deal with. "I am sorry, sire, and I wish it been you in my place."

The heavy face reddened dangerously. "You wished to see your sovereign unseated?"

The immediate area fell completely silent, courtiers holding their breath.

"No, sire, for if it had been you in my saddle, it would have been Sir John on the ground."

King Henry turned and stared down the lists at Sir John Gage, a man ten years his junior and at the peak of his strength and stamina. He began to laugh. "Aye, true enough, lad. But the bridegroom does not joust for fear he break his lance."

Staggering under a jocular slap on the back, Henry would have fallen but for Sir Gilbert's covert assistance. He laughed with the others, for the king had made a joke, but although he was thankful to be back in favor all he could really think of was soaking his bruises in a hot bath.

*　　*　　*

Henry lifted an arm. "A little thinner perhaps but definitely the same shade." Rolling his shoulder muscles, he winced as one of the half-healed abrasions pulled. Injuries that had once taken weeks, or sometimes months, to heal now disappeared in days. "Still, a good set of tournament armor would've come in handy last night."

Last night. . . . He had taken more blood from Vicki and her young friend than he usually took in a month of feedings. She had saved his life, almost at the expense of her own and he was grateful, but it did open up a whole new range of complications. New complications that would just have to wait until the old ones had been dealt with.

He strapped on his watch. 8:10. Maybe Vicki had called back while he was in the shower.

She hadn't.

"Great. Norman Birdwell, York University, and I'll call you back. So call already." He glared at the phone. The waiting was the worst part of knowing that the grimoire was out there and likely to be used.

He dressed. 8:20. Still no call.

His phone books were buried in the hall closet. He dug them out, just in case. No Norman Birdwell. No Birdwell of any kind.

Her message tied him to the apartment. She expected him to be there when she called. He couldn't go out and search on his own. Pointless in any case when she was so close.

8:56. He had most of the glass picked up. The phone rang.

"Vicki?"

"Please do not hang up. You are talking to a compu . . ."

Henry slammed the receiver down hard enough to crack the plastic. "Damn." He tried a quick call out, listened to Vicki's message—for the third time since sunset, and it told him absolutely nothing new—and hung up a little more gently. Nothing appeared to be damaged except for the casing.

9:17. The scrap metal that had once been a television and a coffee table frame were piled in the entryway, ready to go down to the garbage room. He wasn't sure what he was going to do about the couch. Frankly, he didn't care about the couch. Why didn't she call?

9:29. There were stains in the carpet and the balcony still had no door—though he'd blocked the opening with plywood—but essentially all signs of the battle had been erased from the condo. No mindless task remained to keep him from thinking. And somehow he couldn't stop thinking of a woman's broken body hanging from a rusted hook.

"Damn it, Vicki, call!"

The empty space on the bookshelf drew his gaze and the guilt he'd been successfully holding at bay stormed the barricades. The grimoire was his. The responsibility was his. If he'd been stronger. If he'd been faster. If he'd been smarter. Surely with four hundred and fifty years of experience he should be able to outthink one lone mortal with not even a tenth of that.

He looked down at the city regretfully. "I should have. . . ." He let his voice trail off. There was nothing he *could* have done differently. Even had he continued to believe the killer an abandoned child of his kind, even had Vicki not stumbled onto him bending over that corpse, even had he not decided to trust her, it wouldn't have changed last night's battle with the demon, his loss, and the loss of the grimoire. The only thing that could have prevented that would have been his destruction of the grimoire back when he first acquired it in the 1800s, and, frankly, he wasn't sure he could have destroyed it, then or now.

"Although," he acknowledged, right hand wrapped lightly around left forearm, skin even paler than usual against the stark white of the gauze, "had Vicki not worked her way into the equation, I would have died." And there would have been no one to stop the Demon Lord from rising. His lips drew up off his teeth. "Not that *I* seem to be doing much to prevent it."

Why didn't she call?

He began to pace, back and forth, back and forth, before the window.

She'd lost a lot of blood the night before. Had she run into trouble she was too weak to handle?

He remembered the feel of Ginevra's dead flesh under his hands as he cut her down. She'd been so alive. Like Vicki was so alive. . . .

Why didn't she call?

* * *

She'd been conscious now for some time and had been lying quietly, eyes closed, waiting for the pounding at her temples to stop echoing between her ears. Time was of the essence, yes, but sudden movement would have her puking her guts out and she couldn't see where that would help. Better to wait, to gather information, and to move when she might actually have some effect.

She licked her lips and tasted blood, could feel the warm moisture dribbling down from her nose.

Her feet were tied at the ankles. Her arms lashed together almost from wrists to elbows; the binding around her wrists fabric not rope. She'd been dumped on her side, knees drawn up, left cheek down on a hard, sticky surface—probably the floor. Someone had removed her jacket. Her glasses were not on her nose. She fought back the surge of panic that realization brought.

She could hear—or maybe feel—footsteps puttering about behind her and adenoidal breathing coming from the same direction. Norman. From the opposite direction, she could hear short sharp breaths, each exhalation an indignant snort. And Coreen.

So she's still alive. Good. And she sounds angry, not hurt. Even better. Vicki suspected that Coreen was also tied or she wouldn't be so still. *Which, all things considered, is a good thing. Few people get dead faster than amateur heroes. Not,* she added as a flaming spike slammed through the back of her head, *that the professionals are doing so hot.*

She lay there for a moment, playing *if Coreen hadn't interfered* until the new pain faded into the background with the old pain.

The residual stench of the demon was very strong—only in a building used to students could Norman have gotten away with it—overlaid with burning charcoal, candles, air freshener, and toast.

"You know, you could offer me some. I'm starving."

"You'll eat after."

Vicki wasn't surprised to hear that Norman talked with his mouth full. *He probably picks his nose and wears socks with sandals, too. An all-around great guy.*

"After what?"

"After the Demon Lord makes you mine."

"Get real, Birdwell! Demons don't come that powerful!"

Norman laughed.

Cold fingers traced a pattern up and down Vicki's

spine, and she fought to keep herself from flipping over
so that the thing Norman Birdwell had become was no
longer at her exposed back. She'd heard a man laugh
like that once before. The SWAT team had needed
seven hours to take him out and they'd still lost two of
the hostages.

"You'll see," his voice matter-of-fact around the toast.
"First I was just going to have you ripped into little
pieces, real slow. Then I was going to use you as part
of the incantation to call the Demon Lord. Did I tell
you it needed a life? Until you showed up I was going
to grab the kid down the hall." His voice drew closer
and Vicki felt a pointed toe prodding her in the back.
"Now I've decided to use her and keep you for myself."

"You're disgusting, Birdwell!"

"DON'T SAY THAT!"

Concussion or not, Vicki opened her eyes in time to
see Norman dart forward and slap Coreen across the
face. Without her glasses details were a blur, but from
the sound of it, it hadn't been much of a blow.

"Did I hurt you?" he asked, the rage gone as suddenly
as it had appeared.

The bright mass of Coreen's hair swept up and back
as she tossed her head. "No," she told him, chin rising.
Fear had crept into her voice but it was still vastly outweighed by anger.

"Oh." Norman finished his toast and wiped his fingers
on his jeans. "Well, I will."

Vicki could understand and approve of Coreen's
anger. She was furious herself—at Norman, at the situation, at her helplessness. Although she would have preferred to rant and bellow, she held her rage carefully in
check. Releasing it now, when she was bound, would do
neither her, nor Coreen, nor the city any good. She drew
in a deep breath and slowly exhaled. Her head felt as
though it were balanced precariously on the edge of the
world and one false move would sent it tumbling into
infinity.

"Excuse me." She hadn't intended to whisper, but it
was all she could manage.

Norman turned. "Yes?"

"I was wondering . . ." *Swallow, Ride the pain. Continue.* ". . . if I could have my glasses." *Breathe, two, three, while Norman waits patiently. He isn't going anywhere, after all.* "Without them, I can't see what you're doing."

"Oh." She could almost hear his brow furrow even though she couldn't see it. "It only seems fair you should get to see this."

He trotted out of her line of sight and she closed her eyes for a moment to rest them. *Only seems fair? Well, I suppose I should be happy he doesn't want to waste front row seats.*

"Here." He squatted down and very carefully slid the plastic arms back over her ears, settling the bridge gently on her nose. "Better?"

Vicki blinked as the intricate stitching on his black cowboy boot came suddenly into focus. "Much. Thank you." Up close, and considering the features without the expression, he wasn't an unattractive young man. A bit on the thin and gawky side perhaps, but time would take care of both. Time that none of them had, thanks to Norman Birdwell.

"Good." He patted her cheek and the touch, light as it was sent ripples of pain through her head. "I'll tell you what I told her. If you scream, or make any loud noise, I'll kill you both."

"I'm going to go do my teeth now," he continued, straightening up. "I brush after everything I eat." He pulled what looked to be a thick pen out of the pocket protector and unscrewed the cap. It turned out to be a portable toothbrush, with paste in the handle. "You should get one of these," he told her, demonstrating how it worked, his tone self-righteously smug. "*I've* never had a filling."

Fortunately, he didn't wait for a reply.

Some lucky providence had put Coreen directly across the small room, making it thankfully unnecessary for Vicki to move her head. She studied the younger woman for a few seconds, noting the red patch on one pale cheek. Even with her glasses, she seemed to be having trouble focusing. "Are you all right?" she called quietly.

"What do you think?" Coreen didn't bother to modulate her voice. "I'm tied to one of Norman Birdwell's kitchen chairs—with socks!"

Vicki dropped her gaze. At least six socks per leg tied Coreen to the chrome legs of the kitchen chair. Gray and black and brown nylon socks, stretched to their limit and impossible to break. Intrigued, in spite of everything, she gave her own bonds an experimental tug; they didn't respond like socks. As it seemed safer than moving her head, she slid her arms up along the floor until she could see them. Ties. At least four, maybe five—the swirling leaps of paisley and the jarring clashes of color made it difficult to tell for sure—and while it might have had more to do with her own weakness than Norman's skill, for she doubted he'd ever been a boy scout, he certainly seemed to know his knots.

"You were about to jump him, weren't you?"

"What?" Vicki looked up and wished she hadn't as her body protested with alternating waves of dizziness and nausea.

"When we came into the apartment and I . . . I mean. . . . Well, I'm sorry."

It sounded more like a challenge than an apology. "Don't worry about it now." Vicki swallowed, trying not to add to the puddle of drool collecting under her cheek. "Let's just try . . . to get out of this mess."

"What do you think I've been trying to do?" Coreen gave a frantic heave that only resulted in bouncing the chair backward less than half an inch. "I don't believe this! I really don't believe this!"

Hearing the tones of incipient panic, Vicki, in the driest voice she was capable of, said, "It *is* a little like . . . Alfred Hitchcock does *Revenge of the Nerds.*"

Coreen stared at her in astonishment, sniffed, and grinned somewhat shakily. "Or David Cronenberg does *I Dream of Genie,*" she offered in return.

Good girl. It took all the energy Vicki had left to smile approvingly. While there were dangers in Coreen not taking Norman seriously, the dangers were greater if the girl fell apart.

Struggling did more damage to her than to the ties.

She kept struggling anyway. If the world had to end, she'd be damned if she let it go down under the ridiculously high, cowboy booted heel of Norman Birdwell, adding insult to injury.

*   *   *

"Enough!" Henry spun away from the window and hurled himself toward the door. He had a name, he had a place, it was time he joined the hunt. "I should never have waited this long."

At the door, he slowed, grabbed his coat, and managed to appear within the parameters of normality as he exited into the hall. He slid the key into the lock, then headed for the stairs, hating the charade that kept him to a mortal's pace.

In the dim light of the stairwell, he let all pretense drop and moved as quickly as aching muscles would allow.

There were slightly less than two hours until midnight.

He completely forgot that the stairwell was part of the building's random monitoring system.

*   *   *

Vicki drifted up into consciousness thinking, *This has got to stop.* Every time she tried to move, every time she tried to raise her head, she drifted back down into the pit. Occasionally, the blackness claimed her when she was doing nothing more than lying quietly, trying to conserve her strength for another attempt at getting free. *I'm going to have to think of something else.*

All her intermittent struggling had accomplished was to exacerbate her physical condition and to uncover her watch.

Seven minutes after ten. Henry's probably throwing fits. Oh my God, Henry! Her involuntary jerk brought another flash of pain. She ignored it, lost it in sudden horror. *I forgot to warn him about that security guard. . . .*

*   *   *

Although he recognized the necessity of the surveillance cameras, Greg had never liked them. They always made him feel a bit like a peeping Tom. Two or three guards on constant patrol with one manning a central position at the desk, that's the kind of job he'd prefer to work. A camera just couldn't replace a trained man on the scene. But trained men had to be paid and cameras didn't so he was stuck with them.

As the attractive young lady in the whirlpool stepped out and reached for her towel, he politely averted his eyes. Maybe he was just getting old, but those two scraps of fabric were not what he'd call a bathing suit. When he looked back again, that monitor showed only orderly rows of cars in the underground garage.

He sat back in his chair and adjusted the black arm-band he wore in honor of Mrs. Hughes and Owen. The building would be different without them. As the night went on, he kept expecting to see them heading out for their last walk before bed and had to keep reminding himself that he'd never see them again. The young man he'd relieved had raised an eyebrow at the armband and another at the explanation. Young people today had no real concept of respect; not for the dead, not for authority, not for themselves. Henry Fitzroy was one of the few young people he'd met in the last ten years who understood.

Henry Fitzroy. Greg pulled at his lower lip. Last night he'd done a very, very foolish thing. He was embarrassed by it and sorry for it, but not entirely certain he was wrong. As an old sergeant of his used to say, *"If it walks like a duck, and it talks like a duck, and it acts like a duck, odds are good it's a duck."* The sergeant had been referring to Nazis, but Greg figured it applied to vampires as well. While he had his doubts that a young man of Mr. Fitzroy's quality could have committed such an insane murder—there'd been nothing crazy about the look Greg had seen in Mr. Fitzroy's eyes so many weeks ago, it had, in fact, been frighteningly sane—he couldn't believe that a man of Mr. Fitzroy's quality would allow a young lady visiting him to answer the door *a desha-bille.* He'd have gotten up and done it himself. When he'd calmed down enough to think about it, Greg realized that she had to be hiding something.

But what?

A movement in one of the monitors caught his eye and Greg turned toward it. He frowned. Something black had flickered past the fire door leading to the seventh floor too quickly for him to recognize it. He reached for the override and began activating the cameras in the stairwell.

Seconds later, the fifth floor camera picked up Henry Fitzroy running down the stairs two at a time and scowling. He looked like any other young man in reasonable shape—and a bad mood—who'd decided not to waste his time waiting for an elevator. While Greg himself wouldn't have walked from the fourteenth floor, he realized there was nothing supernatural about Henry Fitzroy doing it. Nor in the way he was doing it.

Sighing, he turned the controls back to their random sequencing.

"And what if it doesn't act like a duck all the time?" he wondered aloud.

*　　*　　*

Henry had reached the sixth floor when the abuse his body had taken the night before caught up with him and he had to slow to something more closely approximating a mortal's pace. He snarled as he swung his weight around on the banister, frustrated by the refusal of muscles to respond as they should. Rather than touching down only once on every half flight, he actually had to use every other step.

He was in a *bad* mood when he reached his car and he took the exit ramp from the underground garage much faster than he should have, his exhaust pipe screaming along concrete. The sound forced him to calm. He wouldn't get there any faster if he destroyed his car or attracted the attention of the police.

At the curb, while he waited impatiently for the light to change, he caught a familiar scent.

"A BMW? You've got to be kidding." Tony leaned his forearms through the open window and clicked his tongue. "If that watch is a Rolex," he added softly, "I want my blood back."

Henry knew he owed the boy a great deal, so he tried bury the rage he was feeling. He felt his lips pull back off his teeth and realized he hadn't been significantly successful.

If Tony had doubted his memory of what had happened the night before, Henry's expression would have convinced him for there was very little humanity in it. Had the anger been directed at him, he would've run and not stopped until sunrise and safety. As it was, he pulled his arms back outside the car, just in case. "I thought you might want to talk. . . ."

"Later." If the world survived the night, they'd talk. It wasn't of immediate concern.

"Yeah. Right. Later's good. Say. . . ." Tony frowned. "Is Victory okay?"

"I don't . . ." The light changed. He slammed the car into gear. ". . . know."

Tony stood watching the car speed away, lips pursed, hands shoved deep in his pockets. He rolled a quarter over and over between his fingers.

"This is my home number." Vicki handed him the card *and turned it over so he could see the other number hand-written on the back. "And this is who you call if you're in trouble and you can't get to me."*

"Mike Celluci?" Tony shook his head. *"He don't like me much, Victory."*

"Tough."

"I don't like him much."

"Do I look like I care? Call him anyway."

He pulled the quarter from his pocket and headed to the pay phone on the corner. Four years in a variety of pockets had turned the card limp but the number on the back was still legible. He'd already called the number on the front and wasted a quarter on a stupid machine. Everybody knew Victory never turned the machine on if she was home.

"I gotta talk to Mike Celluci."

"Speaking."

"Victory's in trouble." He was as sure of it as he'd ever been sure of anything in his life.

"Who?"

Tony rolled his eyes at the receiver. And they called them the city's finest. What a dork. "Vicki Nelson. You remember—tall, blonde, pushy, used to be a cop."

"What kind of trouble?"

Good. Celluci sounded worried. "I don't know."

"Where?"

"I don't know." Tony could hear teeth grinding on the other end of the line. If this wasn't so serious, he'd be enjoying himself. "You're the cop, you figure it out."

He hung up before the explosion. He'd done what he could.

Mike Celluci stared at the phone and swore long and loudly in Italian. Upon reflection, he'd recognized the voice as Vicki's little street person and that lent just enough credibility to the message that it couldn't be completely ignored. He dumped a pocket load of little pink slips on the kitchen table and began sorting through them.

"Norman Birdwell. York University." He held it up to the light in a completely futile gesture then tossed it back with the others.

Vicki had never been a grandstander. She'd always played by the rules, made them work for her. She'd never go in to pick up a suspected mass murderer—a suspected psychotic mass murderer—without backup. *But then, she doesn't have backup anymore, does she? And she just might feel like she's got something to prove. . . .*

He'd hit the memory dial to headquarters before he finished the thought.

"This is Celluci. Darrel, I need the number for someone in Administration at York University. I know it's the middle of the night, I want a home number. I *know* I'm off duty. You're not paying my overtime, what the hell are you complaining about?" He balanced the phone under his chin and pulled his shoulder holster up off the back of the chair, shrugging into it as he waited. "So call me at home when you find it. And Darrel, give it top priority. I want that number yesterday."

He reached for his jacket and laid it beside the phone.

He hated waiting. He'd always hated waiting. He dug the pink slip back out of the pile.

Norman Birdwell.

"I don't know what hat you pulled this name out of, Nelson," he growled. "But if I ride to the rescue and you're not in deep shit, bad eyes and insecurity are going to be the least of your problems."

* * *

Norman was talking to the grimoire and had been for some time. His low mumble had become a constant background noise as Vicki drifted in and out of consciousness. Occasionally she heard words, mostly having to do with how the world would now treat Norman the way he deserved. Vicki was all for that.

"Hey, Norman!"

The mumbling stopped. Vicki tried to focus on Coreen. The younger woman looked . . . embarrassed?

Grimoire clutched to his chest, Norman came into her line of sight. She shuddered at the thought of holding that book that closely. The one time she'd touched it back in Henry's apartment had made her skin crawl and the memory still left an unpleasant feeling in her mind.

"Look, Norman, I have really got to go to the bathroom." Coreen's voice was low and intense and left no doubt as to her sincerity and Vicki suddenly found herself wishing she hadn't said that.

"Uh. . . ." Norman obviously had no idea of how to deal with the problem.

Coreen sighed audibly. "Look, if you untie me, I'll walk quietly to the bathroom and then come right back to my chair so you can tie me up again. You can keep me covered with your silly gun the entire time. I *really* have to go."

"Uh. . . ."

"Your Demon Lord isn't going to be too impressed if he shows up and I've peed on his pentagram."

Norman stared at Coreen for a long moment, his hands stroking up and down the dark leather cover of the grimoire. "You wouldn't," he said at last.

"Try me."

It might have been the smile, it might have been the tone of voice, but Norman decided not to risk it.

Vicki drifted off during the untying and came to again as Coreen, once more secured in her chair, said, "What about her?"

Norman shifted his grip slightly on the gun. "She doesn't matter, she'll be dead soon anyway."

Vicki was beginning to be very afraid that he was right. She simply had no reserves left to call on and every time she fought her way up out of the blackness, the world seemed a little further away. *Okay, if I'm dead anyway and I scream and he shoots me, the neighbors will call the police—that thing doesn't have a silencer on it. Of course, he may just whack me on the head again.* That was the last thing she needed. *If I have Coreen scream as well, that may push him over the edge enough that he shoots one of us.*

Coreen, for all the girl believed in vampires and demons and who knew what else, didn't really understand what was about to happen. *Mind you, that's not her fault. I didn't tell her.*

She balanced Coreen's life against the life of the city. It wasn't a decision she had any right to make. She made it anyway. *I'm sorry, Coreen.*

She wet her lips and drew in as deep a breath as she was capable of. "Cor . . ." The butt of the rifle hit the floor inches from her nose, the metal plate slamming against the tiles. The noise and the vibration drove the remainder of her carefully hoarded breath out in an almost silent cry of pain. *Thank God, he had the safety on. . . .*

"Shut up," Norman told her genially.

She didn't really have much choice but to obey as darkness rolled over her once again.

Norman looked around his apartment, exceedingly pleased with himself. Soon all those people who thought him a nobody, a nothing, would pay. He reached out one hand to stroke the book. The book said so.

10:43. Time to start painting the pentagram. It was much more complicated than the form he usually used and he wanted to be sure he got it right.

This was going to be the greatest night of his life.

Fifteen

She knew better than to go near strange men in cars. She'd been raised on horror stories of abduction and rape and young women found weeks later decomposing in irrigation ditches. She answered the summons anyway, her mother's warnings having lost their power from the moment she met the stranger's eyes.

"The administration offices, where are they?"

She knew where the admin offices were, at least, she thought she knew—actually, she wasn't sure what she thought anymore. She wet her lips and offered, "The Ross Building?" She'd seen an office in Ross, maybe more than one.

"Which is where?"

She half turned and pointed. A moment later, she wondered why she was standing in the middle of St. Lawrence Boulevard staring at a set of taillights driving onto the campus—and why she felt a vague sense of disappointment.

Henry scanned the directory board and frowned. Only one office listed might have what he needed: The Office of Student Programs, S302. He sensed a scattering of lives in the building, but he would deal with them as he had to.

11:22. He was running out of time.

The dim lighting was a boon and had anyone been watching they'd have seen only a deeper shadow flickering down the length of the shadowed hall.

The first flight of stairs he found only took him to the

second floor. He found another, found the third floor, and began following the numbers stenciled on the doors. 322, 313, 316 . . . 340? He turned and glared at the fire door he'd just passed through. Surely there had to be a pattern. No one, not even in the twentieth century, numbered a building completely at random.

"I haven't got time for this," he growled.

340, 342, 344, 375a. . . .

A cross corridor carried the numbers off in two directions. Henry paused, there were voices and they were saying things he couldn't ignore.

"Well, what do you expect when you call out the name of a Demon Lord in his consort's temple?"

Temple? Consort? Were there now other groups involved in calling demons or had his assumption that only one person was involved been wrong from the beginning? He didn't have time to check this out. He couldn't afford not to.

Down the cross corridor, around a corner, and the door at the end of the hall showed light behind it. There appeared to be several people talking at once.

"I suppose this means the demon has Elias?"

"Good guess. What are you going to do?"

"What can we do? We wait."

"You can wait," a third voice rose out of the tumult, "but Lexi boots the statue and screams, '*Ashwarn, Ashwarn, Ashwarn, you give him back!*' at the top of her lungs."

Henry paused, hand on the door. There were six lives in the room and no feel of a demonic presence. What was going on?

"Nothing happens."

"What do you mean, nothing?"

"Just what I said, nothing." The young woman sitting at the head of the table spotted Henry standing, blinking on the threshold and smiled. "Hi. You look lost."

They were playing a game. That much was obvious from the piles of brightly colored dice. But a game that called on demons? "I'm looking for student records. . . ."

"Boy are you in the wrong place." A tall young man

scratched at dark stubble. "You need the WOB." At Henry's blank look, he grinned and continued. "The West Office Building, WOB, that's where all that shit is."

"Yeah, but the WOB closes down at five." Carefully placing the little lead figure she'd been holding on the table, one of the other players checked her watch. "It's eight minutes after eleven. There won't be anyone there."

Eight after eleven. More time wasted on fruitless searching.

"Hey, don't look so upset, man, maybe we can help?"

"Maybe we can play?" muttered one of the others. The rest ignored her.

Why not? After all, he was looking for a man who called up demons. The connection was there, however tenuous. "I'm looking for Norman Birdwell."

The young woman at the head of the table curled her lip. "Why?" she asked. "Does he owe you money?"

"You know him?"

"Unfortunately." The group drawled out the word in unison.

They would have laughed, but Henry was at the table before the first sound escaped. They looked at one another in nervous silence instead and Henry could see memories of nine bodies, throats ripped out, rising in their expressions. He couldn't compel a group this large, he could only hope they were still young enough to respond to authority.

"I need his address."

"We, uh, played at his place once. Grace, didn't you write it down?"

They all watched while Grace, the young woman at the head of the table, searched through her papers. She appeared to have written everything down. Henry fought the urge to help her search.

"Is Norman in trouble?"

Henry kept his eyes on the papers, willing the one he needed to be found. "Yes."

The players closest to him edged away, recognizing

the hunter. A second later, with the arrogance of youth, they decided they couldn't possibly be the prey and edged back.

"We, uh, stopped gaming with him 'cause he took the whole thing too seriously."

"Yeah, he started acting like all this stuff was real. Like he was bumping into wizards and warriors and long-legged beasties on every street corner."

"He's such a dork."

"It's just a game."

"It's a game we're not playing," someone pointed out.

"Is Norman in bad trouble?"

"Yes."

They stopped talking after that. They didn't have the concepts to deal with the tone of Henry's voice.

Grace handed him the paper tentatively, although not entirely certain she'd keep her fingers in the deal.

"Wait a minute," the tall young man protested. "I don't like Norman either, but should we be giving out his. . . ." Henry turned to look full at him. He paled and closed his eyes.

As he slammed his car into gear and burned rubber the length of the parking lot, Henry checked his watch. 11:36. So little time.

". . . and one final join here." Norman straightened up and beamed proudly down at his apartment floor. The white outline of the pentagram had almost been obscured by the red and yellow symbols surrounding it. He caressed the open page of the grimoire, tracing with his fingertips the diagram he'd just finished reproducing. "Soon," he told it. "Soon."

The smell of the acrylic paint so close to Vicki's face added to the nausea and made her eyes sting and itch. She no longer had the strength to ignore it, so she endured it instead. Scrubbing out a bit of the pentagram before it dried had seemed like a good idea until she realized that it would only release the Demon Lord to the slaughter that much sooner. But there had to be something she could do. She would not, could not, admit Norman Birdwell had won.

Coreen stared from the pentagram to Norman and back to the drying paint. It was real, all of it, and while she'd always believed, now she began to *believe*. Her mouth suddenly dry and her heart beating so loud she felt sure the skinny geek should be able to hear it, she tried harder to free her right leg. When Norman had tied her back up after taking her to the bathroom, she'd worked a bit of slack into the socks. Ever since, while he'd puttered about doing who knew what, she'd been working them looser, stretching them little by little. Sooner or later, she'd have her leg free. For now, her mind refused to deal with anything beyond that point.

The five candles Norman placed around the pentagram were new. Red and yellow spirals had been much easier to find than black candles of any description. He kept the grimoire with him, tucked under an arm when he needed his hands free, clutched close to his chest when he didn't. He had begun to feel incomplete without it, as if it had become a part of him, even taking it to Canadian Tire that afternoon when he bought the new hibachi. Holding it, he knew that his wildest dreams were about to come true.

The throbbing in his head had become louder, wilder, and more compelling. Its tone varied with his actions . . . or possibly his actions varied with the tones—Norman was no longer entirely sure.

As he pulled the tiny barbecue out of its box and set it up by the balcony door, he checked to see if his audience was impressed. The older woman had closed her eyes again, her glasses having slipped down far enough for him to see over them, but she was still breathing and that was really all that counted. He'd be pissed if she died before he killed her 'cause then he'd have to use Coreen and he had other plans for her. Coreen didn't look impressed either, but she looked scared and that would do for now.

"You're not laughing." He prodded her in the back with the grimoire, noting with pleasure the way she flinched away from its touch, then squatted to set up the three charcoal briquettes.

"There's nothing to laugh at, Norman." Coreen

twisted around in her chair. He was a little behind her and to one side and she hated not being able to see what he was doing. Although she wanted to shriek, she tried to keep her voice from rising too high. *You should talk softly to crazy people*—she'd read that in a book. "Look, this has gone far enough. Ms. Nelson needs a doctor." *A little pleading wouldn't hurt.* "Please, Norman, you let us go and we'll forget we ever saw you."

"Let you go?" It was Norman's turn to laugh at her. He didn't think the Demon Lord could give him anything he'd enjoy so much. He laughed at her the way everyone, all his life, had laughed at him. It grew and grew and she shrank back under the weight of it. He felt it echo in the grimoire, felt his body begin to reverberate with the sound, felt it wrap in and around the pulsing in his head.

"Norman!" It wasn't very loud, but it was enough to cut the laughter off. *All right, so maybe there is power in a name. I've been wrong about other things lately.* Vicki tried to focus on the young man's face, couldn't manage it, and gave up. The insane hysteria of the laughter had stopped. That was the result she'd spent her strength for and she'd have to be content with the victory she'd won.

His brows drawn down into a deep vee, Norman scowled at the woman on the floor. He was glad she was going to die. She'd chased the laughter away. Still scowling, he lit the candles and flicked off the overhead light. Not even Coreen's quick intake of breath at the sudden twilight was enough to put him in a better mood. Not until he got the briquettes burning and the air in the room grew blue with the smoke from a handful of frankincense, did his expression lighten.

Only one thing left to do.

When Vicki next opened her eyes she came closer to panic than she had at any time that night.

When did it get so dark?

She could see five flickering points of light. The rest of the room, Coreen, Norman—gone. And the air . . . it smelled strange, heavy, it hurt to breathe.

Dear God, am I dying?

She tried to move, to fight, to live. Her arms and legs were still bound. That reassured her, slowed her heart and slowed her breathing. If she was tied, she wasn't dead. Not yet.

The lights were candles, could be nothing else, and the air reeked of incense. It must have begun.

She didn't see Norman approach, didn't even realize he was there until he gently pushed her glasses up her nose. His fingers were warm as he wrestled with her arms and pushed the ties back to expose her left wrist. She thought she could see the faint line where Henry had fed the night before and knew she was imagining it. In this light, at this time, she couldn't have seen the wound if her entire hand had been chopped off.

She felt the cold edge of a blade against her skin and its kiss as it opened a vein. And then another. Not the safe horizontal cuts she and Tony had made but vertical cuts that left her wrist awash in darkness and a warm puddle filling the hollow of her palm.

"You have to stay alive through the invocation," Norman told her, pulling her arms away from her body, making them part of the symbols surrounding the pentagram. "So I'm only going to do one wrist. Don't die too fast." She heard the knife clatter down on the floor behind her, and his footsteps move away.

Fucking right I won't. . . . The anger tired her so she let it go. *Essentials only now, never say die.* Especially not when die meant bleeding to death on a dirty floor and delivering her city, not to mention the world, into Armageddon. Sagged over onto her left side, her heart could be no more than four inches off the floor. By concentrating everything she had remaining on her right arm, she managed to get it under her left, elevating the bleeding wrist as high as possible. Maybe not four inches, but it would help to retard the flow.

Pressure'll be low. . . . I could hold on for . . . hours.

It might only be a matter of time, but as much as possible she'd make it her time, not his.

Through her ear pressed against the floor by the weight of her head, all she could hear was a soft rhythmic hissing, like the sound of the ocean in a shell. She lay listening to that, ignoring the chanting rising around her.

*   *   *

He could have identified the specific building in the complex even without the address. The power surrounding it, the expectation of evil, caused every hair on Henry's body to rise. He was out of the car before it had completely skidded to a stop and through the locked door into the lobby a moment later. The reinforced glass was not thick enough to stop the concrete planter he heaved through it.

*   *   *

Norman spat the last discordant word into the air and let his left hand fall down to the open grimoire balanced on his right. His throat hurt, his eyes stung, and he was trembling with excitement, waiting for the telltale shimmer of air that would signify his demon was arriving.

It never came.

One second the pentagram was empty and the throbbing beat out a glorious rhythm inside his head. A second later, with no warning, it was full, and only echoes remained in the silence.

Norman cried out and fell to his knees, the grimoire forgotten as he raised both hands to cover his face.

Coreen whimpered and sagged against her bonds, consciousness fleeing what it couldn't accept.

Vicki attempted to breathe shallowly through her teeth, glad for the first time she couldn't really *see*. Every fear she'd ever held, every nightmare, every terror from childhood to yesterday came with the ill-defined shape in the pentagram. She clamped her teeth down on the urge to wail and used her physical condition—the pain, the weakness—to insulate her from the Demon Lord. *I hurt too much now to be hurt any further.*

The thing in the pentagram seemed amused by that.

Colors ran together in ways that colors could not, creating shades that seared the heart and shades that froze the soul, and they built a creature with blond curls and blue eyes and very, very white teeth. Slender and hermaphroditic, it laid no claim to either sex while claiming both of them.

"Enough," said the Demon Lord, and the terror damped down to a bearable level. It checked the boundaries of its prison and then the lives around it. Coreen, it ignored, but by Vicki's side of the pentagram it squatted and smiled approvingly at the patterns of blood on the floor.

"So, you are the life that opens the way for my power." It smiled and Vicki gave thanks she could see only a shadowy outline of the expression. "But you're not being very cooperative, are you?"

Only the nonresponsiveness of her muscles gave her time to fight the compulsion that she lower her bleeding wrist back to the floor. A sudden shock of recognition lent her strength. "I . . . know you." Not the face, not this creature specifically, but the essence, oh, the essence she knew.

"I know you, too." Something writhed for a second in the Demon Lord's eyes. "And this time, I've won. It's over, Victoria."

She really hated that name. "Not till . . . fat lady sings."

"A joke? In your position? I think that your strength might be better spent pleading for mercy." It stood and dusted its hands against its thighs. "A pity I can't allow you to live. I'd get such pleasure from your reactions to my plans."

All Vicki wanted at that moment was enough saliva left to spit.

It turned to Norman, still cowering by the hibachi. "Stand!"

Scooping up the grimoire, holding the book like a talisman, Norman rose shakily to his feet.

"Release me!"

Norman's lower lip went out and his expression grew decidedly mulish. "No. I called you. I am your master." He had the power, not this thing. He did.

The Demon Lord's laughter blew the windows out of the apartment.

As though there were strings attached to his shoulders

and the Demon Lord was the puppeteer, Norman began
to jerk toward the pentagram. "No," he whined. "I am
the master."

He's fighting, Vicki realized. She would have expected
his will to be swept aside like so many matchsticks. Conceit and self-interest made a stronger defense than she
thought.

*   *   *

As Henry stepped out of the elevator onto the ninth
floor, the smell of blood almost overwhelmed him. It
rose over the pervasive demon-taint and drew him to
the door he needed. The door was locked.

The metal held. The wood of the doorjamb splintered
and gave.

*   *   *

Vicki heard the noise as though it came from a great
distance away. She recognized it, understood its significance, but just couldn't seem to care much.

The Demon Lord heard the noise as well but ignored
it. It kept its attention on Norman who stood inches
from the edge of the pentagram, sweating and shaking
and losing the battle.

The word seemed mostly consonants and it tore at the
ears as it tore at the throat.

The Demon Lord snarled and turned, its patina of
humanity slipping as it moved. When it saw Henry, its
features settled and it smiled. "You call my name,
Nightchild, are you the champion here? Have you come
to save the mortal world from my domination?"

Henry felt it stroke at his mind and swatted the touch
away, his own snarl barely less demonic as he answered.
"Go back to the pit, spawn of Satan! This world is not
yours!"

"Spawn of Satan?" The Demon Lord shook its head.
"You are showing your age, Henry Fitzroy. This world
does not believe in the Dark Lord. I will enjoy teaching
it differently and you cannot stop me from doing exactly
as I wish."

"I will not allow you to destroy this world without a fight." He didn't dare take his eyes from the Demon Lord's to look for Vicki although he knew it was her blood scent that filled the room.

"Fight all you wish." It bowed graciously. "You will lose."

"NO!" Norman stood, splay legged, grimoire tucked under his arm, clutching the AK-47 with enough force to turn his fingers white. "*I* called your name! I AM THE MASTER! YOU WILL NOT IGNORE ME! YOU WON'T! YOU WON'T! YOU WON'T!"

The short burst sprayed across the pentagram, almost cutting the Demon Lord in half. Howling with rage, it lost control of its form, becoming again the maelstrom of darkness it had been at the beginning.

Firearm violation, Vicki thought muzzily, as the slugs tore up the kitchen cabinets behind her.

The noise startled Coreen into full consciousness. With panicked strength she began to fight against her bonds, throwing herself violently from side to side, bouncing the chair legs inches off the floor at a time.

Like night falling in on itself, the Demon Lord reformed and the temperature in the apartment plunged. It smiled, showing great curved teeth it hadn't had before. Once again, Norman began jerking toward it.

The lights came on, throwing the scene into sharp relief, and a voice yelled, "Freeze! Police!"

The first instant of frozen expressions was almost funny, then Henry raised a hand to shield his eyes, the Demon Lord spun about to face a new adversary, and Norman raced toward the door, screaming, "No, it's mine! You can't stop me! It's mine!"

Coreen's leg came free of the socks at last. As Norman passed, she kicked out.

He fought for balance, arms flailing. The grimoire dropped to the floor. A second later, Norman fell into the pentagram.

Then Norman wasn't there anymore, but his scream lingered for a heartbeat or two.

Mike Celluci stood at the light switch, his .38 in one

hand, the other, under no conscious volition, making the sign of the cross. "Jesus H. Christ," he breathed into the sudden silence. "What the hell is going on in here?"

The Demon Lord turned to face him. "But that's it exactly, Detective. *Hell* is going on in here."

This was worse than anything Celluci could have imagined. He hadn't seen the punk with the assault rifle disappear into thin air. He didn't see the thing standing in the middle of the room smiling.

But he had. And he did.

Then he caught sight of Vicki and all the strangeness became of secondary importance.

"Who did this?" he demanded, moving to her side and dropping to one knee. "What is going on in here!" The question came out sounding more than a bit desperate the second time around. While he felt her throat for a pulse, he kept the Demon Lord covered—the direction of the threat obvious after what he'd seen as he came in.

"Pretty much exactly what it looks like," Henry told him. Clearly the stalwart officer of the law was a friend of Vicki's. What he thought he was doing here could be settled later. "That is a Demon Lord. He just destroyed the . . . person who called him and we're in a great deal of trouble."

"Trouble?" Celluci asked, not bothering at the moment with whether he believed all this or not.

"Yes," said the Demon Lord, and stepped out of the pentagram. It effortlessly pulled the gun from Celluci's hand and tossed it out the window.

Celluci watched it go, there being nothing else he could do, then with lips a thin, pale line he bent over Vicki, ignoring the cold sweat that beaded his entire body, ignoring the terror that held his heart in an icy fist, ignoring everything but the one thing he could change. Fighting the knots out of the ties, he bound up her wrist with the first one he got free.

"It won't do any good," the Demon Lord observed. With all attention focused on Vicki, it sidled sideways, whirled around, and dove for the grimoire.

Henry got there first, scooped up the book, and backed away with it. To his surprise, the Demon Lord snarled but let him go. "You have no power," he realized. "You're in this world without power."

"The invocation is not finished," the Demon Lord admitted, its eyes still on the book, "until the woman dies."

"Then the invocation will never be finished." Brute strength forced the bindings off her legs and Celluci threw the ties across the room with unnecessary force.

"It will be finished very soon." the Demon Lord pointed out. "She is dying."

"No she isn't," Celluci growled, easing Vicki's limp body over onto her back.

Yes, I am. Vicki wished she could feel the hand cupping her face, but she hadn't been able to feel anything for some time. Her eyes itched, but she didn't have the strength to blink. She wished it wasn't happening this way. But she'd given it her best shot. Time to rest.

Then the Demon Lord raised its head and looked directly at her, its expression gloating and openly triumphant.

When she died, it won.

The hell it wins. She grabbed onto what life she had left and shook it, hard. *I am not going to die. I am not going to die!*

"I am . . . not . . . going to die. . . ."

"That's what I said." Celluci didn't bother to smile. Neither of them would have believed it. "Listen."

Through the glassless window, up from the street, she could hear sirens growing closer.

"Cavalry?" she asked.

He nodded. "I called in an *officer down* when I reached the building—the place felt like it was under siege. There'll be an ambulance with them. I don't care how much blood you've lost, they can replace it."

"Concussed, too. . . ."

"Your head's hard enough to take it. You're not going to die." He half turned to face the Demon Lord, throwing his conviction over his shoulder at it.

It smiled unpleasantly. "All mortals die in time. I will, of course, try to make it sooner than later."

"Over my dead body," Celluci snarled.

"No need." Henry shook his head. "It can't kill her

or it would have the moment it left the pentagram. Her death is tied to the invocation and it can't affect the invocation. All it can do is wait.

"If you stay," he told it, moving closer, "you'll be fighting every moment. We can't destroy you, but without all your power you'll have no easy time of it."

The Demon Lord watched him move, eyes narrowed.

No, Vicki realized, *it isn't watching him, it's watching the grimoire.*

"So what do you suggest?" it scoffed. "That I surrender? Time is all I need, and time I have in abundance."

Vicki pushed at Celluci's arm, moving him out of his protective position. "A deal. . . . You want . . . the grimoire." If only her tongue wasn't so damned thick. "Go. . . . Break the invocation . . . it's yours."

"In time, I will take the grimoire. You have no idea of how to truly use the knowledge it contains." It made no effort to hide its desire as it stared at the book of demonic lore. "There is nothing in your deal for me."

"Power freely given has more strength than that taken by force." Coreen went deep red as the two men and the Demon Lord turned to stare at her. "Well, it does. Everyone knows it."

"And power freely given is not a power often seen where you come from." Henry added, nodding slowly. The girl had brought up an important point. "It could be the makings of a major coup."

"The name . . . written on the . . . city." The demonkind had proven they were not without ambition.

"Upstart, grasping." The Demon Lord ground out a number of other words in a language that sound like a cat fight and its aspect began to slip again.

"Why wait for this world when you can have another now?" Henry prodded. "You want the grimoire. With it you can control others of your kind. Defeat your enemies. . . ."

"Yessss."

"We give it freely if in exchange you break the invocation and return where you came from. He who called you is no more. Nothing holds you here. Why wait when you can rule?"

With an effort the Demon Lord maintained its shape, holding out hands that were no longer quite hands. "Give it to me. I will make your bargain."

"Swear it on your name."

"I ssso ssssswear."

"And that you'll never use the book against humankind," Coreen added in a rush, before Henry could move.

"It holdsss knowledge only to be usssed againssst demonkind."

Her lower lip went out. "Swear it anyway. On your name."

"I ssswear. I ssswear."

Henry took a step forward and placed the book on what remained of the Demon Lord's hands. Grimoire and Demon Lord disappeared.

Vicki stared to giggle.

Celluci looked down at her and frowned. "What?" he snapped.

"I was just . . . wondering . . . what you're going to . . . put in . . . your report."

*   *   *

"I saw Henry." Tony finished off the last of the gelatin and put the bowl back on the tray. "He came and told me what happened. Said I had a right to know. He's pretty cool. I think he was checking me out."

"Probably," Vicki agreed. "You know a dangerous amount about him."

Tony shrugged. "I'm no threat. Don't matter to me what time a guy gets up."

"Doesn't matter."

He grinned. "That's what I said."

The nurse's shoes squeaked softly against the floor as she came into the room. "Visiting hours are over. You can come again tomorrow."

Tony glanced from the nurse to Vicki and heaved himself to his feet. He paused in the doorway and looked back. "Save me the gelatin."

Vicki grimaced. "It's all yours," she promised.

The nurse puttered about for a few moments, re-

arranged the blankets, checked the IV drip and bandage
that covered Vicki's left arm from hand to elbow. On
her way out, she ran into Mike Celluci on his way in.

"I'm sorry." Drawing herself up to her full height, she
blocked the door. "But visiting hours are over."

Celluci gently moved her aside and, as she started to
bristle, flashed his badge. "Police business," he said, and
closed the door.

He shook his head at heavy purple circles under
Vicki's eyes, clicked his tongue at the IV drip, bent
down, kissed her, and said without straightening, "You
look like shit."

"Actually, I'm feeling much better." She reached up
and pushed the curl of hair back off his forehead. "Yesterday, I *felt* like shit. And speaking of yesterday, where
were you?"

"Writing up my report." He threw himself into the
chair Tony had pulled up beside the bed. "Sure, you can
laugh. That's one part of police work you should be glad
you're free of."

It didn't hurt as much as it used to. In time, she suspected, it would hardly hurt at all. "What did you say?"

"I told the truth." He grinned at her expression.
"Okay, not *all* of it."

"And Norman?"

"He got away while I was trying to keep you alive.
Fortunately the chief remembers you through rose colored glasses and thinks that's a sufficient excuse. There's
a country-wide APB out on him." He shrugged. "It
won't do my arrest record any good, but the killings will
stop and I figure he got what was coming to him."

Vicki wasn't sure that she agreed so she kept silent.
It smacked too much of an eye for an eye. *And the
whole world ends up blind.*

"Your new boyfriend's a little shy."

She had to grin at the tone. "I told you. He's a writer.
He's used to being alone."

"Sure. And I've told you, you're a lousy liar. But I
owe him for taking care of that . . . teenager, so I'll let
it go for now."

Vicki's grin twisted. Coreen had no idea she'd finally

met her vampire and that said vampire had *convinced* her that much of what had happened, hadn't. According to Coreen, Henry's version had left out both the lesser demon and the Demon Lord and had placed all the blame on Norman Birdwell. In a way, Norman was at last getting the recognition he craved.

She reached over with her good arm and poked him in the thigh. "That teenager, as you call her, just paid me a decent wage for that little dustup, so I'll thank you to speak of her with more respect."

Celluci grimaced. "Vicki, she's an airhead. I have no idea how he kept her quiet about, well, you know . . ." He couldn't say it, that would make it too real. ". . . but I shuddered to think of her getting to the press. And now," he heaved himself to his feet and headed for the door. "I'll get out of here so you can get some sleep."

Sleep was a long time coming. She palmed the pills they tried to give her and lay listening to the hospital grow quiet.

It was close to 1:00 when the door opened again.

"You're awake," he said softly.

She nodded, aware he could see her even if she couldn't see him.

"Were you waiting for me?"

She tried to keep her tone light. "Well, I didn't think you'd be here during regular visiting hours." She felt his weight settle on the side of the bed.

"I wasn't sure you'd want to see me."

"Why not?"

"Well, you can't exactly have pleasant memories of the time we shared."

"Not many, no." Some of the memories she found very pleasant, but Vicki wasn't sure she wanted to remind him of that just now. With four hundred and fifty years of experience, he had enough cards already.

Henry frowned, secure in the darkness. She said one thing, but her scent. . . .

"It must have been difficult for you to get in here."

"Hospitals have few shadows," he admitted. "I had hoped I could see you after you got out. . . ?"

"Sure." Would he understand what she was offering? Did she? "We can have dinner."

She couldn't see him smile, but she heard the laugh then felt the cool pressure of his fingers around her hand. "Do you believe in destiny?" he asked.

"I believe in truth. I believe in justice. I believe in my friends. I believe in myself." She hadn't for a while, but now she did again. "And I believe in vampires."

His lips brushed against the skin of her wrist, and the warm touch of his breath when he spoke stood every hair on her body on end.

"Good enough."

BLOOD TRAIL

For DeVerne Jones, who patiently answered hundreds of questions including a few it never occurred to me to ask.

With special thanks to Ken Sagara, whose generosity was responsible for me finishing this manuscript on time, vision intact.

One

The three-quarter moon, hanging low in the night sky, turned even tamed and placid farmland into a mysterious landscape of silver light and shadows. Each blade of grass, toasted golden brown by two months of summer heat, had a thin black replica stretching out behind it. The bushes along the fence bottom, highways for those too timid to brave the open fields, rustled once and then were silent as some nocturnal creature went about its business.

Their summer-shorn fleece turned milky white by the moonlight, a large flock of sheep had settled for the night in one corner of the meadow. Except for the rhythmic motion of a number of jaws and the occasional flick of an ear or twitch of a lamb unable to be still for long, even in sleep, they appeared to be an outcropping of pale stone. An outcropping come suddenly to life as several heads rose at once, aristocratic noses pointed into the breeze.

They were obviously familiar with the creature that bounded over the fence and into the meadow, for although the ewes remained alert they watched it approach with mild curiosity rather than alarm.

The huge black beast paused to mark a fence post, then trotted a few steps into the field and sat down, gazing back at the sheep with a proprietary air. Something in its general outline, in the shape of its head, said wolf just as its coloring, its size, its breadth of chest, and the reaction of the flock said "dog."

Convinced that all was as it should be, it began to

lope along the edge of the fence bottom, plumed tail streaming behind it like a banner, moon-silvered highlights rippling through its thick fur with every movement. Picking up speed, it leapt a thistle—more for the sheer joy of leaping than because the thistle was in its way—and cut diagonally across the lower end of the pasture.

With no more warning than a distant cough, the gleaming black head exploded in a shower of blood and bone. The body, lifted off its feet by the impact, spasmed for a frenzied moment and then lay still.

Bleating in terror at the sudden blood scent, the sheep panicked, racing to the far end of the field and pressed in a huddled noisy mass against the fence. Fortunately, the direction they'd taken had moved them upwind, not down. When nothing further happened, they began to calm and a few of the older ewes moved themselves and their lambs out of the crowding and began to settle once again.

It was doubtful that the three animals who leapt the fence a short time later even noticed the sheep. Huge paws seeming to barely touch ground, they raced to the body. One of them, russet hackles high, started back along the slain animal's trail but a growl from the bigger of the two remaining called it back.

Three pointed muzzles lifted and the howl that lifted with them panicked the sheep yet again. As the sound rose and fell, its primal cadences wiped out any remaining resemblance the three howling might have had to dogs.

Vicki hated August. It was the month in which Toronto proved what a world class city it had become; when the heat and humidity hung on to the car exhaust and the air in the concrete and glass canyon at Yonge and Bloor took on a yellowish-brown hue that left a bitter taste in the back of the throat; when every loose screw in the city decided to take a walk on the wild side and tempers were baked short. The police, in their navy blue pants and hats and heavy boots, hated August for both personal and professional reasons. Vicki had moved quickly out of uniform, and out of the force entirely a year ago, but she still hated August. In fact, as August was now forever linked with her leaving a job she'd loved, this least congenial of months had been blackened beyond redemption.

As she unlocked the door to her apartment, she tried not to smell herself. She'd spent the day, the last three days, working as an order picker in a small coffee processing factory up on Railside Drive. In the last month the company had been plagued with a number of equipment failures that the owners had finally come to realize were sabotage. Desperate—a small specialty company couldn't afford the downtime if they hoped to complete with the multinationals—the owners had hired Vicki to find out what was going on.

"And Vicki Nelson, private investigator, comes through again." She closed the door behind her and thankfully peeled off her damp T-shirt. She'd been able to pinpoint who was jamming the processing machines on her first day but even knowing that, it took her two further days to discover how and to gather enough evidence to bring charges. Tomorrow she'd go in, lay the report on Mr. Glassman's desk and never go near the place again.

Tonight, she wanted a shower, something to eat that didn't smell like coffee, and a long vapid evening spent sucking at the boob tube.

She kicked the filthy T-shirt into a corner as she peeled off her jeans. The only up side about the entire experience was that smelling as she did, she'd gotten a seat on the subway coming home and no one had tried to crowd her.

The hot water had just begun to pound the stink and stiffness away when the phone rang. And rang. She tried to ignore it, to let the shower drown it out, but had little success. She'd always been a compulsive phone answerer. Muttering under her breath, she turned the water off, quickly wrapped herself in towels, and raced for the receiver.

"Oh there you are, dear. What took you so long?"

"It's a very small apartment, Mom." Vicki sighed. She should've known. "Didn't it occur to you at about the seventh ring that maybe I wasn't going to answer the phone?"

"Of course not. I knew you were home or you'd have had your machine plugged in."

She never left her machine on when she was home. She considered it the ultimate in rudeness. Maybe it was time to reconsider. The towel began to unwind and she made a grab for it—a second floor apartment was not high enough up for walking around in skin. "I was in the shower, Mom."

"Good, then I didn't get you away from anything important. I wanted to call you before I left work . . ."

"So that the Life Sciences Department would pay for the call," Vicki added silently. Her mother had been working as a secretary at Queen's University in Kingston for longer than most of the tenured professors and she stretched job perks as far and as often as she could.

". . . and find out when you had vacation this year so maybe we could spend some time together."

Right. Vicki loved her mother but more than three days in her company usually had her ready to commit matricide. "I don't get vacations anymore, Mom. I'm self-employed now and I have to take what jobs come my way. And besides, you were here in April."

"You were in the hospital, Vicki, it wasn't exactly a social visit."

The two vertical scars on her left wrist had faded to fine red lines against the pale skin. It looked like a suicide attempt and it had taken some extremely fancy footwork to avoid telling her mother how she'd actually gotten them. Being set up as a sacrifice for a demon by a sociopathic hacker was not something her mother would deal with well. "As soon as I get a free weekend, I'll come by. I promise. I have to go now, I'm dripping on the carpet."

"Bring that Henry Fitzroy with you. I'd like to meet him."

Vicki grinned. Henry Fitzroy and her mother. That might be worth a weekend in Kingston. "I don't think so, Mom."

"Why not? What's wrong with him? Why was he avoiding me at the hospital?"

"He wasn't avoiding you and there's nothing wrong with him." *Okay, so he died in 1536. It hadn't slowed him down.* "He's a writer. He's a little . . . *unusual.*"

"More unusual than Michael Celluci?"

"Mother!"

She could almost hear her mother's brows rise. "Honey, you may not remember this, but you've dated a number of *unusual* boys in your time."

"I'm not dating boys anymore, Mom. I'm almost thirty-two years old."

"You know what I mean. Remember that young man in high school? I don't recall his name but he kept a harem. . . ."

"I'll call you, Mom."

"Soon."

"Soon," Vicki agreed, rescued the towel again and hung up. "Dated unusual boys in my time. . . ." She snorted and headed back toward the bathroom. All right, a couple of them may have been a bit strange but she was over one hundred percent certain that none of them were vampires.

She turned the water back on and grinned, imagining the scene. *Mom, I'd like you to meet Henry Fitzroy. He drinks blood.* The grin widened as she stepped under the water. Her mother, infinitely practical, would probably ask what type. It took a lot to disrupt her mother's view of the world.

She'd just dumped a pan of scrambled eggs onto a plate when the phone rang again.

"It figures," she muttered, grabbing a fork and crossing into the living room. "Damn thing never rings when I'm not doing anything." Sunset wouldn't be for a couple of hours yet—it wasn't Henry.

"Vicki? Celluci." With so many Michaels on the Metropolitan Toronto Police Force, most of them had gotten into the habit of perpetually referring to themselves by their last names, on duty and off. "You remember the name of Quest's alleged accomplice? The guy who never got charged."

"Good evening, Mike. Nice to hear from you. I'm fine thanks." She shoveled a forkful of egg into her mouth and waited for the explosion.

"Cut the crap, Vicki. He had some woman's name . . . Marion, Maralyn. . . ."

"Margot. Alan Margot. Why?"

Even over the sounds of traffic, she could hear the self-satisfied smile in his voice. "It's classified."

"Listen you son of a bitch, when you pick my brains 'cause you're too lazy to look it up, you don't come back with 'it's classified.' Not if you want to live to collect your pension."

He sighed. "Use the brain you're accusing me of picking."

"You pulled another body out of the lake?"

"Mere moments ago."

So he was still at the site. That explained the background noise. "Same pattern of bruises?"

"Near as I can tell. Coroner just took the body away."

"Nail the bastard."

"That," he told her, "is the plan."

She hung up and slid into her leather recliner, eggs balanced precariously on the arm. Two years ago, the case had been hers. Hers the responsibility of finding the scum who'd beaten a fifteen-year-old girl senseless and then dropped the unconscious body in Lake Ontario. Six weeks of work and they'd picked up a man named Quest, picked him up, charged him, and made it stick. There'd been a another man involved, Vicki had been sure of it, but Quest wouldn't talk and they hadn't been able to lay charges.

This time. . . .

She yanked her glasses off her nose. This time, Celluci would get him, and Vicki Nelson, ex-fair-haired girl of the metro police would be sitting on her duff. The room in front of her blurred into an indistinguishable mass of fuzz-edged colors and she shoved the glasses back on.

"Shit!"

Breathing deeply, she forced herself to calm. After all, what mattered was catching Margot—not who made the collar. She scooped up the remote and flicked on the television. The Jays were in Milwaukee.

"The boys of summer," she sighed, and dug into her cooled eggs, giving herself over to the hypnotic accents of the announcers doing the pregame show. Like most Canadians over a certain age, Vicki was a hockey fan first but it was almost impossible to live in Toronto and not have baseball make inroads into your affections.

It was the bottom of the seventh, the score three to five, the Jays behind two runs, two out and a man on second with Mookie Wilson at bat. Wilson was hitting over three hundred against right-handers and Vicki could see that the Brewers' pitcher was sweating. At which point, the phone rang.

"It figures." She stretched a long arm down and dragged the phone up onto her lap. Sunset had been at eight forty-one. It was now nine oh five. It had to be Henry.

Ball one.

"Yeah, what?"

"Vicki? It's Henry. Are you all right?"

Strike one.

"Yeah, I'm fine. You just called at a bad time."

"I'm sorry, but I have some friends here who need your help."

"My help?"

"Well, they need the help of a private investigator and you're the only one I know."

Strike two.

"They need help right now?" There were only two innings left in the game. How desperate could it be?

"Vicki, it's important." And she could tell by his voice that it was.

She sighed as Wilson popped out to left field, ending the inning, and thumbed the television off. "Well, if it's that important . . ."

"It is."

". . . then I'll be right over." With the receiver halfway back to the cradle, a sudden thought occurred to her and she snapped it back up to her mouth. "Henry?"

He was still there. "Yes?"

"These friends, they aren't vampires are they?"

"No." Through his concern, he sounded a little amused. "They aren't vampires."

*   *   *

Greg gave the young woman a neutral nod as he buzzed her through the security check and into the lobby. Vicki Nelson her name was and she'd dropped by a number of times over the summer while he was on the desk. Although she looked like the kind of person he'd have liked under other circumstances he simply couldn't get over the impressions he'd formed during their initial meeting last spring. It didn't help when observation confirmed that she was not the sort who would normally answer the door half dressed, proving, to his mind, his feeling that she'd been hiding something that night.

But what?

Over the last couple of months his belief that Henry Fitzroy was a vampire had begun to fade. He liked Mr. Fitzroy, respected him, realized that all his idiosyncrasies could stem from being a writer rather than a creature of the night but one last lingering doubt remained.

What had the young woman been hiding that night? And why?

Occasionally, just for his peace of mind, Greg considered asking her outright, but a certain set to her jaw had always stopped him. So he wondered. And he kept an eye on things. Just in case.

Vicki felt a distinct sense of relief as the elevator doors closed behind her. Scrutiny by that particular security guard always made her feel, well, dirty. *Still, it's my own fault. I'm the one who answered the door practically naked.* It had been the only solution she could think of at the time and as it had worked, distracting the old man from his intention of pounding a croquet stake through Henry's heart, she supposed she shouldn't complain about the aftereffects.

She pushed the button for the fourteenth floor and tucked her white golf shirt more securely into her red walking shorts. The little "adventure" last spring had melted off a few pounds and so far she'd managed to keep them from finding their way back. She carried too much muscle to ever be considered slim—a secret desire she'd admitted to no one—but it was nice to have a little more definition at the waist. Squinting in the glare of the fluorescent lights, she studied her reflection in the stainless steel walls of the elevator.

Not bad for an old broad, she decided, shoving the hated glasses up her nose. She wondered briefly if maybe she should have dressed more formally then decided that any friends of Henry Fitzroy, bastard son of Henry the VIII, ex-Duke of Richmond, et cetera, et cetera, were not likely to care if the private investigator showed up in shorts.

When the elevator reached Henry's floor, Vicki settled her purse on her shoulder and put on her professional face. It lasted right up until the condo door swung open and the only creature in the entrance hall was a huge russet-colored dog.

It—no, he—has to be a dog. Vicki extended her hand for him to sniff. *Wolves don't come in that color. Or that size. Do they?* She could have added that wolves don't generally hang out in condominiums in downtown Toronto, but given that it was *Henry's* condo all bets were off.

The animal's eyes were outlined in black, adding to a remarkably expressive face. He enthusiastically sniffed the offered hand, then pushed his head demandingly under Vicki's fingers.

Vicki grinned, pulled the door closed, then obediently began to scratch in the thick ruff behind the pointed ears. "Henry?" she called as a tail heavy enough to knock a grown man to the ground slammed rhythmically into the wall. "You home?"

"In the living room."

Something in the tone of his voice drew her brows down but a saucerlike paw on her instep almost instantly distracted her. "Get off, you great brute." The dog obediently shifted his weight. She grabbed his muzzle lightly in one hand and shook his massive head from side to side. "Come on, fella, they're waiting for us."

He smiled—there really was no other word for it— whirled around and bounded into the living room, Vicki following at a slightly more sedate pace.

Henry stood in his usual place by the huge wall of

windows that looked down on the city. The lights he used on the infrequent occasions he had company picked up the red highlights in his fair hair and turned his hazel eyes almost gold. Actually, Vicki was guessing about the effect on his eyes as she couldn't see details over that great a distance. She never tired of looking at him though, he had a presence that lifted his appearance from merely pleasing to extraordinary and she could certainly understand how poor Lucy and Mina hadn't stood a chance against his well-known fictional counterpart.

He wasn't alone. The young woman fiddling with the CD player turned as Vicki came into the living room and Vicki hid a smile as she found herself being thoroughly and obviously looked over. She took a good long look in return.

A dancer? Vicki wondered. Although small, the girl was sleekly muscled and held herself in a way that could almost be interpreted as challenging. *Don't try it, kid. If I'm not quite twice your age*—the girl could be no older than seventeen or eighteen—*I'm definitely meaner.* The short mane of silver blond hair, Vicki realized with a start, was natural; the brows could have been lightened but not the lashes. While not exactly pretty, the pale hair made for an exotic contrast with the deep tan. *And that sundress certainly leaves little tan to the imagination.*

Their eyes met and Vicki's brows rose. Just for an instant she almost had a grasp of what was really going on, then the instant passed and the girl was looking up through her lashes and smiling shyly.

The large red dog had gone to sit by Henry's side, his head level with Henry's waist, and now the two of them walked forward. Henry wore a carefully neutral expression. The dog looked amused.

"Vicki, I'd like you to meet Rose Heerkens. Her family is having some trouble I think you can help them with."

"Pleased to meet you." Vicki held out her hand and after a quick glance at Henry—*What did he tell her about me?*—the younger woman put hers in it. Very few women are any good at shaking hands, not having been raised to do it, but Vicki was surprised by both a grip that matched her own and a callus-ridged palm.

As Rose released her hold, she extended the motion to indicate the dog now leaning against her legs. "This is Storm."

Storm held up a paw.

Bending over to take it, Vicki grinned. "Pleased to meet you too, Storm."

The big dog gave a short bark and leaned forward, dragging his tongue across Vicki's face with enough force to almost dislodge her glasses.

"Storm, stop it!" With both hands buried in the russet ruff, Rose yanked the dog back. "Maybe she doesn't want to be covered in slobber."

"Oh, I don't mind." She wiped her face off with her palm and resettled her glasses on her nose. "What kind of a dog is he? He's beautiful." Then she laughed, for Storm obviously recognized the compliment and was looking smug.

"Please don't encourage him, Ms. Nelson, he's vain enough already." Rose dug her knee in behind the big dog's shoulder and shoved, knocking him over. "And as for what kind he is—he's a nuisance."

Storm didn't look at all put out by being so unceremoniously dumped. Tongue lolling, he rolled over on his back, all four feet in the air, and looked expectantly up at Vicki.

"Do you want your stomach rubbed, then?"

"Storm." Henry's command brought the animal off the floor, to stand looking remarkably chastened.

Vicki glanced at Henry in astonishment. What was with him?

"Perhaps," he met Vicki's eyes then swept his gaze over the girl and the dog, "we should get on with things."

Vicki found herself moving toward the couch without having made a conscious decision to move. She hated it when he did that. She hated the way she responded to it. And she really hated not being sure if it was the vampire or the prince she was responding to—somehow knuckling under to a supernatural ability seemed less reprehensible than giving in to a medieval petty dictator. *His undead highness and I are going to have to have a little talk about this. . . .*

Tossing her bag down, she settled back against the red velvet upholstery, watching Rose curl up in the armchair and Storm throw himself to the floor at her feet. He looked splendid against the cream colored carpet but the russet fur clashed a little desperately with the crimson of the chair. Henry dropped one denim-clad leg on the arm of the couch and perched beside her, so close that, for a moment, Vicki was aware of him alone.

"It's too soon, Vicki, you lost a lot of blood."

She felt her face flush. It had never occurred to her that he wouldn't want to. . . . It was what they were leading up to, wasn't it? "They put most of it back at the hospital, Henry. I'm fine. Really."

"I believe you." He smiled and she suddenly found the air available in the hallway inadequate.

He's had over four hundred and fifty years to practice that smile, she reminded herself. Breathe.

"We have to be very careful," he continued, placing his hands lightly on her shoulders. "I don't want to hurt you."

It sounded so much like dialogue out of a bad soap opera that Vicki grinned. "Just so long as you remember I haven't got a couple of hundred years to spare," she told him, digging for her apartment keys, "I'll try not to rush you."

That had been almost four months ago, the first time they'd gone out after she'd been released from the hospital. And they still hadn't. Vicki had tried to be patient but there were times, and with him sitting so close this was one of them, when she wanted to kick his feet out from under him and beat him to the floor. With an effort, she brought her attention back to the business at hand.

As everyone appeared to be waiting for her to speak, she arranged her face into her best "the police officer is your friend" expression and turned to Rose. "What is it you need me to help you with?"

Again, Rose glanced at Henry. Although Vicki couldn't see the vampire's response it seemed to reassure the younger woman for she took a deep breath, brushed her hair back off her face with trembling fingers, and said, "In the last month two members of our family have been shot." She had to stop and swallow grief before she could continue. "We need your help, Ms. Nelson, to find the killer."

Murder. Well, that was definitely a little more serious than Vicki had been expecting. And a double murder at that. She pushed her glasses up her nose and let sympathy soften her voice as she asked, "Have the local police not turned up any leads?"

"They don't exactly know."

"What do you mean by 'don't exactly know'?" Vicki could think of several things it might mean and none of them appealed to her.

"Why don't you show her, Rose," Henry said quietly.

Vicki swiveled around to look up at him, her peripheral vision too poor to allow her the luxury of glancing from the corner of her eye. His expression matched his tone. Whatever Rose had to show her was very important. More than slightly apprehensive, she turned around again.

Rose, who had been waiting for her attention, slipped out of her sandals and rose to her feet. Storm, after giving the sandals a quick sniff, padded over to her side. In one quick movement she stripped off the sundress she was wearing, stood naked for a heartbeat, and then, where there had been a pale-haired young woman and a large russet dog there was a red-haired young man and a large white dog.

The young man bore a strong resemblance to the young woman; they shared the same high cheekbones, the same large eyes, the same pointed chins. *And the same lithe dancer's body,* Vicki noted after one quick glance at the obvious difference.

"Werewolves," she heard herself say aloud, amazed at her composure. *Odds are good it's Henry's influence. This is what comes of hanging around with vampires. . . . I'll get the bastard for this.*

The young man, completely undismayed by both her scrutiny and his nakedness, winked.

Vicki, considerably nonplussed, especially when she remembered how she'd been treating the dog—*No, wolf. No, wer. Oh hell.*—earlier, felt herself flushing and glanced away for an instant. When she looked back, she found she'd missed the actual moment of transformation and Rose was tugging her dress back over her head. The young man—Storm?—was resignedly pulling on a pair of bright blue shorts that offered minimal coverage.

Feeling her gaze on him, he looked up, smiled, and advanced with his hand held out. "Hi. I guess further introduction are in order. My name's Peter."

"Uh, hi." Apparently the names changed with the form. A little stunned, Vicki took the offered hand. It had the same pattern of heavy callus that Rose's had. Made sense actually if they ran on four feet part of the time. "You're, uh, Rose's brother?"

"We're twins." He grinned and it reminded Vicki so much of the expression the russet dog had worn that she found herself grinning in return. "She's older; I'm better looking."

"You're noisier," Rose corrected, curling back up in the armchair. "Come and sit down." With a martyred air, Peter did as he was told, throwing himself gracefully down into the same spot he'd occupied as Storm, his back pressed against his sister's knees. "We're sorry about the theatricality of all this, Ms. Nelson," she continued, "but Henry suggested it was the best way to present it, that you . . ."

She hesitated and Henry smoothly finished the sentence. ". . . that you weren't a person who denied the evidence of your own eyes."

Vicki supposed he meant it as a compliment so she contented herself with a quiet snort and an only moderately sarcastic, "Well, you should know."

"You will help us, won't you?" Peter leaned forward, and placed one hand lightly on Vicki's knee. There was nothing sexual in the touch, and the expression accompanying it held only a combination of worry and hope.

Werewolves. Vicki sighed. *First vampires and demons,*

now werewolves. What next? She crossed her legs, dislodging Peter's hand, and settled back into a more comfortable position; odds were good that this was going to be a long story. "Perhaps you'd better start at the beginning."

Two

"At the beginning," Rose repeated, her tone turning the statement into a question. She sighed and pushed a shock of pale hair back off her face. "I guess it started when Silver got shot."

"Silver?" Vicki asked. She had a feeling that if she didn't stay on top of this explanation it was going to get away from her pretty quickly.

"Our aunt," Rose began but Peter cut in when he saw the look on Vicki's face.

"We have two names," he explained. "One for each form." He laid a short-fingered hand against the tanned muscles of his chest. "This is Peter, but it was Storm who met you at the door. And, in her fur-form, Rose is called Cloud. It's easier than explaining to outsiders why all the farm dogs have the same names as members of the family."

"I can imagine it must be," Vicki agreed, pleased that her earlier assumption about the names had been verified. "But doesn't it get a little confusing?"

Peter shrugged. "Why should it? You have more than one name. You're Ms. Nelson to some people, Vicki to others, and you don't find it confusing."

"Not usually, no." Vicki conceded the point. "So your aunt was shot in her . . . uh, wolf form." Well, they were called werewolves so she supposed wolf was the preferred term. It certainly seemed more socially acceptable than dog. *And just think, before Henry came into my life, I never used to worry about things like that. . . .* She'd have to remember to thank him.

"That's right." Peter nodded. "Our family owns a large sheep farm just north of London, Ontario . . ."

The pause dared her to comment but Vicki kept her expression politely interested and her mouth shut.

". . . and Silver was shot in the head when she was out checking the flock."

"At night?"

"Yes."

"We thought about telling the police that someone had shot one of our dogs," Rose continued, "and at the time that's all we thought it was, some dickhead with a gun who had no way of knowing she was anything more. These things happen, people lose dogs all the time." Her voice broke on the last word and Peter butted his head against her knees. She threaded her fingers through his hair and went on. Touch appeared to be important to them, Vicki noted. "But the last thing we need is police roaming around and asking questions, you know, seeing things, so the family decided to deal with it."

Peter's lips drew back off his teeth; long and white, they were his least human feature.

If "the family" had caught up to Silver's killer, Vicki realized, justice would have little to do with the law and the courts. A year ago she would have been appalled at the idea, but a year ago she'd had a badge and things had been a lot simpler. "So what did you tell people who asked where your Aunt Sylvia had gone."

"We told them she'd finally decided to join Uncle Robert up in the Yukon. She always talked about doing it so no one was very surprised. Aunt Nadine—she was Aunt Sylvia's twin. . . ." Rose swallowed again, hard, and Peter pressed closer. "Well, she stayed out of sight for a while. Twin bonds are pretty strong with our people and she kept having to howl. Anyway, Monday night, Ebon—Uncle Jason—was shot in the head while he was out checking on the ewes with fall lambs. No one heard anything and we couldn't find a scent anywhere near the body."

"High velocity rifle, probably with a silencer and a scope," Vicki guessed. She frowned. "Sounds like quite a marksman; to hit a moving target at night. . . ."

"Monday was a full moon," Henry broke in. "There was plenty of light."

"Wouldn't matter with a scope. And there wasn't a full moon the night Silver was killed." She shook her head. "A shot like that, two shots. . . ."

"That isn't all," Rose interrupted, tossing something across the room. "Father found this near the body."

Vicki flailed at the air and the small lump of metal landed in her lap. Silently cursing her lack of depth perception, she dug around in the folds of her shorts and when she fished it out, stared down in puzzlement at what could only be—in spite of its squashed appearance—a silver bullet. She closed her teeth firmly on her instinctive response. *Your uncle was killed by the Lone Ranger?*

Henry reached over her shoulder and plucked the dully gleaming object from her palm, holding it up to the light between finger and thumb. "A silver bullet," he explained, "is one of the traditional ways to kill a werewolf. The silver is a myth. The bullet alone is usually enough to do the job."

"I can imagine." A .30 caliber round—and Vicki knew the slug had to have been at least that large to have maintained any kind of shape at all after traveling through flesh and bone and then impacting into the dirt—fired from a high velocity rifle would have left very little of Ebon's head in the wake of its passing. She turned again to Rose and Peter who had been watching her expressionlessly. "I take it that a similar bullet was not found by your aunt's body or you'd have mentioned it?"

Rose frowned down at her brother then they both shook their heads.

"Doesn't really matter. Even without the bullet, the pattern points to a single marksman." Vicki sighed and leaned forward on the couch, resting her forearms on her thighs. "And here's something else to think about; whoever shot Ebon was shooting specifically at werewolves. If one person knows you're wer, others will too; that's a given. These deaths could be the result of a community. . . ."

"Witch hunt," Henry put in quietly as she paused.

She nodded, not lifting her gaze from the twins, and continued. "You're different and different frightens most people. They could be taking their fear out on you."

Peter exchanged a long look with his sister. "It doesn't have to be that complicated," he said. "Our older brother is a member of the London police force and Barry, his partner, knows he's a wer."

"And his partner is a marksman?" All things considered, it wasn't that wild a guess. Nor would it be unlikely that said partner would own a .30 caliber rifle when any six people in any small town would likely own half a dozen between them.

The twins nodded.

Vicki let her breath out in a long, low whistle. "Messy. Has your brother confronted his partner about this?"

"No, Uncle Stuart won't allow it. He says the pack keeps its trouble within the pack. Aunt Nadine convinced him to call Henry, and Henry convinced them both that we should talk to you. That you might be our only chance. Will you help, Ms. Nelson? Uncle Stuart said we were to agree to whatever you charge."

Peter's hand was back on her knee and he was staring up at her with such single-minded entreaty that she said without thinking, "You want me to find out that Barry didn't do it."

"We want you to find out who did do it," Rose corrected. "Who *is* doing it. Whoever they are." Then, just for an instant, the fear showed through. "Someone is killing us, Ms. Nelson. I don't want to die."

Thus lifting this whole discussion out of the realm of fairy tales. "I don't want you to die either," Vicki told her gently. "But I might not be the best person for the job." She pushed her glasses up her nose and took a deep breath. Both deaths had occurred at night and her eyes simply didn't allow her to function after dark. It was bad enough in the city, but in the country with no streetlights to anchor her, she'd be blind.

On the other hand, what choice did they have? Surely she'd be better than nothing. And her lack of vision didn't affect her mind, or her training, or her years of experience. And this was a job that would count for something, it was important, life or death. *The kind of job Celluci still does.* God damn it! She could work around the disability.

"I can't leave right away." Dawning expressions of relief mixed with hope told her she'd made the right decision. "Unfortunately, I have appointments I can't break. How about Friday?"

"Friday evening," Henry interrupted smoothly. "After sunset. Meanwhile, no one is to go anywhere by themselves. No one. Both Ebon and Silver were shot while they were alone, and that's the only part of the pattern you can change. Make sure the rest of the family understands that. And as much as possible, stay in sight of the house. In fact, as much as you can, stay in sight of nonwer. Whoever is doing this is counting on you not being able to tell anyone, and as long as there are witnesses around you should be safe. Did I miss anything, Vicki?"

"No, I don't think so." He'd missed asking for her opinion before he started his little lecture, but they'd discuss that later. As for his assumption that he'd be going along, well, it solved her transportation problem and created all sorts of new ones that would have to be dealt with—again, later. She wasn't looking forward to "later."

"Over the next two days," she told the twins, "I want you to write me up a list—two lists actually; the people who know what you are on one and the people who might suspect on the other. Get the input of everyone in the family."

"We can do that, no problem." Peter heaved a sigh of relief and bounded to his feet.

Apparently the fact that she and Henry operated as a team had come as no surprise to him. Vicki wondered what Henry had told them before she arrived. "First thing tomorrow," she buried the slug in tissues and sealed it into one of the small freezer bags she always carried in her purse, "I'll drop this off at ballistics and see if they can tell me anything about the rifle it came from."

"But Colin said . . ." Rose began.

Vicki cut her off. "Colin said it would lead to awkward questions. Well, it would in London and, considering your family's situation, it's not the sort of thing you want talked about. Good cops remember the damnedest bits of information and Colin handing around silver bullets could lead to your exposure later on. However," she pitched her voice for maximum reassurance, "this is Toronto. We have a much broader crime base, God forbid, and the fact that *I* was handing around a silver bullet won't mean squat even if someone does remember it."

She paused for breath and tucked the small plastic bag containing the tissues and the slug down into a secure corner of her purse. "Don't expect anything though, this thing is a mess."

"We won't. And we'll tell Aunt Nadine to expect you on Friday night." Peter smiled at her with such complete and utter gratitude that Vicki felt like a heel for even considering refusing to help. "Thanks, Ms. Nelson."

"Yes, thank you." Rose stood as well and added her quieter smile to the brilliance of her brother's. "We really appreciate this. Henry was right."

What Henry was right about *this time* got a little lost in Peter shucking off his shorts. Vicki supposed she'd have to get used to it but at the moment all that naked young man left her a little distracted. The reappearance of Storm came as a distinct relief.

He shook himself briskly and bounded toward the door.

"Why . . ." Vicki began.

Rose understood and grinned. "Because he likes to ride with his head out the car window." She sighed as she stuffed the discarded shorts back into her bag. "He's such lousy company in a car."

"Well, he certainly seems anxious to get going."

"We don't like the city much," Rose explained, her nose wrinkling. "It stinks. Thanks again, Ms. Nelson. We'll see you Friday."

"You're welcome." She watched Henry walk Rose to the door, warn them to be careful, and return to the living room. The look on his face rerouted the accusation of high-handedness she was about to make. "What's wrong?"

Both red-gold brows rose. "My friends are being killed," he reminded her quietly.

Vicki felt herself flush. "I'm sorry," she said. "It's hard to hang onto that amidst all the," she waved a hand as she groped for the word, "strangeness."

"It is, however, the important thing to be hung onto."

"I know. I know." She forced herself not to sound sullen. She shouldn't have had to be reminded of that. "You never thought for a moment that I might say no, did you?"

"I've come to know you over these last few months." His expression softened. "You need to be needed and they need you, Vicki. There aren't too many private investigators they can trust with this."

That was easy to believe. As to her needing to be needed, it was a facetious observation that could easily be ignored. "Are all the wer so," she searched for the right word and settled on, "self-contained? If my family were going through what theirs is, I'd be an emotional wreck."

Somehow he doubted that, but it was still a question that deserved answering. "From the time they're very young, the wer are taught to hide what they are, and not only physically; for the good of the pack you never show vulnerability to strangers. You should consider yourself honored that you got as much as you did. Also, the wer tend to live much more in the present than humans do. They mourn their dead, then they get on with life. They don't carry the burden of yesterday, they don't anticipate tomorrow."

Vicki snorted. "Very poetic. But it makes it nearly impossible for them to deal with this sort of situation, doesn't it?"

"That's why they've come to you."

"And if I wasn't around?"

"Then they'd die."

She frowned. "And why couldn't you save them?"

He moved to his usual place by the window, leaning back against the glass. "Because they won't let me."

"Because you're a vampire?"

"Because Stuart won't allow that kind of challenge to his authority. If he can't save the pack, neither can I. You're female, you're Nadine's problem, and Nadine, at the moment, is devastated by the loss of her twin. If you were wer, you could probably take her position away from her right now, but as you aren't, the two of you should be able to work something out." He shook his head at her expression. "You can't judge them by human standards, Vicki, no matter how human they seem most of the time. And it's too late to back out. You told Rose and Peter you'd help."

Her chin went up. "Did I give you any indication that I might back out?"

"No."

"Damned straight, I didn't." She took a deep breath. She'd worked with the Toronto City Council, she could work with werewolves. At least with the latter all the growling and snapping would mean something. In fact, the wer were likely to be the least of her problems. "There might be difficulties. I mean, with *me* taking this case."

"Like the fact you don't drive." She could hear the smile in his voice.

"No. Real problems."

He turned and spread his arms, the movement causing the hair to glint gold in the lamplight. "So tell me."

It's called retinitis pigmentosa. I'm going blind. I can't see at night. I have almost no peripheral vision. She couldn't tell him. She couldn't handle the pity. Not from him. Not after what she'd gone through with Celluci. *Fuck it.* She shoved her glasses up her nose and shook her head.

Henry dropped his arms. After a moment, when the silence had stretched to uncomfortable dimensions, he said, "I hope you don't mind that I've invited myself along. I thought we made a pretty good team the last time. And, I thought you might need a little help dealing with the . . . strangeness."

She managed an almost realistic laugh. "I do the day work, you cover the night?"

"Just like last time, yes." He leaned back against the glass and watched her turning that over in her mind, worrying it into pieces. She was one of the most stubborn, argumentative, independent women he'd met in four and a half centuries, and he wished she'd confide in him. Whatever the problem was, they could work it out together because whatever the problem was, it couldn't be big enough to keep her from giving everything she had to this case. He wouldn't allow it to be. Friends of his were dying.

"I don't want to die, Ms. Nelson."

I don't want you to die either, Rose. Vicki worried her lower lip between her teeth. If they worked together, he'd find out, eventually. She had to decide if that mattered more than the continuing loss of innocent lives. *And put like that, it's not much of a choice, is it?* If she wasn't their best chance on her own, together she and Henry were. *Screw it. We'll work it out.*

Henry watched her expressions change and smiled. Over his long existence he'd grown very good at reading people, at picking up the delicate nuances that mirrored their inner thoughts. Most of the time, Vicki went right past nuance; her thoughts as easy to read as a billboard.

"So, Friday night after sunset. You can pick me up."

He bowed, the accompanying smile taking the mocking edge off the gesture. "As my lady commands."

Vicki returned the smile, then yawned and stretched, back arched and arms spread out against the red velvet.

Henry watched the pulse beating at the base of her throat. He hadn't fed for three nights and the need was rising in him. Vicki wanted him. He could scent her desire most times they were together, but he'd held back because of the blood loss that she'd taken in the spring. And, he had to admit, held back because he wanted the timing to be right. The one time he'd fed from her had been such a frenzied necessity that she'd missed all the extra pleasures it could bring to both parties involved.

The scent of her life filled the apartment and he walked forward, his pace measured to the beat of her heart. When he reached the couch, he held out his hand.

Vicki took it and hauled herself to her feet. "Thanks."

She yawned again, releasing him to shove a fist in front
of her mouth. "Boy, am I bagged. You wouldn't believe
the time I had to get up this morning and then I spent
the whole day working essentially two jobs in a factory
that had to be eighty degrees C." Dragging her bag up
over her shoulder, she headed for the door. "No need
to see me out. I'll be waiting for you after sunset Friday." She waved cheerfully and was gone.

Henry opened his mouth to protest, closed it, opened
it again, then sighed.

By the time the elevator reached the lobby, Vicki had
managed to stop laughing. The poleaxed look on Henry's face had been priceless and she'd have given a year
of her life to have had a camera. *If his royal undead
highness thinks he's got* this *situation under control, he
can think again.* It had taken almost more willpower
than she had to walk out of that apartment, but it had
been worth it.

"Begin as you mean to go on," she declared under her
breath, wiping sweaty palms against her shorts. "Maybe
Mom's old sayings have more value than I thought."

She was still smiling when she got into the cab, still
flushed with victory, then she leaned back and looked
up at the fuzzy rectangles of light that were Henry's
building. She couldn't see him. Couldn't have even said
for certain which fuzzy rectangle was his. But he was up
there. Looking down at her. Wanting her. Like she
wanted him—and she felt like a teenager whose hormones had just kicked into overdrive.

Why the hell wasn't she up there with him, then?

She let her head drop down against the sweaty leather
of the seat and sighed. "I am *such* an idiot."

"Maybe," the cabbie agreed, turning around with a
gold-toothed grin. "You wanna be a moving idiot? Meter's running."

Vicki glared at him. "Huron Street," she growled.
"South of College. You just drive."

He snorted and faced forward. "Just 'cause you un-
lucky in love, lady, ain't no reason to take it out on me."

The cabbie's muttering blended with the sounds of the

traffic, and all the way down Bloor Street, Vicki could feel Henry's gaze hot on the back of her neck. It was going to be a long night.

The tape ended and Rose fumbled between the seats for a new one with no success. The long drive back from Toronto had left her stiff, tired, and too tense to take her eyes off the road—even if it was only an empty stretch of gravel barely a kilometer from home.

"Hey!" She poked her brother in the back. "Why don't you do something useful and dig out. . . . Storm, hold on!" Her foot slammed down on the brake. With the back end of the small car fishtailing in the gravel and the steering wheel twisting like a live thing in her hands, she fought to regain control, dimly aware of Peter, not Storm, hanging on beside her.

We aren't going to make it! The shadow she'd seen stretched across the road, loomed darker, closer.

Darker. Closer.

Then, just as she thought they might stop in time and relief allowed her heart to start beating again, the front bumper and the shadow met.

Good. They were unhurt. It was no part of his plan to have them injured in a car accident. A pity the change in wind kept him from his regular hunting ground, but it need not stop the hunt entirely. He rested his cheek against the rifle, watching the scene unfold in the scope. They were close to home. One of them would go for help, leaving the other for him.

"I guess Dad was right all along about this old tree being punky. Rotted right off the stump." Peter perched on the trunk, looking like a red-haired Puck in the head-lights. "Think we can move it?"

Rose shook her head. "Not just the two of us. You'd better run home and get help. I'll wait by the car."

"Why don't we both go?"

"Because I don't like leaving the car just sitting here." She flicked her hair back off her face. "It's a five minute run, Peter. I'll be fine. Jeez, you are getting so overprotective lately."

"I am not! It's just. . . ."

They heard the approaching truck at the same time and a heartbeat later Rose and Storm came around the car to face it.

Only the Heerkens farm fronted on this road. Only the Heerkens drove this road at night. His grip tightened on the sweaty metal.

"They spray the oil back of the crossroads today. Stink like anything." Frederick Kleinbein hitched his pants up over the curve of his belly and beamed genially at Rose. "I take long way home to avoid stink. Good thing, eh? We get chain from truck, hitch to tree, and drag tree to side of road." He reached over and lightly grabbed Storm's muzzle, shaking his head from side to side. "Maybe we hitch you to tree, eh? Make you do some work for your living."

"There are none so blind as those who will not see. . . ." There would be no chance of a shot now.

"Thanks, Mr. Kleinbein."

"Ach, why thank me? You do half of work. Truck did other half." He leaned out of the window, mopping his brow with a snowy white handkerchief. "You and that overgrown puppy of yours get home now, eh? Tell your father some of the wood near top is still good to burn. If he doesn't want, I do. And tell him that I return his sump pump before end of month."

Rose stepped back as he put the truck into gear, then forward again as he added something over the sound of the engine that she didn't catch. "What?"

But he only waved a beefy arm and was gone.

"He said," Peter told her, once the red banner of taillights had disappeared and it was safe to change, "Give my regards to your brother. And then he laughed."

"Do you think he saw you as he drove up?"

"Rose, it's a perfectly normal thing for him to say. He might have meant me, he might have meant Colin. After all, Colin used to help him bring in hay. You worry too much."

"Maybe," she acknowledged but silently added as Storm's head went out the window again, *Maybe not.*

He remained where he was, watching, until they drove away, then he slipped the silver bullet from the rifle and into his pocket. He would just have to use it another time.

"Are you sure of this?" The elder Mr. Glassman tapped a manicured nail against the report. "It will hold up in court?"

"No doubt about it. Everything you need is right there." Behind her back the fingers of Vicki's right hand beat a tattoo against her left palm. Every time she faced the elder Mr. Glassman, she found herself standing at parade rest for no reason she could discern. He wasn't a physically imposing man, nor in any way military in bearing so she supposed it must be force of personality. Although he'd been hardly more than a child at the time, he'd managed to not only survive the death camps of the Holocaust but bring his younger brother Joseph safely through the horror as well.

He closed the report and sighed deeply. "Harris." The name put an end to months of petty sabotage, although as he said it, he sounded more weary than angry. "Our thanks for your quick work, Ms. Nelson." He stood and held out his hand.

Vicki took it, noting the strength beneath the soft surface.

"I see your bill is included with the report," he continued. "We'll issue a check at the end of the week. I assume you'll be available for court appearances if necessary?"

"It's part of the service," she assured him. "If you need me, I'll be there."

"Yo, baby-doll!" Harris, spending the last of his lunch break outside in the sun with a couple of cronies, heaved himself to his feet as Vicki left the building. "Packin' it in, eh? Couldn't cut it."

Vicki had every intention of ignoring him.

"Pity that your tight little ass is gonna be wiggling its way somewhere else."

And then again. . . .

He laughed as he saw her reaction and continued to laugh as she crossed the parking lot to stand in front of him. A jock in his younger days, he had the heavy, bulgy build of a man who'd once been muscular, his Blue Jays T-shirt stretched tight over the beer belly he carried around instead of a waist. He was the kind of laughing bigot that everyone tends to excuse.

Don't mind him, it's just his way.

Vicki considered those the most dangerous kind but this time he'd gone beyond excuses. He could complain about people not being able to take a joke all the way to court.

"What's the matter, baby-doll, couldn't leave without a good-bye kiss?" He turned to be sure the two men still sitting by the building appreciated the joke and so missed the expression on Vicki's face.

She'd had a bad night. She was in a bad mood. And she was more than willing to take it out on this racist, sexist son-of-a-bitch. He had a good four inches on her and probably a hundred pounds but she figured she'd have little trouble dusting his ass. *Tempting, but no.* Although her eyes narrowed and her jaw clenched, years of observing due process held her temper in check. *He's not worth the trouble.*

As she turned to leave, Harris swung around and, grinning broadly, reached out and smacked her on the ass.

Vicki smiled. *Oh what the hell. . . .*

Pivoting, she kicked him less hard than she was able on the outside edge of his left knee. He toppled, bellowing with pain, as if both feet had been cut out from under him. A blow just below his ribs drove the air out of his lungs in an anguished gasp and given that she resisted stomping where it would hurt the most, she treated herself to slamming a well-placed foot into his butt as he drew his knees up to his chest. Then she grinned at his buddies and started home again.

He could press charges. But she didn't think he would. He wasn't hurt and she was willing to bet that by the time he got his breath back he'd already be warping the facts to fit his world view—a world view that would not include the possibility of his being taken down by a woman.

She also realized that this wouldn't have been the case if she still carried a badge, police brutality being a rallying cry of his kind.

You know, she shoved her glasses up her nose and ran for the bus she could now see cresting the Eglington Avenue overpass, *I think I could grow to like being a civilian.*

The euphoria faded along with the adrenaline and the crisis of conscience set in barely two blocks from the bus stop. It wasn't so much the violence itself that upset her as her reaction to it; try as she would, she simply couldn't convince herself that Harris hadn't got a small fraction of exactly what he had coming. By the time she was fighting her way to the back of the Dundas streetcar in an attempt to actually make it off at her stop, she was heartily sick of the whole argument.

Violence is never the answer but sometimes, like with cockroaches, it's the only possible response. By physically moving two semi-comatose teenagers out of her way, she made it out the door at the last possible second. *Harris is a cockroach. End of discussion.* It was too damned hot to deal with personal ethics. She promised herself she'd take another crack at it when the weather cooled down.

She could feel the heat of the asphalt through the soles of her sneakers and, walking as quickly as the seething crowds allowed, she turned up Huron Street toward home. Dundas and Huron crossed in the center of Chinatown, surrounded by restaurants and tiny markets selling exotic vegetables and live fish. In hot weather, the metal bins of food garbage heated up and the stench that permeated the area was anything but appetizing. Breathing shallowly through her mouth,

Vicki could completely understand why the wer had hurried out of the city.

As she passed, she checked The Puddle. Tucked up against the curb in a spot where the asphalt had peeled off and a number of the original paving bricks were missing, the puddle collected local runoff as well as assorted organic flotsam. As the temperature rose, foul smelling bubbles occasionally broke through the scummy surface, adding their own bit of joy to the bouquet. Vicki had no idea how deep the puddle was. In five years, she'd never seen it dry. She had a theory that someday, something was going to crawl out of this little leftover bowl of primordial soup and terrorize the neighborhood, so she kept an eye on it. She wanted to be there when it happened.

By the time she reached her apartment, she was covered in a fine sheen of sweat and all she wanted was a cold shower and a colder drink. She suspected it'd be some time before she got either when she could smell the coffee brewing inside as she put her key in the lock.

"It's a hundred and twelve degrees in the shade," she muttered, swinging open the door, "how the hell can you drink hot coffee?"

It was a good thing she didn't expect an answer, because she didn't get one. Snapping the lock back on, she threw her bag down in the hall and went into the tiny living room.

"Nice of you to drop by, Celluci." She frowned. "You look like shit."

"Thank you, Mother Theresa." He raised his mug and drank deeply, barely lifting his head off the back of the recliner. When he finished swallowing, he met her eyes. "We got the son of a bitch."

"Margot?"

Celluci nodded. "Got him cold. We picked the little bastard up at noon."

At noon. While I was proving I was more macho than Billy Harris. For an instant Vicki was so blindly jealous she couldn't speak. That was what she should be doing with her life, making a difference, not making a fool of herself in the parking lot of a coffee factory. Lower lip caught between her teeth, she managed to wrestle the monster back into its pit although she couldn't quite manage the smile.

"Good work." When she'd allowed Mike Celluci back into her life, she'd allowed police work back in. She'd just have to learn to deal with it.

He nodded, his expression showing exhaustion and not much more. Vicki felt some of the tension go out of her shoulders. Either he understood or he was too tired to make a scene. Either way, she could cope. She reached over and took the empty mug from his hand.

"When was the last time you slept?"

"Tuesday."

"Ate?"

"Uh. . . ." He frowned and rubbed his free hand across his eyes.

"Real food." Vicki prodded. "Not something out of a box, covered in powdered sugar."

"I don't remember."

She shook her head and moved into the kitchen. "Sandwich first, then sleep. You'd better not mind cold roast beef, 'cause that's all I've got." As she piled the meat onto bread, she grinned. It was almost like old times. They'd made a pact, she and Celluci, years ago when they'd first gotten involved; if they couldn't take care of themselves, they'd let the other one do it for them.

"This job has enough ways of eating at your soul," she'd told him as he worked the knots out of her back. *"It makes sense to build up a support structure."*

"You sure you just don't want someone to brag to when the job is done?" he snorted.

Her elbow caught him in the solar plexus. She smiled sweetly as he gasped for breath. "That, too."

And as important as someone who'd understood when it went right, was someone who understood when it went wrong. Who didn't ask a lot of stupid questions there were no answers to or give sympathy that poured salt on the wound failure had left.

Someone who'd just make a sandwich and turn down

the bed and then go away while the last set of clean sheets got wrinkled and sweaty.

Six hours later, Celluci stumbled out into the living room and stared blearily at the television. "What inning?"

"Top of the fourth."

He collapsed into the only other chair in the room, Vicki being firmly entrenched in the recliner. "Goals scored?" he asked, scratching at the hair on his chest.

"It's runs, asshole, as you very well know, and it's a no-run game so far."

His stomach rumbled audibly over the sounds of the crowd cheering an easy out at first. "Pizza?"

Vicki tossed him the phone. "It's my place, you're buying."

One lone slice lay congealing in the box and the Jays had actually managed to acquire and hang on to a two-run lead when she told him she was heading for London.

"England?"

"No, Ontario."

"New case?"

"Right first time."

"What's it about?"

I'm looking for the person, or people, involved in shooting a family of sheep-farming werewolves with silver bullets. At least it was real work. Important work. "Uh, I can't tell you right now. Maybe later." *Maybe in a million years. . . .*

Celluci frowned. She was hiding something. He could always tell. "How are you getting there? Train? Bus?" Stretching out his leg, he poked her in the side with a bare foot. "Jogging?"

Vicki snorted. "I'm not the one carrying the love-handles."

In spite of himself, he sucked in his gut.

Vicki grinned as he tried to pretend he hadn't done it, visibly forcing himself to relax. *Pity,* Vicki mused, *because he's just going to get tense again.* "Henry's giving me a lift down tomorrow night."

"Henry?" Celluci kept his voice carefully neutral. She

had, of course, every right to spend time with whoever she wished but there was something about Henry Fitzroy that Celluci most definitely didn't like. Casual inquiries had turned up nothing to make him change his mind—given that they'd turned up nothing at all. "He's involved in this case, is he?" The last of Vicki's cases Henry Fitzroy had been involved with had ended with her half dead at the feet of a grade B movie monster. Celluci had been unimpressed.

Vicki pushed her glasses up her nose. How much to tell him. . . . "He's friends with the people I'm working for."

"Will he be staying after he drops you off?" Correctly interpreting her lowering brows, he added, "Calm down. You know and I know how much trouble a civilian can be around a case. I just want to be sure that you're not complicating things for yourself." He could see that she wasn't convinced of his purity of motive. Tough.

"First of all, Celluci, try to remember that *I* am now a civilian." He snorted and she scowled. "Secondly, he's just giving me a lift and filling me in on some of the background details. He won't be interfering." *He'll be helping. We'll be working together.* She had no intention of letting Mike Celluci know that, not when she didn't know how she felt about it herself. Besides, it would involve an explanation it wasn't her place to give. And if she wanted to work with Henry Fitzroy, it was none of Celluci's damned business.

Celluci read the last thought off her expression and almost got it right. "I was thinking about your career, not your sex life," he growled, tossing back the last inch of tepid beer remaining in the bottle. "Get your mind out of the gutter, Vicki."

"My mind?" It was her turn to snort. She peeled herself out of the recliner, sweaty skin coming away from the vinyl with a painful tearing sound. "I didn't bring it up. But seeing as you have. . . ."

He recognized her next move as a distraction, an attempt to pull his attention away from Henry Fitzroy. As distractions went, it wasn't bad and he decided to cooperate. Time enough later to do a little investigating into the elusive Mr. Fitzroy's background.

Halfway to the bedroom, he asked with mock seriousness—or as close as he could get given his current shortness of breath—"What about the game?"

"They're two runs ahead with an inning an a half to play," Vicki muttered. "Surely they can win this one without us."

As Henry's teeth opened the vein in Tony's wrist he looked up to find the eyes of the younger man locked on him. The pupils dilated and orgasm weighted the lids, but through it all, Tony watched avidly as the vampire drank.

When it was over, and he was sure the coagulant in his saliva had stopped the bleeding, Henry raised himself up on one elbow. "Do you always watch?" he asked.

Tony nodded drowsily. "S'part of the turn on. Seeing you do it."

Henry laughed and pushed a long lock of damp brown hair back off Tony's forehead. He'd been feeding from Tony as often as had been safe for the last five months, ever since Vicki had convinced the young man to help save his life. "And do you watch while I do other things?"

Tony grinned. "I don't remember. You mind?"

"No. It's pleasant not to have to hide what I am."

Letting his gaze drift down the length of Henry's body, Tony yawned. "Not hiding much now," he murmured. "You gonna be around on the weekend?"

"No," Henry told him. "Vicki and I are going to London. Some friends of mine are in trouble."

"More vampires?"

"Werewolves."

"Awesome." The word blurred, his voice barely audible. Then his eyes slid closed as he surrendered to sleep.

It was *very* pleasant not having to hide what he was, Henry reflected, watching the pulse slow in Tony's throat. It had been a long time since he'd had the luxury of removing all masks, and now he had not one but two mortals who knew him for what he was.

He smiled and stroked the soft skin on the inside of Tony's wrist with his thumb. As he couldn't feed from the wer, this trip would finally see him and Vicki . . . better acquainted.

Three

"JAYS LOSE IN NINTH"

"Damn!" Vicki squinted at the headline and decided it wasn't worth thirty cents to discover how the Jays had blown it this time. With no streetcar in sight, she leaned against the newspaper box, immediately regretting it as the box had spent the day basking under an August sun and its metal surface was hot enough to grill steak.

"Well, *that* was *just* what I needed," she growled, rubbing her reddened forearm. Her eyes itched and ached from a combination of the drops and the contortions her ophthalmologist had just put them through, and now she'd fried six square inches of skin. And the streetcar *still* wasn't coming.

"Fuck it. Might as well walk while I can still see the sidewalk." She kicked the newspaper box as she went by and stepped out onto the street, challenging a Camaro crossing Broadview on the yellow light. The driver hit the horn as she dodged the front fender, but the expression she turned toward him closed his teeth on the profane comment he'd been about to add. Obviously not *all* young men driving Camaros had a death wish.

She crossed the Gerrard Street Bridge in a fog, fighting to keep her emotions under control.

Until this morning she'd thought she'd come to grips with the eye disease that had forced her off the Metro Police. She hadn't accepted it graciously, not by any means, but anger and self-pity had stopped being the motivating factors in her life. Many, many people with retinitis pigmentosa were in worse shape than she was but it was hard to keep sight of that when another two degrees of her peripheral vision had degenerated in the last month and what little night sight she had remaining had all but disappeared.

The world was rapidly taking on the enclosed dimensions of a slide show. Snap on the scene in front of her. Turn her head. Snap on the scene in front of her. Turn her head. Snap on the scene in front of her. And could someone please get the lights.

What bloody good am I going to be to a pack of werewolves anyway? How am I supposed to stop a killer I can't see? The more rational part of her mind tried to interject that the wer were hiring her for her detective abilities and her experience, not her eyes, but she was having none of it. *Maybe I'll get lucky and one of them's been trained as a guide dog.*

"Yo! Victory!"

Frowning, she looked around. Her anger had carried her almost to Parliament and Gerrard, farther than she'd expected. "What are you doing in this part of town?"

Tony grinned as he sauntered up. "What happened to, 'Hi, how are ya?' "

Vicki sighed and attempted not to take the day out on Tony. When she'd gone to him for help and together they'd saved Henry, their relationship had changed, moved up a level from cop and kid—not that he'd actually been a kid for some time. Four years ago, when she first busted him, he'd been a scrawny troublemaker of fifteen. Over the years, he'd become her best set of eyes and ears on the street. Now, they seemed to be moving toward something a little more equal, but old habits die hard and she still felt responsible for him.

"All right." She flicked a drop of sweat off her chin. "Hi. How are you?"

"How come," he asked conversationally, falling into step beside her, "when you ask, 'How are you?' it comes out sounding like, 'How much shit are you in?' "

"How much?"

"None."

Vicki turned her head to look at him but he only smiled beatifically, the picture of wronged innocence. He was looking pretty good, she had to admit, his eyes were clear, his hair was clean, and he'd actually begun to gain a little weight. "Good for you. Now back to my first question, what are you doing in this part of town?"

"I got a place here." He dropped that bombshell with all the studied nonchalance a young man of almost twenty could muster.

"You what!" The exclamation was for Tony's benefit, as he so obviously wanted her to make it. Her mood began to lighten under the influence of his pleasure.

"It's just a room in a basement." He shrugged—no big deal. "But I got my own bathroom. I never had one before."

"Tony, how are you paying for this?" He'd always turned the occasional trick, and she hoped like hell he hadn't gone into the business full time—not only because it was illegal but because the specter of AIDS now haunted every encounter.

"I could say it's none of your business. . . ." As her brows drew down, he raised his hands appeasingly. "But I won't. I got a job. Start on Monday. Henry knows this guy who's a contractor and he needed a wiffle."

"A what?"

"Guy who does the joe jobs."

"Henry found you this?"

"Yup. Found me the place too."

All the years she'd known Tony, the most he'd ever been willing to take from her had been the occasional meal and a little cash in return for information. Henry Fitzroy had known him less than five months and had taken over his life. Vicki had to unclench her teeth before she could speak. "Have you been spending a lot of time with Henry?" The question held an edge.

Tony glanced over at her appraisingly, squinting a little in the bright afternoon sun. "Not much. Hear you're gonna be doing some howling with him this weekend though." At her frown, he leaned closer and in an excellent imitation of a monster movie matinee, intoned, "Verevolves."

"And did he discuss the case with you too?"

"Hey, he just mentioned it."

"I'm surprised he didn't invite you along."

"Jeez, Victory," Tony shook his head. "There's just no talking to you in this mood. Get laid or something and lighten up, eh." He waved jauntily and raced to catch the streetcar at the lights.

Vicki's reply got lost in traffic sounds and it was probably just as well.

"Is it something I said?"

Vicki didn't bother to lift her head off the cool glass of the car window. The highway lights were less than useless as illumination so why bother turning to face a man she couldn't see. "What are you talking about?"

Her tone was so aggressively neutral that Henry smiled. He concentrated for a moment on slipping the BMW into the just barely adequate space between two transports then out the other side to a clear section of road where he actually managed to achieve the speed limit for seven or eight car lengths before he caught up to another section of congested traffic. "You haven't said two civil words to me since I picked you up. I was wondering if I'd done something to annoy you."

"No." She shifted position, drummed her fingers on her knee, and took a deep breath. "Yes." Personal differences must not be allowed to influence the case; things were going to be difficult enough already. If they didn't deal with this now, odds were good it'd turn up sometime a lot more dangerous. "I spoke with Tony today."

"Ah." Jealousy, he understood. "You know I must feed from a number of mortals, Vicki, and you yourself chose the other night to. . . ."

She turned to glare at the indistinct outline his body made against the opposite window. "What the hell does that have to do with anything?" Her left fist slammed down on the dash. "For four years I couldn't get Tony to take anything from me but a couple of hamburgers and some spare change. Now all of a sudden you've found him a job and a place to live."

Henry frowned. "I don't understand the problem." He knew her anger was genuine, both her breathing and her heartbeat had accelerated, but if it wasn't the sexual aspect that bothered her. . . . "You don't want Tony to be off the streets?"

"Of course I do, but . . ." . . . *but I wanted to be the one to save him.* She couldn't say that, it sounded so petty. It was also completely accurate. Abruptly anger changed to embarrassment. ". . . but I don't know how you did it," she finished lamely.

The pause and the emotional change were as clear an indication of her thoughts as if she'd spoken them aloud. Four hundred and fifty years having taught discretion if nothing else, Henry wisely responded only to Vicki's actual words. "I was raised to take care of my people."

Vicki snorted, grateful for a chance to change the subject. "Henry, your father was one of the greatest tyrants in history, burning Protestants and Catholics impartially. Disagreement of any kind, personal or political, usually ended in death."

"Granted," Henry agreed grimly. "You needn't convince me. I was there. Fortunately, I wasn't raised by my father." Henry VIII had been an icon for his bastard son to gaze at in awe and more than that, he'd been king in a time when the king was all. "The Duke of Norfolk saw to it that I was taught the responsibilities of a prince." And only fate had prevented the Duke of Norfolk from being the last death of King Henry's reign.

"And Tony is one of 'your people'?"

He ignored the sarcasm. "Yes."

It was as simple as that for him, Vicki realized, and she couldn't deny that Tony had responded to it in a way he'd never responded to her. She was tempted to ask, *"What am I?"* but didn't. The wrong answer would likely throw her into a rage and she had no idea of what the right answer would be. She fiddled with the air-conditioning vents for a moment. "So tell me about werewolves."

Definitely a safer topic.

"Where should I start?"

Vicki rolled her eyes. "How about with the basics? They didn't cover lycanthropy at the police academy."

"All right." Henry drummed his fingers on the steering wheel and thought for a moment. "For starters, you can forget everything you've ever seen at the movies. If you're bitten by a werewolf, all you're going to do is bleed. Humans cannot become wer."

"Which implies that werewolves aren't humans."

"They aren't."

"What are they then, small furry creatures from Alpha Centauri?"

"No, according to the oldest of their legends, they're the direct descendants of a she-wolf and the ancient god of the hunt." He pursed his lips. "That one's pretty much consistent throughout all the packs, although the name of the god changes from place to place. When the ancient Greek and Roman religions began to spread, the wer began calling themselves Diana's chosen, the hunting pack of the goddess. Christianity added the story of Lilith, Adam's first wife, who, when she left the garden, lay with the wolf God created on the fifth day and bore him children."

"What do you believe?"

"That there are more things in heaven and earth than are dreamed up in your philosophy."

Vicki snorted. "What a cop-out," she muttered. "And misquoted."

"How do you know? Remember, I heard the original. Had the hardest time convincing Shakespeare not to call the poor guy Yoluff." He sounded perfectly serious but he had to be pulling her leg. "Yoluff, Prince of Denmark. Can you imagine?"

"No. And I don't really care about mythic wer. I want to know what I can expect tonight."

"What do you know about wolves?"

"Only what I've learned from National Geographic specials on PBS. I suppose we can discount the character assassination indulged in by the Brothers Grimm?"

"Please. Brothers Grimm aside, wer function much the same way wolves do. Each pack is made up of a family group of varying ages, with a dominant male and a dominant female in charge."

"Dominant? How?"

"They run the pack. The family. The farm. They do the breeding."

"The Stuart and Nadine you mentioned the other night?"

"That's right."

Vicki pulled thoughtfully on her lower lip. "For something this important, you'd think that *they'd* have come and spoken to me."

"The dominant pair almost never leave their territory. They're tied to the land in ways we just can't understand."

"You mean, in ways *I* can't understand," she said testily, his tone having made that quite clear.

"Yes." He sighed. "That's what I mean. But before you accuse me of, well, whatever it was you were about to accuse me of, you might consider that four hundred and fifty odd years of experience counts for something."

He had a point. And an unfair advantage. "Sorry. Go on."

"Donald, Rose and Peter's father, used to be the alpha male, so I imagine the hold is still strong on him. Sylvia and Jason are dead and Colin works nights, which makes it difficult to use me as an intermediary. Rose and Peter, while not adults by wer standards, were the only remaining choice."

"And they were, after all, only the icing on a cake you were perfectly capable of baking on your own."

Henry frowned, then smiled as he worked his way through the metaphor. "I didn't think you'd be able to turn them down," he said softly. "Not after you'd seen them."

And what makes you think I'd be able to turn you down, she wondered, but all she said aloud was, "You were telling me about the structure of the pack."

"Yes, well, about thirteen years ago, when Rose and Peter's mother died, their Uncle Stuart and Aunt Nadine took over. Stuart was originally from a pack in Vermont but had been beta male in this pack for some time."

"He'd just wandered in?"

"The young males often leave home. It gives them a

better chance to breed and mixes the bloodlines. Anyway, Donald gave up without a fight. Marjory's death hit him pretty hard."

"Fight?" Vicki asked, remembering the white gleam of Peter's teeth. "You mean that metaphorically, I hope?"

"Not usually. Very few dominant males will just roll over and show their throat and Stuart had already made a number of previous attempts."

Vicki made a bit of a strangled sound in her own throat and Henry reached over and patted her on the shoulder. "Don't worry about it," he advised. "Basically, the wer are just nice, normal people."

"Who turn into wolves." This was not the way Vicki had been raised to think of normal. Still, she was sitting in a BMW with a vampire—things couldn't get much stranger than that. "Do, uh, all you supernatural creatures hang out together or what?"

"What?" Henry repeated, confused.

Vicki pushed her glasses up her nose. It didn't help in the dark but it was a reassuring gesture nevertheless. "Just tell me your doctor's name isn't Frankenstein."

Henry laughed. "It isn't. And I met Perkin Heerkens, Rose and Peter's grandfather, in a perfectly normal way."

Slowly, as the day released its hold on the world, he became aware. First his heartbeat, gaining strength from the darkness, the slow and steady rhythm reassuring him that he'd survived. Then breathing, shallow still for little oxygen reached this far below ground. Finally, he extended his senses up and out, past the small creeping things in the earth to the surface. Only when he was sure that no human lives were near enough to see him emerge, did he begin to dig his way out.

His hiding place was more a collapsed foxhole than anything else, although, if discovered, Henry hoped that the Nazis would believe it a shallow grave. Which, he supposed as he pushed through the loose dirt, was exactly what it would be if the Nazis discovered it. Being unearthed in daylight would kill him more surely than enemy fire.

"I really, really hate this," he muttered as his head broke free and he unhooked the small perforated shield that kept the earth out of his nose and mouth. He dug in only as a last resort, when dawn caught him away from any other shelter. Once or twice he'd almost left it too long and had had to claw the dirt aside with the heat of the sun dancing fire along his back. Burial reminded him too much of the terror of his first awakening, trapped in his common coffin, immortal and alone, hunger clawing at him.

He had all but one leg clear when he caught sight of the animal lying motionless in the pool of darker night under a fir.

Wolves? In the Netherlands? he wondered as he froze. No, not a wolf, for the russet coloring was wrong, but it definitely had wolf in its bloodline and not so very far back. It crouched carefully downwind, ears back flat against its skull, plumed tail tucked in tight against its flanks. It was reacting to the scent of another hunter, preparing to attack to defend its territory.

White teeth gleamed in the darkness and a low growl rumbled deep in the massive throat.

Henry's own lips drew back and he answered the growl.

The animal looked surprised.

And even more surprised a second later when it found its spine pressed against the forest floor and both Henry's hands clamped deep in its ruff. It struggled and snapped, digging at its captor with all four feet. Although the growls continued, it made no louder noises. When it found it couldn't get free, it squirmed around until it managed to lick Henry's wrist with the tip of its tongue.

Cautiously, Henry let it up.

It shook itself vigorously, had a good scratch, and sat, head to one side, studying this strange creature, nose wrinkled and brows drawn down in an expression so like a puzzled frown that Henry had to hide a smile—

showing his teeth at this moment would only start the whole thing off again.

With dominance determined, Henry brushed the worst of the dirt from his heavy workman's clothes and slipped a hand beneath the shirt to check the canvas pouch taped around his waist. He knew the documents were safe, but the faint crackle of the papers reassured him anyway.

He'd need most of the night to reach the village where he'd meet his contact in the Dutch Resistance and as he needed to feed before he arrived—it made working with mortals bearable—he'd better be on his way. Checking his course with the small compass SOE had provided, he started off toward the northeast. The dog rose and followed. He heard it moving through the brush behind him for a time, its movements barely distinguishable from the myriad sounds of a forest at night. As he began to pick up speed, even that trace faded away. He wasn't surprized. A full blood wolf would have trouble keeping up. A dog, regardless of its heritage would have no chance at all.

The German patrol crossed his path about three hours before dawn, not far from the village. As they passed him, standing motionless beside the trail with barely inches to spare, Henry smiled grimly at the skull and crossbones that fronted each cap. Totenkopf. An SS unit used for internal security in occupied territory, especially where the Resistance was active.

The straggler was a barrel-chested young man who somehow managed to strut in spite of the hour and the ground condition, and whose *more-master-race-than-thou* attitude radiated off of him. It seemed safe to assume that his comrades had deliberately let him fall a little behind; there were limits, apparently, even in the SS.

Henry had a certain amount of sympathy for the common soldier in the German army but none whatsoever for the Nazis among them. He took the young man from behind with a savage efficiency that had him off the trail and silenced between one breath and the next. As long as the heart continued to beat, damage to the body was irrelevant. Quickly, for he was vulnerable while he fed,

Henry tore open the left wrist and bent his head to drink. When he finished, he reached up, wrapped one long-fingered hand about the soldier's skull, twisted, and effortlessly broke his neck. Then he froze, suddenly aware of being watched.

The forest froze with him. Even the breeze stilled until the only sound became the soft phut, phut of blood dripping slowly onto leaf mold. Still crouched over the body, muscles tensed and ready, Henry turned to face downwind.

The big dog regarded him steadily for another few seconds, then faded back until not even the vampire's eyes could separate it from the shifting shadows.

The dog shouldn't have been able to track him. Foreboding ran cold fingers along Henry's spine. Swiftly he stood and moved toward the place where the huge animal had disappeared. A heartbeat later he stopped. He could feel the lives of the patrol returning, no doubt searching for the missing soldier.

He would have to deal with the dog another time. Grabbing a handful of tunic and another of trouser, he lifted the corpse up into the crotch of a tree and wedged it there, well above eye level. With one last apprehensive look into the shadows, he continued his journey to the village.

It wasn't difficult to find.

Harsh white light from a half dozen truck-mounted searchlights illuminated the village square. A small group of villagers stood huddled on one side, guarded by a squad of SS. A man who appeared to be the local commander strode up and down between the two, slapping a swagger stick against his leg in the best Nazi approved manner. Except for the slap of the stick against the leather boot top, the scene was surreally silent.

Henry moved closer. He let the sentry live. Until he knew what was going on, another unexplained death could potentially do more harm than good. At the edge of the square he slid into a recessed doorway, waiting in its cover for what would happen next.

The tiny village held probably no more than two hundred people at the very best of times, which these certainly weren't. Its position, near both the border and the rail lines the invaders needed to continue their push north, made it a focal point for the Dutch Resistance. The Resistance had brought Henry, but unfortunately it had also brought the SS.

There were seventy-one villagers in the square, mostly the old, the young, and the infirm. Pulled from their beds, they wore a wide variety of nightclothes and almost identical wary expressions. As Henry watched, two heavily armed men brought in five more.

"These are the last?" the officer asked. On receiving an affirmative, he marched forward.

"We know where the missing members of your families are," he said curtly, his Dutch accented but perfectly understandable. "The train they were to have stopped is not coming. It was a trap to draw them out." He paused for a reaction but received only the same wary stares. Although those of an age to understand were very afraid, they hid it well; Henry's sensitive nose picked up the scent, but the commander had no way of knowing his news had had any effect. The apparent lack of response added an edge to his next words.

"By now they are dead. All of them." A young boy smothered a cry and the commander almost smiled. "But it is not enough," he continued in softer tones, "to merely wipe out resistance. We must wipe out any further thought of resistance. You will all be executed and every building in this place will be burned to the ground as both an example of what happens to those civilians who dare support the Resistance and to those inferiors who dare oppose the Master Race."

"Germans," snorted an old woman, clutching at her faded bathrobe with arthritic fingers. "Talk you to death before they shoot you."

Henry was inclined to agree—the commander definitely sounded like he'd been watching too many propaganda films. This did not lessen the danger. Regardless of what else Hitler had done in his "economic reforms," he'd at least managed to find jobs for every sadistic son-of-a-bitch in the country.

"You." The swagger stick indicated the old woman. "Come here."

Shaking off the restraining hands of friends and relatives and muttering under her breath, she stomped out of the crowd. The top of her head, with its sparse gray hair twisted tightly into an unforgiving bun, came barely up to the commander's collarbone.

"You," he told her, "have volunteered to be first."

With rheumy eyes squinted almost shut in the glare of the searchlights, she raised her head and said something so rude, not to mention biologically impossible, that it drew a shocked, "Mother!" from an elderly man in the clutter of villagers. Just to be sure the commander got the idea, she repeated herself in German.

The swagger stick rose to strike. Henry moved, recognizing as he did so that it was a stupid, impulsive thing to do but unable to stop himself.

He caught the commander's wrist at the apex of the swing, continued the movement and, exerting his full strength, ripped the arm from the socket. Dropping the body, he turned to charge the rest of the squad, swinging his grisly, bleeding trophy like a club, lips drawn back from his teeth so that the elongated canines gleamed.

The entire attack had taken just under seven seconds.

The Nazis were not the first to use terror as a weapon; Henry's kind had learned its value centuries before. It gave him time to reach the first of the guards before any of them remembered they held weapons.

By the time they gathered their wits enough to shoot, he had another body to use as a shield. He heard shouting in Dutch, slippered feet running on packed earth, and then suddenly, thankfully, the searchlights went off.

For the first time since he entered the square, Henry could see perfectly. The Germans could see nothing at all. Completely unnerved, they broke and tried to run, only to find their way blocked by the snarling attack of the largest dog any of them had ever seen.

It was a slaughter after that.

Moments later, standing over his final kill, blood-scent singing along every nerve, Henry watched as the dog that had followed him all night approached stiff-legged, the damp stain on its muzzle more black than red in the darkness. It looked completely feral, like a wolf from the Brothers Grimm.

They were still some feet apart when the sound of boots on cobbles drew both their heads around. Henry moved, but the dog was faster. It dove forward, rolled, and came up clutching a submachine gun in two very human hands. As the storm troopers came into sight, he opened fire. No one survived.

Slinging the gun over one bare shoulder, he turned back to face Henry, scrubbing at the blood around his mouth with the back of one grimy hand. His hair, the exact russet brown of the wolf's pelt, fell in a matted tangle over his forehead and the eyes it partially hid were the eyes that had watched Henry emerge from the earth and later feed.

"I am Perkin Heerkens," he said, his English heavily accented. "If you are Henry Fitzroy, I am your contact."

After four hundred years, Henry had thought that nothing could ever surprise him again. He found himself having to rethink that conclusion.

"They didn't tell me you were a werewolf," he said in Dutch.

Perkin grinned, looking much younger but no less dangerous. "They didn't tell me you were a vampire," he pointed out. "I think that makes us even."

"That is *not* a perfectly normal way to meet someone," Vicki muttered, wishing just for an instant that she was back at home having a nice, *normal,* argument with Mike Celluci. "I mean, you're talking about a vampire in the Secret Service meeting a werewolf in the Dutch Resistance."

"What's so unusual about that?" Henry passed an RV with American license plates and a small orange cat sleeping in the rear window. "Werewolves are very territorial."

"If they were living as part of normal. . . ." She thought for a second and began again. "If they were living as part of human communities, how did they avoid the draft?"

"Conscription was a British-North American phenomenon," Henry reminded her. "Europe was scrambling for survival and it happened so quickly that a few men and women in a few isolated areas were easy to miss. If necessary, they abandoned 'civilization' for the duration of the war and lived off the land."

"All right, what about British and North American werewolves then?"

"There are no British werewolves. . . ."

"Why not?" Vicki interrupted.

"It's an island. Given the human propensity for killing what it doesn't understand, there's not enough space for both humans and wer." He paused for a moment then added, "There may have been wer in Britain once. . . ."

Vicki slumped lower in the seat and fiddled with the vents. *I don't want to die, Ms. Nelson.* "So the wer aren't worldwide?"

"No. Europe as far south as northern Italy, most of Russia, and the more northwestern parts of China and Tibet. As far as I know there are no native North American wer, but I could be wrong. There's been a fair bit of immigration, however."

"All post World War II?"

"Not all."

"So my original question stands. How did they avoid the draft?"

Vicki heard him shrug, shoulders whispering against the thick tweed seatback. "I have no idea but, as most of the wer are completely color-blind, I'd guess they flunked the physical. I do know that the allies used color-blind observers in aerial reconnaissance; because they had to perceive everything by shape they were able to see right through most camouflage. Maybe some of that lot were wer."

"Well, what about you, then? How does a vampire convince the government he should be allowed to do his bit for liberty?" Then she remembered just how convincing Henry could be. "Uh, never mind."

"Actually, I didn't even approach the Canadian government. I stowed away on a troop ship and returned to England where an old friend of mine had risen to a very powerful position. He arranged everything."

"Oh." She didn't ask who the old friend was. She didn't want to know—her imagination was already flashing her scenes of Henry and certain prominent figures in compromising positions. "What happened to the villagers?"

"What?"

"The villagers. Where you met Perkin. Did they all die?"

"No, of course not!"

Vicki couldn't see any *of course not* about it. After all, they'd wiped out an entire squad of SS and the Nazis had disapproved of things like that.

"Perkin and I set it up so that it looked as though they'd been killed in an allied air strike taking out the railway line."

"You called in an air strike?"

She could hear the grin in his voice as he answered.

"Didn't I mention this old friend had risen to a very powerful position?"

"So." One thing still bothered her. "The villagers knew there was a pack of werewolves living amongst them?"

"Not until the war started, no."

"And after the war started?"

"During the war, any enemy of the Nazis was a welcome ally. The British and the Americans even managed to get along."

She supposed that made a certain amount of sense. "And what about after the war?"

"Perkin emigrated. I don't know."

They drove in silence for a while, one of only a few vehicles on the highway now that Toronto had been left behind. Vicki closed her eyes and thought of Henry's story. In some ways the war, for all its complications, had been a simple problem. At least the enemies had been well defined.

"Henry," she asked suddenly, "do you honestly think that a pack of werewolves can live as a part of human society without their neighbors knowing?"

"You're thinking city, Vicki; the Heerkens' nearest neighbors live three miles away. They see people outside the pack when *they* choose to. Besides, if you didn't know me, and you hadn't met that demon last spring, would you believe in werewolves? Would anyone in North America in this century?"

"Someone obviously does," she reminded him dryly. "Although I'd have expected blackmail over murder."

"It would make more sense," Henry agreed.

She sighed and opened her eyes. Here she was, trying to solve the case armed only with a magnifying glass and a vampire, cut off from the resources of the Metro Police. Not that those resources had been any help so far. Ballistics had called just before she left to tell her that the slug had most likely been a standard 7.62mm NATO round; which narrowed her possible suspects down to the entire North Atlantic Treaty Organization as well as almost everyone who owned a hunting rifle. She wasn't looking forward to arriving at the Heerkens farm.

This was the first time she'd ever really gone it alone. What if she wasn't as good as she thought?

"There's a map in the glove compartment." Henry maneuvered the BMW off Highway 2. "Could you get it out for me?"

She found both glove compartment and map by touch and shoved the latter toward her companion.

He returned it. "Multitalented though I may be, I'd rather not try to read a map while driving on strange roads. You'll have to do it."

Fingers tight around the folded paper, Vicki pushed it back at him. "I don't know where we're going."

"We're on Airport Road about to turn onto Oxford Street. Tell me how long we stay on Oxford before we hit Clarke Side Road."

The streetlights provided barely enough illumination to define the windshield. If she strained, Vicki could see the outline of the map. She certainly couldn't find two little lines on it.

"There's a map light under the sun visor," Henry offered.

The map light would be next to useless.

"I can't find it."

"You haven't even looked. . . ."

"I didn't say I wouldn't, I said I couldn't." She'd realized from the moment she'd agreed to leave the safe, known parameters of Toronto that she'd have to tell him the truth about her eyes and couldn't understand how she'd gotten herself backed into that kind of a corner. Tension brought her shoulders up and tied her stomach in knots. Medical explanation or not, it always sounded like an excuse to her, like she was asking for help or understanding. And he'd think of her differently once the "disabled" label had been applied, everyone did. "I have no night sight, little peripheral vision, and am becoming more myopic every time I talk to the damn doctor." Her tone dared him to make something of it.

Henry merely asked, "What's wrong?"

"It's a degenerative eye disease, retinitis pigmentosa. . . ."

"RP," he interrupted. So that was her secret. "I know of it." He kept his feelings from his voice, kept it matter-of-fact. "It doesn't seem to have progressed very far."

Great, just what I need, another expert. Celluci wasn't enough? "You weren't listening," she snarled, twisting the map into an unreadable mess. "I have *no* night sight. It drove me off the force. I am piss useless after dark. You might as well just turn the car around right now if I have to solve this case at night." Although she hid it behind the anger, she was half afraid he'd do just that. And half afraid he'd pat her on the head and say everything was going to be all right—because it wasn't, and never would be again—and she'd try to rip his face off in a moving car and kill them both.

Henry shrugged. He had no intention of playing into what he perceived as self-pity. "I turn into a smoldering pile of carbon compounds in direct sunlight; sounds like you've got a better deal."

"You don't understand."

"I haven't seen the sun in four hundred and fifty years. I think I do."

Vicki shoved her glasses up her nose and turned to glare out the window at a view she couldn't see, unsure of how to react with no outlet for her anger. After a moment she said, "All right, so you understand. So I have a comparatively mild case. So I can still function. I haven't gone blind. I haven't gone deaf. I haven't gone insane. It *still* sucks."

"Granted." He read disappointment at his response and wondered if she realized that she expected a certain amount of effusive sympathy from the people she told. Rejecting that sympathy made her feel strong, compensating for what she perceived as her weakness. He suspected that the disease was the first time she hadn't been able to make everything come out all right through the sheer determination that it would be. "Have you ever thought about taking on a partner? Someone to do the night work?"

Vicki snorted, anger giving way to amusement. "You mean you helping me out as a regular sort of a job? You write romance novels, Henry; you have no experience in this type of thing."

He drew himself up behind the wheel. He was Vampire. King of the Night. The romance novels were just the way he paid the rent. "I wouldn't say. . . ."

"And besides," she interrupted, "I'm barely making enough to keep myself going. They don't call the place Toronto the Good for nothing you know."

"You'd get more jobs if you could work nights."

She couldn't argue with that. It was true.

His voice deepened and Vicki felt the hair on the back of her neck rise. "Just think about it."

Don't use your vampiric wiles on me, you son-of-a-bitch. But her mouth agreed before the thought had finished forming.

They drove the rest of the way to the farm in silence.

When they pulled off the dirt road they'd been following for the last few miles, Vicki could see only a vague fan of light in front of the car. When Henry switched off the headlights, she could see nothing at all. In the sudden silence, the scrabble of claws against the glass beside her head sounded very loud. She didn't quite manage to hold back the startled yell.

"It's Storm," Henry explained—she could hear the

smile in his voice. "Stay put until I come around to guide you."

"Fuck you," she told him sweetly, found the release, and opened the car door.

"Yeah I'm glad to see you, too," she muttered, trying to push the huge head away. His breath was marginally better that of most dogs—*thanks, no doubt, to his other form being able to use a toothbrush*—but only marginally. Finally realizing that without better leverage the odds of moving Storm were slim to none, she sat back and endured the enthusiastic welcome. Her fingers itched to dig through the deep ruff, but the memory of Peter's naked young body held them in check.

"Storm, that's enough."

With one last vigorous sniff, the wer backed out of the way and Vicki felt Henry's hand touch her arm. She shook it off and swung out of the car. Although she could see the waning moon, a hanging, three-quarter circle of silver-white in the darkness, it shed a light too diffuse to do her any good. The blurry rectangles of yellow off to the right were probably the lights of the house and she considered striding off toward them just to prove she wasn't as helpless as Henry might think.

Henry watched the thought cross Vicki's face and shook his head. While he admired her independence, he hoped it wouldn't overwhelm her common sense. He realized that at the moment she felt she had something to prove and could think of no way to let her know she didn't. At least not as far as he was concerned.

He put her bag into her hand, keeping his own hold on it until he saw her fingers close around the grip, then drew her free arm gently through his. "The path curves," he murmured, close to her ear. "You don't want to end up in Nadine's flowers. Nadine bites."

Vicki ignored the way his breath against her cheek caused the hair on the back of her neck to rise and concentrated on walking as though she was not being led. She had no doubt that the wer, in wolf form at least, could see just as well as Henry and she had no intention of undermining her position here by appearing weak to however many of them might be watching.

Head high, she focused on the rectangles of light, attempting to memorize both the way the path felt beneath her sandals and the way it curved from the drive to the house. The familiar concrete and exhaust scents of the city were gone, replaced by what she could only assume was the not entirely pleasant odor of sheep shit. The cricket song she could identify, but the rest of the night sounds were beyond her.

Back in Toronto, every smell, every sound would have meant something. Here, they told her nothing. Vicki didn't like that, not at all; it added another handicap to her failing eyes.

Two sudden sharp pains on her calf and another on her forearm, jolted her out of her funk, reminding her of an aspect of the case she hadn't taken into account.

"Damned bugs!" She pulled her arm free and slapped down at her legs. "Henry, I just remembered something; I hate the country!"

They'd moved into the spill of light from the house and she could just barely make out the smile on his face.

"Too late," he told her, and opened the door.

Vicki's first impression as she stood blinking on the threshold was of a comfortably shabby farmhouse kitchen seething with people and dogs. Her second impression corrected the first: *Seething with* wer. *The people are dogs. Wolves. Oh, hell.*

It was late, nearly eleven. Celluci leaned back in his chair and stared at the one remaining piece of paper on his desk. The Alan Margot case had been wrapped up in record time and he could leave it now to begin its ponderous progress through the courts. Which left him free to attend to a small bit of unfinished business.

Henry Fitzroy.

Something about the man just didn't ring right and Celluci had every intention of finding out what that was. He scooped up the piece of paper, blank except for the name printed in heavy block letters across the top, folded it twice, and placed it neatly in his wallet. Tomorrow he'd run the standard searches on Mr. Fitzroy and if they turned up nothing. . . . His smile was predatory

as he stood. If they turned up nothing, there were ways
to delve deeper.

Some might call what he planned a misuse of authority. Detective-Sergeant Michael Celluci called it looking
out for a friend.

Four

"I'm Nadine Heerkens-Wells. You must be Vicki Nelson."

The woman approaching, hand held out, shared a number of features with Peter and Rose; the same wide-spaced eyes and pointy face, the same thick mane of hair—in this case a dusty black marked with gray—the same short-fingered, heavily callused grip.

Her eyes, however, were shadowed, and lurking behind that shadow was a loss so deep, so intense, that it couldn't be completely hidden and might never be completely erased. Vicki swallowed hard, surprised by the strength of her reaction to the other woman's pain.

On the surface, Vicki had absolutely no doubt she faced the person in charge, and Nadine's expression proved that the welcoming smile had originally developed out of a warning snarl. *Still, I suppose she has no reason to trust me right off, regardless of what Henry's told her.* Keeping her own expression politely unchallenging, Vicki carefully applied as much force to the handshake as she received, despite the sudden inexplicable urge to test her strength. "I hope I'll be able to help," she said in her public service voice, meeting the other woman's gaze squarely.

Force of personality weighted with grief struck her almost a physical blow and her own eyes narrowed in response.

The surrounding wer waited quietly for the dominant female's decision. Henry stood to one side and watched, brows drawn down in a worried frown. For Vicki to

work effectively, the two women had to accept one another as equals, whether they liked it or not.

Nadine's eyes were brown, with a golden sunburst
around the pupil. Deep lines bracketed the corners and
her lids looked bruised.

I can take her, Vicki realized. *I'm younger, stronger.*
I'm . . . out of my mind. She forced the muscles of her
face to relax, denying the awareness of power. "I hadn't
realized London was so far from Toronto," she remarked conversationally, as though the room were not
awash with undercurrents of tension.

"You must be tired from your long drive," Nadine
returned, and only Vicki saw the acknowledgment of
what had just passed between them. "Come in and sit
down."

Then they both looked away.

At that signal, Vicki and Henry found themselves surrounded by hearty handshakes and wet noses and hustled into seats at the huge kitchen table. Henry
wondered if Vicki realized that she'd just been accepted
as a kind of auxiliary member of the pack, much as he
was himself. He'd spent long hours on the phone the
last two nights arguing for that acceptance, convincing
Nadine that from outside the pack Vicki would have
little chance of finding the killer, that Vicki would no
more betray the pack than she'd betray him, knowing as
he did that Nadine's agreement would be conditional on
the actual meeting.

"Shadow, be quiet."

The black pup—about the size of a small German
shepherd—who had been dancing around Vicki's knees
and barking shrilly, suddenly became a small naked boy
of about six or seven who turned to look reproachfully
up at Nadine. "But, Mom," he protested, "you said to
always bark at strangers."

"This isn't a stranger," his mother told him, leaning
forward to brush dusty black hair up off his face, "it's
Ms. Nelson."

He rolled his eyes. "I know *that,* but I don't know
her. That makes her a stranger."

"Don't be a dork, Daniel. Mom says she's okay,"

pointed out one of two identical teenage girls sitting on the couch by the window in a tone reserved solely for younger brothers.

"And she came with Henry," added the other in the exact same tone.

"And if she was a stranger," concluded the first, "you wouldn't have changed in front of her. So she *isn't* a stranger. So shut up."

He tossed his head. "Still don't know her."

"Then get to know her quickly," his mother suggested, turning him back to face Vicki, "so that we can have some peace."

Even though she was watching for it, Vicki missed the exact moment of change when Daniel became Shadow again. One heartbeat a small boy, a heartbeat later, a small dog. . . . *Not that small either, and I can't call them dogs. And yet, they aren't quite wolves.* A cold nose shoved into the back of her knee and she started. *And does that make this, him, a puppy or a cub? Ye gods, but this is going to get complicated.* Trying not to let any of this inner debate show on her face, she reached down and held out her hand.

Shadow sniffed it thoroughly then pushed his head under her fingers. His fur was still downy soft.

"If you start scratching him, Ms. Nelson, you'll be at it all night," one of his sisters told her with a sigh.

Shadow's nose went up and he pointedly turned his back on her, leaning up against Vicki's legs much the way Storm had leaned against Rose that night in Henry's condo. Which reminded Vicki. . . .

"Where's Peter and Rose? Peter. . . ." She paused and shook her head. "I mean, Storm, met the car and I was sure I saw Rose—I mean, Cloud—when I first came in."

"They've gone to get their Uncle Stuart," said the graying man next to Henry. Although he'd taken part in the welcome, those were the first words he'd actually spoken. He extended his hand across the table. An old scar puckered the skin of his forearm. Vicki wasn't positive, but it looked like a bite. "I'm Donald Heerkens, their father."

"I'm Jennifer." The closer of the two girls on the couch broke in before Donald could say any more.

"And I'm Marie."

And how the hell does anyone tell you apart? Vicki wondered. Sitting down, at least, they appeared to be the exact same size and even their expressions looked identical. *Mind you, I'm hardly one to judge. All kids look alike to me at that age. . . .*

The two of them giggled at their uncle's mock scowl.

"So now you've met everyone who's here," Marie continued.

"Everyone except Daddy," Jennifer added, " 'cause like you already met Rose and Peter." The two of them smiled at her in unison. Even their dimples matched.

Daddy must be Stuart, Vicki realized; Nadine's husband, Daniel's father, Donald's brother-in-law, Peter's and Rose's uncle. The dominant male. Meeting *him* should prove to be interesting.

"Nice thing to be ignored in my own home," growled a voice from the door.

Shadow flung himself out from under Vicki's fingers, charged across the kitchen barking like a furry little maniac, and leapt up at the man who'd just come into the house—who caught him, swung him up over his head, and turned Daniel upside down.

Vicki didn't need an introduction. The same force of personality that marked Nadine marked Stuart and he was *definitely* very male. He was also very naked and that added considerable weight to the latter observation. Vicki had to admit she was favorably impressed although at five ten she could probably give him at least four inches. Judging by human standards, which was all she had to work with, Henry's warning aside, he appeared to be younger than his wife by about five years. His hair—all his hair, and there was rather a lot of it all over his body—remained unmarked by gray.

"Stuart. . . ." Nadine pulled a pair of blue sweatpants off the back of her chair and threw them at her husband.

He caught them one-handed, Daniel tucked under the other arm, and stared at them with distaste. Then he turned and looked straight at Vicki. "I don't much like clothing, Ms. Nelson," he told her, obviously as aware of her identity as she was of his. "It stops the change and in this heat it's damned uncomfortable. If you're going to be here for a while, you're going to have to get used to the little we wear."

"It's your house," Vicki told him levelly. "It's not my place to say what you should wear."

He studied her face, then smiled suddenly and she got the impression she'd passed a test of some kind. "Humans usually worry about clothing."

"I save my worry for more important things."

Henry hid a smile. Since they'd met, he'd been trying to figure out if Vicki was infinitely adaptable to circumstances or just so single-minded that anything not leading to her current goal was ignored. In eight months of observation he'd come no closer to an answer.

Tossing the sweatpants in the corner, Stuart held out his hand. "Pleased to meet you, Ms. Nelson."

She returned both smile and handshake, careful not to come on too strong. *Come on too strong to a naked werewolf. Yeah, right.* "And you. Please, call me Vicki."

"Vicki." Then he turned to Henry and by the tiniest of changes, the smile became something else. He held out his hand again. "Henry."

"Stuart." The smile was a warning, not a challenge. Henry recognized it and acknowledged it. It could change to challenge very quickly and neither man wanted that. As long as Henry kept to his place, the situation between them would remain tense but stable.

Uninterested in all this grown-up posturing, Daniel twisted against his father's side, found the grip loose enough to allow change, did, and began to bark. His father put him down just as the screen door opened and Cloud and Storm came in.

For the next few moments, the two older wer allowed themselves to be attacked by their younger cousin, the fight accompanied by much growling and snapping and feigned—at least Vicki assumed they were feigned—yelps of pain. As none of the other adults seemed worried about the battle, Vicki took the time to actually look at her surroundings.

The kitchen furniture was heavy and old and a little shabby from years of use. The wooden table could seat eight easily and twelve without much crowding. Although the chairs had chew marks up each leg they—to judge by the one under Vicki—had been made to endure and still had all four feet planted firmly on the worn linoleum. The lounge that the twins were perched on, tucked under the window by the back door, had probably been bought in the fifties and hadn't been moved from that corner since. The refrigerator looked new, as did the electric stove. In fact, the electric stove looked so new, Vicki suspected it was seldom used. The old woodstove in the far corner would likely be not only a source of winter heat but their main cooking facility. If they cooked. She hadn't thought to ask Henry what the wer ate or if she'd be expected to join in. A sudden vision of a bleeding hunk of meat with a side of steaming entrails as tomorrow's breakfast made her stomach lurch. The north wall was lined with cupboards and the south with doors, leading, Vicki assumed, to the rest of the house.

To her city bred nose, the kitchen quite frankly *smelled*. It smelled of old woodsmoke, of sheep shit—and quite probably sheep, too, if she had any idea of what sheep smelled like—and very strongly of well, wer. It wasn't an unpleasant combination, but it was certainly pungent.

Housework didn't seem to be high on the list of wer priorities. That was fine with Vicki, it wasn't one of her top ten ways to spend time either. Her mother, however, would no doubt have fits at the tufts of hair piled up in every available nook and cranny.

Of course, my mother would no doubt have fits at this entire situation . . .

Peter stood up and dangled a squirming Shadow at shoulder level—front paws in his left hand, rear paws in his right—deftly keeping the pup's teeth away from the more sensitive, protruding, areas of his anatomy.

. . . so it's probably a good thing she isn't here.

Just as she was beginning to wonder if she shouldn't

bring up the reason for her visit, Stuart cleared his throat. Peter released Shadow, smiled a welcome at Vicki and Henry, changed, and curled up on the floor beside his twin. Shadow gave one last excited bark and went over to collapse, panting, on his mother's feet. Everyone else, the two visitors included, turned to face Stuart expectantly.

And all he did was clear his throat. Vicki was impressed again. *If he could bottle that he could make a fortune.*

"Henry assures us that you can be trusted, Ms. Nelson, Vicki." His eyes were a pale Husky blue, startlingly light under heavy black brows. "I'm sure you realize that things would get very unpleasant for us if the world knew we existed?"

"I realize." And she did, which was why she decided not to be insulted at the question. "Although *someone* obviously knows."

"Yes." How a word that was mostly sibilants could be growled Vicki had no idea. But it was. "There are three humans in this territory who know of the pack. An elderly doctor in London, the local game warden, and Colin's partner."

"Colin the police officer." It wasn't really a question. A werewolf on the London Police Force was a phenomenon Vicki was unlikely to forget. She pulled a notebook and a pen from the depths of her purse. "The twins—Rose and Peter, that is—mentioned him."

Donald's expression seemed more confused than proud. "My oldest son. He's the first of us to hold what you could call a job."

"The first to finish high school," Nadine said. At Vicki's expression, she added, "Generally we find school very . . . stressful. Most of us leave as soon as we can." Her lips twisted up into what Vicki could only assume was a smile. "Trouble is, they're making it harder to leave at the same time they're making it harder to stay."

"The world is becoming smaller," Henry said quietly. "The wer are being forced to integrate. Sooner or later, they'll be discovered." He had no doubt as to how his mortal brethren would treat the wer; they'd be considered animals if they were allowed to live at all. When so small a thing as skin color made so large a difference, what chance did the wer have?

Vicki was thinking much the same thing. "Well," her tone brooked no argument, "let's just hope it's later. I personally am amazed you've managed to keep the list down to three."

Stuart shrugged, muscles rippling under the thick mat of black hair that covered his chest. "We keep to ourselves and humans are very good at believing what they wish to believe."

"And seeing what they wish to see," Donald added, the skin around his eyes crinkled with amusement.

"Or not seeing," Marie put in with a giggle.

The assembled wer nodded in agreement—regardless of shape—all save Shadow, who had fallen asleep, chin pillowed on his mother's bare instep.

"What about those who might suspect what you are?" Vicki asked. Murderers were almost always known to the victim. The times they weren't were usually the cases that never got solved.

"There aren't any."

"I beg your pardon?"

"There aren't any," Stuart repeated.

He obviously believed what he said, but Vicki thought he was living in a dream world. A noise from the right pulled her gaze down to the two wer on the floor. Cloud looked as though she wanted to disagree. *Or maybe she wants to go walkies. How the hell can I tell?*

"You do have contact with humans. The younger ones, at least, on a regular basis." Vicki's gesture covered both sets of twins. "What about other kids at school? Teachers?"

"We don't change at *school*," Marie protested.

Jennifer's head bobbed in support, red hair flying. "We *can't* change when we're dressed."

"And as you're dressed at school, you *can't* change at school?" They seemed pleased she was so quick on the uptake. "It must be frustrating. . . ."

Marie shrugged. "It's not so bad."

"Don't you ever want to tell people what you can do? Show them your other shape?"

Stuart's growl sounded very loud and very menacing in the shocked silence that followed. The girls looked as though she'd suggested something obscene. "Okay. I guess not." *Don't judge them by human standards. Try to remember that.* "What about special friends?"

Storm and Cloud were unreadable. Marie and Jennifer looked puzzled. "Boyfriends?"

Both girls wrinkled their noses in identical expressions of disgust.

"Humans don't smell right," Stuart explained, shortly. "That sort of thing never happens."

"They don't smell right?"

"No."

Vicki decided to leave it at that. She really wasn't up for a discussion of werewolf breeding criteria, not at this hour of the night. There were, however, two things that had to be covered. The first still made Vicki uncomfortable and, in almost a year of working for herself, she hadn't come up with a less than blunt way of bringing it up. "About my fee. . . ."

"We can pay it," Stuart told her and only nodded when she mentioned the amount.

"All right, then," she laced her fingers together and stared into the pattern thus formed for a moment, "one more thing. When I find whoever is doing this, what then? We can't take him to court. He can't be held accountable for murder under the law without giving away the existence of your people."

Stuart smiled and, in spite of the heat, Vicki felt a chill run up and down her back. "He will be accountable to our law. To pack law."

"Revenge, then?"

"Why not? He's killed two of us for no reason, no cause. Who has better right to be judge and jury?"

Who indeed?

"There's no other way to stop him from killing again," Henry said quietly. He thought he understood Vicki's hesitation, if only in the abstract. Ethics formed in the sixteenth century had an easier time with justice over law than ethics formed in the twentieth.

What it came down to, Vicki realized, was a question of whose life had more value; the people here in this room or the maniac, singular or collective, who was picking them off one by one? Put like that, it didn't seem to be such a difficult question.

"The three people you have, then, I'd like to check them out."

"We already checked," Donald began but Stuart cut him off.

"It's too late to do anything tonight. We'll get you the information tomorrow."

As Vicki had already been told, they'd attempted to deal with this themselves after Nadine's twin had been shot. She wasn't surprised that they'd done some checking. She wished they hadn't; in her experience, amateurs only muddied the waters. "Did you find anything?"

Stuart sighed and ran both his hands back through his hair. "Only what we already knew; Dr. Dixon is a very old man who hasn't betrayed us in over forty years and isn't likely to start now. Arthur Fortrin went north at the end of July and won't be back until Labor Day weekend. And Colin's partner, Barry, had both the skill and the opportunity."

Vicki tapped her pen against the paper. "That doesn't look good for Barry."

"No," Stuart agreed. "It doesn't."

"Hey, Colin! Wait a minute. . . ."

Colin sighed and leaned against the open door of the truck. There really wasn't anything else he could do; leaping inside and roaring off in a cloud of exhaust fumes would certainly not make things any better. He watched his partner cross the dark parking lot, weaving his way around the scattered cars belonging to the midnight shift, brows drawn down into a deep vee, looking very much like a man who wanted some answers. Exactly the situation Colin had been trying to avoid.

"What is with you, Heerkens?" Barry Wu rocked to a halt and glared. A line of water dribbled down his face from his wet hair and he swiped at it angrily. "First you act like a grade A asshole all shift, then you slink out while I'm in the shower without so much as a 'See you tomorrow,' or a 'Go fuck yourself.' "

"You're my partner, Barry, you're not my mate." As an attempt to lighten the mood, it was a dismal failure; Colin could still smell the anger. He did his best not to react to it, catching the growl in his throat before it rose to an audible level.

"That's right, your partner—let's set aside the fact I thought I was your friend—and as your partner I have a right to know what it is that's got you tied in knots."

"It's pack business. . . ."

"Bullshit! When it affects your job—our job—like it did tonight, it's my business! Three to eleven shift has enough problems without you and your attitude adding to them."

All right. If you really want to know, we think you've murdered two of my family. Except Colin didn't think it, couldn't think it, had to think it. He'd searched Barry's locker, the trunk of his car, even quickly searched his apartment one evening when they went back there for a few beers after work. Nothing beyond the rifles the pack already knew he had. No indication that he'd been casting silver bullets. Nor had his scent been anywhere in the woods. If Barry was responsible for the two deaths, he wasn't leaving evidence lying around. If he wasn't responsible, Colin had found nothing that could clear him.

Colin wanted to confront him. The pack leader had refused to allow it. Torn between pack law and this newer loyalty, Colin had almost reached the point where he couldn't stand it any longer.

He swung up into the truck and slammed the door. "Look" he snarled, "I want to tell you but I can't. Just leave it!" Slamming the truck into gear, he screeched out of the parking lot, knowing full well Barry wouldn't leave it. He'd worry at it and tear at it like Shadow with a slipper until he had it in pieces and could see what it was made of. Colin wasn't looking forward to going to work tomorrow night.

Still, tomorrow night was a long time away and maybe this hotshot Toronto PI Henry Fitzroy had convinced the pack to hire could turn something up.

"When I get out of the city," he told his reflection in the rearview mirror, "I'm going to have a good long howl. I deserve it."

He watched Colin return home, bad mood obvious even through the scope. Finger resting lightly on the trigger, he tracked him from the truck to the house but, although he had a clear line of sight, he couldn't apply the necessary pressure. He told himself it was too dangerous—there were too many others too close—but in his heart he knew it was the uniform. Colin would have to die in his other form.

Shadows moved against the windows, then the kitchen light went off and the farmhouse stood in darkness. Fire would take care of the lot of them, but he doubted he could get close enough to set it.

Staying carefully downwind, he worked his way back to the road and his car, old skills put to new uses. Although tonight's reconnaissance had brought him little new information and no chance of making a kill, his penetration so close to their home had convinced him it would only be a matter of time before he won.

There were, however, the visitors to consider.

Until he found out who, and what, they were, he would not act against them. He would not have the murder of innocents on his conscience.

Henry stood by the bed and watched Vicki sleep. She had one arm thrown up over her head, the other across her stomach. The sheet, like the darkness, did little to hide her from his sight. He watched her breathe, listened to the rhythm of her heart, followed the path of her blood as it pulsed at wrist and throat. Even asleep, her life was like a beacon in the room.

He could feel his hunger growing.

Should he wake her?

She slept with the corners of her mouth curved slightly upward, as though she knew a pleasant secret.

No. There had been enough strangeness for her to deal with for one night. He could wait.

Lightly, very lightly, he drew his finger along the soft skin of her inner arm and whispered, "Tomorrow."

For the first moment after waking, Vicki had no idea where she was. Sunlight painted molten gold across the inside of her lids and, as pretty as it looked, it shouldn't be there. Her bedroom window faced a narrow alley and across that another bedroom window so, even if she'd left the curtains open, which she never did, it couldn't possibly be this bright.

Then she remembered and opened her eyes. The ceiling was a blue blur with a yellow blur across it. Reaching out to the right, her ringers scuttled across the bedside table until they found her glasses. She settled them on her nose and the blurring vanished although the ceiling didn't change significantly. It was still blue. The yellow was a slanting bar of sunlight streaming through the space between the thin cotton curtains. Her room, Sylvia's old room, was obviously on the east side of the house. That settled, Vicki sat up.

The black shape stretched across the lower left corner of the bed gave her a second's panic until she recognized Shadow. Sliding carefully out from under the sheet so as not to wake him, she was just about to stand when she noticed that the bedroom door was wide open and, given the angle of the bed, she'd be fully visible to anyone who walked by.

Fully visible.

Vicki hated wearing pajamas and although she'd brought a T-shirt to sleep in, it had been so hot she hadn't bothered. She supposed she could handle Shadow—mostly because so far she'd avoided thinking of Daniel—but Shadow's cousins or uncle or father— especially Shadow's father—were another kettle of fish entirely and what's more, she could smell coffee so she knew *someone* was up.

Well, I can't stay in bed all day. . . . Girding her loins, metaphorically speaking, she dashed across the small section of open linoleum and eased the door closed.

Shadow scrubbed at his muzzle with one oversized paw but didn't wake. Feeling considerably more secure, Vicki got into a pair of clean underwear and began to hook on her bra. She'd have to have a word with Sha . . . Daniel when he woke up as she knew she'd closed the door last night.

The door opened.

Jennifer, or maybe Marie, came into the room.

It didn't really help that of the two, Vicki was wearing more clothing.

"Hi. Mom sent me up to see if you were awake. Like it's really early still but Aunt Sylvia always said the sun in this room was like an alarm clock. You coming right down?"

"Uh, yes."

"Good." She shook her head at the bra. "Boy am I glad I'll never need one of those things." Glancing around, she sighed volubly. "So that's where the runt got to. If he bugs you just throw him out."

"I'll, uh, do that."

Vicki pushed the door closed again as soon as the bushy tail of the long legged, half-grown wer had cleared the threshold.

Something Henry had said last night as they walked up the stairs together now made sense.

"Inside the pack, the wer have no sense of personal privacy."

She got dressed in record time and decided to skip having a shower. After her father left when she was ten, it had been just her and her mother. With the exception of a year in university residence when she didn't have a choice, she'd lived alone all her adult life. Something told her that all this family togetherness she found herself in the midst of was going to wear thin pretty quickly. . . .

Elbows on the kitchen table, sipping at cup of very good coffee, Vicki tried to look as though a half-naked woman joined her for breakfast every morning.

"The vinyl seats stick," Nadine had explained as she

sat, smoothing her cotton skirt. It had been wrapped so that a single tug would release it.

Apparently Stuart's decision the night before to leave off the despised sweatpants had given the rest of the family the opportunity to dress as they chose. Or not. Given that the heat had already left a damp vee down the back of Vicki's T-shirt, she supposed the "or not" wasn't such a bad idea. She couldn't help but notice the various items of clothing scattered all over the house, ready to be pulled on if an outsider arrived. *"Although if it's someone we don't want to see,"* Nadine had confirmed, *"we just stay in fur-form and ignore them."* Considering the size of the fur-forms, Vicki was willing to bet the wer had no trouble with trespassers.

From where she sat, Vicki could see out the largest of the three kitchen windows. The view included a scruffy expanse of lawn, a weathered building with a slight list to the west that appeared to be a garage, and beyond that, the barnyard. Cloud and Storm were stretched out under the huge willow tree in the center of the lawn. As Vicki watched, Storm lifted his head and yawned. He got slowly to his feet, stretched, and had a vigorous shake, dark russet fur rippling with highlights in the early morning sun. He sniffed at Cloud who ignored him. Dropping into a half crouch, he pushed his muzzle under her jaw and lifted. Her head rose about six inches off the ground and then dropped. She continued to ignore him. He did it again. The third time, Cloud twisted, changed, and Rose grabbed his muzzle with both hands.

"We're at the end of a very long lane." Nadine anticipated Vicki's question. "You can't actually see the house from the road and, with the exception of mail delivery, almost no one uses the road but us."

Out on the lawn, Cloud chased her brother twice around the tree and out of sight.

The sound of claws on linoleum shifted Vicki's attention back into the house but it was only Shadow coming down the stairs and into the kitchen. He sat in front of the refrigerator, had a quick scratch, then changed so he could open the door.

"Ma, there's nothing to eat."

"Don't stand with the fridge door open, Daniel."

He sighed but obediently closed it and Vicki marveled at how universal some things could be . . .

"If you're hungry why don't you go out to the barn and hunt rats?"

. . . and how universal some things were not.

Daniel sighed again and dragged himself over to lean against his mother's shoulder. "Don't know as I'm hungry for rats."

Nadine smiled, brushing the hair back off his forehead. "If you catch one and you don't want to eat it, you can bring it to me."

This apparently solved all problems because it was Shadow who put both front paws up on Nadine's lap and swiped at her face with his tongue before bounding outside. The screen door, Vicki saw, had been hung so that it swung freely in both directions with no latch to prevent a nose or a paw from pushing it open.

"They grow up so fast," Nadine said reflectively, snatching a fly out of the air.

For one horrified moment, with the rats still causing her a little trouble, Vicki was afraid Nadine was going to eat it but the older woman only crushed it and threw it to the floor. All things considered, lousy housekeeping was much easier to deal with. Vicki brushed a fly off the edge of her own mug and tried very hard to be openminded. *Rats. Right. If I don't eat until sundown maybe Henry'll take me to McDonalds.*

"Cloud comes into her first heat this fall," Nadine continued in the same tone, wiping her hand against the fabric of her skirt, "so pretty soon now, Peter'll be leaving."

"Leaving?" Back on the lawn, Shadow was stalking the waving plume of Storm's tail.

"It's too risky to have him stay. We'll probably send him away in early September."

"But . . ."

"When Cloud goes into heat, Storm'll go crazy trying to get to her. Better for all concerned if the males are far away when their littermates—their twins—mature."

Her voice shook a little as she added, "The bonds between twins are very strong with our kind."

"Rose said something similar." Vicki traced the pattern on her mug with the tip of one finger, unsure if
she should say anything about Sylvia's death. The pain
shadowing Nadine's eyes was so intensely personal, sympathy might be seen as an intrusion.

Nadine's nails tapped against the tabletop. "The wer
see death as a natural result of life," she said, reading
Vicki's hesitation. "Our mourning is specific and soon
over. Jason was my brother and I miss him, but with
the loss of my twin, I feel as though I've lost a part
of myself."

"I understand."

"No, you don't. You can't." Then Nadine's voice
twisted into a snarl and her lips lifted off her teeth.
"When you have found this animal with a coward's
weapon, he will pay for the pain he has caused."

It was so easy, Vicki realized, to forget why she was
here; to get caught up in the strangeness and lose sight
of the fact that two people had been murdered. So some
aspects of the case were a little unusual. So what. She
put down her mug, unaware her expression almost exactly mirrored Nadine's. "I'd better get started."

Five

"Why can't I come?" Daniel scowled fiercely up at Peter. "You always took me with you when you went places before."

"It's too dangerous." Peter shimmied the track shorts up over his hips. Vicki tried not to watch and wasn't significantly successful at it. "What if the human who shot Silver and Ebon is out there?"

Lips pulled back off small, pointed teeth. "I'd bite him!"

"He'd shoot you. You're not coming."

"But Peter. . . ."

"No."

"Cloud?"

She growled, her meaning plain.

"Okay, fine." Daniel threw himself down onto the grass. "But if you get in trouble out there, don't go howling for me." He thrust his chin into his cupped hands and only glowered when Cloud gave him a couple of quick licks as she went by.

Vicki fell into step beside Peter and the three of them headed for the nearly overgrown lane behind the barn.

"Hey, Peter!"

Peter turned.

"Ei kee ayaki awro!" The words rose and fell in a singsong cadence, practically dripping with six-year-old indignation.

Peter laughed.

"What did he say?"

"He said I mate with sheep."

It hadn't actually occurred to Vicki that the wer would have a language of their own although now she thought about it, it became obvious. It sounded a bit like Inuit—at least Inuit according to PBS specials on the Arctic; Vicki'd never been farther North than Thunder Bay. When she mentioned this to Peter, he kicked at a clump of yellowed grass.

"I've never heard Inuit but we sure got the same problems. The more we integrate with humans the more we speak their language and lose ours. Grandfather and Grandmother spoke Dutch and English and wer. Father still speaks a little Dutch but only Aunt Sylvia bothered to learn any wer." He sighed. "She taught me and I'm trying to teach Daniel but there's still so much I don't know. The dirt bag that killed her killed my best chance at keeping our language alive."

"You seem to be doing a good job." Vicki waved a hand back toward the willow. "Daniel's certainly using it. . . ." It might not be much comfort but it was all she had to offer so far.

Peter brightened. "True. He's like a little sponge, just soaks it right up. Cloud now," he made a grab for his twin's tail but she whisked it out of his way, "she learned to say Akaywo and gave up."

"Akaywo," Vicki repeated. The word didn't resonate the way it did when Peter said it but it was recognizable. Sort of. "What does it mean?"

"Uh, good hunting mostly. But *that* means hello, good-bye, how's tricks, long time no see."

"Like Aloha."

"Aloha. Alo-ha." Peter lengthened the second syllable until it trembled on the edge of a howl. "Good word. But not one of ours. . . ."

Suddenly, Cloud's ears went up and she bounded off into the underbrush. A second later, Peter shoved his shorts into Vicki's hands and took off after her.

Vicki watched their tails disappear behind a barrier of bushes and weeds and slapped at one of the billions of mosquitoes their passage through the grass had stirred up. "Now what?" she wondered. From all the crashing about, they were still after it, whatever it was. "Hey," she called, "I'll just keep walking to the end of the lane. You can catch up with me there." There was no response but to be honest she didn't expect one.

It was almost comfortable in the lane; a long way from cool but not nearly as hot as it would no doubt get later in the day. Vicki checked her watch. 8:40. *"You can make those calls this morning if you like,"* Nadine had said, *"but you might be better off heading out to the fields and having a look at where it happened before it gets too hot. When it warms up in a couple of hours, no one around here'll be awake to show you the place. Beside, Peter or Rose can tell you all about the three humans while you go."* A good theory if only Peter and Rose, or Peter and Cloud, or even Storm and Cloud— whatever—had stuck around.

She brushed aside a swarm of gnats, crushed another mosquito against her knee, and wondered if Henry was all right. The wer had apparently light-proofed a room for him, but at this point Vicki wasn't entirely certain she'd trust their good intentions. Still, Henry had been here other times and obviously survived.

Pushing her glasses up her nose, sweat having well lubricated the slope, she reached the end of the lane and paused, a little overwhelmed by the vast expanse of land now before her. Up above, the sky stretched on forever, hard-edged and blue. Down below, there was a fence and a field and another fence and a bigger field. There were sheep in both fields. In fact, there were three sheep not twenty feet away on the other side of the first fence.

Two of them were eating, the third stared down the arch of its Roman profile at Vicki.

Vicki had never heard that sheep were dangerous, but then, what did she know, she'd never been this close to a sheep before.

"So," leaning carefully against the fence, she picked a tuft of fleece off a rusty bit of wire and rolled it between her fingers, "I don't suppose you saw anything the night that Jason Heerkens, aka Ebon, was murdered?"

At the sound of her voice, the staring sheep rolled its eyes and danced backward while the other two, still chewing, peeled off to either side and trotted a few feet away.

"So much for interviewing witnesses," she muttered, turning back to look down the lane. "Where the hell are Cloud and Pe . . . Storm?"

As if in answer to her summons, the two wer burst out of the bushes and bounded toward her, tongues lolling, tails waving. Cloud reached the fence first and without pausing sailed over it and came to a dead stop, flattened against the grass on the other side. Storm, only a heartbeat behind, changed in midair, and Peter landed beside his sister in a very human crouch. The sheep, obviously used to this sort of thing, barely bothered to glance up from their grazing.

Vicki, less accustomed, tried to maintain an unruffled expression. Silently, she offered Peter his shorts.

"Thanks." He slid them on with practiced speed. "We almost had him that time."

"Had who?"

"Old groundhog, lives under a pile of cedar rails alongside the lane. He's fast and he's smart, but this time he made it to his den with only about a hair between him and Cloud's teeth."

"Couldn't you just change and move the rails?"

Peter shook his head, bits of bracken flying out of his hair. "That'd be cheating."

"It's not like we're hunting for food," Rose put in, stretching out on the grass. "There'd be no fun in it if we used our hands."

Vicki decided not to point out that there probably wasn't much fun in it for the groundhog either way. She slung her bag over the fence and followed a little more slowly. Rails she might have flag-jumped but wire offered no surface solid enough to push off from. *Besides, if I try to keep up with a couple of teenage werewolves, I'll probably strain something. Besides credibility.*

She pushed her glasses up her nose. "Where to now?"

"Toward the far side of the big pasture." Peter pointed. "Near the woods."

The woods offered sufficient cover for a whole army of assassins.

Vicki picked up her bag. Time to start earning her money. "Who owns the woods?"

"The government, it's crown land." Peter led the way along the fence, Cloud staying close by his side. "We won't cut straight across 'cause these ewes are carrying late fall lambs and we don't want to bother them any more than we have to. Our property ends at the trees," he continued, "but we're butted up against the Fanshawe Conservation Area." He grinned. "We help maintain one of the best deer herds in the county."

"I'm sure. Let me guess, that's how you met the game warden?"

"Uh huh. He came on one of the pack's kills, knew it hadn't been dogs, thought he recognized the spoor as wolf but couldn't figure out what the occasional bare human footprint was doing in there, and tracked us. He was really good. . . ."

"And you, that is, the pack, wasn't being as careful as it could have been." In Vicki's experience, complacency had exposed the majority of the world's secrets.

"Yeah. But Arthur turned out to be an okay guy."

"He could have turned out to be disaster," Vicki pointed out.

Peter shrugged. What was done was done as far as the pack was concerned. They'd taken steps to see it would never happen again and thought no more about it.

"What about the doctor?" She watched Cloud snap at a grasshopper and wondered if the separate forms had separate taste buds.

"Dr. Dixon's ancient history." Peter told her, snatched a high-leaping insect out of the air and popped it in his mouth.

Vicki swallowed a rising wave of nausea. The crunch, crunch, swallow, gave the snack an immediacy the earlier episode with the rats hadn't had. And while it was one thing to see Cloud do it. . . . *Well, I guess that answers my question.* Then she saw the look on Peter's face. *The little shit ate that on purpose to gross me out.* She gave her glasses a push and two steps later plucked a grasshopper off the front of her shorts—fortunately, it was a small one.

A long time ago, on a survival course, an instructor had told Vicki that many insects were edible. She hoped he hadn't been pulling her leg.

Biting down wasn't easy.

Actually, it tastes a bit like a squishy peanut.

The expression on Peter's face made the whole thing worthwhile. The last time she'd impressed a young man to that extent, she'd been considerably younger herself and her mother had gone away for the weekend.

Mike Celluci would maintain that she was insanely competitive. That wasn't true. She merely liked to preserve the status quo and her position at the top of the heap. And no teenage anything was getting the better of her. . . .

"Now, then," she tongued something out of her tooth and swallowed it quickly—there were limits—"you were telling me about Dr. Dixon?"

"Uh, yeah, well. . . ." He shot her a glance out of the corner of one eye but made an obvious decision not to comment. "When our grandparents emigrated from Holland after the war, Grandmother was pregnant with Aunt Sylvia and Aunt Nadine. They got as far as London when she went into labor. We don't normally use doctors, the pack helps if it's needed. I went out to the barn when Daniel was born but Rose watched."

Cloud looked up at the sound of her name. She'd run ahead and was urinating against a fence post.

"Anyway," Peter continued, nostrils flared as they passed the post, "there was this young doctor in the crowd and before Grandfather could carry Grandmother away, he'd hustled the both of them and Father, who was about five, into his office." He snickered. "Boy, did he get a shock. As soon as they were alone, Grandfather changed and almost ripped his throat out. Lucky for the doctor, Aunt Sylvia was wrong—somehow, I don't know—anyway, Dr. Dixon acted like a doctor and Grandfather let him live. He's been taking care of all our doctor stuff ever since."

"Handy man to know." The amount of "doctor stuff" necessary in Canada for government documents alone could be positively staggering. The wer were lucky they'd stumbled onto Dr. Dixon when they had. "So that leaves only Barry Wu."

"Yeah." Peter sighed deeply and scratched at the

patch of red hair in the center of his chest. "But you better talk to Colin about him."

"I intend to. But I'd also like to hear your opinion."

Peter shrugged. "I like him. I hope he didn't do it. It'll kill Colin if he did."

"Have they been partners long?"

"Since the beginning. They went to police school together." They'd reached the second fence. Cloud sailed over it, just as she had the first. Peter slipped his thumbs behind the waistband of his shorts, changed his mind, and started climbing. "Barry's an okay guy. He reacted to us the same way you did . . ." Twisting his head at an impossible angle, he grinned back over his shoulder at her. ". . . kind of shell-shocked but accepting."

Cloud had run on ahead, nose to the ground. About three quarters of the way across the field, she stopped, sat back on her haunches, pointed her nose at the sky, and howled. The sound lifted every hair on Vicki's body and brought a lump into her throat almost too big to swallow. From not very far away came an answer; two voices wrapping about each other in a fey harmony. Then Peter, still in human form, wove in his own song.

The sheep had begun to look distinctly nervous by the time the howl trailed off.

"Father and Uncle Stuart." Peter broke the silence to explain the two additional voices. "They're checking fences." He turned a little red under his tan. "Well, it's almost impossible not to join in. . . ."

As Vicki had felt a faint desire—firmly squelched—to add in her own two cents worth, she nodded understandingly. "Is that where it happened?"

"Yeah. Right here."

At first glance, "right here" looked no different than anywhere else in the field. "Are you sure?"

"Of course, I'm sure. It hasn't rained and the scent's still strong. Besides," one bare foot brushed lightly over the cropped timothy grass, "I was the first one to the body." Cloud pushed up against his legs. He reached down and pulled gently on her ears. "Not something I'm likely to forget."

"No, probably not." Maybe she should have told him

that he'd forget in time but Vicki didn't believe in lying if she could avoid it, even for comfort's sake. The violent death of someone close *should* make a lasting impression. Given that, she gentled her voice to ask, "Are you going to be up to this?"

"Hey, no problem." His hand remained buried in the thick fur behind Cloud's head.

The wer touched a great deal, she realized, and it wasn't just the youngsters. Last night around the kitchen table, the three adults had seldom been out of contact with each other. She couldn't remember the last time she'd spontaneously touched her mother. *And why am I thinking about that now?* She dug out her pad and a pencil. "Let's get started, then."

Ebon had been traveling northeast across the field. The bullet had spun his body around so that the ruin of his head had pointed almost due north. Even without Peter's description, there were enough rust brown stains remaining on the grass to show where what was left of Ebon's head had come to rest. The shot had to have come from the south.

Vicki sat back on her heels and stared south into the wood. *Brilliant deduction, Sherlock.* She stood, rubbing at the imprints of dried grass on her knees. "Where was your aunt shot?"

Peter remained sitting, Cloud's head in his lap. "In the small south field, just off that way." He pointed. The small south field wrapped around a corner of the woods. "Ebon was coming from there."

"Similar shot?"

"Yeah."

Head shots, at night, on moving targets. Whoever he was, he was good. "Which way was the body facing?"

"Like this." Peter shoved Cloud's body around until it was aligned to the northwest. She endured the mauling but didn't look thrilled.

Silver's tracks had been coming from the south and the shot had spun her in an arc identical to Ebon's.

The Conservation Area woods ran east of the small south field.

"I think we can safely assume it's the same guy and he shot from the cover of the trees," Vicki muttered, wishing for a city street and a clear line of sight. Trees shifted and moved about the way buildings never did and, from where Vicki stood, the woods looked like a solid wall of green and brown, with no way of knowing what they hid. A dribble of moisture rolled out of her hair and down the back of her neck. Someone could be watching now, raising the rifle, taking aim. . . . *You're getting ridiculous. The killings have happened at night.* But she couldn't stop a little voice from adding. *So far.*

Her back to the trees and an itching she couldn't control between her shoulder blades, she stood. "Come on."

"Where?" Peter rose effortlessly. Vicki tried not to be annoyed.

"We're going to have a look for the bullet that killed your aunt."

"Why?" He fell into step beside her as Cloud bounded on ahead.

"We're eliminating the possibility of two killers. So far, the pattern of both deaths are identical with only one exception."

"The silver bullet?"

"That's right. If the deaths match on all points, the odds are good there's a single person responsible."

"So if that's the case, how do you find them?"

"You follow the pattern back."

Peter frowned. "I don't think I understand what you mean."

"Common sense, Peter. That's all." She scrambled over another fence. "Everything connects to everything else. I just figure out how."

"After Aunt Sylvia died, the pack went hunting for her killer but we couldn't find any scents in the wood that didn't belong."

"What do you mean, didn't belong?"

"Well, there's a lot of scents in there. We were looking for a strange one." He squirmed a little under Vicki's frown and continued in a less condescending tone. "Anyway, after Uncle Jason was shot, Uncle Stuart wouldn't let anyone go into the woods except Colin."

Good way to lose Colin, Vicki thought, amazed as she

often was at the stupid things otherwise intelligent people could do, but all she said aloud was, "And what did Colin discover?"

"Well, not Barry's scent, and I think that was mostly what he was looking for."

Cloud was making tight circles, nose to the ground, in roughly the center of the field.

"Is that where it happened?"

"Uh huh."

Teeth clenched, Vicki waited for the howl. It didn't come. When she asked Peter why, he shrugged and said, "It happened weeks ago."

"Don't you miss her?"

"Of course we do, but . . ." He shrugged again, unable to explain. Everyone but Aunt Nadine had finished howling for Silver.

Cloud had found the bullet by the time they reached her and had dug it clear with more enthusiasm than efficiency. Her muzzle and paws had acquired a brown patina and the rest of her pelt was peppered with dirt.

"Good nose!" Vicki exclaimed, bending to pick up the slug. *And a good thing there wasn't anything else to learn from the scene,* she added silently, surveying the excavation. A quick wipe on her shorts and she held the prize up in the sunlight. It certainly wasn't lead.

Peter squinted at the metal. "So it's just one guy?"

Vicki nodded, dropping the bullet into her bag. "Odds are good." One marksman. Who lolled at night with a single shot to the head. One executioner.

"And you can find him now?"

"I can start looking."

"We should've found the dirtbag," Peter growled, savagely ripped up a handful of grass. "I mean, we're hunters!"

"Hunting for people is a specialized sort of a skill," Vicki pointed out levelly. The last thing she wanted to do was inspire heroics. "You have to train for it, just like everything else. Now, then," she squinted at the woods then looked back at the two young wer, "I want the both of you to return to the house. I'm going to go in there and have a look around."

"Uh, Ms. Nelson, you don't have much experience in woods, do you?" Rose asked tentatively.

"No. Not especially," Vicki admitted, "but . . . Rose, what the hell do you think you're doing?"

"It's just that, you're from the city and. . . ."

"That's not what I meant!" She positioned herself between the woods and the girl. "You *know* someone is watching your family from those trees. Why are you changing? Why take such a stupid risk?"

Rose rubbed at the dirt on her face. "But there's no one there now."

"You can't know that!" Why the whole damned county wasn't in on the family secret, Vicki had no idea.

"Yes, I can."

"How?"

"It's upwind."

"Upwind? The woods are upwind? You can smell that there's no one there?"

"That's right."

Vicki reminded herself once again not to judge by human standards and decided to drop it. "I think you two should get home."

"Maybe we should stay with you."

"No." Vicki shook her head. "If you're with me, you'll influence what I see." She raised a hand to cut off Peter's protest and added, "Even if you don't intend to. Besides, it's too dangerous."

Peter shrugged. "It's been safe enough since Ebon died."

It took her a moment to understand. "You mean that two members of your family were shot out here and you're still coming in range of the woods? At night?"

"We've been in pairs like Henry said," he protested. "And we've had the wind."

I don't believe this. . . . "From now on, until we know what's going on, *no one* comes out to these fields."

"But we have to keep on eye on the sheep."

"Why?" Vicki snapped, waving a hand toward the flock. "Do they do something?"

"Besides eat and sleep? No, not really. But the reason

there's so few commercial sheep operations in Canada is a problem with predators." Peter's lips drew back off his teeth and under his hair, his ears went back. "We don't *have* problems with predators."

"But you've gotta keep a pretty constant eye out," Rose continued, "so someone's got to come out here."

"Can't you move the sheep closer to the house?"

"We rotate the pastures," Peter explained. "It doesn't quite work like that."

"Bugger the pastures and bugger the sheep," Vicki said, her tone, in direct contrast to her words, reminiscent of a lecture on basic street safety to a kindergarten class. "Your lives are more important. Either leave these sheep alone for a while or move them closer to the house."

Rose and Peter exchanged worried glances.

"It's not just the sheep . . ." Rose began.

"Then what?"

"Well, this is the border of our family's territory. It has to be marked."

"What do you mean, marked?" Vicki asked even though she had a pretty good idea.

Rose waved her hands, her palms were filthy. "You know, marked. Scent marked."

"I would have thought that had been done already."

"Well, yeah, but you've got to keep doing it."

Vicki sighed. "So you're willing to risk your life in order to pee on a post?"

"It's not quite that simple." Rose sighed as well. "But I guess not."

"I guess we could talk to Uncle Stuart . . ." Peter offered.

"You do that," Vicki told him agreeably. "But you do that back at the house. Now."

"But. . . ."

"No." Things had been a little strange for Vicki lately—her eyes, Henry, werewolves—but she was working now and, regardless of the circumstances, that put her back on firm ground. Two shots had been fired from those trees and somewhere in the woods would be the tiny bits of flotsam that even the most meticulous of criminals left behind, evidence that would lead her out of the woods and right down the bastard's throat.

The twins heard the change in her voice, saw the change in her manner, and responded. Cloud stood and shook, surrounding herself for a moment in a nimbus of fine white hairs. Peter heaved himself to his feet, his hand on Cloud's shoulder. He tucked his thumbs behind the waist band of his shorts, then paused. "Would you *mind?*" he asked, gesturing at her shoulder bag with his chin.

Vicki sighed, suddenly feeling old. The distance between thirty-one and seventeen stretched far wider than the distance between thirty-one and four hundred and fifty. "I assume your nose tells you it's still safe?"

"Cross my heart and bite my tail."

"Then give them here," she said, holding out her hand.

He grinned, stripped them off, and tossed them to her. Peter stretched, then Storm stretched, then he and Cloud bounded back toward the house.

Vicki watched until they leapt the closer of the two fences, stuffed Peter's shorts in her bag, and turned toward the woods. The underbrush appeared to reach up to meet the treetops reaching down, every leaf hanging still and sullen in the August heat. Who knew what was in there? She sure as hell didn't.

At the edge of the field she stopped, squared her shoulders, took a deep breath, and pushed forward into the wilderness. Somehow, she doubted this was going to be fun.

Barry Wu blinked a drop of sweat from his eye, squinted through his front sights, and brought the barrel of his .30-06 Springfield down a millimeter.

Normally, he preferred to shoot at good old-fashioned targets set at the greatest distance accuracy would allow but he'd just finished loading a number of low velocity rounds—the kind that reacted ballistically at one hundred yards the way a normal round would react at five—and he wanted to try them out. He'd been reloading his own cartridges since he was about fourteen, but lately he'd been getting into more exotic varieties and these were the first of this type he'd attempted.

A hundred yards away, the lead silhouette of the grizzly waited, scaled in the same five to one ratio as the rounds he planned to put into it.

The bullet slammed into the target with a satisfyingly solid sound and Barry felt a little of the tension drain from his neck and shoulders as the grizzly went down. He worked the bolt, expelling the spent cartridge and moving the next round into the chamber. Shooting had always calmed him. When it was good, and lately it always was, he and the rifle became part of a single unit, one the extension of the other. All the petty grievances of his life could be shot away with a simple pull of the trigger.

All right, not all, he conceded as the moose and the mountain sheep fell in quick succession. *I'm going to have to do something about Colin Heerkens.* The trust necessary for them to do their job was in definite danger. Rising anger caused him to wing the elk, but the white-tailed deer he hit just behind the shoulder.

We clear this up tonight.

He centered the last target and squeezed the trigger.

One way or another.

A hundred yards away, the lead silhouette of the timber wolf slammed flat under the impact of the slug.

Vicki rubbed at a welt on her cheek and waved her other hand about in an ineffectual effort to discourage the swarms of mosquitoes that rose around her with every step. Fortunately, most of them appeared to be males. *Or dieting females,* she amended, trying not to inhale any significant number. Barely a hundred yards into the trees, the field and the sheep had disappeared and looking back the way she'd come, all she could see were more trees. It hadn't been as hard a slog as she'd feared it would be but neither was it a stroll through the park. Fortunately, the sunlight blazed through to the forest floor in sufficient strength to be useful. The world was tinted green, but it was visible.

"Somebody should tidy this place up," she muttered, unhooking her hair from a bit of dead branch. "Preferably with a flamethrower."

She kept to as straight a path as she could, picking out a tree or a bush along the assumed line of fire and then struggling toward it. Somewhere in these woods, she knew she'd find a fixed place where their marksman had a clear line of sight. It hadn't taken her long to realize that this place could only exist up off the forest floor. Which explained why the wer had found nothing; if they hunted like wolves, it was nose to the ground.

Trouble was, every tree she passed had so far been unclimbable. Trees large enough to bear an adult's weight stretched relatively smooth and straight up toward the sun, not branching until there was a chance of some return for the effort.

"So, unless he brought in a ladder . . ." Vicki sighed and scrubbed a drop of sweat off her chin with the shoulder of her T-shirt. She could see what might be higher ground a little to the right of where she thought she should be heading and decided to make for it. Stepping over a fallen branch, she tripped as the smaller branches, hidden under a rotting layer of last year's leaves, gave way under her foot.

"Parking lots." Shoving her glasses back up her nose, she stood and scowled around her at Mother Nature in the height of her summer beauty. "I'm all in favor of parking lots. A couple of layers of asphalt would do wonders for this place." Off to one side a cicada started to buzz. "Shut up," she told it, trudging on.

The higher ground turned out to be the end of a low ridge of rock on which a massive pine had managed to gain, and maintain, a roothold. Brushing aside years of accumulated needles, Vicki sat down just outside the perimeter of its skirts and contemplated her scratched and bitten legs.

This was all Henry's fault. She could have been at home, comfortably settled in front of her eighteen inch, three speed, oscillating fan, watching Saturday morning cartoons, and . . .

". . . and the wer would continue to die." She sighed

and began building the fallen pine needles into little
piles. This was what she'd chosen to do with her life—
to try to make a difference in the sewer the world was
becoming—no point in complaining just because it
wasn't always an easy job. And she had to admit, it was
a job that had gotten a hell of a lot more interesting
since Henry had come into her life. The jury was still
out on whether or not that was a good thing given that
the last time they'd worked together she'd come closer
to getting killed than she ever had in nine years on the
Metro Police.

"And this time, I'm being eaten alive." She rubbed at
a bite on the back of her leg with the rough front of her
sneaker. "Maybe I'm going at this the wrong way.
Maybe I should have started with the people. What the
hell am I going to recognize out here?" Then her hand
froze over a patch of needles and slowly moved back
until the needles were in full sunlight again.

The scorch mark was so faint she had to hold her
head at just the right angle to see it. About two inches
long and half an inch wide, it was a marginally darker
line across the pale brown carpet of dead pine—the
mark a spent cartridge might make against a tinder dry
resting place.

Oh, all right, honesty forced her to admit, *it could've
been caused by any number of other things—like acid
rain or bunny piss.* But it sure looked like a cartridge
scorch to her. *Of course, it could've come from a legitimate hunter out here to blow away whatever it is legitimate hunters blow away.*

There were plenty of bits of bare rock nearby where
the gunman could have stood to retrieve his brass and
plenty of places Vicki had cleared herself but she
searched for tracks anyway. Not expecting to find any
didn't lessen the frustration when she didn't.

Better to find where the shot came from. The ridge
stood barely two and a half feet higher than the forest
floor and the lines of sight hadn't improved. Vicki
looked up. The pine was higher than most of the trees
around it but its branches drooped, heavy with needles,
right to the ground. Then on the north side, she found

a way in to a dimly lit cavern, roofed in living needles, carpeted in dead ones. It was quiet in there, and almost cool, and the branches rose up the trunk as regular as a ladder; which was a good thing because Vicki could barely see.

This was it. This had to be it.

Had she seen the pine from the field? She couldn't remember, trees all looked alike to her.

She peered at a few tiny spurs snapped off close to the trunk, her nose almost resting on the bark. They could have been broken by someone scrabbling for a foothold. *Or they could have been broken by overweight squirrels. There's only one way to be sure.* Settling her glasses more firmly on her face, she swung up onto the first branch.

Climbing wasn't as easy as it looked from the ground; a myriad of tiny branches poked and prodded and generally impeded progress and the whole damn thing moved. Vicki hadn't actually been up a tree since about 1972 and she was beginning to remember why.

If her nose hadn't scraped by an inch from the sneaker print, she probably wouldn't have seen it. Tucked tight up against the trunk on a flattened glob of pine resin, was almost a full square inch of tread signature. Not enough for a conviction, not with every man, woman, and child in the country owning at least one pair of running shoes, but it was a start. The stuff was so soft that removing it from the tree would destroy the print so she made a couple of quick sketches—balanced precariously on one trembling leg—then placed her foot as close to it as possible and heaved herself up.

Her head broke free into direct sunlight. She blinked and swore and when her vision cleared, swore again. "Jesus H. Christ on crutches. . . ."

She'd come farther into the woods than she'd thought. About five hundred yards away, due north, was the spot where Ebon had been shot. A half turn and she could see the small pasture where Silver had been killed, a little closer but still an amazing distance away. If Barry Wu had pulled the trigger, he should have no trouble making the Olympic team *or* bringing home a gold. Vicki knew that some telescopic sights incorporated range finders but even they took both innate skill and years of practice to acquire the accuracy necessary. Throw in a *moving* target at five hundred yards. . . .

She'd once heard that according to all the laws of physics, a human being should not be able to hit a major league fastball. By those same laws of physics, the assassin had hit not one, but two, and hit them out of the ballpark besides.

A quick search turned up rubs in the bark where he'd braced his weapon on the tree.

"Unfortunately," she sighed, leaning her head back against a convenient branch, "discovering how and where brings me no closer to finding the answers to why and who." Closing her eyes for a moment, the sun hot against the lids, she wondered if she'd actually go through with it; if when she found the killer, she'd actually turn him over to the wer for execution. She didn't have an answer. She didn't have an alternative either.

It was time to head back to the house and make some phone calls, although she had a sick feeling that a drive into town and a good look at Constable Barry Wu's sneakers would be more productive.

Climbing down the tree took less time than climbing up but only because gravity took a hand and dropped her seven feet before she landed on a branch thick enough to hold her weight. Heart pounding, she made it the rest of the way to the ground in a slightly less unorthodox fashion.

Had her Swiss army knife contained a saw, she would have attempted to remove that final branch, the one that lifted the climber out of the tree and into the light. Unfortunately, it didn't and whittling off a pine branch two inches in diameter didn't appeal to her. In fact, except for attempting to keep them out of those fields, there wasn't a damn thing she could do to prevent the tree from being used as a vantage point to shoot the wer.

"Never a beaver around when you need one," she muttered, wishing she'd brought an ax. She had, however, uncovered two facts about the murderer. He had to be at least five foot ten, her height—any shorter and his shoulder wouldn't be level with the place where the rifle barrel had rested—and the odds were good that his hair was short and straight. She dragged a handful of needles and a small branch out of her short, straight hair. Had her hair been long or curly, she'd never had made it out of the tree alive.

"Excuse me?"

The shriek was completely involuntary and as she caught it before it passed her lips Vicki figured it didn't count. Her hand on her bag—it had made a useful weapon in the past—she whirled around to confront two puzzled looking middle-aged women, both wearing high-powered binoculars, one of them carrying a canvas bag about a meter long and twenty centimeters wide.

"We were just wondering," said the shorter, "what you were doing up that tree."

Vicki shrugged, waning adrenaline jerking her shoulders up and down. "Oh, just looking around." She waved a not quite nonchalant hand at the canvas bag. "You out here to do a little shooting?"

"In a manner of speaking. Although this is our camera tripod, not a rifle."

"It's illegal to shoot on conservation authority property," added the other woman. She glared at Vicki, obviously still unhappy at having found her up in a tree. "We would report *anyone* we found shooting out here, you can be certain of that."

"Hey." Vicki raised both hands to shoulder height. "I'm unarmed." As neither woman seemed to appreciate her sense of humor, she lowered them again. "You're birders, aren't you?" A recent newspaper nature column had mentioned that *birders* was now the preferred term; *bird-watcher* having gone out of vogue.

Apparently, the column had been correct.

Twenty minutes later, Vicki had learned more about nature photography than she wanted to know; learned that in spite of the high-power binoculars the two women had seen nothing strange on the Heerkens farm—*"We don't look at other people's property, we look at birds."*—and, in fact, didn't even know where the Heerkens farm was; learned that a .30 caliber rifle and scope would easily fit into a tripod bag, allowing it to be carried into the woods without arousing suspicion. Although neither woman had ever come across a hunter, they'd both found spent shell casings and so were always on the look out. With middle-class confidence that no one would ever want to hurt them, they laughed at Vicki's warnings to be careful.

There were two bird-watching clubs in London as well as a photography group run by the YMCA that often came out to the conservation area. Armed with names and phone numbers of people to contact—"Although the members of that *other* club are really nothing more than a group of dilettantes. You'd do much better to join us."—Vicki bade farewell to the birders and tromped off through the bush, willing to bet big money that not everyone with a pair of binoculars kept then trained exclusively on birds and that someone was shooting more than film.

"Henry Fitzroy?" Dave Graham peered over his partner's shoulder at the pile of papers on the desk. "Isn't that the guy that Vicki's seeing?"

"What if it is?" Celluci growled, pointedly turning the entire pile over.

"Nothing, nothing." Dave went around to his side of the desk and sat down. "Did, uh, Vicki ask you to check into his background?"

"No. She didn't."

Dave recognized the tone and knew he should drop it, but some temptations were more than mortal man could resist. "I thought you and Vicki had a relationship based on, what was it, 'trust and mutual respect'?"

Celluci's eyes narrowed and he drummed his fingers against the paper. "Yeah. So?"

"Well . . ." Dave took a long, slow drink of his coffee. "It seems to me that checking up on the other men in her life doesn't exactly fit into those parameters."

Slamming his chair back, Celluci stood. "It's none of your damned business."

"You're right. Sorry." David smiled blandly up at him.

"I'm just looking out for a friend. Okay? He's a writer, god knows what he's been into."

"Right."

Seemingly of their own volition, Celluci's fingers crumpled the uppermost paper into a tightly wadded ball. "She can see who she wants," he ground out through clenched teeth and stomped out of the office.

Dave snickered into his coffee. "Of course she can," he said to the air, "as long as she doesn't see them very often and they meet with your approval." He made plans to be as far out of range as possible when Vicki found out and the shit hit the fan.

By 10:27, Vicki was pretty sure she was lost. She'd already taken twice as long coming out of the woods as she'd spent going in. The trees all looked the same and under the thick summer canopy it was impossible to take any kind of a bearing on the sun. Two paths had petered out into nothing and a blue jay had spent three minutes dive-bombing her, screaming insults. Various rustlings in the underbrush seemed to indicate that the locals found the whole thing pretty funny.

She glared at a pale green moss growing all around a tree.

"Where the hell are the Boy Scouts when you need one?"

Six

Vicki saw no apparent thinning of the woods; one moment she was in them, the next she was stepping out into a field. It wasn't a field she recognized either. There were no sheep, no fences, and no indication of where she might be.

Settling her bag more firmly on her shoulder, she started toward the white frame house and cluster of outbuildings that the other end of the field rolled up against. Maybe she could get directions, or use their phone . . .

". . . or get run off for trespassing by a large dog and a farmer with a pitchfork." She was pretty sure they did that sort of thing in the country, that it was effectively legal, and that it didn't matter because she wasn't going back into those woods. She'd take on half a dozen farmers with pitchforks first.

As she approached, wading knee-deep through grass and goldenrod and thistles, she became convinced that no one had worked this farm for quite some time. The barn had a faded, unused look about it and she could actually smell the roses that climbed all over one wall of the white frame house.

The field ended in a large vegetable garden. Vicki recognized the cabbages, the tomato plants, and the raspberry bushes—nothing else seemed familiar. *Which isn't really surprising.* She picked her way around the perimeter. *My vegetables usually come with a picture of the jolly green. . . .* "Oh. Hello."

"Hello." The elderly man, who had appeared so suddenly in her path, continued to stare, obviously waiting for her to elaborate further.

"I, uh, got lost in the woods."

His gaze started at her sneakers, ran up her scratched and bitten legs, past her walking shorts, paused for a moment on her Blue Jays' T-shirt, flicked over to her shoulder bag, and finally came to rest on her face. "Oh," he said, a small smile lifting the edges of his precise gray mustache.

The single word covered a lot of ground, and the conclusion it drew would've annoyed the hell out of Vicki if it hadn't been so accurate. She held out her hand. "Vicki Nelson."

"Carl Biehn."

His palm was dry and leathery, his grip firm. Over the years, Vicki had discovered she could tell a lot about a man based on how he shook hands with her—or if he'd shake hands at all. Some men still seemed absolutely confused about what to do when the offered hand belonged to a woman. Carl Biehn shook hands with an economy of movement that said he had nothing to prove. She liked him for it.

"You look like you could use some water, Ms. Nelson."

"I could use a lake," Vicki admitted, rubbing at the sweat collected under her chin.

His smile broadened. "Well, no lake, but I'll see what I can do." He led the way around the raspberry bushes and Vicki fell into step beside him. Her first view of the rest of the garden brought an involuntary exclamation of delight.

"Do you like it?" He sounded almost shy.

"It's . . ." She discarded a pile of adjectives as inadequate and finished simply. ". . . the most beautiful thing I've ever seen."

"Thank you." He beamed; first at her and then out over the flower beds where a fallen rainbow, shattered into a thousand brilliant pieces, perched against every possible shade of green. "The Lord has been good to me this summer."

Vicki tensed, but he made no other reference to God.

And thank God for that. She had no idea if her admiration had broken through the elderly man's reserve or if he simply had none when it came to the garden. As they walked between the beds, he introduced the flowers they passed as though they were old friends—here adjusting a stake that held a blood red gladioli upright, there swiftly beheading a dying blossom.

". . . dusty orange beauties are dwarf hemerocallis, day lilies. If you make the effort to plant early, middle, and late varieties, they'll bloom beautifully from June on into September. They're not a fussy grower, not hard to work with, just give them a little phosphate and potash and they'll show their appreciation. Now these shasta daisies over here. . . ."

Having spent most of her life in apartments, Vicki understood next to nothing about gardens or the plants that grew in them but she could—and did—appreciate the amount of work that had gone into creating and maintaining such an oasis of color amid the summer-toasted fields. She also could appreciate the depth of emotion that Carl Biehn lavished on his creation. He wasn't soppy or twee about it but the garden was a living being to him; it showed subtly in his voice, his expressions, his actions. People who cared that much about something outside themselves were rare in Vicki's world and it reinforced her first favorable impression.

An old-fashioned hand pump stood on a cement platform, close by the back door. Carl led the way across the lawn toward it, finishing his enthusiastic monologue about the new heritage roses just as he reached for the handle.

"The cup appears to be missing again, Ms. Nelson. I hope you don't mind."

Vicki grinned. "I may just stick my entire head under if that's all right with you."

"Be my guest."

For all its apparent age, the pump worked smoothly, pulling up clear, cold water with only the slightest taste of iron. Vicki couldn't remember the last time she'd tasted anything as good and the sudden shock of it hitting the back of her head erased much of the morning's stickiness. If the pump had been a little higher off the ground, she'd have stuck her entire body under it.

Flicking her wet hair back off her face, she straightened and indicated the pump. "May I?" When Carl admitted that he wouldn't mind, they changed places. There was more pressure against the handle than Vicki had anticipated and she found herself having to lean into the mechanism. Gardening had obviously kept her elderly benefactor in good condition.

"It really is incredible," she murmured. "I've never seen anything like it."

"You should have seen it last week. Then it was really something." He stood, wiping his hands dry on his pants and gazing proudly out over the vast expanse of color. "Still, I have to admit, it doesn't look bad. Everything out there from A to Zee, from asters to zinnias."

Vicki stepped back as a bumblebee, leg pouches bulging with pollen, flew a slightly wobbly course just past the end of her nose. From this angle, she could look out over the flowers, to the vegetables, to the fields beyond. The contrast was incredible. "It looks like shredded wheat out there. How do you keep the garden watered? It must be almost a full-time job."

"Not at all." He rested one foot up on the cement platform and leaned a forearm across his thigh. "I use an underground irrigation system, developed by the Israelis. I merely turn on the tap and the system does all the work. Just to be on the safe side, however, I've run a water line out into the garden with a hundred feet of hose, in case a specific plant needs a little attention."

She waved a hand between the brown and the green. "I just can't get over the difference."

"Well, sometimes even the Lord needs a little help, his wonders to perform. Have you been saved, Ms. Nelson?"

The question came so unexpectedly, in such a rational tone, that it took Vicki a moment to realize what had been said and a moment beyond that to come up with what she hoped would be a definitive reply. "I'm an Anglican." She wasn't, really, but her mother was, sort of.

"Ah." He nodded, stepping back off the platform. "Church of England." For just a second, caught between the sun and the concrete, the damp sole of his shoe left a print—concentric half circles of tread last seen pressed into pine gum in the crotch of a tree.

Her expression carefully neutral over a sudden surge of adrenaline, Vicki put her own foot up on the platform and bent to tie her shoe. In the heat of the sun, the print dried quickly but it was a definite match.

Unfortunately, so was the print she left behind.

A quick look told her they were wearing the same brand of running shoe. A brand that seemed to cover the feet of half the civilized world.

Shit. Shit. Shit! Good news and bad news. Or bad news and good news, she wasn't quite sure. Evidence no longer pointed directly to the feet of Carl Biehn but her suspect list, based on the sneaker print at least, had just grown by millions. There'd be small differences of course—size, cracks in the rubber, wear patterns—but the possibilities of an easy match had just evaporated.

"Are you all right, Ms. Nelson? Perhaps you should sit down for a moment, out of the sun."

"I'm fine." He was watching her with some concern so she pulled up a smile. "Thank you, Mr. Biehn."

"Well, maybe we'd best see about getting you back where you belong. If I could offer you a lift somewhere. . . ."

"And if you can't, I most certainly will."

Vicki turned. The man standing in the doorway was in his early thirties, of average height, average looks, and above average self-opinion. He leered genially down at her, his pose no doubt intended to show off his manly physique—which, she admitted, wasn't bad. *If you like the squash and health club types.* . . . Which she didn't.

Slipping on a pair of expensive sunglasses, he stepped out into the sunlight, hair gleaming like burnished gold. *I bet he highlights it.* A quick glance showed he wore blue leather deck shoes. Without socks. Vicki hated the look of shoes without socks. Although odds were good he owned a pair of running shoes, she somehow doubted he'd be willing to ruin his manicure by climbing a tree.

Which was a pity as he seemed to be exactly the type of person she'd love to feed to the wer.

Beside her, she heard Carl suppress a sigh.

"Ms. Nelson, may I introduce you to my nephew, Mark Williams."

The younger man grinned broadly at his uncle. "And here I thought your only hobbies were gardening and bird-watching and saving souls." Then he turned the force of his smile on Vicki.

Some expensive dental work there, she thought, picking at a bit of dried pine gum on her T-shirt and trying not to scowl.

"Ms. Nelson got lost in the conservation area," Carl explained tersely. "I was just about to drive her home."

"Oh please, allow me." Mark's voice stopped just short of caressing and more than a little past what Vicki considered insulting. "If I know my uncle, once he gets a lovely woman alone in a car all he'll do is preach."

"Please, don't put yourself out." Her tone made it more a command than a polite reply and Mark looked momentarily nonplussed. "If you wouldn't mind . . ." she continued, turning to Carl. Being preached at would be infinitely preferable to being with Mark. He reminded her of a pimp she'd once busted.

"Not at all." Carl was doing an admirable job of keeping a straight face, but Vicki caught sight of the twinkle in his eye and a suspicious trembling at the ends of his mustache. He waved a hand toward the driveway and indicated Vicki should precede him.

It wasn't hard to connect the car with the man. The late model black jeep with the gold trim, the plush interior, the sunroof, and the rust along the bottom of the doors was practically a simulacrum of Mark. The ten-year-old beige sedan with the recent wax job just as obviously—although not as loudly—said Carl.

Vicki had her hand on the door handle when Mark called, "Hey! I don't even know your first name."

She turned and the air temperature plummeted around her smile. "I know," she told him, and got into the car.

The very expensive stereo system surprised her a little.

"I like to listen to gospel music while I drive," Carl explained, when he saw her looking at enough lights and buttons and switches to fill an airplane cockpit. He stopped the car at the end of the driveway. "Where to?"

Where to, indeed; she had no idea of the address or even the name of the road. "The, uh, Heerkens sheep farm. Are you familiar with it?"

"Yes."

The suppressed emotion in that single word pulled Vicki's brows down. "Is there a problem?"

His knuckles were white around the steering wheel. "Are you family?"

"No. Just the friend of a friend. He thought I needed some time out of the city and brought me here for the weekend." Mike Celluci wouldn't have believed the lie for a moment—he'd often said Vicki was the worst liar he'd ever met—but some of the tension went out of Carl's shoulders and he turned the car out onto the dirt road and headed north.

"I just met them this weekend," she continued matter-of-factly. Experience had taught her that the direct approach worked best with no nonsense people like her host. "Do you know them well?"

Carl's mouth thinned to a tight white line but after a moment he said, "When I first moved here, ten, eleven years ago now, I tried to get to know them. Tried to be a good neighbor. They were not interested."

"Well, they are pretty insular."

"Insular!" His bark of laughter held no humor. "I tried to do my duty as a Christian. Did you know, Ms. Nelson that not one of those children have been baptized?"

Vicki shook her head but before she could say anything, he continued. "I tried to bring that family to God, and do you know what I got for my caring? I was told to get off their property and to stay off if I couldn't leave my God at home."

You're lucky you didn't get bit, Vicki thought. "I bet that made you pretty mad."

"God is not something I carry around like a pocket-book, Ms. Nelson," he told her dryly. "He is a part of everything I do. Yes, it made me angry . . ."

Angry enough to kill? she wondered.

". . . but my anger was a righteous anger, and I gave it to the glory of the Lord."

"And what did the Lord do with it?"

He half turned toward her and smiled. "He put it to work in His service."

Now that *could mean any number of things.* Vicki stared out the window. *How* do *you bring up the subject of werewolves?* "Your nephew mentioned that you're a birder. . . ."

"When I can spare time away from the garden."

"Ever go into the conservation area?"

"On occasion."

"I have a cousin who's a birder." She had nothing of the sort; it was a textbook interrogation lie. "He tells me you can see all sorts of fascinating things out in the woods. He says the unusual and bizarre lurk around every corner."

"Does he? His list must be interesting then."

"What's the most interesting species you've ever identified?"

Gray brows drew down. "I had an Arctic tern once. No idea how it got so far south. I prayed for its safe flight home and as I only saw it the once, I like to think my prayers were answered."

"An Arctic tern?"

"That," he told her without taking his eyes off the road, "was exactly the reaction of the others I told. I never lie, Ms. Nelson. And I never give anyone a chance to call me a liar twice."

She felt as though he'd just slapped her on the wrist. "Sorry." *Well, that got me exactly nowhere.*

"Looks like good hunting out here," she said casually, peering out the car window, watching trees and fields, and more trees and more fields go by. "Do you hunt?"

"No." The single syllable held such abhorrence, such strength of emotion, Vicki had to believe it. "Taking the lives of God's creatures is an abomination."

She squirmed around to face him, wondering how he'd rationalize his diet. "You don't eat meat?"

"Not since 1954."

"Oh." His point. "What about your nephew?"

"In my house he follows my rules. I don't try to run the rest of his life."

Nor do you approve of the rest of his life, Vicki realized. "Has he been staying with you long?"

"No." Then he added, "Mark is my late sister's son. My only living relative."

Which explains why you let the slimebag stay around at all. She sensed his disapproval, but whether it was directed at her or at Mark she couldn't say. "I've, uh, never hunted," she told him, attempting to get back into his good graces. Technically it was the truth. She'd never hunted anything that ran on four legs.

"Good for you. Do you pray?"

"Probably not as much as I should."

That startled him into a smile. "Probably not," he agreed and pulled over at the end of the long lane leading to the Heerkens farm. "If you'll excuse me, this is as far as I can take you."

"Excuse you? You've saved me a long hot walk, I'm in your debt." She slid out of the car and with one finger holding her glasses, leaned back in through the open window. "Thanks for the ride. And the water. And the chance to see your garden."

He nodded solemnly. "You're welcome. Can I convince you to join me at worship tomorrow, Ms. Nelson?"

"No, I don't think so."

"Very well." He seemed resigned. "Be careful, Ms. Nelson; if you endanger your soul you endanger your chance of eternal life."

Vicki could feel his sincerity, knew he wasn't just saying the words, so she nodded and said, "I'll be careful," and stepped back onto the shoulder. She waited where she was until he maneuvered the big car around in a tight three point turn then shifted the weight of her bag on her shoulder, waved, and started toward the lane.

Which was when she saw Storm emerge from the hedgerow about a hundred meters down the road.

Tongue lolling, he trotted toward her, sunlight shimmering in the golden highlights of his fur.

Tires growled against gravel, the big sedan picked up speed, and headed right for the young wer.

Vicki tried to yell—to Storm, to Carl, she wasn't sure—but all that came out of a mouth gone suddenly dry was a strangled croak.

Then, in a spray of dirt and small stones, it was over.

Carl Biehn, his car, and his God, disappeared down the road and Storm danced a welcome around her.

As her heart started beating again, Vicki settled her glasses back on her nose, her free hand absently rubbing the warm fur between Storm's ears. She could have sworn. . . . *I must've got just a little too much sun.*

Finding nothing to interest him in the highly overrated great outdoors, Mark Williams wandered back into the house and pulled a cold beer out of the fridge. "Thank God dear Uncle Carl has nothing against 'alcohol in moderation.' " He laughed and repeated, "Thank God." Hopefully, that blonde bitch was getting an earful of peace and love and the rest of that religious crap from the crazy old coot.

She hadn't been his type anyway. He liked his women smaller, more complacent, willing to be overwhelmed. The kind he could be sure wouldn't go screaming to the police over every little bending of the rules.

"What I like is the kind of woman that doesn't land me in the middle of goddamned nowhere." He took a long swallow of beer and looked out the kitchen window at the fields shimmering in the heat. "Shit." He sighed. "This is all Annette's fault."

If Annette hadn't been ready to blow the sweet little operation he'd been running out of Vancouver, he wouldn't have had to have her killed so quickly that he'd had to hire professional help, and sloppy professional help at that. He shuddered to think of how close he'd come to spending his most productive years behind bars. Fortunately, he'd been able to arrange it so that the hired help had ended up taking the fall. He'd barely been able to close down the business, realize most of the projected profits, and get out of the province before the hired help's family had arrived to demand their share.

"And thus I find myself in the ass-end of civilization." He finished the beer and yawned. It could've been worse; the nights, at least, offered rare sport. Grinning, he tossed the empty into the case. Last night's bit of fun had proven his skills were still as sharp as they'd ever been.

A second yawn threatened to dislocate his jaw. He'd been up until the wee small hours of the morning and been awakened obscenely early. Maybe he should head upstairs for a nap. "Don't want the fingers trembling at a critical moment. Besides," he grabbed another beer to take with him, "there's bugger all else to do until dark."

When an overgrown lilac hedge blocked the line of sight from the road, Vicki silently handed Peter his shorts.

"Thanks. What were you doing with old man Biehn?"

"I came out of the woods on his property." It certainly wasn't going to hurt anything if Peter believed she'd chosen her direction on purpose. "He gave me a ride back."

"Oh. Good thing Uncle Stuart didn't see him."

"Your uncle really ran him off?"

"Oh yeah, and if Aunt Nadine hadn't stopped him, he'd have probably attacked."

Vicki felt her brows go up and she turned her head to look at Peter directly. She gotten used to the disembodied voices of the people walking beside her but occasionally she just had to see expressions. "He'd have attacked over a difference in religion?"

"Is that what old man Biehn said?" Peter snorted. "Jennifer and Marie were six, maybe seven, and Aunt Nadine was pregnant with Daniel. Old man Biehn came over—he dropped by pretty often back then, trying to save our souls, and it was driving us all nuts—and he started talking about hell. I don't know what he said 'cause I wasn't there, but he really scared the girls and they started to howl." Peter's brows drew down and his ears went back. "You don't do that to cubs. Anyway,

Uncle Stuart showed up and that was that. He's never come back."

"He was pretty angry about it," Vicki offered.

"Not as angry as Uncle Stuart."

"But you must see him occasionally. . . ."

Peter looked confused. "Why?"

Vicki thought about that for a moment. *Why, indeed?* She hadn't seen the two young men who lived in the back basement apartment of her building since the day they'd moved in. If in almost three years she hadn't run into them in the hallway, by the only door. . . . *Well, the odds are good you can miss someone indefinitely out here in all this space.* "Never mind."

He shrugged, the fine spray of red-gold hair on his chest glinting in the sun. "Okay."

They'd come to the end of lane and Vicki leaned gracefully against the huge tree that anchored it to the lawn. Mopping her dripping brow, she opened her mouth to ask where everyone was when Peter threw back his head and ran his voice wordlessly up and down a double octave.

"Rose wants to tell you something," he said by way of explanation.

Rose wanted to tell her about Frederick Kleinbein.

"I think she's imagining things," Peter volunteered after his sister finished talking. "What do you think, Ms. Nelson?"

"I think," Vicki told them, "that I'd better go speak to Mr. Kleinbein." She didn't add that she doubted the tree's falling at that time and in such a way had been entirely natural. Off the top of her head, she could think of at least two ways it could be done without leaving a scent for the wer to trace. Had Peter actually left the car, she was pretty certain he'd have returned to find his twin had been shot the same way as Silver and Ebon. Which meant the assassin's pattern wasn't tied to that tree in the woods. Which opened up a whole new can of worms.

Thank God for Frederick Kleinbein. His arrival had no doubt saved Cloud's life and, simultaneously, removed him from the suspect list.

All things considered though, she thought she'd better have a talk with him anyway.

Rose shot a triumphant look at her brother. "He lives just back of the crossroads. I can tell you how to get there if you want to take Henry's car."

"Henry's car?"

"Yeah. It's about three and a half miles, maybe a bit more. It's easy enough for four legs but a bit of a hike for two."

Peter leaned forward, nostrils flared. "What's wrong?"

Nothing's wrong. But, just as I suspected, I'm piss useless out here. You see, I can't. See that is. And I can't drive. How the hell am I supposed to do anything and what the hell can I tell you. . . .

She jumped as Rose reached out and stroked her arm, callused fingers lightly running over sweaty skin. She realized the touch was for comfort, not pity, and stopped herself from jerking the arm away.

"I don't drive," she told them, her voice hard-edged to keep it from shaking. "I can't see well enough."

"Oh, is that all." Peter leaned back relieved. "No problem. We'll drive you. I'll just go get the keys." He flashed her a dazzling grin and loped off to the house.

Oh, is that all? Vicki watched Peter disappear into the kitchen then turned to look at Rose, who smiled, pleased that the problem had been solved. *Don't judge them by human standards.* The phrase was rapidly becoming a litany.

". . . anyway, Uncle Stuart says that if you want the wood, it's yours."

"Good, good. You tell your uncle, I get it when heat breaks." Frederick Kleinbein swiped at his dripping face with the palm of one beefy hand. "So, I have late raspberries that rot because I am too fat and lazy to pick; you interested?"

The twins turned to Vicki, who shrugged. "Just don't ask me to help. I'll stay here in the shade and talk to Mr. Kleinbein." And as Mr. Kleinbein very obviously wanted to talk to her. . . .

"So," he began a moment later, "you are visiting from the city. You know Heerkens for long?"

"Not long at all. I'm a friend of a friend. Do you know them well?"

"Not what you call well. No." He glanced over to where Rose and Peter were barely visible behind a thick row of raspberry canes. "They keep apart that family. Not unfriendly, distant."

"And people respect that?"

"Why not? Farm is paid for. Kids go to school." The finger he waggled in her direction looked like a half cooked sausage. "No law says got to be party animals."

Vicki hid a smile. Party animals—now that was a concept.

He leaned forward, his whole bearing proclaiming he had a secret.

Here it comes, Vicki thought.

"You stay with them so you must know."

She shook her head, fighting to keep her expression vaguely confused. "Know what?"

"The Heerkens . . ."

"Yes?"

". . . the whole family . . ."

She leaned forward herself.

Their noses were practically touching.

". . . nudists."

Vicki blinked and sat back, momentarily speechless.

Frederick Kleinbein sat back as well and nodded sagely, his jowls bobbing an independent emphasis. "They must keep clothes on for you so far." Then his entire face curved upward in a beatific smile. "Too bad, eh?"

"How do you know this?" Vicki managed at last.

The sausage finger waggled again. "I see things. Little things. Careful people, the Heerkens, but sometimes there are glimpses of bodies. That's why the big dogs, to warn them to put on clothes when people come." He shrugged. "Everyone knows. Most peoples, they say bodies are bad and go out of way to avoid Heerkens but me, I say who cares what they do on own land." He waved a hand at the raspberry bushes. "Kids are happy.

What else matters? Besides," this time the smile came accompanied by a decidedly lascivious waggling of impressive eyebrows, "they are very nice bodies."

Vicki had to agree. So the surrounding countryside thought the Heerkens were nudists, did it? She doubted they'd have been able to deliberately create a more perfect camouflage. What people believe defines what people see, and people looking for flesh were not likely to find fur.

And it's a hell of a lot easier to believe in a nudist than a werewolf.

Except that someone, she reminded herself, feeling the weight of the second silver bullet dragging at her bag, *isn't following the party line.*

Although his nephew's jeep was still in the driveway, Mark himself appeared to be nowhere around. Carl sat down at the kitchen table and leaned his head in his hands, thankful for the time alone. The boy was his only sister's only son, flesh of his flesh, blood of his blood, and the only family he had remaining. Family must be more important then personal opinion.

Was it a sin, he wondered, that he couldn't find it in his heart to care for Mark? That he didn't even like him very much?

Carl suspected he was being used as a refuge of some sort. Why else would this nephew he hadn't seen in years suddenly appear on his doorstep for an indefinite stay? The boy—the man—was a sinner, there was no doubt about that. But he was also family and that fact had to outweigh the other.

Perhaps the Lord had sent Mark here, at this time, to be saved. Carl sighed and rubbed at a coffee ring on the table with his thumb. He was an old man and the Lord had asked a great deal of him lately.

Should I ask Mark where he goes at night?

Do I have the strength to know?

Seven

"These are our south fields, this is the conservation area, Mr. Kleinbein lives here, and here's old man Biehn's place." Peter squinted down at his sketch, then dragged another three lines into the dirt. "These are the roads."

"The Old School Road's crooked," Rose pointed out, leaning over his shoulder.

"There's a rock in the way."

"So do it here . . ." She suited the action to the words, smoothing her palm over his road and drawing in a new one with her fingertip. ". . . and you avoid the rock."

Peter snorted. "Then it's at the wrong angle."

"Not really. It still goes from the corner down. . . ."

"Down the wrong way," her brother interrupted.

"Does not!"

"Does so!"

They both had lips and fingers stained with berry juices and Vicki marveled at how easily they could switch from adults to children and back again. She'd decided on the drive back from Mr. Kleinbein's—who had parted from her with a "wink, wink, nudge, nudge" adjuration to keep her eyes open—not to tell them about the local belief that they were nudists. She hadn't quite decided whether or nor she was going to mention it to their Uncle Stuart; mostly because she doubted he'd care.

"You've got to bring the crossroads up here!"

"Do not."

"Do so!"

"It doesn't matter," Vicki told them, stopping the argument cold. The wer, she'd realized while watching them draw the neighborhood on a bald patch of lawn, had very little sense of mapping. Although they probably knew every bush and every fence post on their own territory, the dimensions Peter had drawn were not the dimensions Vicki remembered. She frowned and pushed her glasses back up her nose. "As near as I can tell, here's the tree. And here's where I ended up coming out of the woods."

"But *why* didn't you just follow your back trail?" Rose asked, still confused on that point despite explanations.

Vicki sighed. The wer also had a little trouble dealing with the concept of *getting lost*.

Before they could reopen the subject of noses, a small black head shoved itself under Vicki's hand as Shadow crept forward, trying to get a better look at what was going on.

Peter grabbed him by the scruff of the neck and hauled him back. "Get out of there you, you'll mess it up."

"No, it's all right." Vicki stood, dusting off the seat of her shorts. The grass on the lawn was sparse and bare, so dusty patches were common. "I think I've seen as much as I can here." She should be inside making phone calls; this really wasn't helping.

Shadow squirmed in his cousin's grasp and, when Peter released him, turned into a very excited small boy. "Show Vicki your trick, Peter!"

Under his tan, Peter turned a little red. "I don't think she wants to see it, kiddo."

"Yes she does!" Daniel bounced over to Vicki. "You do, don't you?"

She didn't, but how could she say no in the face of such determined enthusiasm? "Sure I do."

He bounced back over to Peter. "See!"

Peter sighed and surrendered. "All right," he reached out and tugged at the lock of hair falling into Daniel's eyes. "Go and get it."

Barking shrilly, Shadow raced off to the front of the house.

"Is he talking when he does that?" Vicki wondered aloud.

"Not really." Rose's ears pricked forward toward the sound. "Fur-form noises are kind of emoting out loud."

"So Shadow's barking translates into 'Oh boy! Oh boy! Oh boy'?"

The twins looked at each other and laughed. "Close enough," Rose admitted.

Shadow raced back silently, but only, Vicki suspected, because the huge yellow frisbee he carried made barking impossible. He dropped it at Peter's feet—it looked more than a little chewed—and sat back, panting expectantly.

Peter skimmed out of his shorts and scooped up the plastic disk. "You ready?" he asked.

The entire back end of Shadow's body wagged.

Looking not unlike an ancient Greek discus thrower, Peter whipped the frisbee into the air. Shadow took off after it and a heartbeat later so did Storm. Muscles rippling under his russet coat, he raced past the smaller wer, drew his hindquarters under and flung himself into the air, jaws spread, ready to clamp his teeth down on the rim of the disk.

Only to have it snatched out of his grasp by a larger black wer who hit the ground running with both Storm and Shadow in hot pursuit.

Rose giggled, thrust her sundress into Vicki's hands and Cloud took off after them. They raced around the yard for a moment or two then, working as a team, Cloud and Storm cut the larger wer off and jumped it. Shadow, still barking whenever he managed to find a spare breath, threw himself on the mix of tumbling bodies.

A moment later, Nadine looked up out of the pile of multicolored fur, tossed the frisbee to one side and grinned at Vicki. "So, you about ready for lunch?"

"We found tracks, not five hundred yards from the house." The words were almost an unintelligible growl. The silence that followed them took only a few seconds to fill with answering anger.

Nadine crossed the kitchen and clutched at her mate's arm. "Whose?" she demanded. "Whose tracks?"

"We don't know."

"But the scent. . . ."

"Garlic. The trail reeks of nothing but garlic."

"How old?" Peter wanted to know.

"Twelve hours. Maybe a little more. Maybe a little less." Stuart's hair was up and he couldn't remain still, pacing back and forth with jerky steps.

If Ebon had been shot from that tree in the woods, as all evidence seemed to suggest he had, five hundred yards and twelve hours meant the assassin had come within range of the house sometime last night.

"Maybe you'd all better stay at a hotel, in town, until this is over," Vicki suggested, knowing even as the words left her mouth what the reaction was going to be.

"No!" Stuart snapped, turning on her. "This is our territory and we will defend it!"

"He's not after your territory," Vicki pointed out, her own voice rising. "He's after your lives! Take them out of his range, just for a time. It's the only sensible thing to do!"

"We will not run."

"But if he can get that close, you can't protect yourselves from him."

Stuart's eyes narrowed and his words were nearly lost in his snarl. "It will not happen again."

"How do you propose to stop it?" This was worse than arguing with Celluci.

"We will guard. . . ."

"You haven't *been* guarding!"

"He has not been on our territory before!"

Vicki took a deep breath. This was getting nowhere fast. "At least send the children away."

"NO!"

Stuart's response was explosive and Vicki turned to Nadine for help. Surely *she'd* understand the necessity of sending the children to safety.

"The children must stay within the safety of the pack." Nadine held a solemn looking Daniel very tightly, one hand stroking his hair. Daniel, in turn, held tight to his mother.

"This coward with a gun does not run this pack." Stuart yanked his chair out from the table and threw himself down on it. "And his actions will not rule this pack. We will live as we live." He jabbed his finger at Vicki. "You will find him!"

He wasn't angry at her, Vicki realized, but at himself, at his perceived failure to protect his family. Even so, the heat of his gaze forced her to look away. "I will find him," she said, trying not to resent the strength of his rage. *Let's just hope I find him in time.*

Lunch began as an assault; meat ripped and torn between gleaming teeth, an obvious surrogate for an enemy's throat. Fortunately for Vicki's piece of mind, things calmed down fairly quickly, the wer—especially the younger wer—being incapable of sustaining a mood for any length of time when distracted by the more immediate concerns of who forgot to take the butter out of the fridge and just where exactly was the salt.

The entire family ate in human form, more or less in human style.

"It makes it easier on the kids when they go back to school," Nadine explained, putting Daniel's fork into his hand and suggesting that he use it.

The cold mutton accompanying the salad was greasy and not particularly palatable, but Vicki was so relieved it was cooked that she ate it gladly.

"Ms. Nelson went to see Carl Biehn this morning," Peter announced suddenly.

"Carl Biehn?" Donald glanced over at Stuart, whose ears had gone back again, then at Vicki. "Why?"

"It's important I talk to the neighbors," Vicki explained, shooting a look of her own at the dominant male. "I need to know what they might have seen."

"He hasn't been around here for years," Nadine said emphatically. "Not since Stuart ran him off for frightening the girls. Jennifer had nightmares about his *God* for months."

Stuart snorted. "God. He wouldn't know a real God if it bit him on the butt. Old fool's a grasseater."

Vicki blinked. "What?"

"Vegetarian," Rose translated.

"Did he tell you that?"

"Didn't have to." Stuart cracked a bone and sucked out the marrow. "He smells like a grasseater."

Donald tossed a heel of bread onto the table and dusted his hands off against his bare thighs. "He stopped me in town once and pointed out the evils of giving life to animals only to kill them."

"He did it to me once too but I pointed out that killing animals was easier than eating them alive." Peter tossed a radish up into the air, caught it between his teeth, and crunched down with the maximum possible noise.

"Like majorly gross, Peter!" Jennifer made a disgusted face at her cousin, who only grinned and continued devouring his lunch.

"You don't think it's old man Biehn, do you, Vicki?" Rose asked quietly, pitching her voice under the general noise level around the table.

Did she? Living so close, Carl Biehn had opportunity to both accidentally discover the wers' secret and access the tree the shots had come from. He was in good physical condition for a man his age and deeply held religious beliefs were historically a tried and true motive for murder. He had, however, expressed an abhorrence for killing that Vicki believed and, besides a sneaker tread he shared with all and sundry, no evidence linked him to the crimes. The fact that she'd liked him, as subjective as that was, had to be considered. Good cops develop a sensitivity to certain personality types that, no matter how carefully hidden, set off subconscious alarms. Carl Biehn seemed like a decent human being and they were rare.

On the other hand, the next likeliest suspect was a police officer and Vicki didn't want to believe that Barry Wu was responsible. She glanced down the table at Colin who, while larger than his uncle and father, was

still a small, wiry man and probably wouldn't have made
the force under the old size requirements. He looked
like someone had a knife in his heart and was slowly
twisting the blade. He hadn't said two words since he'd
sat down.

Did she think it was old man Biehn? No. Nor did
she want to think it was Colin's partner. Nor could she
completely rule either of them out, not until the murderer was found. A great many people had access to the
woods, however, and in spite of the statistics, the most
obvious suspects didn't always turn out to be guilty.

She turned back to Rose, waiting predator patient for
an answer.

"Until I get more information, I have to suspect everyone, Rose, even Mr. Kleinbein. This is too important
not to."

Having cleared the table of anything remotely like
food, the wer were rising and going their separate ways.
Donald had already changed, padded out to the porch,
and collapsed in a dark triangle of shade. Shadow, with
permission from his mother, had taken a bone into a
corner and, holding it between his front paws, was chewing it into submission.

Vicki stood as Colin did, but he turned and headed
out of the kitchen without acknowledging her in any
way.

"Colin!" Even Vicki stiffened at the command in Stuart's voice and Colin stopped dead, shoulders hunched.
"Vicki wants to talk to you."

Slowly, Colin turned, canines gleaming.

"Colin. . . ." The name was a growl, low and
menacing.

The younger wer hesitated for a moment, then his
shoulders dropped and a curt motion of his head indicated Vicki should follow him.

It was far from gracious, but it would have to do. She
fell into step behind him as he started up the stairs.

"It's too hot to walk outside, so we'll talk in my
room," he said without turning. "Then the kids won't
interrupt."

Vicki wasn't so sure of that, given the wer sense of privacy but, if it made Colin more comfortable, they could talk on the roof for all she cared.

His room was one of three in the addition built on over the woodshed and the door next to his was the first closed door Vicki had seen in the house.

"Henry," Colin said by way of explanation as they passed. "He bolts it from the inside."

"It's not a bedroom. . . ."

"No. It's a storage closet. But it doesn't have a window, and if we shuffle stuff around there's room for a cot."

Vicki brushed her palm over the dark wood and wondered if Henry could sense her in the hallway. Wondered what it was like, lying there in the dark.

"I haven't seen the sun in over four hundred years."

She sighed and entered Colin's room. He threw himself down on the bed, fingers laced behind his head, watching her through narrowed eyes. Despite the outwardly relaxed position, every muscle in his body hummed with tension, ready for fight or flight. Vicki wasn't sure which, nor did she want to find out.

"I used to get the laundry to do mine, too," she told him, nodding at the half dozen clean uniform shirts hanging on the closet door, still in their plastic bags. Pushing a pair of sweatpants off a wooden chair, she sat down. "I had better things to do with my time than iron.

"So," she leaned forward, elbows resting on her knees, "do you think your partner did it?" Colin's eyes narrowed further and his lips drew back but before he could move she added matter-of-factly, "Or do you want to help me prove he didn't?"

Slowly, his eyes never leaving her face, Colin sat up. Vicki accepted his puzzled scrutiny with her blandest expression and waited. The next line was his.

"You don't think Barry did it," he said at last.

"I didn't say that." She rested her chin on her folded hands. "But I don't *want* to believe he did it and you're the best person to prove he didn't. For Chrissakes, Colin, start thinking like a cop, not a . . . a sheepdog." He flinched. "Did he have the opportunity?"

For a moment she wasn't sure he was going to answer her, then he mirrored her position on the edge of the bed and sighed. "Yeah. We were working days both times it happened. He knows the farm and he knows the conservation area. We got off at eleven last night and he could have easily come out here after shift and made those tracks."

"Okay, that's one against, and we know he has the skill. . . ."

"He's going to the next Olympics, he's that good. But if he's casting silver bullets I couldn't find any evidence of it and, believe me, I looked."

"Does he have a motive?"

Colin shook his head. "How should I know? If he's doing it, maybe he's crazy."

"Is he?"

"Is he what?"

"Crazy? You spend eight hours a day with the man. If he's crazy, you should have noticed something." She rolled her eyes at his bewildered expression and used her voice like a club. "Think, damn it! Use your training!"

Colin's ears went back and his breathing sped up but he held himself in check and Vicki could actually see him thinking about it. She was impressed by his control. If a stranger had used that tone on her, she'd have probably done something stupid.

After a moment, he frowned. "I wouldn't swear to this in court," he said slowly, "but I'd bet my life on his sanity."

"You are betting your life on his sanity," Vicki pointed out dryly, "every time you walk out of the station with him. Now we've settled that, why don't we concentrate on proving he *didn't* do it."

"But. . . ."

"But what?" Vicki snapped, getting a little tired of Colin's attitude. She recognized that he was in a terrible position, torn between his family and his partner, but that was no reason to shut off his brain. "Just tell me about the man."

"We, uh, we were at the Police College together." He ran his hands through his hair, the cropped cut accentuating the point of both chin and ears. "I wouldn't even be a cop if it wasn't for Barry, and I guess he wouldn't be one if it wasn't for me. He was the only 'visible ethnic minority' cadet there and I was, well, what I am. We ended up together to survive. When we graduated, we managed to stay together—well, mostly, it's not like we're mated or anything. . . ."

Vicki wasn't surprised by Barry's philosophical reaction to his partner's actual race. In the "us against them" attitude that the job forced police officers to develop, finding out that one of "us" was a werewolf could be dealt with, at least on an individual basis. *Can I depend on my partner to back me up?* was the crucial question, not, *Does my partner bay at the moon?* And now that she thought about it, Vicki had known a number of cops who bayed at the moon.

". . . and the night I got shot. . . ."

"Wait a minute, you what?"

Colin shrugged it off. "We surprised a couple of punks during a holdup. They came out shooting. I took a slug in the leg. It was nothing."

"Wrong. Very wrong." Vicki grinned. "Barry was there?"

"Course he was."

"He saw you bleed?"

"Yeah."

"You probably talked later about dying, about how you thought you were going to be killed?"

"Yeah, but. . . ."

"Why would Barry shoot at the wer with silver bullets—expensive rounds that he'd have to make himself, risking discovery—when he knows that good old lead will do the job?"

"To throw us off his trail?"

"Colin!" Vicki threw her hands up. "That would take a crazy person and you've already told me Barry is sane. Trust your instincts. At least when you've got enough facts to back them up."

Colin opened his mouth, closed it, and then shuddered as if a great weight had been lifted off of him. He leapt to his feet, threw back his head, and howled.

Vicki, who had pretty much forgotten that he was naked, found herself suddenly made very aware of it. The wer might react sexually to scent and therefore not react at all to humans, but humans had a visually based libido and Vicki's had just belted her in the crotch.

Oh, lord, why me? she thought as huge black paws came down on her shoulders and a large pink tongue swept vigorously across her face.

After Colin had galloped off to confront his pack leader—he needed Stuart's permission to finally speak to Barry about what had been going on—Vicki spent the early part of the afternoon on the phone, confirming that the game warden had, indeed, been up north since the beginning of August and had, in fact, been there on the two nights of the murders, his location supported by a bar full of witnesses. That done, and his name crossed off her list, she changed her clothes and had Rose and Peter drive her into London.

Storm spent the entire trip with his head out the window, mouth open, eyes slitted against the wind, ears flat against his skull.

The membership lists of both bird-watching clubs were relatively easy to get. She merely showed the presidents of each her identification and told them she'd been hired to find a distant relative of a very rich man.

"All I have to go on is that they once lived in the London area and enjoyed bird-watching. There's a great deal of money involved if I find them."

"But are you looking for a man or a woman?"

"I don't know," Vicki looked peeved. *"He's lost almost all his marbles and that's all he can remember. Oh, yes, he mumbled something about this relative being a marksman."*

Neither president rose to the bait. If the killer was one of the birders, he or she hadn't mentioned his or her interest in firearms to the executive of either club.

"You don't *have a third cousin named Anthony Carmaletti, do you?"* Vicki crossed her fingers as she asked. If either of them *did* have a third cousin named Anthony Carmaletti it was going to blow her rich, dying relative story right out of the water.

She received one definite no with a twenty minute

lecture on genealogy, one "I'll ask my mother, can you get back to me tomorrow?" from an octogenarian, and both lists. *And Celluci says I'm a lousy liar. Ha.*

"Now what?" Rose asked as she got back into the car after the second stop.

"Now, I need the membership list of the photography club, but I doubt the YMCA will just hand it over, and I need the OPP list of registered firearms, which should be a little easier to get . . ." Cops tended to cooperate with their own. ". . . but right at the moment, I need to talk to Dr. Dixon."

First impressions said Dr. Dixon could not have been the killer. He was a frail old man who wouldn't have made it to the tree, let alone climbed it carrying a high-powered rifle and scope.

They had a short but pleasant visit. Dr. Dixon told Vicki embarrassing stories about Rose and Peter when they were children, which the twins paid no attention to as they were busy in the next room decimating his record collection.

"Opera," the doctor explained when Vicki wondered what was going on. "Every wer I've ever met is crazy about it."

"Every wer?" Vicki asked.

"Every wer *I've* met," he reiterated. "Stuart's old pack in Vermont prefers Italian, but they're close enough to civilization they can afford to be picky. Most of the rest, at least in Canada, particularly the pack just by Algonquin Park and the lot up by Mooseane, are glued to the CBC Sunday afternoons."

"How many packs are there?"

"Well, I just mentioned four, and there's at least two up in the Yukon, one in northern Manitoba. . . ." He frowned. "How the hell should I know? Enough for genetic diversity. Although at some point they seem to have inbred for opera. Can't get enough. I lend this lot records and," he raised his voice, "occasionally they bring them back."

"Next time, Dr. Dixon," Peter called. "We promise."

"Sure you will," he muttered. "If that damned pup's been chewing on them again I'll. . . ."

"Scratch him behind the ears and tell him he's adorable," Rose finished, coming into the room with a half dozen albums under her arm, "just like you always do."

While they were leaving, Vicki paused on the front step and watched Storm race across the lawn after a butterfly.

"What happens when you die?" she asked the doctor.

He snorted. "I rot. Why?"

"I mean, what happens to them? They won't stop needing a doctor just because you're gone."

"When the time is right, I'll tell the young doctor who took over my practice." He laughed suddenly. "She grew up not knowing if she wanted to be a vet or a GP. The wer should be right up her alley."

"Don't wait too long," Vicki warned.

"Don't stick that investigating nose of yours in where it doesn't belong," Dr. Dixon shot back. "I've known the Heerkens family for years, longer than you've been alive. I have no intention of dropping dead and leaving them to face the world alone."

"They *won't* be alone."

He grinned at her defensive tone, but his voice was soft as he said, "No, I don't suppose they will be."

Jennifer and Marie didn't bother coming in for dinner.

"They shared a rabbit about an hour ago," Nadine explained, smiling fondly, sadly, out the window at them. They were curled so tightly around each other that it was difficult to see where one fur-form ended and the other began.

Colin had long since left for work so only the seven of them sat down at the table. Daniel did his best to make up for the missing three.

After dinner, Vicki worked on her notes—impressions of Carl Biehn, Frederick Kleinbein, the birders, the doctor, the new set of tracks—and then she just sat, attempting to put the day and the day's discoveries in order. Order kept escaping her, she had a number of bits and pieces but nothing that definitely fit into the pattern. The opera in the background wasn't a lot of help and the weird harmonics added by her hosts could only be called distracting.

Actually, Vicki could think of a number of other things to call them, but she went to the pond to watch Shadow hunt frogs instead. Under the circumstances, it seemed safer—not only for Shadow but for herself as well.

"Don't let him eat too many," Nadine called over the music as they left, "or he'll make himself sick."

"I'm not at all surprised," Vicki muttered, but she ended up letting him eat both frogs he caught. He'd worked so hard at it, bounding this way and that, barking hysterically, that she felt he deserved them.

Back at the house, dusk seemed to stretch for hours, the crickets and Pavarotti singing duets to the setting sun. Vicki's vision dimmed and the sound of the wind moving in the trees became the sound of death quietly approaching the house: the tap of two twigs, a rifle bolt drawn back. She knew she was allowing her imagination to overrule common sense even while she waited for the gunshot that would tell her it wasn't imagination at all. Finally, the darkness drove her to the kitchen table where the hanging bulb surrounded her with a hard edged circle of sight.

At last, Donald lifted his head and, nostrils flaring, announced, "Henry's up."

Vicki pulled her glasses off and rubbed at her eyes. It was about time. *You know it's been a strange day,* she mused, *when you're looking forward to the arrival of the bloodsucking undead.*

Eight

Usually, when he awoke in a place other than his carefully shielded sanctuary, there would be a moment of near panic while memory fought to reestablish itself. Tonight, he knew even before full consciousness returned, for the unmistakable scent of the wer saturated his tiny chamber.

He stretched and lay still for a moment, senses extended until they touched Vicki's life. The hunger rose to pulse in time with her heartbeat. He would feed tonight.

As Henry made his way downstairs, Mozart's *Don Giovanni* filled the old farmhouse and, he suspected, a good portion of the surrounding countryside. Stereo systems had been one piece of human culture the wer had embraced wholeheartedly. Henry winced as a descant Mozart could never have imagined soared up and over and around the recorded soprano.

Oh, well, I suppose it could be worse. He braced himself against Shadow's enthusiastic welcome. *It could be New Kids on the Block.*

With one hand fondling Shadow's ears, Henry paused on the kitchen's threshold, allowing his eyes to become accustomed to the light. He half expected to see Vicki seated at the table, but the room was empty save for Donald who sat, feet up, watching Jennifer and Marie work their way through a sink full of dishes. Seconds later, this simple domestic scene shattered as Shadow bounded forward and shoved a cold, wet nose against the back of Marie's bare legs. A plate hit the floor, bounced, and lay there forgotten as both twins chased their younger brother out of the house.

"Evening," Donald grunted as Henry bent to pick up the plate. "Don't suppose you know any opera singers?"

He'd known an opera dancer once, almost two hundred years ago, but that wasn't quite the same thing. "Sorry, no. Why?"

"Thought if you knew one, you could bring her out." Donald waved an arm in the air, the gesture encompassing *Don Giovanni*. "Be nice to hear this stuff live for a change."

Henry was about to point out that Toronto wasn't that long a drive and that the Royal Canadian Opera Company, while not Vienna, definitely had its moments when he had a sudden vision of wer at the theater and blanched. "Where is everyone?" he asked instead.

"Tag and Sky . . ."

Stuart and Nadine, Henry translated.

". . . are out hunting, in spite of protests from your Ms. Nelson. You saw the exit of the terrible trio. Colin is at work, and my other two are . . ."

The descant rose above the tenor solo, wrapping the notes almost sideways to each other.

". . . in the living room with their heads between the speakers. They got a couple of old recordings from the doctor today, obscure companies that aren't out yet on CD." He scratched at the mat of red hair on his chest and frowned. "Personally, I think the tenor is a little sharp."

"Why the doctor? Was someone hurt?"

"Everyone is fine." Vicki's voice came from behind him, from the door leading to the bathroom, and her tone added, *so far.* Henry turned as she continued. "I needed to talk to him to make sure he wasn't the killer."

"And are you sure?"

"Quite. It's not him, it's not Colin's partner, and it's not the game warden. Unfortunately, at least another thirty-seven people regularly go wandering through the woods with high-powered binoculars and it could be any one of them. Not to mention an unknown number of nature photographers whose names I don't have yet."

Henry raised a brow and smiled. "Sounds like you've had a productive day."

Vicki snorted. "I've had a day," she amended, shoving her glasses back up her nose. "I'm not really any closer to finding out who *did* do it. And Stuart and Nadine have gone for a little nocturnal hike." Her opinion of that dripped off her voice.

"They're hunters, they. . . ."

"They can hunt at the local supermarket until this is over," she snapped. "Like the rest of us."

"They aren't like the rest of us," Henry reminded her. "You can't judge them by. . . ."

"Leave it! I've had just about as much of that observation as I can take." She sighed at his expression and shook her head. "I'm sorry. I'm just a little frustrated by illogical behavior. Can we go somewhere and talk?"

"Outside?"

She scowled. "It's dark, I won't be able to see, and besides, outside is crawling with bugs. What about my room?"

"What about mine?" While it wasn't large, his was the only room in the house with a door that could be bolted from the inside. If they began in his room, they wouldn't have to move later when it came time to feed. He felt her blood calling him and the plate he still held snapped between his hands. "Oh, hell. Donald, I'm sorry."

Donald only shrugged, a suspiciously knowing smile lurking around the edges of his mouth. "Don't worry about it. We're kinda hard on dishes around here anyway."

Giving thanks that his nature no longer allowed him to blush—his fair Tudor coloring had been the curse of his short life—Henry dropped both halves of the plate in the garbage and turned once again to Vicki. For a change, he found her expression unreadable. "Shall we?" he asked, taking refuge in formality.

Scalloped glass light fixtures illuminated the stairs and the upper hall in the original section of the house but the wer, who could see almost as well in the dark, hadn't bothered extending them down the hall of the addition.

Vicki swore and stopped dead at the edge of the twilight. "Maybe my room is better after all. . . ."

Henry tucked her arm in his and pulled her gently forward. "It isn't far," he said soothingly.

"Don't patronize me," she snapped. "I'm going blind, not senile."

But her fingers tightened against the bend of his elbow and Henry could feel the tension in her step.

The bare forty watt bulb hanging from the center of Henry's closet—it was gross exaggeration to call it a room—threw enough light for Vicki to see Henry's face but the piled junk held shadows layered upon shadows. Dragging his pillow up behind her back, she leaned against the far wall and watched him bolt the door.

He could scent the beginning of her desire.

Slowly, he turned, hunger rising.

"So." She kicked off her sandals and scratched at a mosquito bite. *Nothing like taking care of one itch to distract you from another.* "Sit down and I'll tell you about my day."

He sat. There wasn't much else he could do.

". . . and that's the suspect list as it stands right now."

"You really believe it could be one of these birdwatchers?"

"Or the photographers. Hell, I'd rather it was Carl Biehn or his slimy nephew than some lone hiker we'll never track down."

"You don't think it was Mr. Biehn."

"Get real. He's a nice guy." She sighed. "Course, I have been wrong before and I haven't taken him off the list. Mind you, at this point, I've only got three people who I have taken off the list."

"I don't believe that." Henry picked up the bare leg stretched out on the cot beside him and began kneading her calf, digging his thumbs deep behind the muscle and then rolling it between his palms.

After a half-hearted attempt to drag it out of his grip, Vicki left her leg where it was. "Believe what?"

"That you've been wrong before."

"Yeah. Well. It happens . . ." She had to swallow before she could answer. ". . . occasionally."

Henry knew he could have her now, she'd made her point and would be willing. More than willing—the tiny room all but vibrated to the pounding of her heart. He wrapped iron control around his hunger.

"So." Slapping her lightly on the bottom of the foot, he laid her leg aside. "What did you want me to do?"

Her eyes snapped open and her brows drew down.

Henry waited, his expression one of polite interest.

For a heartbeat, Vicki teetered between anger and amusement. Amusement won and she grinned.

"You can stake out that tree I found. What wind there is—and there's bugger all air moving that I can tell—has changed again so that it's off the fields. If someone shows up with a .30 caliber rifle waiting for a target, grab him and it's case over."

"All right." He began to rise, but she swung her leg across his lap, barring his way.

"Hold it right there . . . and don't raise that eyebrow at me. We keep this up much longer and we'll end up ripping each other's clothes off in the kitchen and embarrassing ourselves. I don't want that to happen, this is one of my favorite T-shirts. Now that we've both exhibited control over our baser natures, what do you say we call it a draw and get on with things?"

"Fair enough." He held out his hand, intending to scoop her up into his arms in the best romantic tradition, but instead found himself yanked down hard against her mouth.

They didn't rip the T-shirt, but they did stretch it a little.

At the end, he took control and when his teeth broke through the skin of her wrist, she cried out, digging the fingers of her free hand hard into his shoulder. She kept moving as he drank and only stilled as he licked the wound clean, the coagulant in his saliva sealing the tiny puncture.

"That was . . . amazing," she sighed a moment later, her breath warm against the top of his head.

"Thank you." The salty smell of her skin filled nose and throat and lungs. "I was pretty amazed myself." He squirmed around until he could see her face. "Tell me, do you always make love with your glasses on?"

She grinned and pushed them higher with an unsteady finger. "Only the first time. After that, I can rely on memory. And for some things, I have a phenomenal memory." She moved, just to feel him move against her. "Are you always this cool?"

"Lower body temperature. Do you mind?"

"It's August and we're in a closet with no ventilation. What do you think?" Her fingernails traced intricate patterns along his spine. "You feel great. This feels great."

"Feels great," he echoed, "but I've got to go." He said it gently, as he sat up, one hand trailing along the slick length of her body. "The nights are short and if you want me to solve this case for you. . . ."

"For the wer," she corrected, yawning, too mellow to react to his smart-ass comment. "Sure, go ahead, eat and run." She snatched her foot back, away from his grab, and watched him dress. "When can we do this again?"

"Not for a while. The blood has to renew."

"You couldn't have taken more than a few mouthfuls; how long is a while?"

Tucking his shirt into his jeans, he leaned down and kissed her, sucking for a moment on her lower lip. "We have lots of time."

"Maybe you do," she muttered, "but I'll be dead in sixty, seventy years tops and I don't want to waste any more of it."

Police Constable Barry Wu glanced over at his partner and wished he knew what the hell was going on. Whatever had been bothering Colin for the last few weeks, getting under his skin and twisting, bothered him no longer—which was great, a depressed werewolf was not the most pleasant companion in a patrol car—but Colin still wouldn't say what the problem had been and Barry didn't like that. If Colin was in some kind of trouble, he should be the first to know. They were partners, for

Chrissakes. "So." He peered up and down Fellner Avenue as they crossed the intersection; it looked quiet. "Everything's all right now?"

Colin sighed. "Like I told you at the beginning of shift, we're working on it. I'll tell you what's happening the moment Stuart releases me." Stuart had proven damned elusive this afternoon, but Colin had every intention of tracking the pack leader down the moment he got off shift and laying Vicki's conclusions before him. Now that loyalties no longer pulled him in two directions, the sooner he could talk this whole thing over with Barry the better.

"But it's about me?" Barry prodded.

"No, I told you, not anymore."

"But it *was* about me?"

"Listen, can you just trust me until tomorrow night? I swear, I'll be able to tell you everything by then."

"Tomorrow night?"

"Yeah."

Barry maneuvered the car around the corner onto Ashland Avenue; on hot summer nights, gangs of kids often hung out around the Arena and the police liked to keep an eye on the place. "All right, sheep-fucker. I can wait."

Colin's lip curled. "You're lucky you're driving."

Barry grinned. "I wouldn't have said it if I hadn't been. . . ."

Henry stood for a moment, staring into the woods, one hand resting on the top rail of the cedar fence. In high summer, the woods seethed with life, with hunters and hunted, far too many for him to separate one from the other. He sensed no human lives near but couldn't be sure if that was due to their absence or to the masking of the smaller lives around them.

Had it been a mistake to feed? he wondered. Hunger would have increased his sensitivity to the presence of blood. *Mind you,* he admitted, smiling at the memory of Vicki moving beneath him, *in the end, I don't think I had much choice.*

In the past, when he stayed with the wer for longer

than three days and it became imperative to feed, he'd drive into London for a couple of hours and hire a prostitute. He didn't mind paying occasionally—spread over time it was still cheaper than buying groceries. Upon a moment's reflection, he decided not to share that thought with Vicki.

The fence was barely a barrier, and a moment later he moved shadow silent through the trees, following the trail Vicki had laid that morning. A small creature crossed his path, then, catching the scent of so large a predator, froze, its heart beating like a trip-hammer. He heard it scurry away once he'd passed and wished it Godspeed; the odds were good it wouldn't survive the night. The wer had come this way, probably on the hunt, but not lately as the spoor had faded to hints and that only where the forest floor retained some dampness.

He ducked under a branch and plucked free a single golden-brown hair from the twig that had captured it. Vicki hadn't done too well in the woods, the evidence of that was all around him—a faint signature of her blood marked much of the trail. Coming as she did from a world of steel and glass, he supposed this was hardly surprising. Tucking the hair safely in his pocket, he continued along her path, allowing his mind to wander with her memory while he walked.

He hadn't intended to come out tonight, but he hadn't been able to sleep so he took that as a sign. Settling back in the tree, drawing in deep breaths of the warm, pine-scented air, he brushed away a rivulet of sweat and squinted at the sky. The stars were a hundred thousand gleaming jewels and the waning moon basked in reflected glory. There would be light enough.

Below and behind him, some large creature blundered about. Perhaps a cow or sheep had wandered into the conservation area from one of the nearby farms. It didn't matter. Now that the wind had changed, his interest lay in the pale rectangles of field beyond the woods. They would come to check the sheep and he would be waiting.

With the barrel of his rifle braced against a convenient limb, he laid his cheek gently against the butt and flicked

on the receiver of his night scope. He'd ordered the
simplest infrared scope from a Bushnell catalog back in
early summer, when he'd first known what he had to do.
It had cost him more than he could really afford, but
the money had been well spent. Nor did he begrudge
the continuing outlay for lithium batteries, replaced before every mission. A man is only as good as his
equipment—his old sergeant had made sure every man
he commanded remembered that.

Under the cross hairs, the ghostly outline of trees
began to show, punctuated here and there by the dim
red heat signatures of small animals. Without bothering
to turn on the emitter, he scanned both fields, registering
nothing more than the sheep. The sheep were innocent.
They had no control over the masters they had. Then
he came back to the trees.

They hunted the conservation area on occasion. He
knew it. Perhaps tonight *they* would hunt and he
would. . . .

He frowned at a flash of red between two trees. Showing too dim for the size, he had no idea what it might
be. Moving slowly, silently, he flicked on the emitter,
playing the beam of infrared light over the area. Although the naked eye could see no difference, his scope
brightened as if he'd turned on a high-powered red
flashlight.

The creature he'd scanned should be. . . .

With an effort, Henry brought himself back to the
woods. It was infinitely pleasanter replaying the earlier
part of the night, but he knew he must be getting close
to the pine. He lifted his head to scan the treetops . . .

. . . and snapped it back snarling as a beam of red
light raked across his eyes.

"Holy shit!" Mark Williams raised his uncle's shotgun
in trembling hands. He didn't know what that was. He
didn't care. He'd had nightmares about things like that,
the kind of nightmares that jerked you awake sweating,
scrabbling for the light, desperately trying to push back
the darkness.

It didn't look human. It didn't look safe.
He pulled the trigger.

The buckshot had spread enough that it did little real damage when it hit, tracing a pattern of holes down the outside of his right hip and thigh. The light had been an annoyance. This was an attack.

Henry had warned Vicki once that his kind held the beast much closer to the surface than mortals did. As blood began to slowly seep into his jeans, he let it loose.

A heartbeat later, a slug hit him in high in the left shoulder and spun him around, lifting him off his feet. His skull cracked hard against the trunk of a tree and he dropped, barely conscious, to the ground.

Through the pain, through the throbbing of his life in his ears, he thought he heard voices, men's voices, one almost hysterical, the other low and intense. He knew it was important that he listen, that he learn, but he couldn't seem to focus. The pain he could deal with. He'd been shot before and knew that even now his body had begun to mend. He fought against the waves of gray, trying to hold onto self, but it was like trying to hold sand that kept seeping out of his grasp.

The voices were gone; where, he had no idea.

Then a hand reached down and turned him gently over. A voice he knew said quietly, "We've got to get him back to the house."

"I don't think he can walk. Go for Donald, he's too heavy for you to carry."

Stuart. He recognized Stuart. That gave him a place to start from. By the time Nadine returned with Donald, he'd managed to grab onto his scattered wits and force them into a semblance of reason. His head felt eggshell fragile, but if he held it carefully, very carefully, he could keep the world from twisting too far off center.

In spite of rough handling, Henry's head had almost cleared by the time the wer got him to the house. A number of gray patches continued to drift up from the swelling at the base of his skull but, essentially, he was back.

He could see Vicki waiting on the porch, peering anx-

iously into the darkness. She looked softer and more
vulnerable than he'd ever seen her. As Stuart and Donald carried him into her reach, she stretched out a hand
and lightly touched his cheek.

Her brows snapped down. "What the fuck happened
to you?"

"Of course I followed you!" Mark Williams gulped a
little more whiskey from the water glass in his hand. "I
get back a little early from a friendly poker game and
see my aged uncle sneaking out of the house in the middle of the night carrying . . ." He waved a hand at the
rifle now lying in pieces on the kitchen table. ". . . that,
off to do God knows what. . . ."

"God knows," Carl interrupted quietly, working the
oily rag along the barrel.

"Fine. God knows. But I don't. And," he slammed
the now empty glass down on the table, "after what I
just went through, I think I deserve an explanation."

Carl stared up at his nephew for a moment, then
sighed. "Sit down."

"Okay. I'll sit." Mark threw himself into a kitchen
chair. "You talk. What the hell were you planning on
hunting out there and what was that thing that attacked me?"

Ever since the Lord had shown him what lived on the
Heerkens farm and had let him know where his duty
lay, Carl Biehn had been afraid he wouldn't be strong
enough. He was an old man, older than he looked, and
the Lord had given one old man a terrible burden to
carry. Mark was not who he would have chosen to help
him bear his cross, but the Lord worked in mysterious
ways and apparently Mark had also been chosen. It
made a certain sense he supposed, the boy was his only
living relative, and by pulling that trigger tonight he'd
proven he had the strength to enter the fray. Perhaps
his own sins would be washed away in the blood of the
ungodly he was to help destroy.

Carl made his decision and took the three rounds he'd
prepared from his vest pocket, standing them on the

table. They gleamed in the overhead light like tiny missiles.

"Holy shit! That's silver!"

"Yes."

Mark stroked one finger down the bullet head and laughed a bit hysterically. "You trying to tell me you're hunting werewolves?"

"Yes."

In the sudden silence the ticking of the kitchen clock sounded unnaturally loud.

The old boy's flipped. He's right out of his tiny little mind. Werewolves. He's crazy.

And then Carl started to talk. Of how he'd been out bird-watching in late spring and seen the first change by accident. How he'd seen the others by design. How he'd recognized a creature of the devil. Realized that this was why none of the cursed family ever entered God's house. Realized they were not God's creatures but Satan's, sent by the Great Deceiver to spread darkness on the earth. Gradually came to know what he must do.

They must be sent back to hell. And they must be sent back in the form that was not a mockery of God's image. It must be done in secret under the cover of the night lest the Lord of Lies try to stop him.

To his surprise, Mark found himself believing. It was the weirdest goddamned story he'd ever heard, but it had the undeniable ring of truth.

"Werewolves," he muttered, shaking his head.

"Creatures of the evil one," his uncle agreed.

"And you're killing them?" *And this is the guy who thinks eating a burger is a sin.*

"I am sending them back to their dark master. Demons cannot actually be killed."

"But you're sending them with silver bullets?"

"Silver is the Lord's metal as it paid for the life of His son."

"Jesus H. Christ."

"Do *not* blaspheme."

Mark looked down at the rifle, now cleaned and reassembled, then back up at his uncle. The man was a moral nut case, something that had to be remembered. A well armed moral nut case and one hell of a shot. "Yeah. Sorry. So, uh, what about that thing in the woods tonight?"

"I don't know." Carl laced his fingers together and sighed. "I shot him to protect you."

Sweat beaded Mark's forehead as he remembered and his heart began to race. For an instant, he thought he might lose control of his bladder again. He'd looked at Death tonight and he'd never forget the feel of icy fingers closing around his life, no matter how badly he might want to. That experience, primal and terrifying, made it easier to believe the rest. "Maybe," he offered, swallowing heavily, "it was Old Nick himself, come to check on his charges."

Carl nodded slowly. "Perhaps, but if so, I will leave him to the Lord."

Easy for you to say. Mark wiped damp hands on his jeans. *It wasn't going for your throat.* "What about the woman?"

"The woman?"

"Yeah, that Nelson babe who wandered by this morning."

"An innocent bystander, nothing more. You will leave her out of this."

But Mark remembered the bits of pine stuck to a Blue Jays T-shirt and wasn't so sure.

"A .30 caliber rifle at that range should've blown your fucking shoulder off." Vicki secured the end of the gauze and frowned down at her handiwork. "There's no way your collarbone should've been able to deflect that shot."

Henry smiled at the incredulous disbelief in Vicki's voice. The pain had fallen to tolerable levels and the damage had been much less than he'd feared. Theoretically, he should be able to regenerate a lost limb but he had no real desire to test the theory. A broken collarbone and a chunk of flesh blown off the top of his shoulder, he could live with. "My kind has stronger bones than yours," he told her, attempting to flex the arm. Vicki made a fist and looked ready to use it, so he stopped.

"Stronger?" She snorted. "Fucking titanium."

"Not quite. Titanium wouldn't have broken." He winced as Donald dug yet another piece of buckshot out of his thigh then turned back to Vicki. "Do you realize your language deteriorates when you're worried?"

"What the hell are you talking about?"

"You've done more swearing in the last hour than you have since we've met."

"Yeah?" She snapped the first aid kit shut with unnecessary force. "Well, I've had more to swear about, haven't I? I don't understand how this happened. You're supposed to be so great at night. What were you thinking about?"

He didn't see any reason to lie. "You. Us. What happened earlier."

Vicki's eyes narrowed. "Isn't that just like a man. Four hundred and fifty fucking years old and he's still thinking with his balls."

"That's the lot." Donald straightened and threw the tweezers into the bowl with the shot. "Few hours and you'll be good as new. Some of the shallower holes are healing already."

"You're pretty good at that," Henry noted, elevating his leg a little to get a better look.

Donald shrugged. "Used to get lots of practice twenty, thirty years ago. Folks were faster on the trigger back then and fur only deflects so much. Used to have a pattern much like that on my butt." Twisting around in a way no human spine could handle, he studied the body part in question. "Seems to be gone now." He picked up the bowl and headed for the door. "If you were one of us, I'd suggest you change a few times to clear out any possible infection. Or lick it. As it is. . . ." He shrugged and was gone.

"I wasn't even going to ask!" Henry protested as Vicki glared down at him.

"Good thing." Lick buckshot holes indeed! She

couldn't hold the glare. It became a grin, then a worried frown as a new problem occurred to her. "Will you need to feed again?"

He shook his head, regretting it almost immediately. "Tomorrow maybe, not tonight."

"After the attack by the demon, you needed to feed right away."

"Trust me, I was in much worse shape after the attack by the demon."

Vicki rested her hand lightly on the flat expanse of Henry's stomach, just where the line of red-gold hair began below his navel. The motion was proprietary without being overtly sexual. "*Can* you feed tomorrow?"

He covered her hand with his good one. "We'll work something out."

She nodded, if not satisfied at least willing to wait. The desire she felt was embarrassing and she hoped like hell Henry's vampiric vibrations were responsible. Overactive hormones were the last thing she needed. "You know, I'm amazed you've managed to survive for four centuries; first the demon, now this, and in only five short months."

"You may not believe this, but until I met you I lived the staid, boring life of a romance writer."

Both her brows rose and her glasses slipped to the end of her nose.

"Oh, all right," he admitted, "the night life was a bit better, but these sorts of things never happened to me."

"Never?"

He grinned as he remembered, although the event had been far from funny at the time. A woman—all right, his preoccupation with a woman—had been responsible for that disaster too. "Well, hardly ever. . . ."

His right knee felt twice its normal size and barely held his weight. A lucky blow from the blacksmith's iron hammer had slammed into the side of the joint. A man would never have walked again. Henry Fitzroy, vampire, had gotten up and run but the damage and the pain held him to a mortal's pace.

He could hear the dogs. They were close.

He should have sensed the trap. Heard or smelled or seen the men waiting in the dark corners of the room. But he'd been so anxious to feed, so anxious to lose himself in the arms of his little Mila, that he never suspected a thing. Never suspected that little Mila, of the sweet smile and soft thighs and hot blood, had confessed her sin to the priest and he had roused the village.

The presence of a vampire outweighed the sanctity of the confessional.

The dogs were gaining. Behind them came the torches and the stakes and the final death.

Had they not placed their faith so strongly in the cross, they would have had him. Only the blacksmith had presence of mind enough to swing as he broke through their circle and made for the door.

His leg twisted and white fire shot through his entire body. The sound of his own blood loud in his ears, he clutched desperately at a tree, fighting to stay upright. He couldn't go on. He couldn't stop.

It hurts. Oh, God, how it hurts.

The dogs were closer.

He couldn't die like this, not after barely a hundred years; hunted down like a beast in the night. His ribs pressed tight around his straining heart, as though they already felt the final pressure of the stake.

The dogs were almost on him. The night had narrowed to their baying and the pain.

He didn't see the cliff.

He missed the rocks at the water's edge by little more than the width of a prayer, then the world turned over and around and he almost drowned before he managed to claw his way back to the air. Unable to fight the current, he gave himself over to it. Fortunately, it was spring and the river ran deep—most of its teeth were safely submerged under three or four feet of water. Most. Not all.

Just before dawn, Henry dragged himself up onto the shore and wedged his battered body as deep as it would go into a narrow stone cleft. It was damp and cold, but the sun would not reach so far and, for the moment, he was safe.

It had never meant more.

"No, sir. Never any trouble from Mr. Fitzroy." Greg squared his shoulders and looked the police officer in the eye. "He's a good tenant."

"No wild parties?" Celluci asked. "Complaints from the neighbors?"

"No sir. Not at all. Mr. Fitzroy is a very quiet gentleman."

"He has no company at all?"

"Oh, he has company, sir." The old security guard's ears burned. "There's a young woman. . . ."

"Tall, short blonde hair, glasses? Early thirties?"

Greg winced a little at the tone. "Yes, sir."

"We know her. Go on."

"Well, there's a boy, late teens. He's kind of scruffy, tough like. Not the kind you'd expect Mr. Fitzroy to have over."

The boy's presence wasn't much of a surprise. It only added another piece to the puzzle, bringing it a step close to completion. "Is that all?"

"All the company, sir, but. . . ."

Celluci pounced on the hesitation. "But what?"

"Well, it's just you never see Mr. Fitzroy in the day-time sir. And when you ask him questions about his past. . . ."

Yes, I've a few questions myself about his past. In fact, Fitzroy had turned out to be more questions than answers. Celluci didn't like that in a man and he liked it even less now that he was beginning to see how he could fill in the blanks.

If Henry Fitzroy thought he could hide what he was, he was due for a nasty surprise.

The old man was asleep; Mark could hear him snoring through the wall that separated their bedrooms.

"The sleep of the just," he murmured, linking his hands behind his head and staring at a watermark on the ceiling. Although he'd agreed to help in his uncle's holy war—*And* that's *one elderly gentleman who's a few pickles short of a barrel.*—nothing had actually been said about what this entailed. Whether or not the werewolves were creatures of the devil was a moot point as far as he was concerned—more importantly, they were creatures apparently outside the law.

He was a businessman; there had to be a way he could make a profit out of that.

If he could capture one of them, he knew a number of people who would be more than willing to purchase such a curiosity. Unfortunately, that idea came with an obvious problem. The creature could just refuse to change—and they appeared to have complete control over the process—ruining any credibility he might have. And in sales, credibility was everything.

"All right, if I can't make a buck out of them live. . . ."

He smiled.

Were*wolves.*

Wolves.

Dead wolves meant pelts. Take the head as well and there'd be a dandy rug.

People were always willing to pay for the unique and the unusual.

Nine

"Has anybody seen Daniel this morning?"

Jennifer glanced up from the burr she was working out of her sister's fur. "He headed up the lane about an hour ago. Said he was going to wait for the mail."

"But it's Sunday." Nadine rolled her eyes. "Honestly, that child and the day of the week. Peter, could you go get him." Her tone fell between an order and a request.

Good sergeants used much the same tone, Vicki reflected; maybe the wer could integrate more easily than she'd expected.

Peter dragged his T-shirt over his head and tossed it at Rose. "You think you can find the car keys before I get back?"

"They're in here somewhere," she muttered, shuffling through yet another pile of papers. "I know they are, I can smell them."

"Don't worry about it," Vicki advised, rescuing a lopsided stack of *Ontario Farmers* from sliding to the floor. "If we don't find them by the time Peter gets back, we'll take Henry's car."

"We'll take the BMW?" Peter kicked his sneakers off. "You know where Henry's keys are?"

Vicki grinned. "Sure, he gave them to me in case we needed to move it."

"All right!" He dropped his shorts on Rose's head. "Don't look too hard," he instructed, then changed and barreled out the door, heading at full speed up the lane.

*   *   *

Mark had intended to just drive by the farm, to see if he could spot any of these alleged werewolves and get a good look at their pelts, but when he saw the shape sitting by the mailbox it seemed like a gift from God.

"And as I have been assured, God is on our side."

So he stopped.

It didn't look like a wolf, but neither did it look quite like a dog. About the size of a small German shepherd, it sat watching him, head cocked to one side, panting a little in the heat. Its pure black coat definitely appeared to have the characteristics of a wolf pelt, with the long silky hairs that women loved to run their hands through.

He stretched an arm out the open window of the car and snapped his fingers. "Here, uh, boy. Comere. . . ."

The creature stood, stretched, and yawned, its teeth showing very white against the black of its muzzle.

Why hadn't he brought a biscuit or a pork chop or something? "Come on." Pity it was black; a more exotic color would fetch a higher price.

And then he saw a flash of red coming up the lane. When it reached the mailbox, he realized that the black must only be about half grown. The red creature was huge with the most beautiful pelt Mark had ever seen. Long thick hair shaded from a deep russet to almost a red-gold in the sunlight. Every time it moved, new highlights flickered along the length of its body. Both muzzle and ears were sharply pointed and its eyes were delineated with darker fur, giving it an almost humanly expressive face.

He knew people who would pay big bucks to own a fur like that.

It studied him for a moment, head high, ignoring the attempts of the smaller one to knock it over. There was something in its gaze that made Mark feel intensely uncomfortable and any doubts he might have had about these creatures being more than they seemed vanished under that steady stare. Then it turned and both creatures headed back down the lane.

"Oh, yes," he murmured, watching them run. "I have

found my fortune." Best of all, if anything went wrong this time, crazy Uncle Carl and his high caliber mission from God would take the rap.

First on the agenda, a drive into London to do a little research.

It didn't take long for Vicki to discover the attraction Henry's BMW held; low on the dashboard, discreetly out of sight from prying eyes and further camouflaged by the mat black finish—on everything including the buttons and the digital display—was a state of the art compact disk player. She was perfectly willing to admire the sound quality, she was even willing to listen to Peter enthuse about woofers and tweeters and internal stabilization somethings, but she was not willing to listen to opera all the way into London, especially not with the two wer singing along.

They compromised and sang along with Conway Twitty instead. As far as the wer were concerned, the Grand Ol' Opry ran a poor second to grand old opera, but it was better than no music at all. Vicki could tolerate country. At least she understood the language, and Rose had a hysterical gift for mimicking twang and heartache.

They cut through the east end of the city, down Highbury Avenue—Highway 126—heading for the 401. The moment they hit traffic, Rose reached over and turned the music off. To Vicki's surprise, Peter, reclining in the back with his head half out the window, made no protest.

"We don't see things quite the same way you do," Rose explained, very carefully changing lanes and passing an eighteen wheeler. "So we have to pay a lot more attention when we drive."

"Most of the world should pay more attention when they drive," Vicki muttered. "Peter, stop kicking the back of my seat."

"Sorry." Peter rearranged his legs. "Vicki, I was wondering, how come you're going to see the OPP on a Sunday? Won't the place be closed down?"

Vicki snorted. "Closed down? Peter, the police don't

ever close down, it's a twenty-four hour a day, seven day a week job. You should know that, your brother's a cop."

"Yeah, but he's city."

"The Ontario Provincial Police are police just like any others . . . except no one keeps messing with the color of their cars." Vicki liked the old black and whites and hadn't approved the Metro Toronto Police cars going bright yellow and then white. "In fact," she continued, "in a lot of places they're the only police. That said, on a hot Sunday afternoon in August, everyone with a good reason to be out of district headquarters should be and I might be able to get the information I need."

"I thought you were just going to go in and ask them for the names of everyone who has a .30 caliber rifle registered?" A Chevy cut in front of them and Rose dropped back a careful three car lengths, muttering, "Dickhead," under her breath.

"I am. But as they have no reason to tell me, a lot is going to depend on how I ask. And who."

Peter snorted. "You're going to try to intimidate some poor rookie, aren't you?"

Vicki pushed her glasses up her nose. "Of course not." It was actually more a combination of a subtle pulling of rank and an invoking of the "We're all in this together" attitude shared by cops all over the world. Granted, she wasn't a cop anymore, but that shouldn't affect the ultimate result.

The OPP District Headquarters overlooked the 401 on the south side of Exidor Road, the red brick building tucked in behind a Ramada Inn. Vicki had the twins wait by the car.

Had she still been a cop, it would've worked. Unfortunately, that she *used* to be a cop, wasn't good enough. Had she not then tried to "intimidate a poor rookie" it might still have worked, but the very intense young woman she spoke to knew Vicki had no right to the information, "working on a case" or not, and, her back up, refused to show it to her.

Things would have gone better with the sergeant if Vicki hadn't lost her temper.

By the time she left the building, most of the anger was self-directed. Her lips had thinned to a tight, white line and her nostrils flared with every breath. She'd handled the whole thing badly and she knew it.

I am not a cop. I cannot expect to be treated like one. The sooner I get that through my fat head, the better. It was a litany easy to forget back in Toronto where everyone knew her and she could still access many of her old privileges, but she'd just been given a nasty preview of what would happen when the people on the Metro force were no longer the men and women she'd served with. Her hands clenched and unclenched as though they were looking for a throat to wrap around.

She started for the car, standing in solitary splendor at the edge of the lot. With every step, she could feel the waves of heat rising up off the pavement, but they were nothing compared to the heat rising off her. *Where the hell are the twins?* She half hoped they'd done something stupid just so she could blow off some steam. With most of the distance to the car covered, she saw them heading across the parking lot from the Ramada Inn carrying bottles of water.

When they met, both wer took one look at her and dropped their eyes.

"It didn't work, did it?" Rose asked tentatively, peering up through her eyelashes. Under her hair, her ears were forward.

"No. It didn't."

"We just went for some water," Peter offered, his posture identical to his sister's. He held out the second of the plastic bottles he carried. "We, uh, brought you one."

Vicki looked from the bottle to the twins and back to the bottle. Finally she snorted and took it. "Thank you." It was cold and it helped. "Oh, chill out. I'm not going to bite you." Which was when she realized that they thought she might.

Which was so absurd that she had to laugh.

Both sets of ears perked up and both twins looked relieved. If they'd been in fur, they probably would have bounced; as they weren't, they merely grinned and drank their water.

Dominant/submissive behavior, Vicki thought draining her bottle. She worried about that a little. If all the wer but the dominant couple were conditioned to be submissive as a response to anger or aggression, that could cause major problems out in the world.

As Rose went around the car to the driver's side, two heavily muscled young men lounging around the Ramada Inn pool began calling out lurid invitations. Rose yawned, turned her back on them, and got into the car.

And then again, Vicki reconsidered, *maybe there's nothing to worry about.*

She tossed her empty bottle into the back seat with Peter. "Let's go get lunch while I come up with another brilliant idea."

Unlike a number of other places, London had managed to grow from a small town serving the surrounding farming community into a fair-sized city without losing its dignity. Vicki approved of what she saw as they drove into the center of town. The city planners had left plenty of parks, from acres of land to tiny playgrounds tucked in odd corners. New development had gone up around mature trees and where that hadn't been possible new trees had been planted. Cicadas sang accompaniment throughout most of the drive and the whole city looked quiet and peaceful, basking in the heat.

Vicki, who liked a little more grit in her cities, strongly suspected that the place would bore her to tears in less than twenty-four hours. Although she emphatically denied sharing the commonly held Torontonian delusion that Toronto occupied the center of the universe, she couldn't imagine working, or living, anywhere else.

"The place is called Bob's Steak House," Peter explained as Rose pulled into a small, nearly empty parking lot. "It's actually up on Clarence Street, but if we leave the car there we have to parallel park."

"Which we're not exactly very good at," Rose added, cutting the engine with a sigh of relief.

Vicki would have been perfectly happy stopping for fast food—all she really demanded at this point was air conditioning—but the twins had argued for a restaurant "where the meat isn't so dead."

A short block east of the lot, Rose rocked to a halt in front of a little corner store and exclaimed, "Baseball stickers!"

Peter nodded. "Make him feel better."

"Is this a coded conversation," Vicki asked of no one in particular, "or can anyone join in?"

"Daniel collects baseball stickers," Rose translated. Her brow furrowed. "No one's quite sure why, but he does. If we bring a few packages back, it'll make up for him not being able to come with us."

"You two go ahead." Vicki rummaged in her bag for the car keys. "I've got this urge to go back and check the car doors."

"I locked mine," Peter told her, paused a moment, and added, "I think."

"Exactly," Vicki grunted. "And I don't want to have to tell Henry that we borrowed his BMW and lost half the pieces."

Rose waved a hand at the empty street. "But there's no one around."

"I have a naturally suspicious nature. Get the stickers. I'll meet you back here."

What's the point of new legislation on Sunday openings, Mark Williams wondered, heading back to the alley where he'd left his jeep, *if the places I need to go are still closed? A truly civilized country wouldn't try to cramp a man's style and . . . hello!*

He sidestepped quickly behind a huge old maple and with one hand resting lightly on the bark, leaned forward to take another look. It *was* Ms. "No First Name" Nelson. He thought he recognized the walk. Few women covered the ground with that kind of an aggressive stride. In fact. . . .

He frowned, watching her check the car doors, wondering why the body language seemed so familiar.

Drives a BMW, eh. Not too shabby.

As she turned away from the car, he ducked back, not wanting to be seen. A number of his most profitable enterprises had begun with him watching and keeping his mouth shut. When he felt enough time had passed, he took another look.

Jesus H. Christ. She's a cop.

For those who took the trouble to learn certain subtle signs, playing spot-the-cop became a game easy to win. Mark Williams had long ago taken the trouble to learn the signs. It never hurt to be prepared and this wasn't the first time that preparation had paid off.

What's she got to do with those werewolves though, that's the question. Maybe the aged uncle hasn't been as clever as he thought. If she's a friend of the family, and a cop. . . .

He came out from behind the tree as she disappeared up a side street at the other end of the parking lot. He couldn't tell if she was packing heat, but then, she could be packing a cannon in that oversized bag of hers and no one would be the wiser. Thinking furiously, he sauntered slowly across the street. If she could prove the aged uncle had been blowing away the neighbor's dogs, she didn't have to bring up the subject of werewolves at all. Uncle Carl would. And Uncle Carl would get locked away in a loonybin. And there would go his own chance to score big.

She was onto something. The pine needles on yesterday's T-shirt proved she'd found the tree and he'd be willing to bet that that little lost waif routine she'd pulled in the aged uncle's flower factory was just a ploy to get close.

He laid his hand against the sun-warmed metal of the BMW.

I'm not going to lose this chance.

She wouldn't appreciate it. She'd say he was interfering, that she could take care of herself, that he should stop being such a patronizing s.o.b. Mike Celluci put down the electric razor and glared at his reflection in the bathroom mirror.

He'd made up his mind. He was going to London.

And Vicki Nelson could just fold that into corners and sit on it.

He had no idea what this Henry Fitzroy had gotten her involved with nor did he really care. London, Ontario probably couldn't come up with something Vicki couldn't handle—as far as he knew, the city didn't have nuclear capabilities. Fitzroy himself, however, that was a different matter.

Yanking a clean golf shirt down over his head, Celluci reviewed all he had learned about this historical romance writer. *Historical romances, for God's sake. What kind of job is that for a man?* He paid his parking tickets on time, he hadn't fought the speeding ticket he'd received a year ago, and he had no criminal record of any kind. His books sold well, he banked at Canada Trust, he paid his taxes, and his charity of choice appeared to be the Red Cross. Not many people knew him and the night guard at his condo both respected and feared him.

All this was fine as far as it went, but a lot of the paper records that modern man carried around with him from birth, were missing from Mr. Fitzroy's life. Not the important things, Celluci admitted, shoving his shirttails down behind the waistband of his pants, but enough of the little things that it set off warning bells. He couldn't dig any deeper, not without having his initial less than ethical investigations come to light, but he could lay his findings before Vicki. She used to be a cop. She'd know what the holes in Fitzroy's background meant.

Organized crime. The police didn't run into it often in Canada, but the pattern fit.

Celluci grinned. Vicki would demand an immediate explanation. He hoped he'd be there to hear Fitzroy try and talk his way out of it.

2:15. Family obligations would keep him in Scarborough until five at the earliest and even at that his sisters would squawk. He shuddered. Two hours of eating burned hamburgers, surrounded by a horde of shrieking nieces and nephews, listening to his brothers-in-law discussing the rising crime statistics and criticizing the police; what a way to spend a Sunday afternoon.

*   *   *

"Okay, so if the gun part of *Rod and Gun Club* refers to the rifle range and stuff," Peter, having convinced Rose that he should have a chance to drive, pulled carefully out of the parking lot, "what's the rod mean?"

"I haven't the faintest idea," Vicki admitted, smoothing the directions out on her knee. The napkin had a few grease stains on it, but the map was actually quite legible. "Maybe they teach fly-tying or something."

"Fly-tying?" Rose repeated.

"That'd take one real small lasso, there, pardner," Peter added, turning north.

Vicki spent the next few blocks explaining what she knew about tying bits of feathers to hooks. As explanations went, it was sketchy. Neither, when asked, did she have any idea why theoretically mature adults would want to stand thigh deep in an ice cold stream being eaten alive by insects so that they could, if lucky, eat something that didn't even look like food when cooked but rather stared up at them off the plate in its full fishy entirety. She was, however, willing to allow that it took all types.

Although Peter drove as meticulously as Rose, he was more easily distracted—any number of bright or moving things pulled his attention from the road.

So once again the wer are inside statistical norms, Vicki thought, squinting through the glare on the windshield, *and we see why teenage girls have fewer accidents than teenage boys.* "Red light, Peter."

"I see it."

It took Vicki a moment to realize they weren't slowing. "Peter. . . ."

His eyes were wide and his canines showed. His right leg pumped desperately at the floor. "The brakes, they aren't catching."

"Shit!"

And then they were in the intersection.

Vicki heard the squeal of tires. The world slowed. She turned, could see the truck, too close already to read the license plate, and knew they didn't have a hope in hell of not being hit. She screamed at Peter to hit the gas and the car lurched forward. The grille of the truck filled the window and then, with an almost delicate precision, it began to push through the rear passenger door. Bits of broken glass danced in the air, refracting the sunlight into a million sharp-edged rainbows.

The world returned to normal speed as the two vehicles spun together across the intersection, tortured metal and rubber shrieking, until the back of the BMW slammed into a light pole and the truck bounced free.

Vicki straightened. Covering her face to protect it had kept her glasses where they belonged. Thankfully, she pushed them up her nose, then reached over and turned off the ignition. For the first sudden instant of silence, her heart was the only sound she could hear, booming in her ears like an entire percussion section, then, from a distance, as though the volume were slowing being turned up, came voices, horns, and, farther away still, sirens. She ignored it all.

Peter had his head down on the steering wheel, pillowed on his folded arms. Vicki unsnapped her seat belt and gripped his shoulder lightly.

"Peter?"

The lower half of his face dripped blood but, as far as she could tell, it came from his nose.

"The brakes," he panted. "They—they didn't work."

"I know." She tightened her grip slightly. He was beginning to tremble and although he deserved it, although they all deserved it, this was not the time for hysterics. "Are you all right?"

He blinked, glanced down the length of his body, then back at her. "I think so."

"Good. Take off your seat belt and see if your door will open." Her tone was an echo of the one Nadine had used that morning and Peter responded to it without questions. Giving thanks for learned behaviors, Vicki pulled herself up on her knees and leaned over into the back to check on Rose.

The rear passenger side door had buckled, but essentially held. The inner covering and twisted pieces of the actual mechanisms it contained spread across three quarters of the seat which now tilted crazily up toward the roof. The rear window had blown out. The side window had blown in. Most of the glass had crumbled into a million tiny pieces, but here and there sizable shards had been driven into the upholstery.

A triangular blade about eight inches long trembled just above Rose's fetal curl, its point buried deep in the door lining. Glass glittered in her pale hair like ice in a snow field and her arms and legs were covered with a number of superficial cuts.

Vicki reached over and yanked the glass dagger free. A 1976 BMW didn't have plastic-coated safety glass.

"Rose?"

She slowly uncurled. "Is it over?"

"It's over."

"Am I alive?"

"You're alive." Although she wouldn't have been had she been sitting on the other side of the car.

"Peter. . . ."

"Is fine."

"I want to howl."

"Later," Vicki promised. "Right now, unlock your door so Peter can get it open."

While Peter helped his sister from the back, Vicki clambered over the gearshift and out the driver's door, dragging her bag behind her, and throwing it up on her shoulder the moment she was clear, its familiar weight a reassurance in the chaos. A small crowd had gathered and more cars were stopping. One of them, she was pleased to note, belonged to the London Police and other sirens could be heard coming closer.

With the twins comforting each other and essentially unharmed, Vicki made her way around the car to check on the driver of the truck. Blood ran down one side of his face from a cut over his left eye and the right side of his neck was marked by a angry red friction burn from the shoulder strap of his seat belt.

"Jesus Christ, lady," he moaned as she stopped beside him. "Just look at my truck." Although the massive bumper had absorbed most of the impact, the grille had been driven back into the radiator. "Man, I didn't even have fifty klicks on this thing yet. My wife is going to have my ass." He reached down and lightly touched the one whole headlight. "Quartz-halogen. Seventy-nine bucks a pop."

"Is everyone all right here?"

Vicki knew what she'd see before she turned; she'd used that exact tone too many times herself. The London police constable was an older man, gray hair, regulation mustache, regulation neutral expression. His younger partner was with the twins, and the two uniforms from the second car were taking charge of traffic and crowd control. She could hear Peter beginning to babble about the brake failure and decided to let him be for the moment. A little bit of hysteria would only help convince the police they were telling the truth. People who were too calm were often perceived as having something to hide.

"As far as I can tell," she said, "we're all fine."

His brows rose. "And you are?"

"Oh. Sorry. Vicki Nelson. I was a detective with the Metro Toronto Police until my eyes went." It didn't even hurt to say it anymore. Maybe she was in shock. "I was in the BMW." She dug out her ID and passed it over.

"You were driving?"

"No, Peter was."

"It's your car?"

"No, a friend's. He lent it to us for the day. When Peter tried to stop for the light, the brakes had gone. We couldn't stop." She waved a hand at the truck. "He didn't have a chance of missing us."

"Right out in front of me," the driver of the truck agreed, swiping at the blood on his cheek. "Not even fifty klicks on this baby. And the whole front end'll have to be repainted." He sighed deeply, his belly rising and falling. "The wife is going to have my ass."

"They were working earlier?"

"We stopped just down the road without any . . ." The world slid a little sideways. ". . . trouble."

"I think you'd better sit down." The constable's hand was around her elbow.

"I'm fine," Vicki protested.

He smiled slightly. "You've got a purple lump the size

of a goose egg on your temple. Offhand, I'd say you're not quite fine."

She touched her temple lightly and brilliant white stars shot inward from her fingertips. All of a sudden, it hurt. A lot. Her whole body hurt. And she had no memory of how or when it had happened. "I'm getting too old for this shit," she muttered, letting the constable lead her to the side of the road.

"Tell me about it." He lowered her gently to the curb. "You just sit there for a minute. We'll have the ambulance people take a look at you."

Everything appeared to be about six inches beside where it should be. "I think," she said slowly. "That might not be a bad idea. The ownership, insurance, everything, is in the glove compartment."

He nodded and headed for the car. Vicki stopped keeping track of things for a while.

When the ambulance attendants suggested she go to the hospital, she didn't put up much of a fight, only pulled Dr. Dixon's phone number from the depths of her bag, asked that he be called immediately, and insisted on Rose and Peter coming with her. The police, who had soon recognized the family resemblance between the twins and one of their own people, overruled the protests of the attendants and helped all three of them into the back of the ambulance.

"We're not charging you with anything," the older constable told her, handing up the tow truck driver's card, "but we will be checking with the mechanics about those brakes. This is the garage he's taking the car to."

Vicki nodded carefully and stowed the card in her bag.

As the ambulance pulled away, the tow truck driver looked down at the wreck of the BMW and shook his head. "Good thing they weren't driving domestic."

"Storm. Storm!"

Storm gave Cloud one last frenzied lick and looked up at Dr. Dixon.

"Go into the kitchen and get me a glass of water, please." Vicki made a motion to rise out of her chair, but the old man waved her back. "No, I want Storm to go. Run the water good and cold. If there's ice in the freezer, you'd better use it.''

Nails clicking against the hardwood, Storm left the room. The sound continued down the hall and then stopped. Vicki assumed he'd changed. Cloud, her fur stuck up in damp spikes from Storm's tongue, shook herself briskly then lay her head down on her front paws and closed her eyes.

Dr. Dixon sighed. "She's getting too close," he said softly to Vicki, "and her twin's beginning to sense it."

Vicki frowned. "She's getting too close to what?"

"Her first heat. I imagine he'll be sent away as soon as this trouble's over. I only hope it isn't too late."

"Too late?" Vicki echoed, remembering Nadine had spoken of Cloud's first heat on Saturday morning.

"Usually it happens in late September, early October, that way if there's a pregnancy, the baby, or babies, will be born in early summer, ensuring a good food supply for the last few months of gestation and the first few months of life." He chuckled. "The wer aren't born with teeth, but they come up damn soon after. Of course, all this meant more when they lived solely by hunting, but the basic biology still rules. Thank God the baby's changes are tied to the mother's for the first couple of years."

Vicki dropped her hand on the old man's arm. The hospital had cleared her of any damage except a nasty bump but her head hurt and she knew she was missing something. "Dr. Dixon, what the hell are you talking about?"

"Huh?" He turned to look at her and shook his head. "I'm sorry, I'm old, I forgot you've only known the wer for a short time." His voice took on a lecturing tone, slow and precise. "Cloud is nearing sexual maturity. Her scent is changing. Storm is responding. Didn't you notice the way he was licking her?"

"I thought that was for comfort, to clean the cuts."

"It was, partially, but I didn't like the look of what it was turning into. That's why I sent him to the kitchen."

"But he's her brother," Vicki protested.

"Which is why the family will be sending him away.

It's hard on twins. You simply can't keep them together during a first heat; he'd injure himself trying to get to her. When he's older, he'll be able to control his response but this first time, this first time for both of them. . . ." Dr. Dixon let his voice trail off and shook his head.

He remained silent as Peter came back into the room.

"I brought you some water, too," he said, handing Vicki the second glass he carried.

She thanked him. She needed a drink. Water would have to do. She watched carefully as Storm flopped down and rested his muzzle across Cloud's back, sighed deeply, and appeared to go instantly to sleep. It all looked perfectly innocent to her. She glanced at Dr. Dixon. He didn't look worried, so apparently this was within the parameters of acceptable behavior.

The tableau shattered a moment later when a car door slammed outside and both wer leapt up and raced for the front of the house, barking excitedly.

"Their father," Dr. Dixon explained. "I called him as we were leaving the hospital. No sense worrying him before that and now he can take you back to the farm."

"Do they know it's going to happen?" Vicki asked. "That he's going to be sent away?"

Dr. Dixon looked momentarily puzzled. "Who? Oh. Cloud and Storm? Rose and Peter?" At her nod, he sighed. "They know intellectually that it's what happens, but for all they're wer, they're still teenagers and they don't believe it will happen to them." He shook his head. "Teenagers. You couldn't pay me enough to go through that again."

Vicki reached over and clinked her glass against his. "Amen," she said. "Amen."

Brows lowered, Mike Celluci worked his fingers around the steering wheel. He'd left his sister's later than he'd planned and felt lucky to get away at all. No one had warned him that their Aunt Maria would be at the "little family barbecue," probably because they knew he'd refuse to come.

"Well, surely you didn't expect Grandma to come on

her own, Mike. I mean the woman is eighty-three years old."

If they'd mentioned Grandma was coming he'd have driven out to get her himself. A trip to Dufferin and St. Clair beat the hell out of an afternoon with Aunt Maria. Although he'd tried, it had been impossible to avoid her for the entire afternoon and eventually he'd had to endure the litany he'd heard from her at every meeting practically since puberty.

When are you getting married, Michele? You can't forget, you're the last of the Cellucis, Michele. I told your father, my brother, rest his soul, that a man needs many sons to carry on the name but he didn't listen. Daughters, he had three daughters. When are you getting married, Michele?

This afternoon he'd managed to keep his temper, but only barely. If his grandmother hadn't stepped in. . . .

"And the last thing I need now is a fucking traffic jam on the four-oh-goddamed-one." He had his light and siren in the glove compartment. The urge to slap it on the roof and go tearing up the paved shoulder, around the Sunday evening traffic, was intense.

He wanted to be in London before dark, but he wasn't going to make it. If traffic didn't open up, he doubted he'd be there before eleven. Time wasn't a problem, he had three days off, but he wanted to confront Vicki tonight.

He'd called Dave Graham, to let him know where he was heading, and ended up slamming the receiver down when the other man started to laugh.

"Jealous," he growled, scowling up at the setting sun. It wasn't funny. Vicki had to be told what kind of person she'd gotten involved with. He'd do the same for any friend.

Suddenly, he grinned. Maybe he should introduce Vicki to Aunt Maria; the old lady'd never know what hit her.

"What are you so nervous about?"

Vicki jumped, whirled, and glared up at Henry. "Don't *do* that!"

"Do wha. . . . Sweet Jesu, Vicki, what happened?" He reached out to touch the purple and green lump on her temple but stopped when she flinched back.

"There was an accident."

"An accident?" He glanced around, nostrils flared. "Where is everyone?"

"Outside." Vicki took a deep breath and released it slowly. "We agreed I should be the one to tell you." Peter had wanted to, but Vicki had overruled him; he'd been through enough for one day.

Henry frowned. There were strange undercurrents in Vicki's voice he didn't understand. "Has someone else been shot?"

"No, not that." She glanced out the window. Although the sun had set, the sky was still a deep sapphire blue. "The wer have been staying out of those fields, patrolling around the house; it seems to be working for now. No, this involves something else."

"Something that involves . . ." He flicked his gaze over to the lump and she nodded. ". . . and me."

"In a manner of speaking. The brakes failed on the BMW today. We—Peter, Rose, and I—were broad-sided by a truck. The car, well, the car was pretty badly damaged."

"And the three of you? You weren't badly hurt?"

"If we had been," Vicki snapped, "I'd have more to worry about than totaling your car." She winced. "Sorry. It's been a day."

Henry smiled. "Another one." He cupped her chin lightly with his right hand and looked up into her eyes. "No concussion?"

"No. Peter got a bloody nose and Rose has a few cuts from flying bits of glass. We were lucky." His hazel eyes appeared almost green in the lamplight. She could feel his hand on her skin through every nerve in her body, which was strange because as far as she could remember her chin had never been an erogenous zone before. She moved back and his hand dropped.

"You were *very* lucky," Henry agreed, pulling out a chair and settling into it. He wasn't sure if Vicki was responding to his hunger—his own injuries would heal faster if he fed—or if his hunger rose with her response, but for the moment he ignored both possibilities. "I don't understand about the brakes, though. I had a full service check done in the spring and they were fine. I've hardly driven the car since."

Vicki dropped into a chair beside him. "The garage was closed today, it being Sunday and all, so I'll talk to the mechanic tomorrow." She leaned her elbows on the table and peered into his face. "You're being very understanding about this. If someone trashed *my* BMW, I'd be furious."

"Four hundred and fifty years gives you a different perspective on possessions," he explained. "You learn not to grow too attached to *things.*"

"Or people?" Vicki asked quietly.

His smile twisted. "No, I've never managed to learn that. Although every now and then, I make the attempt."

Vicki couldn't imagine watching everyone she cared about grow old and die while she went on without them and she wondered where Henry found the strength. Which set her to wondering. . . .

"How are *you* tonight?" She plucked gently at the sling around his left arm.

"Bruised thigh, bruised head, shoulder's healing." It was frustrating more than painful. Especially with her blood so close.

"You've got that look on your face."

"What look?"

"Like you're listening to something."

To her heartbeat. To the sound of her blood as it pulsed just under the skin. "I'd better go."

She stood with him.

"No, Vicki."

Just in time she remembered not to raise her brows. "No, Vicki? Henry, you need to feed, I need to relax. I'm a grown woman and if I think I can spare you another few mouthfuls of my precious bodily fluids, you have no room for argument."

Henry opened his mouth, closed it again, and surrendered. Healing had used up whatever reserves he had and the hunger was too strong to fight. At least that's what he told himself as they climbed the stairs.

"How dare you! How fucking dare you!" Barry Wu couldn't remember ever being so furious. "You god-damned fucking son of a bitch, you actually believed I'd do something like that!"

Colin was trying desperately hard to keep his own temper, but he could feel himself responding to Barry's anger. He'd been pulled out of the car for special duty tonight, and this was the first chance they'd had to talk. "If you'd listen—I said I didn't believe you did it!"

Barry slammed his palm down on the hood of Colin's truck. "But you didn't believe I didn't! It took a fucking Toronto PI to convince you!"

"You've got to admit the evidence. . . ."

"I don't have to admit shit!" He stomped off half a dozen paces, whirled around, and stomped back. "And another thing, where the fuck do you get off searching my place?"

"What? I was supposed to just sit on my ass and wait for the guy to strike again?"

"You could've fucking told me!"

"I *couldn't* fucking tell you!"

"Hey!"

Neither of them had heard the car pull up. They spun simultaneously, shoulder to shoulder, dropped into a defensive position, and went for their guns.

Which neither of them are wearing. Celluci lifted a sardonic eyebrow. *How lucky for all three of us.* "You two might want to find another place to have your disagreement. Police officers screaming profanities at each other in the station parking lot looks bad to civilians." If he remembered correctly, a sergeant had once said the same to him and Vicki.

Neither Barry nor Colin wasted a moment wondering how the stranger had known they were police officers even out of uniform. They were young. They hadn't been on the force very long. They weren't stupid.

"No, sir!" they replied in unison, almost but not quite coming to attention.

Celluci hid a smile. "I'm looking for someone. A woman. Her name is Vicki Nelson. She's a private investigator from Toronto. She's working for some people who own a sheep farm north of the city. I figure by now she'll have contacted the police, for information if nothing else. Can you help?"

Colin stepped toward the car, trying to paste a neutral expression over concern. "Excuse me, sir, but why are you looking for her? Is she in trouble?"

Jackpot first try. She's probably had this poor kid breaking into police files for her. "I'm a friend. I have information about the man she's traveling with."

"About Henry?" The concern broke through. Information about Henry could mean trouble.

Barry frowned at the tone but moved forward, ready if Colin needed him.

"You *know* him?"

"Uh, yeah, I do." Barry looked a little surprised at the change in Colin's voice and more surprised when he continued with, "I'm Colin Heerkens. Henry and Vicki are out at my family's farm," and then proceeded to give detailed directions. There was an undercurrent of amusement about Colin's whole attitude that made Barry very nervous.

As the car pulled away, Colin gave a shout of laughter and slapped Barry on the back. "Come on," he yanked open the truck door and climbed in, "you're not going to want to miss this!"

"Miss what?"

"What happens when he gets to the farm."

"What happens?"

Colin rolled his eyes. "Christ, Barry, I know your nose isn't worth much but I don't believe you didn't smell that. That guy was so jealous he was practically green." He leaned over and opened the passenger door. "You know, if you'd learn to read nonverbal clues you'd be a better cop."

"Yeah?" Barry swung up into the truck. "And if I'd wanted to be in the canine corps, I'd have joined it." He settled back against the seat cushions and buckled in. "I still want to know what happens when he gets to the farm."

"Beats me." Colin shot him a grin as he pulled out onto the street. "But it oughta be interesting."

"You think this is pretty funny, don't you?"

"We think most of you humans are pretty funny. Laugh a minute."

"Sheep-fucker."

"Yellow peril."

"You know, Colin, your uncle's probably not going to be too thrilled by you sending this guy out to the farm." Barry drummed his fingers against the dash and shot a look at his partner. "I mean, you lot aren't big on company just generally and right now. . . ."

Colin frowned. "You know, you're right. I guess I was reacting to his scent and the situation. Uncle Stuart's going to have my throat." He sucked in a deep breath through his teeth. "I guess I just didn't think."

"It's your least endearing trait." And one that would keep him from promotion; keep him on the street, in uniform. Barry doubted that Colin would ever rise any higher than constable and sometimes he wondered how the wer would manage when he moved on.

"Barry, I did *want* to tell you."

"I know. Forget it." And he knew that Colin could, the wer lived very much in the here-and-now. It would take a little longer for him.

Ten

This is ridiculous. It's 11:30. Vicki's likely asleep. Celluci
sat in his car and stared at the dark bulk of the farmhouse.
Or at least in bed. He decided not to take that thought
any further. *The lights are on in the kitchen. Someone's up.
I could at least make sure this is the right. . . .* "Jesus!"

The white head staring in the driver's side window
belonged to the biggest dog he'd ever seen. It looked to
be part shepherd, part malamute, and, if he didn't know
better, he'd swear, part wolf. It didn't look angry, just
curious and its eyes. . . . Unable to decide if the eyes
were as strange as he thought or if the glass was dis-
torting them somehow, he cracked open the window
enough for the head, but not the shoulders, and kept his
finger on the switch in case the beast should lunge.

Not so much as a whisker crossed the edge of the
window, but the wet black nose twitched once, twice as
the cool air inside the car flowed out into the night.

The eyes were strange; it wasn't just the glass. Celluci
wasn't quite sure what the difference was but he'd never
seen a dog of any kind with eyes that looked so human.

Suddenly, the big dog whirled and ran barking for the
house, its pale form flickering like a negative image
against the night.

Realizing his choice had just been made for him, Celluci shut off the engine. He'd been announced. He might
as well go in.

"Vicki. Come on, Vicki. Wake up."
Vicki tried to ignore both the voice and the hand gen-

tly shaking her shoulder but, in spite of her best efforts, her body betrayed her and began losing its hold on sleep. Finally she surrendered, muttered an obscenity, and groped for her glasses. Cool fingers gripped her wrist, guiding her search. She didn't bother opening her eyes until she actually had the glasses in place—not much point when she wouldn't be able to see anything anyway.

In the dim spill of light from the hallway, she could just barely make out the darker outline of a man. It had to be Henry, not only was he the only adult male in the house who habitually wore clothes, but the temperature of his touch was a dead giveaway.

"Henry, I'm flattered but I'm exhausted. Get lost."

She could hear the smile in his reply. "Next time I'll be able to do more of the work. But that wasn't why I woke you. We've got company and I think you'd better get up."

"What time is it?"

"11:33."

Vicki really disliked digital watches, only race horses and defense attorneys needed to time life to the second. "I just got to sleep. Can't it wait until morning?"

"I don't think so."

"All right." She sighed and swung her legs out from under the sheet. "Who is it?"

"Detective-Sergeant Michael Celluci."

"Say what!"

"Detec . . ."

"I heard you the first time. Close the door and turn on the light."

He did as she requested, shielding his eyes against the sudden glare.

The clothes she'd worn this afternoon would have to do, Celluci had certainly seen her look worse. "Are you sure?"

"Very. Cloud checked out the car when it first pulled up. She said she could smell a gun, so I took a quick look. It's Michael Celluci. Keeping in mind how we met, I'm not likely to forget him."

Vicki had very little memory of how Henry and Celluci had met, but considering that she was tired and bleeding and about to become a demonic sacrifice at the time, that was hardly surprising. "What the hell is *he* doing here?"

"I don't know." Henry leaned back against the wall and waited while she pulled a T-shirt over her head before he continued. "But I thought you might like to be there when we found out."

"Be there?" She stuffed her feet into sandals and stood, running both hands through her hair rather than search for a brush. "You couldn't pay me enough to miss this explanation and if something isn't very wrong that I *have* to know about immediately—and I'll be damned if I can think of what that might be—I'll have a few words to say in return."

Because Henry had every intention of living for another four hundred and fifty years, he kept his initial response to that clamped firmly behind his teeth.

"Detective-Sergeant Michael Celluci, ma'am. Is Vicki Nelson here?"

"Yes, she's here. Henry's gone to wake her."

"That isn't necessary." Henry must've seen him approaching the house and recognized him. *He's got eyes like an owl if that's the case, I couldn't see my hand a foot in front of my face out there, cloud cover's got everything blocked off.* "It's late. Now I know this is the right place, I can return tomorrow."

"Nonsense." The woman stepped back out of the way and motioned him into the kitchen. "You've driven all the way from Toronto, you might as well wait. She'll be right down."

If they'd gone to get her up, he didn't really have a choice. The only thing worse than having Vicki dragged out of bed, would be having her dragged out of bed and not staying around to explain why. Slipping his shield and his ID back into his pocket, he followed a gesture into a chair, keeping a wary eye on the huge white dog who watched him from across the room. *This is ridiculous. One more night isn't going to make a difference. And she's not going to be happy about being woken up.*

A red dog came out and sat beside the white. It

looked less than happy to see him. It also looked larger
although, considering the size of the first, Celluci found
that difficult to believe. He shifted a little in his chair.
"What, uh, kind of dogs are they?"

"They're descended from an obscure European hunting breed. You've probably never heard of it."

"Something like wolfhounds?"

"Something like, yes." She pulled out a chair and sat
down, pinning him under a curiously intent gaze. "My
name is Nadine Heerkens-Wells, my husband and I run
this farm. Vicki is working for us at the moment. Is there
something I should know, Detective?"

"No, ma'am. This doesn't concern you." In fact, Celluci was having a little trouble dealing with a friendship
between the man he perceived Henry Fitzroy to be and
this woman. Although physically she was quite striking,
with her widow's peak and sharp, almost exotic features,
the quality of her surroundings said poor white trash.
Her wrinkled sleeveless dress looked as if it had just
been picked up off the floor and thrown on. *And there's
enough stuff scattered around to dress a half a dozen
people, provided they're not too fussy about the condition
of their clothes.* None of the furniture could be less than
ten years old, clumps of hair had piled up in every corner, and the whole kitchen had a kind of shabby ambience that indicated money was scarce.

*Of course, all their spare cash could be going into
dog food.*

He heard footsteps on the stairs and stood, turning to
face the door leading into the hall.

"All right, Celluci, what's wrong?" Vicki stopped
barely a handspan from his chest and glared up into his
face. "Someone had better be dying. . . ." Her tone
added, *or someone's going to be.*

"What the hell happened to your head?"

"My what? Oh that. I was in a car accident this afternoon. I guess I hit the dash." The fingers on her right
hand patted the air over the purple and green swelling.
"The hospital says it's just a bump. Looks bad but no
real damage." Her eyes narrowed, glasses sliding down
her nose with the motion. "Your turn."

Henry, standing just inside the kitchen, hid a smile. Vicki obviously thought Celluci was entitled to hear about the accident; while she was telling him, the challenge dropped from her voice and posture. The moment she finished, it was back.

Celluci drew in a deep breath and let it out slowly. "Can we talk somewhere privately?"

"Privately?"

He glanced over her shoulder at Henry. "Yeah. Privately. As in I'd like to speak with you alone."

Vicki frowned. She'd seen that look before. Politely translated, it meant he was ready to make an arrest. Why he should be aiming it at Henry. . . . "We'll go out to your car."

"I thought you couldn't see in the dark?"

"I know what you look like." She grabbed his arm just above the elbow and propelled him toward the kitchen door, throwing an "I won't be long" to the room in general as they left.

The moment they were clear of the house, Peter stretched and said, "I wonder why she didn't want to use the living room?"

Henry grinned. "Where you could've heard every word they said?"

"Well. . . ."

"Vicki has a pretty good idea of how well the wer can hear." He walked to the window and stared across the dark lawn at Celluci's car. "And she *knows* how well I can."

"Well?"

He tapped his fingers against the steering wheel. Where to start? "It's about your friend, Mr. Fitzroy."

Vicki snorted. "No kidding."

"I did some checking into his background . . ."

"You *what?*"

He ignored the interruption and continued. ". . . and there're a number of discrepancies I think you should know about."

"And I suppose you had a good *reason* for abusing

police privilege?" The tension in her jaw pulled at her temple, sharpening the pain and spreading it out over her skull, but Vicki didn't dare unclench her teeth. If Celluci had discovered Henry's secret, she had to know about it and couldn't risk it getting lost in a screaming fight. *Later.*

Celluci could hear the suppressed anger in her voice, could see the tightening of her lips in the pale oval of her face. He had no idea why she was hanging onto her temper but he knew it wouldn't last so he'd better use the time he had.

"Your *reason*, Celluci."

"You think what happened last spring wasn't reason enough?"

"Not if you just started searching now, no, I don't."

"What makes you think I just started searching now?"

He could see the lighter slash of her smile. It didn't look friendly.

"You drive all the way from Toronto, you barge into a strange house at 11:30 at night, you have me roused from sleep and dragged from bed, and I'm supposed to believe this is information you've had for months? Cop a plea, Celluci, the evidence is against you."

"Look," he turned to face her, "your friend isn't what you think he is."

"What do I think he is?" This didn't sound good.

"Oh, I don't know." Celluci drove both hands up through his hair. "Hell, yes I do. You think he's some sort of exotic literary figure, who can wine you and dine you and offer you moonlit nights of romance . . ."

Vicki felt her jaw drop.

". . . but he's got holes in his background you could drive a truck through. Everything points to only one answer; he's got to be deeply involved in organized crime."

"Organized crime?" Her voice came out flat, no inflection.

"It's the only solution that fits all the facts."

She sputtered. She just couldn't help it. She just couldn't hold it in any longer.

Celluci leaned toward her, trying to read her expression. When she got over the initial shock, she'd want to hear what he'd found.

Vicki managed to repeat *organized crime* one more time before she lost it.

He watched her laugh and wondered if he should smack her. He could always use hysteria as an excuse.

Finally, she managed to get hold of herself.

"Are you ready to listen?" he asked through gritted teeth.

Vicki shook her head, reached up and brushed the long curl of hair back off his forehead—she didn't have to see it to know it was there. "Leaving aside your reasons for the moment, you couldn't be more wrong. Trust me, Mike. Henry Fitzroy is not involved in organized crime. At any level, of any kind."

"You're sleeping with him, aren't you?"

So much for his reasons. *You are mine* resonated over, under, and through that question. Unfortunately, she couldn't deal with his archaic perceptions right now; this was too potentially dangerous for Henry. "What does that have to do with this?"

"You wouldn't be willing to believe. . . ."

"Bullshit! I'm perfectly willing to believe that you're a chauvinistic, possessive bastard and I sleep with you." So much for good intentions.

He hadn't intended to be so loud, but his voice practically echoed in the confines of the car. "Vicki, I'm telling you, beyond a certain point, Henry Fitzroy has no. . . . What the hell was that?"

"Was what?" Vicki peered out the windows but couldn't see past the night. She shoved her glasses up her nose. It didn't help.

"Something ran past out there. It might have been one of those big dogs. It looked like it might be hurt."

"Shit!" She was out of the car and racing toward the house before the final explosive "t" had passed her lips. The darkness was absolute save for the faint square of light that was the kitchen window. *It's a big building. How can I miss it?* Then she remembered Henry warning her the first night about the curve in the path. Too late. She stumbled and fell, burying her hands in the loose dirt of the garden.

"Come on." Celluci heaved her to her feet and kept a tight hold on her arm. "If it's that important, I'll be your eyes."

They pounded through the kitchen door together, just in time to see a massive russet shape crash to the floor, the fur on its chest a darker, more deadly shade of red.

"Too big to be Storm," Vicki panted, fighting free of Celluci's grip. "Has to be. . . ."

And then there wasn't any question as outlines blurred and blood began pumping from an ugly gash across the right side of Donald's ribs.

Vicki and Nadine hit the floor beside the wounded wer at roughly the same time. Nadine, who had grabbed a first aid kit from over the kitchen sink, was expertly pinching the torn edges of flesh together and wrapping them in place.

"We do most of our own doctoring," she said, in response to Vicki's silent question.

All things considered, it made sense. The presence of Dr. Dixon didn't carry much weight against an entire history with no physicians. "Doesn't look like a gunshot wound." Together they got the gauze around Donald's neck. "Looks like he got hit with a chunk of flying rock."

Nadine snorted. "Comforting."

"I thought," Vicki grunted, holding Donald's weight while Nadine continued to wind the gauze, "that you'd all agreed to stay out of those fields."

"It isn't that easy to overcome a territorial imperative."

"It isn't that easy to overcome a .30 caliber slug either."

"What the hell are you two *talking* about?" Celluci took a step forward. "What the *hell* is going on around here?"

"Later, Mike. I think he's going to need a hospital."

"I think you're right. Cloud!"

To Celluci's astonishment, the big white dog galloped out of the room. "What's it going to do? Call 911?"

"Yes," Vicki snapped, pushing at her glasses with the back of a bloody hand.

Henry started across the kitchen. Someone was going to have to take care of Michael Celluci and, as much as he might wish otherwise, it looked like it was going to have to be him. *No need for concern, Detective, it's just werewolves.* Coercion would be safer than explanation; get him outside and twist his mind until he no longer knew exactly what he'd seen.

Unfortunately, by the time Henry had covered the four meters to Celluci, the situation had changed again.

Stuart, who had seen a stranger's car parked at the end of the lane, had grabbed a pair of shorts from the barn and changed before coming to the house. A voice and a pair of hands could often make a difference in an unplanned confrontation, but now he wished he'd stayed with tooth and claw. A member of his pack was down and the blood scent drew his lips back from his teeth.

"What's going on?" he growled.

"Donald got hit. Vicki thinks it was a ricochet. There's an ambulance coming." Nadine shot the words out without looking up.

"He changed?"

"As he went out."

Stuart turned to face the stranger, hackles rising, ears tight against his head. "And this one saw?"

"Yeah, *this one* saw." Celluci's jaw jutted out at a dangerous angle. "And I want some explanations of *what* I saw and I want them now."

"Don't push, Detective." Henry could see that Stuart was close to the edge and was facing Celluci's aggression the way he'd face a challenge from a dominant male of his own kind.

"Stay out of this, Fitzroy!" His fingers curled into fists, Celluci locked eyes with the man in the doorway. He'd taken as much abuse as he was going to. Dogs *did not* change into men. "I want answers *now.*"

The growl was a warning and something deep in Celluci's hindbrain recognized it as such. He didn't listen. "Well? I'm waiting!" He didn't have to wait long. His tottering world view fell and shattered as thumbs were shoved behind shorts, shorts hit the floor, and a great black beast that seemed mostly teeth leapt suddenly for his throat. Then something pushed him back and Henry and the beast were on the floor.

Henry had thrown his good shoulder under the charge and managed to force Stuart's fur-form down. With only one arm, however, he couldn't keep him there without injuring him. *At least his anger's been redirected. . . .*

Celluci knew a man couldn't possibly move as fast as Henry Fitzroy was moving. The beast lunged and Fitzroy was somewhere else. Instantly. Or as near as made no difference. Again. And again. And again. With barely a heartbeat between. And through it all came the deep-throated growl of an enraged animal, building to a savage crescendo with each attack.

A deadly little dance, Henry realized as teeth snapped closed on the air beside his hip. Even with one bad arm he knew he could force the wer to submit—he was stronger and faster, but then what? Defeat the dominant male and rule the pack. *No thank you,* he thought as they scrabbled through another movement. But he could feel himself responding to the scents and the sounds and the anger and wondered how much longer he'd be able to maintain control. *There has to be a way to break through. . . .*

Suddenly, it was no longer his problem.

With Donald still on the floor, the red wer attacking had to be Storm. Henry backed quickly out of the way while the two rolled snarling and snapping then sprang apart, circled, and charged together again.

Enough! Celluci dropped to one knee and pulled his gun from his ankle holster. He wasn't thinking exactly clearly, he had no real idea of what he was going to shoot—*this is someone's kitchen for Chrissakes!*—but he felt more in control with the weight of the weapon in his hand.

Then Storm yelped and threw himself down on his back, all four feet in the air and the edge of one ear split. Long white teeth closed around his throat.

Celluci raised the gun.

A high-pitched, piercing howl cut through the chaos and everyone froze, looking like they'd been playing a demented game of statues. Then, in near unison, they turned. Shadow sat just inside the hall door, muzzle raised and throat working as his howl undulated mournfully up and down the scale. It lasted just over a minute, bouncing off the walls, reverberating through bone and blood, impossible to ignore, and then trailing off into a series of hiccuping yelps.

Nadine responded first, leaving Donald with Vicki and racing across the room to gather Shadow up into her arms. He pushed closer and tried to bury his head under her breasts. She lifted his head and gazed anxiously down into his eyes. "What is it, baby? What's wrong?"

Given encouragement to speak, and therefore to change, Daniel peered over his mother's shoulder and wailed. "That man's going to shoot my papa!"

All heads now turned to follow Daniel's pointing finger—all except Storm who had been pinned by one of his uncle's huge paws and was now having his bitten ear vigorously licked.

Vicki sat back on her knees, one hand resting lightly on the thick pad of gauze wrapped around Donald's chest, monitoring the rise and fall of his labored breathing with her fingertips. She rolled her eyes and sighed. "Oh for Chrissake, Celluci, put the penis substitute away."

A shout of laughter from outside the screen door was the immediate and unexpected response. Everyone turned yet again as Colin and Barry came into the kitchen, Colin saying, "I told you we'd miss all the good stuff if we stopped for gas."

"I'm sure I saw this once in an old Marx Brothers' movie," Vicki muttered to no one in particular. She raised her voice. "People, what are the odds we could pull ourselves together before the ambulance arrives?"

Colin glanced around the kitchen, nostrils flaring as they caught the varied scents, smile vanishing as he saw the body on the floor. "Dad!" He threw himself to his knees, pushing Vicki away. "What happened to my father?"

"Ricochet. Our marksman missed."

"Is he . . . ?"

"At least one busted rib and some torn up muscle. I don't know about internal injuries."

"Why is he just lying here? We've got to get him to a hospital!" He put his hands under his father's shoulders.

Vicki lifted them away. "Calm down, there's an ambulance coming."

"If you're being shot at in human form now, we'll *have* to report it," Barry put in, touching Colin lightly on the back.

"He wasn't," Vicki told him, getting to her feet. "He changed when he hit the house. You must be Barry Wu."

"Yes, ma'am."

"I want to talk to you."

"Yes, ma'am. Later. Uh, if he changed in the house, then. . . ." His gaze flickered to Celluci and back.

Vicki sighed. "Yes, he saw." She turned to Celluci, wiping her bloody fingers on her shorts. "Please put the gun away, Mike."

Breathing heavily, he looked down at the gun as if he'd never seen it before.

"Put it away, Mike."

He looked up at her and his brows drew down into a deep vee. "This is crazy," he said.

"There's a perfectly simple explanation," she told him, moving closer. She'd jump him if she had to. With luck, he'd hesitate before shooting her and she'd be able to disarm him.

"Okay." He tossed the curl of hair back off his forehead. "Let's hear it."

Vicki glanced back at Nadine who shrugged.

"Go ahead," she said. "If you think he can handle it."

Vicki thought they didn't have much choice, at least not until they got that gun back where it belonged.

"Your simple explanation?" Celluci prodded.

Squaring her shoulders, she met his eyes and said, as matter-of-factly as she was able, "Werewolves."

"Werewolves," he repeated blankly, then he bent and slipped the .38 into its holster, twitching the leg of his jeans back into place before he straightened. He looked down at Shadow, rubbing himself up against his father's fur, at Storm and Cloud who were doing much the same, and then over at Henry.

"You, too?" he asked.

Henry shook his head. "No."

Celluci nodded. "Good." He drew in a deep breath and then he started to swear. In Italian. He kept it up for almost three minutes and managed to dredge up words and phrases he hadn't used since childhood. Most of them, he screamed at Vicki who waited patiently for him to run down.

Henry, who spoke fluent if slightly archaic Italian, noted, moderately impressed, that he only repeated himself in order to add adjectives to the profanity.

His vocabulary ran out just as the lights of the ambulance turned in at the top of the lane.

The moment they showed, Nadine took charge. "Cloud! Get Shadow back upstairs and make sure he and the twins stay there. Storm stay in fur-form; your ear is still bleeding. Tag, get some clothes on."

Tag? Vicki repeated silently as Stuart scooped up a pair of sweatpants. *Stuart's fur-form name is Tag?*

"Colin," Nadine continued, closing the hall door behind Cloud and Shadow, "you follow them into town in case he needs blood. Vicki, could you go in the ambulance? If he wakes up. . . ."

"No problem."

She'd told the others and asked Vicki—Henry noted the distinction with some amusement.

As the paramedics carried Donald out on the stretcher, Celluci grabbed Vicki's arm and pulled her to one side.

"I'm going to follow you in. We have to talk."

"I'll be looking forward to it."

"Good." He drew his lips back off his teeth in a parody of a smile. No one in the room, vampire or wer, could have done it better.

Eleven

"Because the hospital has to report gunshot wounds, you should know that."

Colin glanced over at Barry and the two Ontario Provincial Police constables standing talking by the nurses' station. "You said it was a ricochet."

Vicki rolled her eyes. "Colin. . . ."

"Okay, sorry. It's just, well, what am I going to tell them?"

"You aren't going to tell them anything." She smothered a yawn with her fist. "I am. Trust me. I've been at this longer than you have, I know the things a police department wants to hear and the way they want to hear them."

"Vicki." Celluci leaned forward and tapped her on the shoulder. "I hate to burst your bubble, but you are quite possibly the worst liar I know."

She turned to face him, pushing her glasses up her nose. "Lie to the police? I wouldn't think of it. Every word out of my mouth is going to be the truth."

"So there's been someone taking potshots out of those woods for a while now?"

"Well, I'm not sure three shots counts as *potshots*, Constable."

"Still should've been reported, ma'am. If someone's firing a hunting rifle out in the conservation area we'd like to know about it."

"The family figured it was just because Arthur Fortrin was out of town," Colin put in.

Given a little direction, Colin was remarkably good at half-truths. *But then, he'd have to be,* Vicki realized. *All things considered.*

The OPP constable looked dubious. "I don't think the absence of one game warden's going to make much difference. And *you* should've known better." He snapped his occurrence book shut. "Tell your family next time they hear a shot, to call us immediately. Maybe we can spot the guy's car."

"I'll tell them. . . ." Colin shrugged.

"Yeah, I know, but will they listen." The constable sighed and glanced over at Vicki. He didn't think much of a Toronto private detective messing around in his neck of the woods, although her police background did lend credibility. His warning to be careful died in his throat when he caught her eye. She looked like a person who could take care of herself—and anything else that crossed her path. "So," he turned back to Colin, "this have anything to do with your Aunt Sylvia leaving?"

Colin snorted. "Well, she did say it was the last straw."

"Didn't she head up to the Yukon?"

"Yeah, her brother, my Uncle Robert, has a place just outside Whitehorse. She said it was getting too crowded around here."

"Your Uncle Jason just took off too, didn't he?"

"Yeah, Father accused Aunt Sylvia of starting an exodus and threatened to lock Peter, Rose, and I in the house until things calmed down."

"Well, frankly I was surprised he stayed around as long as he did. Man needs a place of his own." The OPP constable poked Colin in the ribs with his pen. "When'll you be moving out?"

"When I feel suicidal enough to live on my own cooking."

Both men laughed and the conversation turned to a general discussion of food.

Vicki realized that the wer were perhaps not as isolated as she'd originally thought. Colin leaving the farm and taking a job had brought them to the attention of the police if nothing else. Fortunately, the police tended to take care of their own. As for the shooting; she knew there wasn't much the OPP could do. She could only hope that a few extra patrols up and around the area would give her time to find this psycho before anyone else got killed. The wer would just have to recognize their higher visibility and be more careful when they changed for a while. It seemed a small price to pay.

". . . anyway, Donald's fine. The hospital released him into Dr. Dixon's care—that's one persuasive old man—and he'll probably be able to come home tomorrow. Apparently because he was shot in one form and then changed there's no danger of infection. Colin's on his way back, but I thought I should call and fill you in. Oh, and Nadine, I'll be spending the night in town."

"Explanations?"

"Uh-huh."

"Do you trust him with this?"

"I trust Mike Celluci with my life."

"Good. Because you're trusting him with ours."

Vicki half turned so she could see Celluci leaning on the hospital wall across from the phones. He looked tired but impassive, with all professional barriers raised. "It'll be okay. Can I speak to Henry?"

"Hang on." Nadine held the receiver out to the vampire. "You were right," she told him as he took it.

He didn't appear particularly gratified by this information. If Celluci's face was impassive, Henry's was stone. "Vicki?"

"Hi. I thought I should tell you, I'm staying in town tonight. I need a little time alone."

"Alone?"

"Well, away."

"I can't say as I'm surprised. You and Mr. Celluci have a great deal to discuss."

"Tell me about it. Do me a favor?"

"Anything." Before she could speak, he reconsidered and added. "Almost anything."

"Stay around the house tonight."

"Why?"

"Because it's 3:40 in the morning and sunrise is around 6:00."

"Vicki, I have been avoiding the dawn for a long time. Don't patronize me."

Okay. Maybe she deserved that. "Look, Henry, it's late, you've only got one good arm—at best one and a half—I've had a very rough day, and it isn't over yet. Please, give me one less person to worry about over the next few hours. We know this guy is coming right up to the house and we don't know for sure just where exactly Donald was shot."

"You didn't ask him?"

"I didn't get the chance. Look," she sagged against the wall, "let's just assume that the farm is under a state of siege and act accordingly. Okay?"

"You're asking me to do this for your peace of mind?"

She drew in a deep breath and let it out slowly. She had no right to ask him such a thing for such a reason. "Yes."

"All right. I'll sit quietly in the kitchen and work on an outline for my next book."

"Thank you. And keep the wer in the house. Even if you have to nail the doors shut." She slid a finger and thumb up under the edge of her glasses and rubbed the bridge of her nose. "I mean, how many times do I have to tell them to stay out of those fields?"

"An enemy they can't see or smell isn't very real to them."

She snorted. "Well, death is. I'll see you tomorrow night."

"Count on it. Vicki? Is he likely to be difficult?"

She shot another glance at Celluci, who was attempting to cover a massive yawn. "He excels at being difficult, but I can usually make him see reason if I thump him hard enough."

After she hung up, she rested her head for a few seconds on the cool plastic top of the phone. She couldn't remember the last time she'd wanted to sleep this badly.

"Come on." Celluci pulled her arm through his and steered her out into the parking lot where the heat hit them like a moist and semi-solid wall. "I know a cheap, clean motel out by the airport where they don't care what time you show up as long as you pay cash."

"How the hell did you find a place like that?" The yawn threatened to split her head in two and the pain came down on her bruised temple with hobnailed boots. "Never mind. I don't want to know." She slid into the car and let her head fall back against the seat. "I know you're dying to begin the interrogation—why don't I just start at the beginning and tell it in my own words?" If she had a nickel for every time she'd said that to a witness, she'd be a rich woman.

Eyes closed, she started with Rose and Peter in Henry's condo. She finished, with Donald being shot, as they pulled in at the motel. The only thing she left out was Henry's actual nature. That wasn't her story to tell.

To her surprise, Celluci's only response was, "Wait in the car. I'll go get us a room."

As she had no intention of moving farther or more often than she had to, she ignored his tone and waited. Fortunately, the keys he returned with were to a room on the ground floor. At this point, she doubted her ability to climb stairs.

"Why so quiet?" she asked at last, easing herself gently down on one of the double beds. "I was expecting another fine set of Italian hysterics at the very least."

"I'm thinking." He sat on the other bed, unbuckled his holster, and laid it carefully on the bedside table. "A concept I know you're unfamiliar with."

Except he didn't know *what* he was thinking. There were a number of things Vicki wasn't telling him and exhaustion had distanced the events of the night so they felt as though they'd happened to someone else. He couldn't believe he'd actually pulled his gun. It was easier to believe in werewolves.

"Werewolves," he muttered. "What next?"

"Sleep?" Vicki suggested hopefully, her voice slurred.

"Does this have anything to do with what happened last spring?"

"Sleeping?" Something about that didn't make sense but she couldn't quite get her brain around it.

"Never mind." He pulled her glasses off her face and set them down beside his gun, then quickly undressed her. She let him. She hated sleeping in her clothes and didn't have the energy to get rid of them herself.

"Goodnight, Vicki."

"Night, Mike. Don't worry." She fought with her mouth to get the last words out. "It'll all make sense in the morning."

He leaned over and pulled the sheet up around her shoulders. "Somehow, I doubt it," he told her softly, although he suspected she could no longer hear him.

Henry stood and stared up at the night, trying to decide how he felt. Jealousy was an emotion his kind learned to deal with early on or they didn't survive long. *You are mine!* sounded very dramatic, especially when accompanied by a swirling cape and ominous music, but real life just didn't work that way.

The trouble, therefore, had to be Celluci. "The man throws his life out like a challenge," Henry muttered. He wasn't at all surprised Stuart had attacked the detective—dominant males usually came to blows. His continuing presence probably hadn't helped. Although he had a special status within the family, while he was around Stuart remained on edge, instincts demanding that one of them submit. It was the alpha male's responsibility to protect the pack and his frustration at having to call in outside help had no doubt destabilized Stuart further.

"Given Celluci's attitude and Stuart's state of mind, a fight had been inevitable. Storm's intervention, on the other hand, had been a complete surprise to everyone involved, including Storm. Cloud must be getting very close for her twin to be behaving so irrationally.

Which brought them back around, more or less, to Vicki.

Henry grinned. If Celluci was a wer, he'd piss a circle around her, telling the world, *This is mine!* And then Vicki would get up and walk out of it.

"I'm not jealous of him," he told the night, aware as he spoke that it was almost a lie.

"Can we love?" The process had begun although the final change had not yet been made.

Christina turned to him, dark eyes veiled behind the ebony fan of her lashes. "Do you doubt it?" she asked, and came into his arms.

He had loved half a dozen times in the centuries since and each time it had shone like a beacon in the long darkness of his life.

Was it happening again? He wasn't sure. He only knew he wanted to tell Mike Celluci, "The day is yours, but the night is *mine.*"

Celluci would be as unlikely to agree to such a division as Vicki would.

"You cannot resent what they do in the daylight hours." Christina laid his head upon her breast and lightly stroked his hair. *"For if you do, it will fester in your heart and twist your nature and you will become one of those creatures of darkness they are right to fear. Fear is what kills us."*

Perhaps, when the wer were safe, he would ask her, "Will you give me your nights?"

Perhaps.

He wanted to touch her, hold her . . . no . . . he wanted to catch her up and throw her down and reestablish his claim on her. The intensity of his desire frightened him, stopped him. Confused, he sat on the edge of his bed, watching her sleep, listening to the soft sound of her breathing play a counterpoint to the helicopter roar of cheap air-conditioning.

They'd never had an exclusive relationship. They'd both had other lovers. *She'd* had other lovers.

Mike Celluci forced his hands to relax against his bare thighs and took a deep breath of the chilled air. Nothing had changed between him and Vicki since Henry Fitzroy came on the scene.

Suddenly, he couldn't stop thinking about the first

eight months after she'd left the force. They'd had one
last bitter fight and then no contact at all as the days
dragged into weeks and the world had become more and
more impossible to deal with. Until she was gone, he
hadn't realized how important a part of his life she'd
been. And it wasn't the sex he'd missed. He'd missed
conversations and arguments—even considering that
most of their conversations became arguments—and just
having someone around who'd get the joke. He'd lost
his best friend and had barely learned to live with the
loss when fate had thrown them together again.

No one should have to go through that twice.

But Fitzroy wasn't taking her anywhere.

Was he?

"Look, if you think that after last night I'm going
meekly back to Toronto, think again. I'm driving you
back to the farm. Get in the car."

Vicki sighed and surrendered. She recognized Celluci's
*"There's more going on here than meets the eye and I'm
going to get to the bottom of it regardless of how you
feel"* tone, and it was just too hot to keep arguing. Besides, if he didn't drive her, someone would have to
come out from the farm to get her and that didn't seem
entirely fair.

And he already knew about the wer, so what harm
would it do with Henry safely locked away?

"So," he started the engine and flipped the air-
conditioning on full, "what are the odds your furry
friend is going to go for my throat again?"

"Depends. What are the odds you're going to act like
a jackass?"

He frowned. "Did I?"

Vicki shook her head. *Just when you think he has no
redeeming characteristics. . . .* "Well," she said aloud,
"you did challenge Stuart's authority in his own house."

"I was a little upset, werewolves are a new concept
for me. I wasn't myself."

"You were definitively yourself," Vicki corrected with
a smile. "But I think that under normal circumstances
Stuart will be able to deal with that."

They stopped for breakfast at a hotel down the road and Vicki allowed Celluci to pump her about the case while they ate, giving the waitress only one bad moment when Vicki exclaimed, ". . . and to blow the top of his head off from that distance was one hell of a shot!" just as she put the plates down. If Celluci noticed she talked around Henry's involvement, he didn't mention it. She couldn't decide if he was being tactful or deep.

"You do realize," Celluci said, mashing the last of his hash browns into the leftover yoke on his plate, "that there're two of them out there? One with a shotgun and one with a rifle?"

She shook her head, setting down her empty coffee mug with just a little too much force. "I don't think so; this has all the earmarks of being a one-person setup. I know, I know," she raised her hand and cut off his protest, "Henry got shot at twice." Henry's injuries had been considerably downplayed over the course of the conversation. "But one man can operate two guns and up until now there's been no evidence of a second player."

Celluci snorted. "There's been bugger all evidence, period."

"But the tracks, the tree, the type of shot, all point to a single obsessed personality. I think he," she spread her hands as Celluci's brows went up, "or she, just kept the shotgun handy in case anyone got too close."

"Like your *writer* friend." His tone made it perfectly clear what he thought about both Henry *and* Henry wandering around in the woods playing the great detective.

"Henry Fitzroy can take care of himself."

"Oh, obviously." He stood and tossed a twenty down on the table. "That's why he got shot. Twice. Still, I'm amazed you let an amateur wander around out there at night, considering the danger."

"I didn't know about the shotgun," she protested as they left the coffee shop, then wished she could recall the words the moment they left her mouth. "Henry's a grown man," she muttered getting into the car. "I didn't *let* him do anything."

"That's a surprise."

"I'm not going to discuss him with you."

"Did I say I wanted to?" He pulled out of the parking lot and headed north. "You've gotten yourself involved with a pack of werewolves, Vicki. For the moment, that makes organized crime seem just a little tame."

"Henry is *not* involved in organized crime."

"All right. Fine. It makes whatever he is involved with seem just a little tame."

Vicki pushed her glasses up her nose and slouched down in the seat. *That's all you know,* she thought. She recognized the set of Celluci's jaw and knew that although he might be temporarily distracted by the wer, he wasn't going to let his suspicions about Henry drop. *Fine. Henry can deal with it. In four hundred odd years, this can't be the first time.* While she had no intention of getting caught in the cross fire, she would be perfectly willing to bash their heads together if it became necessary.

"Look," she said just before they reached Highbury Avenue, "if you're going to hang around, you might as well make yourself useful."

He scowled suspiciously. "Doing what?"

"Turn right. You're going to pay a visit to the OPP for me."

She had to give him credit for brains, he understood the reason for the visit immediately.

"You haven't got the firearms registration list, have you? Why the hell not?"

"Well . . ." Vicki flicked the air-conditioner vents back and forth a time or two. "The OPP and I had a little misunderstanding." She hated admitting even that much, knowing that Celluci would blow it all out of proportion.

"I'll bet," he grunted and, to her surprise, let it drop.

Twenty minutes later when he came out of the station, he made up for his silence.

"A little misunderstanding?" He slammed the car door and twisted around to glare at her. "Vicki, you may have destroyed any chance of provincial cooperation with local police forces for now and for always. What the hell did you say?"

She told him.

He shook his head. "I'm amazed the Duty Sergeant let you leave the building alive."

"I take it then that you didn't get the list."

"Dead on, Sherlock, but I did get an earful concerning proper police procedure."

"Damn it! I need that list."

"Should've thought of that before you made the crack about his mother." Celluci stopped the car at the parking lot exit. "Which way?"

"Left." Vicki waited until he'd maneuvered the car around the turn and into traffic before she added. "I want you to pick up a membership list from the Y."

"Have you alienated them, too?"

She supposed it was a legitimate question, all things considered. "No, but I have no right to ask them for the list and they have no reason to hand it over. You, however, are a cop." She poked him in the biceps. "Nice people, like those at the Y, are used to trusting the police. If *you* ask them for their firstborn child, they'll hand the little nipper over."

"You want me to lie for you?"

Vicki smiled at him, showing her teeth. "You're always bragging about how good you are at it."

The nice people at the YMCA proved fully as cooperative as Vicki had suggested and Celluci threw the membership list of the photography club on her lap as he climbed into the car.

"Anything else," he grumbled, starting the engine.

"You're the one who decided to stick around," Vicki pointed out, scanning the membership for names she recognized. No one looked familiar, so she folded it carefully and put it in her purse. "That's it for this morning. Let's head out to the farm, I'm desperate for a change of clothes." Although she'd had a lovely long shower behind the locked door of the motel bathroom, she was still wearing yesterday's shorts and shirt and they were both a bit the worse for wear.

"I was wondering what that smell was."

"Piss off, Celluci. You sure you can find your way out of the city?"

He could. Although he had to start from the police station to do it.

They drove in silence for a while, Vicki half dozing as she stared out the window at the passing fields and trees and trees and fields and. . . .

Suddenly she straightened. "I think you missed the turn."

"What are you talking about?"

"I don't remember seeing that ruined schoolhouse before."

"Just because you didn't see it. . . ."

"Look, I've been out this way three times now. Twice," she used the word to cut off his next comment, "in the daylight when I could see. I think you missed the turn."

"You might be right," he conceded, searching the surrounding farmland for landmarks. "Should we turn around now or cut east at the next opportunity?"

"Well, county roads are usually laid out on a simple grid pattern. As long as we head south at the first opportunity we should be fine."

"The next east it is, then."

Vicki slid down in the seat and braced her knees against the dashboard. They both knew it would make more sense to turn around now and look for the correct crossroad, but Vicki was comfortable and relaxed for the first time in days and didn't think a few extra moments would make a difference. She understood Mike Celluci. He had come to represent the natural in the face of the supernatural, and that meant she could let her guard down in a way she couldn't with either Henry or the wer. If they turned and went back, the interlude would only be over that much earlier.

She didn't dare guess what Celluci's reasons were for driving on.

The side road they turned onto petered out in a farmyard after six kilometers. The farmer, not bothering to hide his amusement, gave them directions while his dog marked a rear tire. They'd driven past the south turnoff, thinking it was only a lane.

"This thing has more potholes than Spadina Avenue,"

Vicki grunted, blocking the ceiling's attempt to smack her in the head. "Do you think maybe you could slow down?"

"Just watch for the red barn."

The red barn had either fallen or faded; it certainly wasn't where the farmer had said. They finally turned east on the second crossroad, which after two kilometers swung around a gentle, banked curve and headed due south.

"We're going to end up back in London at this rate."

Celluci sighed. "Hasn't anyone out here ever heard of street signs? There's a building up ahead. Let's see if we can get some coherent directions this time."

They'd turned into the driveway before Vicki recognized the white farm house.

"Lost again, Ms. Nelson?" Carl Biehn approached the passenger side of the car, brushing dirt off his hands.

Vicki smiled up at him. "Not this time, Mr. Biehn." She hooked a thumb back over her shoulder. "*He* was driving."

Carl bent so he could see into the car and nodded at Celluci who nodded back and said, "We seem to have taken a wrong turn."

"Easy to do in the country," the older man told him, straightening.

Vicki thought he looked tired. His eyes were ringed in purple shadows and the lines running past the corners of his mouth had deepened. "Trouble in the garden?" she asked, and wondered why he started.

"No. No trouble." He rubbed at a bit of mud dried to the edge of his thumb, his hands washing around and around themselves.

"Well, well, well. Lost again, Ms. Nelson?" The words were identical, but the tone sat just this side of insult. "I think you'll have to face the fact that some people aren't cut out for country life."

Vicki considered returning a smile as false as the one Mark Williams offered her but decided not to bother. She didn't like him; she didn't care if he knew it.

He pushed past his uncle and leaned into the car, resting one hand on the bottom edge of the open window.

"I see this morning you've managed to lead someone else astray." His left hand stretched across Vicki into the car. "Mark Williams."

"Celluci. Michael Celluci."

They shook briefly. Vicki found herself tempted to take a bite out of the tanned arm as it withdrew. She restrained herself; time spent with the wer had obviously influenced her thinking. *Besides, odds are I'd catch something disgusting.*

"What happened to your head?" He sounded concerned.

"I had an accident." And it was none of his business.

"You weren't badly hurt?" Carl looked down over his nephew's shoulder, brow furrowed.

"Just a bump," Vicki assured him. He nodded, satisfied, and she shot Mark a look that warned against further questions.

"We're trying to get to the Heerkens farm." Celluci wore his neutral expression—not friendly, not unfriendly, just there. Vicki had one like it. She didn't bother to put it on.

"No problem. Three or four kilometers down this road and the first left. Their lane's about two K in." He laughed companionably. His breath spilled into the car, smelling like mint. "And about two K long once you get there."

"Nothing wrong with privacy," Celluci said mildly.

"Nothing at all," the other man agreed. He stood and spread his hands, the gold hair on his forearms glinting in the sun. "I'm all for it myself."

I bet you are, Vicki thought. *And wouldn't I just love a look at the dirty little secrets your privacy hides. Probably good for five to ten just for starters. . . .*

"Ms. Nelson?" Carl had stopped rubbing at the dirt but he still appeared disturbed. "Will you be staying with the Heerkens long?"

"I hope not."

"That sounds almost like a prayer."

She sighed. "Maybe it is." She was staying until she nailed the bastard with the rifle and if prayer would help then she had nothing against it. Pushing her glasses up her nose, she turned to wave as Celluci did a three point turn in the driveway and headed back to the road.

Carl raised a strained hand in a reserved salute but Mark, who knew full well he hadn't been included in the farewell gesture, responded with a flamboyant movement of his arm.

"Well?"

"Well, what?" He half turned toward her, brows up. "You aren't actually asking my opinion, are you?"

"Celluci."

He pursed his lips and turned back to face the road. "The older man's upset by something, probably the younger—pity you can't choose your relatives. Given what you told me over breakfast and what I observed just now, my brilliant powers of deduction conclude you like Mr. Biehn, who I admit seems to be a decent sort, but you don't like Mr. Williams."

Vicki snorted. "Don't tell me you do?"

"He didn't seem so bad. Hey! Don't assault the driver."

"Then don't bullshit me."

Celluci grinned. "What? You want your opinion confirmed? That's gotta be a first."

Vicki waited. She knew he wouldn't miss an opportunity to tell her what he thought.

"I think," he continued right on cue, "that Mark Williams would sell his own mother if he figured he could make a profit from the deal. I guarantee he's up to something else; his kind always are."

Vicki shoved at her glasses even though they were sitting firmly at the top of her nose. It'd be a cold day in hell before Mark Williams had the discipline to become the kind of marksman who was picking off the wer.

Carl Biehn turned away the moment the car left the drive. He'd always been able to find peace in the garden but this morning it had eluded him. He kept hearing, over and over, the cry of the creature he had wounded in the night. It was not one of God's creatures so its pain should have no power to move him but he couldn't block the cry from his mind or his heart.

The Lord tested him, to see if his resolve was strong. Evil must not be pitied, it must be cast out.

"Two cops." Mark Williams pursed his lips thoughtfully. "She seems to have brought in reinforcements." It was too bad yesterday's accident hadn't removed the problem but, as he always said, nothing ventured, nothing gained. Even if Ms. Nelson's friend was here to investigate the crash, he'd been very careful to leave nothing on the car that would incriminate him.

On the other hand, with the two of them rummaging about, he'd better get a move on or between the police and his trigger-happy uncle, there'd be nothing left of his lovely little plan.

"Are you going to fight with my father again?"

"Not unless he fights with me."

Daniel turned and looked up at Stuart, who had risen as Vicki and Celluci came in and was now standing behind his chair growling low in his throat. "Daddy?"

Stuart ignored him. The two men locked eyes.

"Daddy? Can I bite him for you?"

Stuart started and glanced down at his son. "Can you what?"

"Can I bite him for you?" Daniel bared small white teeth.

"Daniel, you don't just go around biting people. You've been taught better than that."

The youngest wer narrowed his eyes. "You were going to," he pointed out.

"That's different."

"Why?"

"You'll understand when you're older."

"Understand what?"

"Well. . . ." He shot a helpless look at Celluci who spread his hands, equally at a loss for an answer. "It's a . . . man thing."

Daniel snorted. "I never get to bite anybody," he

complained, kicked the screen door open, and stomped out into the yard.

Although laughter might be the spark in the tinder, Vicki couldn't help herself. She collapsed back onto the sagging couch, holding her sides and gasping for breath. "A man thing," she managed to wheeze finally, and started up harder than ever.

The two men looked down at her and then at each other, expressions identical.

"Stuart Heerkens-Wells."

"Michael Celluci."

"Is she with you?"

"Never saw her before in my life."

When Vicki came downstairs from changing her clothes, only Nadine was in the kitchen.

"Where is everyone?" she asked, shoving her glasses up her nose and setting her bag on the floor.

"Well, my daughters are out in the barn chasing rats, my son is hopefully wearing himself out chasing that frisbee. . . ."

Vicki peered out the kitchen window and saw, to her surprise, Celluci throwing the frisbee for Shadow. "What's *he* still doing here?"

"I think he's waiting for you."

Vicki sighed. "You know, when we turned in the lane, I thanked him for his help and told him to get lost. I wonder what made me think he'd listen?"

"He's a man. I think you're expecting too much of him. Anyway, Rose and Peter are getting dressed to take you back into town and Tag's gone to check the flock."

Which reminded Vicki of something she'd meant to ask. "Tag? He doesn't look much like a Tag."

"Maybe not now," Nadine agreed, "but he was the youngest and the smallest in a set of triplets and I guess it suited him then."

"The smallest?"

Nadine grinned. "Yes, well, he grew."

Just then Celluci came into the kitchen leaving Shadow out on the lawn, tongue lolling, frisbee safe under both front paws. "Good, you're ready. Let's get going, it's almost noon. I hear Henry Fitzroy's still in bed." He kept himself from sneering but only just.

"He had a busy night."

"Didn't we all."

Then it hit her. "Going where?"

"Back into town. You need to check with the mechanic—unless you don't care if Peter's charged with operating an unsafe vehicle—someone somewhere has to know who has the skill to make those shots so I suggest we go where the boys are, and Donald has to be picked up and brought home."

"Yeah? So?" She folded her arms across her chest. "What does any of that have to do with you?"

"I've decided to stick around." He inclined his head toward Nadine. "No extra charge."

Vicki bit off the *Fuck you!* before she actually vocalized it. It almost choked her, but her pride, measured against the lives of the wer, meant nothing. On the other hand, in spite of what he thought, Mike Celluci did not have a direct line to truth and he had no right to butt in.

"What's up?" Peter followed his sister into the kitchen and looked from Vicki to Celluci, nostrils flared. There were some strange scents in the air.

"Vicki's just deciding who's going to be driving into town," Nadine told him.

"Rose," Peter said promptly. "I'm still traumatized from yesterday."

Rose rolled her eyes. "You want to sit with your head out the window."

He grinned. "That, too."

"I'm driving because we're taking my car."

The twins turned as one to look at Vicki.

I should tell him to go home and this time make it stick, even if I have to break a few bones. I don't need his high-handed help.

Reading her indecision, Peter moved a step closer, and lowered his voice. "Uh, Vicki, about *him* being around, I don't think Henry's going to approve."

Her eyes narrowed to slits. What the hell did Henry have to do with this? She grabbed her purse up off the floor and headed for the door. "What are you standing around for?" she snapped as she passed Celluci. "I thought you were driving."

Celluci glanced speculatively at Peter, then followed.

"What was all that about?" Peter wondered as the twins hurried to catch up. "Why did Aunt Nadine start laughing?"

"You really don't know?"

"No. I really don't."

Rose sighed and shook her head. "Peter, you are such a dork sometimes."

"Am not."

"Are too."

They'd have continued the argument all the way into London if Vicki hadn't threatened to muzzle them both.

Twelve

"There's your problem."

Vicki peered down into the engine of Henry's BMW. Nothing looked obviously wrong. "Where's the problem?"

"There." The mechanic pointed with the screwdriver he held. "Brake line, up by the master cylinder."

"There's something wrong with the brake line?"

"Yeah. Holed."

"What do you mean, holed?"

The mechanic sighed. His expression said *"Women!"* as clearly as if he'd spoken the word aloud. "Holed. Like, not solid."

"Someone put a hole in it?" It took a moment for the implications of that to sink in. Had the stakes just gone up? Had the killer become aware of her involvement and decided to do something about it? She frowned; that didn't fit the established pattern. Suddenly the air in the garage, already redolent with iron and oil and gasoline, grew thicker and harder to breathe.

"Didn't say someone did it. See here?" He lifted the black rubber hose on the end of his screwdriver. "Rubbed against that piece of metal. Rubbed just right between the ribs and broke through." Shrugging, he let the hose drop. "Happens. Brakes work for a while but lose fluid. Lose enough fluid and. . . ." A greasy finger cut a line across his throat.

"Yes, I know." Vicki straightened. "I was there. So you'll be telling the police . . . ?"

"Accident. Tough luck. Nobody's fault." He shrugged

again and turned to shake his head at the destroyed side of the car. "Hard to believe everyone walked away. Lucky."

Very lucky, Vicki realized. Death had missed her by less than a couple of feet and if Rose had been riding on the passenger side, she wouldn't have survived. Holding her glasses on her nose, Vicki bent over the brakeline again; something didn't look right.

"Why the hell would anyone build a car so that the brake line rubbed?"

She could hear the shrug in the mechanic's voice. "Could be 'cause it's an old car. Built in '76, things go wrong. Could've been a mistake on the line. No two cars are exactly alike."

All right, it made sense, bad luck and nothing more had put her and Rose and Peter in the car when that little mistake had paid off. *Jesus, if you can't count on a BMW. . . .*

Except. . . . There were two spots bracketing the tear where the yellow markings on the hose showed brighter, places where accumulated dirt could have rubbed off on someone's fingers as they gave that little mistake a helping hand. Careful not to touch the rubber, Vicki pressed her finger against the protruding bit of metal that had done the actual damage. While not exactly sharp, it held a definite edge.

"Suppose you wanted to hole someone's brake line and yet made it look like an accident," she gestured down into the engine, "how long would it take you to duplicate that?"

The mechanic looked speculative. "Not long."

They'd been in the restaurant for an hour and a half. Plenty of time.

Intrigued by the idea, he reached down into the car. "I'd grab it here . . ."

"Don't touch it!"

He jerked back as though stung. "You don't think. . . ."

"I don't think I want to take any chances. I want you to call the police. I have the number of the officer at the scene if you don't."

"No. I got it."

"Good. Tell him you've found suspicions of tampering and, if nothing else, they should take prints." She had her own small kit, not exactly high tech but certainly up to lifting prints off greasy hoses. If, however, police technology could be brought to bear, so much the better.

"Why don't you call?"

"Because you're the expert."

He scowled at her for a moment then sighed and said, "Okay, lady. You win. I'll call."

"Now," she suggested.

"Okay. Now. You don't touch nothing while I'm gone."

"Fine. And you don't touch anything until the ident man has come and gone."

The scowl returned. He went two steps, stopped, and looked back. "Someone tried to kill you, eh?"

"Maybe." Or Peter. Or Rose.

He shook his head, his expression hovering between respect and disgust. "Bet it isn't the first time." He continued to the office without waiting for a reply.

Vicki rubbed her right thumb against the faint scars on her left wrist, saw again the inhuman smile, and heard the demon say, *"So you are to be the sacrifice."* A trickle of sweat that had nothing to do with the heat ran down between her breasts and behind it, she could feel her heart begin to race. Death had been so close that a shadow of it remained long after the substance had been defeated. With practiced skill, she pushed the memory away and buried it deep.

The world outside the memory seemed strange for a moment then she shook her head and forced herself back to the present. Out by the car, Rose was telling Celluci some kind of story that involved a great deal of arm waving, Peter hovering protectively at her side. When Celluci laughed at something Rose said, Vicki saw Peter's shoulders stiffen.

"Peter! Could you come here, please?"

Reluctantly, he came.

She nodded toward the car. "What are the odds that

you could pick up someone's scent off a rubber brake-line?"

Peter glanced down into the engine and wrinkled his nose. "Slim to none. The smell of the brake fluid is kind of strong. Why?"

Vicki saw no point in lying, the wer already knew they were under the threat of death. "I think someone engineered yesterday's accident."

"Wow. Henry's going to be pissed."

"Henry?"

"Well, they totaled his car."

"And almost killed us," Vicki reminded him.

"Oh. Yeah."

The office door opened and the mechanic walked back into the garage. He didn't look thrilled. "Okay. I called. He says someone'll come around. Later." He glared at the car and then up at Vicki. "He says he wants to talk to you. Don't leave town."

"I wouldn't dream of it. Thanks, you've been a big help."

He returned her smile with a snort and pointedly bent to work on a late model blue Saab that had seen better days.

Vicki recognized a dismissal when she saw it. As there was nothing more she could do here, she even decided to pay attention to it. "Come on, Peter."

Frowning thoughtfully, Peter followed her out of the garage.

"What?" she asked as they crossed the parking lot to Celluci's car.

"It's probably nothing, but while you were talking to Mr. Sunshine I had a sniff around the edges of the hood. I mean, if someone messed with the brakes they had to get the hood open first." He took a deep breath. "Anyway, for just a second there, I thought I caught a scent I recognized. Then I lost it. Sorry."

"Would you know it again?"

"I think so."

"Okay, if you do come across it, tell me immediately. This guy is dangerous."

"Hey," he protested. "I know. It's my dad that got shot."

Vicki wondered if she should tell him that the person who'd shot his father and the person who'd tampered with Henry's car weren't likely to be the same man—the actions were far too different—and in her book this new threat, with no pattern to make it predictable, was a lot more dangerous. She decided against it. What good would it do?

Celluci watched until Peter and Rose had gone inside then he backed out of Dr. Dixon's driveway and headed downtown. "It's hard not to like them, isn't it?"

"What's not to like?"

"This from the woman who once said that teenagers should be against the law?"

"Well, they're not exactly your typical teenagers, are they?"

Celluci glanced sideways at her. "All right, what's bothering you? You've been in a mood since we left the garage."

Vicki shoved her glasses up her nose and sighed. "I was just thinking . . ."

"That's a first."

She ignored him. ". . . that if someone's taking the trouble to try to kill me, I must know something I'm not aware of knowing. The killer thinks I'm getting too close."

"Or you weren't the target, Rose and Peter were. You were just there."

"No, there's already a system set up to kill the wer, why change it? It's still working. I have a feeling this was aimed at me."

"A hunch?"

"Call it what you like, but if you call it woman's intu- ition, I'll rip your face off."

As he had no intention of saying anything so blatantly suicidal, he ignored the threat. "So let's go over what you do know."

"Shouldn't take that long." Knees braced against the dash, Vicki ticked the points off on her fingers. "I know

Barry Wu didn't do it. I know Dr. Dixon didn't do it. I know Arthur Fortrin didn't do it. *Anyone* else might have, up to and including a chance acquaintance either of those three might have bragged to in a bar. Once Barry tells me who around London is capable of that kind of shot, well, I'll make some comparisons with those lists of the people who use the conservation area regularly. Hopefully we can decode these directions to his apartment before he leaves for work."

Celluci plucked the sheet of paper off her lap, scanned it, and tossed it back. He had complete faith in his ability to find his way around in spite of the morning's scenic tour of the countryside. "And if Barry doesn't know?"

"Someone knows. I'll find them." She smoothed the map out on her leg. "Oh, and it isn't Frederick Kleinbein either."

"Who?"

"Technically, I guess you could call him their nearest neighbor. He informed me that the Heerkens have a deep, dark secret." She grinned. "They're nudists, you know."

"Nudists?"

"So he tells me. Apparently, the locals prefer to believe in nudists over werewolves."

He shot her a sour look. "Hardly surprising. I am, however, surprised it hasn't brought flocks of young men out armed with telephoto lenses."

"I got the impression the 'dogs' took care of that problem."

Celluci who had been on the receiving end of one of those "dogs" in action could see how it might discourage a casual voyeur.

Vicki interpreted his grunt as agreement and went on. "The only other people I've really talked to are Carl Biehn and Mark Williams."

It took him a moment to place the names. "The two guys this morning?"

"That's right."

"So maybe it's them."

"Not likely." She snorted. "Can you see someone like Williams taking the time and trouble to become a marksman? Uh uh. The way I read him, it's instant gratification or he's not interested."

"And the older man? The uncle?"

Vicki sighed. "He's a vegetarian."

"He's not eating the wer, Vicki, he's just killing them."

"And he's a deeply religious man."

"So are a lot of nut cakes. It's not mutually exclusive."

"And he gardens."

"*And* you like him."

She sighed again, flicking the air-conditioning vent open and closed. "Yeah. And I like him. He seems like such a basically decent person."

"Another feeling?"

"Piss off, Celluci." Between the bright sunlight, yesterday's injury, and the lack of sleep, she was developing one mother of a headache. "Having a slime-bag for a nephew is hardly grounds to accuse someone of multiple murders. I am, however, going to ask Barry to check out Mr. Williams for priors, just in case. If *you* want to be helpful, and the wind is in the right direction, you can spend tonight watching the tree."

"Thank you very much. Just what I always wanted to do, spend the night out in the woods being eaten alive by mosquitoes." *While you and Henry are comfy cozy inside? Not fucking likely.* He glanced over at her and then back at the road. "Who says he'll go back to it?"

"It's part of his pattern when the wind's off the field."

"Then why don't you cut it down?"

"I've thought about it."

"While you're thinking about that, here's another one. If you know he keeps going back to that tree, why haven't *you* staked it out?"

"How? *You* know I can't see a damned thing after dark. Besides, Henry went out. . . ."

"You sent a civilian!"

"He volunteered!" Vicki snapped, ignoring the fact that she herself was now a civilian.

"And did he volunteer to get shot?"

"Henry's a grown man. He knew the risks."

"A grown man. Right. And that's another thing, according to his driver's license, Fitzroy is only twenty-four years old." He took his eyes off the road long enough to glare at her. "You're almost eight years older than he is, or doesn't that . . . What's so funny?"

Although the vibrations were doing nasty things to the inside of her head, Vicki couldn't stop laughing. *Eight whole years. Good God.* Finally, the frigid silence on the other side of the car got through and she managed to get ahold of herself. *Eight whole years.* . . . She took her glasses off and wiped her eyes on the shoulder of her shirt. "Mike, you have no idea of how little that matters."

"Obviously not," Celluci grunted through gritted teeth.

"Hey! Are we in hot pursuit or something? You just accelerated through a yellow light." Vicki took one look at the set of his jaw and decided the time had come to change the subject. "What could I possibly know that's worth killing to protect?"

It wasn't the most graceful of conversational transitions but Celluci grabbed at it. He suddenly did *not* want to know what she'd been laughing at. At a full twelve years older than Henry fucking Fitzroy, he didn't think his ego was up to it. "If I were you, I'd have Carl Biehn and his nephew pulled in for questioning."

"On what grounds?"

"Someone thinks you're getting too close and they're the only *someones* you've talked to who haven't been cleared."

"Well, you're not me." Vicki scratched at a mosquito bite on the back of her calf. "And in case you've missed the point, not only is this not a police case but we can't get the police involved."

"They're already involved, or have you forgotten last night's reported gunshot wound?"

"Queen Street. Turn here. Barry's apartment building is number 321." Pushing her glasses up her nose, she added. "The police only think they're involved. They haven't a clue about what's really going on."

"And you don't think they'll find out?" he asked while swinging wide around the corner to avoid a small boy on a bicycle.

Vicki spread her hands. "How are they going to find out? You going to tell them?"

"They'll investigate."

"Sure they will. The OPP'll swing around by the conservation area a little more frequently for a couple of weeks and then something more important than an accidental shooting'll come up for them to allot man-hours to."

"But it wasn't an accident," Celluci pointed out, making an effort and keeping his temper.

"*They* don't know that." Vicki forced herself to relax. Clenched teeth just made her temple throb and had no effect on the thickhead sitting next to her. "Nor are they going to find out."

"Well, they're going to have to get involved when you find out who's doing the killing. Or," he continued sarcastically, "had you planned on arranging an accident that would take care of everything?"

"There." She pointed. "Three twenty-one. Sign says visitor's parking is in the rear."

The silence around the words spoke volumes.

"Jesus Christ, Vicki. You *aren't* going to bring this to trial, are you?"

She studied the toes of her sneakers.

"Answer me, damn it!" He slammed on the brakes and, almost before the car had stopped, grabbed her shoulder, twisting her around to face him.

"Trial?" She jerked her shoulder free. God, he was so dense sometimes. "And what happens to the wer at a trial?"

"The law . . ."

"They don't want the law, Celluci, they want justice and if the killer goes to trial they won't get it. You know as well as I do that the victim goes on trial with the accused. What kind of a chance would the wer have? If you're not white, or you're poor, or, God forbid, you're a woman, the system sees you as less than human. The wer *aren't* human! How do you think the system is going to see them? And what kind of a life would they have after it was finished with them?"

He couldn't believe what he was hearing. "Are you trying to convince me or are you trying to convince yourself?"

"Shut up, Celluci!" He was deliberately not understanding. *His own neat little world view gets screwed and he can't adapt. That's not my fault.*

His voice rose in volume to match hers. "I'm not going to stand around and watch you throw away everything you've believed in for so long."

"Then leave!"

"You're willing to be judge and jury—who's to be the executioner? Or are you going to do *that,* too?"

They stared at each other for moment then Vicki closed her eyes. The pounding of her heart became rifle fire and on the inside of her lids she saw Donald, bleeding, then one by one the rest of the pack, sprawled where the bullets dropped them, their fur splattered with blood, and only she was left to mourn. She drew in a long shuddering breath, and then another, and then she opened her eyes.

"I don't know," she said quietly. "I'll do what I have to."

"And if that includes murder?"

"Leave it, Mike. Please. I said I didn't know."

He forced both hands up through his hair, closing his lips around all but one of the things he wanted to say. He even managed to keep his voice sounding reasonably calm. "You used to know."

"Life used to be a lot simpler. Besides," she unhooked the seat belt, gave a shaky and totally unconvincing laugh, and opened the car door. "I haven't even caught the son-of-a-bitch yet. Let's worry about this shit when it hits the fan."

Celluci followed her into Barry Wu's building, concern and anger in about equal proportions grinding together inside his head. *Life used to be a lot simpler.* He sure couldn't argue with that.

"Most of all, you need a good set of knives."

"I have the knives."

"Pah. New knives. Factory edges are crap."

"I'll have them sharpened this afternoon."

"Pah." The elderly man pulled a torn envelope out of the mess of papers on the kitchen table and scribbled an address on the back of it. "Go here," he commanded as he passed it to his visitor, "last place in town that might do a decent job."

Mark Williams folded the paper in half and tucked it in his wallet. A few questions asked around the fur trade had gotten him the old man's name. A fifty had bought him a couple of hours of instruction. Considering what the pelts were going to net him, he considered it money well spent.

"Okay. Listen up. We go over this one more time and if you go slow you shouldn't have any trouble. Your first cut is along the length of the belly—almost a seam there anyway—then . . ."

"The problem is, there isn't anyone else. In fact, I'm not positive I could make those shots myself. Not at night." Barry stuck his head out of the bedroom where he was getting dressed for work. "I haven't done much scope work."

"What about one of the special weapons and tactics people?"

His eyebrows drew down. "You mean a cop?"

Celluci sighed. In his opinion, young men always looked petulant when they tried to scowl. "You trying to tell me London's never had a bad cop?"

"Well . . . no . . . but it's not like we're Toronto or anything." He disappeared back into the bedroom and emerged a moment later, uniform shirt hanging open and carrying his boots. "I guess I could ask around," he offered, perching on the edge of the one remaining empty chair. The apartment was a little short of furniture although both the television and stereo system were first rate. "But frankly, I don't think any of those guys could do it either." He took a deep breath. "I know it sounds like bragging but even considering my lack of scope work, none of them are in my league."

Vicki picked Barry's police college graduation picture

up from its place of honor on top of the television. Only one of the earnestly smiling faces in the photograph belonged to a visible minority; Barry Wu. *Plus five women and a werewolf. What a great mix.* All the women were white. Technically, so was the werewolf. *And the police wonder why community relations are falling apart.* Actually, she had to admit, the police knew why community relations were falling apart, they just couldn't come up with the quick fix solution everybody wanted in the face of such a long-term problem. Unfortunately, "it'll take time" wasn't much of an answer when time was running out.

"I'm surprised the S.W.A.T. boys haven't scooped you up." She carefully set the picture back down. It was still strange thinking of herself and *the police* as separate units.

He smiled a little self-consciously. "I've been warned the moment I come back with Olympic gold, I'm theirs." The smile faded as he bent to lace his boots. "I guess I'd better check them out, hadn't I?"

"Well, if you can find out what their best marksmen were doing on the nights of the murders, it would help."

"Yeah." He sighed. "Pity we didn't have some big hostage crisis those nights that'd clear them."

"Pity," Vicki agreed, and hid a totally inappropriate smile. The boy—young man—had been completely serious.

"I just can't believe that someone'd be shooting at Colin's family. I mean," he sat up and began buttoning his shirt, fingers trembling with indignation, "they're probably the nicest people I know."

"It doesn't bother you that these people turn into animals?" Celluci asked.

Barry stiffened. "They don't turn into animals," he snapped. "Just because they have a fur-form doesn't make them animals. And anyway, most of the animals I've met lately have been on two legs! And besides, Colin's a great cop. Once he picks up a suspect's scent the perp's had it. You couldn't ask for a better guy to back you up in a tight situation, and what's more, the wer practically invented the concept of the team-player."

"I only wondered if it bothered you," Celluci told him mildly.

"No." Savagely shoving his shirttails into his pants, Barry turned faintly red. "Not anymore. I mean, once you get to know a guy, you can't hate him just because he's a werewolf."

Words of wisdom for our time, Vicki thought. "Back to the shooting . . ."

"Yeah, I think I know someone who might be able to help. Bertie Reid. She's a real buff, you know, one of those people who can quote facts and figures at you from the last fifty years. If there's someone in the area capable of making those shots, she'll know it. Or she'll be able to find it out."

"Does she shoot?"

"Occasionally small arms but not the high caliber stuff anymore. She must be over seventy."

"Do you know her address?"

"No, I don't, and her phone number is unlisted—I heard her mention it one day at the range—but she's not hard to find. She drops by the Grove Road Sportsman's Club most afternoons, sits up in the clubroom, has a few cups of tea and criticizes everyone's shooting." He glanced up from the piece of paper he was writing the directions on. "She told me I kept my forward arm too tense." Flexing the arm in question, he added, "She was right."

"Why don't you practice at the police range?" Celluci asked.

Barry looked a little sheepish as he handed over the address of the club. "I do occasionally. But I always end up with an audience and, well, the targets there all look like people. I don't like that."

"I never cared for it much myself," Vicki told him, dropping the folded piece of paper in her purse. It might be realistic, certainly anything a cop would have to shoot would be people-shaped, but the yearly weapons qualifying always left her feeling slightly ashamed of her skill.

They accompanied Barry down to the parking lot, watched him shrug into a leather jacket—"I'd rather sweat than leave my elbows on the pavement."—and a helmet with a day-glow orange strip down the back, carefully pack his cap under the seat of his motorcycle, and roar away.

Vicki sighed, carefully leaning back on the hot metal of Celluci's car. "Please tell me I was never that gung ho."

"You weren't," Celluci snorted. "You were worse." He opened the car door and eased himself down onto the vinyl seat. There hadn't been any shade to park in, not that he would have seen it given the conversation they'd been involved in when they arrived. Swearing under his breath as his elbow brushed the heated seatback, he unlocked Vicki's door and was busying himself with the air conditioning when she got in.

The echoes of their fight hung in the car. Neither of them spoke, afraid it might begin again.

Celluci had no desire to do a monologue on the dangers of making moral judgments and he knew that as far as Vicki was concerned the topic was closed. *But if she thinks I'm leaving before this is over, she can think again.* He didn't have to be back at work until Thursday and after that, if he had to, he'd use sick time. It was more than Henry Fitzroy now, Vicki needed saving from herself.

For the moment, they'd maintain the truce.

"It's almost 2:30 and I'm starved. How about stopping for something to eat?"

Vicki glanced up from Barry's scribbled directions and gratefully acknowledged the peace offering. "Only if we eat in the car on the way."

"Fine." He pulled out onto the street. "Only if it's not chicken. In this heat the car'll suck up the smell of the Colonel and I'll never be free of it."

They stopped at the first fast food place they came to. Sitting in the car, eating french fries and waiting for Vicki to get out of the washroom, Celluci's attention kept wandering to a black and gold jeep parked across the street. He knew he'd seen it before but not where, only that the memory carried vaguely unpleasant connotations.

The driver had parked in front of an ancient shoe

repair shop. A faded sign in the half of the window Celluci could see proclaimed, *You don't look neat if your shoes are beat.* He puzzled over the fragment of memory until the answer walked out of the shop.

"Mark Williams. No wonder I had a bad feeling about it." Williams had the kind of attitude Celluci hated. He'd take out-and-out obnoxiousness over superficial charm any day. He grinned around a mouthful of burger. *Which certainly explains my relationship with Vicki.*

Whistling cheerfully, Williams came around to the driver's side of the jeep, opened the door, and tossed a bulky brown paper package onto the passenger seat before climbing in himself.

Had he been in his own jurisdiction, Celluci might have gone over for a chat, just on principle; let the man know he was being watched, try to find out what was in the package. He strongly believed in staying on top of the kind of potential situations Mark Williams represented. As it was, he sat and watched him drive away.

With the jeep gone, a second sign became visible in the shoe shop window.

Knives sharpened.

"Bertie Reid?" The middle-aged man sitting behind the desk frowned. "I don't think she's come in yet but . . ." The phone rang and he rolled his eyes as he answered. "Grove Road Sportsman's Club. That's correct, tomorrow night in the pistol range. No, ma'am, there'll be no shooting while the function is going on. Thank you. Hope to see you there. Damn phones," he continued as he hung up. "Alexander Graham Bell should've been given a pair of cement overshoes and dropped off the continental shelf. Now then, where were we?"

"Bertie Reid," Vicki prompted.

"Right." He glanced up at the wall clock. "It's only just turned three, Bertie's not likely to be here for another hour. If you don't mind my askin', what's a couple of Toronto PI's want with Bertie anyway?"

More than a little amused by his assumption that her ID covered Celluci as well, Vicki gave him her best professional smile, designed to install confidence in the general public. "We're looking for some information on competition shooting and Barry Wu told us that Ms. Reid was our best bet."

"You know Barry?"

"We make it our business to work closely with the police." Celluci had no problem with being perceived as Vicki's partner. Better that than flashing his badge all over London—behavior guaranteed to be unpopular with his superiors in Toronto.

"And so do we." His voice grew defensive. "Gun club members take responsibility for their weapons. Every piece of equipment that comes into this place is registered with both the OPP and local police and we keep no ammunition on the premises. It's the assholes who think a gun is a high-powered pecker extension—begging your pardon—who start blasting away in restaurants and school yards or who accidentally blow away Uncle Ralph while showing off their new .30 caliber toy, not our people."

"Not that it's better to be shot on purpose than by accident," Vicki pointed out acerbically. Still, she acknowledged his point. If the entire concept of firearms couldn't be stuffed back into Pandora's box, better the glamour be removed and they become just another tool or hobby. Personally, however, she'd prefer worldwide gun control legislation so tight that everyone from manufacturers to consumers would give up rather than face the paperwork, and the punishment for the use of a gun while committing a crime would fit the crime . . . and they could use the bastard's own weapon then bury it with the body. She'd developed this philosophy when she saw what a twelve gauge shotgun at close range could do to the body of a seven-year-old boy.

"Do you mind if we wait for Ms. Reid to arrive?" Celluci asked, before the man at the desk could decide if Vicki's words had been agreement or attack. He figured he'd already gone through his allotment of impassioned diatribes for the day.

Frowning slightly, the man shrugged. "I guess it won't hurt if Barry sent you. He's the club's pride and joy, you know; nobody around here comes close to being in his league. He'll be going to the next Olympics and, if there's any justice in the world, coming back with gold. Damn!" As he reached for the phone, he motioned toward the stairs. "Clubroom's on the second floor, you can wait for Bertie up there."

The clubroom had been furnished with a number of brown or gold institutional sofas and chairs, a couple of good sized tables, and a trophy case. A small kitchen in one corner held a large coffee urn, a few jars of instant coffee, an electric kettle and four teapots in varying sizes. The room's only inhabitant at 3:00 on a Monday afternoon was a small gray cat curled up on a copy of the *Shooter's Bible* who looked up as Vicki and Celluci came in then pointedly ignored them.

From behind the large windows in the north wall came the sound of rifle fire.

Celluci glanced outside then picked up a pair of binoculars from one of the tables and pointed them down-range at the targets. "Unless they're cleverly trying to throw us off the trail," he said a moment later passing them to Vicki, "neither of these two are the marksman we're looking for."

Vicki set the binoculars back on the table without bothering to use them. "Look, Celluci, there's no reason for both of us to be stuck here until four. Why don't you swing around by Dr. Dixon's, take the twins and their father home, and then come back and pick me up."

"While you do what?"

"Ask a few questions around the club then talk to Bertie. Nothing you'd need to baby-sit me during."

"Are you trying to get rid of me?" he asked, leaning back against the cinder block wall.

"I'm trying to be considerate." She watched him fold his arms and stifled a sigh. "Look, I know how much you hate waiting for things and I doubt there's enough going on around here to keep both of us busy for an hour."

As much as he disliked admitting it, she had a point. "We could talk," he suggested warily.

Vicki shook her head. Another *talk* with Michael Celluci was the last thing she needed right now. "When it's over, we'll talk."

He reached out and pushed her glasses up her nose. "I'll hold you to that." It sounded more like a threat than a promise. "Call the farm when you want me to start back. No point in me arriving in the middle of things."

"Thanks, Mike."

"No problem."

"Now why did I do that?" she wondered once she had the clubroom to herself. "I know exactly what he's going to do." The chairs were more comfortable than they looked and she sank gratefully into the gold velour. "He only agreed to go so he could pump the wer about Henry without me around to interfere." Did she *want* him to find out about Henry?

"He's already been searching into Henry's background," she told the cat. "Better he finds out under controlled conditions than by accident."

It was a perfectly plausible reason and Vicki decided to believe it. She only hoped Henry would.

Thirteen

"I'm sorry, you just missed him. He's gone back to bed."

"Gone back to bed?" Celluci glanced down at his watch. "It's ten to four in the afternoon. Is he sick?"

Nadine shook her head. "Not exactly, but his allergies were acting up, so he took some medicine and went upstairs to lie down." She placed the folded sheet carefully in the laundry basket, reminding herself to inform Henry of his allergies when darkness finally awakened him.

"I'd hoped for a chance to talk to him."

"He said he'd be up around dusk. The pollen count doesn't seem to be as high after dark." As she spoke, she reached out to take the next piece of clean laundry from the line and overbalanced. Instantly, Celluci's strong grip on her elbow steadied her. *Almost a pity he isn't a wer,* she thought, simultaneously thanking him and shaking off his hand. *And it's a very good thing Stuart is out in the barn.* "If you stay for supper," she continued, "you can talk to Henry later."

Allergies. Henry Fitzroy did not look like the type of man to be laid low by allergies. As much as Celluci wanted to believe that a writer, and a romance writer yet, was an ineffectual weakling living in a fantasy world, he couldn't deny the feeling of strength he got from the man. He was still more than half convinced the writing covered connections to organized crime. After all, how long could it take to write a book? There'd be plenty of time left over to get involved in a great many unsavory things.

Unfortunately, he couldn't wait around indefinitely.

"Thank you for the invitation, but . . ."

"Detective?"

He turned toward the summons.

"It's Ms. Nelson. On the phone for you."

"If you'll excuse me?"

Nadine nodded, barely visible under the folds of a slightly ragged fitted sheet. Nocturnal changes were hard on the linens.

Wondering what had gone wrong, Celluci went into the house and followed the redheaded teenager into a small office just off the kitchen. The office was obviously the remains of a larger room, left over when indoor plumbing and a bathroom had been put into the farmhouse.

"Thank you, uh . . ." He'd met the younger set of twins not fifteen minutes before, when they'd appeared to help Peter and Rose get Donald upstairs and into bed, but he had no idea which one this was.

"Jennifer." She giggled and tossed her mane of russet hair back off her face. "I'm the prettier one."

"Pardon me." Celluci smiled down at her. "I'll remember that for next time."

She giggled again and fled.

Still smiling, he picked up the old black receiver—probably the original phone from when the line had been put in thirty years before. "Celluci."

Vicki, who'd learned her phone manners in the same school, had no problem with the lack of pleasantries. She seldom used them herself. "I just found out that Bertie Reid won't be in until five at the earliest."

"You going to wait?"

"I don't see as I have an option."

"Shall I come in?"

"No point, really. Stay around the farm so I can reach you and try to keep the we . . . Heerkens from going out to those south fields."

"Should be safe enough in the daytime."

"I don't care. No one else gets shot if I have to leash the lot of them."

She hung up without asking about Henry. Celluci

found that a little surprising, as though she'd known he wouldn't be around. Of course, she could just be showing more tact than usual, but he doubted it.

Mulling over possibilities, he returned to the yard and Nadine. "It looks like I'll be staying around for a while, the woman Vicki needs to speak with is going to be late."

"No problem." Which wasn't the exact truth, but in Nadine's opinion, Stuart needed to work on tolerating non-wer dominants. This Toronto detective would be good practice for the next time Stuart had to go into the co-op; the last time had almost been a disaster. It was getting hard enough to keep their existence a secret without Stuart wanting to challenge every alpha male he met. And while she recognized her mate's difficulty in accepting outsiders as protectors of the pack, it was done and he was just going to have to learn to live with it. *Or we all die without it. Like Silver.* She passed Celluci a handful of clothespins. "Put these in that basket, please."

Frowning a little at her sudden sadness, Celluci complied, wondering if he should say something. And if so, what?

"Mom?" The perfect picture of six-year-old dejection, Daniel dragged himself around the corner of the house and collapsed against the step. "I wanna go to the pond, but there's no one to take me. Daddy's got his head stuck in a tractor and he says Peter and Rose gotta fix that fence up by the road and Uncle Donald's sick and Colin's gone to work and Jennifer and Marie are taking care of Uncle Donald . . ." He let his voice trail off and sighed deeply. "I was wondering . . . ?"

"Not right now, sweetie." She reached down and stroked his hair back out of his eyes. "Maybe later."

Daniel's ebony brows drew down. "But I wanna go now. I'm hot."

"I can take him." Celluci spread his hands as Nadine turned to look at him. "I don't have anything else to do." Which was true as far as it went. It had also occurred to him that children, of any species, often knew more than adults suspected. If Fitzroy was an old family friend then Daniel might be able to fill in some of those irritating blanks.

"Can you swim?" Nadine asked at last.

"Like a fish."

"*Please,* Mom."

She weighed her child's comfort against her child's safety with this virtual stranger. In all fairness, last night couldn't be weighed against him. Males were not accountable for their actions when their blood was up.

"Mommy!"

And the challenge had, essentially, given him a position of sorts within the pack. "All right."

Daniel threw his arms around her legs with what came very close to a bark of joy, and bounded away, throwing an excited, "Come on!" back over his shoulder at Celluci, who followed at a more sedate pace.

"Hey!"

He turned, barely managing to snag the towel before it hit him in the face.

Nadine grinned, tongue protruding just a little from between very white teeth. "You'll probably need that. And don't let him eat any frogs. He'll spoil his dinner."

"I dunno. He's been coming for my whole life."

Translation: three or four years. "Does he come very often?"

"Sure. Lots of times."

"Do you like him?"

Daniel turned around and walked backward down the path, peering up at Celluci through a wild shock of dusty black hair. "Course I do. Henry brings me stuff."

"Like what?"

"Action figures. You know, like superheros and stuff." He frowned. "They chew up awful easy though." A bare heel slammed into a hummock of grass and, arms windmilling, he sat down. He growled at the offending obstacle then, having warned it against further attempts to trip him, accepted Celluci's offered hand.

"Are you okay?"

"Sure." He ran a little bit ahead then came back, just to prove he was all right. "I've fallen farther than that."

Celluci slapped at a mosquito. "Is the pond far?" He pulled the squashed insect out of the hair of his arm and wiped the mess on his jeans.

"Nope." Three jumps proved that an overhanging branch was still too high and he moved on.

"Is it part of the farm?"

"Uh-huh. Grandpa had it dugged a gizillion years ago. When Mommy was little," he added, just in case Celluci had no idea how long a gizillion years was.

"Does Henry take you swimming?"

"Nah. I'm not allowed to swim at night 'less everybody's there."

"Isn't Henry ever here in the daytime?"

Daniel sighed and stared up at Celluci like he was some kind of idiot. "Course he is. It's daytime now."

"But he's asleep."

"Yeah." A butterfly distracted him and he bounded off after it until it flew high up into one of the poplars bordering the path and stayed there.

"Why doesn't he ever take you swimming in the daytime."

"Cause he's asleep."

"Just when you want to go swimming?"

Daniel wrinkled his nose and looked up from the bug he was investigating. "No."

The security guard at Fitzroy's building had already told Celluci that Henry Fitzroy seemed to live his life at night. Working nights and sleeping days wasn't that unusual but added to all the other bits and pieces—or to the lack of bits and pieces—it certainly didn't help allay suspicion. "Does Henry ever bring anyone with him?"

"Course. Brought Vicki."

"Anyone else?"

"Nope."

"Do you know what Henry does when he's at home?"

Daniel knew he wasn't supposed to tell that Henry was a vampire, just as he wasn't to tell about his family being werewolves. It was one of the earliest lessons he'd been taught. But the policeman knew about the furforms and he was a friend of Vicki's and she knew about

Henry. So maybe he did, too. Daniel decided to play it safe. "I'm not supposed to tell."

That sounded promising. "Not supposed to tell what?"

Daniel scowled. This grown-up was real dull, all he wanted to do was talk and that meant no fur-form. Vicki had been lots more fun; she'd thrown sticks for him to chase. "You mad at Henry 'cause he's with your mate?"

"She's not my mate," Celluci snapped, before he considered the wisdom of answering the question at all.

"You smell like she is." His brow furrowed. "She doesn't though."

He had to ask. "And what does she smell like?"

"Herself."

This is not the type of conversation to have with a six-year-old, Celluci reminded himself as the path opened out into a small meadow, the pond shimmering blue-green in a hollow at the far end.

"Oh, boy! Ducks!" Daniel tore out of his shorts and raced across the field, barking shrilly, tail thrashing from side to side. The half dozen ducks waited until he was almost at the pond before taking wing. He plunged in after them, splashing and barking until they were out of sight behind the trees then sat down in the shallows, had a quick drink, and looked back, panting, to see if his companion had witnessed his routing of the enemy.

Celluci laughed and scooped up the discarded shorts. "Well done!" he called. He'd felt a superstitious prickling up his spine when the boy had first changed, but it hadn't been able to maintain itself against the rest of the scene. Crossing the meadow, he decided to leave Henry for the rest of the afternoon and just enjoy himself.

"Is it deep?" he asked, arriving at the pond.

" 'Bout as deep as you near the middle," Daniel told him after a moment's study.

Over six feet was pretty deep for such a little guy. "Can you swim?"

Daniel licked a drip of water off his nose. "Course I can," he declared indignantly. "I can dog paddle."

*   *   *

"Think we'll get this done by supper time?" Rose asked, scrubbing a dribble of sweat off her forehead.

"I didn't think Uncle Stuart gave us an option," Peter panted, leaning on the mallet. "He's sure been growly lately."

"In case you'd forgotten, the family's under attack. He has a good reason."

"Sure, but that doesn't mean he has to growl at me."

Rose only shrugged and started stomping the earth tightly around the base of the metal fence post. She hated the amount of clothing she had to wear for this—shoes, jeans, shirt—but fences couldn't be fixed in a sundress, especially not when every section seemed determined to support at least one raspberry bush.

"I mean," Peter clipped an eight-inch length of wire off the bale and began reattaching the lower part of the fence to the post, "everything you do, he snaps at you."

Everything you *do, you mean.* Rose sighed and kept her mouth shut. She'd been feeling so strange herself lately, she certainly wasn't going to criticize her twin.

He squinted up at the sun, burning yellow-white in the late afternoon sky, and fought the urge to pant. "What a day to be working outside. I don't believe how hot it is."

"At least you can work without a shirt on."

"So could you."

"Not right next to the road."

"Why not?" He grinned. "There's never any traffic along here and besides, they're so little no one'll be able to see them anyway."

"Peter!"

"Peter!" he echoed, as she took a swing at him. "Okay, if you don't like that idea, why don't you trot back to the house and get us some water."

Rose snorted. "Right. While you lean on the fence and watch the world go by."

"No." He bent and picked up the brush shears. "While I clear the crap from around the next post."

She looked from the post to her brother, then turned and started walking back to the house. "You better have that done . . ." she warned, over her shoulder.

"Or what?"

"Or . . . Or I'll bite your tail off!" She laughed as Peter cowered at their favorite childhood threat, and then she broke into a run, feeling his gaze on her back until she left the field and started down the lane.

Peter yanked at the waistband of his jeans. They were too tight, too constrictive, too hot. He wanted . . . Actually, he didn't know what he wanted anymore.

"This has been one hell of a summer," he muttered, moving along the fence. He missed his Aunt Sylvia and his Uncle Jason. With the two older wer gone, it seemed like he and Rose had no choice but to become adults in their place.

He suddenly wanted to howl but worked off some of his frustrations in hacking at the brush instead. Maybe he should get a life outside the pack, like Colin had. He tossed that idea almost the instant he had it. Colin didn't have a twin and Peter couldn't imagine living without Rose beside him. They almost hadn't made it through grade eleven when class schedules kept them apart for most of the day. The guidance counselor had no idea how close she'd come to being bitten when she refused to change things. She'd said it was time they broke free of an unhealthy emotional dependency. Peter beheaded a few daisies, working the shears like two-handed scissors. *That's all she knew. Maybe if humans developed a little emotional dependency the world wouldn't be so fucked up.*

The sound of an approaching car brought him over to the fence where he could get a look at the driver. The black and gold jeep slowed as it drew even with him, stopped a few feet down the road, then backed up spraying gravel. It was the same jeep that had been parked at the end of the lane Sunday morning when he'd gone to the mailbox to fetch Shadow. Hackles rising, he put down the shears and jumped the fence. Time to find out why this guy was hanging around.

Mark Williams couldn't believe his luck. Not only was there a solitary werewolf right up by the road where he could get to it, but it was one of the redheads. One of the young redheads. And in his experience, teenage anythings could be easily manipulated into impulsive, reckless behavior.

Even in jeans and running shoes, the creature had a certain wolflike grace, and as Mark watched it jump the fence and start toward the car he became convinced that this was the other version of the animal he'd seen by the mailbox yesterday. The set of its head, the expression of wary curiosity, was, given the variation in form, identical.

He rolled down the window, having already determined how to take advantage of this chance meeting. He'd always believed he did his best work off the cuff.

"You one of the Heerkens?"

"Yeah. What of it?"

"You may have noticed me around a bit lately."

"Yeah."

Mark recognized the stance. The creature wanted to be a hero. *Well, keep your pants on, you'll get your chance.* "I've, uh, had my eye on your little problem."

"What problem's that?"

He pointed his finger and said, "Bang. Hear you lost two members of your family this month. I have, uh . . ." The sudden noise startled him, especially when he realized what it was. The creature was growling, the sound beginning deep in its throat and emerging clearly as threat. Mark pulled his arm into the car and kept one finger on the window control. No point taking unnecessary chances. "I have information that might help you catch the person responsible. Are you interested?"

Russet brows drew down. "Why tell me?"

Mark smiled, being careful not to show his teeth. "Do you see anyone else to tell? I thought you might want to do something about it."

The growling faded and stopped. "But . . ."

"Never mind." Mark shrugged. *Careful now, it's almost hooked.* . . . "If you'd rather sit safely at home while other people save your family. . . ." He started to raise the window.

"No! Wait! Tell me."

Got him. "My uncle, Carl Biehn . . ."

"The grasseater?"

The disgust in the interruption couldn't be missed.

Mark hid a grin. He'd been about to say his uncle had seen something through his binoculars while bird-watching but hurriedly rewrote the script to take advantage of the prejudice of a predator for a vegetarian. Even if it did throw his uncle to the wolves. So to speak. "Yeah. The grasseater. He's the one. But no one'll believe you if you just *tell* them, so meet me in his old barn tonight after dark and I'll give you the proof."

"*I* don't believe you."

"Suit yourself. But just in case you decide your family's worth a bit of your time, I'll be in the barn at sunset. I suppose you can tell your . . . people anyway." He sighed deeply, shaking his head. "But you *know* that without proof they won't believe you—A grasseater? Ha!—not any more than you believe me and if you don't come, you'll have missed your only chance. Not something I'd like to have on my conscience."

Mark raised the window and drove away before the creature had a chance to sort out the convolutions of that last sentence and ask more questions. A number of things could go wrong with the plan, but he was pretty sure he'd read the beast correctly and the risk fell within acceptable limits.

He glanced in the rearview mirror to see the creature still standing by the side of the road. Pretty soon it would convince itself that, regardless of the stranger's motives, it couldn't hurt to check out the proof. In the way of the young, it wouldn't bother telling anyone else, not until it was sure.

"Come on, save the world. Be a hero. Impress the girls." Mark patted the bundle of leg-hold traps on the seat beside him. "Make me rich."

Rose got back to the fence with the jug of water just as the dust trail behind the car began to settle. She'd seen Peter talking to someone but hadn't been able to either see or smell who it was.

"Hey!" she called. "You standing in the road for a reason?"

Peter started.

"Peter? What's wrong?"

"Nothing." He shook himself and came back over the fence. "Nothing's wrong."

Rose frowned. *That* was a blatant lie. About to call him on it, she remembered the advice Aunt Nadine had given her when she'd mentioned Peter's recent moodiness. *"Let him have a little space, Rose. It's hard for boys around this age."* They'd never had secrets from each other before, but perhaps Aunt Nadine was right.

"Here." She held out the jug. "Maybe this will make you feel better."

"Maybe." But he doubted it. Then their fingers touched and he felt the light caress sizzle up his arm and resonate though his entire body. The world went away as he drank in her scent, musky and warm and so very, very close. He swayed. He felt the jug pulled from his lax grip and then the freezing cold splash of water over his head and torso.

Rose tried not to laugh. He looked furious but that she could deal with. "I thought you were going to faint," she offered, backing up a step.

"If we could change," Peter growled, tossing his head and spraying water from his hair, "I'd chase you into the next county and when I caught you I'd . . ."

"You'd what?" she taunted, dancing out of his reach, suddenly conscious of a strange sense of power. If only she weren't wearing so many clothes.

"I'd . . ." A rivulet of water worked its way past the waistband of his jeans. "I'd . . . damn it, Rose, that's cold! I'd bite your tail off, that's what I'd do!"

She laughed then, it was impossible not to, and the moment passed.

"Come on." She picked up the mallet and headed toward the fence. "Let's get this done before Uncle Stuart bites both our tails off."

Peter grabbed the bale of wire and followed. "But I'm all wet," he muttered, rubbing at the moisture beading the hair on his chest.

"Quit complaining. Mere moments ago, you were too hot."

She lifted the mallet over her head and the smell of her sweat washed down over him. Peter felt his ears begin to burn and all at once, he came to a decision. He would go to Carl Biehn's barn tonight.

He toyed with the idea of telling his Uncle Stuart and then discarded it. One of two things would happen, either he'd dismiss the information about the grasseater out of hand and want to know what this human was up to, or he'd believe the information and want to receive the proof himself. Either way, he, Peter, would be out of the action. *That* wasn't going to happen.

He'd tell Uncle Stuart when he had the proof. Present it to him as a fait accompli. That would show the older wer he was someone to be reckoned with. Not a child any longer. Peter's head filled with visions of challenging the alpha male and winning. Of running the pack. Of winning the right to mate.

His nostrils flared. If he came back with the information that saved the family, it couldn't help but impress Rose.

"You the young woman who's waiting to see me?"

Vicki came awake with a start and glanced down at her watch. It was 6:10. "Damn!" she muttered, shoving her glasses back up her nose. Her mouth tasted like the inside of a sewer.

"Here, maybe this'll help."

Vicki stared down at the cup of tea that had suddenly appeared in her hand and thought, *Why not?*

A moment later she had her answer.

Because I hate tea. Why did I do that?

She very carefully set the cup down and forced her scattered wits to regroup. *This is the clubroom at the Grove Road Sportman's Club. So this little old lady in blue jeans must be . . .*

"Bertie Reid?"

"In the flesh. Such as remains of it." The older woman smiled, showing a mouthful of teeth too regular to be real. "And you must be Vicki Nelson, Private Investigator." The smile broadened, the face around it compressing into an even tighter network of fine lines. "I hear you need my help."

"Yeah." Vicki stretched, apologized, and watched as

Bertie settled carefully into one of the gold velour chairs, teacup balanced precisely on one knee. "Barry Wu tells me that if anyone in this city can help, it's you."

She looked pleased. "He said that? What a sweetie. Nice boy, Barry, bound to be in the medals at the next Olympics."

"So everyone says."

"No, everyone says he'll take the gold. I don't. I don't want to jinx the boy before he gets there, neither do I want him to feel badly if he comes home with the silver. Second best in the entire world is nothing to feel badly about and all those armchair athletes who sneer at second deserve a good swift kick in the butt." She took a deep breath and a long draught of tea. "Now then, what did you want to know?"

"Is there anyone around London, not just at this club, who can shoot with anything approaching Barry Wu's accuracy?"

"No. Was there anything else?"

Vicki blinked. "No?" she repeated.

"Not that I know of. Oh, there're a couple of kids who might be decent if they practiced and one or two old-timers who occasionally show a flash of what they once had but people with Barry's ability and the discipline necessary to develop it are rare." She grinned and saluted with the cup. "That's why they only give out one gold."

"Shit!"

The old woman studied Vicki's face for a moment, then put down the teacup and settled back in the chair, crossing one denim clad leg over the other, the lime green laces in her hightops the brightest spot of color in the room. "How much do you know about competition shooting?"

"Not much," Vicki admitted.

"Then tell me why you're asking that question, and I'll tell you if you're asking the right one."

Vicki took off her glasses and scrubbed at her face with her hands. It didn't make things any clearer. In fact, she realized as the movement pulled at the bruise on her temple, it was a pretty stupid thing to do. She shoved her glasses back on and scrambled in her bag for the bottle of pills they'd given her at the hospital. *There was a time I could make love to a vampire, walk away from major car accident, rush a client to the hospital, stay up until dawn, and spend the day arguing ethics with Celluci, no problem. I must be getting old.* She took the pill dry. The only alternative was another mouthful of tea and she didn't think she was up to that.

"Cracked my head," she explained as she tossed the small plastic bottle back in her bag.

"In the line of duty?" Bertie asked, looking intrigued.

"Sort of." Vicki sighed. Somehow in the last couple of minutes, she'd come to the conclusion that Bertie was right. Without knowing more about competition shooting, she *couldn't* know if she was asking the right questions. Her voice low to prevent the only other occupant of the clubroom from overhearing, she presented an edited version of the events that had brought her to London.

Bertie whistled softly at the description of the shots that killed "two of the family dogs," then she said, "Let me be sure I've got this straight, five hundred yards on a moving target at night from twenty feet up in a pine tree?"

"As much as five, maybe as little as three."

"As little as three?" Bertie snorted. "And both dogs were killed with a single, identical head shot? Come on." Setting the teacup aside, she heaved herself out of the chair, pale blue eyes gleaming behind the split glass of her bifocals.

"Where are we going?"

"My place. One shot like that might have been a fluke, luck, nothing more. But two, two means a trained talent and you don't acquire skill like that overnight. Like I said before, there's damned few people in the world who can do that kind of shooting and this marksman of yours didn't spring full grown from the head of Zeus. I think I can help you find him, but we've got to go to my place to do it. That's where all my reference material is. This lot wouldn't know a book if it bit them on the butt." She waved a hand around the clubroom. The fortyish man sitting at one of the tables stroking the cat looked startled and waved back. "Gun magazines, that's all they ever read. I keep telling them they need a library. Probably leave them mine when I die and it'll spend ten or twenty years sitting around getting outdated then they'll throw it out. Did you drive?"

"No . . ."

"No? I thought every PI owned a sexy red convertible. Never mind. We'll take my car. I live pretty close." A sudden flurry of shots caught her attention and she strode over to the window. "Ha! I told him not to buy a Winchester if he wants to compete this fall. He'll be months getting used to that offset scope. Fool should've listened. Robert!"

The man at the table looked even more startled at being directly addressed. "Yes?"

"If Gary comes up tell him I said, I told you so."

"Uh, sure, Bertie."

"His wife's down in the pistol range," Bertie confided to Vicki as they headed out the door. "They come by most evenings after work. He hates guns but he loves her so they compromised; she only shoots targets, he doesn't watch."

Bertie's car was a huge old Country Squire station wagon, white, with wood-colored panels. The eight cylinders roared as they headed out onto the highway and then settled down into a steady seventy-five kilometers an hour purr.

Vicki tried not to fidget at the speed—or lack of it—but the passing time gnawed at her. Hopefully Donald's wound would remind the wer of why they had to stay close to the house after dark, but she wasn't counting on it. As long as the wer insisted on their right to move around their land, every sunset, every extra day she spent solving this case, put another one of them in danger. If she couldn't convince them to stay safe, and so far she'd had remarkably little luck at that, she had to find this guy as fast as possible.

A car surged past, horn honking.

"I wanted to get a bumper sticker that read, 'Honk at me and I'll shoot your tires out' but a friend talked me out of it." Bertie sighed. "Waste of diminishing natural resources driving that speed." She dropped another five kilometers as she spoke, just to prove her point.

Vicki sighed as well, but her reasons were a little different.

Fourteen

Bertie Reid lived in a small bungalow about a ten-minute drive from the range.

Ten minutes had anyone else been driving, Vicki sighed silently as she got out of the car and followed the older woman into the house. "May I use your phone, I'd better call—*oh, hell, what do I call Celluci?*—my driver and let him know where I am."

"Phone's right there." She pointed into the living room. "I'll just go put the kettle on for tea. Unless you'd rather have coffee."

"I would actually."

"It's only instant."

"That's fine. Thank you." Vicki was not a coffee snob and anything was better than tea.

The phone, a white touch-tone, sat on of a pile of newspapers beside an overstuffed floral armchair with a matching footstool. A pole lamp with three adjustable lights rose up behind the chair and the remote for the television lay on one wide arm, partially buried under an open *TV Guide.*

Obviously the command center. Vicki punched in the Heerkens number and looked around the living room while she waited for someone at the farm to answer. The room bulged with books, on shelves, on the floor, on the other pieces of furniture, classics, romances—she spotted two by Elizabeth Fitzroy, Henry's pseudonym—mysteries, nonfiction. Vicki had seen bookstores with a less eclectic collection.

"Hello?"

"Rose? It's Vicki Nelson. Is Mike Celluci still there?"

"Uh-huh, Aunt Nadine invited him to dinner. I'll get him."

Dinner. Vicki shook her head. That should prove interesting, a little alpha male posturing over the hot dogs. She heard voices in the background, then someone lifted the receiver.

"Great timing, we just sat down. You ready to be picked up?"

"No, not yet. Ms. Reid arrived late. I'm at her place now and likely to be for some time. She doesn't know who the marksman is, but she thinks we can find out."

"How?"

"Anyone as good as this guy is has to have left some kind of a record and if someone made a record of it, she says she has a copy. But," she glanced around the living room, nothing appeared to be shelved in any particular order, "it may take a while to find it."

"Do you want me to come in?"

"No." The less time she spent with him, the less likely he'd restage the afternoon's fight and she just didn't want to deal with that right now. Letting Celluci tie her in knots wouldn't help anyone. Her job was to find the killer and stop him, not argue the ethics of the case. "I'd rather you stayed there and kept an eye on things."

"What about Henry?"

What about Henry? She wondered how his absence had been explained. Celluci swore he always knew when she lied so she chose her words carefully. "He hasn't any training."

"Christ, Vicki, these are werewolves; *I* haven't any training." In her mind's eye she saw him tossing the curl of hair back off his forehead. "And that wasn't what I meant."

"Listen, Mike, I told you what I think of your organized crime theory and I haven't got time to pander to your bruised male ego right now. You and Henry work it out." The best defense is a good offense—she didn't know where she'd first heard it but it made sense. "I'll call you when I get done." She could hear him speaking as she hung up. He didn't sound happy. *Odds are he'll repeat it later so I haven't missed anything.*

The early evening sunlight stretched long golden fingers into the living room. Almost two and a half hours remained until dark. Vicki found herself wishing she could push that pulsing golden ball down below the horizon, releasing Henry from the hold of day. Henry understood, unlike Mike Celluci who was trying to apply rules to a game no one was playing.

And wasn't I just thinking it was nice to have Celluci around, lending an aura of normality to all this? When did my life get so complicated?

"Cream and sugar?" Bertie called from the kitchen.

Vicki shook her head, trying to clear the cobwebs. "Just cream," she said, moving toward the voice. Nothing to do but keep going and hope it all untangled itself in the end.

The second bedroom had been turned into a library, with bookshelves on three of the four walls and filing cabinets on the fourth. A huge paper-piled desk took up much of the central floor space. The desk caught Vicki's eye.

"It's called a partnership desk," Bertie told her, caressing a gleaming edge of dark brown wood with a fingertip. "It's really two desks in a single piece of furniture." She lifted a pile of newspapers off one of the chairs and motioned for Vicki to sit down. "Ruth and I bought it almost twenty-five years ago now. If you don't count the cars or the house, it's the most expensive thing we ever bought."

"Ruth?" Vicki asked, leveling a space on the desk blotter for her coffee.

The older woman picked up a framed photograph off one of the bookshelves, smiled down at it for an instant, then passed it over. "Ruth was my partner. We were together for thirty-two years. She died three years ago. Heart attack." Her smile held more grief than humor. "There hasn't seemed to be much point in housecleaning without her around. You'll have to excuse the mess."

Vicki returned the picture. "It's hard to lose someone

close," she said softly, thinking that Nadine's eyes had held the same stricken look when she'd spoken of her twin. "And I'd be the last person to criticize housecleaning. As long as you can find things when you need them."

"Yes, well . . ." Bertie set the photograph of Ruth carefully back on the shelf and waved a hand at the rows and rows of titles; *History of Marksmanship, Rifle Shooting as a Sport, Position Rifle Shooting, The Complete Book of Target Shooting.* "Where do we start?"

Reaching into her purse, Vicki drew out the lists of those who used the conservation area with any frequency—both sets of birders, the nature photography club—and laid it on the desk. "I thought we'd start at the top and compare these names with first the Canadian Olympic teams, then regional award winners, then down to local winners."

Bertie bent over and scanned the lists. "Be easier though if you knew who had registered weapons in this group. Doesn't the OPP have . . . ?"

"Yes."

The older woman looked a little startled at the tone and the muscles moved around her mouth, but Vicki's expression helped her to hold back her curiosity. After a moment she asked, "Just the Canadian teams?"

"To start with, yes." Vicki took a long swallow of coffee and wondered if she should apologize. After all, it had been her own damned fault she didn't have that registration list. "If they turn up empty, we'll start on other countries. If you have . . ."

"I have every Olympic shooting team for the last forty years as well as the American nationals, most of the regionals, and local competitions from Pennsylvania, Michigan, and New York."

The Canadian teams were in seven fat red binders. Even ignoring all the statistics, the photocopies of newspaper articles, and the final results, the daunting number of names to wade through started Vicki's head throbbing again.

If this were a television show, I'd have found a bit of shirt caught in that tree that could have belonged to only one man, there'd have been a car chase, a fight, time out to go to the bathroom, and everything wrapped up in a nice, neat tidy package in less than an hour. She laid the first list of birders beside the first binder and pushed her glasses up her nose. *Welcome to the real world.*

A half a dozen times during dinner, Peter changed his mind about telling the rest of the family what he knew. A half a dozen times, he changed it back. They deserved to know. But if *he* could present them with the proof. . . . Back and forth. Forth and back.

A part of him just wanted to dump the whole thing on the older wer and let them take care of it but Rose's knee bumping randomly against his under the table kept knocking that thought out of his head. He hardly tasted a mouthful of his food because every time he inhaled, the only thing he could smell was his twin and the only thing he could think of was proving himself to her.

"Peter! The bread?"

"Sorry, Aunt Nadine." He couldn't remember her asking for the bread but her tone made it obvious she had. As he passed the plate of heavy black bread up the table he realized that whatever else he decided, he couldn't tell his aunt. To say *I think I might know who killed your twin* without having the proof so she could act would just be worrying at the wound. Besides, she thought he was still a cub and treated him not much different than Daniel. He had to prove to her that he was a man. He hadn't noticed before, but Aunt Nadine smelled very much like Rose.

He couldn't tell his father. His father was wounded. He couldn't even talk it over with his father because his father didn't do anything without talking it over with Uncle Stuart first.

Uncle Stuart. Peter tore at a piece of meat as Uncle Stuart accepted the saltshaker from Rose. *He didn't have to touch her. Thinks he's so . . . so shit hot. Thinks he knows everything. Well, I know something he doesn't.*

"Whacha angry about, Peter?"

Peter glared at his young cousin. "I'm not angry."

Daniel shrugged. "Smell angry. You going to jump on Daddy again?"

"I said I'm *not* angry."

"Peter." Stuart leaned around Daniel, brows down and teeth bared.

Peter fought the urge to toss his head back, exposing his throat. His ears were tight against the sides of his skull, the torn edge throbbing in time with his pulse. "I didn't do anything!" he growled, shoving away from the table and stomping out of the kitchen. *You just wait*, he thought as he stripped and changed. *I'll show you.*

Rose made as if to follow but Nadine reached out and pushed her back into her chair. "No," she said.

Stuart sighed and scratched at a scar over his eyebrow, the result of his first challenge fight as an adult male. This had to happen when there was a stranger with the family. He looked over at Celluci who was calmly wiping ketchup off his elbow—Daniel had been overly enthusiastic with the squeeze bottle again—and then at Nadine. Arrangements to separate Rose and Peter would have to be made this evening. They couldn't put it off any longer.

Storm skulked around the barn, looking for rats to take out his bad temper on. He didn't find any. That didn't help his mood. He chased a flock of starlings into the air but he didn't manage to sink his teeth into any of them. Flopping down in the shade beside Celluci's car, he worried at a bit of matted fur on his shoulder.

Life sucks, he decided.

It would be almost two hours until dark. Hours until he could prove himself. Hours until he could take that human's throat in his teeth and shake the truth out of him. He imagined the reactions of his family, of Rose, when he walked in and declared, *I know who the killer is.* Or better yet, when he walked in and threw the body down on the floor.

Then faintly, over the smell of steel and gas and oil, he caught a whiff of a familiar scent. He rose. On the passenger side of Celluci's car, up along the edge of the window was an area that smelled very clearly of the man in the black and gold jeep.

He frowned and licked his nose.

Then he remembered.

The scent he'd caught at the garage, the trace clinging to the hood release of Henry's wrecked car, was, except for intensity, identical to the scent here and now.

This changed things. Tonight's meeting could only be a trap. Storm scratched at the ground and whined a little in his excitement. This was great. This alone would convince everyone to take him seriously.

"Peter?"

He pricked up his ears. That was his uncle's voice, over by the house, not calling him, talking about him. Storm inched forward, until he could see around the front of the car but not be seen. Fortunately for eavesdropping, he was downwind.

His uncle and Detective Celluci were sitting on the back porch.

"He's all right," Stuart continued. "He's just, well, a teenager."

Celluci snorted. "I understand. Teenagers."

The two men shook their heads.

Storm growled softly. So they could dismiss him with one word could they? Say *teenager* like it was some kind of disease. Like it explained everything. Like he was still a child. His hackles rose and his lips curled back, exposing the full gleaming length of his fangs. He'd show them.

Tonight.

". . . course, up until the early 60s, most shooters thought that no one would ever shoot a score above 1150 in an international style competition but then in 1962, a fellow named Gary Anderson shot 1157 in free-rifle. Well, there were some jaws hitting the floor that day and most folks believed he'd never be beat." Bertie shook her head at the things most folks believed. "They were wrong, of course. That 1150 was just what they call a psychological factor and once Gary broke it, well, it got shot all to shit. So to speak. I'll just make another pot of tea. You sure you don't want more coffee?"

"No, thanks." Since she'd left the force, Vicki's caffeine tolerance had dropped and she could feel the effect of the three cups she'd already had. Her nerves were stretched so tightly, she could almost hear them ring every time she moved. Leaving Bertie in the kitchen, she hurried to the living room and the phone.

The evening had passed unnoticed while she'd been comparing lists of names. The sun, a disk so huge and red and clearly defined against the sky that it looked fake, trembled on the edge of the horizon. Vicki checked her watch. 8:33. Thirty-five minutes to sunset. Thirty-five minutes to Henry.

He said his arm would be healed by tonight so maybe he and Celluci could stake out that tree together and she could get Peter to drive in and pick her up. She snickered at the vision that idea presented as she sat down in the armchair and flicked on one of the lights. She'd definitely had too much coffee.

The surnames of eleven Olympic shooters had matched with members in the local clubs. Time for the next step.

"Hello, Mrs. Scott? My name is Terri Hanover, I'm a writer, and I'm doing an article on Olympic contestants. I was wondering if you were related to a Brian Scott who was a member of the Canadian rifle team at the '76 Olympics in Montreal? No? But you went to Montreal. . . . That's very interesting but, unfortunately, I really need to talk to the contestants themselves." Vicki stifled a sigh. "Sorry to bother you. Goodnight."

One down. Ten to go. Lies to get at truth.

Hi, there. My name is Vicki Nelson and I'm a private investigator. Have you or any members of your family been shooting werewolves?

She pushed her glasses up her nose and punched in the next number without any real hope of success.

For Henry the moment of sunset came like the moment between life and death. Or perhaps, death and life. One instant he wasn't. The next, awareness began to lift the shroud of day from his senses. He lay still, listening to his heartbeat, his breathing, the rustle of the sheet against the hairs on his chest as his lungs filled and emptied. He felt the weave of the fabric beneath him, the mattress beneath that, the bed beneath both. The scent of wer wiped out even the scent of self but, all things considered, that didn't surprise him. Redefined for another night, he opened his eyes and sat up, extending his senses beyond his sanctuary.

Vicki wasn't in the house. Mike Celluci was.

Wonderful. Why hadn't she gotten rid of him? And for that matter, where *was* she?

He flexed his arm and peered down at the patch of new skin along the top of his shoulder. Although still a little tender, the flesh dimpled where the new muscle fiber had yet to add bulk, the wound had essentially healed. The day had given him back his strength and the hunger had faded to a whisper he could easily ignore.

As he dressed, he considered Detective-Sergeant Celluci. The wer had obviously accepted him, for Henry could feel no fear or anger in his sensing of the mortal. While he still thought that burning the memory of the wer and the witnessed change out of Celluci's mind was the safest plan, he couldn't make a decision without knowing how things had progressed over the course of the day. He wished he knew what suspicions the man harbored about him, what he'd said to Vicki last night, and what Vicki had said in return.

"Only one way to find out." He threw open the door and stepped out into the hall. Mike Celluci was in the kitchen. He'd join him there.

Just before the sun slid below the horizon, Storm leapt the fence behind the barn and using the fence bottom as cover, moved away from the house. If his uncle saw him, he'd call him back. If Rose saw him, she'd demand an explanation of where he thought he was going without her. Both would mean disaster so he used every trick he'd learned in stalking prey to stay hidden.

It didn't matter how long it took, the human would wait for him. He was sure of that. His ears flattened and his eyes gleamed. The human would get more than he bargained for.

"No luck?"

"No." Vicki rubbed her eyes and sighed. "And I've

about had it for tonight. I don't think I can face those lists again without at least twelve hours sleep."

"No reason why you should," Bertie told her, clearing away the sandwich plates. "And it's not like it's an emergency or anything. Surely those people can keep their dogs tied up for a few days."

"It's not that simple."

"Why not?"

"Because it never is." A facetious explanation, but she didn't have a better one. Even if she'd been able to discuss it, Vicki doubted she could do justice to the territorial imperatives of the wer—not when it involved such incredibly stupid actions as presenting oneself as a target. She checked her watch and dug another two pain killers out of her purse, swallowing them dry. At eleven, Colin would be off shift. In an hour or so she'd head over to the police department and catch a ride back to the farm with him. In the meantime. . . .

"If you can put up with me for a little while longer, I think I'd better get started on the non-Canadian teams."

Bertie looked dubious. "I don't mind. If you think you're up to it. . . ."

"I have to be." Vicki dragged herself up out of the depths of the armchair, which seemed to be dragging back. "The people I talked to tonight will probably mention the call." She raised her voice so she could hear herself over the percussion group that had set up inside her skull. "I have to move quickly before our marksman spooks and goes to ground." She gave her head a quick shake, trying to settle things back where they belonged. The percussion group added a brass section, her knees buckled, and she clutched desperately at the nearest bookcase for support, knocking three books off the shelf and onto the floor.

With the bookcase still supporting most of her weight, she bent to pick them up and froze.

"Are you all right?" Bertie's worried question seemed to come from very far away.

"Yeah. Fine." She straightened slowly, holding the third book which had fallen faceup at her feet. *MacBeth*.

This morning Carl Biehn had been wringing his hands,

trying to scrub off a bit of dirt. Like Lady MacBeth, she thought, hefting the book, and wondered what had happened to make the old man so anxious. But Lady MacBeth's scrubbing had been motivated by guilt not anxiety. What was Carl Biehn feeling guilty about?

Something his slimy nephew had done? Possibly, but Vicki doubted it. She'd bet on Carl Biehn being the type of man who took full responsibility for his actions and expected everyone else to do the same. If he felt guilty, he'd done something.

Vicki still couldn't believe he was a murderer. And she knew that her belief had nothing to do with it.

Most murders are committed by someone the victim knows.

Strongly held religious beliefs had justified arbitrary bloodbaths throughout history.

It wouldn't hurt to check him out. Just to make sure.

He hadn't been on any of the Canadian teams but Biehn was a European name and although he didn't have an accent, that didn't mean much.

"Are you *sure* you're all right?" Bertie asked as Vicki turned to face her. "You're looking, well, kind of peculiar."

Vicki placed the copy of *MacBeth* back on the shelf. "I need to look at the European shooting teams. Germans, Dutch . . ."

"I think you'd be better off sitting down with a cold compress. Can't it wait until tomorrow?"

There was no reason why it couldn't.

"No." Vicki stopped herself before she shook her head, the vision of the old man's hands washing themselves over and over caught in her mind. "I don't think it can."

Storm tested the wind as he crouched at the edge of the woods, watching the old Biehn barn. The man from the black and gold jeep was alone in the building. The grasseater remained in the house.

The most direct route was straight across the field but even with the masking darkness, Storm had no intention of being that exposed. Not far to the south an old fence bottom ran from the woods to the road, passing only twenty meters from the barn on its way, the scraggly line of trees and bushes breaking the night into irregular patterns. Secure in the knowledge that even another wer would have difficulty spotting him, Storm moved quickly along its corridor of shifting shadows.

Although he longed to give chase, he ignored the panicked flight of a flushed cottontail. Tonight he hunted larger game.

Neither the East nor West Germans had ever had a Carl Biehn on their shooting teams. Vicki sighed as she flipped through the binder looking for the lists from the Netherlands. When she closed her eyes, all she could see were little black marks on sheets of white.

The way people move around these days, Biehn could come from anywhere. Maybe I should do this alphabetically. Alphabetically . . . She stared blankly down at the page, not seeing it, and her heart began to beat unnaturally loud.

Rows of flowers stretched before her and a man's voice said, *"Everything from A to Zee."*

Zee. Canadians pronounced the last letter of the alphabet as Zed. Americans said Zee.

She reached for the binder that held the information on the U. S. Olympic teams, already certain of what she'd find.

Henry stood in the shadows of the lower hall and listened to Celluci patiently explain to Daniel that it was now too dark to play catch with the frisbee. He hadn't thought the mortal the type who cared for children but then, he hadn't thought much about this mortal at all. Obviously, he would have to rectify that.

The man was close to Vicki, a good friend, a colleague, a lover. If only through Vicki, they would continue to come into contact. Their relationship must therefore be defined, for the safety of them both.

Like most of his kind, Henry preferred to keep his

dealings with the mortal world to a minimum and those
dealings under his control. Mike Celluci was not the sort
of man he would normally associate with. He was too . . .

Henry frowned. Too honest? Too strong? Was this
where a prince had fallen then, avoiding the honest and
the strong for the weak and the rogue? In his life, he
had commanded the loyalty of men like this one. He
was not now less than he had been. He stepped out into
the light.

Mike Celluci didn't hear Henry's approach, but he felt
something at his back and turned. For a moment, he
didn't recognize the man who stood just inside the
kitchen door. Power and presence acquired over centuries hit him with almost physical force and when the
hazel eyes met his and he saw they considered him wor-
thy, he had to fight the totally irrational urge to drop to
one knee.

What the hell is going on here? He shook his head
to clear it, recognized Henry Fitzroy, and to cover his
confusion, snarled, "I want to talk to you."

The phone rang, freezing them where they stood.

A moment later Nadine came into the kitchen,
glanced from one to the other and sighed. "It's Vicki.
She sounds a little strange. She wants to talk to . . ."

Celluci didn't wait to hear a name, but even as he
stomped into the office and snatched up the receiver, he
had to acknowledge that Henry Fitzroy had allowed him
to take the call; that without Fitzroy's implicit permission, he wouldn't have been able to move. *If that man's
nothing but a romance writer, I'm a . . .* He couldn't
think of a sufficiently strong comparison. "What?"

"Where's Henry?"

"Why?" He knew better than to take his anger out
on Vicki. He did it anyway. "Want to make kissy-face
over the phone?"

"Fuck off, Celluci." Exhaustion colored the words.
"Carl Biehn was a member of the American shooting
team in the 1960 Summer Olympics in Rome."

Anger no longer had a place in the conversation, so
he ignored it. "You've found your marksman, then."

"Looks that way." She didn't sound happy about it.

"Vicki, this information has to go to the police."

"Just put Henry on. I don't even know why I'm talking to you."

"If you don't report this, I will."

"No. You won't."

He'd been about to say that their friendship, that the wer, couldn't come before the law but the cold finality in her voice stopped him. For a moment, he felt afraid. Then he just felt tired. "Look, Vicki, I'll come and get you. We won't do anything until we talk."

A sudden burst of noise from the kitchen drowned out her reply and, tucking the phone under one arm, he moved to the door to close it. Then he stopped. And he listened.

And he knew.

Good cops don't ever laugh at intuition, too often a life hangs in the balance.

"The situation's changed." He cut Vicki off, not hearing what she said. "You'll have to make it back here on your own. Peter's missing."

Storm crept across the open twenty meters from the fence bottom to the barn crouched so low the fur on his stomach brushed the ground. When he reached the stone foundation of the barn wall, he froze.

The boards were old and warped and most had a line of light running between them. He changed—to get his muzzle out of the way, not because one form had better vision than the other—and placed one eye up against a crack.

A kerosene lantern burned on one end of a long table, illuminating the profile of the man from the jeep as he stood, back to the door, fiddling with something Peter couldn't see. A shotgun leaned against the table edge, in easy reach.

Under the man-scent, the smell of the lantern, and the lingering odor of the animals the barn had once held there was a strong scent of oiled steel, more than the gun alone could possibly account for. Peter frowned, changed, and padded silently around to the big front doors. One stood slightly ajar, wide enough for him to slip through in either form but angled so that he couldn't charge straight into the barn and attack the man at the table. His lips curled his teeth and his throat vibrated with an unvoiced growl. The human underestimated him; a wer that didn't want to be heard, wasn't. He could get in, turn, and attack before the human could reach the gun, let alone aim and fire it.

He moved forward. The scent of oiled steel grew stronger. The dirt floor shifted under his front paw and he froze. Then he saw the traps. Three of them, set in the opening angle of the door, in hollows dug out of the floor then covered with something too light to set them off or hinder their movement when the jaws snapped shut. He couldn't be sure, but it smelled like the moss stuff Aunt Nadine put in the garden.

He could jump them easily, but the floor beyond had been disturbed as well and he couldn't tell for certain where safe footing began. Nor could he change and spring the traps without becoming a target for the shotgun.

Nose to the walls, he circled the building. Every possible entry had the same scent.

Every possible entry but one.

High on the east wall, almost hidden behind the branches of a young horse-chestnut tree was a small square opening used, back when the barn had held cattle, for passing hay bales into the loft. As a rule, the wer didn't climb trees, but that didn't mean they couldn't and callused fingers and toes found grips that mere human hands and feet might not have been able to use.

Moving carefully along a dangerously narrow limb, Peter checked out the hole, found no traps, and slipped silently through, congratulating himself on outwitting his enemy.

The old loft smelled only of stale hay and dust. Crouched low, Peter padded along a huge square cut beam until he could see down into the barn. He was almost directly over the table which contained, besides the lantern, a brown paper package, a notebook, and a heavy canvas apron.

The man from the jeep checked his watch and stood, head cocked, listening.

The whole setup was a trap and a trap set specifically for fur-form.

There could no longer be any question about it, this was the man who was killing his family. A man who knew them well enough to judge correctly what form he'd wear tonight.

Peter grinned and his eyes gleamed in the lantern light. He'd never felt so alive. His entire body thrummed. He had no intention of disappointing the human; he wanted fur-form, he'd get it. Tooth and claw would take him down. Moving to the edge of the beam, he changed and launched himself snarling through the air, landing with all four feet on the back of the human below.

Together, they crashed to the ground.

For one brief instant, Mark Williams had been pleased to see the shape that dropped out of the loft. He'd called the creature's reactions correctly right down the line. Except he hadn't thought about the loft or realized exactly what he'd be facing.

More terrified than he'd ever been in his life, he fought like a man possessed. He'd once seen a German shepherd kill a gopher by grabbing the back of its neck and crushing the spine. That wasn't going to happen to him. He felt claws tear through his thin shirt and into his skin, hot breath on his ear, and managed to twist around and shove one forearm between the beast's open jaws while his other hand groped frantically around on the floor for the fallen gun.

Storm tossed back his head, releasing the arm, and dove forward for the suddenly exposed throat.

Mark saw death approaching. Then he saw it pause.

Shit, man. I can't just rip out some guy's throat! What am I doing? Abruptly, the blood lust was gone.

With his legs up under the belly of the beast, Mark heaved.

Completely disoriented, Storm hit the ground with a heavy thud and scrambled to regain his feet. The floor moved under his left rear paw. Steel jaws closed.

The snap, the yelp of pain and fear combined, brought Mark slowly to his knees. He smiled as he saw the russet wolf struggling against the trap, twisting and snarling in a panicked effort to get free. His smile broadened as the struggles grew weaker and creature finally lay panting on the floor.

No! Please, no! He couldn't change. Not while his foot remained held in the trap. *It hurts. Oh, God, it hurts.* He could smell his own blood, his own terror. *I can't breathe! It hurts.*

Dimly, Storm knew the trap was the lesser danger. That the human approaching, teeth showing, was far, far more deadly. He whined and his front paws scrabbled against the ground but he couldn't seem to rise. His head suddenly become too heavy to lift.

"Got you now, you son of a bitch." The poison had been guaranteed. Mark was pleased to see he'd got his money's worth. Wincing, he reached over his shoulder and his hand came away red. Staying carefully out of range, just in case, he spat on the floor by the creature's face. "I hope it hurts like hell."

Maybe . . . if I howl . . . they'll hear me. . . .

Then the convulsions started and it was too late.

Fifteen

". . . I don't know! He's been acting so strangely lately!"

Stuart and Nadine exchanged glances over Rose's head. Nadine opened her mouth to speak but her mate's expression caused her to close it again. Now was not the time for explanations.

"Rose." Celluci came out of the office and walked quickly across the kitchen, until he could gaze directly into the girl's face. "This is important. Besides the family, Vicki, Mr. Fitzroy, and myself, who did Peter talk with today?"

He knows something, Henry thought. *I should never have let him take that call.*

Rose frowned. "Well, he talked to the mechanic at the garage, Dr. Dixon, Dr. Levin—the one who took over from Dr. Dixon, she was at his house for a while—um, Mrs. Von Thorne, next door to Dr. Dixon, and somebody driving by up on the road, but I didn't see who."

"Did you see the car?"

"Yeah. It was black, mostly, with gold trim and fake gold spokes on the wheels." Her nose wrinkled. "A real poser's car." Then her expression changed again as she read Celluci's reaction. "That's the one you were waiting for, wasn't it? Wasn't it?" She stepped toward him, teeth bared. "Where's Peter? What's happened to my brother?"

"I think," Stuart said flatly, coming around from behind his niece, "you'd better tell us what you know."

Only Henry had some idea of the conflict Celluci was

going through and he had no sympathy for it. The question of law versus justice could have only one answer. He watched the muscles on Celluci's back tense and heard his heartbeat quicken.

Everything in Celluci's training said he leave them with an ambiguous answer and take care of this himself. If werewolves expected to be treated like the rest of society, within the law, then they couldn't act outside the law. And if the only way he could do his duty was to fight his way out of this house. . . . his hands curled into fists.

A low growl began to build in Stuart's throat.

And Rose's.

And Nadine's.

Henry stepped forward. He'd had enough.

Then Daniel began to whimper. He threw himself on his mother's legs and buried his face in her skirt. "Peter's gonna get killed!" The fabric did little to muffle the howl of a six-year-old child who only understood one small part of what was going on.

Celluci looked down at Daniel, who seemed to have an uncanny knack for bringing the focus back to the important matters, then over at Rose. "Can't you let me take care of this?" he asked softly.

She shook her head, panic beginning to build. "You don't understand."

"You *can't* understand," Nadine added, clutching at Daniel so tightly he squirmed in her grasp.

Celluci saw the pain in the older woman's eyes, pain that cut and twisted and would continue far longer than anyone should be forced to endure. His decision might possibly keep that pain from Rose.

"Carl Biehn was an Olympic marksman. His nephew, Mark Williams, drives a black and gold jeep."

Rose's eyes widened. "If he was talking to Peter this afternoon . . ." She whirled, her sundress hit the floor, and Cloud streaked out of the kitchen and into the night.

"Rose, no!" Unencumbered by the need to change, Henry raced after her before Stuart, still caught in challenge with Celluci, began to react.

Jesus Christ! Nobody moves that fast! Celluci grabbed

Stuart's arm as Henry disappeared into the night. "Wait!" he barked. "I need you to show me the way to Carl Biehn's farm."

"Let me go, human!"

"Damn it, Stuart, the man's got guns. He's taken Henry out once already! Charging in will only get everyone shot. We can get there before them in my car."

"Don't count on it." Stuart laughed but the sound held no humor. "And this is our hunt. You have no right to be there."

"Take him, Stuart!" Nadine's tone left no room for her mate to argue. "Think of after."

The male wer snarled but after an instant he yanked his arm free of Celluci's hold and started for the door, "Come on, then."

After? Celluci wondered as the two of them charged across the lawn. *Mary, Mother of God, they want me there to explain the body. . . .*

"What is taking him so long!" Vicki shoved at her glasses and turned away from the living room window. With the sun down she could see nothing past her reflection on the glass but that didn't stop her from pacing the length of the room and back then peering out into the darkness again.

"He has to come all the way from Adelaide and Dundas," Bertie pointed out. "It's going to take him a few minutes."

"I *know* that!" She sighed and took a deep breath. "I'm sorry. I had no right to snap at you. It's just that . . . well, if it wasn't for my damned eyes, I'd be driving myself. I'd be halfway there by now!"

Bertie pursed her lips and looked thoughtful. "You don't trust your partner to deal with it?"

"Celluci's not a partner, he's a friend. I don't have a partner. Exactly." And although Henry could be counted on to keep Celluci from doing anything stupid, who would save Peter, or watch the wer, or grab the murdering bastard—Vicki always saw him with Mark Williams' face, convinced that he had been the reason for the deaths even if he hadn't pulled the trigger—

and . . . and then what? "I *have* to be there! How can
I *know* it's justice if I'm not there?"

Realizing that some questions weren't meant to be
answered, Bertie wisely kept silent. Questions of her
own would have to wait.

"Damn it, I told him it was an emergency!" Vicki
whirled back to the window and squinted into the night.
"Where is he?" With an hour left in the shift, and Colin
already back in the station, it hadn't been hard for Vicki
to convince the duty sergeant to release him for a family
emergency. "Why the . . . There!" Headlights turned up
the driveway.

Vicki snatched up her bag and ran for the door, shouting back over her shoulder, "Don't talk about this to
anyone. I'll be in touch."

Outside, and effectively blind, she aimed for the headlights and narrowly missed being run down by one of
London's old blue and white police cars. She grabbed
for the rear door as it screeched to a stop and threw
herself into the back seat.

Barry slammed the car into reverse and laid rubber
back down the length of the driveway while Colin
twisted around and snarled, "What the hell is going on?"

Vicki pushed her glasses back into place and clutched
at the seat as the car took a corner on two wheels.

"Carl Biehn was an Olympic marksman by way of
Korea and the marines."

"That grasseater?"

"He may be," Vicki snapped, "but his nephew . . ."

"Was charged with fraud in '86, possession of stolen
goods in '88, and accessory to murder nine months ago,"
Barry broke in. "No convictions. Got off on a technicality all three times. I ran him this afternoon."

"And the emergency," Colin growled, teeth bared.

"Peter's missing."

Grasses and weeds whipped at his legs; trees flickered
past in the periphery of his sight, unreal shadow images
barely seen before they were gone; the barrier of a fence
became no barrier at all as he vaulted the wire net and
landed still running. Henry had always known that the

wer were capable of incredible bursts of speed but he never knew how fast until that night. Making no effort to elude him, Cloud merely raced toward her twin, not far ahead but far enough that he feared he could never catch her.

With her moonlight-silvered shape remaining so horribly just out of reach, Henry would have traded his immortal life for the ability to shapechange given to his kind by tradition. All else being equal, four legs were faster and more sure than two.

All else, therefore, could not be equal.

He hadn't run like this in many years, and he threw all he was into the effort to close the gap. This was a race he had to win, for if one couldn't be saved, the other had to be.

Spraying dirt and gravel in a great fan-shaped tail, Celluci fought the car through the turn at the end of the lane without losing speed. The suspension bottomed out as they drove into and out of a massive pothole and the oil pan shrieked a protest as it dragged across a protruding rock. The constant machine gun staccato of stones thrown up against the undercarriage of the car made conversation impossible.

Stuart kept up a continuous deep-throated growl.

Over it all, Celluci kept hearing the voice of memory. *"You're willing to be judge and jury—who's to be the executioner? Or are you going to do that, too?"*

He very much feared he was about to get his answer and he prayed Vicki would arrive too late to be a part of it.

By the time Cloud reached the open door of the barn, Henry ran right at her tail. Another step, maybe two and he could stop her, just barely in time.

Then Cloud caught the scent of her twin and, snarling, sprang forward.

As her feet left the packed dirt, Henry saw with horror where she'd land. Saw the false floor. Saw the steel jaws beneath. With all he had left, he threw himself at her in a desperate flying tackle.

He knew as he grabbed her that it wasn't going to be quite enough so he twisted and shielded the struggling wer with his body as they hit the floor and rolled.

Two traps sprang shut, one closing impotently on a few silver-white hairs, the other cheated entirely of a prize.

From the floor, Henry took in a kaleidoscope of images—the russet body lying motionless on the table, the mortal standing over it, covered neck to knees with a canvas apron, the slender knife gleaming dully in the lamplight—and by the time he rose to a crouch, one arm still holding the panting Cloud, he knew. Anger, red and hot, surged through him.

Then Cloud squirmed free and attacked.

For the second time that night Mark Williams looked death in the face; only this time, he knew it wouldn't pause. He screamed and fell back against the table, felt hot breath against his throat and the kiss of one ivory fang then suddenly, nothing. Self preservation took over and without stopping to think, he grabbed for the shotgun.

Henry fought with Cloud, fought with his own blood lust. *She's a seventeen-year-old girl, barely more than a child. She must not be allowed to kill.* The wer no longer lived apart from humans and their values. What point victory now if she spent the rest of her life with that kind of a stain on her soul? Over and over, as she tried to tear herself out of his grip, he said the only words he knew would get through to her.

"He's still alive, Cloud. Storm is still alive."

Finally she stilled, whimpered once, then turned toward the table, muzzle raised to catch her brother's scent. A second whimper turned to a howl.

With her attention now fixed on Storm rather than death, Henry stood. "Stay where you are," he commanded and Cloud dropped to the floor, trembling with the need to get to her twin but unable to disobey. As he lifted his head, he came face-to-face with both barrels of the shotgun.

"So, he's still alive, is he?" Both the gun and the laugh were shaky. "I couldn't feel a heartbeat. You sure?"

Henry could hear the slow and labored beating of Storm's heart, could feel the blood struggling to keep moving through passages constricted by poison. He allowed his own blood lust to rise. "I know life," he said, stepping forward. "And I know death."

"Yeah?" Mark wet his lips. "And I know Bo Jackson. Hold it right there."

Henry smiled. "No." Vampire. Prince of Darkness. Child of the Night. It all showed in Henry's smile.

The table against his back made retreat impossible; Mark had no choice but to stand fast. Sweat beaded on his forehead and dribbled down the side of his nose. This was the demon he'd shot in the forest. Man-shaped but nothing manlike in its expression. "I—I don't know what you are," he stammered, forcing his trembling fingers to maintain their grip on the gun, "but I know you can be hurt."

One more step would move the barrel of the weapon around enough so that Cloud would be out of the line of fire. *One more step,* Henry told himself fueling the hunger with rage, *and this* thing *is mine.* He raised his foot.

The barn door slammed back, crashing against the wall and breaking the tableau.

"Drop it!" Celluci commanded from the doorway.

Stuart snarled a counterpoint beside him, the effort of will it took to hold his attack while Cloud remained in danger sending tremors rippling across the muscles of his back. Her howl had yanked him from the car before it had quite stopped and pulled him unthinking into the barn in human form where the clothes he wore confined his shape.

The shotgun barrel dipped then rose again. "I don't think so."

"What the hell is going on out here?" Carl Biehn demanded, rifle covering the two men standing in the open doorway. He'd heard the car race down the driveway; heard it stop, spraying gravel; heard the howl and known that Satan's creatures were involved. It had taken him only a moment to snatch up his rifle and he'd arrived at the barn just behind the men from the car. He

still didn't know what was going on, but his nephew
needed his help, that much was obvious. "Put the safety
on and toss your revolver to the ground." He gestured
with the rifle. "Over there, away from everyone."

Teeth gritted, Celluci did as he was told. He couldn't
see as he had an option. The snap of steel jaws closing
as the gun hit the floor startled everyone about equally.

"Traps," Stuart said, pointing. "There and there." The
dirt floor just beyond his bare foot had been disturbed.
"And here."

Mark smiled. "Pity you don't take longer strides."

"Now move over there," Carl commanded, "by the
others so I can get a . . ." As they picked their way
between the traps and into the lamplight, he recognized
Stuart and his eyes narrowed. All day he had prayed for
an answer to his doubts and now the Lord delivered the
leader of the ungodly into his hands. Then he saw Cloud,
still crouched behind Henry, ignoring everything but the
body on the table.

Then he saw Storm.

He lowered the rifle from his shoulder to his hip, holding it balanced by the pistol grip, finger still resting on
the trigger. Keeping the muzzle carefully pointed toward
the group of intruders now clustered together at one side
of the barn, he moved to stand beside the table. "What,"
he repeated, "is going on here? How did this creature
die?"

"He's not dead!" Rose threw herself into Stuart's
arms. "He's not dead, Uncle Stuart! He's not."

"I know, Rose. And we'll save him." He stroked her
hair, glaring at the younger human who stared at her as
though he'd never seen skin before. She needed comfort
but, if they were to save themselves and Storm, too,
better she have the use of tooth and claw. Silently he
cursed the clothing that held him to human form.
"Change now," he told her. "Watch. Be ready."

"Stop that!" The rifle swung from Stuart to Cloud and
back again. "You will do no more devil's tricks!"

Cloud whined but Stuart buried his hand in the thick
fur behind her head and said quietly, "Wait."

Carl swallowed hard. The pain in the creature's eyes

as it, no, she, gazed up at him added itself to the cry of the creature he had wounded and the weight of doubt settled heavier around his heart. The work of the Lord should not bring pain. He turned and gazed down at Storm with horrified fascination. "I asked you a question, nephew."

Mark put a little more distance between himself and Henry before he answered—coincidentally moving himself closer to the door, just in case—fighting the silent command that called him to *look at me.* "I assume," he said with a forced grin, "that as we've been assured my guest isn't dead you want to know, how did you put it, 'What the hell is going on here?' It's simple, really. I decided to combine your policy of holy extermination with a profit-making plan of my own."

"You do *not* find profit in doing the Lord's work!" Suddenly unsure of so many other things, this belief, at least, Carl held to firmly.

"Bullshit! You reap your rewards in heaven, I want mine . . . Hold it right there!" He gestured with the shotgun and Henry froze. "I don't know what you are, but I'm pretty damned sure both barrels at this range will blow you to hell and gone and I'd be more than willing to prove it." White showed all around his eyes and he was breathing heavily, sweat burning in the scratches on his back.

Celluci glanced at Henry's profile and wondered what the other man could see that had him so terrified. He wondered, but he really didn't want to know. In his opinion their best chance lay with Carl Biehn, who looked confused and somehow, in spite of his unquestionable ability with the rifle, fragile and old. "This has gone too far," he said calmly, making his voice the voice of reason, laying it over the tension like a balm. "Whatever you thought when you started this, things have changed. It's up to you to end it."

"Shut up!" Mark snapped. "We don't need your two cents worth."

Carl lifted his hand from where it lay almost in benediction on Storm's head and took a firmer grip on the rifle. "And what do you plan to do now?" he asked pointedly, desperation tinting his voice, the question echoing prayers that had remained unanswered.

"You said yourself the devil's creatures must die. That one," Mark nodded at Storm, "has been taken care of. This one," Cloud whined again and pressed close to Stuart's legs, "I could use as well. Pity we can't get the big one to change before he dies."

Stuart snarled and tensed to spring.

"No!" Henry's command snapped Stuart back on his heels, furious and impotent. With both weapons pointing at them from different angles, an attack, whether it succeeded or not, would be fatal to at least one of their company. There had to be another way and they had to find it quickly for although Storm's heart still fought to survive, Henry could hear how much it had weakened, how tenuously it clung to life.

"You keep your goddamned mouth shut," Mark suggested. His hands were sweating around the shotgun but even with his uncle covering their "guests" he dared not wipe his palms. He was well aware that the moment the shooting started and it no longer had anything to lose that creature would charge. This had to be carefully choreographed so that he and his pelts came out in one piece. And if he couldn't bring Uncle Carl around . . . *Poor old man, he wasn't entirely sane, you know.* "All right, the lot of you, turn around and line up facing that wall."

"Why, Mark?"

"So that I can cover them and you can send them back to hell where they belong." With a sudden flash of inspiration, he added, "God's will be done."

Carl's head came up. "God's will be done." It was not for him to question the will of God.

"Mr. Biehn." Celluci wet his lips. Time to lay all the cards on the table. "I'm a Detective-Sergeant with the Metropolitan Toronto Police Department. My badge is in the front left-hand pocket of my pants."

"You're with the police?" The rifle barrel dipped toward the floor.

"He's consorting with Satan's creatures!" Mark

snapped. The cop would die by a rifle bullet. *Poor Uncle Carl . . .*

The rifle barrel came up. "The police are not immune to the temptations of the devil." He peered at Celluci. "Have you been saved?"

"Mr. Biehn, I'm a practicing Catholic, and I will recite for you the 'Lord's Prayer,' the 'Apostles' Creed,' and three 'Hail Marys,' if you like." Celluci's voice grew gentle, the voice of a man who could be trusted. "I understand why you've been shooting these people. I really do. But hasn't it occurred to you that God has plans you're not aware of and maybe, just maybe, you're wrong?" As they were still alive, it had obviously occurred to him; Celluci attempted to make the most of it. "Why don't you put down that gun, and we'll talk, you and I, see if we can't find a way out of this mess." And then, up out of the depths of childhood when his tiny, black-clad grandmother had made him learn a Bible verse every Sunday, he added, " 'For there is nothing covered that shall not be revealed; neither hid, that shall not be known.' "

"St. Luke, chapter twelve, verse two." Carl shuddered and Mark saw that he was losing him.

"Even the devil quotes scripture, Uncle."

"And if he is not the devil, what then?" A muscle jumped in the old man's cheek. "Would you murder an officer of the law?"

"Man's law, Uncle, not God's law!"

"Answer my question!"

"Yes, answer him, Mark. Would you commit murder? Break a commandment?" Now, Celluci used his voice like a chisel, hoping to expose the rotten core. "Thou shalt not kill. What about that?"

Mark had escaped death twice already this night. From the moment he'd recognized the creature that had attacked him in the woods, he'd known that escaping death a third time would take more than luck. In order for him to live, everyone in the barn would have to die. And he was *going* to live. This goddamned bastard of a fucking cop was manipulating the one thing he needed to pull his ass out of the fire and still be able to make a profit. The old man as a live stooge was preferable to the old man as a dead excuse.

"Uncle Carl . . ." Stress the relationship. Remind him of where the blood ties lay, of family loyalty. "These are not God's creatures. You said so yourself."

Carl looked down at Cloud and shuddered. "They are *not* God's creatures." Then he raised his tormented eyes to Celluci's face. "But what of him?"

"Condemned by his own actions. Willingly consorting with Satan's minions."

"But if he is a police officer, the law . . ."

"Don't worry, Uncle Carl." Mark didn't bother to hide the sudden rush of relief. If the old man was concerned about repercussions, then he'd already decided to take action. It was in the bag. "I can make the whole thing look like an accident. Just be careful when you kill the white wolf—dog, whatever—that you don't ruin the pelt."

Just a little too late, he realized he'd said the wrong thing.

The old man shuddered and then straightened, as though he were shouldering a terrible weight. "So much I'm unsure of, but this I know; whatever happens tonight will be for the grace of God. You will not profit from it." He swung the rifle around until it pointed at Mark. "Put down the gun and get over there with them."

Mark opened his mouth and closed it, but no sound came out.

"What are you going to do?" Celluci asked, voice and expression carefully neutral.

"I don't know. But *he* isn't going to be a part of it."

"You can't do this to me." Mark found his tongue. "I'm family. Your own flesh and blood."

"Put down the gun and go over there with them." Carl knew now where he'd made his mistake, where he'd left the path the Lord had shown him. The burden was his to bear alone, he should never have shared it.

"No." Mark shot a horrified glance at Henry, whose expression invited him to come as close as he liked. "I can't . . . I won't . . . you can't make me."

Carl gestured with the rifle. "I can."

Mark saw the death he'd been holding off approaching as Henry's smile broadened. "NO!" He swung the shotgun around at the one who drove him to it.

Carl Biehn saw the muzzle come around and prepared to die. He couldn't, not even to save himself, shoot his only sister's only son. *Into your hands, I commend my spir . . .*

Cloud reacted without thinking and flung herself through the air. Her front paws hit the middle of the old man's chest and the shot sprayed harmlessly over the east wall as the two of them hit the ground together.

Then Henry moved.

One moment, almost ten feet between them. The next, Henry ripped the shotgun out of Mark's grasp and threw it with such force it broke through the wall of the barn. His fingers closed around the mortal's throat and tightened, blood welling around his fingertips where his nails pierced the skin.

"No!" Celluci charged forward. "You can't!"

"I'm not going to," Henry said quietly. And he backed his burden up; one step, two. The trap snapped closed and Henry released his grip.

The arm that stopped Celluci was an impassable barrier. He couldn't move it. He couldn't get around it.

It took a moment for the pain to penetrate through the terror. With both hands at his throat, Mark pulled his eyes from Henry's face and looked down. Soft leather deck shoes had done little to protect against the steel bite; his blood welled up thick and red. He cried out, a hoarse, strangled sound, and dropped to his knees, pushing at the hinge with nerveless fingers. Then the convulsions started. Three minutes later, he was dead.

Henry dropped his arm.

Mike Celluci looked from the body to Henry and said, through a mouth dry with fear. "You aren't human, are you?"

"Not exactly, no." The two men stared at each other.

"Are you going to kill me, too?" Celluci asked at last.

Henry shook his head and smiled. It wasn't the smile Mark Williams took with him into death. It was the smile of a man who had survived for four hundred and fifty years by knowing when he could turn his back. He did so now, joining Cloud and Stuart beside Storm's body.

Now what? Celluci wondered. *Do I just go away and forget all this happened? Do I deal with the body? What?* Technically, he'd just been a witness to a murder. "Hang on, if Storm's still alive, maybe . . ."

"You've seen enough death to recognize it, Detective."

Fitzroy was right. He *had* seen enough death to know he saw it sprawled at his feet on the dirt floor; not even the flickering lamplight could hide it. "But why so quickly?"

"He," Stuart snarled, "was only human." The last word sounded like a curse.

"Jesus H. Christ, what happened?"

Celluci whirled around, hands curling into fists, even though—or perhaps because—he recognized the voice. "What the hell are you doing here? You're stone blind in the dark!"

Vicki ignored him.

Colin pushed past her, into the barn, desperate to get to his brother.

Barry moved to follow. One step, two, and the floor shifted under his foot. He felt the impact of steel teeth slamming into a leather police boot all the way up his leg. "Colin!"

Colin stopped and half turned back toward his partner, caught in the beam of the flashlight Vicki had pulled from her purse, his face twisted with the need to be in two places at once.

Vicki couldn't make him choose. "Go," she commanded. "I'll take care of Barry."

He went.

Dropping carefully to one knee, Vicki trained the light on Barry's foot. The muscles of his leg trembled where they rested against her shoulder. Tucking the flashlight securely under her chin, she studied the construction of the steel jaws. "Can you tell if it's gone through the boot?"

She heard him swallow. "I don't know."

"Okay. I don't think it has, but I'll have to get it off to be sure." Her fingers had barely touched the metal before Celluci slapped them aside.

"Poisoned," he said before she could protest, and slipped a rusty iron bar in at the hinge. "Hold his leg steady."

Both sole and reinforced toe had taken a beating but had held. Barry sagged against Vicki's arm, relief finally allowing a reaction. *I could have died,* he thought and swallowed hard. The heat had little to do with the sweat that plastered his shirt to his back. *I could have died.* His foot hurt. It didn't seem to matter. *I could have died.* He took a deep breath. *But I didn't.*

"Are you all right?" Vicki asked, playing the circular definition of her vision over his face.

He nodded, straightened, and took a step. Then another slightly less shaky one back to her side. "Yeah. I'm okay."

Vicki smiled at him and swept the flashlight beam over the interior of the barn. There was a body on the floor. Carl Biehn sat on a barrel of some kind looking stunned. Everyone else—Colin, Cloud, Henry, Stuart—was with Storm."

"Is Storm . . . ?"

"He's alive," Celluci told her. "Apparently Williams caught him in another one of those traps. Which are buried all over this place so walk only where I tell you."

"Williams?"

"Is dead." Celluci jerked his head in the direction of Carl Biehn and said to Barry, "Get over there. Watch him."

Barry nodded, thankful for some direction, and limped across the barn.

All the long way here in the back of the police car, Vicki had thought only about arriving in time to make a difference. Now she was here, it was over, and the flashlight showed her only broken scenes suspended in darkness. "Mike, what happened?"

For a second, he weighed the alternatives, then he quickly laid out the facts, attempting to keep them uncolored by emotions he himself wasn't certain of. He watched her face carefully when he told her what Henry had done but she let nothing show he could use.

"And Peter? I mean, Storm?" she asked when he finished.

"I don't know."

Sixteen

Vicki launched herself toward the blur of light, the dim figures moving through it taking on solid form as she came closer. If Storm died, she didn't think she'd be able to forgive herself. If only she hadn't been so stupidly wrong about Carl Biehn, so sure he couldn't be the killer. She felt Celluci take her arm and allowed herself to be guided the last few feet, flashlight hanging forgotten in her hand.

Cloud had her front paws up on the table and was desperately licking her brother's face, her tongue alternately smoothing and spiking the fur on his muzzle. Stuart's arms were around Storm's shoulders, supporting his weight. Colin stroked trembling fingers down the russet back, whimpering low in his throat.

Henry . . . Vicki squinted at Henry, bent over one of Storm's back legs. As she watched, he straightened and spat.

"The poison's spread through his system. I'd kill him if I tried to take it all."

Colin began to make a noise, low in his throat, not quite a howl, not quite a moan.

"Get him to Dr. Dixon." Cloud ignored her. The rest turned to stare.

"We can't move him, Vicki," Henry told her softly. "He's trembling on the edge right now. It would be so easy to tip him over."

"If only we could get him to change," Stuart rested his cheek on the top of Storm's head, the anger in his voice only emphasizing the pain in his expression.

Vicki remembered what the doctor had said about the change somehow neutralizing infection. She supposed poison could be considered a type of infection. "He can't change because he isn't conscious?"

Stuart nodded, tears marking the russet fur with a darker pattern.

"Then what about forcing an unconscious change?"

"You don't know anything about us, human."

"I know as much as I need to." Vicki's heart began to pound as she gathered up everything Dr. Dixon had told her, added it to her own observations, and knew she had something that might work. "If he won't change on his own, maybe he'll change for Rose. Twins are linked. Dr. Dixon said it, Nadine said it, hell, you can see it. And Rose and Peter are . . ." She couldn't think of a way to phrase it, not with Rose—Cloud—right there. *Oh, hell, no way around it.* "As Rose goes into heat, she's pulling Peter with her. Their reactions are linked more now than they ever have been. If Rose, not Cloud, would, uh, well, maybe it would pull Storm over into Peter."

Stuart raised his head. "Do you realize what might happen? How strong a bond this is with our kind?"

Vicki sighed. "Look, even if it works, he's too sick to do anything and besides . . ." She reached out and stroked one finger down the limp length of Storm's front leg. *Incest or death, what a choice.* ". . . isn't it better than the alternative?"

"Yes. Oh, yes." Rose didn't wait for Stuart to reply. She threw herself down beside her twin, gathering him as close as she could, rubbing her face over his.

Stuart released Storm and straightened, one hand resting lightly on his nephew's shoulder. "Call him," he said, his voice resigned, his expression watchful. He would not allow this to go any further than it had to. "Bring him back to us, Rose." *But try not to lose yourself.* The last thing they needed now was Rose going into heat without Nadine around to protect her. Breeding reaction had destroyed packs in the past.

"Peter?"

The fine hair along her spine rising, Vicki could feel

the power in a name. *This is who you are,* it said. *Come back to us.*

"Peter, oh, please. Please, Peter don't leave me!"

For agonizing moments it looked as though nothing was happening. Rose continued to call, the grief, the pain, the longing, the love enough to raise the dead. Surely it must have some effect on one not yet gone.

"He moved," Henry said suddenly. "I saw his nostrils twitch."

"He's got the scent," Stuart said, and he and Colin both shifted uncomfortably.

Then it happened. Slowly enough this time that Vicki always after swore she'd seen the exact moment of change.

Peter tossed his head and moaned, his skin gray and clammy, left foot horribly cut by the steel jaws of the trap.

Rose pressed kisses on his lips, his throat, his eyes, until her uncle moved her bodily off the table and shook her, hard. She burst into tears and buried her face on Peter's chest, both hands tightly wrapped around one of his.

"His heartbeat is stronger." Henry listened to it struggling, forcing the sluggish blood to flow. "His life has a better hold. I think it's safe to move him now."

"In a minute." Vicki took a deep breath. It felt like the first in some time and even the dusty, kerosene scented air of the barn smelled sweet. *Jesus Christ, how the hell are we going to explain this to the police?* "Here's what we're going to do. . . ."

"Excuse me."

She started and for a moment didn't recognize the old man who crept forward into the lamplight, Barry Wu trailing behind like an anxious shadow.

Carl Biehn reached out a trembling hand and lightly brushed the silver spray of Rose's hair. She rubbed her nose on the back of her wrist and looked up, eyes narrowing when she saw who it was.

"I know it won't be enough," he said, speaking only to her, the words rough-edged with pain, "but I realize now I was wrong. In spite of all I'd done to you and yours, even in the midst of your grief, you saved my life at the risk of your own. *That* is the way of the Lord." He had to pause to clear his throat. "I wanted to thank you, and say I'm sorry even though I know I have no right to your forgiveness."

He turned away then, and Vicki met his eyes.

They were red rimmed with weeping but surprisingly clear. Although pain had become a part of them, no doubt lingered. This was a man who had made his peace with himself. Vicki heard the voice of memory say, *"He's a decent human being and they're rare."* She nodded, once. He echoed it and moved past, bowed but somehow still possessing a quiet dignity.

"Okay people, we're going to keep this as uncomplicated as possible." She blinked rapidly to clear her eyes and shoved at her glasses. "This is what happened. The police already know someone has been taking potshots at the Heerkens dogs—and the Heerkens—and that I'm looking into it. Obviously Peter found something out . . ."

"He spoke with Mark Williams this afternoon," Celluci told her, wondering how far he was going to let this vaguely surreal explanation go on.

"Great. Suspicious, he headed over here. Meanwhile, I found out the same information, called, discovered that Peter was missing, pulled Colin off shift, and started out here. Meanwhile, you," she pointed at Celluci, "and you," the finger moved to Stuart, "raced to the rescue. We stick to the truth as far as we can. Now then, Henry, you weren't here."

Henry nodded. Staying clear of police investigations had always been one of his tenets of survival.

"Colin, you and Barry, get Peter into the back of your car. Rose, stay with him. Don't let him change again. And Rose, you weren't here either. The boys picked you up on their way back into town as you were running along the road, trying to get here, furious that Stuart and Celluci wouldn't take you with them. Got that?"

Rose sniffed again and nodded, letting go of her twin only long enough to pull on the T-shirt Stuart stripped off and gave her. It fell to mid-thigh and would do as clothing until they reached the doctor's where the entire family kept something to wear.

Gently Colin lifted his brother and, with Peter's head lolling in the hollow of his throat, made for the door, Rose close at his side, her hands chasing each other up and down her twin's body.

"Wait by the car," Vicki called, sending Barry after them. "There're a few more things you'll have to know."

"Like what you're planning to do about the corpse," Celluci snapped, running both hands up through his hair, his patience nearly at an end. "I don't know if you've taken a good look at it, but someone obviously helped it achieve its current condition, which is going to be just a little hard to explain. Or were you just going to bury it in the woods and conveniently forget about it? And what about Mr. Biehn? Where does he fit into this fairy tale you're wea . . . ?"

The gunshot, even strangely muffled as it was, jerked Celluci around. Stuart growled and fought to get himself free of the confining sweatpants. Even Henry whirled to face the sound, and from outside the barn came questioning exclamations and running footsteps.

Vicki only closed her eyes and tried not to listen, tried to think of flowers spread across an August morning like a fallen rainbow.

"He went into the corner, put the rifle muzzle in his mouth and pulled the trigger with his toe."

She felt Celluci's hands on her shoulders and opened her eyes.

"You knew he was going to do that, didn't you?"

She shrugged as well as she was able considering his grip. "I suspected."

"No, you knew!" He started to shake her. "Why the hell didn't you stop him?"

She brought her arms up between his and broke his hold. They stood glaring at each other for a moment and when she thought he'd actually hear her, she said, "He couldn't live with what he'd done, Mike. Who was I to say he had to?" Sliding her glasses up her nose, she looked past him and drew a long shuddering breath. "We're not done yet. Is there a can of kerosene around for that lamp?"

"Here, by the table." Stuart bent to lift the five gallon can.

"No, don't touch it."

Celluci knew at that moment what she was going to do and knew this was his last chance to stop her, to bring this entire night back under the cover of the law. He strongly suspected that if he tried, both Henry and Stuart would align themselves firmly on her side. Trouble was, if it came to choosing sides. . . .

Vicki dug a pair of leather driving gloves out of the bottom of her purse and as though she was reading his mind asked him, as she pulled them on. "Did you want to add something, Celluci?"

Slowly, realizing he had no choice at all, he shook his head, forgetting that she couldn't see him. He'd decided where he stood back at the farmhouse when he'd passed on the information she'd given him. She knew that as well as he did. *Maybe better.*

Gloves in place, Vicki bent and carefully picked up the can. It felt nearly full. She unscrewed the cap, and paused. She needed both hands on the can but would be unable to see without her flashlight the moment she left the immediate area of the lamp. "God damn it all to . . ."

Celluci found himself looking at Henry, whose expression so clearly said, *It's up to you,* that it took a moment before he realized it hadn't been said out loud. *Up to me. Right. As if I had a choice.* But he walked forward and picked up the flashlight anyway.

Vicki squinted up into his face, but the light was too bad to make out nuances. *Not that Celluci tends to do nuances.* It was enough he was there; it helped. *Let's get on with it.*

She walked along the beam of light toward Mark Williams' body, pouring the kerosene carefully on the packed earth floor as she went, thankful that her grip on the can hid the trembling of her fingers. The law had meant everything to her once. "As far as anyone will be able to piece together, there was a fight, probably because Carl Biehn walked in on whatever it was his nephew was doing to Peter. During the fight, Mark Williams stepped in one of his own grisly little bits of ironmongery. Out of grief, or guilt, or God knows what, Carl Biehn shot himself. Unfortunately, at some point during the fight, the can of kerosene got knocked over."

The light slid across the body. It was evident that Mark Williams had died in great pain, the mark of Henry's fingers still apparent on his neck. Vicki couldn't find it in her to be sorry. The only thing she'd felt for Mark Williams in life had been contempt and his death hadn't changed that. *As soon feel sorry for squashing a cockroach,* she thought, setting the can down beside the corpse and tipping it over.

"What about Carl Biehn? "

"Leave him alone. Let him lie where he chose." She walked back along the light to the table and picked up the lantern. The dancing flame made patterns against the darkness that continued to dance in her vision after she looked away. "Also unfortunately, at some time during the fight, the lantern shattered."

The force with which the lantern hit the floor eloquently expressed the emotions that lurked behind her matter-of-fact tones.

The kerosene in the shattered reservoir caught first, and then the path Vicki had poured.

"Take a good look, Mike, Stuart. This what you saw when you arrived." She took a deep breath and peeled off the gloves, shoving them down into the depths of her bag. "Plus Peter's body, lying naked on the table. The two of you rushed in, grabbed Peter, and got out. The flames were then too high for you to go back. Now, I suggest *we* get out of here, as this barn is ancient, tinder dry, and likely to go up in very little time."

With a hungry woosh, Mark Williams' clothes caught, the burning kerosene outlining his body in flame.

She paused at the door, her hand dropping from Celluci's guiding arm, and looked back. A splash of orange had to be fire climbing the surface of the north wall. They couldn't stop it now, even if they wanted to. She wondered for an instant just who *they* were, then squared her shoulders and went out to talk to Colin and Barry by their car.

"When we arrived," she told them, "Celluci and Stuart had Peter lying out on the grass. The barn was burning. Forget everything else. You put Peter in the car, called in the fire, and headed back to town, picking Rose up on the way."

"But what about . . ." Barry didn't sound happy.

Vicki stood quietly, waiting. She couldn't see his face but she had a good idea of what must be going through his mind.

She heard him sigh. "There isn't any other way, is there? Not without exposing the wer and . . ." She heard Henry in his pause, heard him decide not to voice his suspicions. ". . . other things."

"No, there isn't any other way. And don't let anyone get a good look at your boot."

She watched their taillights pull away, saw them speed down the highway, then turned and walked back to the three men—the vampire, the werewolf, and the cop—outlined in the flickering flames from the burning building. There would be ash and not much more remaining when the fire burned out.

As though his turn had now come to read her mind, Celluci said dryly, "If they sift the ashes, any competent forensic team could poke a thousand holes in your story."

"Why should they investigate? With you and me and two of the local city police on the scene, I think they'll be happy to take our word for it."

He had to admit she was likely right. Three cops and an ex-cop with nothing to gain from lying—and covering for a family of werewolves would not likely occur to anyone—they'd wrap it up and write it off and get on to something they could solve.

"Still, there are a lot of loose ends," Stuart said thoughtfully.

Vicki snorted. "Police prefer loose ends. Wrap it up too neatly and they'll think you're handing them a package." The night was sultry, without a breath of wind, and the barn was now burning brightly, but Vicki hugged her arms close. They'd won, she should feel happy, relieved, something. All she felt was empty.

"Hey." Henry wished he could see her eyes. All he could see were the flames reflected on her glasses. "You all right?"

"Yeah. I'm fine. Why wouldn't I be?"

He reached out and slid her glasses up her nose. "No reason."

She grinned, a little shakily. "You'd better get going. I don't know how long it'll take the fire trucks and the OPP to get out here."

"Will you be back to the farmhouse?"

"As soon as the police are finished with me."

He shot a look at Celluci but managed to hold back the comment.

Vicki sighed. "Go," she told him.

He went.

Celluci took his place.

Vicki sighed again. "Look, if you're about to treat me to another lecture on ethics or morals, I'm not in the mood."

"Actually, I was wondering if a grass fire was part of your plan? Maybe as a diversion? We're starting to get some sparks and the field behind the barn is awfully dry."

Flames were racing across the roof now, the entire structure wrapped in red and gold.

The last thing she wanted to do was more damage. "There's a water hookup in the garden with plenty of hose. Just wet the field down."

"Well, how the hell was I supposed to know?"

"You could have looked! Jesus H. Christ, do I have to do everything?"

"No, thanks. You've done quite enough!" He wanted to recall the words the moment he said them but to his surprise, Vicki started to laugh. It didn't sound like hysteria, it just sounded like laughter. "What?"

It was a moment before she could speak and even then, the threat of another outbreak seemed imminent. "I was just thinking that it's all over but the shouting."

"Yeah? So?"

"So?" She waved one hand helplessly in the air as she went off again. "So, now it's over."

"You will come back and see us again? When you need to get out of the city?"

"I will." Vicki grinned. "But right at the moment, the peace and quiet of the city seems pretty inviting."

Nadine snorted. "I don't know how you stand it. Bad smells and too many strangers on your territory. . . ." Although she still bore the mark of her twin's loss, in the last twenty-four hours the wound had visibly healed. Whether it was due to the deaths of Mark Williams and Carl Biehn or the saving of Peter's life, Vicki wasn't sure. Neither did she want to know.

Rose had also changed, with less of the child she'd been and more of the woman she was becoming showing in her face. Nadine kept her close, snarling when any of the males approached.

Vicki moved toward the door where Henry stood waiting for her, tension stretching between him and Stuart in almost a visible line.

"In the barn, before you arrived," Henry'd explained earlier, "I gave him an order he had no choice but to obey.

"You vampired him?"

"If you like. We're both pretending it didn't happen, but it'll take him some time to forget that it did."

Shadow, his black fur marked with dust, crawled out from under the wood stove, his jaws straining around a huge soup bone. He trotted to the door and dropped it at Vicki's feet.

"It's my best bone," Daniel told her solemnly. "I want you to have it so you don't forget me."

"Thank you, Daniel." The bone disappeared into the depths of Vicki's bag. She reached out and picked a bit of fluff from the top of his head. "I think that I can pretty much guarantee that I'll never, ever forget you."

Daniel squirmed, then Shadow threw himself at her knees, barking excitedly.

Oh, what the hell, Vicki thought, crouched down and

did what she'd done to Storm way back in the beginning, digging her fingers deep into the thick, soft fur of his ruff and giving him a good scratch.

It was hard to say which of them enjoyed it more.

Celluci leaned against the car and tossed the keys from hand to hand. It was an hour and a half after sunset and he wanted to get going; after the last two days, plain, old, big city crime would be a welcome relief.

He still wasn't certain why he'd offered Vicki and Henry a ride back to Toronto. No, that wasn't entirely true. He knew why he'd offered Vicki a lift, he just wasn't sure why he'd included Henry in the package. Granted, the man's BMW would be another week in the shop, at least, but that wasn't really much of a reason.

"What the hell is taking them so long?" he muttered.

As if in answer, the back door opened and Shadow bounded out, tail beating the air. Vicki and Henry followed, accompanied by all the rest of the family except Peter, who had remained at Dr. Dixon's.

Vicki had been right about the police investigation. The whole thing was just so weird and the witnesses so credible that the OPP had jumped to pretty much exactly the conclusions Vicki had outlined and were willing to write off the rest. Mark Williams' police record hadn't hurt either, especially when a report of his latest business venture had come in from Vancouver.

Celluci braced himself as Shadow leapt up on his chest, licked his face twice, then raced off to run noisy circles around the group approaching across the lawn. Werewolves. He'd never be able to look at anyone quite the same way again. If werewolves existed, who knew what other mythical creatures might turn up.

Vicki seemed to have taken the whole thing in stride, but then, he'd always known she was a remarkable woman. An obnoxious, arrogant, opinionated woman much of the time, but still, remarkable. On the other hand, he thought as he closed his fist around the keys, Vicki had known Henry since Easter so maybe none of this was new to her. Who knew what the two of them had been involved with?

During the gratitude and the good-byes, Stuart approached, hand held out. "Thank you for your help."

The tone wasn't exactly gracious, but Celluci understood about pride. He smiled, careful to keep his teeth covered, and took the offered hand. "You're welcome."

The grip started firmly enough but soon progressed so that the veins in both forearms were standing out against the muscle and Celluci, in spite of being nearly ten inches taller and proportionally heavier, began to worry about his knuckles popping.

Nadine, having caught scent of the competition, nudged Vicki and they both turned to watch.

"Do they keep this up until one of them breaks a hand?" Vicki wondered dryly, squinting at the joined silhouette straining in the fan of light from the car.

"Hard to tell with males," Nadine told her in much the same tone. "Their bodies seem to be able to go on for hours once their brains have shut off."

Vicki nodded. "I've noticed that."

If the sudden release came with any visible signals passing between the two men, Vicki didn't see them. One moment they were locked in stylized hand-to-hand combat, the next they were clapping each other on the shoulders like the best of friends. She figured that the correct internal pressure had finally been reached, tripping a switch and allowing life to go on—but she wasn't going to ask because she really didn't want to know.

While Stuart demanded to know what his mate was laughing at, Celluci found himself unexpectedly preoccupied by a logistics problem; who was going to sit beside him in the front seat on the way home. It seemed a childish thing to worry about but although the seat should by rights go to Vicki—she was the taller and entitled to the greater leg room—he didn't want Henry Fitzroy sitting behind him in the dark for the three hour drive.

Vicki took the decision away from him. Running her fingers along the car until she found the rear door handle, she opened it, tossed her bag in and climbed in after it, carefully removing Shadow—who'd been trying to get a few more licks in—before she closed the door. She'd known Mike Celluci for eight years and she had a pretty good idea of what was going through his head concerning this. If he thought she was going to run interference between him and Henry, he could think again.

Henry kept his face expressionless as he slid into the front seat and buckled his seat belt.

Shadow chased the car to the end of the lane then sat by the mailbox barking until they were out of sight.

By the time they reached the 401, Celluci couldn't stand the silence a moment longer. "Well," he cleared his throat, "are all your cases that *interesting?*"

Vicki grinned. She knew he'd break first. "Not all of them," she said, "but then I have a pretty exclusive clientele."

"That's one word for it," Celluci grunted. "What's going to happen with Rose and Peter, did they say?"

"As soon as Peter's better, Stuart's sending him to stay with his family in Vermont. Rose is pretty broken up about it."

"At least he's alive to send away."

"True enough."

"Rose is probably going to spend the next week howling in her room while the three adult males make themselves scarce."

"Three males? You mean her father . . ."

"Apparently it's a pretty strong biological imperative."

"Yeah, but . . ."

"Don't get your shorts in a knot, Celluci, Nadine'll make sure nothing happens."

"Only the alpha female gets to breed," Henry said matter-of-factly.

"Yeah? Great." Celluci drummed his fingers on the steering wheel and shot a sideways glance at the other man. "I'm still not sure where you fit in."

Henry raised a red-gold brow. "Well, in this particular instance, I acted as intermediary. Usually though, I'm just a friend." And then, because he couldn't resist, he added, "Sometimes I help Vicki out with the night work."

"Yeah. I bet you do." The engine roared as Celluci

gunned the car past a transport. "And you probably had more to do with that . . . that . . . thing, we ran into last spring than either of you are telling me."

"Perhaps."

"Perhaps nothing." Celluci ran one hand up through his hair. "Look, Vicki, you can get involved with as many ghoulies and ghosties and things that go bump in the night," he shot another look at Henry, "as you want. But from now on keep me out of it."

"No one invited you into it," Henry pointed out quietly before Vicki could respond.

"You should be damned glad I showed up!"

"Should we?"

"Yeah, you should."

"Perhaps you'd care to elaborate on that, Detective-Sergeant."

"Perhaps I would."

Vicki sighed, settled back, and closed her eyes. It was going to be a long ride home.